THE
Best American Mystery Stories
OF THE CENTURY

THE
Best American
Mystery Stories
OF THE CENTURY

Tony Hillerman EDITOR

Otto Penzler SERIES EDITOR

WITH AN INTRODUCTION
BY TONY HILLERMAN

HOUGHTON MIFFLIN COMPANY

BOSTON · NEW YORK

ISSN 1094-8384
ISBN 0-618-01267-2
ISBN 0-618-01271-0 (pbk.)

Printed in the United States of America

Book design by Robert Overholtzer

DOC   20 19 18 17 16 15 14

Contents

Foreword

As a fan of mystery fiction for what is now approaching a half century (good grief! can it be?), I have read what some might regard as an inordinate number of short stories. It is impossible to count the thousands, but it *is* possible to count the great ones.

For me, it has always been the short story. It started when I was just a kid and loved the surprise endings of O. Henry, the bizarre situations of a Sherlock Holmes adventure, and the deliciously creepy nightmares of Edgar Allan Poe. My appreciation of the short form was enhanced when I discovered the quirky humor of Damon Runyon and Ring Larder, clearly at their peak in a twenty-page sidesplitter. Finally, my devotion was complete when I learned that Stanley Ellin needed a full month to polish his little masterpieces, explaining their meticulous perfection.

Most classic detective stories rely on a single clue, or gimmick, or bit of legerdemain, or realization (the "aha" moment); the rest is embellishment. The old-fashioned detective novel, when it was good, created a universe with a population about whom the reader cared. An antisocial act, usually murder, occurred to disrupt the comfortable progress of that universe, and the remainder of the narrative illustrated the consequences of that crime on the population and the efforts made to apprehend the villain. With the identification of the perpetrator of the very bad deed (or deeds, as it was common for the culprit to commit additional crimes in order to cover up the first one), the universe was restored to its original peaceful state. And the villain was always caught because, no matter how brilliant he was, he invariably made one small mistake, which was spotted by the hero detective (but rarely by the reader).

Because the entire denouement relied on the uncovering of that single element to complete the jigsaw puzzle, it is clear that many of those novels could have been told in short story form with no loss of cleverness by the protagonist. Some of those novels, stripped to their essentials, became the brilliant short stories included in this volume.

But do not misunderstand me. Originality and felicitousness of language, development of memorable characters, even the texture of a created universe, cannot all be condensed into a short story. The best mystery novels, just as the best in all literature, are far richer than their plots. The story line is merely a single element, albeit a vital one, of any good crime novel, just as it is of any novel. In many cases, the tighter constrictions of the short story enable, or even force, an author into an economy of words that produces a crisper, superior work.

Searching for these gems of storytelling led me to *Ellery Queen's Mystery Magazine* as a young reader in my twenties. Making its first appearance in 1941, it is still being published, carrying the banner of the mystery story longer than any magazine in history.

By the 1940s, the pulp magazines had begun their plunge into oblivion. These nickel and dime story magazines, which once numbered more than a thousand titles a month, served as the training field for scores of writers who went on to distinguished careers as novelists and screenwriters. Called "pulps" because of the cheap newsprint on which they were printed, they were the major reading material for masses of America's readers. The rest read the "slicks," which were produced on superior paper, were illustrated throughout, often partially in color, and paid writers tremendous fees. While a writer for *Black Mask, Dime Detective,* or *The Shadow,* for example, might be paid a penny or two a word (if he was a big name), such mainstream authors as F. Scott Fitzgerald and John P. Marquand were paid $10,000 for stories in *The Saturday Evening Post* or *Scribner's.*

The slicks, too, were dying at the same rate as the pulps. The increased availability and popularity of radio shifted America's use of its leisure time, and the creation of the inexpensive paperbacks completed the task. The introduction of television on a large scale in the 1950s pretty much finished the publication of short fiction in any medium that was designed to be read by millions.

Ellery Queen's Mystery Magazine battled terrific odds by offering a digest-sized periodical containing only mystery fiction, thereby giving up that substantial portion of readers who preferred more diversity. By commissioning new stories from the best mystery writers on both sides of the Atlantic, and reprinting classic (though frequently forgotten) fiction, the magazine flourished.

It is a tribute to Frederic Dannay, one half of the writing team of Ellery Queen, that he devoted so much time and energy to the risky venture. His was not a celebrity endorsement or franchised name on a masthead. For nearly half a century, Dannay edited stories, corresponded with authors, suggested new (and usually better) story titles, and had his hand in every phase of the editorial content of what can only be regarded as *his* magazine.

Dannay was also a superb anthologist, breaking ground in a variety of fashions. Perhaps the finest anthology of mystery stories ever conceived and executed is his *101 Years' Entertainment,* which I read in a Modern Library edition as a teenager. It introduced me to so many of the detectives and authors who became a major part of my reading life that I still regard it as one of the half dozen most influential books in my development as a lifelong addict of the written word.

It is largely Dannay's tireless efforts to preserve distinguished mystery fiction in his numerous anthologies (more than two hundred bear his name as editor) that rescued so many first-rate writers from obscurity, lifting a story from the futurelessness of an ephemeral magazine appearance to the enduring substance of a hardcover book.

I doubt that any good stories escaped Dannay's eye, making it dramatically easier to produce this volume of the century's greatest American mystery stories. It would have been virtually impossible to locate every fiction magazine of the twentieth century in order to identify which works were appropriate for consideration, much less read them all.

Other anthologies proved useful, too, of course, notably *The Best Detective Stories of the Year* series, begun in 1946 (and now defunct) by Dutton; the annual theme anthologies produced under the aegis of the Mystery Writers of America; and numerous solo efforts, but nothing approaches the contributions made by Frederic Dannay.

Having read many hundreds of these anthologies over the years, I had a pretty good idea of many of the stories that deserved consideration for inclusion in this important volume. Or I thought I did. The memory can play nasty tricks. Stories that I remembered with tremendous affection turned out, on rereading, to be disappointing, sometimes astonishingly so. Where was my taste, I wondered, when I reread two or three collections of stories by an author I'd once admired and couldn't find a single story that held my interest or that had even one important thought or original use of language?

What surprised me is how few pulp stories hold up today. Most are dated, both in outlook and in language. Characters are seldom multidimensional, dialogue is stilted as everyone tries to be tougher than a two-dollar steak. Chandler, arguably the greatest mystery writer who ever lived, transcends his venue, of course, and so does Hammett, and even the purple prose of Woolrich remains intensely readable a half century or more after it was written. But the fast-paced adventures of Carroll John Daly, Raoul Whitfield, Frank Gruber, Frederick Nebel, Norbert Davis, and Erle Stanley Gardner, once read with such avidity, don't stay in the memory a day later. They remain entertaining, like a television sitcom, but they lack the timeless magic of significant writers. In spite of their enormous popularity for three decades (the 1920s, 1930s, and 1940s), there are few examples in the present volume.

An entirely different problem arose when I weighed the work of the truly wonderful authors. How many Chandler stories deserved to be included here? A half dozen, maybe, or more. And how many of Woolrich? A full dozen? And Stanley Ellin? Half his opera sounded about right. But we decided to limit the collection to no more than one story by an author, enabling readers to sample a rainbow of styles and subgenres. No one will stop you from searching out more stories by the authors you enjoy the most.

Another surprise, though it probably shouldn't have been, is how many of the best mystery, crime, and suspense stories were produced by authors not generally regarded as "mystery writers." Ernest Hemingway, William Faulkner, John Steinbeck, Damon Runyon, O. Henry, Joyce Carole Oates, Ring Lardner, James Thurber, and others dipped their toes into the mystery waters and, as they did with their other work, excelled.

The process of list-making is, obviously, subjective. There are no scientific instruments that can tell a reader which of Harlan Ellison's two Edgar-winning short stories is better. It is a coin toss, and it can't be anything else. Let's just live with it.

Reducing the list of distinguished stories from several thousand stories to a few hundred required a good deal of rereading and weeding. Getting that list down to a manageable number from which Tony Hillerman made the final selection was like self-surgery. Each story eliminated after a certain point was like another incision, one painfully deeper than another.

Some Edgar winners made the final cut, and some did not. For the life of me, I cannot fathom how some Edgar committees, filled with smart and caring and honorable people, could have selected some of the stories they did while ignoring obviously superior ones. And yet ESPN recently chose the fifty greatest athletes of the century and actually picked Secretariat ahead of Mickey Mantle. Such choices are clearly subjective.

So here they are. Are these truly the best American mystery stories of the century? Almost. Tony Hillerman left out some I'd have wanted, but it would have been boring if we had agreed on everything.

And while I've been reading mystery fiction for about four decades, Tony Hillerman has been reading it even longer. He was clearly the right person to serve as the editor for this distinguished collection. He has been, for three decades, the quintessential American mystery writer, as well as being a most learned scholar.

His first book, *The Blessing Way,* was published by Harper and Row in 1970 and was nominated for an Edgar. His third book, *Dance Hall of the Dead,* won that prestigious award, the Oscar of the mystery world, as the best novel of the year. Since then, his sensitive and intelligent portrayals of the Navajo Indians and the two policemen who served as their guardians, Joe Leaphorn and Jim Chee, have been given every imaginable accolade (and it's not hype to state unequivocally that they are fully deserved). They have also enjoyed the ultimate testament to their ability to reach readers in a meaningful way — frequent appearances on the bestseller list. As final acknowledgment of his preeminence in the mystery writing world, the Mystery Writers of America selected him to be a Grand Master, joining the elite company of such giants as Raymond Chandler, James M. Cain, Ed McBain, Ross Macdonald, and Elmore Leonard.

Finally, the careful consideration that went into the selection of these stories should go unnoticed. This very large volume should be a joyful experience, a bountiful cornucopia of delights into which the reader can slip at any moment for a time of pleasure. Will you disagree with some of the choices? We expect so. However, because this is my bit of preamble, I hide behind the collaborative effort. If you approve of the choices, thank you. If you don't, it's only because Tony left out the stories that you'd have wanted to see included.

— Otto Penzler

Introduction

If I, alone, were stuck with the Herculean task of selecting the best mystery stories of the twentieth century, I'm afraid they would be clustered in periods. I'd give you a lot of tales from the years between the wars when thousands of good writers were supporting their families with yarns spun for the pulps. I'd pick out a dozen or so from those slick magazines that paid living-wage prices for short stories until television destroyed both them and national literacy. Finally, I'd give you another bunch from the 1990s, when enough folks had been turned off by the tube to produce a new market for the short story form. In other words I would impose upon you my personal taste.

Fortunately, Otto Penzler was also involved in the selection process. To those of you who bring a mature love of mystery and detective fiction to this book, the Penzler name means the Mysterious Press, the Mysterious Bookshops, and other key contributions to the field, recognized by an Edgar for the *Encyclopedia of Mystery and Detection* and an Ellery Queen Award from the Mystery Writers of America for lifetime achievement in the publishing world. Penzler helped select works that give us a broader outlook than I'd have managed on my own. All the eras in which the American mystery took its special form, wresting leadership from the British, defying the academicians, and — more than any other genre — making popular American literature dominant worldwide are represented between these covers.

For a quick glimpse of the progress that American popular literature has made in the twentieth century, first read "The Problem of Cell 13," published in 1905, and then jump ahead ninety-three years to "Poachers." I'm asking you to skip O. Henry's "A Retrieved Reformation" and Willa Cather for the moment. O. Henry, being a genius of the short form, was too far ahead of his time to be typical, while Futrelle's tale is a fine example of what American writers were doing at the turn of the century.

At that time, American mystery writers generally copied the British, who were copying Edgar Allan Poe. They produced puzzles involving the wealthy educated leisure class. That was logical because the educated leisure class included the folks with the ability to read, the time to do it, and the money to buy the stories. Was Futrelle himself upper-class? He drowned (heroically saving others) when the *Titanic* hit an iceberg, and he wasn't traveling steerage class. Thus it's no accident that "The Thinking Machine" character he invented reminds one of Sherlock Holmes and that his characters aren't likely candidates for AFL-CIO membership.

But in 1905 the characters in mysteries were not important. Only the puzzle mattered. Now, skip ahead to 1998 and "Poachers." In Tom Franklin's story, the puzzle matters hardly at all. Here you meet real people — three orphaned and brutish brothers who live as predators in the wet woods of the Gulf Coast south, the old widower who loves them, and the sheriff who pitied them all. Who killed two of these brutal boys and blinded the third? You never really know. If you care, you can take your pick. In any case, the muddy river, the endless rain, the half-wild hunting dogs, are more important than the plot.

Futrelle and most of his contemporaries produced puzzling whodunits as pastimes for the educated few. But, even as he wrote, the market was changing. Pulitzer, Hearst, Greeley, McCormick, Nelson, and a host of other publishers were building their empires with the so-called "Penny Press," published for blue-collar workers. Public education was making the hod carriers, farmers, miners, maids, and millers as literate as lords and ladies.

Many of these newspapers of the "Yellow Journalism" days published short mystery stories, helping set the stage for the golden years of the pulp magazines. By the second decade of the century (and on through the third and fourth), virtually every drugstore in the nation big enough to have its own soda fountain had a magazine rack made glorious and alive by the gaudy reds, yellows, greens, and blues favored by the publishers of such journals as *Black Mask, Hollywood Detective, Spicy Detective,* and so on. They usually boasted "bodice-ripper" illustrations and promised as much blood, violence, and raunch in their headlines as the mores of the times would allow.

With the pulps, American writers made the big break from the British. The pay scale ranged from two cents a word downward (though a really spectacular yarn might merit three cents a word). As a young fellow making $1.25 per ten-hour hay-baling day when I first paid a dime for a detective pulp, two cents a word sounded generous. Personally, I rated only rejection slips from the pulps, but many of the writers herein did well with them — especially Dashiell Hammett and Raymond Chandler.

The pulps took the mystery story out of the parlors and drawing rooms and onto the "mean streets" among the people who were actually the victims of the crime. One of the old rules had been "the butler didn't do it," implying that the criminal, as well as the victim, must be an upper-crust person — someone the well-bred reader would care about. Such rules made no sense when neither you, nor those for whom you were writing, had ever seen a butler.

By midcentury the American mystery genre was generally being written in American English. It had left the manicured lawns of the manor houses behind to focus on those folks I like to call "real people." Local color had crept in (though rarely as emphatically as in "Poachers"), as well as social issues. The tales of pure ratiocination still thrived in the form of U.S. versions of the polite British "cozies." The segment of American fiction devoted to crime and its solution was not only booming, it was developing in a variety of channels. Most important of all — certainly for me — mystery fiction was elbowing its way from the shelves that bookstores reserve for mere tales to the front, where the novels are stocked.

In this volume, you'll encounter many writers who had a hand in this movement — including the great Raymond Chandler. I consider Chandler the Thomas Paine of this twentieth-century American revolution. That analogy makes Professor Jacques Barzun and Wendell Hertig Taylor the spokesmen for the counterrevolution in their landmark *A Catalogue of Crime,* but the first blast fired by the Tories came from Edmund Wilson, who in the 1940s was America's most portentous literary critic. Someone had called his attention to *The Maltese Falcon,* which I consider Hammett's masterwork. Wilson rated it on the level of newspaper serial comic strips and wrote a *New Yorker* essay denouncing the entire mystery-detection field as trash that served only to worsen the wartime paper shortage. Then, persuaded by a friend that to be fair he should read an Agatha Christie, he did, and wrote "Who Cares Who Killed Roger Ackroyd?" While I agree that's a fair enough question, I disagree with his summary judgment that the entire genre was devoid of value.

(Those too young to remember Wilson might like to know that he's the fellow most responsible for introducing Americans to Marcel Proust and James Joyce, causing untold thousands of college students to suffer through *Remembrance of Things Past* and Joyce's stream of consciousness.)

Chandler's rebuttal "The Simple Art of Murder" was published by *The Atlantic Monthly* in 1944, a sort of declaration of independence from the British detective form and an argument that mystery fiction was as likely to have social importance as any other work of fiction — the implication being that literature didn't have to be boring.

"The British may not always be the best writers in the world," he said, "but they are incomparably the best dull writers." One of Chandler's points was that many American writers had been copying this British business of turning out mystery stories in which the whole purpose was the puzzle — avoiding character development or any real effort at realistic settings or situations. S. S. Van Dine, America's best-selling mystery writer of the 1920s and 1930s, created Philo Vance, probably the most insufferable snob in all of literature, and gave him an upper-class British accent and foreign cigarettes. Van Dine even used phony footnotes to underline Philo's intellectual superiority.

Chandler argues that unless the plots really worked in such books (and they rarely did), the reader received nothing for his two dollars. Dorothy Sayers had just published an essay stating that detective fiction could never attain "the loftiest levels of literary achievement" because it was literature of escape and not "literature of expression." Chandler rated this critical jargon as nonsense. This isn't the place to reprint "The Simple Art of Murder," but as you read this book you'll note that Chandler's position — that detective fiction could, and should, include the same elements that deemed novels "literature of expression" — was adopted by most of the writers who followed him.

In their introductory essay to *A Catalogue of Crime* in 1971, Barzun and Taylor fired their broadside in favor of preserving mystery fiction in its classical form. Mystery stories should be "tales of ratiocination," written for those who wish to entertain themselves with amusing intellectual exercises. They should be set in quiet havens without intrusions of realism to distract the reader from the puzzle. Detective fiction, said Barzun, is a tale, not a novel. It should deal with the intellect, not with emotions. It should not pretend to have social importance. "The characters it presents are not persons but types, as in the gospels: the servant, the rich man, the camel driver (now a chauffeur)."

As you will note in the short stories that follow, the argument didn't end in the 1970s. It still hasn't. It never will. There will always be room under the tent for the classic form and the novel form, with untold variations in between. I'd guess that approximately half of the audience for mysteries today still prefers the puzzle to the novel. What's important is the example Chandler gave us with his own novels. His use of the work of a private detective to illuminate the corruption of society has attracted into the genre many mystery writers who wish to produce "literature of expression" and shoot for lofty literary goals. Driven out of the so-called mainstream of American writing by the academic critics and the academic trends — minimalism, deconstructionism, and whatever is next — we have found a home in the mystery form.

— Tony Hillerman

1903

O. HENRY

....

A Retrieved Reformation

Criminal: Jimmy Valentine

A GUARD CAME to the prison shoe shop, where Jimmy Valentine was assiduously stitching uppers, and escorted him to the front office. There the warden handed Jimmy his pardon, which had been signed that morning by the governor.

Jimmy took it in a tired kind of way. He had served nearly ten months of a four-year sentence. He had expected to stay only about three months, at the longest. When a man with as many friends on the outside as Jimmy Valentine had is received in the "stir" it is hardly worth while to cut his hair.

"Now, Valentine," said the warden, "you'll go out in the morning. Brace up, and make a man out of yourself. You're not a bad fellow at heart. Stop cracking safes, and live straight."

"Me?" said Jimmy, in surprise. "Why, I never cracked a safe in my life."

"Oh, no," laughed the warden. "Of course not. Let's see, now. How was it you happened to get sent up on that Springfield job? Was it because you wouldn't prove an alibi for fear of compromising somebody in extremely high-toned society? Or was it simply a case of a mean old jury that had it in for you? It's always one or the other with you innocent victims."

"Me?" said Jimmy, still blankly virtuous. "Why, Warden, I never was in Springfield in my life!"

"Take him back, Cronin," smiled the warden, "and fix him up with outgoing clothes. Unlock him at seven in the morning, and let him come to the bullpen. Better think over my advice, Valentine."

At a quarter past seven on the next morning Jimmy stood in the warden's outer office. He had on a suit of the villainously fitting, ready-made clothes and a pair of the stiff, squeaky shoes that the state furnishes to its discharged compulsory guests.

The clerk handed him a railroad ticket and the five-dollar bill with which the law expected him to rehabilitate himself into good citizenship and prosperity. The warden gave him a cigar, and shook hands. Valentine, 9762, was chronicled on the books "Pardoned by Governor," and Mr. James Valentine walked out into the sunshine.

Disregarding the song of the birds, the waving green trees, and the smell of the flowers, Jimmy headed straight for a restaurant. There he tasted the first sweet joys of liberty in the shape of a broiled chicken and a bottle of wine — followed by a cigar a grade better than the one the warden had given him.

From there he proceeded leisurely to the depot. He tossed a quarter into the hat of a blind man sitting by the door, and boarded his train. Three hours set him down in a little town near the state line. He went to the café of one Mike Dolan and shook hands with Mike, who was alone behind the bar.

"Sorry we couldn't make it sooner, Jimmy, me boy," said Mike. "But we had that protest from Springfield to buck against, and the governor nearly balked. Feeling all right?"

"Fine," said Jimmy. "Got my key?"

He got his key and went upstairs, unlocking the door of a room at the rear. Everything was just as he had left it. There on the floor was still Ben Price's collar button that had been torn from that eminent detective's shirt when they had overpowered Jimmy to arrest him.

Pulling out from the wall a folding bed, Jimmy slid back a panel in the wall, and dragged out a dust-covered suitcase. He opened this and gazed fondly at the finest set of burglar's tools in the East. It was a complete set, made of specially tempered steel, the latest designs in drills, punches, braces and bits, jimmies, clamps, and augers, with two or three novelties invented by Jimmy himself, in which he took pride.

In half an hour Jimmy went downstairs and through the café. He was now dressed in tasteful and well-fitting clothes, and carried his dusted and cleaned suitcase in his hand.

"Got anything on?" asked Mike Dolan, genially.

"Me?" said Jimmy, in a puzzled tone. "I don't understand. I'm representing the New York Amalgamated Short Snap Biscuit Cracker and Frazzled Wheat Company."

This statement delighted Mike to such an extent that Jimmy had to take a seltzer-and-milk on the spot. He never touched "hard" drinks.

A week after the release of Valentine, 9762, there was a neat job of safe burglary done in Richmond, Indiana, with no clue to the author. A scant $800 was all that was secured.

Two weeks after that a patented, improved, burglar-proof safe in Logansport was opened like a cheese to the tune of $1500.

That began to interest the rogue-catchers. Then an old-fashioned bank-safe in Jefferson City became active and threw out of its crater an eruption of banknotes amounting to $5000.

The losses were now high enough to bring the matter up into Ben Price's class of work. By comparing notes, a remarkable similarity in the methods of the burglaries was noticed. Ben Price investigated the scenes of the robberies, and was heard to remark: "That's Dandy Jim Valentine's autograph. He's resumed business. Look at that combination knob — jerked out as easy as pulling up a radish in wet weather. He's got the only clamps that can do it. And look how clean those tumblers were punched out! Jimmy never has to drill but one hole. Yes, I guess I want Mr. Valentine. He'll do his bit next time without any short-time or clemency foolishness."

Ben Price knew Jimmy's habits. He had learned them while working up the Springfield case. Long jumps, quick getaways, no confederates, and a taste for good society — these ways had helped Mr. Valentine to become noted as a successful dodger of retribution. It was given out that Ben Price had taken up the trail of the elusive cracksman, and other people with burglar-proof safes felt more at ease.

One afternoon Jimmy Valentine and his suitcase climbed out of the mailback in Elmore, a little town five miles off the railroad down in the black-jack country of Arkansas. Jimmy, looking like an athletic young senior just home from college, went down the broad sidewalk toward the hotel.

A young lady crossed the street, passed him at the corner, and entered a door over which was the sign "The Elmore Bank." Jimmy Valentine looked into her eyes, forgot what he was, and became another man. She lowered her eyes and colored slightly. Young men of Jimmy's style and looks were scarce in Elmore.

Jimmy collared a boy loafing on the steps of the bank as if he were one of the stockholders and began to ask him questions about the town, feeding him dimes at intervals. By and by the young lady came out, looking royally unconscious of the young man with the suitcase, and went her way.

"Isn't that young lady Miss Polly Simpson?" asked Jimmy, with specious guile.

"Naw," said the boy. "She's Annabel Adams. Her pa owns this bank. What'd you come to Elmore for? Is that a gold watch-chain? I'm going to get a bulldog. Got any more dimes?"

Jimmy went to the Planters' Hotel, registered as Ralph D. Spencer, and engaged a room. He leaned on the desk and declared his platform to the clerk. He said he had come to Elmore to look for a location to go into business. How was the shoe business, now, in the town? He had thought of the shoe business. Was there an opening?

The clerk was impressed by the clothes and manner of Jimmy. He, himself, was something of a pattern of fashion to the thinly gilded youth of Elmore, but he now perceived his shortcomings. While trying to figure out Jimmy's manner of trying his four-in-hand he cordially gave information.

Yes, there ought to be a good opening in the shoe line. There wasn't an exclusive shoe store in the place. The dry goods and general stores handled them. Business in all lines was fairly good. Hoped Mr. Spencer would decide to locate in Elmore. He would find it a pleasant town to live in, and the people very sociable.

Mr. Spencer thought he would stop over in the town a few days and look over the situation. No, the clerk needn't call the boy. He would carry up his suitcase himself; it was rather heavy.

Mr. Ralph Spencer, the phoenix that arose from Jimmy Valentine's ashes — ashes left by the flame of a sudden and alterative attack of love — remained in Elmore, and prospered. He opened a shoe store and secured a good run of trade.

Socially he was also a success, and made many friends. And he accomplished the wish of his heart. He met Miss Annabel Adams and became more and more captivated by her charms.

At the end of a year the situation of Mr. Ralph Spencer was this: he had won the respect of the community, his shoe store was flourishing, and he and Annabel were engaged to be married in two weeks. Mr. Adams, the typical, plodding, country banker, approved of Spencer. Annabel's pride in him almost equalled her affection. He was as much at home in the family of Mr. Adams and that of Annabel's married sister as if he were already a member.

One day Jimmy sat down in his room and wrote this letter, which he mailed to the address of one of his old friends in St. Louis:

Dear Old Pal:
    I want you to be at Sullivan's place, in Little Rock, next Wednesday night, at nine o'clock. I want you to wind up some little matters for me. And, also, I want to make you a present of my kit of tools. I know you'll be glad to get them — you couldn't duplicate the lot for a thousand dollars. Say, Billy, I've quit the old business — a year ago. I've got a nice store. I'm making an honest living, and I'm going to marry the finest girl on earth two weeks from now. It's the only life, Billy — the straight one. I wouldn't touch a dollar of another man's money now for a million. After I get married I'm going to sell out and go West, where there won't be so much danger of having old scores brought up against me. I tell you, Billy, she's an angel. She believes in me; and I wouldn't do another crooked thing for the whole world. Be sure to be at Sully's, for I must see you.
                                                            Your old friend,
                                                            Jimmy

On the Monday night after Jimmy wrote this letter, Ben Price jogged unobtrusively into Elmore in a livery buggy. He lounged about town in his quiet way until he found out what he wanted to know. From the drug store across the street from Spencer's shoe store he got a good look at Ralph D. Spencer.

Going to marry the banker's daughter, are you, Jimmy? said Ben to himself, softly. Well, I don't know!

The next morning Jimmy took breakfast at the Adamses. He was going to Little Rock that day to order his wedding suit and buy something nice for Annabel. That would be the first time he had left town since he came to Elmore. It had been more than a year now since those last professional "jobs," and he thought he could safely venture out.

After breakfast quite a family party went downtown together — Mr. Adams, Annabel, Jimmy, and Annabel's married sister and her two little girls, aged five and nine. They came by the hotel where Jimmy still boarded, and he ran up to his room and brought down his suitcase. Then they went on to the bank. There stood Jimmy's horse and buggy and Dolph Gibson, who was going to drive him over to the railroad station.

All went inside the high, carved-oak railings into the banking room — Jimmy included, for Mr. Adams' future son-in-law was welcome anywhere. The clerks were pleased to be greeted by the good-looking, agreeable young man who was going to marry Miss Annabel.

Jimmy set his suitcase down. Annabel, whose heart was bubbling with happiness and lively youth, put on Jimmy's hat and picked up the suitcase. "Wouldn't I make a nice drummer?" said Annabel. "My, Ralph, how heavy it is. Feels like it was full of gold bricks."

"Lot of nickel-plated shoehorns in there," said Jimmy coolly, "that I'm going to return. Thought I'd save express charges by taking them up. I'm getting economical."

The Elmore Bank had just put in a new safe and vault. Mr. Adams was very proud of it, and insisted on an inspection by everyone. The vault was a small one, but it had a new patented door. It fastened with three solid steel bolts thrown simultaneously with a single handle, and had a time lock.

Mr. Adams beamingly explained its workings to Mr. Spencer, who showed a courteous but not too intelligent interest. The two children, May and Agatha, were delighted by the shining metal and funny clock and knobs.

While they were thus engaged, Ben Price sauntered in and leaned on his elbow, looking casually inside between the railings. He told the teller he didn't want anything; he was just waiting for a man he knew.

Suddenly there were screams from the women, and a commotion. Unperceived by the elders, May, the nine-year-old girl, in a spirit of play, had shut Agatha in the vault. She had then shot the bolts and turned the knob of the combination as she had seen Mr. Adams do.

The old banker sprang to the handle and tugged at it.

"The door can't be opened," he groaned. "The clock hasn't been wound nor the combination set."

Agatha's mother screamed again, hysterically.

"Hush!" said Mr. Adams, raising his trembling hand. "All be quiet for a moment. Agatha!" he called as loudly as he could. "Listen to me." During the following silence they could just hear the faint sound of the child wildly shrieking in the dark vault in a panic of terror.

"My precious darling!" wailed the mother. "She will die of fright! Open the door! Oh, break it open! Can't you men do something?"

"There isn't a man nearer than Little Rock who can open that door," said Mr. Adams, in a shaky voice. "My God! Spencer, what shall we do? That child — she can't stand it long in there. There isn't enough air, and, besides, she'll go into convulsions from fright."

Agatha's mother, frantic now, beat the door of the vault with her hands. Somebody wildly suggested dynamite. Annabel turned to Jimmy, her large eyes full of anguish, but not yet despairing. To a woman nothing seems quite impossible to the powers of the man she worships.

"Can't you do something, Ralph — *try*, won't you?"

He looked at her with a queer, soft smile in his keen eyes.

"Annabel," he said, "give me that rose you are wearing, will you?"

Hardly believing that she heard him aright, she unpinned the bud from the bosom of her dress and placed it in his hand. Jimmy stuffed it into his vest pocket, threw off his coat, and pulled up his shirt sleeves. With that act Ralph D. Spencer passed away and Jimmy Valentine took his place.

"Get away from the door, all of you," he commanded.

He set his suitcase on the table and opened it out flat. From that time on he seemed to be unconscious of the presence of anyone else. He laid out the shining, queer implements swiftly and orderly, whistling softly to himself as he always did when at work. In a deep silence and immovable, the others watched him as if under a spell.

In a minute Jimmy's pet drill was biting smoothly into the steel door. In ten minutes — breaking his own burglarious record — he threw back the bolts and opened the door.

Agatha, almost collapsed, but safe, was gathered into her mother's arms.

Jimmy Valentine put on his coat, and walked outside the railings toward the front door. As he went he thought he heard a faraway voice that he once knew call "Ralph!" But he never hesitated.

At the door a big man stood somewhat in his way.

"Hello, Ben!" said Jimmy, still with his strange smile. "Got around at last, have you? Well, let's go. I don't know that it makes much difference, now."

Then Ben Price acted strangely.

"Guess you're mistaken, Mr. Spencer," he said. "Don't believe I recognize you. Your buggy's waiting for you, ain't it?"

And Ben Price turned and strolled down the street.

1905

WILLA CATHER

....

Paul's Case

IT WAS Paul's afternoon to appear before the faculty of the Pittsburgh High School to account for his various misdemeanors. He had been suspended a week ago, and his father had called at the Principal's office and confessed his perplexity about his son. Paul entered the faculty room suave and smiling. His clothes were a trifle outgrown, and the tan velvet on the collar of his open overcoat was frayed and worn; but for all that there was something of the dandy about him, and he wore an opal pin in his neatly knotted black four-in-hand, and a red carnation in his buttonhole. This latter adornment the faculty somehow felt was not properly significant of the contrite spirit befitting a boy under the ban of suspension.

Paul was tall for his age and very thin, with high, cramped shoulders and a narrow chest. His eyes were remarkable for a certain hysterical brilliancy, and he continually used them in a conscious, theatrical sort of way, peculiarly offensive in a boy. The pupils were abnormally large, as though he were addicted to belladonna, but there was a glassy glitter about them which that drug does not produce.

When questioned by the Principal as to why he was there, Paul stated, politely enough, that he wanted to come back to school. This was a lie, but Paul was quite accustomed to lying; found it, indeed, indispensable for overcoming friction. His teachers were asked to state their respective charges against him, which they did with such a rancor and aggrieved-ness as evinced that this was not a usual case. Disorder and imperti-nence were among the offenses named, yet each of his instructors felt that it was scarcely possible to put into words the real cause of the trou-ble, which lay in a sort of hysterically defiant manner of the boy's; in the contempt which they all knew he felt for them, and which he seemingly made not the least effort to conceal. Once, when he had been making a synopsis of a paragraph at the blackboard, his English teacher had stepped to his side and attempted to guide his hand. Paul had started back with a shudder and thrust his hands violently behind him. The astonished woman could scarcely have been more hurt and embarrassed had he struck at her. The insult was so involuntary and definitely personal as to be unforgettable. In one way and another, he had made all his teachers, men and women alike, conscious of the same feeling of physical aversion. In one class he habitually sat with his hand shading his eyes; in another he always looked out of the window during the recitation; in another he made a running commentary on the lecture, with humorous intent.

His teacher felt this afternoon that his whole attitude was symbolized by his shrug and his flippantly red carnation flower, and they fell upon him without mercy, his English teacher leading the pack. He stood through it smiling, his pale lips parted over his white teeth. (His lips were continually twitching, and he had a habit of raising his eyebrows that was contemptuous and irritating to the last degree.) Older boys than Paul had broken down and shed tears under the ordeal, but his set smile did not once desert him, and his only sign of discomfort was the nervous trembling of the fingers that toyed with the buttons of his overcoat, and an occasional jerking of the other hand which held his hat. Paul was always smiling, always glancing about him, seeming to feel that people might be watching him and trying to detect something. This conscious expression, since it was as far as possible from boyish mirthfulness, was usually attributed to insolence or "smartness."

As the inquisition proceeded, one of his instructors repeated an impertinent remark of the boy's, and the Principal asked him whether he thought that a courteous speech to make to a woman. Paul shrugged his shoulder slightly and his eyebrows twitched.

"I don't know," he replied. "I didn't mean to be polite or impolite, either. I guess it's a sort of way I have, of saying things regardless."

The Principal asked him whether he didn't think that a way it would be well to get rid of. Paul grinned and said he guessed so. When he was told that he could go, he bowed gracefully and went out. His bow was like a repetition of the scandalous red carnation.

His teachers were in despair, and his drawing master voiced the feeling of them all when he declared there was something about the boy which none of them understood. He added: "I don't really believe that smile of his comes altogether from insolence; there's something sort of haunted about it. The boy is not strong, for one thing. There is something wrong about the fellow."

The drawing master had come to realize that, in looking at Paul, one saw only his white teeth and the forced animation of his eyes. One warm afternoon the boy had gone to sleep at his drawing board, and his master had noted with amazement what a white, blue-veined face it was; drawn and wrinkled like an old man's about the eyes, the lips twitching even in his sleep.

His teachers left the building dissatisfied and unhappy; humiliated to have felt so vindictive toward a mere boy, to have uttered this feeling in cutting terms, and to have set each other on, as it were, in the gruesome game of intemperate reproach. One of them remembered having seen a miserable street cat set at bay by a ring of tormentors.

As for Paul, he ran down the hill whistling the Soldiers' Chorus from *Faust,* looking wildly behind him now and then to see whether some of his teachers were not there to witness his lightheartedness. As it was now late in the afternoon and Paul was on duty that evening as usher at Carnegie Hall, he decided that he would not go home to supper.

When he reached the concert hall the doors were not yet open. It was chilly outside, and he decided to go up into the picture gallery — always deserted at this hour — where there were some of Raffelli's gay studies of Paris streets and an airy blue Venetian scene or two that always exhilarated him. He was delighted to find no one in the gallery but the old guard, who sat in the corner, a newspaper on his knee, a black patch over one eye and the other closed. Paul possessed himself of the place and walked confidently up and down, whistling under his breath. After a while he sat down before a blue Rico and lost himself. When he bethought him to look at his watch, it was after seven o'clock, and he rose with a start and ran downstairs, making a face at Augustus Cæsar, peering out from the castroom, and an evil gesture at the Venus of Milo as he passed her on the stairway.

When Paul reached the ushers' dressing room half a dozen boys were there already, and he began excitedly to tumble into his uniform. It was one of the few that at all approached fitting, and Paul thought it very becoming — though he knew the tight, straight coat accentuated his narrow chest, about which he was exceedingly sensitive. He was always excited while he dressed, twangling all over to the tuning of the strings and the preliminary flourishes of the horns in the music room; but to-night he seemed quite beside himself, and he teased and plagued the boys until, telling him that he was crazy, they put him down on the floor and sat on him.

Somewhat calmed by his suppression, Paul dashed out to the front of the house to seat the early comers. He was a model usher. Gracious and smiling he ran up and down the aisles. Nothing was too much trouble for him; he carried messages and brought programs as though it were his greatest pleasure in life, and all the people in his section thought him a charming boy, feeling that he remembered and admired them. As the house filled, he grew more and more vivacious and animated, and the color came to his cheeks and lips. It was very much as though this were a great reception and Paul were the host. Just as the musicians came out to take their places, his English teacher arrived with checks for the seats which a prominent manufacturer had taken for the season. She betrayed some embarrassment when she handed Paul the tickets, and a *hauteur* which subsequently made her feel very foolish. Paul was startled for a moment, and had the feeling of wanting to put her out; what business had she here among all these fine people and gay colors? He looked her over and decided that she was not appropriately dressed and must be a fool to sit downstairs in such togs. The tickets had probably been sent her out of kindness, he reflected, as he put down a seat for her, and she had about as much right to sit there as he had.

When the symphony began Paul sank into one of the rear seats with a long sigh of relief, and lost himself as he had done before the Rico. It was not that symphonies, as such, meant anything in particular to Paul, but the first sigh of the instruments seemed to free some hilarious spirit within him; something that struggled there like the Genius in the bottle found by the Arab fisherman. He felt a sudden zest of life; the lights danced before his eyes and the concert hall blazed into unimaginable splendor. When the soprano soloist came on, Paul forgot even the nastiness of his teacher's being there, and gave himself up to the peculiar intoxication such personages always had for him. The soloist chanced to be a German woman, by no means in her first youth, and the mother of many children; but she wore a satin gown and a tiara, and she had that indefinable air of achievement, that world-shine upon her, which always blinded Paul to any possible defects.

After a concert was over, Paul was often irritable and wretched until he got to sleep — and tonight he was even more than usually restless. He had the feeling of not being able to let down; of its being impossible to give up this delicious excitement which was the only thing that could be called living at all. During the last number he withdrew and, after hastily changing his clothes in the dressing room, slipped out to the side door where the singer's carriage stood. Here he began pacing rapidly up and down the walk, waiting to see her come out.

Over yonder the Schenley, in its vacant stretch, loomed big and square through the fine rain, the windows of its twelve stories glowing like those of a lighted cardboard house under a Christmas tree. All the actors and singers of any importance stayed there when they were in the city, and a number of the big manufacturers of the place lived there in the winter. Paul had often hung about the hotel, watching the people go in and out, longing to enter and leave schoolmasters and dull care behind him forever.

At last the singer came out, accompanied by the conductor, who helped her into her carriage and closed the door with a cordial *auf wiedersehen* — which set Paul to wondering whether she were not an old sweetheart of his. Paul followed the carriage over to the hotel, walking so rapidly as not to be far from the entrance when the singer alighted and disappeared behind the swinging glass doors which were opened by a Negro in a tall hat and a long coat. In the moment that the door was ajar, it seemed to Paul that he, too, entered. He seemed to feel himself go after her up the steps, into the warm, lighted building, into an exotic, a tropical world of shiny, glistening surfaces and basking ease. He reflected upon the mysterious dishes that were brought into the dining room, the green bottles in buckets of ice, as he had seen them in the supper party pictures of the Sunday supplement. A quick gust of wind brought the rain down with sudden vehemence, and Paul was startled to find that he was still outside in the slush of the gravel driveway; that his boots were letting in the water and his scanty overcoat was clinging wet about him; that the lights in front of the concert hall were out, and that the rain was driving in sheets between him and the orange glow of the windows above him. There it was, what he wanted — tangibly before him, like the fairy world of a Christmas pantomime; as the rain beat in his face, Paul wondered whether he were destined always to shiver in the black night outside, looking up at it.

He turned and walked reluctantly toward the car tracks. The end had to come some time; his father in his night-clothes at the top of the stairs, explanations that did not explain, hastily improvised fictions that were forever tripping him up, his upstairs room and its horrible yellow wallpaper, the creaking bureau with the greasy plush collarbox, and over his painted wooden bed the pictures of George Washington and

John Calvin, and the framed motto, "Feed my Lambs," which had been worked in red worsted by his mother, whom Paul could not remember.

Half an hour later, Paul alighted from the Negley Avenue car and went slowly down one of the side streets off the main thoroughfare. It was a highly respectable street, where all the houses were exactly alike, and where business men of moderate means begot and reared large families of children, all of whom went to Sabbath school and learned the shorter catechism, and were interested in arithmetic; all of whom were as exactly alike as their homes, and of a piece with the monotony in which they lived. Paul never went up Cordelia Street without a shudder of loathing. His home was next to the house of the Cumberland minister. He approached it tonight with the nerveless sense of defeat, the hopeless feeling of sinking back forever into ugliness and commonness that he had always had when he came home. The moment he turned into Cordelia Street he felt the waters close above his head. After each of these orgies of living, he experienced all the physical depression which follows a debauch; the loathing of respectable beds, of common food, of a house permeated by kitchen odors; a shuddering repulsion for the flavorless, colorless mass of everyday existence; a morbid desire for cool things and soft lights and fresh flowers.

The nearer he approached the house, the more absolutely unequal Paul felt to the sight of it all; his ugly sleeping chamber; the cold bathroom with the grimy zinc tub, the cracked mirror, the dripping spigots; his father, at the top of the stairs, his hairy legs sticking out from his nightshirt, his feet thrust into carpet slippers. He was so much later than usual that there would certainly be inquiries and reproaches. Paul stopped short before the door. He felt that he could not be accosted by his father tonight; that he could not toss again on that miserable bed. He would not go in. He would tell his father that he had no car fare, and it was raining so hard he had gone home with one of the boys and stayed all night.

Meanwhile, he was wet and cold. He went around to the back of the house and tried one of the basement windows, found it open, raised it cautiously, and scrambled down the cellar wall to the floor. There he stood, holding his breath, terrified by the noise he had made; but the floor above him was silent, and there was no creak on the stairs. He found a soap-box, and carried it over to the soft ring of light that streamed from the furnace door, and sat down. He was horribly afraid of rats, so he did not try to sleep, but sat looking distrustfully at the dark, still terrified lest he might have awakened his father. In such reactions, after one of the experiences which made days and nights out of the dreary blanks of the calendar, when his senses were deadened, Paul's head was always singularly clear. Suppose his father had heard him getting in at the window and had come down and shot him for a burglar? Then, again, suppose his father had come down, pistol in hand, and he had cried out in time to save himself, and his father had been horrified to think how nearly he had killed him? Then, again, suppose a day should come when his father would remember that night, and wish there had been no warning cry to stay his hand? With this last supposition Paul entertained himself until daybreak.

The following Sunday was fine; the sodden November chill was broken by the last flash of autumnal summer. In the morning Paul had to go to church and Sabbath school, as always. On seasonable Sunday afternoons the burghers of Cordelia Street usually sat out on their front "stoops," and talked to their neighbors on the next stoop, or called to those across the street in neighborly fashion. The men sat placidly on gay cushions placed upon the steps that led down to the sidewalk, while the women, in their Sunday "waists," sat in rockers on the cramped porches, pretending to be greatly at their ease. The children played in the streets; there were so many of them that the place resembled the recreation grounds of a kindergarten. The men on the steps — all in their shirt sleeves, their vests unbuttoned — sat with their legs well apart, their stomachs comfortably protruding, and talked of the prices of things, or told anecdotes of the sagacity of their various chiefs and overlords. They occasionally looked over the multitude of squabbling children, listened affectionately to their high-pitched, nasal voices, smiling to see their own proclivities reproduced in their offspring, and interspersed their legends of the iron kings with remarks about their sons' progress at school, their grades in arithmetic, and the amounts they had saved in their toy banks. On this last Sunday of November, Paul sat all the afternoon on the lowest step of his "stoop," staring into the street, while his sisters, in their rockers, were talking to the minister's daughters next door about how many shirtwaists they had made in the last week, and how many waffles someone had eaten at the last church supper. When the weather was warm, and his father was in a particularly jovial frame of mind, the girls made lemonade, which was always brought out in a red-glass pitcher, ornamented with forget-me-nots in blue enamel. This the girls thought very fine, and the neighbors joked about the suspicious color of the pitcher.

Today Paul's father, on the top step, was talking to a young man who shifted a restless baby from knee to knee. He happened to be the young man who was daily held up to Paul as a model, and after whom it was his father's dearest hope that he would pattern. This young man was of a ruddy complexion, with a compressed, red mouth, and faded near-sighted eyes, over which he wore thick spectacles, with gold bows that curved about his ears. He was clerk to one of the magnates of a great steel corporation, and was looked upon in Cordelia Street as a young man with a future. There was a story that, some five years ago — he was now barely twenty-six — he had been a trifle "dissipated," but in order to curb his appetites and save the loss of time and strength that a sowing of wild oats might have entailed, he had taken his chief's advice, oft reiterated to his employees, and at twenty-one had married the first woman whom he could persuade to share his fortunes. She happened to be an angular schoolmistress, much older than he, who also wore thick glasses, and who had now borne him four children, all near-sighted, like herself.

The young man was relating how his chief, now cruising in the Mediterranean, kept in touch with all the details of the business, arranging his office hours on his yacht just as though he were at home, and "knocking off work enough to keep two stenographers busy." His father told, in turn, the plan his corporation was considering, of putting in an electric railway plant at Cairo. Paul snapped his teeth; he had an awful apprehension that they might spoil it all before he got there. Yet he rather liked to hear these legends of the iron kings, that were told and retold on Sundays and holidays; these stories of palaces in Venice, yachts on the Mediterranean, and high play at Monte Carlo appealed to his fancy, and he was interested in the triumphs of cash boys who had become famous, though he had no mind for the cash-boy stage.

After supper was over, and he had helped to dry the dishes, Paul nervously asked his father whether he could go to George's to get some help in his geometry, and still more nervously asked for car fare. This latter request he had to repeat, as his father, on principle, did not like to hear requests for money, whether much or little. He asked Paul whether he could not go to some boy who lived nearer, and told him that he ought not to leave his school work until Sunday; but he gave him the dime. He was not a poor man, but he had a worthy ambition to come up in the world. His only reason for allowing Paul to usher was that he thought a boy ought to be earning a little.

Paul bounded upstairs, scrubbed the greasy odor of the dishwater from his hands with the ill-smelling soap he hated, and then shook over his fingers a few drops of violet water from the bottle he kept hidden in his drawer. He left the house with his geometry conspicuously under his arm, and the moment he got out of Cordelia Street and boarded a downtown car, he shook off the lethargy of two deadening days, and began to live again.

The leading juvenile of the permanent stock company which played at one of the downtown theaters was an acquaintance of Paul's, and the boy had been invited to drop in at the Sunday night rehearsals whenever he could. For more than a year Paul had spent every available moment loitering about Charley Edwards's dressing room. He had won a place among Edwards's following not only because the young actor, who could not afford to employ a dresser, often found him useful, but because he recognized in Paul something akin to what churchmen termed "vocation."

It was at the theater and at Carnegie Hall that Paul really lived; the rest was but a sleep and a forgetting. This was Paul's fairy tale, and it had for him all the allurement of a secret love. The moment he inhaled the gassy, painty, dusty odor behind the scenes, he breathed like a prisoner set free, and felt within him the possibility of doing or saying splendid, brilliant things. The moment the cracked orchestra beat out the overture from *Martha*, or jerked at the serenade from *Rigoletto*, all stupid and ugly things slid from him, and his senses were deliciously, yet delicately fired.

Perhaps it was because, in Paul's world, the natural nearly always wore the guise of ugliness, that a certain element of artificiality seemed to him necessary in beauty. Perhaps it was because his experience of life elsewhere was so full of Sabbath-school picnics, petty economies, wholesome advice as to how to succeed in life, and the inescapable odors of cooking, that he found this existence so alluring, these smartly clad men and women so attractive, that he was so moved by these starry apple orchards that bloomed perennially under the limelight.

It would be difficult to put it strongly enough how convincingly the stage entrance of that theater was for Paul the actual portal of Romance. Certainly none of the company ever suspected it, least of all Charley Edwards. It was very like the old stories that used to float about London of fabulously rich Jews, who had subterranean halls, with palms, and fountains, and soft lamps and richly appareled women who never saw the disenchanting light of London day. So, in the midst of that smoke-palled city, enamored of figures and grimy toil, Paul had his secret temple, his wishing-carpet, his bit of blue-and-white Mediterranean shore bathed in perpetual sunshine.

Several of Paul's teachers had a theory that his imagination had been perverted by garish fiction; but the truth was, he scarcely ever read at all. The books at home were not such as would either tempt or corrupt a youthful mind, and as for reading the novels that some of his friends urged upon him — well, he got what he wanted much more quickly from music; any sort of music, from an orchestra to a barrel organ. He needed only the spark, the indescribable thrill that made his imagination master of his senses, and he could make plots and pictures enough of his own. It was equally true that he was not stage-struck — not, at any rate, in the usual acceptation of that expression. He had no desire to become an actor, any more that he had to become a musician. He felt no necessity to do any of these things; what he wanted was to see, to be in the atmosphere, float on the wave of it, to be carried out, blue league after blue league, away from everything.

After a night behind the scenes, Paul found the schoolroom more than ever repulsive; the bare floors and naked walls; the prosy men who never wore frock coats, or violets in their buttonholes; the women with their dull gowns, shrill voices, and pitiful seriousness about prepositions that govern the dative. He could not bear to have the other pupils think, for a moment, that he took these people seriously; he must convey to them that he considered it all trivial, and was there only by way of a joke, anyway. He had autograph pictures of all the members of the stock company which he showed his classmates, telling them the most incredible stories of his familiarity with these people, of his acquaintance with the soloists who came to Carnegie Hall, his suppers with them and the flowers he sent them. When these stories lost their effect, and his audience grew listless, he would bid all the boys good-by, announcing that he was going to travel for a while; going to Naples, to California, to Egypt. Then, next Monday, he would slip back, conscious and nervously smiling, his sister was ill, and he would have to defer his voyage until spring.

Matters went steadily worse with Paul at school. In the itch to let his instructors know how heartily he despised them, and how thoroughly he was appreciated elsewhere, he mentioned once or twice that he had no time to fool with theorems; adding — with a twitch of the eyebrows and a touch of that nervous bravado which so perplexed them — that he was helping the people down at the stock company; they were old friends of his.

The upshot of the matter was, that the Principal went to Paul's father, and Paul was taken out of school and put to work. The manager at Carnegie Hall was told to get another usher in his stead; the doorkeeper at the theater was warned not to admit him to the house; and Charley Edwards remorsefully promised the boy's father not to see him again.

The members of the stock company were vastly amused when some of Paul's stories reached them — especially the women. They were hard-working women, most of them supporting indolent husbands or brothers, and they laughed rather bitterly at having stirred the boy to such fervid and florid inventions. They agreed with the faculty and with his father, that Paul's was a bad case.

The east-bound train was plowing through a January snowstorm; the dull dawn was beginning to show gray when the engine whistled a mile out of Newark. Paul started up from the seat where he had lain curled in uneasy slumber, rubbed the breath-misted window glass with his hand, and peered out. The snow was whirling in curling eddies above the white bottom-lands, and the drifts lay already deep in the fields and along the fences, while here and there the long dead grass and dried weed stalks protruded black above it. Lights shone from the scattered houses, and a gang of laborers who stood beside the track waved their lanterns.

Paul had slept very little and he felt grimy and uncomfortable. He had made the all-night journey in a day coach because he was afraid if he took a Pullman he might be seen by some Pittsburgh business man who had noticed him in Denny & Carson's office. When the whistle woke him, he clutched quickly at his breast pocket, glancing about him with an uncertain smile. But the little, clay-bespattered Italians were still sleeping, the slatternly women across the aisle were in open-mouthed oblivion, and even the crumby, crying babies were for the nonce stilled. Paul settled back to struggle with his impatience as best he could.

When he arrived at the Jersey City station, he hurried through his breakfast, manifestly ill at ease and keeping a sharp eye about him. After he reached the Twenty-third Street station, he consulted a cabman, and had himself driven to a men's furnishing establishment which was just opening for the day. He spent upward of two hours there, buying with endless reconsidering and great care. His new street suit he put on in the fitting room; the frock coat and dress clothes he had bundled into the cab with his new shirts. Then he drove to a hatter's and a shoe house. His next errand was at Tiffany's, where he selected silver-mounted brushes and a scarfpin. He would not wait to have his silver marked, he said. Lastly, he stopped at a trunk shop on Broadway, and had his purchases packed into various traveling bags.

It was a little after one o'clock when he drove up to the Waldorf, and, after settling with the cabman, went into the office. He registered from Washington; said his mother and father had been abroad, and that he had come down to await the arrival of their steamer. He told his story plausibly and had no trouble, since he offered to pay for them in advance, in engaging his rooms; a sleeping-room, sitting room and bath.

Not once, but a hundred times Paul had planned his entry into New York. He had gone over every detail of it with Charley Edwards, and in his scrapbook at home there were pages of description about New York hotels, cut from the Sunday papers.

When he was shown to his sitting room on the eighth floor, he saw at a glance that everything was as it should be; there was but one detail in his mental picture that the place did not realize, so he rang for the bell-boy and sent him down for flowers. He moved about nervously until the boy returned, putting away his new linen and fingering it delightedly as he did so. When the flowers came, he put them hastily into water, and then tumbled into a hot bath. Presently he came out of his white bathroom, resplendent in his new silk underwear, and playing with the tassels of his red robe. The snow was whirling so fiercely outside his windows that he could scarcely see across the street; but within, the air was deliciously soft and fragrant. He put the violets and jonquils on the tabouret beside the couch, and threw himself down with a long sigh, covering himself with a Roman blanket. He was thoroughly tired; he had been in such haste, he had stood up to such a strain, covered so much ground in the last twenty-four hours, that he wanted to think how it had all come about. Lulled by the sound of the wind, the warm air, and the cool fragrance of the flowers, he sank into deep, drowsy retrospection.

It had been wonderfully simple; when they had shut him out of the theater and concert hall, when they had taken away his bone, the whole thing was virtually determined. The rest was a mere matter of opportunity. The only thing that at all surprised him was his own courage — for he realized well enough that he had always been tormented by fear, a sort of apprehensive dread that, of late years, as the meshes of the lies he had told closed about him, had been pulling the muscles of his body tighter and tighter. Until now, he could not remember a time when he had not been dreading something. Even when he was a little boy, it was always there — behind him, or before, or on either side. There had always been the shadowed corner, the dark place into which he dared not look, but from which something seemed always to be watching him — and Paul had done things that were not pretty to watch, he knew.

But now he had a curious sense of relief, as though he had at last thrown down the gauntlet to the thing in the corner.

Yet it was but a day since he had been sulking in the traces; but yesterday afternoon that he had been sent to the bank with Denny & Carson's deposit, as usual — but this time he was instructed to leave the book to be balanced. There was above two thousand dollars in checks, and nearly a thousand in the bank notes which he had taken from the book and quietly transferred to his pocket. At the bank he had made out a new deposit slip. His nerves had been steady enough to permit of his returning to the office, where he had finished his work and asked for a full day's holiday tomorrow, Saturday, giving a perfectly reasonable pretext. The bank book, he knew, would not be returned before Monday or Tuesday, and his father would be out of town for the next week. From the time he slipped the bank notes into his pocket until he boarded the night train for New York, he had not known a moment's hesitation.

How astonishingly easy it had all been; here he was, the thing done; and this time there would be no awakening, no figure at the top of the stairs. He watched the snowflakes whirling by his window until he fell asleep.

When he awoke, it was four o'clock in the afternoon. He bounded up with a start; one of his precious days gone already! He spent nearly an hour in dressing, watching every stage of his toilet carefully in the mirror. Everything was quite perfect; he was exactly the kind of boy he had always wanted to be.

When he went downstairs, Paul took a carriage and drove up Fifth Avenue toward the Park. The snow had somewhat abated; carriages and tradesmen's wagons were hurrying soundlessly to and fro in the winter twilight; boys in woolen mufflers were shoveling off the doorsteps; the avenue stages made fine spots of color against the white street. Here and there on the corners whole flower gardens blooming behind glass windows, against which the snowflakes stuck and melted; violets, roses, carnations, lilies of the valley — somehow vastly more lovely and alluring that they blossomed thus unnaturally in the snow. The Park itself was a wonderful stage winter-piece.

When he returned, the pause of the twilight had ceased, and the tune of the streets had changed. The snow was falling faster, lights streamed from the hotels that reared their many stories fearlessly up into the storm, defying the raging Atlantic winds. A long, black stream of carriages poured down the avenue, intersected here and there by other streams, tending horizontally. There were a score of cabs about the entrance of his hotel, and his driver had to wait. Boys in livery were running in and out of the awning stretched across the sidewalk, up and down the red velvet carpet laid from the door to the street. Above, about, within it all, were the rumble and roar, the hurry and toss of thousands of human beings as hot for pleasure as himself, and on every side of him towered the glaring affirmation of the omnipotence of wealth.

The boy set his teeth and drew his shoulders together in a spasm of realization; the plot of all dramas, the text of all romances, the nerve-stuff of all sensations was whirling about him like the snow flakes. He burnt like a faggot in a tempest.

When Paul came down to dinner, the music of the orchestra floated up the elevator shaft to greet him. As he stepped into the thronged corridor, he sank back into one of the chairs against the wall to get his breath. The lights, the chatter, the perfumes, the bewildering medley of color — he had, for a moment, the feeling of not being able to stand it. But only for a moment; these were his own people, he told himself. He went slowly about the corridors, through the writing rooms, smoking rooms, reception rooms, as though he were exploring the chambers of an enchanted palace, built and peopled for him alone.

When he reached the dining room he sat down at a table near a window. The flowers, the white linen, the many-colored wine glasses, the gay toilettes of the women, the low popping of corks, the undulating repetitions of the *Blue Danube* from the orchestra, all flooded Paul's dream with bewildering radiance. When the roseate tinge of his champagne was added — that cold, precious, bubbling stuff that creamed and foamed in his glass — Paul wondered that there were honest men in the world at all. This was what all the world was fighting for, he reflected; this was what all the struggle was about. He doubted the reality of his past. Had he ever known a place called Cordelia Street, a place where fagged-looking business men boarded the early car? Mere rivets in a machine they seemed to Paul — sickening men, with combings of children's hair always hanging to their coats, and the smell of cooking in their clothes. Cordelia Street — Ah, that belonged to another time and country! Had he not always been thus, had he not sat here night after night, from as far back as he could remember, looking pensively over just such shimmering textures, and slowly twirling the stem of a glass like this one between his thumb and middle finger? He rather thought he had.

He was not in the least abashed or lonely. He had no especial desire to meet or to know any of these people; all he demanded was the right to look on and conjecture, to watch the pageant. The mere stage properties were all he contended for. Nor was he lonely later in the evening, in his loge at the Opera. He was entirely rid of his nervous misgivings, of his forced aggressiveness, of the imperative desire to show himself different from his surroundings. He felt now that his surroundings explained him. Nobody questioned the purple; he had only to wear it passively. He had only to glance down at his dress coat to reassure himself that here it would be impossible for anyone to humiliate him.

He found it hard to leave his beautiful sitting room to go to bed that night, and sat long watching the raging storm from his turret window. When he went to sleep, it was with the lights turned on in his bedroom; partly because of his old timidity, and partly so that, if he should wake in the night, there would be no wretched moment of doubt, no horrible suspicion of yellow wallpaper, or of Washington and Calvin above his bed.

On Sunday morning the city was practically snowbound. Paul breakfasted late, and in the afternoon he fell in with a wild San Francisco boy, a freshman at Yale, who said he had run down for a "little flyer" over Sunday. The young man offered to show Paul the night side of the town, and the two boys went off together after dinner, not returning to the hotel until seven o'clock the next morning. They had started out in the confiding warmth of a champagne friendship, but their parting in the elevator was singularly cool. The freshman pulled himself together to make his train, and Paul went to bed. He awoke at two o'clock in the afternoon, very thirsty and dizzy, and rang for ice water, coffee and the Pittsburgh papers.

On the part of the hotel management, Paul excited no suspicion. There was this to be said for him, that he wore his spoils with dignity and in no way made himself conspicuous. His chief greediness lay in his ears and eyes, and his excesses were not offensive ones. His dearest pleasures were the gray winter twilights in his sitting room; his quiet enjoyment of his flowers, his clothes, his wide divan, his cigarette and his sense of power. He could not remember a time when he had felt so at peace with himself. The mere release from the necessity of petty lying, lying every day and every day, restored his self-respect. He had never lied for pleasure, even at school; but to make himself noticed and admired, to assert his difference from other Cordelia Street boys; and he felt a good deal more manly, more honest, even, now that he had no need for boastful pretensions, now that he could, as his actor friends used to say, "dress the part." It was characteristic that remorse did not occur to him. His golden days went by without a shadow, and he made each as perfect as he could.

On the eighth day after his arrival in New York, he found the whole affair exploited in the Pittsburgh papers, exploited with a wealth of detail which indicated that local news of a sensational nature was at a low ebb. The firm of Denny & Carson announced that the boy's father had refunded the full amount of his theft, and that they had no intention of prosecuting. The Cumberland minister had been interviewed, and expressed his hope of yet reclaiming the motherless lad, and Paul's Sabbath-school teacher declared that she would spare no effort to that end. The rumor had reached Pittsburgh that the boy had been seen in a New York hotel, and his father had gone East to find him and bring him home.

Paul had just come in to dress for dinner; he sank into a chair, weak in the knees, and clasped his head in his hands. It was to be worse than jail, even; the tepid waters of Cordelia Street were to close over him finally and forever. The gray monotony stretched before him in hopeless, unrelieved years; Sabbath school, Young Peoples' Meeting, the yellow-papered room, the damp dish-towels; it all rushed back upon him with sickening vividness. He had the old feeling that the orchestra had suddenly stopped, the sinking sensation that the play was over. The sweat broke out on his face, and he sprang to his feet, looked about him with his white, conscious smile, and winked at himself in the mirror. With something of the childish belief in miracles with which he had so often gone to class, all his lessons unlearned, Paul dressed and dashed whistling down the corridor to the elevator.

He had no sooner entered the dining room and caught the measure of the music, than his remembrance was lightened by his old elastic power of claiming the moment, mounting with it, and finding it all sufficient. The glare and glitter about him, the mere scenic accessories had again, and for the last time, their old potency. He would show himself that he was game, he would finish the thing splendidly. He doubted, more than ever, the existence of Cordelia Street, and for the first time he drank his wine recklessly. Was he not, after all, one of these fortunate beings? Was he not still himself, and in his own place? He drummed a nervous accompaniment to the music and looked about him, telling himself over and over that it had paid.

He reflected drowsily, to the swell of the violin and the chill sweetness of his wine, that he might have done it more wisely. He might have caught an outbound steamer and been well out of their clutches before now. But the other side of the world had seemed too far away and too uncertain then; he could not have waited for it; his need had been too sharp. If he had to choose over again, he would do the same thing to-morrow. He looked affectionately about the dining room, now gilded with a soft mist. Ah, it had paid indeed!

Paul was awakened next morning by a painful throbbing in his head and feet. He had thrown himself across the bed without undressing, and had slept with his shoes on. His limbs and hands were lead heavy, and his tongue and throat were parched. There came upon him one of those fateful attacks of clear-headedness that never occurred except when he was physically exhausted and his nerves hung loose. He lay still and closed his eyes and let the tide of realities wash over him.

His father was in New York; "stopping at some joint or other," he told himself. The memory of successive summers on the front stoop fell upon him like a weight of black water. He had not a hundred dollars left; and he knew now, more than ever, that money was everything, the wall that stood between all he loathed and all he wanted. The thing was winding itself up; he had thought of that on his first glorious day in New York, and had even provided a way to snap the thread. It lay on his dressing table now; he had got it out last night when he came blindly up from dinner — but the shiny metal hurt his eyes, and he disliked the look of it, anyway.

He rose and moved about with a painful effort, succumbing now and again to attacks of nausea. It was the old depression exaggerated; all the world had become Cordelia Street. Yet somehow he was not afraid of anything, was absolutely calm; perhaps because he had looked into the dark corner at last, and knew. It was bad enough, what he saw there; but somehow not so bad as his long fear of it had been. He saw everything clearly now. He had a feeling that he had made the best of it, that he had lived the sort of life he was meant to live, and for half an hour he sat staring at the revolver point. But he told himself that was not the way, so he went downstairs and took a cab to the ferry.

When Paul arrived at Newark, he got off the train and took another cab, directing the driver to follow the Pennsylvania tracks out of the town. The snow lay heavy on the roadways and had drifted deep in the open fields. Only here and there the dead grass or dried weed stalks projected, singularly black, above it. Once well into the country, Paul dismissed the carriage and walked, floundering along the tracks, his mind a medley of irrelevant things. He seemed to hold in his brain an actual picture of everything he had seen that morning. He remembered every feature of both his drivers, the toothless old woman from whom he had bought the red flowers in his coat, the agent from whom he had got his ticket, and all of his fellow passengers on the ferry. His mind, unable to cope with vital matters near at hand, worked feverishly and deftly at sorting and grouping these images. They made for him a part of the ugliness of the world, of the ache in his head, and the bitter burning on his tongue. He stooped and put a handful of snow into his mouth as he walked, but that, too, seemed hot. When he reached a little hillside, where the tracks ran through a cut some twenty feet below him, he stopped and sat down.

The carnations in his coat were drooping with the cold, he noticed; all their red glory over. It occurred to him that all the flowers he had seen in the show windows that first night must have gone the same way, long before this. It was only one splendid breath they had, in spite of their brave mockery at the winter outside the glass. It was a losing game in the end, it seemed, this revolt against the homilies by which the world is run. Paul took one of the blossoms carefully from his coat and scooped a little hole in the snow, where he covered it up. Then he dozed a while, from his weak condition, seeming insensible to the cold.

The sound of an approaching train woke him, and he started to his feet, remembering only his resolution, and afraid lest he should be too late. He stood watching the approaching locomotive, his teeth chattering, his lips drawn away from them in a frightened smile; once or twice he glanced nervously sidewise, as though he were being watched. When the right moment came, he jumped. As he fell, the folly of his haste occurred to him with merciless clearness, the vastness of what he had left undone. There flashed through his brain, clearer than ever before, the blue of Adriatic water, the yellow of Algerian sands.

He felt something strike his chest — his body was being thrown swiftly through the air, on and on, immeasurably far and fast, while his limbs gently relaxed. Then, because the picture-making mechanism was crushed, the disturbing visions flashed into black, and Paul dropped back into the immense design of things.

1905

JACQUES FUTRELLE

....

The Problem of Cell 13

PRACTICALLY ALL THOSE LETTERS remaining in the alphabet after Augustus S.F.X. Van Dusen was named were afterward acquired by that gentleman in the course of a brilliant scientific career, and, being honorably acquired, were tacked on to the other end. His name, therefore, taken with all that belonged to it, was a wonderfully imposing structure. He was a Ph.D., an LL.D., an F.R.S., an M.D., and an M.D.S. He was also some other things — just what he himself couldn't say — through recognition of his ability by various foreign educational and scientific institutions.

In appearance he was no less striking than in nomenclature. He was slender with the droop of the student in his thin shoulders and the pallor of a close, sedentary life on his clean-shaven face. His eyes wore a perpetual, forbidding squint — the squint of a man who studies little things — and when they could be seen at all through his thick spectacles, were mere slits of watery blue. But above his eyes was his most striking feature. This was a tall, broad brow, almost abnormal in height and width, crowned by a heavy shock of bushy, yellow hair. All these things conspired to give him a peculiar, almost grotesque, personality.

Professor Van Dusen was remotely German. For generations his ancestors had been noted in the sciences; he was the logical result, the mastermind. First and above all he was a logician. At least thirty-five years of the half century or so of his existence had been devoted exclusively to proving that two and two always equal four, except in unusual cases, where they equal three or five, as the case may be. He stood broadly on the general proposition that all things that start must go somewhere, and was able to bring the concentrated mental force of his forefathers to bear on a given problem. Incidentally it may be remarked that Professor Van Dusen wore a No. 8 hat.

The world at large had heard vaguely of Professor Van Dusen as The Thinking Machine. It was a newspaper catchphrase applied to him at the time of a remarkable exhibition at chess; he had demonstrated then that a stranger to the game might, by the force of inevitable logic, defeat a champion who had devoted a lifetime to its study. The Thinking Machine! Perhaps that more nearly described him than all his honorary initials, for he spent week after week, month after month, in the seclusion of his small laboratory from which had gone forth thoughts that staggered scientific associates and deeply stirred the world at large.

It was only occasionally that The Thinking Machine had visitors, and these were usually men who, themselves high in the sciences, dropped in to argue a point and perhaps convince themselves. Two of these men, Dr. Charles Ransome and Alfred Fielding, called one evening to discuss some theory which is not of consequence here.

"Such a thing is impossible," declared Dr. Ransome emphatically, in the course of the conversation.

"Nothing is impossible," declared The Thinking Machine with equal emphasis. He always spoke petulantly. "The mind is master of all things. When science fully recognizes that fact a great advance will have been made."

"How about the airship?" asked Dr. Ransome.

"That's not impossible at all," asserted The Thinking Machine. "It will be invented sometime. I'd do it myself, but I'm busy."

Dr. Ransome laughed tolerantly.

"I've heard you say such things before," he said. "But they mean nothing. Mind may be master of matter, but it hasn't yet found a way to apply itself. There are some things that can't be *thought* out of existence, or rather which would not yield to any amount of thinking."

"What, for instance?" demanded The Thinking Machine.

Dr. Ransome was thoughtful for a moment as he smoked.

"Well, say prison walls," he replied. "No man can *think* himself out of a cell. If he could, there would be no prisoners."

"A man can so apply his brain and ingenuity that he can leave a cell, which is the same thing," snapped The Thinking Machine.

Dr. Ransome was slightly amused.

"Let's suppose a case," he said, after a moment. "Take a cell where prisoners under sentence of death are confined — men who are desperate and, maddened by fear, would take any chance to escape — suppose you were locked in such a cell. Could you escape?"

"Certainly," declared The Thinking Machine.

"Of course," said Mr. Fielding, who entered the conversation for the first time, "you might wreck the cell with an explosive — but inside, a prisoner, you couldn't have that."

"There would be nothing of that kind," said The Thinking Machine. "You might treat me precisely as you treated prisoners under sentence of death, and I would leave the cell."

"Not unless you entered it with tools prepared to get out," said Dr. Ransome.

The Thinking Machine was visibly annoyed and his blue eyes snapped.

"Lock me in any cell in any prison anywhere at any time, wearing only what is necessary, and I'll escape in a week," he declared, sharply.

Dr. Ransome sat up straight in the chair, interested. Mr. Fielding lighted a new cigar.

"You mean you could actually *think* yourself out?" asked Dr. Ransome.

"I would get out," was the response.

"Are you serious?"

"Certainly I am serious."

Dr. Ransome and Mr. Fielding were silent for a long time.

"Would you be willing to try it?" asked Mr. Fielding, finally.

"Certainly," said Professor Van Dusen, and there was a trace of irony in his voice. "I have done more asinine things than that to convince other men of less important truths."

The tone was offensive and there was an undercurrent strongly resembling anger on both sides. Of course it was an absurd thing, but Professor Van Dusen reiterated his willingness to undertake the escape and it was decided upon.

"To begin now," added Dr. Ransome.

"I'd prefer that it begin tomorrow," said The Thinking Machine, "because —"

"No, now," said Mr. Fielding, flatly. "You are arrested, figuratively, of course, without any warning locked in a cell with no chance to communicate with friends, and left there with identically the same care and attention that would be given to a man under sentence of death. Are you willing?"

"All right, now, then," said The Thinking Machine, and he arose.

"Say, the death cell in Chisholm Prison."

"The death cell in Chisholm Prison."

"And what will you wear?"

"As little as possible," said The Thinking Machine. "Shoes, stockings, trousers, and a shirt."

"You will permit yourself to be searched, of course?"

"I am to be treated precisely as all prisoners are treated," said The Thinking Machine. "No more attention and no less."

There were some preliminaries to be arranged in the matter of obtaining permission for the test, but all three were influential men and everything was done satisfactorily by telephone, albeit the prison commissioners, to whom the experiment was explained on purely scientific grounds, were sadly bewildered. Professor Van Dusen would be the most distinguished prisoner they had ever entertained.

When The Thinking Machine had donned those things which he was to wear during his incarceration he called the little old woman who was his housekeeper, cook, and maidservant all in one.

"Martha," he said, "it is now twenty-seven minutes past nine o'clock. I am going away. One week from tonight, at half past nine, these gentlemen and one, possibly two, others will take supper with me here. Remember Dr. Ransome is very fond of artichokes."

The three men were driven to Chisholm Prison, where the warden was awaiting them, having been informed of the matter by telephone. He understood merely that the eminent Professor Van Dusen was to be his prisoner, if he could keep him, for one week; that he had committed no crime, but that he was to be treated as all other prisoners were treated.

"Search him," instructed Dr. Ransome.

The Thinking Machine was searched. Nothing was found on him; the pockets of the trousers were empty; the white, stiff-bosomed shirt had no pocket. The shoes and stockings were removed, examined, then replaced. As he watched all these preliminaries, and noted the pitiful, childlike physical weakness of the man — the colorless face, and the thin, white hands — Dr. Ransome almost regretted his part in the affair.

"Are you sure you want to do this?" he asked.

"Would you be convinced if I did not?" inquired The Thinking Machine in turn.

"No."

"All right, I'll do it."

What sympathy Dr. Ransome had was dissipated by the tone. It nettled him, and he resolved to see the experiment to the end; it would be a stinging reproof to egotism.

"It will be impossible for him to communicate with anyone outside?" he asked.

"Absolutely impossible," replied the warden. "He will not be permitted writing materials of any sort."

"And your jailers, would they deliver a message from him?"

"Not one word, directly or indirectly," said the warden. "You may rest assured of that. They will report anything he might say or turn over to me, anything he might give them."

"That seems entirely satisfactory," said Mr. Fielding, who was frankly interested in the problem.

"Of course, in the event he fails," said Dr. Ransome, "and asks for his liberty, you understand you are to set him free?"

"I understand," replied the warden.

The Thinking Machine stood listening, but had nothing to say until this was all ended, then:

"I should like to make three small requests. You may grant them or not, as you wish."

"No special favors, now," warned Mr. Fielding.

"I am asking none," was the stiff response. "I should like to have some tooth powder — buy it yourself to see that it is tooth powder — and I should like to have one five-dollar and two ten-dollar bills."

Dr. Ransome, Mr. Fielding, and the warden exchanged astonished glances. They were not surprised at the request for tooth powder, but were at the request for money.

"Is there any man with whom our friend would come in contact that he could bribe with twenty-five dollars?"

"Not for twenty-five hundred dollars," was the positive reply.

"Well, let him have them," said Mr. Fielding. "I think they are harmless enough."

"And what is the third request?" asked Dr. Ransome.

"I should like to have my shoes polished."

Again the astonished glances were exchanged. This last request was the height of absurdity, so they agreed to it. These things all being attended to, The Thinking Machine was led back into the prison from which he had undertaken to escape.

"Here is Cell Thirteen," said the warden, stopping three doors down the steel corridor. "This is where we keep condemned murderers. No one can leave it without my permission; and no one in it can communicate with the outside. I'll stake my reputation on that. It's only three doors back of my office and I can readily hear any unusual noise."

"Will this cell do, gentlemen?" asked The Thinking Machine. There was a touch of irony in his voice.

"Admirably," was the reply.

The heavy steel door was thrown open, there was a great scurrying and scampering of tiny feet, and The Thinking Machine passed into the gloom of the cell. Then the door was closed and double-locked by the warden.

"What is that noise in there?" asked Dr. Ransome, through the bars.

"Rats — dozens of them," replied The Thinking Machine, tersely.

The three men, with final good nights, were turning away when The Thinking Machine called:

"What time is it exactly, Warden?"

"Eleven-seventeen," replied the warden.

"Thanks. I will join you gentlemen in your office at half past eight o'clock one week from tonight," said The Thinking Machine.

"And if you do not?"

"There is no 'if' about it."

Chisholm Prison was a great, spreading structure of granite, four stories in all, which stood in the center of acres of open space. It was surrounded by a wall of solid masonry eighteen feet high, and so smoothly finished inside and out as to offer no foothold to a climber, no matter how expert. Atop this fence, as a further precaution, was a five-foot fence of steel rods, each terminating in a keen point. This fence in itself marked an absolute deadline between freedom and imprisonment, for, even if a man escaped from his cell, it would seem impossible for him to pass the wall.

The yard, which on all sides of the prison building was twenty-five feet wide, that being the distance from the building to the wall, was by day an exercise ground for those prisoners to whom was granted the boon of occasional semi-liberty. But that was not for those in Cell 13. At all times of the day there were armed guards in the yard, four of them, one patrolling each side of the prison building.

By night the yard was almost as brilliantly lighted as by day. On each of the four sides was a great arc light which rose above the prison wall and gave to the guards a clear sight. The lights, too, brightly illuminated the spiked top of the wall. The wires which fed the arc lights ran up the side of the prison building on insulators and from the top story led out to the poles supporting the arc lights.

All these things were seen and comprehended by The Thinking Machine, who was only enabled to see out his closely barred cell window by standing on his bed. This was on the morning following his incarceration. He gathered, too, that the river lay over there beyond the wall somewhere, because he heard faintly the pulsation of a motor boat and high up in the air saw a river bird. From that same direction came the shouts of boys at play and the occasional crack of a batted ball. He knew then that between the prison wall and the river was an open space, a playground.

Chisholm Prison was regarded as absolutely safe. No man had ever escaped from it. The Thinking Machine, from his perch on the bed, seeing what he saw, could readily understand why. The walls of the cell, though built he judged twenty years before, were perfectly solid, and the window bars of new iron had not a shadow of rust on them. The window itself, even with the bars out, would be a difficult mode of egress because it was small.

Yet, seeing these things, The Thinking Machine was not discouraged. Instead, he thoughtfully squinted at the great arc light — there was bright sunlight now — and traced with his eyes the wire which led from it to the building. That electric wire, he reasoned, must come down the side of the building not a great distance from his cell. That might be worth knowing.

Cell 13 was on the same floor with the offices of the prison — that is, not in the basement, nor yet upstairs. There were only four steps up to the office floor, therefore the level of the floor must be only three or four feet above ground. He couldn't see the ground directly beneath his window, but he could see it further out toward the wall. It would be an easy drop from the window. Well and good.

Then The Thinking Machine fell to remembering how he had come to the cell. First, there was the outside guard's booth, a part of the wall. There were two heavily barred gates there, both of steel. At this gate was one man always on guard. He admitted persons to the prison after much clanking of keys and locks, and let them out when ordered to do so. The warden's office was in the prison building, and in order to reach that official from the prison yard one had to pass a gate of solid steel with only a peephole in it. Then coming from that inner office to Cell 13, where he was now, one must pass a heavy wooden door and two steel doors into the corridors of the prison; and always there was the double-locked door of Cell 13 to reckon with.

There were then, The Thinking Machine recalled, seven doors to be overcome before one could pass from Cell 13 into the outer world, a free man. But against this was the fact that he was rarely interrupted. A jailer appeared at his cell door at six in the morning with a breakfast of prison fare; he would come again at noon, and again at six in the afternoon. At nine o'clock at night would come the inspection hour. That would be all.

"It's admirably arranged, this prison system," was the mental tribute paid by The Thinking Machine. "I'll have to study it a little when I get out. I had no idea there was such great care exercised in the prisons."

There was nothing, positively nothing, in his cell, except his iron bed, so firmly put together that no man could tear it to pieces save with sledges or a file. He had neither of these. There was not even a chair, or a small table, or a bit of tin or crockery. Nothing! The jailer stood by when he ate, then took away the wooden spoon and bowl which he had used.

One by one these things sank into the brain of The Thinking Machine. When the last possibility had been considered he began an examination of his cell. From the roof, down the walls on all sides, he examined the stones and the cement between them. He stamped over the floor carefully time after time, but it was cement, perfectly solid. After the examination he sat on the edge of the iron bed and was lost in thought for a long time. For Professor Augustus S.F.X. Van Dusen, The Thinking Machine, had something to think about.

He was disturbed by a rat, which ran across his foot, then scampered away into a dark corner of the cell, frightened by its own daring. After a while The Thinking Machine, squinting steadily into the darkness of the corner where the rat had gone, was able to make out in the gloom many little beady eyes staring at him. He counted six pair, and there were perhaps others; he didn't see very well.

Then The Thinking Machine, from his seat on the bed, noticed for the first time the bottom of his cell door. There was an opening there of two inches between the steel bar and the floor. Still looking steadily at this opening, The Thinking Machine backed suddenly into the corner where he had seen the beady eyes. There was a great scampering of tiny feet, several squeaks of frightened rodents, and then silence.

None of the rats had gone out the door, yet there were none in the cell. Therefore there must be another way out of the cell, however small. The Thinking Machine, on hands and knees, started a search for this spot, feeling in the darkness with his long, slender fingers.

At last his search was rewarded. He came upon a small opening in the floor, level with the cement. It was perfectly round and somewhat larger than a silver dollar. This was the way the rats had gone. He put his fingers deep into the opening; it seemed to be a disused drainage pipe and was dry and dusty.

Having satisfied himself on this point, he sat on the bed again for an hour, then made another inspection of his surroundings through the small cell window. One of the outside guards stood directly opposite, beside the wall, and happened to be looking at the window of Cell 13 when the head of The Thinking Machine appeared. But the scientist didn't notice the guard.

Noon came and the jailer appeared with the prison dinner of repulsively plain food. At home The Thinking Machine merely ate to live; here he took what was offered without comment. Occasionally he spoke to the jailer who stood outside the door watching him.

"Any improvements made here in the last few years?" he asked.

"Nothing particularly," replied the jailer. "New wall was built four years ago."

"Anything done to the prison proper?"

"Painted the woodwork outside, and I believe about seven years ago a new system of plumbing was put in."

"Ah!" said the prisoner. "How far is the river over there?"

"About three hundred feet. The boys have a baseball ground between the wall and the river."

The Thinking Machine had nothing further to say just then, but when the jailer was ready to go he asked for some water.

"I get very thirsty here," he explained. "Would it be possible for you to leave a little water in a bowl for me?"

"I'll ask the warden," replied the jailer, and he went away.

Half an hour later he returned with water in a small earthen bowl.

"The warden says you may keep this bowl," he informed the prisoner. "But you must show it to me when I ask for it. If it is broken, it will be the last."

"Thank you," said The Thinking Machine. "I shan't break it."

The jailer went on about his duties. For just the fraction of a second it seemed that The Thinking Machine wanted to ask a question, but he didn't.

Two hours later this same jailer, in passing the door of Cell No. 13, heard a noise inside and stopped. The Thinking Machine was down on his hands and knees in a corner of the cell, and from that same corner came several frightened squeaks. The jailer looked on interestedly.

"Ah, I've got you," he heard the prisoner say.

"Got what?" he asked, sharply.

"One of these rats," was the reply. "See?" And between the scientist's long fingers the jailer saw a small gray rat struggling. The prisoner brought it over to the light and looked at it closely.

"It's a water rat," he said.

"Ain't you got anything better to do than to catch rats?" asked the jailer.

"It's disgraceful that they should be here at all," was the irritated reply. "Take this one away and kill it. There are dozens more where it came from."

The jailer took the wriggling, squirmy rodent and flung it down on the floor violently. It gave one squeak and lay still. Later he reported the incident to the warden, who only smiled.

Still later that afternoon the outside armed guard on the Cell 13 side of the prison looked up again at the window and saw the prisoner looking out. He saw a hand raised to the barred window and then something white fluttered to the ground, directly under the window of Cell 13. It was a little roll of linen, evidently of white shirting material, and tied around it was a five-dollar bill. The guard looked up at the window again, but the face had disappeared.

With a grim smile he took the little linen roll and the five-dollar bill to the warden's office. There together they deciphered something which was written on it with a queer sort of ink, frequently blurred. On the outside was this:

"Finder of this please deliver to Dr. Charles Ransome."

"Ah," said the warden, with a chuckle. "Plan of escape number one has gone wrong." Then, as an afterthought: "But why did he address it to Dr. Ransome?"

"And where did he get the pen and ink to write with?" asked the guard.

The warden looked at the guard and the guard looked at the warden. There was no apparent solution of that mystery. The warden studied the writing carefully, then shook his head.

"Well, let's see what he was going to say to Dr. Ransome," he said at length, still puzzled, and he unrolled the inner piece of linen.

"Well, if that — what — what do you think of that?" he asked, dazed.

The guard took the bit of linen and read this:
"*Epa cseot d'net niiy awe htto n'si sih. T.*"

The warden spent an hour wondering what sort of a cipher it was, and half an hour wondering why his prisoner should attempt to communicate with Dr. Ransome, who was the cause of his being there. After this the warden devoted some thought to the question of where the prisoner got writing materials, and what sort of writing materials he had. With the idea of illuminating this point, he examined the linen again. It was torn apart of a white shirt and had ragged edges.

Now it was possible to account for the linen, but what the prisoner had used to write with was another matter. The warden knew it would have been impossible for him to have either pen or pencil, and, besides, neither pen nor pencil had been used in this writing. What, then? The warden decided to investigate personally. The Thinking Machine was his prisoner; he had orders to hold his prisoners; if this one sought to escape by sending cipher messages to persons outside, he would stop it, as he would have stopped it in the case of any other prisoner.

The warden went back to Cell 13 and found The Thinking Machine on his hands and knees on the floor, engaged in nothing more alarming than catching rats. The prisoner heard the warden's step and turned to him quickly.

"It's disgraceful," he snapped, "these rats. There are scores of them."

"Other men have been able to stand them," said the warden. "Here is another shirt for you — let me have the one you have on."

"Why?" demanded The Thinking Machine, quickly. His tone was hardly natural, his manner suggested actual perturbation.

"You have attempted to communicate with Dr. Ransome," said the warden severely. "As my prisoner, it is my duty to put a stop to it."

The Thinking Machine was silent for a moment.

"All right," he said, finally. "Do your duty."

The warden smiled grimly. The prisoner arose from the floor and removed the white shirt the warden had brought. The warden took the white shirt eagerly, and then and there compared the pieces of linen on which was written the cipher with certain torn places in the shirt. The Thinking Machine looked on curiously.

"The guard brought *you* those, then?" he asked.

"He certainly did," replied the warden triumphantly. "And that ends your first attempt to escape."

The Thinking Machine watched the warden as he, by comparison, established to his own satisfaction that only two pieces of linen had been torn from the white shirt.

"What did you write this with?" demanded the warden.

"I should think it a part of your duty to find out," said The Thinking Machine, irritably.

The warden started to say some harsh things, then restrained himself and made a minute search of the cell and of the prisoner instead. He found absolutely nothing; not even a match or toothpick which might have been used for a pen. The same mystery surrounded the fluid with which the cipher had been written. Although the warden left Cell 13 visibly annoyed, he took the torn shirt in triumph.

"Well, writing notes on a shirt won't get him out, that's certain," he told himself with some complacency. He put the linen scraps into his desk to await developments. "If that man escapes from that cell I'll — hang it — I'll resign."

On the third day of his incarceration The Thinking Machine openly attempted to bribe his way out. The jailer had brought his dinner and was leaning against the barred door, waiting, when The Thinking Machine began the conversation.

"The drainage pipes of the prison lead to the river, don't they?" he asked.

"Yes," said the jailer.

"I suppose they are very small."

"Too small to crawl through, if that's what you're thinking about," was the grinning response.

There was silence until The Thinking Machine finished his meal. Then:

"You know I'm not a criminal, don't you?"

"Yes."

"And that I've a perfect right to be freed if I demand it?"

"Yes."

"Well, I came here believing that I could make my escape," said the prisoner, and his squint eyes studied the face of the jailer. "Would you consider a financial reward for aiding me to escape?"

The jailer, who happened to be an honest man, looked at the slender, weak figure of the prisoner, at the large head with its mass of yellow hair, and was almost sorry.

"I guess prisons like these were not built for the likes of you to get out of," he said, at last.

"But would you consider a proposition to help me get out?" the prisoner insisted, almost beseechingly.

"No," said the jailer, shortly.

"Five hundred dollars," urged The Thinking Machine. "I am not a criminal."

"No," said the jailer.

"A thousand?"

"No," again said the jailer, and he started away hurriedly to escape further temptation. Then he turned back. "If you should give me ten thousand dollars I couldn't get you out. You'd have to pass through seven doors, and I only have the keys to two."

Then he told the warden all about it.

"Plan number two fails," said the warden, smiling grimly. "First a cipher, then bribery."

When the jailer was on his way to Cell 13 at six o'clock, again bearing food to The Thinking Machine, he paused, startled by the unmistakable scrape, scrape of steel against steel. It stopped at the sound of his steps, then craftily the jailer, who was beyond the prisoner's range of vision, resumed his tramping, the sound apparently that of a man going away from Cell 13. As a matter of fact he was in the same spot.

After a moment there came again the steady scrape, scrape, and the jailer crept cautiously on tiptoes to the door and peered between the bars. The Thinking Machine was standing on the iron bed working at the bars of the little window. He was using a file, judging from the backward and forward swing of his arms.

Cautiously the jailer crept back to the office, summoned the warden in person, and they returned to Cell 13 on tiptoes. The steady scrape was still audible. The warden listened to satisfy himself and then suddenly appeared at the door.

"Well?" he demanded, and there was a smile on his face.

The Thinking Machine glanced back from his perch on the bed and leaped to the floor, making frantic efforts to hide something. The warden went in, with hand extended.

"Give it up," he said.

"No," said the prisoner, sharply.

"Come, give it up," urged the warden. "I don't want to have to search you again."

"No," repeated the prisoner.

"What was it — a file?" asked the warden.

The Thinking Machine was silent and stood squinting at the warden with something very nearly approaching disappointment on his face — nearly, but not quite. The warden was almost sympathetic.

"Plan number three fails, eh?" he asked, good-naturedly. "Too bad, isn't it?"

The prisoner didn't say.

"Search him," instructed the warden.

The jailer searched the prisoner carefully. At last, artfully concealed in the waistband of the trousers, he found a piece of steel about two inches long, with one side curved like a half moon.

"Ah," said the warden, as he received it from the jailer, "from your shoe heel," and he smiled pleasantly.

The jailer continued his search and on the other side of the trousers waistband found another piece of steel identical with the first. The edge showed where they had been worn against the bars of the window.

"You couldn't saw a way through those bars with these," said the warden.

"I could have," said The Thinking Machine firmly.

"In six months, perhaps," said the warden, good-naturedly.

The warden shook his head slowly as he gazed into the slightly flushed face of his prisoner.

"Ready to give it up?" he asked.

"I haven't started yet," was the prompt reply.

Then came another extensive search of the cell. Carefully the two men went over it, finally turning out the bed and searching that. Nothing. The warden in person climbed upon the bed and examined the bars of the window where the prisoner had been sawing. When he looked he was amused.

"Just made it a little bright by hard rubbing," he said to the prisoner, who stood looking on with a somewhat crestfallen air. The warden grasped the iron bars in his strong hands and tried to shake them. They were immovable, set firmly in the solid granite. He examined each in turn and found them all satisfactory. Finally he climbed down from the bed.

"Give it up, Professor," he advised.

The Thinking Machine shook his head and the warden and jailer passed on again. As they disappeared down the corridor The Thinking Machine sat on the edge of the bed with his head in his hands.

"He's crazy to try to get out of that cell," commented the jailer.

"Of course he can't get out," said the warden. "But he's clever. I would like to know what he wrote that cipher with."

It was four o'clock next morning when an awful, heart-racking shriek of terror resounded through the great prison. It came from a cell, somewhere about the center, and its tone told a tale of horror, agony, terrible fear. The warden heard and with three of his men rushed into the long corridor leading to Cell 13.

As they ran there came again that awful cry. It died away in a sort of wail. The white faces of prisoners appeared at cell doors upstairs and down, staring out wonderingly, frightened.

"It's that fool in Cell Thirteen," grumbled the warden.

He stopped and stared in as one of the jailers flashed a lantern. "That fool in Cell Thirteen" lay comfortably on his cot, flat on his back with his mouth open, snoring. Even as they looked there came again the piercing cry, from somewhere above. The warden's face blanched a little as he started up the stairs. There on the top floor he found a man in Cell 43, directly above Cell 13, but two floors higher, cowering in a corner of his cell.

"What's the matter?" demanded the warden.

"Thank God you've come," exclaimed the prisoner, and he cast himself against the bars of his cell.

"What is it?" demanded the warden again.

He threw open the door and went in. The prisoner dropped on his knees and clasped the warden about the body. His face was white with terror, his eyes were widely distended, and he was shuddering. His hands, icy cold, clutched at the warden's.

"Take me out of this cell, please take me out," he pleaded.

"What's the matter with you, anyhow?" insisted the warden, impatiently.

"I heard something — something," said the prisoner, and his eyes roved nervously around the cell.

"What did you hear?"

"I — I can't tell you," stammered the prisoner. Then, in a sudden burst of terror: "Take me out of this cell — put me anywhere — but take me out of here."

The warden and the three jailers exchanged glances.

"Who is this fellow? What's he accused of?" asked the warden.

"Joseph Ballard," said one of the jailers. "He's accused of throwing acid in a woman's face. She died from it."

"But they can't prove it," gasped the prisoner. "They can't prove it. Please put me in some other cell."

He was still clinging to the warden, and that official threw his arms off roughly. Then for a time he stood looking at the cowering wretch, who seemed possessed of all the wild, unreasoning terror of a child.

"Look here, Ballard," said the warden, finally, "if you heard anything, I want to know what it was. Now tell me."

"I can't, I can't," was the reply. He was sobbing.

"Where did it come from?"

"I don't know. Everywhere — nowhere. I just heard it."

"What was it — a voice?"

"Please don't make me answer," pleaded the prisoner.

"You must answer," said the warden, sharply.

"It was a voice — but — but it wasn't human," was the sobbing reply.

"Voice, but not human?" repeated the warden, puzzled.

"It wounded muffled and — and far away — and ghostly," explained the man.

"Did it come from inside or outside the prison?"

"It didn't seem to come from anywhere — it was just here, here, everywhere. I heard it. I heard it."

For an hour the warden tried to get the story, but Ballard had become suddenly obstinate and would say nothing — only pleaded to be placed in another cell, or to have one of the jailers remain near him until daylight. These requests were gruffly refused.

"And see here," said the warden, in conclusion, "if there's any more of this screaming I'll put you in the padded cell."

Then the warden went his way, a sadly puzzled man. Ballard sat at his cell door until daylight, his face, drawn and white with terror, pressed against the bars, and looked out into the prison with wide, staring eyes.

That day, the fourth since the incarceration of The Thinking Machine, was enlivened considerably by the volunteer prisoner, who spent most of his time at the little window of his cell. He began proceedings by throwing another piece of linen down to the guard, who picked it up dutifully and took it to the warden. On it was written:

"Only three days more."

The warden was in no way surprised at what he read; he understood that The Thinking Machine meant only three days more of his imprisonment, and he regarded the note as a boast. But how was the thing written? Where had The Thinking Machine found his new piece of linen? Where? How? He carefully examined the linen. It was white, of fine texture, shirting material. He took the shirt which he had taken and carefully fitted the two original pieces of the linen to the torn places. This third piece was entirely superfluous; it didn't fit anywhere, and yet it was unmistakably the same goods.

"And where — where does he get anything to write with?" demanded the warden of the world at large.

Still later on the fourth day The Thinking Machine, through the window of his cell, spoke to the armed guard outside.

"What day of the month is it?" he asked.

"The fifteenth," was the answer.

The Thinking Machine made a mental astronomical calculation and satisfied himself that the moon would not rise until after nine o'clock that night. Then he asked another question:

"Who attends to those arc lights?"

"Man from the company."

"You have no electricians in the building?"

"No."

"I should think you could save money if you had your own man."

"None of my business," replied the guard.

The guard noticed The Thinking Machine at the cell window frequently during that day, but always the face seemed listless and there was a certain wistfulness in the squint eyes behind the glasses. After a while he accepted the presence of the leonine head as a matter of course. He had seen other prisoners do the same thing; it was the longing for the outside world.

That afternoon, just before the day guard was relieved, the head appeared at the window again, and The Thinking Machine's hand held something out between the bars. It fluttered to the ground and the guard picked it up. It was a five-dollar bill.

"That's for you," called the prisoner.

As usual, the guard took it to the warden. That gentleman looked at it suspiciously; he looked at everything that came from Cell 13 with suspicion.

"He said it was for me," explained the guard.

"It's a sort of a tip, I suppose," said the warden. "I see no particular reason why you shouldn't accept —"

Suddenly he stopped. He had remembered that The Thinking Machine had gone into Cell 13 with one five-dollar bill and two ten-dollar bills; twenty-five dollars in all. Now a five-dollar bill had been tied around the first pieces of linen that came from the cell. The warden still had it, and to convince himself he took it out and looked at it. It was five dollars; yet here was another five dollars, and The Thinking Machine had only had ten-dollar bills.

"Perhaps somebody changed one of the bills for him," he thought at last, with a sigh of relief.

But then and there he made up his mind. He would search Cell 13 as a cell was never before searched in this world. When a man could write at will, and change money, and do other wholly inexplicable things, there was something radically wrong with his prison. He planned to enter the cell at night — three o'clock would be an excellent time. The Thinking Machine must do all the weird things he did sometime. Night seemed the most reasonable.

Thus it happened that the warden stealthily descended upon Cell 13 that night at three o'clock. He paused at the door and listened. There was no sound save the steady, regular breathing of the prisoner. The keys unfastened the double locks with scarcely a clank, and the warden entered, locking the door behind him. Suddenly he flashed his dark lantern in the face of the recumbent figure.

If the warden had planned to startle The Thinking Machine he was mistaken, for that individual merely opened his eyes quietly, reached for his glasses, and inquired, in a most matter-of-fact tone:

"Who is it?"

It would be useless to describe the search that the warden made. It was minute. Not one inch of the cell or the bed was overlooked. He found the round hole in the floor, and with a flash of inspiration thrust his thick fingers into it. After a moment of fumbling there he drew up something and looked at it in the light of his lantern.

"Ugh!" he exclaimed.

The thing he had taken out was a rat — a dead rat. His inspiration fled as a mist before the sun. But he continued the search. The Thinking Machine, without a word, arose and kicked the rat out of the cell into the corridor.

The warden climbed on the bed and tried the steel bars in the tiny window. They were perfectly rigid; every bar of the door was the same.

Then the warden searched the prisoner's clothing, beginning at the shoes. Nothing hidden in them! Then the trousers waistband. Still nothing! Then the pockets of the trousers. From one side he drew out some paper money and examined it.

"Five one-dollar bills," he gasped.

"That's right," said the prisoner.

"But the — you had two tens and a five — what the — how do you do it?"

"That's my business," said The Thinking Machine.

"Did any of my men change this money for you — on your word of honor?"

The Thinking Machine paused just a fraction of a second.

"No," he said.

"Well, do you make it?" asked the warden. He was prepared to believe anything.

"That's my business," again said the prisoner.

The warden glared at the eminent scientist fiercely. He felt — he knew — that this man was making a fool of him, yet he didn't know how. If he were a real prisoner he would get the truth — but, then, perhaps, those inexplicable things which had happened would not have been brought before him so sharply. Neither of the men spoke for a long time, then suddenly the warden turned fiercely and left the cell, slamming the door behind him. He didn't dare to speak, then.

He glanced at the clock. It was ten minutes to four. He had hardly settled himself in bed when again came that heart-breaking shriek through the prison. With a few muttered words, which, while not elegant, were highly expressive, he relighted his lantern and rushed through the prison again to the cell on the upper floor.

Again Ballard was crushing himself against the steel door, shrieking, shrieking at the top of his voice. He stopped only when the warden flashed his lamp in the cell.

"Take me out, take me out," he screamed. "I did it, I did it, I killed her. Take it away."

"Take what away?" asked the warden.

"I threw the acid in her face — I did it — I confess. Take me out of here."

Ballard's condition was pitiable; it was only an act of mercy to let him out into the corridor. There he crouched in a corner, like an animal at bay, and clasped his hands to his ears. It took half an hour to calm him sufficiently for him to speak. Then he told incoherently what had happened. On the night before at four o'clock he had heard a voice — a sepulchral voice, muffled and wailing in tone.

"What did it say?" asked the warden, curiously.

"Acid — acid — acid!" gasped the prisoner. "It accused me. Acid! I threw the acid, and the woman died. Oh!" It was a long, shuddering wail of terror.

"Acid?" echoed the warden, puzzled. The case was beyond him.

"Acid. That's all I heard — that one word, repeated several times. There were other things, too, but I didn't hear them."

"That was last night, eh?" asked the warden. "What happened to-night — what frightened you just now?"

"It was the same thing," gasped the prisoner. "Acid — acid — acid!" He covered his face with his hands and sat shivering. "It was acid I used on her, but I didn't mean to kill her. I just heard the words. It was some-thing accusing me — accusing me." He mumbled, and was silent.

"Did you hear anything else?"

"Yes — but I couldn't understand — only a little bit — just a word or two."

"Well, what was it?"

"I heard 'acid' three times, then I heard a long, moaning sound, then — then — I heard 'number eight hat.' I heard that twice."

"Number eight hat," repeated the warden. "What the devil — num-ber eight hat? Accusing voices of conscience have never talked about number eight hats, so far as I ever heard."

"He's insane," said one of the jailers, with an air of finality.

"I believe you," said the warden. "He must be. He probably heard something and got frightened. He's trembling now. Number eight hat! What the —"

When the fifth day of The Thinking Machine's imprisonment rolled around the warden was wearing a hunted look. He was anxious for the end of the thing. He could not help but feel that his distinguished pris-oner had been amusing himself. And if this were so, The Thinking Ma-chine had lost none of his sense of humor. For on this fifth day he flung down another linen note to the outside guard, bearing the words "Only two days more." Also he flung down half a dollar.

Now the warden knew — he *knew* — that the man in Cell 13 didn't have any half dollars — he *couldn't* have any half dollars, no more than he could have pen and ink and linen, and yet he did have them. It was a condition, not a theory; that is one reason why the warden was wearing a hunted look.

That ghastly, uncanny thing, too, about "acid" and "number eight hat" clung to him tenaciously. They didn't mean anything, of course, merely the ravings of an insane murderer who had been driven by fear to confess his crime, still there were so many things that "didn't mean anything" happening in the prison now since The Thinking Machine was there.

On the sixth day the warden received a postal stating that Dr. Ransome and Mr. Fielding would be at Chisholm Prison on the following evening, Thursday, and in the event Professor Van Dusen had not yet escaped — and they presumed he had not because they had not heard from him — they would meet him there.

"In the event he had not yet escaped!" The warden smiled grimly. Escaped!

The Thinking Machine enlivened this day for the warden with three notes. They were on the usual linen and bore generally on the appointment at half past eight o'clock Thursday night, which appointment the scientist had made at the time of his imprisonment.

On the afternoon of the seventh day the warden passed Cell 13 and glanced in. The Thinking Machine was lying on the iron bed, apparently sleeping lightly. The cell appeared precisely as it always did from a casual glance. The warden would swear that no man was going to leave it between that hour — it was then four o'clock — and half past eight o'clock that evening.

On his way back past the cell the warden heard the steady breathing again, and coming closer to the door looked in. He wouldn't have done so if The Thinking Machine had been looking, but now — well, it was different.

A ray of light came through the high window and fell on the face of the sleeping man. It occurred to the warden for the first time that his prisoner appeared haggard and weary. Just then The Thinking Machine stirred slightly and the warden hurried on up the corridor guiltily. That evening after six o'clock he saw the jailer.

"Everything all right in Cell Thirteen?" he asked.

"Yes, sir," replied the jailer. "He didn't eat much, though."

It was with a feeling of having done his duty that the warden received Dr. Ransome and Mr. Fielding shortly after seven o'clock. He intended to show them the linen notes and lay before them the full story of his woes, which was a long one. But before this came to pass the guard from the river side of the prison yard entered the office.

"The arc light in my side of the yard won't light," he informed the warden.

"Confound it, that man's a hoodoo," thundered the official. "Everything has happened since he's been here."

The guard went back to his post in the darkness, and the warden phoned to the electric light company.

"This is Chisholm Prison," he said through the phone.

"Send three or four men down here quick, to fix an arc light."

The reply was evidently satisfactory, for the warden hung up the receiver and passed out into the yard. While Dr. Ransome and Mr. Fielding sat waiting the guard at the outer gate came in with a special-delivery letter. Dr. Ransome happened to notice the address, and, when the guard went out, looked at the letter more closely.

"By George!" he exclaimed.

"What is it?" asked Mr. Fielding.

Silently the doctor offered the letter. Mr. Fielding examined it closely.

"Coincidence," he said. "It must be."

It was nearly eight o'clock when the warden returned to his office. The electricians had arrived in a wagon, and were now at work. The warden pressed the buzz-button communicating with the man at the outer gate in the wall.

"How many electricians came in?" he asked, over the short phone. "Four? Three workmen in jumpers and overalls and the manager? Frock coat and silk hat? All right. Be certain that only four go out. That's all."

He turned to Dr. Ransome and Mr. Fielding.

"We have to be careful here — particularly," and there was broad sarcasm in his tone, "since we have scientists locked up."

The warden picked up the special-delivery letter carelessly, and then began to open it.

"When I read this I want to tell you gentlemen something about how — Great Caesar!" he ended, suddenly, as he glanced at the letter. He sat with mouth open, motionless, from astonishment.

"What is it?" asked Mr. Fielding.

"A special-delivery letter from Cell Thirteen," gasped the warden. "An invitation to supper."

"What?" and the two others arose, unanimously.

The warden sat dazed, staring at the letter for a moment, then called sharply to a guard outside in the corridor.

"Run down to Cell Thirteen and see if that man's in there."

The guard went as directed, while Dr. Ransome and Mr. Fielding examined the letter.

"It's Van Dusen's handwriting; there's no question of that," said Dr. Ransome. "I've seen too much of it."

Just then the buzz on the telephone from the outer gate sounded, and the warden, in a semitrance, picked up the receiver.

"Hello! Two reporters, eh? Let 'em come in." He turned suddenly to the doctor and Mr. Fielding. "Why, the man *can't* be out. He must be in his cell."

Just at that moment the guard returned.

"He's still in his cell, sir," he reported. "I saw him. He's lying down."

"There, I told you so," said the warden, and he breathed freely again. "But how did he mail that letter?"

There was a rap on the steel door which led from the jail yard into the warden's office.

"It's the reporters," said the warden. "Let them in," he instructed the guard; then to the two other gentlemen: "Don't say anything about this before them, because I'd never hear the last of it."

The door opened, and the two men from the front gate entered.

"Good evening, gentlemen," said one. That was Hutchinson Hatch; the warden knew him well.

"Well?" demanded the other, irritably. "I'm here."

That was The Thinking Machine.

He squinted belligerently at the warden, who sat with mouth agape. For the moment that official had nothing to say. Dr. Ransome and Mr. Fielding were amazed, but they didn't know what the warden knew. They were only amazed; he was paralyzed. Hutchinson Hatch, the reporter, took in the scene with greedy eyes.

"How — how — how did you do it?" gasped the warden, finally.

"Come back to the cell," said The Thinking Machine, in the irritated voice which his scientific associates knew so well.

The warden, still in a condition bordering on trance, led the way.

"Flash your light in there," directed The Thinking Machine.

The warden did so. There was nothing unusual in the appearance of the cell, and there — there on the bed lay the figure of The Thinking Machine. Certainly! There was the yellow hair! Again the warden looked at the man beside him and wondered at the strangeness of his own dreams.

With trembling hands he unlocked the cell door and The Thinking Machine passed inside.

"See here," he said.

He kicked at the steel bars in the bottom of the cell door and three of them were pushed out of place. A fourth broke off and rolled away in the corridor.

"And here, too," directed the erstwhile prisoner as he stood on the bed to reach the small window. He swept his hand across the opening and every bar came out.

"What's this in bed?" demanded the warden, who was slowly recovering.

"A wig," was the reply. "Turn down the cover."

The warden did so. Beneath it lay a large coil of strong rope, thirty feet or more, a dagger, three files, ten feet of electric wire, a thin, powerful pair of steel pliers, a small tack hammer with its handle, and — and a derringer pistol.

"How did you do it?" demanded the warden.

"You gentlemen have an engagement to supper with me at half past nine o'clock," said The Thinking Machine.

"Come on, or we shall be late."

"But how did you do it?" insisted the warden.

"Don't ever think you can hold any man who can use his brain," said The Thinking Machine. "Come on; we shall be late."

It was an impatient supper party in the rooms of Professor Van Dusen and a somewhat silent one. The guests were Dr. Ransome, Alfred Fielding, the warden, and Hutchinson Hatch, reporter. The meal was served to the minute, in accordance with Professor Van Dusen's instructions of one week before; Dr. Ransome found the artichokes delicious. At last the supper was finished and The Thinking Machine turned full on Dr. Ransome and squinted at him fiercely.

"Do you believe it now?" he demanded.

"I do," replied Dr. Ransome.

"Do you admit that it was a fair test?"

"I do."

With the others, particularly the warden, he was waiting anxiously for the explanation.

"Suppose you tell us how —" began Mr. Fielding.

"Yes, tell us how," said the warden.

The Thinking Machine readjusted his glasses, took a couple of preparatory squints at his audience, and began the story. He told it from the beginning logically; and no man ever talked to more interested listeners.

"My agreement was," he began, "to go into a cell, carrying nothing except what was necessary to wear, and to leave that cell within a week. I had never seen Chisholm Prison. When I went into the cell I asked for tooth powder, two ten- and one five-dollar bills, and also to have my shoes blacked. Even if these requests had been refused it would not have mattered seriously. But you agreed to them.

"I knew there would be nothing in the cell which you thought I might use to advantage. So when the warden locked the door on me I was apparently helpless, unless I could turn three seemingly innocent things to use. They were things which would have been permitted any prisoner under sentence of death, were they not, warden?"

"Tooth powder and polished shoes, yes, but not money," replied the warden.

"Anything is dangerous in the hands of a man who knows how to use it," went on The Thinking Machine. "I did nothing that first night but sleep and chase rats." He glared at the warden. "When the matter was broached I knew I could do nothing that night, so suggested next day. You gentlemen thought I wanted time to arrange an escape with outside assistance, but this was not true. I knew I could communicate with whom I pleased, when I pleased."

The warden stared at him a moment, then went on smoking solemnly.

"I was aroused next morning at six o'clock by the jailer with my breakfast," continued the scientist. "He told me dinner was at twelve and supper at six. Between these times, I gathered, I would be pretty much to myself. So immediately after breakfast I examined my outside surroundings from my cell window. One look told me it would be useless to try to scale the wall, even should I decide to leave my cell by the window, for my purpose was to leave not only the cell, but the prison. Of course, I could have gone over the wall, but it would have taken me longer to lay my plans that way. Therefore, for the moment, I dismissed all idea of that.

"From this first observation I knew the river was on that side of the prison, and that there was also a playground there. Subsequently these surmises were verified by a keeper. I knew then one important thing — that anyone might approach the prison wall from that side if necessary without attracting any particular attention. That was well to remember. I remembered it.

"But the outside thing which most attracted my attention was the feed wire to the arc light which ran within a few feet — probably three or four — of my cell window. I knew that would be valuable in the event I found it necessary to cut off that arc light."

"Oh, you shut it off tonight, then?" asked the warden.

"Having learned all I could from that window," resumed The Thinking Machine, without heeding the interruption, "I considered the idea of escaping through the prison proper. I recalled just how I had come into the cell, which I knew would be the only way. Seven doors lay between me and the outside. So, also for the time being, I gave up the idea of escaping that way. And I couldn't go through the solid granite walls of the cell."

The Thinking Machine paused for a moment and Dr. Ransome lighted a new cigar. For several minutes there was silence, then the scientific jailbreaker went on:

"While I was thinking about these things a rat ran across my foot. It suggested a new line of thought. There were at least half a dozen rats in the cell — I could see their beady eyes. Yet I had noticed none come under the cell door. I frightened them purposely and watched the cell door to see if they went out that way. They did not, but they were gone. Obviously they went another way. Another way meant another opening.

"I searched for this opening and found it. It was an old drain pipe, long unused and partly choked with dirt and dust. But this was the way the rats had come. They came from somewhere. Where? Drain pipes usually lead outside prison grounds. This one probably led to the river, or near it. The rats must therefore come from that direction. If they came a part of the way, I reasoned that they came all the way, because it was extremely unlikely that a solid iron or lead pipe would have any hole in it except at the exit.

"When the jailer came with my luncheon he told me two important things, although he didn't know it. One was that a new system of plumbing had been put in the prison seven years before: another that the river was only three hundred feet away. Then I knew positively that the pipe was a part of an old system; I knew, too, that it slanted generally toward the river. But did the pipe end in the water or on land?

"This was the next question to be decided. I decided it by catching several of the rats in the cell. My jailer was surprised to see me engaged in this work. I examined at least a dozen of them. They were perfectly dry; they had come through the pipe, and, most important of all, they were *not house rats, but field rats.* The other end of the pipe was on land, then, outside the prison walls. So far, so good.

"Then, I knew that if I worked freely from this point I must attract the warden's attention in another direction. You see, by telling the warden that I had come there to escape you made the test more severe, because I had to trick him by false scents."

The warden looked up with a sad expression in his eyes.

"The first thing was to make him think I was trying to communicate with you, Dr. Ransome. So I wrote a note on a piece of linen I tore from my shirt, addressed it to Dr. Ransome, tied a five-dollar bill around it, and threw it out the window. I knew the guard would take it to the warden, but I rather hoped the warden would send it as addressed. Have you that first linen note, Warden?"

The warden produced the cipher.

"What the deuce does it mean, anyhow?" he asked.

"Read it backward, beginning with the *T* signature and disregard the division into words," instructed The Thinking Machine.

The warden did so.

"*T-h-i-s*, this," he spelled, studied it a moment, then read it off, grinning:

"This is not the way I intend to escape."

"Well, now what do you think o' that?" he demanded, still grinning.

"I knew that would attract your attention, just as it did," said The Thinking Machine, "and if you really found out what it was it would be a sort of gentle rebuke."

"What did you write it with?" asked Dr. Ransome, after he had examined the linen and passed it to Mr. Fielding.

"This," said the erstwhile prisoner, and he extended his foot. On it was the shoe he had worn in prison, though the polish was gone — scraped off clean. "The shoe blacking, moistened with water, was my ink; the metal tip of the shoelace made a fairly good pen."

The warden looked up and suddenly burst into a laugh, half of relief, half of amusement.

"You're a wonder," he said, admiringly. "Go on."

"That precipitated a search of my cell by the warden, as I had intended," continued The Thinking Machine. "I was anxious to get the warden into the habit of searching my cell, so that finally, constantly finding nothing, he would get disgusted and quit. This at last happened, practically."

The warden blushed.

"He then took my white shirt away and gave me a prison shirt. He was satisfied that those two pieces of the shirt were all that was missing. But while he was searching my cell I had another piece of that same shirt, about nine inches square, rolled into a small ball in my mouth."

"Nine inches of that shirt?" demanded the warden. "Where did it come from?"

"The bosoms of all stiff white shirts are of triple thickness," was the explanation. "I tore out the inside thickness, leaving the bosom only two thicknesses. I knew you wouldn't see it. So much for that."

There was a little pause, and the warden looked from one to another of the men with a sheepish grin.

"Having disposed of the warden for the time being by giving him something else to think about, I took my first serious step toward freedom," said Professor Van Dusen. "I knew, within reason, that the pipe led somewhere to the playground outside; I knew a great many boys played there; I knew that rats came into my cell from out there. Could I communicate with some one outside with these things at hand?

"First was necessary, I saw, a long and fairly reliable thread, so — but here," he pulled up his trousers legs and showed that the tops of both stockings, of fine, strong lisle, were gone. "I unraveled those — after I got them started it wasn't difficult — and I had easily a quarter of a mile of thread that I could depend on.

"Then on half of my remaining linen I wrote, laboriously enough I assure you, a letter explaining my situation to this gentleman here," and he indicated Hutchinson Hatch. "I knew he would assist me — for the value of the newspaper story. I tied firmly to this linen letter a ten-dollar bill — there is no surer way of attracting the eye of anyone — and wrote on the linen: 'Finder of this deliver to Hutchinson Hatch, *Daily American,* who will give another ten dollars for the information.

"The next thing was to get this note outside on that playground where a boy might find it. There were two ways, but I chose the best. I took one of the rats — I became adept in catching them — tied the linen and money firmly to one leg, fastened my lisle thread to another, and turned him loose in the drain pipe. I reasoned that the natural fright of the rodent would make him run until he was outside the pipe and then out on earth he would probably stop to gnaw off the linen and money.

"From the moment the rat disappeared into that dusty pipe I became anxious. I was taking some many chances. The rat might gnaw the string, of which I held one end; other rats might gnaw it; the rat might run out of the pipe and leave the linen and money where they would never be found; a thousand other things might have happened. So began some nervous hours, but the fact that the rat ran on until only a few feet of the string remained in my cell made me think he was outside the pipe. I had carefully instructed Mr. Hatch what to do in case the note reached him. The question was: would it reach him?

"This done, I could only wait and make other plans in case this one failed. I openly attempted to bribe my jailer, and learned from him that he held the keys to only two of seven doors between me and freedom. Then I did something else to make the warden nervous. I took the steel supports out of the heels of my shoes and made a pretense of sawing the bars of my cell window. The warden raised a pretty row about that. He developed, too, the habit of shaking the bars of my cell window to see if they were solid. They were — then."

Again the warden grinned. He had ceased being astonished.

"With this one plan I had done all I could and could only wait to see what happened," the scientist went on. "I couldn't know whether my note had been delivered or even found, or whether the mouse had gnawed it up. And I didn't dare to draw back through the pipe that one slender thread which connected me with the outside.

"When I went to bed that night I didn't sleep, for fear there would come the slight signal twitch at the thread which was to tell me that Mr. Hatch had received the note. At half past three o'clock, I judge, I felt this twitch, and no prisoner actually under sentence of death ever welcomed a thing more heartily."

The Thinking Machine stopped and turned to the reporter.

"You'd better explain just what you did," he said.

"The linen note was brought to me by a small boy who had been playing baseball," said Mr. Hatch. "I immediately saw a big story in it, so I gave the boy another ten dollars, and got several spools of silk, some twine, and a roll of light, pliable wire. The professor's note suggested that I have the finder of the note show me just where it was picked up, and told me to make my search from there, beginning at two o'clock in the morning. If I found the other end of the thread I was to twitch it gently three times, then a fourth.

"I began the search with a small-bulb electric light. It was an hour and twenty minutes before I found the end of the drain pipe, half-hidden in weeds. Then I found the end of the lisle thread, twitched it as directed and immediately I got an answering twitch.

"Then I fastened the silk to this and Professor Van Dusen began to pull it into his cell. I nearly had heart disease for fear the string would break. To the end of the silk I fastened the twine, and when that had been pulled in I tied on the wire. Then that was drawn into the pipe and we had a substantial line, which rats couldn't gnaw, from the mouth of the drain into the cell."

The Thinking Machine raised his hand and Hatch stopped.

"All this was done in absolute silence," said the scientist. "But when the wire reached my hand I could have shouted. Then we tried another experiment, which Mr. Hatch was prepared for. I tested the pipe as a speaking tube. Neither of us could hear very clearly, but I dared not speak loud for fear of attracting attention in the prison. At last I made him understand what I wanted immediately. He seemed to have great difficulty in understanding when I asked for nitric acid, and I repeated the word 'acid' several times.

"Then I heard a shriek from a cell above me. I knew instantly that someone had overheard, and when I heard you coming, Mr. Warden, I feigned sleep. If you had entered my cell at that moment that whole plan of escape would have ended there. But you passed on. That was the nearest I ever came to being caught.

"Having established this improvised trolley it is easy to see how I got things in the cell and made them disappear at will. I merely dropped them back into the pipe. You, Mr. Warden, could not have reached the connecting wire with your fingers; they are too large. My fingers, you see, are longer and more slender. In addition I guarded the top of that pipe with a rat — you remember how."

"I remember," said the warden, with a grimace.

"I thought that if anyone were tempted to investigate that hole the rat would dampen his ardor. Mr. Hatch could not send me anything useful through the pipe until next night, although he did send me change for ten dollars as a test, so I proceeded with other parts of my plan. Then I evolved the method of escape which I finally employed.

"In order to carry this out successfully it was necessary for the guard in the yard to get accustomed to seeing me at the cell window. I arranged this by dropping linen notes to him, boastful in tone, to make the warden believe, if possible, one of his assistants was communicating with the outside for me. I would stand at my window for hours gazing out, so the guard could see, and occasionally I spoke to him. In that way I learned that the prison had no electricians of its own, but was dependent upon the lighting company if anything should go wrong.

"That cleared the way to freedom perfectly. Early in the evening of the last day of my imprisonment, when it was dark, I planned to cut the feed wire which was only a few feet from my window, reaching it with an acid-tipped wire I had. That would make that side of the prison perfectly dark while the electricians were searching for the break. That would also bring Mr. Hatch into the prison yard.

"There was only one more thing to do before I actually began the work of setting myself free. This was to arrange final details with Mr. Hatch through our speaking tube. I did this within half an hour after the warden left my cell on the fourth night of my imprisonment. Mr. Hatch again had serious difficulty in understanding me, and I repeated the word 'acid' to him several times, and later on the words 'number eight hat' — that's my size — and these were the things which made a prisoner upstairs confess to murder, so one of the jailers told me next day. This prisoner heard our voices, confused of course, through the pipe, which also went to his cell. The cell directly over me was not occupied, hence no one else heard.

"Of course the actual work of cutting the steel bars out of the window and door was comparatively easy with nitric acid, which I got through the pipe in tin bottles, but it took time. Hour after hour on the fifth and sixth and seventh days the guard below was looking at me as I worked on the bars of the window with the acid on a piece of wire. I used the tooth powder to prevent the acid spreading. I looked away abstractedly as I worked and each minute the acid cut deeper into the metal. I noticed that the jailers always tried the door by shaking the upper part, never the lower bars; therefore I cut the lower bars, leaving them hanging in place by thin strips of metal. But that was a bit of daredeviltry. I could not have gone that way so easily."

The Thinking Machine sat silent for several minutes.

"I think that makes everything clear," he went on. "Whatever points I have not explained were merely to confuse the warden and jailers. These things in my bed I brought in to please Mr. Hatch, who wanted to improve the story. Of course, the wig was necessary in my plan. The special-delivery letter I wrote and directed in my cell with Mr. Hatch's fountain pen, then sent it out to him and he mailed it. That's all, I think."

"But your actually leaving the prison grounds and then coming in through the outer gate to my office?" asked the warden.

"Perfectly simple," said the scientist. "I cut the electric light wire with acid, as I said, when the current was off. Therefore when the current was turned on the arc didn't light. I knew it would take some time to find out what was the matter and make repairs. When the guard went to report to you the yard was dark, I crept out the window — it was a tight fit, too — replaced the bars by standing on a narrow ledge, and remained in a shadow until the force of electricians arrived. Mr. Hatch was one of them.

"When I saw him I spoke and he handed me a cap, a jumper, and overalls, which I put on within ten feet of you, Mr. Warden, while you were in the yard. Later Mr. Hatch called me, presumably as a workman, and together we went out the gate to get something out of the wagon. The gate guard let us pass out readily as two workmen who have just passed in. We changed our clothing and reappeared, asking to see you. We saw you. That's all."

There was silence for several minutes. Dr. Ransome was first to speak.

"Wonderful!" he exclaimed. "Perfectly amazing."

"How did Mr. Hatch happen to come with the electricians?" asked Mr. Fielding.

"His father is manager of the company," replied The Thinking Machine.

"But what if there had been no Mr. Hatch outside to help?"

"Every prisoner has one friend outside who would help him escape if he could."

"Suppose — just suppose — there had been no old plumbing system there?" asked the warden, curiously.

"There were two other ways out," said The Thinking Machine, enigmatically.

Ten minutes later the telephone bell rang. It was a request for the warden.

"Light all right, eh?" the warden asked, through the phone. "Good. Wire cut beside Cell Thirteen? Yes, I know. One electrician too many? What's that? Two came out?"

The warden turned to the others with a puzzled expression.

"He only let in four electricians; he has let out two and says there are three left."

"I was the odd one," said The Thinking Machine.

"Oh," said the warden. "I see." Then through the phone: "Let the fifth man go. He's all right."

1914

FREDERICK IRVING ANDERSON

··

Blind Man's Buff

"GODAHL, ATTEND!" said that adept in smart crime to himself as he paused at the curb. "You think you are clever; but there goes your better."

He had to step into the street to make way for the crowd that overflowed the pavement — men and women, newsboys, even unhorsed actors leaving their pillars for the time for the passing sensation, the beginning of the homing matinée crowds — all elbowing for a place about a tall, slender man in black who, as he advanced, gently tapped a cane point before him. What attracted the vortex, however, was not so much the man himself as the fact that he wore a black mask. The mask was impenetrable. People said he had no eyes. It was Malvino the Magician, born to eternal darkness. From a child, so the story went, his fingers had been schooled with the same cruel science they ply in Russia to educate the toes of their ballet dancers — until his fingers saw for him.

Head erect, shoulders squared, body poised with the precision of a skater — his handsome, clear-cut features, almost ghastly in contrast to the band of silk ribbon that covered the sockets where sight should have been — he advanced with military step in the cleared circle that ever revolved about him, his slender cane shooting out now and again with the flash of a rapier to tap-tap-tap on the flags. Why pay for an orchestra chair to witness his feats of legerdemain? Peopling silk hats with fecund families of rabbits, or even discovering a hogshead of boiling water in an innocent bystander's vest pocket, was as nothing to this theatric negotiation of Broadway in the rush hour of late Saturday afternoon. Malvino the Magician seemed oblivious to everything save the subtle impulses of that wand of a cane.

He stopped, suddenly alert to some immediate impression. The vague features relaxed; the teeth shone.

"Ah! Godahl, my friend!" he cried. He turned and advanced deliberately through the crowd that opened a path in front of him. Those wonderful hands reached out and touched Godahl on the arm, without hesitation as to direction.

Godahl could not repress a smile. Such a trick was worth a thousand dollars a week to the front of the house; and nobody knew better than the Great Malvino the value of advertising. That was why he walked Broadway unattended twice a day.

When he spoke it was in French. "I am sickened of them all," he said, sweeping his cane in a circle to indicate the gaping crowd straining to catch his words. "See! We have at hand a public chauffeur with nothing better to do than to follow in the wake of the Great Malvino. Godahl, my friend, you are at leisure? Then we will enter."

And Godahl, playing his cards with enjoyment and admiration as well, permitted the blind man to open the door and help him — Godahl, possessing five senses — into the cab; pleased doubly, indeed, to note that the magician had managed to steal his wallet in the brief contact. "To the park!" ordered Malvino, showing his teeth to the crowd as he shut the door.

Godahl had known Malvino first in Rome. The great of the earth gravitate toward each other. No one knew how great Godahl was except himself. He knew that he had never failed. No one knew how great Malvino was except Godahl. Once he had attempted to imitate Malvino and had almost failed. The functions of the third finger of his left hand lacked the wonderful coordination possessed by the magician. Malvino knew Godahl as an entertaining cosmopolitan, of which the world possesses far too few.

"I would exercise my Eng-lish," said the mask, "if you will be so good, my friend. Tell me — you know the lake shore in that city of Chicago?"

"As a book," said Godahl. "You are about to parade there — eh?"

"I am about to parade there," replied Malvino, imitating the accents of the other. "Therefore I would know it — as a book. Read it to me — slowly — page by page, my friend. I walk there shortly."

Godahl possessed, first of all, a marvelous faculty of visualizing. It was most necessary, almost as much so in fact for him in his profession as for Malvino in his — Malvino without eyes. In a matter-of-fact manner, like a mariner charting some dangerous channel, he plotted the great thoroughfare from the boulevard entrance to the auditorium. The

other listened attentively, recording every word. He had made use of
Godahl in this way before and knew the value of that man's observa-
tions. Then suddenly, impatiently, "One moment; there is another thing
— of immediate need. The Pegasus Club? We are passing it at this moment — eh? You are one of the — what is it they say? — ah, yes, the
fifty little millionaires — ha-ha! — yes?"

Godahl looked out of the window. Indeed, they were passing the club
now. They had been proceeding slowly, turning this way and that,
halted now and again or hurried on by traffic policemen, until they
were merely a helpless unit in the faltering tide of Fifth Avenue; it was
past five in the evening and all uptown New York was on the move,
afoot and awheel.

It was said of Malvino that he would suffer himself to be whirled
round twenty times on being set down in some remote neighborhood
of a strange city, and with the aid of his cane find his way back to his
hotel with the surety of a pigeon. But even that faculty did not explain
how he knew they were passing a certain building, the Pegasus Club, at
this moment. Unless, thought Godahl — who was better pleased to
study the other's methods than to ask questions — unless the sly fox
had it recorded in his strange brain map that carriage wheels rattled
over cart tracks a hundred yards below this point. Godahl smiled. It was
simple after all.

"I perform for your club Tuesday night. One thousand dollars they
will pay me — the monkey who sees without eyes! My friend, it is good
to be a monkey, even for such as these, who — but —" He paused and
laid his hand on his companion's arm. "If I could but see the color that
is called blue once! They tell me it is cool. They cannot make me feel
how cool it is. You will go to sea with me next summer and tell me
about it — eh? Will you not, my friend? But three of these — what you
call the fifty little millionaires — you will tell me why they are called
that, three of these came to me in my hotel and would grasp my hand.
And why not? I would grasp the hand of the devil himself if he but offered it. They are surprised. They would blindfold my poor eyes — my
poor eyes, Godahl! — blindfold them again, and again offer me their
hands, thinking Malvino a charlatan. Ha-ha! Again I must shake hands
with them! One wears a ring, with a great greasy stone. See! I have it
here with me. It is bottleglass. Yet would this barbarian wear it until I in
pity took it from him."

Godahl burst into a laugh. So this was the thief! Colwell, one of the

so-called fifty little millionaires who gave the Pegasus Club its savor —
who exhibited their silk hats and ample bootsoles in the plate-glass
windows every Sunday afternoon — had been crying over the loss of a
ring stone: a garish green affair for which he had paid hugely abroad.

"I am a marvelous man, eh, friend Godahl?"

"Indeed yes!" agreed the other, smiling.

"Malvino the Magician sought Godahl, his friend, this afternoon.
Petroff, my manager, he walks ten steps behind me, in the crowd. He
taps three times with his stick. Three steps to the right. Ha! There is
Godahl! The *canaille* applaud; even Godahl must smile. My friend,
Tuesday night Petroff is too clumsy. You will be my manager; but you
must be somewhere else."

"Indeed not!" cried Godahl warmly; and to himself, "What does he
drive at?"

"Indeed yes!" said the blind man, laying his hand again on the other's
arm. "I ask it of you. You will be in other places. If you but say yes you
will take me to sea in June and tell me what is the color blue. Listen!
First, Malvino will play the monkey. Then I am to be locked in a room
for five minutes. At the end of five minutes, if I am gone, that which I
have is mine — even to their wallets — fat wallets like this one of yours,
which I now return intact."

Godahl accepted the return of his wallet absent-mindedly.

"It is what Mr. Colwell calls a sporting proposition. See! I have it in
writing. It is in addition to the $1,000. That I already possess. Now these
fifty little millionaires, friend Godahl — are they all like the three who
came to me in my hotel? The one with the slippery stone in his ring —
the stone that I have — that one had $8,000 — forty thousand francs
— in one wallet in $1,000-notes. Does the American nation make new
money especially for such as these? The notes were new, the imprint
still crisp, like the face of my watch. Forty thousand francs in one wallet! I know, because I had the wallet as he talked. No, my friend. I have it
not now. I put it back. Ha-ha! What? And there are fifty of them like
that. I am to carry away what I can find! Godahl, it is told that the very
servants of the club own rows of brick houses and buy consols at correct times. But fifty little millionaires! And Malvino is to be locked in a
room, alone! I have it in writing."

A passing street lamp looked in and caught Godahl in the act of
blinking.

"Godahl, my friend, if you will tell me what I must know, then I will teach you what you wish to know. You wish to know many things, eh? I can tell, for I always feel your eyes when you are by. Tell me now, every inch of the way. Play it is the lake front in that city of Chicago."

Godahl chuckled. He did not love the fifty little millionaires. Those marvelous fingers! Malvino was playing with them in the air now in his earnestness. They could rob a poor box! Godahl, smiling grimly, began to draw the map his friend desired. Three steps up from the street, then the first glass door. Inside, two vestibules. Past them, on the right, the smoking room and lounge, a log fire at each end. On the left the street parlor, a great table in the center, and heavy chairs, all upholstered — none far from the walls. Between the rooms, on the left wall, the electric-switch panel. Would he play with light and darkness? It would be as well to hold the secret of this panel. On the floors, deep carpets —

"Deep carpets!" repeated the magician. "It is well I know. I do not like deep carpets. And this room, where I shall be left alone behind locked doors —"

"It would have to be the cloakroom, on the left of the main entrance," said Godahl. Yes, that would be the only available room for such a test. No other rooms off the street parlor could be locked, as there were no doors. In this cloakroom there were two doors: one on the main corridor and one on the first vestibule. There was a small window, but it was not to be thought of for one of Malvino's girth. The doors were massive, of oak; and the locks — Godahl remembered the locks well, having had need to examine them on a recent occasion — were tumbler locks. It would be rare business to see a man, even a magician, leave the cloakroom without help. And that, too, was in the bond — this sporting proposition.

"The locks have five tumblers," laughed Godahl, more and more amused.

"Let there be fifty!" whispered the other contemptuously. "Tell me, my observing friend, who counts the tumblers of a lock from the outside, do these doors open in or out?"

"In," said Godahl — and the long fingers closed on his wrist in a twinkling.

"In, you say?"

"In!" repeated Godahl; and he made a mental note to study the peculiar characteristics of doors that open in.

Malvino buried himself in his furs. The car sped on through the winding thoroughfares of the park, and Godahl fell to counting the revolving flashes of the gas lamps as they rushed by.

"This is the one place in your great city where I find joy," said the blind man at length. "There are no staring crowds; I can pick my thoughts; and the pavements are glass. Outside of these walls your city is a rack that would torture me. Tell me, why is blue so cool? June will be too late for the Mediterranean. We will start before. If you will but tell me, friend Godahl, so that I can feel it, I will give you the half — no! I will not. What is money to you? Are you quite sure about the doors opening in? Yes? That is good. Godahl, if I could see I think I would be like you — looking on and laughing. Let me tell you something of doors that open in — what! We are traveling at an unlawful speed! Mr. Officier — indeed, yes, the Great Malvino! Pity his poor eyes! Here is money falling from your hair! You are not a frugal man — so careless!"

The park policeman who had stopped them to warn them against speed stood staring at the crisp bill the blind man had plucked from his hair, as the taxicab sped forward again. Malvino directed the driver to his hotel through the speaking tube, and a few minutes later they were set down there. Godahl declined dinner with his queer friend.

"I have here your wallet once more, friend Godahl!" laughed the blind magician. "The fifty little millionaires! Ha-ha! You promise? You will not be there when I am there?"

"You have my stickpin," said Godahl. "I believe you are collecting bogus stones. That one is bogus, but it was thought to be a fine gift by a friend who is now dead."

The other, with evident disappointment, returned the pilfered stickpin. "You promise! You will not be there when I am there, my friend?"

Godahl held the blue-white hand in his own for a moment as they parted. "No, I promise you," he said; and he watched his queer friend walk away — Malvino erect, smiling, unfaltering in his fine stride, conscious to the last dregs of the interest he excited on all sides. He shunned the elevator and started up the broad marble stairs, his slender cane tap-tap-tapping, lighting the way for his confident tread.

Godahl dined at his club — looking on and laughing, as Malvino had said with a directness that rather startled the easy rogue into wakefulness. Godahl's career had defied innuendo; his was not an art, but a science, precise, infallible. But several times that afternoon in the somber shadows of their cab he had felt, with a strange thrill, that black impenetrable mask turn on him as though an inner vision lighted those darkened orbs.

Frankly, he avoided afflicted persons in the pursuit of his trade, not because of compunction, which troubled him not at all, but because a person lacking in any of the five senses was apt to be uncannily alert in some one of the remaining four. He was intensely a materialist, a gambler who pinned his faith to marked cards, never to superstition. He believed intuition largely a foolish fetish, except as actuated by the purely physical cravings; yet he recognized a strange clarity in the mental outlook of the afflicted that seemed unexplainable by any other means.

Malvino, too, played with marked cards. After all, magic is but the clever arrangement of properties. But why had Malvino picked him? Why had Malvino confided in him at all? There were a dozen other members of the Pegasus Club who would have served as well, so far as furnishing the business of the affair; who would have entered the game as a huge joke. To hold up the fifty little millionaires in their upholstered wallow would surely set the whole town by the ears. Something of the sort was needed to bring the ribald crew back to earth. But, thought Godahl, if the task were to be done he would much prefer to do it himself, not look on as a supernumerary.

Malvino, of course, was a thief. The only reason he did not practice his profession was that he found the business of playing the monkey paid better. Then, too, as a thief he must bury his talents; and there is nothing so sweet to the Latin as applause. Malvino could not keep his fingers quiet. Godahl had permitted himself to be stripped in their ride through sheer enjoyment of observation. There is nothing too small to be learned and learned well. Nevertheless, it had irritated him to think that this master had whispered in his ear familiarly. It smacked too much of kinship. Godahl knew no kin!

As he swept the magnificent dining room with his eyes, however, he could not repress a chuckle of sheer delight. It would be a hundred-day jest. They all conformed pretty well to type — a type against which the finer sensibilities of Godahl revolted. In the beginning the Pegasus had been the coming together of a few kindred souls — modest, comfortable, homelike; a meeting place of intellectual men who took their chiefest pleasure in the friction of ideas. In this way the organization had come to have a name, even among the many clubs of the city.

Godahl had adopted it as his home, and — he cynically paraphrased it — he might be without honor in his own country, but never in his own home. He had always been pleased to think that when he entered here he left the undesirable something outside, like the dust of his shoes on the doormat. Not that he lacked the lust of the game or a conscious pride in that slick infallibility which had made him a prince for whom other men went poor. There are times and places for all things. And this had been home.

Until, one by one, this tribe had crept in, overturned traditions, substituted the brass of vulgar display for the gold of the fine communion they did not profess to understand, much less to practice. A newspaper wag had finally dubbed them the Club of the Fifty Little Millionaires, and the name had stuck. It happened that a handful of them had been brooded in the same coop, that of a copper king who had begun at the slagpile and ended in philanthropy. As the newcomers gained ascendency the old sect of friends gradually drifted away. The pace was too fast for them.

There was truth in what Malvino had said of the servants; and there is nothing quite so unappetizing as the contempt of those who serve one meat and drink. But Godahl, looking on and laughing, still preserved the habit of picking his meals here with discriminating taste — though now he was less particular about wiping his feet on the doormat than formerly. He even indulged in play occasionally, and while he played he listened to the talk about things worth knowing.

Tonight the talk was all Malvino at the particular rubber where he chose to play. It was to be a rare occasion. True, they were to pay the magician roundly for the séance and had offered him, besides, a sporting proposition in the shape of written permission to carry off all his fingers could lift, but they chose to interpret sport according to their own lights. Two centuries ago it was sport in merry England to tie a gamecock to a stump and shy brickbats at it. The game was conducted according to rules carefully worked out, and was popular with all concerned — except the gamecock.

Godahl, at length getting his fill, rose in disgust and passed out. At the corner the street lamp winked at him in its knowing way, and Godahl, forgetting the gorge that had risen in him, returned the wink, smiling.

Colwell, the master of ceremonies, was venturing to a chosen few that a certain faker would be ineligible for dates on a kerosene circuit in Arkansas before the evening was over, when the telephone boy brought him a message from the Victoria. Malvino had started, and was driving to avoid the inevitable crowd that dogged his steps.

The committee was giving a last touch to its properties — a camera and flashlight apparatus arranged behind a screen — when there came the familiar tap-tap-tapping of the cane on the marble steps. If the lilt of his gait were any criterion the mask was in fine fettle.

"So," he was whispering, "three steps up from the street — two vestibules — and deep carpets. Deep carpets are bad!"

As he passed through the first vestibule this strange, impassive figure in dead black ran his fingers along the wall. There was the door, indeed, by which he would escape.

"Malvino the Magician!" cried a flunkey in gold lace as the inner doors swung open. Colwell was there, with extended hand. The hand of the other closed on it without hesitation, holding it for a moment.

"You speak no French? No? It is — most unfortunate. I speak things — and I am most awkward in your tongue. Is there the color blue here? I would touch it before I play."

He waved his cane toward the entrance. "The corridor? It is empty — yes? It is so in the bond. Thus," he cried, his teeth glowing at the circle of faces before him, "thus am I to take away that which is mine — is it not?"

Colwell elevated a knowing eyebrow at his companions. Colwell had not been a plumber's assistant for nothing in the days of his youth. He had plugged the key slots with molten lead. Once closed it would require the aid of a carpenter, not a locksmith — not even a magical locksmith — to negotiate the doors of the cloakroom. Colwell did not begrudge his walletful of small change at auction bridge, but he was decidedly averse to letting it fall into the hands of this blind beggar.

They helped him out of his coat. "My cane, too!" he said as he handed the cane to Colwell. It was of ebony, as thin as a baton and without ornament of any kind, save a platinum top. "It is — my faithful Achates! It is — a little brother to my poor senses. It is wonderful —" He swayed slightly and put out a hand to steady himself against Colwell. "But tonight, gentlemen, in your honor Malvino disarms himself, for the — how is it? — the fifty little millionaires — ha-ha! — who are so good as to receive me.

"Am I," he continued, "to have the honor of shaking the hands of the gentlemen? I do not know." He paused as though embarrassed, shrugged his shoulders deprecatingly, and then, smiling: "Myself, as a person, is not present if you so desire — only my talents, which you buy and pay for. Ah, I am awkward in your tongue. Sometimes, gentlemen, I am the guest, sometimes I am only the monkey, with his tricks. You understand? I thank you, sir. Saunders, of Texas Union? Ah, of the landed gentry of this great country! I am indeed pleasured."

A smile went the rounds. Saunders, of Texas Union, who was shaking the hand of the mask with one hand and discreetly feeling the muscles under the black-sleeved arm with the other, had been a puddler at Homestead until his talents for ragtime rescued him from oblivion and gave him Texas Union as a pocket piece. He brought forward Jones, of Pacific Cascade; Welton, of Tonopah Magnet; Smithers, of Excelsior Common; Jamieson, of Alleghany Western — and so on down the line. The guest, in his naïveté, seemed under the impression that the handles to the names referred to ancestral acres. These men had been named in the daily papers so often in connection with their pet manipulations in the market that they themselves had come to accept the nomenclature, using it much as an Englishman would say Kitchener of Khartoum or Marlborough of Blenheim.

So the mask was passed round the room. He was well worth seeing at close range. He accepted each hand with a steely grip; concentrated the vague blackness of his mask on each face, and spoke briefly and in halting phrases. In laying aside his cane he seemed to have lost something of the poise that distinguished the Great Malvino on the street or on the stage; and he leaned heavily on a shoulder here, on an arm there, as he was passed from one to another. There was a tremor of excitement in the room. A diversion had been promised; but what it was to be the honorable gentlemen of the committee had kept to themselves and their confederates. Colwell, Saunders, and Mason — of Independent Guano — whispered together for a moment; and when the circle of introductions was complete the guest was led to the center of the room. He took his place at the head of the big table, exploring it nervously with his fingers while he waited for the company to be seated.

What followed was somewhat tame, and they expressed themselves to that effect occasionally behind their hands. They had seen the same thing before; a two-dollar bill gave the veriest street loafer the same privilege every afternoon and evening at the Victoria, except for a few parlor pieces the magician reserved for private entertainments. But even the makings of these were to be had for a few pennies in any one of the numerous shops on Sixth Avenue devoted to the properties of magic. It was merely quickness of hand against slowness of eye. It is said that the persistency of vision amounts to one-hundredth of a second. These fingers found ample room to work in that slit of time. Yet the circle looked on languidly, like an audience at a championship fistfight tolerating the preliminaries.

The performer had borrowed a pack of cards bearing the unbroken

seal of the club, and was playing a solitary game of whist, cards faced —
a trick of Malvino's, by the way, which has never been satisfactorily explained — when suddenly the barons of Tonopah, Alleghany, and so
forth, sat up with a thrill of anticipation. It was evident to all, except
perhaps the performer himself, that the apex of the evening was at
hand. Mason softly opened the electric-switch cabinet; Colwell and
Saunders moved carelessly toward the table, taking up positions on
each hand of the mask, as though for a better view of the game.

Then came blank, overwhelming darkness! There was the scuffle of
feet; the snapping impact of body against body; a gasp; a half-uttered
cry of pain; then: "Confound him!" It was the voice of Colwell, breathing hard. "He's like a bull — Gad! Can't you —"

Then another voice — that of Saunders: "Steady, I've got him!
Ready?"

The unseen struggle ceased suddenly. There were several in that
thrilled circle that grew sick. It seemed evident that the honorable gentlemen of the committee had overpowered the magician, were about to
strip him of his mask, to show him up as the charlatan who had too
long duped a city. They wanted their money's worth. Colwell was
laughing, short, sharp; he had the mask now — they could hear the
silken ribbon rip as it came away.

"Now! Mason, let him have it!"

The words ended in a roar of mingled rage and pain; there came a
sharp snap-snap — as of bones coming away from their sockets; and simultaneously the muffled explosion and the blinding glare of the camera flashlight. And in the one-hundredth of a second of incandescence
there was indelibly imprinted on the vision of the audience the figure of
the magician holding two men at arm's length, each by the wrist, their
features hideously contorted. Then dead darkness fell, in the midst of
which hung the imprinted scene in silhouette against a phosphorescent
pall.

Someone thought of the lights. It was the magician himself. This curious circumstance was not noted until later. The switch clicked and the
chandeliers sprang into being again. Colwell held the torn mask in his
hand. Every eye, still straining for sight after the shock of the flashlight,
sought the blind face of the performer. It was horribly blind now,
stripped of its silk ribbon. Covering the eye-sockets he stumbled across
the room, almost fell against the table. His uncertain hand sought
Colwell's arm, traveled down its length, and took from the fingers the
torn mask and replaced it. The master of ceremonies gazed at the ca-

daverous face, fascinated. The room was deathly silent. The magician flashed his teeth in a poor attempt at a smile. His voice, when he spoke, was in whispers as crisp as leaves.

"Ah — my poor eyes! I do not sell — gentlemen, I am clumsy with your words. Let me not offend those who are my friends among you when I say I do not sell you my private self — it is only the monkey in me you can buy."

Colwell and Saunders were making efforts to soothe their arms, which were suffering exquisitely. Several men pushed forward, ashamed, to bridge the embarrassment with their apologies to the magician, who stared at them imperturbably with the mask. Things gradually came to rights, except for the honorable gentlemen of the committee, who took the first chance to retire with their troubles. The hands of the mask were like steel and when he wrenched the bones in their sockets he had not dealt lightly.

"We proceed," said the magician with a deprecating wave of his hand. "The room! I am to be your prisoner. It is so written."

The few members who knew of Colwell's precautions of plugging the key slots with lead thought wryly of the fact now. If this thing went any further the Pegasus Club would be the butt of the town!

"We will forget that," said Welton, of Tonopah Magnet, assuming leadership in a movement to make amends. "Besides," he added with a laugh, "we haven't given you a chance to go through our pockets yet. You would have to escape empty-handed."

"Your pardon!" said the mask with a grand bow. "I have already taken the opportunity."

So saying he displayed the contents of his capacious pockets. He had at least a score of wallets and several rolls of banknotes. The room exploded in a cry of amazement. Then the truth flashed upon them. When they passed the guest from hand to hand his nimble fingers had been busy substituting wads of paper for wallets.

"The hour is late," he continued, feeling the face of his watch. "I must be gone in five minutes. The room — if you will."

Welton, of Tonopah Magnet, roaring with laughter, took the magician — they admitted now he was at least that — and led him to the door of the cloakroom.

"One favor!" said the mask at the threshold. "My coat — my hat — my faithful cane. Ah! I thank you. I bid you good night!"

The naïveté of the words was masterly. Welton, of Tonopah Magnet, drew the door shut with a slam and the lock clicked. He faced the others and turned his trousers pockets inside out comically. He was not worrying about the safety of his cash, but he did admire the deftness of those fingers.

"I am glad to say he left my watch," he said, and he put his watch on the table. It was lacking five minutes of midnight. "What gets me," he continued, turning toward the closed door, "is how we are going to get the poor devil out without a battering ram! Colwell has most certainly earned everlasting fame by his brilliant entertainment this evening."

The keys were useless now that the spring locks had snapped shut on the prisoner. Someone suggested sending for the engineer, but one and all agreed that the game must be played out in common decency. They all retired to the lounging room to give the blind beggar five minutes to find out the trick that had been played on him.

At the end of five minutes they sent for the engineer, and that grimy individual appeared, loaded down with tools; he expressed it as his reverend opinion that a damned fine door was about to be turned into scrap. There was one chance — that a gasoline torch might blow the lead from the keyslot. But, no — the molten metal only completed the upsetting of the fine mechanism. There was nothing to do but to cut around the lock with a compass saw.

"Cheer up, Malvino!" said Welton through the door. "We will be with you in another minute."

Just then Godahl ran in from the street. He threw his hat and coat to an attendant.

"Ha! The devil to pay — eh?" he cried excitedly. "I just this minute heard of it; and I rushed here."

"What?" said a number of voices at once.

The usually exquisite Godahl was somewhat disheveled and his eyes were red.

"Malvino!" cried he, staring at them as though perplexed at their blandness. "Do you mean to say you don't know why he didn't show up this evening?"

"Didn't show up! What do you mean?"

"You really don't know?" cried Godahl, his eyes blazing.

"No! What? Tell us the answer!" said someone with a laugh.

"The police found him bound and gagged in a deserted cab in Central Park. They've got him in Bellevue Hospital now, raving. By Gad! If I —"

The room laughed. Even the grimy engineer boring a hole to start his compass saw looked over his shoulder and grinned at Godahl.

"Don't excite yourself, Godahl," said Welton, of Tonopah Magnet. "Somebody's been stringing you. We've got Malvino here now. Gad, I wish we didn't have him! You're just in time to help us out of a devil of a mess. That humorist Colwell has plugged the locks with lead; and we can't get the blind beggar out without sawing the door down. He's sweating blood in there now."

"In there?" cried Godahl, pushing his way through the ring round the engineer.

"In there!" repeated Welton. "The kleptomaniac has got a cool ten thousand of mine."

"No!"

"Yes!" said Welton, mimicking Godahl's tone. "You didn't know there was that much money in the world, eh?"

"Let me get this straight," said Godahl, laying a hand on the engineer's arm to stop his work. "You think you have Malvino locked in there with your wallets? I tell you Malvino hasn't been within a mile of this place tonight!"

"I'll lay you a thousand on it!" cried Welton.

"Tut! Tut! Believe me, you are betting on the wrong card." Godahl's eyes danced.

"I lay you a thousand on it!" reiterated the Tonopah magnate. "We'll have to let Malvino hold my stake until we get him out. Gad, he went through me so clean I couldn't swear at this minute that I've got on socks!"

"You are betting on a sure thing?"

"I'm taking candy from a child," retorted Welton.

"I take you!" cried Godahl, his eyes twinkling. "Anybody else want any candy? I warn you!"

There were several. It wasn't every day in the week that they could get Godahl on the hip.

"I warn you again," said Godahl as he accepted the markers, "that Malvino is not in that room. If anybody is there, it is an impostor. You can prove it in a minute by telephoning Bellevue."

The biting saw completed its half circle about the lock; the door swung open. The room was empty!

Several volunteers ran to the rear door. Their sharp chorus of amazement started the crowd tumbling after them. The rear door was off its hinges! It stood propped against the jamb. A child could see what had happened. The prisoner, laden with the cash of the fifty little million-aires, had simply drawn the bolts of the two hinges and lifted the door out of its frame. On the floor was a wad of handbills like those the rogue had left in his dupes' pockets in place of their wallets. They read: "Malvino! He Has No Eyes! Watch His Fingers!"

The fifty little millionaires gazed at each other dumbfounded, feeling their pockets the while. The Infallible Godahl fell into a chair, roaring with laughter. He threw back his head, kicked out his heels, buried his hands wrist deep in the crisp bills that lined his pockets — all in cold, hard cash! On the whole, he had never spent a more profitable evening.

As for Malvino the Magician, that charlatan could be mighty thankful that it was not he whom the honorable gentlemen of the committee had subjected to manhandling. For Malvino had the eyes of a hawk. So much Godahl had ascertained earlier in the evening when he, in the guise of a murderous cabby, was subjecting the Italian to the indignity of a gag.

MELVILLE DAVISSON POST

....

Naboth's Vineyard

ONE HEARS a good deal about the sovereignty of the people in this republic; and many persons imagine it a sort of fiction, and wonder where it lies, who are the guardians of it, and how they would exercise it if the forms and agents of the law were removed. I am not one of those who speculate upon this mystery, for I have seen this primal ultimate authority naked at its work. And, having seen it, I know how mighty and how dread a thing it is. And I know where it lies, and who are the guardians of it, and how they exercise it when the need arises.

There was a great crowd, and for the whole country was in the courtroom. It was a notorious trial.

Elihu Marsh had been shot down in his house. He had been found lying in a room, with a hole through his body that one could put his thumb in. He was an irascible old man, the last of his family, and so, lived alone. He had rich lands, but only a life estate in them, the remainder was to some foreign heirs. A girl from a neighboring farm came now and then to bake and put his house in order, and he kept a farm hand about the premises.

Nothing had been disturbed in the house when the neighbors found Marsh; no robbery had been attempted, for the man's money, a considerable sum, remained on him.

There was not much mystery about the thing, because the farm hand had disappeared. This man was a stranger in the hills. He had come from over the mountains some months before, and gone to work for Marsh. He was a big blond man, young and good looking; of better blood, one would say, than the average laborer. He gave his name as Taylor, but he was not communicative, and little else about him was known.

The country was raised, and this man was overtaken in the foothills of the mountains. He had his clothes tied into a bundle, and a long-barreled fowling-piece on his shoulder. The story he told was that he and Marsh had settled that morning, and he had left the house at noon, but that he had forgotten his gun and had gone back for it; had reached the house about four o'clock, gone into the kitchen, got his gun down from the dogwood forks over the chimney, and at once left the house. He had not seen Marsh, and did not know where he was.

He admitted that this gun had been loaded with a single huge lead bullet. He had so loaded it to kill a dog that sometimes approached the house, but not close enough to be reached with a load of shot. He affected surprise when it was pointed out that the gun had been discharged. He said that he had not fired it, and had not, until then, noticed that it was empty. When asked why he had so suddenly determined to leave the country, he was silent.

He was carried back and confined in the county jail, and now he was on trial at the September term of the circuit court.

The court sat early. Although the Judge, Simon Kilrail, was a landowner and lived on his estate in the country some half dozen miles away, he rode to the courthouse in the morning, and home at night, with his legal papers in his saddle-pockets. It was only when the court sat that he was a lawyer. At other times he harvested his hay and grazed his cattle, and tried to add to his lands like any other man in the hills, and he was as hard in a trade and as hungry for an acre as any.

It was the sign and insignia of distinction in Virginia to own land. Mr. Jefferson had annulled the titles that George the Third had granted, and the land alone remained as a patent of nobility. The Judge wished to be one of these landed gentry, and he had gone a good way to accomplish it. But when the court convened he became a lawyer and sat upon the bench with no heart in him, and a cruel tongue like the English judges.

I think everybody was at this trial. My Uncle Abner and the strange old doctor, Storm, sat on a bench near the center aisle of the courtroom, and I sat behind them, for I was a half-grown lad, and permitted to witness the terrors and severities of the law.

The prisoner was the center of interest. He sat with a stolid countenance like a man careless of the issues of life. But not everybody was concerned with him, for my Uncle Abner and Storm watched the girl who had been accustomed to bake for Marsh and red up his house.

She was a beauty of her type; dark haired and dark eyed like a gypsy, and with an April nature of storm and sun. She sat among the witnesses with a little handkerchief clutched in her hands. She was nervous to the point of hysteria, and I thought that was the reason the old doctor watched her. She would be taken with a gust of tears, and then throw up her head with a fine defiance; and she kneaded and knotted and worked the handkerchief in her fingers. It was a time of stress and many witnesses were unnerved, and I think I should not have noticed this girl but for the whispering of Storm and my Uncle Abner.

The trial went forward, and it became certain that the prisoner would hang. His stubborn refusal to give any reason for his hurried departure had but one meaning, and the circumstantial evidence was conclusive. The motive, only, remained in doubt, and the Judge had charged on this with so many cases in point, and with so heavy a hand, that any virtue in it was removed. The Judge was hard against this man, and indeed there was little sympathy anywhere, for it was a foul killing — the victim an old man and no hot blood to excuse it.

In all trials of great public interest, where the evidences of guilt overwhelmingly assemble against a prisoner, there comes a moment when all the people in the courtroom, as one man, and without a sign of the common purpose, agree upon a verdict; there is no outward or visible evidence of this decision, but one feels it, and it is a moment of the tensest stress.

The trial of Taylor had reached this point, and there lay a moment of deep silence, when this girl sitting among the witnesses suddenly burst into a very hysteria of tears. She stood up shaking with sobs, her voice choking in her throat, and the tears gushing through her fingers.

What she said was not heard at the time by the audience in the courtroom, but it brought the Judge to his feet and the jury crowding about her, and it broke down the silence of the prisoner, and threw him into a perfect fury of denials. We could hear his voice rise above the confusion, and we could see him struggling to get to the girl and stop her. But what she said was presently known to everybody, for it was taken down and signed; and it put the case against Taylor, to use a lawyer's term, out of court.

The girl had killed Marsh herself. And this was the manner and the reason of it: She and Taylor were sweethearts and were to be married. But they had quarreled the night before Marsh's death and the following morning Taylor had left the country. The point of the quarrel was some remark that Marsh had made to Taylor touching the girl's reputation. She had come to the house in the afternoon, and finding her lover gone, and maddened at the sight of the one who had robbed her of him, had taken the gun down from the chimney and killed Marsh. She had then put the gun back into its place and left the house. This was about two o'clock in the afternoon, and about an hour before Taylor returned for his gun.

There was a great veer of public feeling with a profound sense of having come at last upon the truth, for the story not only fitted to the circumstantial evidence against Taylor, but it fitted also to his story and it disclosed the motive for the killing. It explained, too, why he had refused to give the reason for his disappearance. That Taylor denied what the girl said and tried to stop her in her declaration, meant nothing except that the prisoner was a man, and would not have the woman he loved make such a sacrifice for him.

I cannot give all the forms of legal procedure with which the closing hours of the court were taken up, but nothing happened to shake the girl's confession. Whatever the law required was speedily got ready, and she was remanded to the care of the sheriff in order that she might come before the court in the morning.

Taylor was not released, but was also held in custody, although the case against him seemed utterly broken down. The Judge refused to permit the prisoner's counsel to take a verdict. He said that he would withdraw a juror and continue the case. But he seemed unwilling to release any clutch of the law until some one was punished for this crime.

It was on our way, and we rode out with the Judge that night. He talked with Abner and Storm about the pastures and the price of cattle, but not about the trial, as I hoped he would do, except once only, and then it was to inquire why the prosecuting attorney had not called either of them as witnesses, since they were the first to find Marsh, and Storm had been among the doctors who examined him. And Storm had explained how he had mortally offended the prosecutor in his canvass, by his remark that only a gentleman should hold office. He did but quote Mr. Hamilton, Storm said, but the man had received it as a deadly insult, and thereby proved the truth of Mr. Hamilton's expression, Storm added. And Abner said that as no circumstance about Marsh's death was questioned, and others arriving about the same time had been called, the prosecutor doubtless considered further testimony unnecessary.

The Judge nodded, and the conversation turned to other questions. At the gate, after the common formal courtesy of the country, the Judge asked us to ride in, and, to my astonishment, Abner and Storm accepted his invitation. I could see that the man was surprised, and I thought annoyed, but he took us into his library.

I could not understand why Abner and Storm had stopped here, until I remembered how from the first they had been considering the girl, and it occurred to me that they thus sought the Judge in the hope of getting some word to him in her favor. A great sentiment had leaped up for this girl. She had made a staggering sacrifice, and with a headlong courage, and it was like these men to help her if they could.

And it was to speak of the woman that they came, but not in her favor. And while Simon Kilrail listened, they told this extraordinary story: They had been of the opinion that Taylor was not guilty when the trial began, but they had suffered it to proceed in order to see what might develop. The reason was that there were certain circumstantial evidences, overlooked by the prosecutor, indicating the guilt of the woman and the innocence of Taylor. When Storm examined the body of Marsh he discovered that the man had been killed by poison, and was dead when the bullet was fired into his body. This meant that the shooting was a fabricated evidence to direct the suspicion against Taylor. The woman had baked for Marsh on this morning, and the poison was in the bread which he had eaten at noon.

Abner was going on to explain something further, when a servant entered and asked the Judge what time it was. The man had been greatly impressed, and he now sat in a profound reflection. He took his watch out of his pocket and held it in his hand, then he seemed to realize the question and replied that his watch had run down. Abner gave the hour, and said that perhaps his key would wind the watch. The Judge gave it to him, and he wound it and laid it on the table. Storm observed my Uncle with, what I thought, a curious interest, but the Judge paid no attention. He was deep in his reflection and oblivious to everything. Finally he roused himself and made his comment.

"This clears the matter up," he said. "The woman killed Marsh from the motive which she gave in her confession, and she created this false evidence against Taylor because he had abandoned her. She thereby avenged herself desperately in two directions. . . . It would be like a woman to do this, and then regret it and confess."

He then asked my Uncle if he had anything further to tell him, and although I was sure that Abner was going on to say something further when the servant entered, he replied now that he had not, and asked for the horses. The Judge went out to have the horses brought, and we remained in silence. My Uncle was calm, as with some consuming idea, but Storm was as nervous as a cat. He was out of his chair when the door was closed, and hopping about the room looking at the law books standing on the shelves in their leather covers. Suddenly he stopped and plucked out a little volume. He whipped through it with his forefinger, smothered a great oath, and shot it into his pocket, then he crooked his finger to my Uncle, and they talked together in a recess of the window until the Judge returned.

We rode away. I was sure that they intended to say something to the Judge in the woman's favor, for, guilty or not, it was a fine thing she had done to stand up and confess. But something in the interview had changed their purpose. Perhaps when they had heard the Judge's comment they saw it would be of no use. They talked closely together as they rode, but they kept before me and I could not hear. It was of the woman they spoke, however, for I caught a fragment.

"But where is the motive?" said Storm.

And my Uncle answered, "In the twenty-first chapter of the Book of Kings."

We were early at the county seat, and it was a good thing for us, because the court-room was crowded to the doors. My Uncle had got a big record book out of the county clerk's office as he came in, and I was glad of it, for he gave it to me to sit on, and it raised me up so I could see. Storm was there, too, and, in fact, every man of any standing in the country.

The sheriff opened the court, the prisoners were brought in, and the Judge took his seat on the bench. He looked haggard like a man who had not slept, as, in fact, one could hardly have done who had so cruel a duty before him. Here was every human feeling pressing to save a woman, and the law to hang her. But for all his hagridden face, when he came to act, the man was adamant.

He ordered the confession read, and directed the girl to stand up. Taylor tried again to protest, but he was forced down into his chair. The girl stood up bravely, but she was white as plaster, and her eyes dilated. She was asked if she still adhered to the confession and understood the consequences of it, and, although she trembled from head to toe, she spoke out distinctly. There was a moment of silence and the Judge was about to speak, when another voice filled the court-room. I turned about on my book to find my head against my Uncle Abner's legs.

"I challenge the confession!" he said.

The whole court-room moved. Every eye was on the two tragic figures standing up: the slim, pale girl and the big, somber figure of my Uncle. The Judge was astounded.

"On what ground?" he said.

"On the ground," replied my Uncle, "that the confession is a lie!"

One could have heard a pin fall anywhere in the whole room. The girl caught her breath in a little gasp, and the prisoner, Taylor, half rose and then sat down as though his knees were too weak to bear him. The Judge's mouth opened, but for a moment or two he did not speak, and I could understand his amazement. Here was Abner assailing a confession which he himself had supported before the Judge, and speaking for the innocence of a woman whom he himself had shown to be guilty and taking one position privately, and another publicly. What did the man mean? And I was not surprised that the Judge's voice was stern when he spoke.

"This is irregular," he said. "It may be that this woman killed Marsh, or it may be that Taylor killed him, and there is some collusion between these persons, as you appear to suggest. And you may know something to throw light on the matter, or you may not. However that may be, this is not the time for me to hear you. You will have ample opportunity to speak when I come to try the case."

"But you will never try this case!" said Abner.

I cannot undertake to describe the desperate interest that lay on the people in the courtroom. They were breathlessly silent; one could hear the voices from the village outside, and the sounds of men and horses that came up through the open windows. No one knew what hidden thing Abner drove at. But he was a man who meant what he said, and the people knew it.

The Judge turned on him with a terrible face.

"What do you mean?" he said.

"I mean," replied Abner, and it was in his deep, hard voice, "that you must come down from the bench."

The Judge was in a heat of fury.

"You are in contempt," he roared. "I order your arrest. Sheriff!" he called.

But Abner did not move. He looked the man calmly in the face.

"You threaten me," he said, "but God Almighty threatens you." And he turned about to the audience. "The authority of the law," he said, "is in the hands of the electors of this county. Will they stand up?"

I shall never forget what happened then, for I have never in my life seen anything so deliberate and impressive. Slowly, in silence, and without passion, as though they were in a church of God, men began to get up in the courtroom.

Randolph was the first. He was a justice of the peace, vain and pompous, proud of the abilities of an ancestry that he did not inherit. And his superficialities were the annoyance of my Uncle Abner's life. But whatever I may have to say of him hereafter I want to say this thing of him here, that his bigotry and his vanities were builded on the foundations of a man. He stood up as though he stood alone, with no glance about him to see what other men would do, and he faced the Judge calmly above his great black stock. And I learned then that a man may be a blusterer and a lion.

Hiram Arnold got up, and Rockford, and Armstrong, and Alkire, and Coopman, and Monroe, and Elnathan Stone, and my father, Lewis, and Dayton and Ward, and Madison from beyond the mountains. And it seemed to me that the very hills and valleys were standing up.

It was a strange and instructive thing to see. The loudmouthed and the reckless were in that courtroom, men who would have shouted in a political convention, or run howling with a mob, but they were not the persons who stood up when Abner called upon the authority of the people to appear. Men rose whom one would not have looked to see — the blacksmith, the saddler, and old Asa Divers. And I saw that law and order and all the structure that civilization had builded up, rested on the sense of justice that certain men carried in their breasts, and that those who possessed it not, in the crisis of necessity, did not count.

Father Donovan stood up; he had a little flock beyond the valley river, and he was as poor, and almost as humble as his Master, but he was not afraid; and Bronson, who preached Calvin, and Adam Rider, who traveled a Methodist circuit. No one of them believed in what the other taught; but they all believed in justice, and when the line was drawn, there was but one side for them all.

The last man up was Nathaniel Davisson, but the reason was that he was very old, and he had to wait for his sons to help him. He had been time and again in the Assembly of Virginia, at a time when only a gentleman and landowner could sit there. He was a just man, and honorable and unafraid.

The Judge, his face purple, made a desperate effort to enforce his authority. He pounded on his desk and ordered the sheriff to clear the courtroom. But the sheriff remained standing apart. He did not lack for courage, and I think he would have faced the people if his duty had been that way. His attitude was firm, and one could mark no uncertainty upon him, but he took no step to obey what the Judge commanded.

The Judge cried out at him in a terrible voice.

"I am the representative of the law here. Go on!"

The sheriff was a plain man, and unacquainted with the nice expressions of Mr. Jefferson, but his answer could not have been better if that gentleman had written it out for him.

"I would obey the representative of the law," he said, "if I were not in the presence of the law itself!"

The Judge rose. "This is revolution," he said; "I will send to the Governor for the militia."

It was Nathaniel Davisson who spoke then. He was very old and the tremors of dissolution were on him, but his voice was steady.

"Sit down, your Honor," he said, "there is no revolution here, and you do not require troops to support your authority. We are here to support it if it ought to be lawfully enforced. But the people have elevated you to be the Bench because they believed in your integrity, and if they have been mistaken they would know it." He paused, as though to collect his strength, and then went on. "The presumptions of right are all with your Honor. You administer the law upon our authority and we stand behind you. Be assured that we will not suffer our authority to be insulted in your person." His voice grew deep and resolute. "It is a grave thing to call us up against you, and not lightly, nor for a trivial reason shall any man dare to do it." Then he turned about. "Now, Abner," he said, "what is this thing?"

Young as I was, I felt that the old man spoke for the people standing in the courtroom, with their voice and their authority, and I began to fear that the measure which my Uncle had taken was high-handed. But he stood there like the shadow of a great rock.

"I charge him," he said, "with the murder of Elihu Marsh! And I call upon him to vacate the Bench."

When I think about this extraordinary event now, I wonder at the calmness with which Simon Kilrail met this blow, until I reflect that he had seen it on its way, and had got ready to meet it. But even with that preparation, it took a man of iron nerve to face an assault like that and keep every muscle in its place. He had tried violence and had failed with it, and he had recourse now to the attitudes and mannerisms of a judicial dignity. He sat with his elbows on the table, and his clenched fingers propping up his jaw. He looked coldly at Abner, but he did not speak, and there was silence until Nathaniel Davisson spoke for him. His face and his voice were like iron.

"No, Abner," he said, "he shall not vacate the Bench for that, nor upon the accusation of any man. We will have your proofs, if you please."

The Judge turned his cold face from Abner to Nathaniel Davisson, and then he looked over the men standing in the courtroom.

"I am not going to remain here," he said, "to be tried by a mob, upon the *viva voce* indictment of a bystander. You may nullify your court, if you like, and suspend the forms of law for yourselves, but you cannot nullify the constitution of Virginia, nor suspend my right as a citizen of that commonwealth."

"And now," he said, rising, "if you will kindly make way, I will vacate this courtroom, which your violence has converted into a chamber of sedition."

The man spoke in a cold, even voice, and I thought he had presented a difficulty that could not be met. How could these men before him undertake to keep the peace of this frontier, and force its lawless elements to submit to the forms of law for trail, and deny any letter of those formalities to this man? Was the grand jury, and the formal indictment, and all the right and privilege of an orderly procedure for one, and not for another?

It was Nathaniel Davisson who met this dangerous problem.

"We are not concerned," he said, "at this moment with your rights as a citizen; the rights of private citizenship are inviolate, and they remain to you, when you return to it. But you are not a private citizen. You are our agent. We have selected you to administer the law for us, and your right to act has been challenged. Well, as the authority behind you, we appear and would know the reason."

The Judge retained his imperturbable calm.

"Do you hold me a prisoner here?" he said.

"We hold you an official in your office," replied Davisson, "not only do we refuse to permit you to leave the courtroom, but we refuse to permit you to leave the Bench. This court shall remain as we have set it up until it is our will to readjust it. And it shall not be changed at the pleasure or demand of any man but by us only, and for a sufficient cause shown to us."

And again I was anxious for my Uncle, for I saw how grave a thing it was to interfere with the authority of the people as manifested in the forms and agencies of the law. Abner must be very sure of the ground under him.

And he was sure. He spoke now, with no introductory expressions, but directly and in the simplest words.

"These two persons," he said, indicating Taylor and the girl, "have each been willing to die in order to save the other. Neither is guilty of this crime. Taylor has kept silent, and the girl has lied, to the same end. This is the truth: There was a lovers' quarrel, and Taylor left the country precisely as he told us, except the motive, which he would not tell lest the girl be involved. And the woman, to save him, confesses to a crime that she did not commit.

"Who did commit it?" He paused and included Storm with a gesture. "We suspected this woman because Marsh had been killed by poison in his bread, and afterwards mutilated with a shot. Yesterday we rode out with the Judge to put those facts before him." Again he paused. "An incident occurring in that interview indicated that we were wrong; a second incident assured us, and still later, a third convinced us. These incidents were, first, that the Judge's watch had run down; second, that we found in his library a book with all the leaves in it uncut, except at one certain page; and, third, that we found in the county clerk's office an unindexed record in an old deed book." There was deep quiet and he went on:

"In addition to the theory of Taylor's guilt or this woman's, there was still a third; but it had only a single incident to support it, and we feared to suggest it until the others had been explained. This theory was that some one, to benefit by Marsh's death, had planned to kill him in such a manner as to throw suspicion on this woman who baked his bread, and finding Taylor gone, and the gun above the mantel, yielded to an afterthought to create a further false evidence. It was overdone!

"The trigger guard of the gun in the recoil caught in the chain of the assassin's watch and jerked it out of his pocket; he replaced the watch, but not the key which fell to the floor, and which I picked up beside the body of the dead man."

Abner turned toward the Judge.

"And so," he said, "I charge Simon Kilrail with this murder; because the key winds his watch; because the record in the old deed book is a conveyance by the heirs of Marsh's lands to him at the life tenant's death; and because the book we found in his library is a book on poisons with the leaves uncut, except at the very page describing that identical poison with which Elihu Marsh was murdered."

The strained silence that followed Abner's words was broken by a voice that thundered in the courtroom. It was Randolph's.

"Come down!" he said.

And this time Nathaniel Davisson was silent.

The Judge got slowly on his feet, a resolution was forming in his face, and it advanced swiftly.

"I will give you my answer in a moment," he said.

Then he turned about and went into his room behind the Bench. There was but one door, and that opening into the court, and the people waited.

The windows were open and we could see the green fields, and the sun, and the far-off mountains, and the peace and quiet and serenity of autumn entered. The Judge did not appear. Presently there was the sound of a shot from behind the closed door. The sheriff threw it open, and upon the floor, sprawling in a smear of blood, lay Simon Kilrail, with a dueling pistol in his hand.

1917

SUSAN GLASPELL

....

A Jury of Her Peers

WHEN Martha Hale opened the storm door and got a cut of the north wind, she ran back for her big woolen scarf. As she hurriedly wound that round her head her eye made a scandalized sweep of her kitchen. It was no ordinary thing that called her away — it was probably farther from ordinary than anything that had ever happened in Dickson County. But what her eye took in was that her kitchen was in no shape for leaving: her bread all ready for mixing, half the flour sifted and half unsifted.

She hated to see things half done; but she had been at that when the team from town stopped to get Mr. Hale, and then the sheriff came running in to say his wife wished Mrs. Hale would come too — adding, with a grin, that he guessed she was getting scarey and wanted another woman along. So she had dropped everything right where it was.

"Martha!" now came her husband's impatient voice. "Don't keep folks waiting out here in the cold."

She again opened the storm door, and this time joined the three men and the one woman waiting for her in the big two-seated buggy.

After she had the robes tucked around her she took another look at the woman who sat beside her on the back seat. She had met Mrs. Peters the year before at the county fair, and the thing she remembered about her was that she didn't seem like a sheriff's wife. She was small and thin and didn't have a strong voice. Mrs. Gorman, sheriff's wife before Gorman went out and Peters came in, had a voice that somehow seemed to be backing up the law with every word. But if Mrs. Peters didn't look like a sheriff's wife, Peters made it up in looking like a sheriff. He was to a dot the kind of man who could get himself elected sheriff — a heavy man with a big voice, who was particularly genial with the law-abiding, as if to make it plain that he knew the difference between criminals and non-criminals. And right there it came into Mrs. Hale's mind, with a stab, that this man who was so pleasant and lively with all of them was going to the Wrights' now as a sheriff.

"The country's not very pleasant this time of year," Mrs. Peters at last ventured, as if she felt they ought to be talking as well as the men.

Mrs. Hale scarcely finished her reply, for they had gone up a little hill and could see the Wright place now, and seeing it did not make her feel like talking. It looked very lonesome this cold March morning. It had always been a lonesome-looking place. It was down in a hollow, and the poplar trees around it were lonesome-looking trees. The men were looking at it and talking about what had happened. The county attorney was bending to one side of the buggy, and kept looking steadily at the place as they drew up to it.

"I'm glad you came with me," Mrs. Peters said nervously, as the two women were about to follow the men in through the kitchen door.

Even after she had her foot on the doorstep, her hand on the knob, Martha Hale had a moment of feeling she could not cross that threshold. And the reason it seemed she couldn't cross it now was simply because she hadn't crossed it before. Time and time again it had been in her mind, "I ought to go over and see Minnie Foster" — she still thought of her as Minnie Foster, though for twenty years she had been Mrs. Wright. And then there was always something to do and Minnie Foster would go from her mind. But *now* she could come.

The men went over to the stove. The women stood close together by the door. Young Henderson, the county attorney, turned around and said:

"Come up to the fire, ladies."

Mrs. Peters took a step forward, then stopped. "I'm not — cold," she said.

The men talked for a minute about what a good thing it was the sheriff had sent his deputy out that morning to make a fire for them, and then Sheriff Peters stepped back from the stove, unbuttoned his outer coat, and leaned his hands on the kitchen table in a way that seemed to mark the beginning of official business. "Now, Mr. Hale," he said in a sort of semi-official voice, "before we move things about, you tell Mr. Henderson just what it was you saw when you came here yesterday morning."

The county attorney was looking around the kitchen.

"By the way," he said, "has anything been moved?" He turned to the sheriff. "Are things just as you left them yesterday?"

Peters looked from cupboard to sink; from that to a small worn rocker a little to one side of the kitchen table.

"It's just the same."

"Somebody should have been left here yesterday," said the county attorney.

"Oh — yesterday," returned the sheriff, with a little gesture as of yesterday having been more than he could bear to think of. "When I had to send Frank to Morris Center for that man who went crazy — let me tell you, I had my hands full *yesterday*. I knew you could get back from Omaha by today, George, and as long as I went over everything here myself —"

"Well, Mr. Hale," said the county attorney, in a way of letting what was past and gone go, "tell just what happened when you came here yesterday morning."

Mrs. Hale, still leaning against the door, had that sinking feeling of the mother whose child is about to speak a piece. Lewis often wandered along and got things mixed up in a story. She hoped he would tell this straight and plain, and not say unnecessary things that would just make things harder for Minnie Foster. He didn't begin at once, and she noticed that he looked queer — as if standing in that kitchen and having to tell what he had seen there yesterday morning made him almost sick.

"Harry and I had started to town with a load of potatoes," Mrs. Hale's husband began.

Harry was Mrs. Hale's oldest boy. He wasn't with them now, for the very good reason that those potatoes never got to town yesterday and he was taking them this morning, so he hadn't been home when the sheriff stopped to say he wanted Mr. Hale to come over to the Wright place and tell the county attorney his story there, where he could point it all out.

"We came along this road," Hale was going on, with a motion of his hand to the road over which they had just come, "and as we got in sight of the house I says to Harry, 'I'm goin' to see if I can't get John Wright to take a telephone.' You see," he explained to Henderson, "unless I can get somebody to go in with me they won't come out this branch road except for a price *I* can't pay. I'd spoke to Wright about it once before; but he put me off, saying folks talked too much anyway, and all he asked was peace and quiet — guess you know about how much he talked himself. But I thought maybe if I went to the house and talked about it before his wife, and said all the womenfolks liked the telephones, and that in this lonesome stretch of road it would be a good thing — well, I

said to Harry that that was what I was going to say — though I said at
the same time that I didn't know as what his wife wanted made much
difference to John —".

Now, there he was! — saying things he didn't need to say. Mrs. Hale
tried to catch her husband's eye, but fortunately the county attorney interrupted with:

"Let's talk about that a little later, Mr. Hale. I do want to talk about
that, but I'm anxious now to get along to just exactly what happened
when you got here."

When he began this time, it was very deliberately and carefully:

"I didn't see or hear anything. I knocked at the door. And still it was
all quiet inside. I knew they must be up — it was past eight o'clock. So I
knocked again, louder, and I thought I heard somebody say, 'Come in.' I
wasn't sure — I'm not sure yet. But I opened the door — this door,"
jerking a hand toward the door by which the two women stood, "and
there, in that rocker" — pointing to it — "sat Mrs. Wright."

Everyone in the kitchen looked at the rocker. It came into Mrs. Hale's
mind that that rocker didn't look in the least like Minnie Foster — the
Minnie Foster of twenty years before. It was a dingy red, with wooden
rungs up the back, and the middle rung was gone, and the chair sagged
to one side.

"How did she — look?" the county attorney was inquiring.

"Well," said Hale, "she looked — queer."

"How do you mean — queer?"

As he asked it he took out a notebook and pencil. Mrs. Hale did not
like the sight of that pencil. She kept her eye fixed on her husband, as if
to keep him from saying unnecessary things that would go into that
notebook and make trouble.

Hale did speak guardedly, as if the pencil had affected him too.

"Well, as if she didn't know what she was going to do next. And kind
of — done up."

"How did she seem to feel about your coming?"

"Why, I don't think she minded — one way or other. She didn't pay
much attention. I said, 'Ho' do, Mrs. Wright? It's cold, ain't it?' And she
said, 'Is it?' — and went on pleatin' at her apron.

"Well, I was surprised. She didn't ask me to come up to the stove, or
to sit down, but just set there, not even lookin' at me. And so I said: 'I
want to see John.' And then she laughed. I guess you would call it a
laugh.

"I thought of Harry and the team outside, so I said, a little sharp,

'Can I see John?' 'No,' says she — kind of dull like. 'Ain't he home?' says
I. Then she looked at me. 'Yes,' says she, 'he's home.' 'Then why can't I
see him?' I asked her, out of patience with her now. "Cause he's dead,'
says she, just as quiet and dull — and fell to pleatin' her apron. 'Dead?'
says I, like you do when you can't take in what you've heard.

"She just nodded her head, not getting a bit excited, but rockin' back
and forth.

"'Why — where is he?' says I, not knowing *what* to say.

"She just pointed upstairs — like this" — pointing to the room above.

"I got up, with the idea of going up there myself. But this time I —
didn't know what to do. I walked from there to here; then I says: 'Why,
what did he die of?'

"'He died of a rope round his neck,' says she; and just went on pleatin'
at her apron."

Hale stopped speaking, and stood staring at the rocker, as if he were
still seeing the woman who had sat there the morning before. Nobody
spoke; it was as if everyone were seeing the woman who had sat there
the morning before.

"And what did you do then?" the county attorney at last broke the silence.

"I went out and called Harry. I thought I might — need help. I got
Harry in, and we went upstairs." His voice fell almost to a whisper.
"There he was — lying over the —"

"I think I'd rather have you go into that upstairs," the county attorney interrupted, "where you can point it all out. Just go on now with
the rest of the story."

"Well, my first thought was to get that rope off. It looked —"

He stopped, his face twitching.

"But Harry, he went up to him, and he said, 'No, he's dead all right,
and we'd better not touch anything.' So we went downstairs. She was
still sitting that same way. 'Has anybody been notified?' I asked. 'No,'
said she, unconcerned.

"'Who did this, Mrs. Wright?' said Harry. He said it businesslike, and
she stopped pleatin' at her apron. 'I don't know,' she says. 'You don't
know?' says Harry. 'Weren't you sleepin' in the bed with him?' 'Yes,' says
she, 'but I was on the inside.' 'Somebody slipped a rope round his neck
and strangled him, and you didn't wake up?' says Harry. 'I didn't wake
up,' she said after him.

"We may have looked as if we didn't see how that could be, for after a
minute she said, 'I sleep sound.'

"Harry was going to ask her more questions, but I said maybe that weren't our business; maybe we ought to let her tell her story first to the coroner or the sheriff. So Harry went fast as he could over to High Road — the Rivers' place, where there's a telephone."

"And what did she do when she knew you had gone for the coroner?" The attorney got his pencil in his hand all ready for writing.

"She moved from that chair to this one over here" — Hale pointed to a small chair in the corner — "and just sat there with her hands held together and looking down. I got a feeling that I ought to make some conversation, so I said I had come in to see if John wanted to put in a telephone; and at that she started to laugh, and then she stopped and looked at me — scared."

At sound of a moving pencil the man who was telling the story looked up.

"I dunno — maybe it wasn't scared," he hastened; "I wouldn't like to say it was. Soon Harry got back, and then Dr. Lloyd came, and you, Mr. Peters, and so I guess that's all I know that you don't."

He said that last with relief, and moved a little, as if relaxing. Everyone moved a little. The county attorney walked toward the stair door.

"I guess we'll go upstairs first — then out to the barn and around."

He paused and looked around the kitchen.

"You're convinced there was nothing important here?" he asked the sheriff. "Nothing that would — point to any motive?"

The sheriff too looked all around, as if to re-convince himself.

"Nothing here but kitchen things," he said, with a little laugh for the insignificance of kitchen things.

The county attorney was looking at the cupboard — a peculiar, ungainly structure, half closet and half cupboard, the upper part of it being built in the wall, and the lower part just the old-fashioned kitchen cupboard. As if its queerness attracted him, he got a chair and opened the upper part and looked in. After a moment he drew his hand away sticky.

"Here's a nice mess," he said resentfully.

The two women had drawn nearer, and now the sheriff's wife spoke.

"Oh — her fruit," she said, looking to Mrs. Hale for sympathetic understanding. She turned back to the county attorney and explained: "She worried about that when it turned so cold last night. She said the fire would go out and her jars burst."

Mrs. Peters' husband broke into a laugh.

"Well, can you beat the women! Held for murder, and worrying about her preserves!"

The young attorney set his lips.

"I guess before we're through she may have something more serious than preserves to worry about."

"Oh, well," said Mrs. Hale's husband, with good-natured superiority, "women are used to worrying over trifles."

The two women moved a little closer together. Neither of them spoke. The county attorney seemed suddenly to remember his manners — and think of his future.

"And yet," said he, with the gallantry of a young politician, "for all their worries, what would we do without the ladies?"

The women did not speak, did not unbend. He went to the sink and began washing his hands. He turned to wipe them on the roller towel — whirled it for a cleaner place.

"Dirty towels! Not much of a housekeeper, would you say, ladies?"

He kicked his foot against some dirty pans under the sink.

"There's a great deal of work to be done on a farm," said Mrs. Hale stiffly.

"To be sure. And yet" — with a little bow to her — "I know there are some Dickson County farmhouses that do not have such roller towels."

"Those towels get dirty awful quick. Men's hands aren't always as clean as they might be."

"Ah, loyal to your sex, I see," he laughed. He stopped and gave her a keen look. "But you and Mrs. Wright were neighbors. I suppose you were friends, too."

Martha Hale shook her head.

"I've seen little enough of her of late years. I've not been in this house — it's more than a year."

"And why was that? You didn't like her?"

"I liked her well enough," she replied with spirit. "Farmers' wives have their hands full, Mr. Henderson. And then —" She looked around the kitchen.

"Yes?" he encouraged.

"It never seemed a very cheerful place," said she, more to herself than to him.

"No," he agreed; "I don't think anyone would call it cheerful. I shouldn't say she had the homemaking instinct."

"Well, I don't know as Wright had, either," she muttered.

"You mean they didn't get on very well?" he was quick to ask.

"No; I don't mean anything," she answered, with decision. As she turned a little away from him, she added: "But I don't think a place would be any the cheerfuller for John Wright's bein' in it."

"I'd like to talk to you about that a little later, Mrs. Hale," he said. "I'm anxious to get the lay of things upstairs now."

He moved toward the stair door, followed by the two men.

"I suppose anything Mrs. Peters does'll be all right?" the sheriff inquired. "She was to take in some clothes for her, you know — and a few little things. We left in such a hurry yesterday."

The county attorney looked at the two women whom they were leaving alone there among the kitchen things.

"Yes — Mrs. Peters," he said, his glance resting on the woman who was not Mrs. Peters, the big farmer woman who stood behind the sheriff's wife. "Of course Mrs. Peters is one of us," he said, in a manner of entrusting responsibility. "And keep your eye out, Mrs. Peters, for anything that might be of use. No telling; you women might come upon a clue to the motive — and that's the thing we need."

Mr. Hale rubbed his face after the fashion of a showman getting ready for a pleasantry.

"But would the women know a clue if they did come upon it?" he said; and, having delivered himself of this, he followed the others through the stair door.

The women stood motionless and silent, listening to the footsteps, first upon the stairs, then in the room above.

Then, as if releasing herself from something strange, Mrs. Hale began to arrange the dirty pans under the sink, which the county attorney's disdainful push of the foot had deranged.

"I'd hate to have men comin' into my kitchen," she said testily — "snoopin' round and criticizin'."

"Of course it's no more than their duty," said the sheriff's wife, in her manner of timid acquiescence.

"Duty's all right," replied Mrs. Hale bluffly; "but I guess that deputy sheriff that come out to make the fire might have got a little of this on." She gave the roller towel a pull. "Wish I'd thought of that sooner! Seems mean to talk about her for not having things slicked up, when she had to come away in such a hurry."

She looked around the kitchen. Certainly it was not "slicked up." Her eye was held by a bucket of sugar on a low shelf. The cover was off the wooden bucket, and beside it was a paper bag — half full.

Mrs. Hale moved toward it.

"She was putting this in there," she said to herself — slowly.

She thought of the flour in her kitchen at home — half sifted. She had been interrupted, and had left things half done. What had interrupted Minnie Foster? Why had that work been left half done? She made a move as if to finish it — unfinished things always bothered her — and then she glanced around and saw that Mrs. Peters was watching her — and she didn't want Mrs. Peters to get that feeling she had got of work begun and then — for some reason — not finished.

"It's a shame about her fruit," she said, and walked toward the cupboard that the county attorney had opened, and got on the chair, murmuring: "I wonder if it's all gone."

It was a sorry enough looking sight, but "Here's one that's all right," she said at last. She held it toward the light. "This is cherries, too." She looked again. "I declare I believe that's the only one."

With a sigh, she got down from the chair, went to the sink, and wiped off the bottle.

"She'll feel awful bad, after all her hard work in the hot weather. I remember the afternoon I put up my cherries last summer."

She set the bottle on the table, and, with another sigh, started to sit down in the rocker. But she did not sit down. Something kept her from sitting down in that chair. She straightened — stepped back, and, half turned away, stood looking at it, seeing the woman who had sat there "pleatin' at her apron."

The thin voice of the sheriff's wife broke in upon her: "I must be getting those things from the front room closet." She opened the door into the other room, started in, stepped back. "You coming with me, Mrs. Hale?" she asked nervously. "You — you could help me get them."

They were soon back — the stark coldness of that shut-up room was not a thing to linger in.

"My!" said Mrs. Peters, dropping the things on the table and hurrying to the stove.

Mrs. Hale stood examining the clothes the woman who was being detained in town had said she wanted.

"Wright was close!" she exclaimed, holing up a shabby black skirt that bore the marks of much making over. "I think maybe that's why she kept so much to herself. I s'pose she felt she couldn't do her part; and then, you don't enjoy things when you feel shabby. She used to wear pretty clothes and be lively — when she was Minnie Foster, one of the town girls, singing in the choir. But that — oh, that was twenty years ago."

With a carefulness in which there was something tender, she folded the shabby clothes and piled them at one corner of the table. She looked up at Mrs. Peters, and there was something in the other woman's look that irritated her.

"She don't care," she said to herself. "Much difference it makes to her whether Minnie Foster had pretty clothes when she was a girl."

Then she looked again, and she wasn't so sure; in fact, she hadn't at any time been perfectly sure about Mrs. Peters. She had that shrinking manner, and yet her eyes looked as if they could see a long way into things.

"This all you was to take in?" asked Mrs. Hale.

"No," said the sheriff's wife; "she said she wanted an apron. Funny thing to want," she ventured in her nervous little way, "for there's not much to get you dirty in jail, goodness knows. But I suppose just to make her feel more natural. If you're used to wearing an apron — . She said they were in the bottom drawer of this cupboard. Yes — here they are. And then her little shawl that always hung on the stair door."

She took the small gray shawl from behind the door leading upstairs.

Suddenly Mrs. Hale took a quick step toward the other woman.

"Mrs. Peters!"

"Yes, Mrs. Hale?"

"Do you think she — did it?"

A frightened look blurred the other thing in Mrs. Peters' eyes.

"Oh, I don't know," she said, in a voice that seemed to shrink away from the subject.

"Well, I don't think she did," affirmed Mrs. Hale stoutly. "Asking for an apron, and her little shawl. Worryin' about her fruit."

"Mr. Peters says — ." Footsteps were heard in the room above; she stopped, looked up, then went on in a lowered voice: "Mr. Peters says — it looks bad for her. Mr. Henderson is awful sarcastic in a speech, and he's going to make fun of her saying she didn't — wake up."

For a moment Mrs. Hale had no answer. Then, "Well, I guess John Wright didn't wake up — when they was slippin' that rope under his neck," she muttered.

"No, it's *strange*," breathed Mrs. Peters. "They think it was such a — funny way to kill a man."

"That's just what Mr. Hale said," said Mrs. Hale, in a resolutely natural voice. "There was a gun in the house. He says that's what he can't understand."

"Mr. Henderson said, coming out, that what was needed for the case was a motive. Something to show anger — or sudden feeling."

"Well, I don't see any signs of anger around here," said Mrs. Hale. "I don't —"

She stopped. It was as if her mind tripped on something. Her eye was caught by a dish towel in the middle of the kitchen table. Slowly she moved toward the table. One half of it was wiped clean, the other half messy. Her eyes made a slow, almost unwilling turn to the bucket of sugar and the half empty bag beside it. Things begun — and not finished.

After a moment she stepped back, and said, in that manner of releasing herself: "Wonder how they're finding things upstairs? I hope she had it a little more red up there. You know" — she paused, and feeling gathered — "it seems kind of *sneaking:* locking her up in town and coming out here to get her own house to turn against her!"

"But, Mrs. Hale," said the sheriff's wife, "the law is the law."

"I s'pose 'tis," answered Mrs. Hale shortly.

She turned to the stove, worked with it a minute, and when she straightened up she said aggressively:

"The law is the law — and a bad stove is a bad stove. How'd you like to cook on this?" — pointing with the poker to the broken lining. She opened the oven door and started to express her opinion of the oven; but she was swept into her own thoughts, thinking of what it would mean, year after year, to have that stove to wrestle with. The thought of Minnie Foster trying to bake in that oven — and the thought of her never going over to see Minnie Foster —

She was startled by hearing Mrs. Peters say:

"A person gets discouraged — and loses heart."

The sheriff's wife had looked from the stove to the pail of water which had been carried in from outside. The two women stood there silent, above them the footsteps of the men who were looking for evidence against the woman who had worked in that kitchen. That look of seeing into things, of seeing through a thing to something else, was in the eyes of the sheriff's wife now. When Mrs. Hale next spoke to her, it was gently:

"Better loosen up your things, Mrs. Peters. We'll not feel them when we go out."

Mrs. Peters went to the back of the room to hang up the fur tippet she was wearing. A moment later she exclaimed, "Why, she was piecing a quilt," and held up a large sewing basket piled high with quilt pieces.

Mrs. Hale spread some of the blocks out on the table.

"It's log-cabin pattern," she said, putting several of them together. "Pretty, isn't it?"

They were so engaged with the quilt that they did not hear the footsteps on the stairs. Just as the stair door opened Mrs. Hale was saying:

"Do you suppose she was going to quilt it or just knot it?"

The sheriff threw up his hands.

"They wonder whether she was going to quilt it or just knot it!" he said.

There was a laugh for the ways of women, a warming of hands over the stove, and then the county attorney said briskly:

"Well, let's go right out to the barn and get that cleared up."

"I don't see as there's anything so strange," Mrs. Hale said resentfully, after the outside door had closed on the three men — "our taking up our time with little things while we're waiting for them to get the evidence. I don't see as it's anything to laugh about."

"Of course they've got awful important things on their minds," said the sheriff's wife apologetically.

They returned to an inspection of the block for the quilt. Mrs. Hale was looking at the fine, even sewing, and preoccupied with thoughts of the woman who had done that sewing, when she heard the sheriff's wife say, in a queer tone:

"Why, look at this one."

She turned to take the block held out to her.

"The sewing," said Mrs. Peters, in a troubled way. "All the rest of them have been so nice and even — but — this one. Why, it looks as if she didn't know what she was about!"

Their eyes met — something flashed to life, passed between them; then, as if with an effort, they seemed to pull away from each other. A moment Mrs. Hale sat there, her hands folded over that sewing which was so unlike all the rest of the sewing . Then she had pulled a knot and drawn the threads.

"Oh, what are you doing, Mrs. Hale?" asked the sheriff's wife.

"Just pulling out a stitch or two that's not sewed very good," said Mrs. Hale mildly.

"I don't think we ought to touch things," Mrs. Peters said, a little helplessly.

"I'll just finish up this end," answered Mrs. Hale, still in that mild, matter-of-fact fashion.

She threaded a needle and started to replace bad sewing with good. For a little while she sewed in silence. Then, in that thin, timid voice, she heard:

"Mrs. Hale!"

"Yes, Mrs. Peters?"

"What do you suppose she was so — nervous about?"

"Oh, *I* don't know," said Mrs. Hale, as if dismissing a thing not important enough to spend much time on. "I don't know as she was — nervous. I sew awful queer sometimes when I'm just tired."

She cut a thread, and out of the corner of her eye looked up at Mrs. Peters. The small, lean face of the sheriff's wife seemed to have tightened up. Her eyes had that look of peering into something. But next moment she moved, and said in her indecisive way:

"Well, I must get those clothes wrapped. They may be through sooner than we think. I wonder where I could find a piece of paper — and string."

"In that cupboard, maybe," suggested Mrs. Hale, after a glance around.

One piece of the crazy sewing remained unripped. Mrs. Peters' back turned, Martha Hale now scrutinized that piece, compared it with the dainty, accurate sewing of the other blocks. The difference was startling. Holding this block made her feel queer, as if the distracted thoughts of the woman who had perhaps turned to it to try and quiet herself were communicating themselves to her.

Mrs. Peters' voice roused her.

"Here's a bird-cage," she said. "Did she have a bird, Mrs. Hale?"

"Why, I don't know whether she did or not." She turned to look at the cage Mrs. Peters was holding up. "I've not been here in so long." She sighed. "There was a man last year selling canaries cheap — but I don't know as she took one. Maybe she did. She used to sing real pretty herself."

"Seems kind of funny to think of a bird here." She half laughed — an attempt to put up a barrier. "But she must have had one — or why would she have a cage? I wonder what happened to it."

"I suppose maybe the cat got it," suggested Mrs. Hale, resuming her sewing.

"No; she didn't have a cat. She's got that feeling some people have about cats — being afraid of them. When they brought her to our house yesterday, my cat got in the room, and she was real upset and asked me to take it out."

"My sister Bessie was like that," laughed Mrs. Hale.

The sheriff's wife did not reply. The silence made Mrs. Hale turn around. Mrs. Peters was examining the bird-cage.

"Look at this door," she said slowly. "It's broke. One hinge has been pulled apart."

Mrs. Hale came nearer.

"Looks as if someone must have been — rough with it."

Again their eyes met — startled, questioning, apprehensive. For a moment neither spoke nor stirred. Then Mrs. Hale, turning away, said brusquely:

"If they're going to find any evidence, I wish they'd be about it. I don't like this place."

"But I'm awful glad you came with me, Mrs. Hale." Mrs. Peters put the bird-cage on the table and sat down. "It would be lonesome for me — sitting here alone."

"Yes, it would, wouldn't it?" agreed Mrs. Hale, a certain very determined naturalness in her voice. She had picked up the sewing, but now it dropped in her lap, and she murmured in a different voice: "But I tell you what I *do* wish, Mrs. Peters. I wish I had come over sometimes when she was here. I wish — I had."

"But of course you were awful busy, Mrs. Hale. Your house — and your children."

"I could've come," retorted Mrs. Hale shortly. "I stayed away because it weren't cheerful — and that's why I ought to have come. I" — she looked around — "I've never liked this place. Maybe because it's down in a hollow and you don't see the road. I don't know what it is, but it's a lonesome place, and always was. I wish I had come over to see Minnie Foster sometimes. I can see now —" She did not put it into words.

"Well, you mustn't reproach yourself," counseled Mrs. Peters. "Somehow, we just don't see how it is with other folks till — something comes up."

"Not having children makes less work," mused Mrs. Hale, after a silence, "but it makes a quiet house — and Wright out to work all day — and no company when he did come in. Did you know John Wright, Mrs. Peters?"

"Not to know him. I've seen him in town. They say he was a good man."

"Yes — good," conceded John Wright's neighbor grimly. "He didn't drink, and kept his word as well as most, I guess, and paid his debts. But he was a hard man, Mrs. Peters. Just to pass the time of day with him —" She stopped, shivered a little. "Like a raw wind that gets to the bone." Her eye fell upon the cage on the table before her, and she added, almost bitterly: "I should think she would've wanted a bird!"

Suddenly she leaned forward, looking intently at the cage. "But what do you s'pose went wrong with it?"

"I don't know," returned Mrs. Peters; "unless it got sick and died."

But after she said it she reached over and swung the broken door. Both women watched it as if somehow held by it.

"You didn't know — her?" Mrs. Hale asked, a gentler note in her voice.

"Not till they brought her yesterday," said the sheriff's wife.

"She — come to think of it, she was kind of like a bird herself. Real sweet and pretty, but kind of timid and — fluttery. How — she — did — change."

That held her for a long time. Finally, as if struck with a happy thought and relieved to get back to everyday things, she exclaimed:

"Tell you what, Mrs. Peters, why don't you take the quilt in with you? It might take up her mind."

"Why, I think that's a real nice idea, Mrs. Hale," agreed the sheriff's wife, as if she too were glad to come into the atmosphere of a simple kindness. "There couldn't possibly be any objection to that, could there? Now, just what will I take? I wonder if her patches are in here — and her things."

They turned to the sewing basket.

"Here's some red," said Mrs. Hale, bringing out a roll of cloth. Underneath that was a box. "Here, maybe her scissors are in here — and her things." She held it up. "What a pretty box! I'll warrant that was something she had a long time ago — when she was a girl."

She held it in her hand a moment; then, with a little sigh, opened it.

Instantly her hand went to her nose.

"Why — !"

Mrs. Peters drew nearer — then turned away.

"There's something wrapped up in this piece of silk," faltered Mrs. Hale.

Her hand not steady, Mrs. Hale raised the piece of silk. "Oh, Mrs. Peters!" she cried, "it's —"

Mrs. Peters bent closer.

"It's the bird," she whispered.

"But, Mrs. Peters!" cried Mrs. Hale. "*Look* at it! Its *neck* — look at its neck! It's all — other side *too.*"

The sheriff's wife again bent closer.

"Somebody wrung its neck," said she, in a voice that was slow and deep.

And then again the eyes of the two women met — this time clung together in a look of dawning comprehension, of growing horror. Mrs. Peters looked from the dead bird to the broken door of the cage. Again their eyes met. And just then there was a sound at the outside door.

Mrs. Hale slipped the box under the quilt pieces in the basket, and sank into the chair before it. Mrs. Peters stood holding to the table. The county attorney and the sheriff came in.

"Well, ladies," said the county attorney, as one turning from serious things to little pleasantries, "have you decided whether she was going to quilt it or knot it?"

"We think," began the sheriff's wife in a flurried voice, "that she was going to — knot it."

He was too preoccupied to notice the change that came in her voice on that last.

"Well, that's very interesting, I'm sure," he said tolerantly. He caught sight of the cage. "Has the bird flown?"

"We think the cat got it," said Mrs. Hale in a voice curiously even.

He was walking up and down, as if thinking something out.

"Is there a cat?" he asked absently.

Mrs. Hale shot a look up at the sheriff's wife.

"Well, not *now,*" said Mrs. Peters. "They're superstitious, you know; they leave."

The county attorney did not heed her. "No sign at all of anyone having come in from the outside," he said to Peters, in the manner of continuing an interrupted conversation. "Their own rope. Now let's go upstairs again and go over it, piece by piece. It would have to have been someone who knew just the —"

The stair door closed behind them and their voices were lost.

The two women sat motionless, not looking at each other, but as if peering into something and at the same time holding back. When they spoke now it was as if they were afraid of what they were saying, but as if they could not help saying it.

"She liked the bird," said Martha Hale, low and slowly. "She was going to bury it in that pretty box."

"When I was a girl," said Mrs. Peters, under her breath, "my kitten — there was a boy took a hatchet, and before my eyes — before I could get there —" She covered her face an instant. "If they hadn't held me back I would have" — she caught herself, looked upstairs where footsteps were heard, and finished weakly — "hurt him."

Then they sat without speaking or moving.

"I wonder how it would seem," Mrs. Hale at last began, as if feeling her way over strange ground — "never to have had any children around." Her eyes made a slow sweep of the kitchen, as if seeing what that kitchen had meant through all the years. "No, Wright wouldn't like the bird," she said after that — "a thing that sang. She used to sing. He killed that too." Her voice tightened.

Mrs. Peters moved uneasily.

"Of course we don't know who killed the bird."

"I knew John Wright," was Mrs. Hale's answer.

"It was an awful thing was done in this house that night, Mrs. Hale," said the sheriff's wife. "Killing a man while he slept — slipping a thing round his neck that choked the life out of him."

Mrs. Hale's hand went out to the bird-cage.

"His neck. Choked the life out of him."

"We don't *know* who killed him," whispered Mrs. Peters wildly. "We don't *know*."

Mrs. Hale had not moved. "If there had been years and years of — nothing, then a bird to sing to you, it would be awful — still — after the bird was still."

It was as if something within her not herself had spoken, and it found in Mrs. Peters something she did not know as herself.

"I know what stillness is," she said, in a queer, monotonous voice. "When we homesteaded in Dakota, and my first baby died — after he was two years old — and me with no other then —"

Mrs. Hale stirred.

"How soon do you suppose they'll be through looking for the evidence?"

"I know what stillness is," repeated Mrs. Peters, in just that same way. Then she too pulled back. "The law has got to punish crime, Mrs. Hale," she said in her tight little way.

"I wish you'd seen Minnie Foster," was the answer, "when she wore a white dress with blue ribbons, and stood up there in the choir and sang."

The picture of that girl, the fact that she had lived neighbor to that girl for twenty years, and had let her die for lack of life, was suddenly more than she could bear.

"Oh, I *wish* I'd come over here once in a while!" she cried. "That was a crime! That was a crime! Who's going to punish that?"

"We mustn't take on," said Mrs. Peters, with a frightened look toward the stairs.

"I might 'a' *known* she needed help! I tell you, it's *queer*, Mrs. Peters. We live close together, and we live far apart. We all go through the same things — it's all just a different kind of the same thing! If it weren't — why do you and I *understand?* Why do we *know* — what we know this minute?"

She dashed her hand across her eyes. Then, seeing the jar of fruit on the table, she reached for it and choked out:

"If I was you I wouldn't *tell* her her fruit was gone! Tell her it *ain't.* Tell her it's all right — all of it. Here — take this in to prove it to her! She — she may never know whether it was broke or not."

Mrs. Peters reached out for the bottle of fruit as if she were glad to take it — as if touching a familiar thing, having something to do, could keep her from something else. She got up, looked about for something to wrap the fruit in, took a petticoat from the pile of clothes she had brought from the front room, and nervously started winding that round the bottle.

"My!" she began, in a high, false voice, "it's a good thing the men couldn't hear us! Getting all stirred up over a little thing like a — dead canary." She hurried over that. "As if that could have anything to do with — with — My, wouldn't they *laugh?*"

Footsteps were heard on the stairs.

"Maybe they would," muttered Mrs. Hale — "maybe they wouldn't."

"No, Peters," said the county attorney incisively, "it's all perfectly clear, except the reason for doing it. But you know juries when it comes to women. If there was some definite thing — something to show. Something to make a story about. A thing that would connect up with this clumsy way of doing it."

In a covert way Mrs. Hale looked at Mrs. Peters. Mrs. Peters was looking at her. Quickly they looked away from each other. The outer door opened and Mr. Hale came in.

"I've got the team round now," he said. "Pretty cold out there."

"I'm going to stay here awhile by myself," the county attorney suddenly announced. "You can send Frank out for me, can't you?" he asked the sheriff. "I want to go over everything. I'm not satisfied we can't do better."

Again, for one brief moment, the two women's eyes found one another.

The sheriff came up to the table.

"Did you want to see what Mrs. Peters was going to take in?"

The county attorney picked up the apron. He laughed. "Oh, I guess they're not very dangerous things the ladies have picked out."

Mrs. Hale's hand was on the sewing basket in which the box was concealed. She felt that she ought to take her hand off the basket. She did not seem able to. He picked up one of the quilt blocks which she had piled on to cover the box. Her eyes felt like fire. She had a feeling that if he took up the basket she would snatch it from him.

But he did not take it up. With another little laugh, he turned away.

"No; Mrs. Peters doesn't need supervising. For that matter, a sheriff's wife is married to the law. Ever think of it that way, Mrs. Peters?"

Mrs. Peters was standing beside the table. Mrs. Hale shot a look up at her; but she could not see her face. Mrs. Peters had turned away. When she spoke, her voice was muffled.

"Not — just that way," she said.

"Married to the law!" chuckled Mrs. Peters' husband. He moved toward the door into the front room, and said to the county attorney:

"I just want you to come in here a minute, George. We ought to take a look at these windows."

"Oh — windows," said the county attorney scoffingly.

"We'll be right out, Mr. Hale," said the sheriff to the farmer.

Hale went to look after the horses. The sheriff followed the county attorney into the other room. Again — for one final moment — the two women were alone in that kitchen.

Martha Hale sprang up, her hands tight together, looking at that other woman, with whom it rested. At first she could not see her eyes, for the sheriff's wife had not turned back since she turned away at that suggestion of being married to the law. But now Mrs. Hale made her turn back. Here eyes made her turn back. Slowly, unwillingly, Mrs. Peters turned her head until her eyes met the eyes of the other woman. There was a moment when they held each other in a steady, burning look in which there was no evasion nor flinching.

Then Martha Hale's eyes pointed the way to the basket in which was hidden the thing that would make certain the conviction of the other woman — that woman who was not there and yet who had been there with them all through that hour.

For a moment Mrs. Peters did not move. And then she did it. With a rush forward, she threw back the quilt pieces, got the box, tried to put it in her handbag. It was too big. Desperately she opened it, started to take the bird out. But there she broke — she could not touch the bird. She stood there helpless, foolish.

There was the sound of a knob turning in the inner door. Martha Hale snatched the box from the sheriff's wife, and got it in the pocket of her big coat just as the sheriff and the county attorney came back.

"Well, Henry," said the county attorney facetiously, "at least we found out that she was not going to quilt it. She was going to — what is it you call it, ladies?"

Mrs. Hale's hand was against the pocket of her coat.

"We call it — knot it, Mr. Henderson."

1925

DASHIELL HAMMETT

....

The Gutting of Couffignal

WEDGE-SHAPED Couffignal is not a large island, and not far from the mainland, to which it is linked by a wooden bridge. Its western shore is a high, straight cliff that jumps abruptly up out of San Pablo Bay. From the top of this cliff the island slopes eastward, down to a smooth pebble beach that runs into the water again, where there are piers and a club-house and moored pleasure boats.

Couffignal's main street, paralleling the beach, has the usual bank, hotel, moving-picture theater, and stores. But it differs from most main streets of its size in that it is more carefully arranged and preserved. There are trees and hedges and strips of lawn on it, and no glaring signs. The buildings seem to belong beside one another, as if they had been designed by the same architect, and in the stores you will find goods of a quality to match the best city stores.

The intersecting streets — running between rows of neat cottages near the foot of the slope — become winding hedged roads as they climb toward the cliff. The higher these roads get, the farther apart and larger are the houses they lead to. The occupants of these higher houses are the owners and rulers of the island. Most of them are well-fed old gentlemen who, the profits they took from the world with both hands in their younger days now stowed away at safe percentages, have bought into the island colony so they may spend what is left of their lives nursing their livers and improving their golf among their kind. They admit to the island only as many storekeepers, working-people, and similar riffraff as are needed to keep them comfortably served.

That is Couffignal.

It was some time after midnight. I was sitting in a second-story room in Couffignal's largest house, surrounded by wedding presents whose value would add up to something between fifty and a hundred thousand dollars.

Of all the work that comes to a private detective (except divorce work, which the Continental Detective Agency doesn't handle) I like weddings as little as any. Usually I manage to avoid them, but this time I hadn't been able to. Dick Foley, who had been slated for the job, had been handed a black eye by an unfriendly pickpocket the day before. That let Dick out and me in. I had come up to Couffignal — a two-hour ride from San Francisco by ferry and auto stage — that morning, and would return the next.

This had been neither better nor worse than the usual wedding detail. The ceremony had been performed in a little stone church down the hill. Then the house had begun to fill with reception guests. They had kept it filled to overflowing until some time after the bride and groom had sneaked off to their eastern train.

The world had been well represented. There had been an admiral and an earl or two from England; an ex-president of a South American country; a Danish baron; a tall young Russian princess surrounded by lesser titles, including a fat, bald, jovial and black-bearded Russian general who had talked to me for a solid hour about prize fights, in which he had a lot of interest, but not so much knowledge as was possible; an ambassador from one of the Central European countries; a justice of the Supreme Court; and a mob of people whose prominence and near-prominence didn't carry labels.

In theory, a detective guarding wedding presents is supposed to make himself indistinguishable from the other guests. In practice, it never works out that way. He has to spend most of his time within sight of the booty, so he's easily spotted. Besides that, eight or ten people I recognized among the guests were clients or former clients of the Agency, and so knew me. However, being known doesn't make so much difference as you might think, and everything had gone off smoothly.

Shortly after dark a wind smelling of rain began to pile storm clouds up over the bay. Those guests who lived at a distance, especially those who had water to cross, hurried off for their homes. Those who lived on the island stayed until the first raindrops began to patter down. Then they left.

The Hendrixson house quieted down. Musicians and extra servants left. The weary house servants began to disappear in the direction of their bedrooms. I found some sandwiches, a couple of books and a comfortable armchair, and took them up to the room where the presents were now hidden under grey-white sheeting.

Keith Hendrixson, the bride's grandfather — she was an orphan — put his head in at the door.

"Have you everything you need for your comfort?" he asked.

"Yes, thanks."

He said good night and went off to bed — a tall old man, slim as a boy.

The wind and the rain were hard at it when I went downstairs to give the lower windows and doors the up-and-down. Everything on the first floor was tight and secure, everything in the cellar. I went upstairs again.

Pulling my chair over by a floor lamp, I put sandwiches, books, ash tray, gun and flashlight on a small table beside it. Then I switched off the other lights, set fire to a Fatima, sat down, wriggled my spine comfortably into the chair's padding, picked up one of the books, and prepared to make a night of it.

The book was called *The Lord of the Sea,* and had to do with a strong, tough and violent fellow named Hogarth, whose modest plan was to hold the world in one hand. There were plots and counterplots, kidnappings, murders, prison-breakings, forgeries and burglaries, diamonds large as hats and floating forts larger than Couffignal. It sounds dizzy here, but in the book it was as real as a dime.

Hogarth was still going strong when the lights went out.

In the dark, I got rid of the glowing end of my cigarette by grinding it in one of the sandwiches. Putting the book down, I picked up gun and flashlight, and moved away from the chair.

Listening for noises was no good. The storm was making hundreds of them. What I needed to know was why the lights had gone off.

I waited. My job was to watch the presents. Nobody had touched them yet. There was nothing to get excited about.

Minutes went by, perhaps ten of them.

The floor swayed under my feet. The windows rattled with a violence beyond the strength of the storm. The dull boom of a heavy explosion blotted out the sounds of wind and falling water. The blast was not close at hand, but not far enough away to be off the island.

Crossing to the window, peering through the wet glass, I could see nothing. I should have seen a few misty lights far down the hill. Not being able to see them settled one point. The lights had gone out all over Couffignal, not only in the Hendrixson house.

That was better. The storm could have put the lighting system out of whack, could have been responsible for the explosion — maybe.

Staring through the black window, I had an impression of great excitement down the hill, of movement in the night. But all was too far away for me to have seen or heard even had there been lights, and all too vague to say what was moving. The impression was strong but worthless. It didn't lead anywhere. I told myself I was getting feebleminded, and turned away from the window.

Another blast spun me back to it. This explosion sounded nearer than the first, maybe because it was stronger. Peering through the glass again, I still saw nothing. And still had the impression of things that were big moving down there.

Bare feet pattered in the hall. A voice was anxiously calling my name. Turning from the window again, I pocketed my gun and snapped on the flashlight. Keith Hendrixson, in pajamas and bathrobe, looking thinner and older than anybody could be, came into the room.

"Is it —"

"I don't think it's an earthquake," I said, since that is the first calamity your Californian thinks of. "The lights went off a little while ago. There have been a couple of explosions down the hill since the —"

I stopped. Three shots, close together, had sounded. Rifleshots, but of the sort that only the heaviest of rifles could make. Then, sharp and small in the storm, came the report of a far-away pistol.

"What is it?" Hendrixson demanded.

"Shooting."

More feet were pattering in the halls, some bare, some shod. Excited voices whispered questions and exclamations. The butler, a solemn, solid block of a man, partly dressed, and carrying a lighted five-pronged candlestick, came in.

"Very good, Brophy," Hendrixson said as the butler put the candlestick on the table. "Will you try to learn what is the matter?"

"I have tried, sir. The telephone seems to be out of order, sir. Shall I send Oliver down to the village?"

"No-o. I don't suppose it's that serious. Do you think it is anything serious?" he asked me.

I said I didn't think so, but I was paying more attention to the outside than to him. I had heard a thin screaming that could have come from a distant woman, and a volley of small-arms shots. The racket of the storm muffled these shots, but when the heavier firing we had heard before broke out again, it was clear enough.

To have opened the window would have been to let in gallons of water without helping us to hear much clearer. I stood with an ear tilted to the pane, trying to arrive at some idea of what was happening outside.

Another sound took my attention from the window — the ringing of the doorbell. It rang loudly and persistently.

Hendrixson looked at me. I nodded.

"See who it is, Brophy," he said.

The butler went solemnly away, and came back even more solemnly. "Princess Zhukovski," he announced.

She came running into the room — the tall Russian girl I had seen at the reception. Her eyes were wide and dark with excitement. Her face was very white and wet. Water ran in streams down her blue waterproof cape, the hood of which covered her dark hair.

"Oh, Mr. Hendrixson!" She had caught one of his hands in both of hers. Her voice, with nothing foreign in its accents, was the voice of one who is excited over a delightful surprise. "The bank is being robbed, and the — what do you call him? — marshal of police has been killed!"

"What's that?" the old man exclaimed, jumping awkwardly, because water from her cape had dripped down on one of his bare feet. "Weegan killed? And the bank robbed?"

"Yes! Isn't it terrible?" She said it as if she were saying wonderful. "When the first explosion woke us, the general sent Ignati down to find out what was the matter, and he got down there just in time to see the bank blown up. Listen!"

We listened, and heard a wild outbreak of mixed gunfire.

"That will be the general arriving!" she said. "He'll enjoy himself most wonderfully. As soon as Ignati returned with the news, the general armed every male in the household from Aleksandr Sergyeevich to Ivan the cook, and led them out happier than he's been since he took his division to East Prussia in 1914."

"And the duchess?" Hendrixson asked.

"He left her at home with me, of course, and I furtively crept out and away from her while she was trying for the first time in her life to put water in a samovar. This is not the night for one to stay at home!"

"H-m-m," Hendrixson said, his mind obviously not on her words. "And the bank!"

He looked at me. I said nothing. The racket of another volley came to us.

"Could you do anything down there?" he asked.

"Maybe, but —" I nodded at the presents under their covers.

"Oh, those!" the old man said. "I'm as much interested in the bank as in them; and, besides, we will be here."

"All right!" I was willing enough to carry my curiosity down the hill. "I'll go down. You'd better have the butler stay in here, and plant the chauffeur inside the front door. Better give them guns if you have any. Is there a raincoat I can borrow? I brought only a light overcoat."

Brophy found a yellow slicker that fitted me. I put it on, stowed gun and flashlight conveniently under it, and found my hat while Brophy was getting and loading an automatic pistol for himself and a rifle for Oliver, the mulatto chauffeur.

Hendrixson and the princess followed me downstairs. At the door I found she wasn't exactly following me — she was going with me.

"But, Sonya!" the old man protested.

"I'm not going to be foolish, though I'd like to," she promised him. "But I'm going back to my Irinia Androvana, who will perhaps have the samovar watered by now."

"That's a sensible girl!" Hendrixson said, and let us out into the rain and the wind.

It wasn't weather to talk in. In silence we turned downhill between two rows of hedging, with the storm driving at our backs. At the first break in the hedge I stopped, nodding toward the black blot a house made.

"That is your —"

Her laugh cut me short. She caught my arm and began to urge me down the road again.

"I only told Mr. Hendrixson that so he would not worry," she explained. "You do not think I am not going down to see the sights."

She was tall. I am short and thick. I had to look up to see her face — to see as much of it as the rain-grey night would let me see.

"You'll be soaked to the hide, running around in this rain," I objected.

"What of that? I am dressed for it."

She raised a foot to show me a heavy waterproof boot and a woolen-stockinged leg.

"There's no telling what we'll run into down there, and I've got work to do," I insisted. "I can't be looking out for you."

"I can look out for myself."

She pushed her cape aside to show me a square automatic pistol in one hand.

"You'll be in my way."

"I will not," she retorted. "You'll probably find I can help you. I'm as strong as you, and quicker, and I can shoot."

The reports of scattered shooting had punctuated our argument, but now the sound of heavier firing silenced the dozen objections to her company that I could still think of. After all, I could slip away from her in the dark if she became too much of a nuisance.

"Have it your own way," I growled, "but don't expect anything from me."

"You're so kind," she murmured as we got under way again, hurrying now, with the wind at our backs speeding us along.

Occasionally dark figures moved on the road ahead of us, but too far away to be recognizable. Presently a man passed us, running uphill — a tall man whose nightshirt hung out of his trousers, down below his coat, identifying him as a resident.

"They've finished the bank and are at Medcraft's!" he yelled as he went by.

"Medcraft is the jeweler," the girl informed me.

The sloping under our feet grew less sharp. The houses — dark but with faces vaguely visible here and there at windows — came closer together. Below, the flash of a gun could be seen now and then.

Our road put us into the lower end of the main street just as a staccato rat-tat-tat broke out.

I pushed the girl into the nearest doorway, and jumped in after her.

Bullets ripped through walls with the sound of hail tapping on leaves.

That was the thing I had taken for an exceptionally heavy rifle — a machine gun.

The girl had fallen back in a corner, all tangled up with something. I helped her up. The something was a boy of seventeen or so, with one leg and a crutch.

"It's the boy who delivers papers," Princess Zhukovski said, "and you've hurt him with your clumsiness."

The boy shook his head, grinning as he got up.

"No'm, I ain't hurt none, but you kind of scared me, jumping on me."

She had to stop and explain that she hadn't jumped on him, that she had been pushed into him by me, and that she was sorry and so was I.

"What's happening?" I asked the newsboy when I could get a word in.

"Everything," he boasted, as if some of the credit were his. "There must be a hundred of them, and they've blowed the bank wide open, and now some of 'em is in Medcraft's, and I guess they'll blow that up, too. And they killed Tom Weegan. They got a machine gun on a car in the middle of the street."

"Where's everybody — all the merry villagers?"

"Most of 'em are up behind the Hall. They can't do nothing, though, because the machine gun won't let 'em get near enough to see what they're shooting at, and that smart Bill Vincent told me to clear out, 'cause I've only got one leg, as if I couldn't shoot as good as the next one, if I only had something to shoot with!"

"That wasn't right of them," I sympathized. "But you can do something for me. You can stick here and keep your eye on this end of the street, so I'll know if they leave in this direction."

"You're not just saying that so I'll stay here out of the way, are you?"

"No," I lied. "I need somebody to watch. I was going to leave the princess here, but you'll do better."

"Yes," she backed me up, catching the idea. "This gentleman is a detective, and if you do what he asks you'll be helping more than if you were up with the others."

The machine gun was still firing, but not in our direction now.

"I'm going across the street," I told the girl. "If you —"

"Aren't you going to join the others?"

"No. If I can get around behind the bandits while they're busy with the others, maybe I can turn a trick."

"Watch sharp now!" I ordered the boy, and the princess and I made a dash for the opposite sidewalk.

We reached it without drawing lead, sidled along a building for a few yards, and turned into an alley. From the alley's other end came the smell and wash and the dull blackness of the bay.

While we moved down this alley I composed a scheme by which I hoped to get rid of my companion, sending her off on a safe wild-goose chase. But I didn't get a chance to try it out.

The big figure of a man loomed ahead of us.

Stepping in front of the girl, I went on toward him. Under my slicker I held my gun on the middle of him.

He stood still. He was larger than he had looked at first. A big, slope-shouldered, barrel-bodied husky. His hands were empty. I spotted the flashlight on his face for a split second. A flat-cheeked, thick-featured face, with high cheekbones.

"Ignati!" the girl exclaimed over my shoulder.

He began to talk what I supposed was Russian to the girl. She laughed and replied. He shook his big head stubbornly, insisting on something. She stamped her foot and spoke sharply. He shook his head again and addressed me.

"General Pleshskev, he tell me bring Princess Sonya to home."

His English was almost as hard to understand as his Russian. His tone puzzled me. It was as if he was explaining some absolutely necessary thing that he didn't want to be blamed for, but that nevertheless he was going to do.

While the girl was speaking to him again, I guessed the answer. This big Ignati had been sent out by the general to bring the girl home, and he was going to obey his orders if he had to carry her. He was trying to avoid trouble with me by explaining the situation.

"Take her," I said, stepping aside.

The girl scowled at me, laughed.

"Very well, Ignati," she said in English, "I shall go home," and she turned on her heel and went back up the alley, the big man close behind her.

Glad to be alone, I wasted no time in moving in the opposite direction until the pebbles of the beach were under my feet. The pebbles ground harshly under my heels. I moved back to more silent ground and began to work my way as swiftly as I could up the shore toward the center of action. The machine gun barked on. Smaller guns snapped. Three concussions, close together — bombs, hand grenades, my ears and my memory told me.

The stormy sky glared pink over a roof ahead of me and to the left. The boom of the blast beat my eardrums. Fragments I couldn't see fell around me. That, I thought, would be the jeweler's safe blowing apart.

I crept on up the shore line. The machine gun went silent. Lighter guns snapped, snapped, snapped. Another grenade went off. A man's voice shrieked pure terror.

Risking the crunch of pebbles, I turned down to the water's edge again. I had seen no dark shape on the water that could have been a boat. There had been boats moored along this beach in the afternoon. With my feet in the water of the bay I still saw no boat. The storm could have scattered them, but I didn't think it had. The island's western height shielded this shore. The wind was strong here, but not violent.

My feet sometimes on the edge of the pebbles, sometimes in the water, I went on up the shore line. Now I saw a boat. A gently bobbing black shape ahead. No light was on it. Nothing I could see moved on it. It was the only boat on that shore. That made it important.

Foot by foot, I approached.

A shadow moved between me and the dark rear of a building. I froze. The shadow, man-size, moved again, in the direction from which I was coming.

Waiting, I didn't know how nearly invisible, or how plain, I might be against my background. I couldn't risk giving myself away by trying to improve my position.

Twenty feet from me the shadow suddenly stopped.

I was seen. My gun was on the shadow.

"Come on," I called softly. "Keep coming. Let's see who you are."

The shadow hesitated, left the shelter of the building, drew nearer. I couldn't risk the flashlight. I made out dimly a handsome face, boyishly reckless, one cheek dark-stained.

"Oh, how d'you do?" the face's owner said in a musical baritone voice. "You were at the reception this afternoon."

"Yes."

"Have you seen Princess Zhukovski? You know her?"

"She went home with Ignati ten minutes or so ago."

"Excellent!" He wiped his stained cheek with a stained handkerchief, and turned to look at the boat. "That's Hendrixson's boat," he whispered. "They've got it and they've cast the others off."

"That would mean they are going to leave by water."

"Yes, he agreed, "unless — Shall we have a try at it?"

"You mean jump it?"

"Why not?" he asked. "There can't be very many aboard. God knows there are enough of them ashore. You're armed. I've a pistol."

"We'll size it up first," I decided, "so we'll know what we're jumping."

"That is wisdom," he said, and led the way back to the shelter of the buildings.

Hugging the rear walls of the buildings, we stole toward the boat.

The boat grew clearer in the night. A craft perhaps forty-five feet long, its stern to the shore, rising and falling beside a small pier. Across the stern something protruded. Something I couldn't quite make out.

Leather soles scuffled now and then on the wooden deck. Presently a dark head and shoulders showed over the puzzling thing in the stern.

The Russian lad's eyes were better than mine.

"Masked," he breathed in my ear. "Something like a stocking over his head and face."

The masked man was motionless where he stood. We were motionless where we stood.

"Could you hit him from here?" the lad asked.

"Maybe, but night and rain aren't a good combination for sharp-shooting. Our best bet is to sneak as close as we can, and start shooting when he spots us."

"That is wisdom," he agreed.

Discovery came with our first step forward. The man in the boat grunted. The lad at my side jumped forward. I recognized the thing in the boat's stern just in time to throw out a leg and trip the young Russian. He tumbled down, all sprawled out on the pebbles. I dropped behind him.

The machine gun in the boat's stern poured metal over our heads.

"No good rushing that!" I said. "Roll out of it!"

I set the example by revolving toward the back of the building we had just left.

The man at the gun sprinkled the beach, but sprinkled it at random, his eyes no doubt spoiled for night-seeing by the flash of his gun.

Around the corner of the building, we sat up.

"You saved my life by tripping me," the lad said coolly.

"Yes. I wonder if they've moved the machine gun from the street, or if —"

The answer to that came immediately. The machine gun in the street mingled its vicious voice with the drumming of the one in the boat.

"A pair of them!" I complained. "Know anything about the layout?"

"I don't think there are more than ten or twelve of them," he said, "although it is not easy to count in the dark. The few I have seen are completely masked — like the man in the boat. They seem to have disconnected the telephone and light lines first and then to have destroyed the bridge. We attacked them while they were looting the bank, but in front they had a machine gun mounted in an automobile, and we were not equipped to combat on equal terms."

"Where are the islanders now?"

"Scattered, and most of them in hiding, I fancy, unless General Pleshskev has succeeded in rallying them again."

I frowned and beat my brains together. You can't fight machine guns and hand grenades with peaceful villagers and retired capitalists. No matter how well led and armed they are, you can't do anything with them. For that matter, how could anybody do much against that tough a game?

"Suppose you stick here and keep your eye on the boat," I suggested. "I'll scout around and see what's doing farther up, and if I can get a few good men together, I'll try to jump the boat again, probably from the other side. But we can't count on that. The getaway will be by boat. We can count on that, and try to block it. If you lie down you can watch the boat around the corner of the building without making much of a target of yourself. I wouldn't do anything to attract attention until the break for the boat comes. Then you can do all the shooting you want."

"Excellent!" he said. "You'll probably find most of the islanders up behind the church. You can get to it by going straight up the hill until you come to an iron fence, and then follow that to the right."

"Right."

I moved off in the direction he had indicated.

At the main street I stopped to look around before venturing across. Everything was quiet there. The only man I could see was spread out face-down on the sidewalk near me.

On hands and knees I crawled to his side. He was dead. I didn't stop to examine him further, but sprang up and streaked for the other side of the street.

Nothing tried to stop me. In a doorway, flat against a wall, I peeped out. The wind had stopped. The rain was no longer a driving deluge, but a steady down-pouring of small drops. Couffignal's main street, to my senses, was a deserted street.

I wondered if the retreat to the boat had already started. On the sidewalk, walking swiftly toward the bank, I heard the answer to that guess.

High up on the slope, almost up to the edge of the cliff, by the sound, a machine gun began to hurl out its stream of bullets.

Mixed with the racket of the machine gun were the sounds of smaller arms, and a grenade or two.

At the first crossing, I left the main street and began to run up the hill. Men were running toward me. Two of them passed, paying no attention to my shouted, "What's up now?"

The third man stopped because I grabbed him — a fat man whose breath bubbled, and whose face was fish-belly white.

"They've moved the car with the machine gun on it up behind us," he gasped when I had shouted my question into his ear again.

"What are you doing without a gun?" I asked.

"I — I dropped it."

"Where's General Pleshskev?"

"Back there somewhere. He's trying to capture the car, but he'll never do it. It's suicide!"

Other men had passed us, running downhill, as we talked. I let the white-faced man go, and stopped four men who weren't running so fast as the others.

"What's happening now?" I questioned them.

"They's going through the houses up the hill," a sharp-featured man with a small mustache and a rifle said.

"Has anybody got word off the island yet?" I asked.

"Can't," another informed me. "They blew up the bridge first thing."

"Can't anybody swim?"

"Not in that wind. Young Catlan tried it and was lucky to get out again with a couple of broken ribs."

"The wind's gone down," I pointed out.

The sharp-featured man gave his rifle to one of the others and took off his coat.

"I'll try it," he promised.

"Good! Wake up the whole country, and get word through to the San Francisco police boat and to the Mare Island Navy Yard. They'll lend a hand if you tell 'em the bandits have machine guns. Tell 'em the bandits have an armed boat waiting to leave in. It's Hendrixson's."

The volunteer swimmer left.

"A boat?" two of the men asked together.

"Yes. With a machine gun on it. If we're going to do anything, it'll have to be now, while we're between them and their getaway. Get every man and every gun you can find down there. Tackle the boat from the roofs if you can. When the bandits' car comes down there, pour it into it. You'll do better from the buildings than from the street."

The three men went on downhill. I went uphill, toward the crackling of firearms ahead. The machine gun was working irregularly. It would pour out its rat-tat-tat for a second or so, and then stop for a couple of seconds. The answering fire was thin, ragged.

I met more men, learned from them that the general, with less than a dozen men, was still fighting the car. I repeated the advice I had given the other men. My informants went down to join them. I went on up.

A hundred yards farther along, what was left of the general's dozen broke out of the night, around and past me, flying downhill, with bullets hailing after them.

The road was no place for mortal man. I stumbled over two bodies, scratched myself in a dozen places getting over a hedge. On soft, wet sod I continued my uphill journey.

The machine gun on the hill stopped its clattering. The one in the boat was still at work.

The one ahead opened again, firing too high for anything near at hand to be its target. It was helping its fellow below, spraying the main street.

Before I could get closer it had stopped. I heard the car's motor racing. The car moved toward me.

Rolling into the hedge, I lay there, straining my eyes through the spaces between the stems. I had six bullets in a gun that hadn't yet been fired.

When I saw wheels on the lighter face of the road, I emptied my gun, holding it low.

The car went on.

I sprang out of my hiding-place.

The car was suddenly gone from the empty road.

There was a grinding sound. A crash. The noise of metal folding on itself. The tinkle of glass.

I raced toward those sounds.

Out of a black pile where an engine sputtered, a black figure leaped — to dash off across the soggy lawn. I cut after it, hoping that the others in the wreck were down for keeps.

I was less than fifteen feet behind the fleeing man when he cleared a hedge. I'm no sprinter, but neither was he. The wet grass made slippery going.

He stumbled while I was vaulting the hedge. When we straightened out again I was not more than ten feet behind him.

Once I clicked my gun at him, forgetting I had emptied it. Six cartridges were wrapped in a piece of paper in my vest pocket, but this was not time for loading.

A building loomed ahead. My fugitive bore off to the right, to clear the corner.

To the left a heavy shotgun went off.

The running man disappeared around the house corner.

"Sweet God!" General Pleshskev's mellow voice complained. "That with a shotgun I should miss all of a man at that distance!"

"Go round the other way!" I yelled, plunging around the corner.

His feet thudded ahead. I could not see him. The general puffed around from the other side of the house.

"You have him?"

"No."

In front of us was a stone-faced bank, on top of which ran a path. On either side of us was a high and solid hedge.

"But, my friend," the general protested. "How could he have — ?"

A pale triangle showed on the path above — a triangle that could have been a bit of shirt showing above the opening of a vest.

"Stay here and talk!" I whispered to the general, and crept forward.

"It must be that he has gone the other way," the general carried out my instructions, rambling on as if I were standing beside him, "because if he had come my way I should have seen him, and if he had raised himself over either of the hedges or the embankment, one of us would surely have seen him against . . ."

He talked on and on while I gained the shelter of the bank on which the path sat, while I found places for my toes in the rough stone facing.

The man on the road, trying to make himself small with his back in a bush, was looking at the talking general. He saw me when I had my feet on the path.

He jumped, and one hand went up.

I jumped, with both hands out.

A stone, turning under my foot, threw me sidewise, twisting my ankle, but saving my head from the bullet he sent at it.

My outflung left arm caught his legs as I spilled down. He came over on top of me. I kicked him once, caught his gun arm, and had just decided to bite it when the general puffed up over the edge of the path and prodded the man off me with his shotgun.

When it came my turn to stand up, I found it not so good. My twisted ankle didn't like to support its share of my hundred-and-eighty-some pounds. Putting most of my weight on the other leg, I turned my flashlight on the prisoner.

"Hello, Flippo!" I exclaimed.

"Hello!" he said without joy in the recognition.

He was a roly-poly Italian youth of twenty-three or -four. I had helped send him to San Quentin four years ago for his part in a payroll stick-up. He had been out on parole for several months now.

"The prison board isn't going to like this," I told him.

"You got me wrong," he pleaded. "I ain't been doing a thing. I was up here to see some friends. And when this thing busted loose I had to hide, because I got a record, and if I'm picked up I'll be railroaded for it. And now you got me, and you think I'm in on it!"

"You're a mind reader," I assured him, and asked the general, "Where can we pack this bird away for awhile, under lock and key?"

"In my house there is a lumber room with a strong door and not a window."

"That'll do it. March, Flippo!"

General Pleshskev collared the youth, while I limped along behind them, examining Flippo's gun, which was loaded except for the one shot he had fired at me, and reloading my own.

We had caught our prisoner on the Russian's grounds, so we didn't have far to go.

The general knocked on the door and called out something in his language. Bolts clicked and grated, and the door was swung open by a heavily mustached Russian servant. Behind him the princess and a stalwart older woman stood.

We went in while the general was telling his household about the capture, and took the captive up to the lumber room. I frisked him for his pocketknife and matches — he had nothing else that could help him get out — locked him in and braced the door solidly with a length of board. Then we went downstairs again.

"You are injured!" the princess, seeing me limp across the floor, cried.

"Only a twisted ankle," I said. "But it does bother me some. Is there any adhesive tape around?"

"Yes," and she spoke to the mustached servant, who went out of the room and presently returned, carrying rolls of gauze and tape and a basin of steaming water.

"If you'll sit down," the princess said, taking these things from the servant.

But I shook my head and reached for the adhesive tape.

"I want cold water, because I've got to go out in the wet again. If you'll show me the bathroom, I can fix myself up in no time."

We had to argue about that, but I finally got to the bathroom, where I ran cold water on my foot and ankle, and strapped it with adhesive tape, as tight as I could without stopping the circulation altogether. Getting my wet shoe on again was a job, but when I was through I had two firm legs under me, even if one of them did hurt some.

When I rejoined the others I noticed that the sound of firing no longer came up the hill, and that the patter of rain was lighter, and a grey streak of coming daylight showed under a drawn blind.

I was buttoning my slicker when the knocker sounded on the front door. Russian words came through, and the young Russian I had met on the beach came in.

"Aleksandr, you're —" the stalwart older woman screamed, when she saw the blood on his cheek, and fainted.

He paid no attention to her at all, as if he was used to having her faint.

"They've gone in the boat," he told me while the girl and two men servants gathered up the woman and laid her on an ottoman.

"How many?" I asked.

"I counted ten, and I don't think I missed more than one or two, if any."

"The men I sent down there couldn't stop them?"

He shrugged.

"What would you? It takes a strong stomach to face a machine gun. Your men had been cleared out of the buildings almost before they arrived."

The woman who had fainted had revived by now and was pouring anxious questions in Russian at the lad. The princess was getting into her blue cape. The woman stopped questioning the lad and asked her something.

"It's all over," the princess said. "I am going to view the ruins."

That suggestion appealed to everybody. Five minutes later all of us, including the servants, were on our way downhill. Behind us, around us, in front of us, were other people going downhill, hurrying along in the drizzle that was very gentle now, their faces tired and excited in the bleak morning light.

Halfway down, a woman ran out of a crosspath and began to tell me something. I recognized her as one of Hendrixson's maids.

I caught some of her words.

"Presents gone. . . . Mr. Brophy murdered. . . . Oliver. . . ."

*   *   *

"I'll be down later," I told the others, and set out after the maid.

She was running back to the Hendrixson house. I couldn't run, couldn't even walk fast. She and Hendrixson and more of his servants were standing on the front porch when I arrived.

"They killed Oliver and Brophy," the old man said.

"How?"

"We were in the back of the house, the rear second story, watching the flashes of the shooting down in the village. Oliver was down here, just inside the front door, and Brophy in the room with the presents. We heard a shot in there, and immediately a man appeared in the doorway of our room, threatening us with two pistols, making us stay there for perhaps ten minutes. Then he shut and locked the door and went away. We broke the door down — and found Brophy and Oliver dead."

"Let's look at them."

The chauffeur was just inside the front door. He lay on his back, with his brown throat cut straight across the front, almost back to the vertebræ. His rifle was under him. I pulled it out and examined it. It had not been fired.

Upstairs, the butler Brophy was huddled against a leg of one of the tables on which the presents had been spread. His gun was gone. I turned him over, straightened him out, and found a bullet hole in his chest. Around the hole his coat was charred in a large area.

Most of the presents were still here. But the most valuable pieces were gone. The others were in disorder, lying around any which way, their covers pulled off.

"What did the one you saw look like?" I asked.

"I didn't see him very well," Hendrixson said. "There was no light in our room. He was simply a dark figure against the candle burning in the hall. A large man in a black rubber raincoat, with some sort of black mask that covered his whole head and face."

As we went downstairs again I gave Hendrixson a brief account of what I had seen and heard and done since I had left him. There wasn't enough of it to make a long tale.

"Do you think you can get information about the others from the one you caught?" he asked, as I prepared to go out.

"No. But I expect to bag them just the same."

Couffignal's main street was jammed with people when I limped into it again. A detachment of Marines from Mare Island was there, and men from a San Francisco police boat. Excited citizens in all degrees of partial nakedness boiled around them. A hundred voices were talking at once, recounting their personal adventures and braveries and losses and what they had seen. Such words as machine gun, bomb, bandit, car, shot, dynamite, and killed sounded again and again, in every variety of voice and tone.

The bank had been completely wrecked by the charge that had blown the vault. The jewelry store was another ruin. A grocer's across the street was serving as a field hospital. Two doctors were toiling there, patching up damaged villagers.

I recognized a familiar face under a uniform cap — Sergeant Roche of the harbor police — and pushed through the crowd to him.

"Just get here?" he asked as we shook hands. "Or were you in on it?"

"In on it."

"What do you know?"

"Everything."

"Who ever heard of a private detective that didn't," he joshed as I led him out of the mob.

"Did you people run into an empty boat out in the bay?" I asked when we were away from audiences.

"Empty boats have been floating around the bay all night," he said.

I hadn't thought of that.

"Where's your boat now?" I asked.

"Out trying to pick up the bandits. I stayed with a couple of men to lend a hand here."

"You're in luck," I told him. "Now sneak a look across the street. See the stout old boy with the black whiskers? Standing in front of the druggist's."

General Pleshskev stood there, with the woman who had fainted, the young Russian whose bloody cheek had made her faint, and a pale, plump man of forty-something who had been with them at the reception. A little to one side stood big Ignati, the two menservants I had seen at the house, and another who was obviously one of them. They were chatting together and watching the excited antics of a red-faced property owner who was telling a curt lieutenant of Marines that it was his own personal private automobile that the bandits had stolen to mount their machine gun on.

"Yes," said Roche, "I see your fellow with the whiskers."

"Well, he's your meat. The woman and two men with him are also your meat. And those four Russians standing to the left are some more of it. There's another missing, but I'll take care of that one. Pass the word to the lieutenant, and you can round up those babies without giving them a chance to fight back. They think they're safe as angels."

"Sure, are you?" the sergeant asked.

"Don't be silly!" I growled, as if I had never made a mistake in my life.

I had been standing on my one good prop. When I put my weight on the other to turn away from the sergeant, it stung me all the way to the hip. I pushed my back teeth together and began to work painfully through the crowd to the other side of the street.

The princess didn't seem to be among those present. My idea was that, next to the general, she was the most important member of the push. If she was at their house, and not yet suspicious, I figured I could get close enough to yank her in without a riot.

Walking was hell. My temperature rose. Sweat rolled out on me.

"Mister, they didn't none of 'em come down that way."

The one-legged newsboy was standing at my elbow. I greeted him as if he were my pay check.

"Come on with me," I said, taking his arm. "You did fine down there, and now I want you to do something else for me."

Half a block from the main street I led him up on the porch of a small yellow cottage. The front door stood open, left that way when the occupants ran down to welcome police and Marines, no doubt. Just inside the door, beside a hall rack, was a wicker porch chair. I committed unlawful entry to the extent of dragging that chair out on the porch.

"Sit down, son," I urged the boy.

He sat, looking up at me with a puzzled freckled face. I took a firm grip on his crutch and pulled it out of his hand.

"Here's five bucks for rental," I said, "and if I lose it I'll buy you one of ivory and gold."

And I put the crutch under my arm and began to propel myself up the hill.

It was my first experience with a crutch. I didn't break any records. But it was a lot better than tottering along on an unassisted bum ankle.

The hill was longer and steeper than some mountains I've seen, but the gravel walk to the Russian's house was finally under my feet.

I was still some dozen feet from the porch when Princess Zhukovski opened the door.

"Oh!" she exclaimed, and then, recovering from her surprise, "your ankle is worse!"

She ran down the steps to help me climb them. As she came I noticed that something heavy was sagging and swinging in the right-hand pocket of her grey flannel jacket.

With one hand under my elbow, the other arm across my back, she helped me up the steps and across the porch. That assured me she didn't think I had tumbled to the game. If she had, she wouldn't have trusted herself within reach of my hands. Why, I wondered, had she come back to the house after starting downhill with the others?

While I was wondering we went into the house, where she planted me in a large and soft leather chair.

"You must certainly be starving after your strenuous night," she said. "I will see if —"

"No, sit down," I nodded at a chair facing mine. "I want to talk to you."

She sat down, clasping her slender white hands in her lap. In neither face nor pose was there any sign of nervousness, not even of curiosity. And that was overdoing it.

"Where have you cached the plunder?" I asked.

The whiteness of her face was nothing to go by. It had been white as marble since I had first seen her. The darkness of her eyes was as natural. Nothing happened to her other features. Her voice was smoothly cool.

"I am sorry," she said. "The question doesn't convey anything to me."

"Here's the point," I explained. "I'm charging you with complicity in the gutting of Couffignal, and in the murders that went with it. And I'm asking you where the loot has been hidden."

Slowly she stood up, raised her chin, and looked at least a mile down at me.

"How dare you? How dare you speak so to me, a Zhukovski!"

"I don't care if you're one of the Smith Brothers!" Leaning forward, I had pushed my twisted ankle against a leg of the chair, and the resulting agony didn't improve my disposition. "For the purpose of this talk you are a thief and a murderer."

Her strong slender body became the body of a lean crouching animal. Her white face became the face of an enraged animal. One hand — claw now — swept to the heavy pocket of her jacket.

Then, before I could have batted an eye — though my life seemed to depend on my not batting it — the wild animal had vanished. Out of it — and now I know where the writers of the old fairy stories got their ideas — rose the princess again, cool and straight and tall.

She sat down, crossed her ankles, put an elbow on an arm of her chair, propped her chin on the back of that hand, and looked curiously into my face.

"However," she murmured, "did you chance to arrive at so strange and fanciful a theory?"

"It wasn't chance, and it's neither strange nor fanciful," I said. "Maybe it'll save time and trouble if I show you part of the score against you. Then you'll know how you stand and won't waste your brains pleading innocence."

"I should be grateful," she smiled, "very!"

I tucked my crutch in between one knee and the arm of my chair, so my hands would be free to check off my points on my fingers.

"First — whoever planned the job knew the island — not fairly well, but every inch of it. There's no need to argue about that. Second — the car on which the machine gun was mounted was local property, stolen from the owner here. So was the boat in which the bandits were supposed to have escaped. Bandits from the outside would have needed a car or a boat to bring their machine guns, explosives, and grenades here, and there doesn't seem to be any reason why they shouldn't have used that car or boat instead of stealing a fresh one. Third — there wasn't the least hint of the professional bandit touch on this job. If you ask me, it was a military job from beginning to end. And the worst safe-burglar in the world could have got into both the bank vault and the jeweler's safe without wrecking the buildings. Fourth — bandits from the outside wouldn't have destroyed the bridge. They might have blocked it, but they wouldn't have destroyed it. They'd have saved it in case they had to make their getaway in that direction. Fifth — bandits figuring on a getaway by boat would have cut the job short, wouldn't have spread it over the whole night. Enough racket was made here to wake up California all the way from Sacramento to Los Angeles. What you people did was to send one man out in the boat, shooting, and he didn't go far. As soon as he was at a safe distance, he went overboard, and swam back to the island. Big Ignati could have done it without turning a hair."

That exhausted my right hand. I switched over, counting on my left.

"Sixth — I met one of your party, the lad, down on the beach, and he was coming from the boat. He suggested that we jump it. We were shot at, but the man behind the gun was playing with us. He could have wiped up out in a second if he had been in earnest, but he shot over our heads. Seventh — that same lad is the only man on the island, so far as I know, who saw the departing bandits. Eighth — all of your people that

I ran into were especially nice to me, the general even spending an hour talking to me at the reception this afternoon. That's a distinctive amateur crook trait. Ninth — after the machine gun car had been wrecked I chased its occupant. I lost him around this house. The Italian boy I picked up wasn't him. He couldn't have climbed up on the path without my seeing him. But he could have run around to the general's side of the house and vanished indoors there. The general liked him, and would have helped him. I know that, because the general performed a downright miracle by missing him at some six feet with a shotgun. Tenth — you called at Hendrixson's house for no other purpose than to get me away from there."

That finished the left hand. I went back to the right.

"Eleventh — Hendrixson's two servants were killed by someone they knew and trusted. Both were killed at close quarters and without firing a shot. I'd say you got Oliver to let you into the house, and were talking to him when one of your men cut his throat from behind. Then you went upstairs and probably shot the unsuspecting Brophy yourself. He wouldn't have been on his guard against you. Twelfth — but that ought to be enough, and I'm getting a sore throat from listing them."

She took her chin off her hand, took a fat white cigarette out of a thin black case, and held it in her mouth while I put a match to the end of it. She took a long pull at it — a draw that accounted for a third of its length — and blew the smoke down at her knees.

"That would be enough," she said when all these things had been done, "if it were not that you yourself know it was impossible for us to have been so engaged. Did you not see us — did not everyone see us — time and time again?"

"That's easy!" I argued. "With a couple of machine guns, a trunkful of grenades, knowing the island from top to bottom, in the darkness and in a storm, against bewildered civilians — it was duck soup. There are nine of you that I know of, including two women. Any five of you could have carried on the work, once it was started, while the others took turns appearing here and there, establishing alibis. And that is what you did. You took turns slipping out to alibi yourselves. Everywhere I went I ran into one of you. And the general! That whiskered old joker running around leading the simple citizens to battle! I'll bet he led 'em plenty! They're lucky there are any of 'em alive this morning!"

She finished her cigarette with another inhalation, dropped the stub on the rug, ground out the light with one foot, sighed wearily, and asked:

"And now what?"

"Now I want to know where you have stowed the plunder."

The readiness of her answer surprised me.

"Under the garage, in a cellar we dug secretly there some months ago."

I didn't believe that, of course, but it turned out to be the truth.

I didn't have anything else to say. When I fumbled with my borrowed crutch, preparing to get up, she raised a hand and spoke gently:

"Wait a moment, please. I have something to suggest."

Half standing, I leaned toward her, stretching out one hand until it was close to her side.

"I want the gun," I said.

She nodded, and sat still while I plucked it from her pocket, put it in one of my own, and sat down again.

"You said a little while ago that you didn't care who I was," she began immediately. "But I want you to know. There are so many of us Russians who once were somebodies and who now are nobodies that I won't bore you with the repetition of a tale the world has grown tired of hearing. But you must remember that this weary tale is real to us who are its subjects. However, we fled from Russia with what we could carry of our property, which fortunately was enough to keep us in bearable comfort for a few years.

"In London we opened a Russian restaurant, but London was suddenly full of Russian restaurants, and ours became, instead of a means of livelihood, a source of loss. We tried teaching music and languages, and so no. In short, we hit on all the means of earning our living that other Russian exiles hit upon, and so always found ourselves in overcrowded, and thus unprofitable, fields. But what else did we know — could we do?

"I promised not to bore you. Well, always our capital shrank, and always the day approached on which we should be shabby and hungry, the day when we should become familiar to readers of your Sunday papers — charwomen who had been princesses, dukes who now were butlers. There was no place for us in the world. Outcasts easily become outlaws. Why not? Could it be said that we owed the world any fealty? Had not the world sat idly by and seen us despoiled of place and property and country?

"We planned it before we had heard of Couffignal. We could find a small settlement of the wealthy, sufficiently isolated, and, after establishing ourselves there, we would plunder it. Couffignal, when we found it, seemed to be the ideal place. We leased this house for six months, having just enough capital remaining to do that and to live properly here while our plans matured. Here we spent four months establishing ourselves, collecting our arms and our explosives, mapping our offensive, waiting for a favorable night. Last night seemed to be that night, and we had provided, we thought, against every eventuality. But we had not, of course, provided against your presence and your genius. They were simply others of the unforeseen misfortunes to which we seem eternally condemned."

She stopped, and fell to studying me with mournful large eyes that made me feel like fidgeting.

"It's no good calling me a genius," I objected. "The truth is you people botched your job from beginning to end. Your general would get a big laugh out of a man without military training who tried to lead an army. But here are you people with absolutely no criminal experience trying to swing a trick that needed the highest sort of criminal skill. Look at how you all played around with me! Amateur stuff! A professional crook with any intelligence would have either let me alone or knocked me off. No wonder you flopped! As for the rest of it — your troubles — I can't do anything about them."

"Why?" very softly. "Why can't you?"

"Why should I?" I made it blunt.

"No one else knows what you know." She bent forward to put a white hand on my knee. "There is wealth in that cellar beneath the garage. You may have whatever you ask."

I shook my head.

"You aren't a fool!" she protested. "You know —"

"Let me straighten this out for you," I interrupted. "We'll disregard whatever honesty I happen to have, sense of loyalty to employers, and so on. You might doubt them, so we'll throw them out. Now I'm a detective because I happen to like the work. It pays me a fair salary, but I could find other jobs that would pay more. Even a hundred dollars more a month would be twelve hundred a year. Say twenty-five or thirty thousand dollars in the years between now and my sixtieth birthday.

"Now I pass up about twenty-five or thirty thousand of honest gain because I like being a detective, like the work. And liking work makes you want to do it as well as you can. Otherwise there'd be no sense to it. That's the fix I am in. I don't know anything else, don't enjoy anything else, don't want to know or enjoy anything else. You can't weigh that against any sum of money. Money is good stuff. I haven't anything against it. But in the past eighteen years I've been getting my fun out of chasing crooks and tackling puzzles, my satisfaction out of catching crooks and solving riddles. It's the only kind of sport I know anything about, and I can't imagine a pleasanter future than twenty-some years more of it. I'm not going to blow that up!"

She shook her head slowly, lowering it, so that now her dark eyes looked up at me under the thin arcs of her brows.

"You speak only of money," she said. "I said you may have whatever you ask."

That was out. I don't know where these women get their ideas.

"You're still all twisted up," I said brusquely, standing now and adjusting my borrowed crutch. "You think I'm a man and you're a woman. That's wrong. I'm a man hunter and you're something that has been running in front of me. There's nothing human about it. You might just as well expect a hound to play tiddlywinks with the fox he's caught. We're wasting time anyway. I've been thinking the police or Marines might come up here and save me a walk. You've been waiting for your mob to come back and grab me. I could have told you they were being arrested when I left them."

That shook her. She had stood up. Now she fell back a step, putting a hand behind her for steadiness, on her chair. An exclamation I didn't understand popped out of her mouth. Russian, I thought, but the next moment I knew it had been Italian.

"Put your hands up."

It was Flippo's husky voice. Flippo stood in the doorway, holding an automatic.

I raised my hands as high as I could without dropping my supporting crutch, meanwhile cursing myself for having been too careless, or too vain, to keep a gun in my hand while I talked to the girl.

So this is why she had come back to the house. If she freed the Italian, she had thought, we would have no reason for suspecting that he hadn't been in on the robbery, and so we would look for the bandits among his friends. A prisoner, of course, he might have persuaded us of his innocence. She had given him the gun so he could either shoot his way clear, or, what would help her as much, get himself killed trying.

While I was arranging these thoughts in my head, Flippo had come up behind me. His empty hand passed over my body, taking away my own gun, his, and the one I had taken from the girl.

"A bargain, Flippo," I said when he had moved away from me, a little to one side, where he made one corner of a triangle whose other corners were the girl and I. "You're out on parole, with some years still to be served. I picked you up with a gun on you. That's plenty to send you back to the big house. I know you weren't in on this job. My idea is that you were up here on a smaller one of your own, but I can't prove that and don't want to. Walk out of here, alone and neutral, and I'll forget I saw you."

Little thoughtful lines grooved the boy's round, dark face.

The princess took a step toward him.

"You heard the offer I just now made him?" she asked. "Well, I make that offer to you, if you will kill him."

The thoughtful lines in the boy's face deepened.

"There's your choice, Flippo," I summed up for him. "All I can give you is freedom from San Quentin. The princess can give you a fat cut of the profits in a busted caper, with a good chance to get yourself hanged."

The girl, remembering her advantage over me, went at him hot and heavy in Italian, a language in which I know only four words. Two of them are profane and the other two obscene. I said all four.

The boy was weakening. If he had been ten years older, he'd have taken my offer and thanked me for it. But he was young and she — now that I thought of it — was beautiful. The answer wasn't hard to guess.

"But not to bump him off," he said to her, in English, for my benefit. "We'll lock him up in there where I was at."

I suspected Flippo hadn't any great prejudice against murder. It was just that he thought this one unnecessary, unless he was kidding me to make the killing easier.

The girl wasn't satisfied with his suggestion. She poured more hot Italian at him. Her game looked sure-fire, but it had a flaw. She couldn't persuade him that his chances of getting any of the loot away were good. She had to depend on her charms to swing him. And that meant she had to hold his eye.

He wasn't far from me.

She came close to him. She was singing, chanting, crooning Italian syllables into his round face.

She had him.

He shrugged. His whole face said yes. He turned —

I knocked him on the noodle with my borrowed crutch.

The crutch splintered apart. Flippo's knees bent. He stretched up to his full height. He fell on his face on the floor. He lay there, dead still, except for a thin worm of blood that crawled out of his hair to the rug.

A step, a tumble, a foot or so of hand-and-knee scrambling put me within reach of Flippo's gun.

The girl, jumping out of my path, was halfway to the door when I sat up with the gun in my hand.

"Stop!" I ordered.

"I shan't," she said, but she did, for the time at least. "I am going out."

"You are going out when I take you."

She laughed, a pleasant laugh, low and confident.

"I'm going out before that," she insisted good-naturedly.

I shook my head.

"How do you purpose stopping me?" she asked.

"I don't think I'll have to," I told her. "You've got too much sense to try to run while I'm holding a gun on you."

She laughed again, an amused ripple.

"I've got too much sense to stay," she corrected me. "Your crutch is broken, and you're lame. You can't catch me by running after me, then. You pretend you'll shoot me, but I don't believe you. You'd shoot me if I attacked you, of course, but I shan't do that. I shall simply walk out, and you know you won't shoot me for that. You'll wish you could, but you won't. You'll see."

Her face turned over her shoulder, her dark eyes twinkling at me, she took a step toward the door.

"Better not count on that! " I threatened.

For answer to that she gave me a cooing laugh. And took another step.

"Stop, you idiot!" I bawled at her.

Her face laughed over her shoulder at me. She walked without haste to the door, her short skirt of grey flannel shaping itself to the calf of each grey wool-stockinged leg as its mate stepped forward.

Sweat greased the gun in my hand.

When her right foot was on the doorsill, a little chuckling sound came from her throat.

"Adieu!" she said softly.

And I put a bullet in the calf of her left leg.

She sat down — plump! Utter surprise stretched her white face. It was too soon for pain.

I had never shot a woman before. I felt queer about it.

"You ought to have known I'd do it!" My voice sounded harsh and savage and like a stranger's in my ears. "Didn't I steal a crutch from a cripple?"

RING LARDNER

....

Haircut

I GOT *another* barber that comes over from Carterville and helps me
out Saturdays, but the rest of the time I can get along all right alone.
You can see for yourself that this ain't no New York City and besides
that, the most of the boys works all day and don't have no leisure to
drop in here and get themselves prettied up.

You're a newcomer, ain't you? I thought I hadn't seen you round before. I hope you like it good enough to stay. As I say, we ain't no New
York City or Chicago, but we have pretty good times. Not as good,
though, since Jim Kendall got killed. When he was alive, him and Hod
Meyers used to keep this town in an uproar. I bet they was more
laughin' done here than any town its size in America.

Jim was comical, and Hod was pretty near a match for him. Since
Jim's gone, Hod tries to hold his end up just the same as ever, but it's
tough goin' when you ain't got nobody to kind of work with.

They used to be plenty fun in here Saturdays. This place is jam-
packed Saturdays, from four o'clock on. Jim and Hod would show
up right after their supper, round six o'clock. Jim would set himself
down in that big chair, nearest the blue spittoon. Whoever had been
settin' in that chair, why they'd get up when Jim come in and give it
to him.

You'd of thought it was a reserved seat like they have sometimes in a
theayter. Hod would generally always stand or walk up and down, or
some Saturdays, of course, he'd be settin' in his chair part of the time,
gettin' a haircut.

Well, Jim would set there a w'ile without openin' his mouth only to
spit, and then finally he'd say to me, "Whitey" — my right name, that is,
my right first name, is Dick, but everybody round here calls me Whitey

— Jim would say, "Whitey, your nose looks like a rosebud tonight. You must of been drinkin' some of your aw de cologne."

So I'd say, "No, Jim, but you look like you'd been drinkin' somethin' of that kind or somethin' worse."

Jim would have to laugh at that, but then he'd speak up and say, "No, I ain't had nothin' to drink, but that ain't sayin' I wouldn't like somethin'. I wouldn't even mind if it was wood alcohol."

Then Hod Meyers would say, "Neither would your wife." That would set everybody to laughin' because Jim and his wife wasn't on very good terms. She'd of divorced him only they wasn't no chance to get alimony and she didn't have no way to take care of herself and the kids. She couldn't never understand Jim. He *was* kind of rough, but a good fella at heart.

Him and Hod had all kinds of sport with Milt Sheppard. I don't suppose you've seen Milt. Well, he's got an Adam's apple that looks more like a mushmelon. So I'd shavin' Milt and when I'd start to shave down here on his neck, Hod would holler, "Hey, Whitey, wait a minute! Before you cut into it, let's make up a pool and see who can guess closest to the number of seeds."

And Jim would say, "If Milt hadn't of been so hoggish, he'd of ordered a half a cantaloupe instead of a whole one and it might not of stuck in his throat."

All the boys would roar at this and Milt himself would force a smile, though the joke was on him. Jim certainly was a card!

There's his shavin' mug, settin' on the shelf, right next to Charley Vail's. "Charles M. Vail." That's the druggist. He comes in regular for his shave, three times a week. And Jim's is the cup next to Charley's. "James H. Kendall." Jim won't need no shavin' mug no more, but I'll leave it there just the same for old time's sake. Jim certainly was a character!

Years ago, Jim used to travel for a canned goods concern over in Carterville. They sold canned goods. Jim had the whole northern half of the state and was on the road five days out of every week. He'd drop in here Saturdays and tell his experiences for that week. It was rich.

I guess he paid more attention to playin' jokes than makin' sales. Finally the concern let him out and he come right home here and told everybody he'd been fired instead of sayin' he'd resigned like most fellas would of.

It was a Saturday and the shop was full and Jim got up out of that chair and says, "Gentlemen, I got an important announcement to make. I been fired from my job."

Well, they asked him if he was in earnest and he said he was and nobody could think of nothin' to say till Jim finally broke the ice himself. He says, "I been sellin' canned goods and now I'm canned goods myself."

You see, the concern he'd been workin' for was a factory that made canned goods. Over in Carterville. And now Jim said he was canned himself. He was certainly a card!

Jim had a great trick that he used to play w'ile he was travelin'. For instance, he'd be ridin' on a train and they'd come to some little town like, well, like, we'll say, like Benton. Jim would look out the train window and read the signs on the stores.

For instance, they'd be a sign, "Henry Smith, Dry Goods." Well, Jim would write down the name and the name of the town and when he got to wherever he was goin' he'd mail back a postal card to Henry Smith at Benton and not sign no name to it, but he'd write on the card, well, somethin' like "Ask your wife about that book agent that spent the afternoon last week," or "Ask your Missus who kept her from gettin' lonesome the last time you was in Carterville." And he'd sign the card, "A Friend."

Of course, he never knew what really come of none of those jokes, but he could picture what *probably* happened and that was enough. Jim didn't work very steady after he lost his position with the Carterville people. What he did earn, doin' odd jobs round town, why he spent pretty near all of it on gin and his family might of starved if the stores hadn't of carried them along. Jim's wife tried her hand at dressmakin', but they ain't nobody goin' to get rich makin' dresses in this town.

As I say, she'd of divorced Jim, only she seen that she couldn't support herself and the kids and she was always hopin' that some day Jim would cut out his habits and give her more than two or three dollars a week.

They was a time when she would go to whoever he was workin' for and ask them to give her his wages, but after she done this once or twice, he beat her to it by borrowin' most of his pay in advance. He told it all round town, how he had outfoxed his Missus. He certainly was a caution!

But he wasn't satisfied with just outwittin' her. He was sore the way she had acted, tryin' to grab off his pay. And he made up his mind he'd get even. Well, he waited till Evans's Circus was advertised to come to town. Then he told his wife and two kiddies that he was goin' to take them to the circus. The day of the circus, he told them he would get the tickets and meet them outside the entrance to the tent.

Well, he didn't have no intentions of bein' there or buyin' tickets or nothin'. He got full of gin and laid round Wright's poolroom all day. His wife and kids waited and waited and of course he didn't show up. His wife didn't have a dime with her, or nowhere else, I guess. So she finally had to tell the kids it was all off and they cried like they wasn't never goin' to stop.

Well, it seems, w'ile they was cryin', Doc Stair came along and he asked what was the matter, but Mrs. Kendall was stubborn and wouldn't tell him, but the kids told him and he insisted on takin' them and their mother in to the show. Jim found this out afterwards and it was one reason why he had it in for Doc Stair.

Doc Stair come here about a year and a half ago. He's a mighty handsome young fella and his clothes always look like he has them made to order. He goes to Detroit two or three times a year and w'ile he's there he must have a tailor take his measure and then make him a suit to order. They cost pretty near twice as much, but they fit a whole lot better than if you just bought them in a store.

For a w'ile everybody was wonderin' why a young doctor like Doc Stair should come to a town like this where we already got old Doc Gamble and Doc Foote that's both been here for years and all the practice in town was already divided between the two of them.

Then they was a story got round that Doc Stair's gal had throwed him over, a gal up in the Northern Peninsula somewheres, and the reason he come here was to hide himself away and forget it. He said himself that he thought they wasn't nothin' like general practice in a place like ours to fit a man to be a good all round doctor. And that's why he'd came.

Anyways, it wasn't long before he was makin' enough to live on, though they tell me that he never dunned nobody for what they owed him, and the folks here certainly has got the owin' habit, even in my business. If I had all that was comin' to me for just shaves alone, I could go to Carterville and put up at the Mercer for a week and see a different picture every night. For instance, they's old George Purdy — but I guess I shouldn't ought to be gossipin'.

Well, last year, our coroner died, died of the flu. Ken Beatty, that was his name. He was the coroner. So they had to choose another man to be coroner in his place and they picked Doc Stair. He laughed at first and said he didn't want it, but they made him take it. It ain't no job that anybody would fight for and what a man makes out of it in a year would just about buy seeds for their garden. Doc's the kind, though, that can't say no to nothin' if you keep at him long enough.

But I was goin' to tell you about a poor boy we got here in town — Paul Dickson. He fell out of a tree when he was about ten years old. Lit on his head and it done somethin' to him and he ain't never been right. No harm in him, but just silly. Jim Kendall used to call him cuckoo; that's a name Jim had for anybody that was off their head, only he called people's head their bean. That was another of his gags, callin' head bean and callin' crazy people cuckoo. Only poor Paul ain't crazy, but just silly.

You can imagine that Jim used to have all kinds of fun with Paul. He'd send him to the White Front Garage for a left-handed monkey wrench. Of course they ain't no such a thing as a left-handed monkey wrench.

And once we had a kind of a fair here and they was a baseball game between the fats and the leans and before the game started Jim called Paul over and sent him way down to Schrader's hardware store to get a key for the pitcher's box.

They wasn't nothin' in the way of gags that Jim couldn't think up, when he put his mind to it.

Poor Paul was always kind of suspicious of people, maybe on account of how Jim had kept foolin' him. Paul wouldn't have much to do with anybody only his own mother and Doc Stair and a girl here in town named Julie Gregg. That is, she ain't a girl no more, but pretty near thirty or over.

When Doc first came to town, Paul seemed to feel like here was a real friend and he hung around Doc's office most of the w'ile; the only time he wasn't there was when he'd go home to eat or sleep or when he seen Julie Gregg doin' her shoppin'.

When he looked out Doc's window and seen her, he'd run downstairs and join her and tag along with her to the different stores. The poor boy was crazy about Julie and she always treated him mighty nice and made him feel like he was welcome, though of course it wasn't nothin' but pity on her side.

Doc done all he could to improve Paul's mind and he told me once that he really thought the boy was gettin' better, that they was times when he was as bright and sensible as anybody else.

But I was goin' to tell you about Julie Gregg. Old Man Gregg was in the lumber business, but got to drinkin' and lost the most of his money and when he died, he didn't leave nothin' but the house and just enough insurance for the girl to skimp along on.

Her mother was a kind of a half invalid and didn't hardly ever leave the house. Julie wanted to sell the place and move somewheres else after the old man died, but the mother said she was born here and would die here. It was tough on Julie, as the young people round this town — well, she's too good for them.

She's been away to school and Chicago and New York and different places and they ain't no subject she can't talk on, where you take the rest of the young folks here and you mention anything to them outside of Gloria Swanson or Tommy Meighan and they think you're delirious. Did you see Gloria in *Wages of Virtue?* You missed somethin'!

Well, Doc Stair hadn't been here more than a week when he come in one day to get shaved and I recognized who he was as he had been pointed out to me, so I told him about my old lady. She's been ailin' for a couple years and either Doc Gamble or Doc Foote, neither one, seemed to be helpin' her. So he said he would come out and see her, but if she was able to get out herself, it would be better to bring her to his office where he could make a complete examination.

So I took her to his office and w'ile I was waiting' for her in the reception room, in come Julie Gregg. When somebody comes in Doc Stair's office, they's a bell that rings in his inside office so he can tell they's somebody to see him.

So he left my old lady inside and come out to the front office and that's the first time him and Julie met and I guess it was what they call love at first sight. But it wasn't fifty-fifty. This young fella was the slickest lookin' fella she'd ever seen in this town and she went wild over him. To him she was just a young lady that wanted to see the doctor.

She'd came on about the same business I had. Her mother had been doctorin' for years with Doc Gamble and Doc Foote and with no results. So she'd heard they was a new doc in town and decided to give him a try. He promised to call and see her mother that same day.

I said a minute ago that it was love at first sight on her part. I'm not only judgin' by how she acted afterwards but how she looked at him that first day in his office. I ain't no mind reader, but it was wrote all over her face that she was gone.

Now Jim Kendall, besides bein' a jokesmith and a pretty good drinker, well, Jim was quite a lady-killer. I guess he run pretty wild durin' the time he was on the road for them Carterville people, and besides that, he'd had a couple little affairs of the heart right here in town. As I say, his wife could of divorced him, only she couldn't.

But Jim was like the majority of men, and women, too, I guess. He wanted what he couldn't get. He wanted Julie Gregg and worked his head off tryin' to land her. Only he'd of said bean instead of head.

Well, Jim's habits and his jokes didn't appeal to Julie and of course he was a married man, so he didn't have no more chance than, well, than a rabbit. That's an expression of Jim's himself. When somebody didn't have no chance to get elected or somethin', Jim would always say they didn't have no more chance than a rabbit.

He didn't make no bones about how he felt. Right in here, more than once, in front of the whole crowd, he said he was stuck on Julie and anybody that could get her for him was welcome to his house and his wife and kids included. But she wouldn't have nothin' to do with him; wouldn't even speak to him on the street. He finally seen he wasn't gettin' nowheres with his usual line so he decided to try the rough stuff. He went right up to her house one evenin' and when she opened the door he forced his way in and grabbed her. But she broke loose and before he could stop her, she run in the next room and locked the door and phoned to Joe Barnes. Joe's the marshal. Jim could hear who she was phonin' to and he beat it before Joe got there.

Joe was an old friend of Julie's pa. Joe went to Jim the next day and told him what would happen if he ever done it again.

I don't know how the news of this little affair leaked out. Chances is that Joe Barnes told his wife and she told somebody else's wife and they told their husband. Anyways, it did leak out and Hod Meyers had the nerve to kid Jim about it, right here in this shop. Jim didn't deny nothin' and kind of laughed it off and said for us all to wait: that lots of people had tried to make a monkey out of him, but he always got even.

Meanw'ile everybody in town was wise to Julie's bein' wild mad over the Doc. I don't suppose she had any idea how her face changed when him and her was together; of course she couldn't of, or she'd kept away from him. And she didn't know that we was all noticin' how many times she made excuses to go up to his office or pass it on the other side of the street and look up in his window to see if he was there. I felt sorry for her and so did most other people.

Hod Meyers kept rubbin' it into Jim about how the Doc had cut him out. Jim didn't pay no attention to the kiddin' and you could see he was plannin' one of his jokes.

One trick Jim had was the knack of changin' his voice. He could make you think he was a girl talkin' and he could mimic any man's voice. To show you how good he was along this line, I'll tell you the joke he played on me once.

You know, in most towns of any size, when a man is dead and needs a shave, why the barber that shaves him soaks him five dollars for the job; that is, he don't soak *him,* but whoever ordered the shave. I just charge three dollars because personally I don't mind much shavin' a dead person. They lay a whole lot stiller than live customers. The only thing is that you don't feel like talkin' to them and you get kind of lonesome.

Well, about the coldest day we ever had here, two years ago last winter, the phone rung at the house w'ile I was home to dinner and I answered the phone and it was a woman's voice and she said she was Mrs. John Scott and her husband was dead and would I come out and shave him.

Old John had always been a good customer of mine. But they live seven miles out in the country, on the Streeter road. Still I didn't see how I could say no.

So I said I would be there, but would have to come in a jitney and it might cost three or four dollars besides the price of the shave. So she, or the voice, it said that was all right, so I got Frank Abbott to drive me out to the place and when I got there, who should open the door but old John himself! He wasn't no more dead than, well, than a rabbit.

It didn't take no private detective to figure out who had played me this little joke. Nobody could of thought it up but Jim Kendall. He certainly was a card!

I tell you this incident just to show you how he could disguise his voice and make you believe it was somebody else talkin'. I'd of swore it was Mrs. Scott had called me. Anyways, some woman.

Well, Jim waited till he had Doc Stair's voice down pat; then he went after revenge.

He called Julie up on a night when he knew Doc was over in Carterville. She never questioned but what it was Doc's voice. Jim said he must see her that night; he couldn't wait no longer to tell her somethin'. She was all excited and told him to come to the house. But he said he was expectin' an important long distance call and wouldn't she please forget her manners for once and come to his office. He said they couldn't nothin' hurt her and nobody would see her and he just *must* talk to her a little w'ile. Well, poor Julie fell for it.

Doc always keeps a night light in his office, so it looked to Julie like they was somebody there.

Meanw'ile Jim Kendall had went to Wright's poolroom, where they was a whole gang amusin' themselves. The most of them had drank plenty of gin, and they was a rough bunch even when sober. They was always strong for Jim's jokes and when he told them to come with him and see some fun they give up their card games and pool games and followed along.

Doc's office is on the second floor. Right outside his door they's a flight of stairs leadin' to the floor above. Jim and his gang hid in the dark behind these stairs.

Well, Julie come up to Doc's door and rung the bell and they was nothin' doin'. She rung it again and she rung it seven or eight times. Then she tried the door and found it locked. Then Jim made some kind of a noise and she heard it and waited a minute, and then she says, "Is that you, Ralph?" Ralph is Doc's first name.

They was no answer and it must of came to her all of a sudden that she'd been bunked. She pretty near fell downstairs and the whole gang after her. They chased her all the way home, hollerin', "Is that you, Ralph?" and "Oh, Ralphie, dear, is that you?" Jim says he couldn't holler it himself, as he was laughin' too hard.

Poor Julie! She didn't show up here on Main Street for a long, long time afterward.

And of course Jim and his gang told everybody in town, everybody but Doc Stair. They was scared to tell him, and he might of never knowed only for Paul Dickson. The poor cuckoo, as Jim called him, he was here in the shop one night when Jim was still gloatin' yet over what he'd done to Julie. And Paul took in as much of it as he could understand and he run to Doc with the story.

It's a cinch Doc went up in the air and swore he'd make Jim suffer. But it was a kind of a delicate thing, because if it got out that he had beat Jim up, Julie was bound to hear of it and then she'd know that Doc knew and of course knowin' that he knew would make it worse for her than ever. He was goin' to do somethin', but it took a lot of figurin'.

Well, it was a couple of days later when Jim was here in the shop again, and so was the cuckoo. Jim was goin' duck-shootin' the next day and had come in lookin' for Hod Meyers to go with him. I happened to know that Hod had went over to Carterville and wouldn't be home till the end of the week. So Jim said he hated to go alone and he guessed he would call it off. Then poor Paul spoke up and said if Jim would take him he would go along. Jim thought a w'ile and then he said, well, he guessed a half-wit was better than nothin'.

I suppose he was plottin' to get Paul out in the boat and play some joke on him, like pushin' him in the water. Anyways, he said Paul could go. He asked him had he ever shot a duck and Paul said no, he'd never even had a gun in his hands. So Jim said he could set in the boat and watch him and if he behaved himself, he might lend him his gun for a couple of shots. They made a date to meet in the mornin' and that's the last I seen of Jim alive.

Next mornin', I hadn't been open more than ten minutes when Doc Stair come in. He looked kind of nervous. He asked me had I seen Paul Dickson. I said no, but I knew where he was, out duck-shootin' with Jim Kendall. So Doc says that's what he had heard, and he couldn't understand it because Paul had told him he wouldn't never have no more to do with Jim as long as he lived.

He said Paul had told him about the joke Jim had played on Julie. He said Paul had asked him what he thought of the joke and the Doc had told him that anybody that would do a thing like that ought not to be let live.

I said it had been a kind of a raw thing, but Jim just couldn't resist no kind of a joke, no matter how raw. I said I thought he was all right at heart, but just bubblin' over with mischief. Doc turned and walked out.

At noon he got a phone call from old John Scott. The lake where Jim and Paul had went shootin' is on John's place. Paul had came runnin' up to the house a few minutes before and said they'd been an accident. Jim had shot a few ducks and then give the gun to Paul and told him to try his luck. Paul hadn't never handled a gun and he was nervous. He was shakin' so hard that he couldn't control the gun. He let fire and Jim sunk back in the boat, dead.

Doc Stair, bein' the coroner, jumped in Frank Abbott's flivver and rushed out to Scott's farm. Paul and old John was down on the shore of the lake. Paul had rowed the boat to shore, but they'd left the body in it, waitin' for Doc to come.

Doc examined the body and said they might as well fetch it back to town. They was no use leavin' it there or callin' a jury, as it was a plain case of accidental shootin'.

Personally I wouldn't never leave a person shoot a gun in the same boat I was in unless I was sure they knew somethin' about guns. Jim was a sucker to leave a new beginner have his gun, let alone a half-wit. It probably served Jim right, what he got. But still we miss him round here. He certainly was a card!

Comb it wet or dry?

1925

WILBUR DANIEL STEELE

Blue Murder

AT MILL CROSSING it was already past sunset. The rays, redder for what autumn leaves were left, still laid fire along the woods crowning the stony slopes of Jim Bluedge's pastures; but then the line of the dusk began and from that level it filled the valley, washing with transparent blue the buildings scattered about the bridge, Jim's house and horse sheds and hay barns, Frank's store, and Camden's blacksmith shop.

The mill had been gone fifty years, but the falls which had turned its wheel still poured in the bottom of the valley, and when the wind came from the Footstool way their mist wet the smithy, built of the old stone on the old foundations, and their pouring drowned the clink of Camden's hammer.

Just now they couldn't drown Camden's hammer, for he wasn't in the smithy; he was at his brother's farm. Standing inside the smaller of the horse paddocks behind the sheds he drove in stakes, one after another, cut green from saplings, and so disposed as to cover the more glaring of the weaknesses in the five-foot fence. From time to time, when one was done and another to do, he rested the head of his sledge in the pocket of his leather apron (he was never without it; it was as though it had grown on him, lumpy with odds and ends of his trade — bolts and nails and rusty pliers and old horseshoes) and, standing so, he mopped the sweat from his face and looked up at the mountain.

Of the three brothers he was the dumb one. He seldom had anything to say. It was providential (folks said) that of the three enterprises at the Crossing one was a smithy; for while he was a strong, big, hungry-muscled fellow, he never would have had the shrewdness to run the store or the farm. He was better at pounding — pounding while the fire reddened and the sparks flew, and thinking, and letting other people wonder what he was thinking of.

Blossom Bluedge, his brother's wife, sat perched on the top bar of the paddock gate, holding her skirts around her ankles with a trifle too much care to be quite unconscious, and watched him work. When he looked at the mountain he was looking at the mares, half a mile up the slope, grazing in a line as straight as soldiers, their heads all one way. But Blossom thought it was the receding light he was thinking of, and her own sense of misgiving returned and deepened.

"You'd have thought Jim would be home before this, wouldn't you, Cam?" Her brother-in-law said nothing. "Cam, look at me!"

It was nervousness, but it wasn't all nervousness — she was the prettiest girl in the valley; a small part of it was mingled coquetry and pique.

The smith began to drive another stake, swinging the hammer from high overhead, his muscles playing in fine big rhythmical convulsions under the skin of his arms and chest, covered with short blond down. Studying him cornerwise, Blossom muttered, "Well, don't look at me, then!"

He was too dumb for any use. He was as dumb as this: when all three of the Bluedge boys were after her a year ago, Frank, the storekeeper, had brought her candy: chocolates wrapped in silver foil in a two-pound Boston box. Jim had laid before her the Bluedge farm and with it the dominance of the valley. And Camden! To the daughter of Ed Beck, the apple grower, Camden had brought a box of apples! — and been bewildered, too, when, for all she could help it, she had had to clap a hand over her mouth and run into the house to have her giggle.

A little more than just bewildered, perhaps. Had she, or any of them, ever speculated about that? . . . He had been dumb enough before; but that was when he had started being as dumb as he was now.

Well, if he wanted to be dumb let him be dumb. Pouting her pretty lips and arching her fine brows, she forgot the unimaginative fellow and turned to the ridge again. And now, seeing the sun was quite gone, all the day's vague worries and dreads — held off by this and that — could not be held off longer. For weeks there had been so much talk, so much gossip and speculation and doubt.

"Camden," she reverted suddenly. "Tell me one thing, did you hear —"

She stopped there. Some people were coming into the kitchen yard, dark forms in the growing darkness. Most of them lingered at the porch, sitting on the steps and lighting their pipes. The one that came out was Frank, the second of her brothers-in-law. She was glad. Frank wasn't like Camden, he would talk. Turning and taking care of her skirts, she gave him a bright and sisterly smile.

"Well, Frankie, what's the crowd?"

Far from avoiding the smile, as Camden's habit was, the storekeeper returned it with a brotherly wink for good measure. "Oh, they're tired of waiting down the road, so they come up here to see the grand arrival." He was something of a man of the world; in his calling he had acquired a fine turn for skepticism. "Don't want to miss being on hand to see what flaws they can pick in 'Jim's five hundred dollars' wuth of expiriment.'"

"Frank, ain't you the least bit worried over Jim? So late?"

"Don't see why."

"All the same, I wish either you or Cam could've gone with him."

"Don't see why. Had all the men from Perry's stable there in Twinshead to help him get the animal off the freight, and he took an extra rope and the log chain and the heavy wagon, so I guess no matter how wild and woolly the devil is he'll scarcely be climbing in over the tailboard. Besides, them Western horses ain't such a big breed, even a stallion."

"All the same — (look the other way, Frankie) —" Flipping her ankles over the rail, Blossom jumped down beside him. "Listen, Frank, tell me something, did you hear — did you hear the reason Jim's getting him cheap was because he killed a man out West there, what's-its-name, Wyoming?"

Frank was taking off his sleeve protectors, the pins in his mouth. It was Camden, at the bars, speaking in his sudden deep rough way, "Who the hell told you that?"

Frank got the pins out of his mouth. "I guess what it is, Blossie, what's mixed you up is his having that name 'Blue Murder.'"

"No, sir! I got some sense and some ears. You don't go fooling me."

Frank laughed indulgently and struck her shoulder with a light hand.

"Don't you worry. Between two horsemen like Jim and Cam —"

"Don't Cam me! He's none of my horse. I told Jim once —" Breaking off, Camden hoisted his weight over the fence and stood outside, his feet spread and his hammer in both hands, an attitude that would have looked a little ludicrous had any one been watching him.

Jim had arrived. With a clatter of hoofs and a rattle of wheels he was in the yard and come to a standstill, calling aloud as he threw the lines over the team, "Well, friends, here we are."

The curious began to edge around, closing a cautious circle. The dusk had deepened so that it was hard to make anything at any distance of Jim's "expiriment" but a blurry silhouette anchored at the wagon's tail. The farmer put an end to it, crying from his eminence, "Now, now, clear out and don't worry him; give him some peace tonight, for Lord's sake! Git!" He jumped to the ground and began to whack his arms, chilled with driving, only to have them pinioned by Blossom's without warning.

"Oh, Jim, I'm so glad you come. I been so worried; gi' me a kiss!"

The farmer reddened, eyeing the crowd of witnesses. He felt awkward and wished she could have waited. "Get along, didn't I tell you fellows?" he cried with a trace of the Bluedge temper. "Go wait in the kitchen then: I'll tell about everything soon's I come in. Well, now — wife —"

"What's the matter?" she laughed, an eye over her shoulder. "Nobody's looking that matters. I'm sure Frank don't mind. And as for Camden —"

Camden wasn't looking at them. Still standing with his hammer two-fisted and his legs spread, his chin down and his thoughts to himself (the dumbhead) he was looking at Blue Murder, staring at the other dumbhead, which, raised high on the motionless column of the stallion's neck, seemed hearkening with an exile's doubt to the sounds of this new universe, tasting with wide nostrils the taint of equine strangers, and studying with eyes accustomed to far horizons these dark pastures that went up in the air.

Whatever the smith's cogitations, presently he let the hammer down and said aloud, "So you're him, eh?"

Jim had put Blossom aside, saying, "Got supper ready? I'm hungry!" Excited by the act of kissing and the sense of witnesses to it, she fussed her hair and started kitchenward as he turned to his brothers.

"Well, what do you make of him?"

"Five hundred dollars," said Frank. "However, it's your money."

Camden was shorter. "Better put him in."

"All right; let them bars down while I and Frank lead him around."

"No, thanks!" The storekeeper kept his hands in his pockets. "I just cleaned up, thanks. Cam's the boy for horses."

"He's none o' my horses!" Camden wet his lips, shook his shoulders, and scowled. "Be damned, no!" He never had the right words, and it made him mad. Hadn't he told Jim from the beginning that he washed his hands of this fool Agricultural College squandering, "and a man-killer to the bargain"?

"Unless," Frank put in shyly, "unless Cam's scared."

"Oh, is Cam scared?"

"Scared?" And still, to the brothers' enduring wonder, the big dense fellow would rise to that boyhood bait. "Scared? The hell I'm scared of any horse ever wore a shoe! Come on, I'll show you! I'll show you!"

"Well, be gentle with him, boys; he may be brittle." As Frank sauntered off around the shed he whistled the latest tune.

In the warmth and light of the kitchen he began to fool with his pretty sister-in-law, feigning princely impatience and growling with a wink at the assembled neighbors, "When do we eat?"

But she protested, "Land, I had everything ready since five, ain't I? And now, if it ain't you, it's them to wait for. I declare for men!"

At last one of the gossips got in a word.

"What you make of Jim's purchase, Frank?"

"Well, it's Jim's money, Darred. If I had the running of his farm —" Frank began drawing up chairs noisily, leaving it at that.

Darred persisted. "Don't look to me much like an animal for women and children to handle, not yet awhile."

"Cowboys han'les 'em, Pa." That was Darred's ten-year-old, big-eyed.

Blossom put the kettle back, protesting, "Leave off, or you'll get me worried to death; all your talk. . . . I declare, where are those bad boys?" Opening the door she called into the dark, "Jim! Cam! Land's sake!"

Subdued by distance and the intervening sheds, she could hear them at their business — sounds muffled and fragmentary, soft thunder of hoofs, snorts, puffings, and the short words of men in action: "Aw, leave him be in the paddock tonight." . . . "With them mares there, you damn fool?". . . "Damn fool, eh? Try getting him in at that door and see who's the damn fool!" . . . "Come on, don't be so scared." . . . "Scared eh?"

Why was it she always felt that curious tightening of all her powers of attention when Camden Bluedge spoke? Probably because he spoke so rarely, and then so roughly, as if his own thickness made him mad.

"Last call for supper in the dining car, boys!" she called, and closed the door. Turning back to the stove she was about to replace the tea water for the third time when, straightening up, she said, "What's that?"

No one else had heard anything. They looked at one another.

"Frank, go — go see what — go tell the boys to come in."

Frank hesitated, feeling foolish, then went to the door.

Then everyone in the room was out of his chair.

There were three sounds. The first was human and incoherent. The second was incoherent, too, but it wasn't human. The third was a crash, a ripping and splintering of wood.

When they got to the paddock they found Camden crawling from beneath the wreckage of the fence where a gap was opened on the pasture side. He must have received a blow on the head, for he seemed dazed. He didn't seem to know they were there. At a precarious balance — one hand at the back of his neck — he stood facing up the hill, gaping after the diminuendo of floundering hoofs, invisible above.

So seconds passed. Again the beast gave tongue, a high wild horning note, and on the black of the stony hill to the right of it a faint shower of sparks blew like fireflies where the herding mares wheeled. It seemed to awaken the dazed smith. He opened his mouth. "Almighty God!" Swinging, he flung his arms toward the shed. "There! There!"

At last someone brought a lantern. They found Jim Bluedge lying on his back in the corner of the paddock near the door to the shed. In the lantern light, and still better in the kitchen when they had carried him in, they read the record of the thing when Camden, dumb in good earnest now, seemed unable to tell them with anything but his strange, unfocused stare.

The bloody offense to the skull would have been enough to kill the man, but it was the second, full on the chest above the heart, that told the tale. On the caved grating of the ribs, already turning blue under the yellowish down, the iron shoe had left its mark, and when, laying back the rag of shirt, they saw that the toe of the shoe was upward and the cutting calkends down they knew all they wanted to know of that swift, black episode.

No outlash here of heels in fright. Here was a forefoot. An attack aimed and frontal; an onslaught reared, erect; beast turned biped; red eyes mad to white eyes aghast. . . . And only afterward, when it was done, the blood-fright that serves the horses for conscience; the blind rush across the enclosure; the fence gone down. . . .

No one had much to say. No one seemed to know what to do.

As for Camden, he was no help. He simply stood propped on top of his legs where someone had left him. From the instant when with his "Almighty God!" he had been brought back to memory, instead of easing its hold as the minutes passed, the event to which he remained the only living human witness seemed minute by minute to tighten its grip. It set its sweat-beaded stamp on his face, distorted his eyes, and tied his tongue. He was no good to anyone.

As for Blossom, even now — perhaps more than ever now — her dependence on physical touch was the thing that ruled her. Down on her knees beside the lamp they had set on the floor, she plucked at one of the dead man's shoes monotonously, and as it were idly swaying the toe like an inverted pendulum from side to side. That was all. Not a word. And when Frank, the only one of the three with any sense, got her up finally and led her away to her room, she clung to him.

It was lucky that Frank was a man of affairs. His brother was dead, and frightfully dead, but there was tomorrow for grief. Just now there were many things to do. There were people to be gotten rid of. With short words and angry gestures he cleared them out, all but Darred and a man named White, and to these he said, "Now, first thing, Jim can't stay here." He ran and got a blanket from a closet. "Give me a hand and we'll lay him in the icehouse overnight. Don't sound good, but it's best, poor fellow. Cam, come along!"

He waited a moment, and as he studied the wooden fool the blood poured back into his face. "Wake up, Cam! You great big scared stiff, you!"

Camden brought his eyes out of nothingness and looked at his brother. A twinge passed over his face, convulsing the mouth muscles. "Scared?"

"Yes, you're scared!" Frank's lip lifted, showing the tips of his teeth. "And I'll warrant you something: if you wasn't the scared stiff you was, this hellish damn thing wouldn't have happened, maybe. Scared! you a blacksmith! Scared of a horse!"

"Horse!" Again that convulsion of the mouth muscles, something between irony and an idiot craft. "Why don't you go catch 'im?"

"Hush it! Don't waste time by going loony now, for God's sake. Come!"

"My advice to anybody —" Camden looked crazier than ever, knotting his brows. "My advice to anybody is to let somebody else go catch that — that —" Opening the door he faced out into the night, his head sunk between his shoulders and the fingers working at the ends of his hanging arms; and before they knew it he began to swear. They could hardly hear because his teeth were locked and his breath soft. There were all the vile words he had ever heard in his life, curses and threats and abominations, vindictive, violent, obscene. He stopped only when at a sharp word from Frank he was made aware that Blossom had come back into the room. Even then he didn't seem to comprehend her return but stood blinking at her, and at the rifle she carried, with his distraught bloodshot eyes.

Frank comprehended. Hysteria had followed the girl's blankness. Stepping between her and the body on the floor, he spoke in a persuasive, unhurried way. "What you doing with that gun, Blossie? Now, now, you don't want that gun, you know you don't."

It worked. Her rigidity lessened appreciably. Confusion gained.

"Well, but — Or, Frank — well, but when we going to shoot him?"

"Yes, yes, Blossie — now, yes — only you best give me that gun; that's the girlie." When he had got the weapon he put an arm around her shoulders. "Yes, yes, course we're going to shoot him; what you think? Don't want an animal like that running round. Now first thing in the morning —"

Hysteria returned. With its strength she resisted his leading.

"No, now! Now! He's gone and killed Jim! Killed my husband! I won't have him left alive another minute! I won't! Now! No, sir, I'm going myself, I am! Frank, I am! Cam!"

At his name, appealed to in that queer screeching way, the man in the doorway shivered all over, wet his lips, and walked out into the dark.

"There, you see?" Frank was quick to capitalize anything. "Cam's gone to do it. Cam's gone, Blossie . . . Here, one of you — Darred, take this gun and run give it to Camden, that's the boy."

"You sure he'll kill him, Frank? You sure?"

"Sure as daylight. Now you come along back to your room like a good girl and get some rest. Come, I'll go with you."

When Frank returned to the kitchen ten minutes later, Darred was back.

"Well, now, let's get at it and carry out poor Jim, he can't lay here. . . . Where's Cam gone now, damn him!"

"Cam? Why, he's gone and went."

"Went where?"

"Up the pasture like you said."

"Like I —" Frank went an odd color. He walked to the door. Between the light on the sill and the beginnings of the stars where the woods crowned the mountain was all one blackness. One stillness, too. He turned on Darred. "But, look, you never gave him that gun, even."

"He didn't want it."

"Lord's sake; what did he say?"

"Said nothing. He'd got the log chain out of the wagon and when I caught him he was up hunting his hammer in under that wreck at the fence. Once he found it he started off up. 'Cam,' says I, 'here's a gun; want it?' He seemed not to. Just went on walking on up."

"How'd he look?"

"Look same's you seen him looking. Sick."

"The damned fool!"

Poor dead Jim! Poor fool Camden! As the storekeeper went about his business and afterward when, the icehouse door closed on its tragic tenant and White and Darred had gone off home, he roamed the yard, driven here and there, soft-footed, waiting, hearkening — his mind was for a time not his own property but the plaything of thoughts diverse and wayward. Jim, his brother, so suddenly and so violently gone. The stallion. That beast that had kicked him to death. With anger and hate and pitiless impatience of time he thought of the morrow, when they would catch him, take their revenge with guns and clubs. Behind these speculations, covering the background of his consciousness and stringing his nerves to endless vigil, spread the wall of the mountain: silent from instant to instant but devising under its black silence (who-could-know-what instant to come), a neigh, a yell, a spark-line of iron hoofs on rolling flints, a groan. And still behind that and deeper into the borders of the unconscious, the storekeeper thought of the farm that had lost its master, the rich bottoms, the broad, well-stocked pastures, the fat barns, and the comfortable house whose chimneys and gable ends fell into changing shapes against the stars as he wandered here and there. . . . Jim gone. . . . And Camden, at any moment. . . .

His face grew hot. An impulse carried him a dozen steps. "I ought to go up. Ought to take the gun and go up." But there shrewd sanity put on the brakes. "Where's the use? Couldn't find him in this dark. Besides, I oughtn't to leave Blossom here alone."

With that he went around toward the kitchen, thinking to go in. But the sight of the lantern, left burning out near the sheds, sent his ideas off on another course. At any rate, it would give his muscles and nerves something to work on. Taking the lantern and entering the paddock, he fell to patching the gap into the pasture, using broken boards from the wreck. As he worked his eyes chanced to fall on footprints in the dung-mixed earth — Camden's footprints, leading away beyond the little ring of light. And beside them, taking off from the landing-place of that prodigious leap, he discerned the trail of the stallion. After a moment he got down on his knees where the earth was softest, holding the lantern so that its light fell full.

He gave over his fence-building. Returning to the house his gait was no longer that of the roamer; his face, caught by the periodic flare of the swinging lantern, was the face of another man. In its expression there was a kind of fright and a kind of calculating eagerness. He looked at the clock on the kitchen shelf, shook it, and read it again. He went to the telephone and fumbled at the receiver. He waited till his hand quit shaking, then removed it from the hook.

"Listen, Darred," he said, when he had got the farmer at last, "get White and whatever others you can and come over first thing it's light. Come a-riding and bring your guns. No, Cam ain't back."

He heard Blossom calling. Outside her door he passed one hand down over his face, as he might have passed a washrag, to wipe off what was there. Then he went in.

"What's the matter with Blossie? Can't sleep?"

"No, I can't sleep. Can't think. Can't sleep. Oh, Frankie!"

He sat down beside the bed.

"Oh, Frankie, Frankie, hold my hand!"

She looked almost homely, her face bleached out and her hair in a mess on the pillow. But she would get over that. And the short sleeve of the nightgown on the arm he held was edged with pretty lace.

"Got your watch here?" he asked. She gave it to him from under the pillow. This, too, he shook as if he couldn't believe it was going.

Pretty Blossom Beck. Here, for a wonder, he sat in her bedroom and held her hand. One brother was dead and the other was on the mountain.

But little by little, as he sat and dreamed so, nightmare crept over his brain. He had to arouse and shake himself. He had to set his thoughts resolutely in other roads. . . . Perhaps there would be even the smithy. The smithy, the store, the farm. Complete. The farm, the farmhouse, the room in the farmhouse, the bed in the room, the wife in the bed. Complete beyond belief. If . . . Worth dodging horror for. If . . .

"Frank, has Cam come back?"

"Cam? Don't you worry about Cam. . . . Where's that watch?"

Far from rounding up their quarry in the early hours after dawn, it took the riders, five of them, till almost noon simply to make certain that he wasn't to be found — not in any of the pastures. Then, when they discovered the hole in the fence far up in the woods beyond the crest, where Blue Murder had led the mares in a break for the open country of hills and ravines to the south, they were only at the beginning.

The farmers had left their work undone at home and, as the afternoon lengthened and with it the shadows in the hollow places, they began to eye one another behind their leader's back. Yet they couldn't say it; there was something in the storekeeper's air today, something zealous and pitiless and fanatical, that shut them up and pulled them plodding on.

Frank did the trailing. Hopeless of getting anywhere before sundown in that unkempt wilderness of a hundred square miles of scrub, his companions slouched in their saddles and rode more and more mechanically, knee to knee, and it was he who made the casts to recover the lost trail and, dismounting to read the dust, cried back: "He's still with 'em," and with gestures of imperious excitement beckoned them on.

"Which you mean?" Darred asked him once. "Cam or the horse?"

Frank wheeled his beast and spurred back at the speaker. It was extraordinary. "You don't know what you're talking about!" he cried, with a causelessness and a disordered vehemence which set them first staring, then speculating. "Come on, you dumbheads; don't talk — ride!"

By the following day, when it was being told in all the farmhouses, the story might vary in details and more and more as the tellings multiplied, but in its fundamentals it remained the same. In one thing they certainly all agreed: they used the same expression — "It was like Frank was drove. Drove in a race against something, and no sparing the whip."

They were a good six miles to the south of the fence. Already the road back home would have to be followed three parts in the dark.

Darred was the spokesman. "Frank, I'm going to call it a day."

The others reined up with him but the man ahead rode on. He didn't seem to hear. Darred lifted his voice. "Come on, call it a day, Frank. Tomorrow, maybe. But you see we've run it out and they're not here."

"Wait," said Frank over his shoulder, still riding on into the pocket.

White's mount — a mare — laid back her ears, shied, and stood trembling. After a moment she whinnied.

It was as if she had whinnied for a dozen. A crashing in the woods above them to the left and the avalanche came — down-streaming, erupting, wheeling, wheeling away with volleying snorts, a dark rout.

Darred, reining his horse, began to shout, "Here they go this way, Frank!" But Frank was yelling, "Up here, boys! This way, quick!"

It was the same note, excited, feverish, disordered, breaking like a child's. When they neared him they saw he was off his horse, rifle in hand, and down on his knees to study the ground where the woods began. By the time they reached his animal the impetuous fellow had started up into the cover, his voice trailing, "Come on; spread out and come on!"

One of the farmers got down. When he saw the other three keeping their saddles he swung up again.

White spoke this time. "Be darned if I do!" He lifted a protesting hail, "Come back here, Frank! You're crazy! It's getting dark!"

It was Frank's own fault. They told him plainly to come back and he wouldn't listen.

For a while they could hear his crackle in the mounting underbrush. Then that stopped, whether he had gone too far for their ears or whether he had come to a halt to give his own ears a chance. . . . Once, off to his right, a little higher up under the low ceiling of the trees that darkened moment by moment with the rush of night, they heard another movement, another restlessness of leaves and stones. Then that was still.

Darred ran a sleeve over his face and swung down. "God alive, boys!"

It was the silence. All agreed there — the silence and the deepening dusk.

The first they heard was the shot. No voice. Just the one report. Then after five breaths of another silence a crashing of growth, a charge in the darkness under the withered scrub, continuous and diminishing.

They shouted, "Frank!" No answer. They called, "Frank Bluedge!"

Now, since they had to, they did. Keeping contact by word, and guided partly by directional memory (and mostly in the end by luck), after a time they found the storekeeper in a brake of ferns, lying across his gun.

They got him down to the open, watching behind them all the while. Only then, by the flares of successive matches, under the noses of snorting horses, did they look for the damage done.

They remembered the stillness and the gloom; it must have been quite black in there. The attack had come from behind — equine and pantherine at once, and planned and cunning. A deliberate lunge with a forefoot again: the shoe which had crushed the backbone between the shoulder blades was a foreshoe, that much they saw by the match flares in the red wreck.

They took no longer getting home than they had to, but it was longer than they would have wished. With Frank across his own saddle, walking their horses and with one or another ahead to pick the road (it was going to rain, and even the stars were lost), they made no more than a creeping speed.

None of them had much to say on the journey. Finding the break in the boundary fence and feeling through the last of the woods, the lights of their farms began to show in the pool of blackness below, and Darred uttered a part of what had lain in the minds of them all during the return: "Well, that leaves Cam."

None followed it up. None cared to go any closer than he was to the real question. Something new, alien, menacing and pitiless had come into the valley of their lives with that beast they had never really seen; they felt its oppression, every one, and kept the real question back in their minds:

"Does it leave Cam?"

It answered itself. Camden was at home when they got there.

He had come in a little before them, empty-handed. Empty-headed, too. When Blossom, who had waited all day, part of the time with neighbor women who had come in and part of the time alone to the point of going mad — when she saw him coming down the pasture, his feet stumbling and his shoulders dejected, her first feeling was relief. Her first words, however, were, "Did you get him, Cam?" And all he would answer was, "Gi' me something to eat, can't you? Gi' me a few hours' sleep, can't you? Then wait!"

He looked as if he would need more than a few hours' sleep. Propped on his elbows over his plate it seemed as though his eyes would close before his mouth would open.

His skin was scored by thorns and his shirt was in ribbons under the straps of his iron-sagged apron, but it was not by these marks that his twenty-odd hours showed: it was by his face. While yet his eyes were open and his wits still half awake, his face surrendered. The flesh relaxed into lines of stupor, a putty-formed, putty-colored mask of sleep.

Once he let himself be aroused. This was when, to an abstracted query as to Frank's whereabouts, Blossom told him Frank had been out with four others since dawn. He heaved clear of the table and opened his eyes at her showing the red around the rims.

He spoke with the thick tongue of a drunkard. "If anybody but me lays hand on the stallion I'll kill him. I'll wring his neck."

Then he relapsed into his stupidity, and not even the arrival of the party bringing his brother's body seemed able to shake him so far clear of it again.

At first, when they had laid Frank on the floor where on the night before they had laid Jim, he seemed hardly to comprehend.

"What's wrong with Frank?"

"Some more of Jim's 'expiriment.'"

"Frank see him? He's scared, Frank is. Look at his face there."

"He's dead, Cam."

"Dead, you say? Frank dead? Dead of fright, is that it?"

Even when, rolling the body over, they showed him what was what, he appeared incapable of comprehension, of amazement, of passion, or of any added grief. He looked at them all with a kind of befuddled protest. Returning to his chair and his plate, he grumbled, "Le' me eat first, can't you? Can't you gi' me a little time to sleep?"

"Well, you couldn't do much tonight anyway, I guess." At White's words Blossom opened her mouth for the first time.

"No, nothing tonight, Cam. Cam! Camden! Say! Promise!"

"And then tomorrow, Cam, what we'll do is to get every last man in the valley, and we'll go at this right. We'll lay hand on that devil —"

Camden swallowed his mouthful of cold steak with difficulty. His obsession touched, he showed them the rims of his eyes again.

"You do and I'll wring your necks. The man that touches that animal before I do gets his neck wrang. That's all you need to remember."

"Yes, yes — no — that is —" Poor Blossom. "Yes, Mr. White, thanks; no, Cam's not going out tonight. . . . No, Cam, nobody's going to interfere — nor nothing. Don't worry there. . . ."

Again poor Blossom! Disaster piled too swiftly on disaster; no discipline but instinct left. Caught in fire and flood and earthquake and not knowing what to come, and no creed but "save him who can!" — by hook or crook of wile or smile. With the valley of her life emptied out, and its emptiness repeopled monstrously and pressing down black, on the roof under which (now that Frank was gone to the icehouse, too, and the farmers back home) one brother was left of three — she would tread softly, she would talk or she would be dumb, as her sidelong glimpses of the awake-asleep man's face above the table told her was the instant's need; or if he would eat, she would magic out of nothing something, anything; or if he would sleep, he could sleep, so long as he slept in that house where she could know he was sleeping.

Only one thing. If she could touch him. If she could touch and cling.

Lightning filled the windows. After a moment the thunder came avalanching down the pasture and brought up against the clapboards of the house. At this she was behind his chair. She put out a hand. She touched his shoulder. The shoulder was bare, the shirt ripped away; it was caked with sweat and with the blackening smears of scratches, but for all its exhaustion and dirt it was flesh alive — a living man to touch.

Camden blundered up. "What the hell!" He started off two steps and wheeled on her. "Why don't you get off to bed, for Goll sake!"

"Yes, Cam, yes — right off, yes."

"Well, I'm going, I can tell you. For Goll sake. I need some sleep!"

"Yes, that's right, yes, Cam, good night, Cam — only — only you promise — promise you won't go out — nowheres."

"Go out? Not likely I won't! Not likely! Get along!"

It took her no time to get along then — quick and quiet as a mouse.

Camden lingered to stand at one of the windows where the lightning came again, throwing the black barns and paddocks at him from the white sweep of the pastures crowned by woods.

As it had taken her no time to go, it took Blossom no time to undress and get in bed. When Camden was on his way to his room he heard her calling, "Cam! Just a second, Cam!"

In the dark outside her door he drew one hand down over his face, wiping off whatever might be there. Then he entered.

"Yes? What?"

"Cam, set by me a minute, won't you? And Cam, oh, Cam, hold my hand."

As he slouched down, his fist enclosing her fingers, thoughts awakened and ran and fastened on things. They fastened, tentatively at first, upon the farm. Jim gone. Frank gone. The smithy, the store, and the farm. The whole of Mill Crossing. The trinity. The three in one. . . .

"Tight, Cam, for pity's sake! Hold it tight!"

His eyes, falling to his fist, strayed up along the arm it held. The sleeve, rumpled near the shoulder, was trimmed with pretty lace.

"Tighter, Cam!"

A box of apples. That memory hidden away in the cellar of his mind. Hidden away clamped down in the dark, till the noxious vapors, the murderous vapors of its rotting had filled the shut-up house he was. . . . A box of red apples for the apple-grower's girl . . . the girl who sniggered and ran away from him to laugh at him. . . .

And there, by the unfolding of a devious destiny, he sat in that girl's bedroom, holding that girl's hand. Jim who had got her, Frank who had wanted her lay side by side out there in the icehouse under the lightning. While he, the "dumb one" — the last to be thought of with anything but amusement and the last to be feared — his big hot fist inclosing her imprecating hand now, and his eyes on the pretty lace at her shoulder — He jumped up with a gulp and a clatter of iron.

"What the —" He flung her hand away. "What the hell!" He swallowed. "Damn you, Blossie Beck!" He stared at her with repugnance and mortal fright. "Why, you — you — you —"

He moderated his voice with an effort, wiping his brow. "Good night. You must excuse me, Blossie; I wasn't meaning — I mean — I hope you sleep good. I shall. . . . Good night!"

In his own brain was the one word "Hurry!"

She lay and listened to his boots going along the hall and heard the closing of his door. She ought to have put out the lamp. But even with the shades drawn, the lightning around the edges of the window unnerved her; in the dark alone it would have been more than she could bear.

She lay so till she felt herself nearing exhaustion from the sustained rigidity of her limbs. Rain came and with the rain, wind. Around the eaves it neighed like wild stallions; down the chimneys it moaned like men.

Slipping out of bed and pulling on a bathrobe she ran from her room, barefooted, and along the hall to Camden's door.

"Cam!" she called. "Oh, Cam!" she begged. "Please, please!"

And now he wouldn't answer her.

New lightning, diffused through all the sky by the blown rain, ran at her along the corridor. She pushed the door open. The lamp was burning on the bureau but the room was empty and the bed untouched.

Taking the lamp she skittered down to the kitchen. No one there. . . .

"Hurry!"

Camden had reached the woods when the rain came. Lighting the lantern he had brought, he made his way on to the boundary fence. There, about a mile to the east of the path the others had taken that day, he pulled the rails down and tumbled the stones together in a pile. Then he proceeded another hundred yards, holding the lantern high and peering through the streaming crystals of the rain.

Blue Murder was there. Neither the chain nor the sapling had given way. The lantern and, better than the lantern, a globe of lightning, showed the tethered stallion glistening and quivering, his eyes all whites at the man's approach.

"Gentle, boy; steady, boy!" Talking all the while in the way he had with horses, Camden put a hand on the taut chain and bore with a gradually progressive weight, bringing the dark head nearer. "Steady, boy; gentle there, damn you; gentle!"

Was he afraid of horses? Who was it said he was afraid of horses?

The beast's head was against the man's chest, held there by an arm thrown over the bowed neck. As he smoothed the forehead and fingered the nose with false caresses, Camden's "horse talk" ran on — the cadence one thing, the words another.

"Steady, Goll damn you; you're going to get yours. Cheer up, cheer up, the worst is yet to come. Come now! Come easy! Come along!"

When he had unloosed the chain he felt for and found with his free hand his hammer hidden behind the tree. Throwing the lantern into the brush, where it flared for an instant before dying, he led the stallion back as far as the break he had made in the fence. Taking a turn with the chain around the animal's nose, like an improvised hackamore, he swung from the stone pile to the slippery back. A moment's shying, a sliding caracole of amazement and distrust, a crushing of knees, a lash of the chain-end, and that was all there was to that. Blue Murder had been ridden before. . . .

In the smithy, chambered in the roaring of the falls and the swish and shock of the storm, Camden sang as he pumped his bellows, filling the cave beneath the rafters with red. The air was nothing, the words were mumbo jumbo, but they swelled his chest. His eyes, cast from time to time at his wheeling prisoner, had lost their look of helplessness and surly distraction.

"Shy, you devil!" He wagged his exalted head. "Whicker, you hellion! Whicker all you want to, stud horse! Tomorrow they're going to get you, the dumb fools! Tomorrow they can have you. I got you tonight!"

He was more than other men; he was enormous. Fishing an iron shoe from that inseparable apron pocket of his, he thrust it into the coals and blew and blew. He tried it and it was burning red. He tried it again and it was searing white. Taking it out on the anvil he began to beat it, swinging his hammer one-handed, gigantic. So in the crimson light, ir-radiating iron sparks, he was at his greatest. Pounding, pounding. A man in the dark of night with a hammer about him can do wonders; with a horseshoe about him he can cover up a sin. And if the dark of night in a paddock won't hold it, then the dark of under-growth on a mountainside will. . . .

Pounding, pounding; thinking, thinking, in a great halo of hot stars. Feeding his hungry, his insatiable muscles.

"Steady now, you blue bastard! Steady, boy!"

What he did not realize in his feverish exaltation was that his muscles were not insatiable. In the thirty-odd hours past they had had a feast spread before them and they had had their fill. . . . More than their fill.

As with the scorching iron in his tongs he approached the stallion, he had to step over the nail-box he had stepped over five thousand times in the routine of every day.

A box of apples, eh? Apples to snigger at, eh? But whose girl are you now? . . . Scared, eh?

His foot was heavier of a sudden than it should have been. This five thousand and first time, by the drag of the tenth of an inch, the heel caught the lip of the nail box.

He tried to save himself from stumbling. At the same time, instinctively, he held the iron flame in his tongs away.

There was a scream out of a horse's throat; a whiff of hair and burnt flesh.

There was a lash of something in the red shadows. There was another sound and another wisp of stench. . . .

When, guided by the stallion's whinnying, they found the smith next day, they saw by the cant of his head that his neck was broken, and they perceived that he, too, had on him the mark of a shoe. It lay up one side of his throat and the broad of a cheek. It wasn't blue this time, however, it was red. It took them some instants in the sunshine pouring through the wide door to comprehend this phenomenon. It wasn't sunk in by a blow this time; it was burned in, a brand.

Darred called them to look at the stallion, chained behind the forge.

"Almighty God!" The words sounded funny in his mouth. They sounded the funnier in that they were the same ones the blundering smith had uttered when, staring uphill from his clever wreckage of the paddock fence, he had seen the mares striking sparks from the stones where the stallion struck none. And he, of all men, a smith!

"Almighty God!" called Darred. "What can you make of these here feet?"

One fore-hoof was freshly pared for shoeing; the other three hoofs were as virgin as any yearling's on the plains. Blue Murder had never been shod. . . .

1928

BEN RAY REDMAN

....

The Perfect Crime

THE WORLD'S GREATEST DETECTIVE complacently sipped a port some years older than himself and intently gazed across the table at his most intimate acquaintance; for many years the detective had not permitted himself the luxury of friends. Gregory Hare looked back at him, waiting, listening.

"There is no doubt about it," Trevor reiterated, putting down his glass, "the perfect crime is a possibility; it requires only the perfect criminal."

"Naturally," assented Hare with a shrug, "but the perfect criminal . . ."

"You mean he is a mythical fellow, not apt to be met with in the flesh?"

"Exactly," said Hare, nodding his big head.

Trevor sighed, sipped again, and adjusted the eyeglasses on his thin, sharp nose. "No, I admit I haven't encountered him as yet, but I am always hopeful."

"Hoping to be done in the eye, eh?"

"No, hoping to see the perfect methods of detection tested to the limits of their possibilities. You know, a gifted detector of crime is something more than an inspired policeman with a little bloodhound blood in his veins, something more than a precise scientist; he's an art critic as well, and no art critic likes to be condemned to a steady diet of second-rate stuff."

"Quite."

"Second-rate stuff is bad enough, but it's not the worst. Think of the third, fourth, fifth, and heaven-knows-what-rate crimes that come along every day! And even the masterpieces, the 'classics,' are pretty poor daubs when you look at them closely: a bad tone here and a wrong line there; something false, something botched."

"Most murderers are rather foolish," interjected Hare.

"Foolish! Of course they are. You should know, man, you've defended enough of them. The trouble is that murder almost never evokes the best efforts of the best minds. As a rule it is the work of an inferior mind, cunningly striving towards a perfection that is beyond its reach, or of a superior mind so blinded by passion that its faculties are temporarily impaired. Of course, there are your homicidal maniacs, and they are often clever, but they lack imagination and variety; sooner or later their inability to do anything but repeat themselves brings them up with a sharp jerk."

"Repetition is dullness," murmured Hare, "and dullness, as somebody has remarked, is the one unforgivable sin."

"Right," agreed Trevor. "It is, and plenty of murderers have suffered for it. But they have suffered from vanity almost as often. Practically every murderer, unless he has been accidentally impelled to crime, is an egregious egotist. You know that as well as I do. His sense of power is tremendous, and as a rule he can't keep his mouth shut."

Dr. Harrison Trevor's glasses shone brightly, and he plucked continually at the black cord depending from them as he jerked out his sentences with rapidity and precision. He was on his own ground, and he knew what he was talking about. For twenty years criminals had been his specialty and his legitimate prey. He had hunted them through all lands, and he hunted them successfully. Upstairs, in a chiffonier drawer in his bedroom, there was a large red-leather box holding visible symbols of that success: small decorations of gold and silver and bright ribbons bore mute witness to the gratitude that various European governments had felt, on notable occasions, towards the greatest man hunter of his generation. If Trevor was a dogmatist on murder he was entitled to be one.

Hare, on the other hand, was a good and respectful listener, but, being a criminal lawyer of long experience, he was a man with ideas of his own; and he always expressed them when there was no legal advantage to be gained by withholding them. He expressed one now, when he drawled softly, "All murderers are great egotists, are they? How about great detectives?"

Trevor blinked, then smiled coldly, clutching at his black cord. "Most detectives are asses, I grant you, complete asses and vain as peacocks;

very few of them are great. I know only three. One of them is now in Vienna, the second is in Paris, and the third is . . ."

Hare raised his hand in interruption and said, "The third, or rather the first, is in this room."

The greatest detective in the world nodded briskly. "Of course. There's no point in false modesty, is there?"

"None at all. And it might be a little difficult to maintain such an attitude so soon after the Harrington case. The poor chap was put out of his misery week before last, wasn't he?"

Trevor snorted. "Yes, if you want to call him a poor chap; he was a deliberate murderer. But let's get back to that perfect crime of ours."

"Of yours, you mean," Hare corrected him politely. "I haven't subscribed to the possibility of it as yet. And how would you know about a perfect crime if it ever were committed? The criminal would never be discovered."

"If he had any artistic pride, he would leave a full account of it to be published after his death. Besides, you are forgetting the perfect methods of detection."

Hare whistled softly. "There's a pretty theoretical problem for you. What would happen when the perfect detector set out to catch the perfect criminal? Rather like the immovable object and the irresistible force business, and just about as sensible. The fly in the ointment, of course, is that there is no such thing as perfection."

Dr. Trevor sat up rigidly and glared at the speaker. "There is perfection in the detection of crime."

"Well, perhaps there is." Hare laughed amiably, "You should know, Trevor. But I think what you really mean is that there is a perfect method for detecting imperfect crimes."

The doctor's rigidity had vanished, and now he was smiling with as much geniality as he ever displayed. "Perhaps that is what I do mean, perhaps it is. But there is a little experiment that I should like to try, just the same."

"And that is?"

"And that is, or rather would be, the experiment of exercising all my intelligence in the commission of a crime, then, forgetting every detail of it utterly, using my skill and knowledge to solve the riddle of my own creation. Should I catch myself, or should I escape myself? That's the question."

"It would be a nice sporting event," agreed Hare, "but I'm afraid it's one that can't be pulled off. The little trifle of forgetting is the difficulty. But it would be interesting to see the outcome."

"Yes, it would," said the other, speaking rather more dreamily than was his habit, "but we can never see quite as far as we should like to. My Japanese man, Tanaka, has a saying that he resorts to whenever he is asked a difficult question. He simply smiles and answers, '*Fuji san ni nobottara sazo tōku made miemashō.*' It means, I believe, that if one were to ascend Mount Fuji one could see far. The trouble is that, as in the case of so many problems, we can't climb the mountain."

"Wise Tanaka. But tell me, Trevor, what is your conception of a perfect crime?"

"I'm afraid it isn't precisely formulated; but I have a rough outline in my mind, and I'll give it to you as well as I can. First, though, let's go up to the library; we shall be more comfortable there, and it will give Tanaka a chance to clear the table. Bring your cigar, and come along."

Together the two men climbed the narrow staircase, the host leading. Dr. Trevor's house was a compact, brick building in the East Fifties, not far from Madison Avenue. Its picturesqueness was rather uncharacteristic of its owner, but its neatness was entirely like him. It was not a large house according to the standards of wealthy New York, but it was a perfectly appointed one, and considerably more spacious than it looked from the street, for the doctor had built on an addition that completely covered the plot which had once been the back yard; and this new section, as well as housing the kitchen and servants' quarters below, held a laboratory and workroom two stories high. An industrial or research chemist might have coveted the equipment of that room; and the filing cases that completely lined the encircling gallery would have furnished any newspaper with a complete reference department. A door opened from the library into the laboratory, and the library itself came close to being the ideal chamber of every student. Dr. Harrison Trevor's house was, in short, an ideal bachelor's establishment, and he had never been tempted to transform it into anything else. More than one male visitor had found reason to remark, "Old Trevor does well for himself."

The same idea flitted across Hare's mind as he puffed at his host's excellent cigar and tasted the liqueur that Tanaka had placed on the table beside his chair. He, too, enjoyed the pleasures of bachelorhood, but he had never learned the knack of enjoying them quite so thoroughly. He would make a few improvements in the routine of his life; he could afford them.

"The perfect crime must, of course, be a murder." Trevor's voice broke the silence that had followed their entrance into the library.

Hare shifted his bulk a little and inquired, "Yes? Why?"

"Because it is, according to our accepted standards, the most reprehensible of all crimes and, therefore, according to my interests, the best. Human life is what we prize most and do our best to protect; to take human life with an art that eludes all detection is unquestionably the ideal criminal action. In it there is a degree of beauty possible in no other crime."

"Humph!" grunted Hare, "you make it sound pleasant."

"I am speaking at once as an amateur and as a professor crime. You have heard surgeons talk of 'beautiful cases.' Well, that is my attitude precisely; and in my cases invariably, as in most of theirs, the patient dies."

"I see."

Trevor blinked, tugged at his eyeglass cord, and then continued. "The crime must be murder, and it must be murder of a particular kind, the purest kind. Now what is the 'purest' kind? Let us see. The *crime passionel* can be ruled out at once, for it is almost impossible that it should be perfect. Passion does not make for art; hot blood begets innumerable blunders. What about the murder for gain? Murderers of this kind make murder a means, not an end in itself; they kill not for the sake of eliminating the victim but in order to profit by the victim's death. No, we can't look to murder for profit as the type that might produce our perfect crime."

The sharp-nosed doctor paused and held his cigar for a moment between his thin lips. Hare studied his face curiously; the man's complete lack of emotion in discussing such matters was not wholly pleasant, he reflected.

Trevor put down his cigar. "Now, how about political and religious murders? They can be counted out almost immediately, for the simple reason that the murderer in such cases is always convinced that he is either serving the public or serving God and, therefore, seldom makes any attempt to conceal his guilt. But there is another class to be considered — those who kill for the sheer joy of killing, those who are dominated by the blood lust. Offhand you would think that their killing would be of the purest type. But as I have said before, the maniac invariably repeats himself, and his repetition leads to his discovery. And even more important is the consideration that the artist must possess the faculty of choice, and that the born killer has no choice. His actions are not willed by himself, they are compelled; whereas the perfect crime must be a work of art, not of necessity."

"You seem to have written off all the possibilities pretty well," remarked Hare.

The doctor shook his head quickly. "Not all. There is one type of murder left, and it is the kind we are looking for: the murder of elimination, the murder in which the sole and pure object is to remove the victim from the world, to get rid of a person whose continued existence is not desirable to the murderer."

"But that brings you back to your *crime passionel,* doesn't it? Practically all murders of jealousy, for example, are murders of elimination, aren't they?"

"In a sense, yes, but not in the purest sense. And, as I have said before, passion can never produce the perfect crime. It must be studied, carefully meditated, and performed in absolutely cold blood. Otherwise it is sure to be imperfect."

"You do go at this in a rather fish-blooded way," remarked the good listener as the doctor paused for a moment.

"Of course I do, and that is the only way the perfect crime could be committed. Now I can imagine a pure murder of elimination that would be ideal so far as motives and circumstances were concerned. Suppose you had spent fifteen years establishing a certain reading of a dubious passage in one of Pindar's odes."

"Ha, ha!" interrupted Hare jocosely. "Suppose I had."

"And suppose," continued Dr. Harrison Trevor, not noticing the interruption, "that another scholar had managed to build up an argument which completely invalidated your interpretation. Suppose, further, that he communicated his proofs to you, and that he had as yet mentioned them to no one else. There you would have a perfect motive and a perfect set of circumstances; only the method of the murder would remain to be worked out."

Gregory Hare sat bolt upright. "Good God, man! What do you mean, 'the method of the murder'?"

The doctor blinked. "Why, don't you understand? You would have excellent reasons for eliminating your rival and thereby saving your own interpretation of the text from confutation; and no one, once your victim was dead and the proofs destroyed, could suspect that you had any such motive. You could work with perfect freedom, you could concentrate on two essentials: the method of the murder and, of course, the disposition of the body."

"The disposition of the body?" Hare seemed to echo the speaker's last words involuntarily.

"To be sure; that is a very important item, most important in fact. But I flatter myself," and here the doctor chuckled softly, "that I have done some very valuable research work along that line."

"You have, eh?" murmured Hare. "And what have you found out?"

"I'll tell you later," Trevor assured him, "and I don't think I would tell any other man alive, because it's really too simple and too dangerous. But at the moment I want to impress on you that the disposition of the body is perhaps the most important step of all in the commission of the perfect crime. The absence of a *corpus delicti* is curiously troublesome to the police. Harrington should really have managed to get rid of West's body, although it probably wouldn't have kept him from sitting in the electric chair two weeks ago. He was too careless."

Hare again sat up sharply and exclaimed, "Was he? Speaking of that, it was the Harrington case that I chiefly wanted to talk to you about to-night."

"Oh, was it? Well, we can get around to that in a minute. And, by the way, that came pretty close to being a murder of elimination, if you like; but the money element figured in it, big money, and gold is apt to have a fairly strong smell when it is mixed up with crime. Harrington's motive was easily traced, but his position made it impossible to touch him until we had our case absolutely water-tight."

"Water-tight, eh? That's what I want to hear about. You see I was abroad until last week, and didn't even know Harrington had been arrested until just before I sailed. The North African newspapers aren't so informative. I was particularly interested, you see, because I knew both men fairly well, and West's wife even better."

"Oh, yes, his wife, gorgeous woman. They were separated, and she's been in Europe for the last two and a half years."

"Yes, I know she has — most of the time."

"All the time. She hasn't been in the United States during that period."

"Hasn't she? Well, I last saw her at Monte Carlo, but that's not important at the moment. I want to hear how you tracked down Harrington."

Dr. Harrison Trevor smiled complacently, adjusted his eyeglasses, and then launched forth in his characteristic manner. "It was really simplicity itself. The only flaw was that Harrington finally confessed. That rather annoyed me, for we didn't need a confession; the circumstantial evidence was complete."

"Circumstantial?"

"Of course. You know as well as I do that most convictions for murder are based on circumstantial evidence. One doesn't send out invitations for a killing."

"No, of course not. Sorry."

"Well, as you probably know, Ernest West, Wall Street operator and multimillionaire (as the papers had it), was found shot through the heart one night a little more than a year ago. He had a shack down on Long Island, near Smithtown, that he used as a base for duck shooting and fishing. The only servant he kept there was an old housekeeper, a local inhabitant; he liked to lead the simple life when he could. Never even used to take a chauffeur down with him. The evening he was killed the housekeeper was absent, spending the night with a sick daughter of hers in Jamaica. She testified that West had sent her off, saying that he could pick up a light supper and breakfast for himself. She turned up the next morning, and nearly died of the shock. West was shot in what was a kind of gun room where he kept all his gear and a few books — cosy sort of place and the best room in the house. There was no sign of a struggle. He was sitting slumped in a big armchair. The bullet that killed him was a .25 caliber. Furst, of the Homicide Bureau, called me up as soon as the regulars failed to locate any scent, and I went down there immediately. West was an important man, you know." The doctor tugged self-consciously at his black cord. "I went down there at once, and I discovered various things. First of all, the house was isolated, and there was no one in the neighborhood who could give any useful evidence whatsoever. The body had been discovered by a messenger boy with a telegram at about seven-thirty; medical examination indicated that the murder had been committed about an hour before. Inside the house I found only one item that I thought useful. After going over the dust and so forth which I swept up from the gun-room floor, I had several tiny thread ends that had pretty obviously come from a tweed suit; and those threads could not be matched in West's wardrobe. But they might have been months old, so I didn't concentrate on them at first. Outside the house there was more to go on. The ground was damp, and two sets of footprints were visible: a man's and a woman's . . ."

"A woman's?" Hare was all attention now.

"Yes, the housekeeper's, of course."

"Oh, yes, the housekeeper's."

"Certainly. But it was difficult to identify them, for the reason that the man, apparently through nervousness, had walked up and down the lane leading to the road several times before finally leaving the scene of his crime; and he had trampled over almost every one of the woman's footprints, scarcely leaving one intact."

"That was odd, wasn't it?

"Very, at first glance, but really simple enough when you think it over. The murderer had hurried out of the house after firing the fatal shot; then he hesitated. He was flurried and couldn't make up his mind as to his next step, even though he had an automobile waiting for him at the end of the lane. So he walked up and down for a few minutes, to calm his nerves and collect his ideas. It was a narrow lane, and the obliteration of the other tracks was at once accidental and inevitable."

"He had a car waiting?"

"Yes, a heavy touring car. Its tire marks were plain, as were those of the public hack that West had ordered for his housekeeper that afternoon. And there was one interesting feature about the marks. There was a big, hard blister on one of the shoes, and it left a perfectly defined indentation in the mud every time it came around."

"I see. And both sets of footprints ended at the same spot?"

"Naturally. The hack stopped for the woman just where the murderer later parked his car."

"Hum." Hare had now lighted a new cigar, and he puffed at it reflectively before asking, "And you are quite sure the woman did not get into the car with the man?"

Trevor stared at the speaker blankly and exclaimed, "You must be wool gathering, Hare. The woman was the housekeeper, and she went off in a public hack at least two hours before the crime was committed. In any event, Harrington confirmed the correctness of all my deductions when he finally confessed." Dr. Harrison Trevor was obviously nettled.

"Oh, yes, of course he did; I'd forgotten. Sorry. Let's hear how you nabbed him."

For a moment the detective looked at his companion doubtfully, as though he feared the other might be baiting him; for Hare's questions had not been of the sort that his alert mind usually asked. He seemed to have something up his sleeve. But Trevor thrust his suspicions aside and returned to the pleasant task of describing his triumph.

"With the bullet, the footprints, the tire marks, and the threads, I had considerable to go on. All I had to do was to relate them unmistakably to one man, and I had my murderer. But the trail soon let into quarters where we had to move cautiously. With my material evidence in front of me, I set out to fasten upon some individual who might have had a motive for killing West. So far as anyone could say, he had no enemies; but on the other hand he had few friends. He believed in the maxim that he travels fastest who travels alone. However, he had nipped some men pretty badly in the Street; and it was upon his financial operations that I soon concentrated my attention. There, with the facilities for investigation at my command, I discovered some very interesting facts. During the three weeks prior to West's death the common stock of Elliott Light and Power had risen fifty-seven points; four days after he had been shot it had dropped back no less than sixty-three points. Investigation showed that on the day West was murdered Harrington was short one hundred and thirty-odd thousand shares of that particular stock. He had been selling it short all the way up, and West had been buying all that was offered. Harrington's resources, great as they were, weren't equal to his rival's. He knew that unless he could break Elliott Common wide open he was a ruined man, and he took the one sure way to do it that he could think of. He eliminated West. It was murder for millions."

Trevor paused impressively; Hare did not say a word.

"That's about all there is to the story; the rest of it was routine sleuthing. One of my men found four tires, three in perfect condition, which had been taken from Harrington's touring car and replaced on the day following the murder. They had been put in a loft of the garage on Harrington's country place. Three perfect tires, mind you; and on the fourth there was a large, hard blister. Harrington's shoes fitted the footprints in West's lane, and the thread ends matched the threads in one of Harrington's suits. And, to top it all off, after the man was arrested, we found a .25, pearl-handled revolver in his wall safe. One shot had been fired, and the weapon hadn't been cleaned since. Harrington's chauffeur testified that his master had taken out the big touring car alone on the afternoon of the murder: the man remembered the date because it had been his wife's birthday. It was all very simple, and even such elements of interest as it possessed were lessened by Harrington's confession. The press made much too much of a stir abut my part in the affair." The doctor smiled deprecatingly. "It was really no mystery at all, and if the men involved had not been so rich and so prominent the case would have been virtually ignored. But we nailed him just in time; he was sailing for Europe the following week."

"What kind of a revolver did you say it was?" Hare asked the question so abruptly that Trevor started before answering.

"Why, it was a .25, pearl-handled and nickel-finished. Rather a dainty weapon altogether; Harrington was a bit apologetic about owning such a toy."

"I should think he might have been. Was the handle slightly chipped on the right side?"

Trevor leaned forward suddenly. "Yes, it was. How the devil did you know?"

"Why it got chipped when Alice dropped it on a rock at Davos. The four of us were target shooting back of the hotel."

"Alice!" exclaimed Trevor. "What Alice? And what do you mean by the four of you?"

Hare answered quietly, "Alice West, my dear fellow. You see, it was her gun. And the four of us were West, Alice, Harrington, and myself; we were all staying at the same hotel in Switzerland four years ago."

"Her gun?" The doctor was speaking excitedly now. "You mean she gave it to him?"

"I doubt it, much as she loved him," drawled Hare. "He probably took it away from her, too late."

"You're talking in riddles," snapped the detective. "What do you mean?"

"Simply that that little weapon helped to execute the wrong man," said Hare wearily.

"The wrong man!"

"Well, that's one way of putting it; but in this case I am very much afraid that the right 'man' was a woman."

Trevor's apparent excitement had vanished abruptly, and now he was as calm as a sphinx. "Tell me exactly what you mean," he demanded.

Hare put aside the butt of his cigar. "It all began back in Davos, four years ago. Harrington fell in love with Alice West, and she fell in love with him. West played dog in the manger: he wouldn't let his wife divorce him and he wouldn't divorce her. They separated, of course, but that didn't help Alice and Harrington towards getting married. I was on the inside of the affair from the first, you see; accidentally to begin with, and afterwards because they all made me their confidant in various degrees. West behaved like a swine, because he really didn't love the woman any more. He simply had made up his mind that no other man was going to have her, legally at least. And he stuck to it — until she killed him."

"She killed him?" The great detective spoke softly.

"I'm as sure of it as though I had seen her do it. To begin with, it was her revolver that fired the shot, as you have proved to me. I've seen it a hundred times when we were firing at bottles and what not for fun. There was no reason for Harrington to borrow it; he had a nice little armory of his own, hadn't he?"

"Yes, we did find a couple of heavy service revolvers and an automatic."

"Exactly. He never would have used a toy like that in a thousand years; and besides he would never have committed a murder. He was too level-headed. Alice, on the other hand, is an extremely hysterical type; I've seen her go completely off her head with anger. Beautiful, Lord, yes! But dangerous, and in the last analysis a coward. She's proved that. I never did envy Harrington."

"But she was in Europe, man, when the murder was committed."

"She was not, Trevor. She was in Montreal that very month, to my certain knowledge, and Montreal isn't so far from Long Island. Harry Sands ran into her at the Ritz there; they were reminiscing about it at Monte Carlo the last time I saw her. She was in Europe before and after the murder, but she wasn't there when it happened. Anyway, that's not the whole story."

"Well, what is it?" Trevor's mouth was grim.

Hare's fingers were playing with a silver match box, and he hesitated a minute before answering. Then he spoke quickly and to the point.

"The rest of it is this. As I told you, Alice is hysterical, and during the past few years drink and dope haven't helped her any. Well, one night at Monte, just before I left, she went off the deep end. We had been talking about her husband's death, and I had been speculating as to who could have done it. Harrington hadn't been arrested then. And I'd been asking her, too, if she and Harrington weren't going to get married soon. She dodged that question, obviously embarrassed. Then suddenly she burst out into a wild tirade against the dead man, called him every name under heaven, and finally dived into her evening bag and fished out a letter. It was addressed to her, and the post mark was more than a year old; it was almost broken at the creases from having been read over and over again. She shoved it at me, and insisted that I read it. It was from West, and it was a cruel letter if I've ever read one. It was the letter of a cat to a mouse, of a jailer to his prisoner: West had her where he wanted her, and he intended to keep her there. He didn't miss a trick when it came to rubbing it in. It was so bad that I didn't want to finish it, but she made me. When I gave it back to her her eyes were blazing; and she grabbed my hand and cried, 'What would you do to a man like that?' I hemmed and hawed for a minute, and she answered herself by exclaiming, 'Kill him! Kill him! Wouldn't you?' As calmly as I could I pointed out to her that someone had already done just that; and she burst into a fit of the wickedest laughter I've ever heard. Then she calmed down, powdered her nose, and said quietly, 'It's funny that you can shoot the heads off all the innocent bottles you like and no one says a word, but if you kill a human snake they hang you for it. And I don't want to hang, thank you very much.'"

Hare paused as though he were very tired, and then he added, "That's about all there was to it; it wasn't very nice. I left for Africa the next day, and I scarcely ever saw the papers there. But I hadn't any doubts as to who had bumped off Ernest West."

While the minute hand on the mantel clock jumped three times there was silence in the book-lined room. Then Trevor spoke, and his voice was strained. "So you think I made a mistake?"

Hare looked him straight in the eye. "What do you think?"

The detective took refuge in another question. "Have you any theory as to what really happened?"

"It's hard to say exactly, but I'm sure she did it. Her reference to the bottles showed that she knew what weapon had been used; she must have done in a thousand bottles with it at various times. My guess is that she and Harrington went down to see West together, to see if they couldn't make him change his mind after all, and that they failed. Then she pulled out that little toy of hers. She always carried it around in her bag. I use to tell her it was a bad habit. She shot West before he could move; she was a better shot than Harrington, he could never have found the man's heart. Then they left the house and drove off in Harrington's car; but first of all he went back and thoughtfully trampled out every one of her footprints and, just to make sure he wasn't missing any, he walked over the housekeeper's as well. There were three sets of tracks there, Trevor, not two; I'll bet on that. Then Harrington took the gun away from her — if he hadn't taken it before — and drove her to wherever she wanted to go. She left him; she left him to stand the gaff if he was suspected, and it was like him to do what he did. He loved her if any man ever loved a woman; and she loved him in her own way, but it wasn't the best way in the world. She loved her own white neck considerably more." Hare smiled a wry smile. "She had forgotten that New York State doesn't go in for hanging. Altogether it is not a pretty tale. But Harrington, poor devil, wanted to save the woman even if she wasn't worth it. You see, to him she was."

"It's impossible!" Trevor snapped out the words as if despite himself.

"What is?"

"That I made a mistake."

"We all make mistakes, my dear fellow."

"I don't." The tight mouth was tighter than ever.

"Well, it's a shame, but what's done is done." Hare shrugged his shoulders.

Trevor looked at him with cold eyes. "Obviously you do not understand. My reputation does not permit of mistakes. I simply can't make them. That's all."

Hare mustered a genial smile; he was genuinely sorry that Trevor was so distressed and he sought to reassure him. "But your reputation isn't going to suffer. The facts won't come out. Alice West will be dead of dope inside of two years, if I'm any judge, and no one else knows."

"You do."

"Yes, I do; but we can forget about that."

Trevor nodded nervously. "Yes, we must. Do you understand, Hare, we *must*."

Hare studied him quizzically. "Don't worry, old chap, your reputation's safe with me; I'll keep my mouth shut."

Trevor nodded again, more nervously and more emphatically. "Yes, yes, I know you will, of course. I know you will."

"And how about a drink?" Hare swung himself out of his chair.

"On the table there. Help yourself. I'm going into the laboratory for a minute."

The doctor disappeared through the low door, and Hare busied himself with the decanters and the bottles in a preoccupied manner. He was sorry that Trevor was so upset; but what colossal egotism! Perhaps he should have held his tongue; nothing had been gained. He would never mention the subject again. It was a stiff drink of brandy that Hare finally poured himself, and he held it up to the light studying it, with his back to the laboratory door. But he never drank it; for he dropped the glass as he felt the lean fingers at his throat and the chloroform pad smothering his mouth and nostrils. He managed to say only the two words, "My God . . ."

About fifteen minutes later, Dr. Harrison Trevor peered cautiously over the banister of his own stairway. There was no one below, and he descended swiftly. In the kitchen Tanaka heard the front door slam, and almost immediately afterwards his master's voice calling him from the first-floor landing. Tanaka responded briskly.

"Mr. Hare has just left," said the doctor, "and he forgot his cigarette case. Run after him; he may still be in sight."

Tanaka sped upon his errand. Yes, there on the corner was a tall man, obviously Hare *san*; but he was getting into a taxi. Tanaka ran, but before he was half way down the block Hare *san* had driven off. Tanaka returned to report failure.

"Too bad," said his master, who met him on the landing. "But it doesn't really matter. Telephone Mr. Hare's apartment and tell his man that Mr. Hare left his case here, and that he is not to worry about it. You can take it to him in the morning."

Tanaka went downstairs to obey orders; and his master was left to wonder at the coincidence of the man who looked like Hare getting into the taxi. The accidental evidence might prove useful, but it was quite unnecessary, quite unnecessary; he had no need of accidental aid. At the door of his library the detective paused and surveyed the scene with a critical eye: everything was in place, comfortably, conventionally, indisputably in place. There were no fragments of the broken tumbler on the floor; only a dark, wet spot on the carpet that was drying rapidly. Brandy and soda would leave no stain. Dr. Harrison Trevor smiled a chilly smile and then walked resolutely toward the laboratory where his task awaited him. Once the door had been locked behind him, his first act was to switch on the electric ventilator fan which carried off all obnoxious odors through a concealed flue. After that he worked on into the morning hours.

The disappearance of Mr. Gregory Hare, eminent criminal lawyer, within a week after his return from abroad, furnished the front pages of the newspapers with rather more than a nine days' wonder. It was Dr. Trevor who was the first to insist upon foul play; and it was Dr. Trevor who worked fervently upon the case, with all the assistance that the police could give him. Naturally he was deeply concerned, for Hare had been an intimate acquaintance, and he had been among the last to see the man alive; but the body was never found, and there was no evidence to go on with. Tanaka repeated what he knew, reiterating the story of the taxi; and a patrolman on fixed post confirmed the Japanese's testimony. The tall gentleman had come from the direction of Dr. Trevor's house, and had driven off just as the servant had come running after him. All of which helped not at all. A certain "Limping" Louie, whom Hare, years before when he was District Attorney, had sent up for a long term, was dragged in by the police net; but he had a perfect alibi. The mystery remained a mystery.

Dr. Trevor and Inspector Furst were discussing the case one afternoon, long after it had been abandoned. Furst still toyed with the idea that it might not have been murder, but the doctor was positive.

"I'm absolutely sure of it, Furst, absolutely sure. Hare was killed."

"Well," said the Inspector, "if you are so sure, I'm inclined to agree. You've never made a mistake."

1933

JAMES M. CAIN

....

The Baby in the Icebox

OF COURSE there was plenty pieces in the paper about what happened out at the place last Summer, but they got it all mixed up, so I will now put down how it really was, and specially the beginning of it, so you will see it is not no lies in it.

Because when a guy and his wife begin to play leapfrog with a tiger, like you might say, and the papers put in about that part and not none of the stuff that started it off, and then one day say X marks the spot and next day say it wasn't really no murder but don't tell you what it was, why I don't blame people if they figure there was something funny about it or maybe that somebody ought to be locked up in the booby-hatch. But there wasn't no booby-hatch to this, nothing but plain onriness and a dirty rat getting it in the neck where he had it coming to him, as you will see when I get the first part explained right.

Things first began to go sour between Duke and Lura when they put the cats in. They didn't need no cats. They had a combination auto camp, filling-station, and lunchroom out in the country a ways, and they got along all right. Duke run the filling-station, and got me in to help him, and Lura took care of the lunchroom and shacks. But Duke wasn't satisfied. Before he got this place he had raised rabbits, and one time he had bees, and another time canary birds, and nothing would suit him now but to put in some cats to draw trade. Maybe you think that's funny, but out here in California they got every kind of a farm there is, from kangaroos to alligators, and it was just about the idea that a guy like Duke would think up. So he begun building a cage, and one day he showed up with a truckload of wildcats.

I wasn't there when they unloaded them. It was two or three cars waiting and I had to gas them up. But soon as I got a chance I went back there to look things over. And believe me, they wasn't pretty. The guy that sold Duke the cats had went away about five minutes before, and Duke was standing outside the cage and he had a stick of wood in his hand with blood on it. Inside was a dead cat. The rest of them was on a shelf, that had been built for them to jump on, and every one of them was snarling at Duke.

I don't know if you ever saw a wildcat, but they are about twice as big as a house cat, brindle gray, with tufted ears and a bobbed tail. When they set and look at you they look like a owl, but they wasn't setting and looking now. They was marching around, coughing and spitting, their eyes shooting red and green fire, and it was an ugly sight, specially with that bloody dead one down on the ground. Duke was pale, and the breath was whistling through his nose, and it didn't take no doctor to see he was scared to death.

"You better bury that cat," he says to me. "I'll take care of the cars."

I looked through the wire and he grabbed me. "Look out!" he says. "They'd kill you in a minute."

"In that case," I says, "how do I get the cat out?"

"You have to get a stick," he says, and shoves off.

I was pretty sore, but I begun looking around for a stick. I found one, but when I got back to the cage Lura was there. "How did that happen?" she says.

"I don't know," I says, "but I can tell you this much: If there's any more of them to be buried around here, you can get somebody else to do it. My job is to fix flats, and I'm not going to be no cat undertaker."

She didn't have nothing to say to that. She just stood there while I was trying the stick, and I could hear her toe snapping up and down in the sand, and from that I knowed she was choking it back, what she really thought, and didn't think no more of this here cat idea than I did.

The stick was too short. "My," she says, pretty disagreeable, "that looks terrible. You can't bring people out here with a thing like that in there."

"All right," I snapped back. "Find me a stick."

She didn't make no move to find no stick. She put her hand on the gate. "Hold on," I says. "Them things are nothing to monkey with."

"Huh," she says. "All they look like to me is a bunch of cats."

There was a kennel back of the cage, with a drop door on it, where they was supposed to go at night. How you got them back there was bait them with food, but I didn't know that then. I yelled at them, to drive them back in there, but nothing happened. All they done was yell back.

Lura listened to me a while, and then she give a kind of gasp like she couldn't stand it no longer, opened the gate, and went in.

Now believe me, that next was a bad five minutes, because she wasn't hard to look at, and I hated to think of her getting mauled up by them babies. But a guy would of had to of been blind if it didn't show him that she had a way with cats. First thing she done, when she got in, she stood still, didn't make no sudden motions or nothing, and begun to talk to them. Not no special talk. Just "Pretty pussy, what's the matter, what they been doing to you?" — like that. Then she went over to them.

They slid off, on their bellies, to another part of the shelf. But she kept after them, and got her hand on one, and stroked him on the back. Then she got a-hold of another one, and pretty soon she had give them all a pat. Then she turned around, picked up the dead cat by one leg, and come out with him. I put him on the wheelbarrow and buried him.

Now, why was it that Lura kept it from Duke how easy she had got the cat out and even about being in the cage at all? I think it was just because she didn't have the heart to show him up to hisself how silly he looked. Anyway, at supper that night, she never said a word. Duke, he was nervous and excited and told all about how the cats had jumped at him and how he had to bean one to save his life, and then he give a long spiel about cats and how fear is the only thing they understand, so you would of thought he was Martin Johnson just back from the jungle or something.

But it seemed to me the dishes was making quite a noise that night, clattering around on the table, and that was funny, because one thing you could say for Lura was: she was quiet and easy to be around. So when Duke, just like it was nothing at all, asks me by the way how did I get the cat out, I heared my mouth saying, "With a stick," and not nothing more. A little bird flies around and tells you, at a time like that. Lura let it pass. Never said a word. And if you ask me, Duke never did find out how easy she could handle the cats, and that ain't only guesswork, but on account of something that happened a little while afterward, when we got the mountain-lion.

A mountain-lion is a cougar, only out here they call them a mountain-lion. Well, one afternoon about five o'clock this one of ours squat down on her hunkers and set up the worst squalling you ever listen to. She kept it up all night, so you wanted to go out and shoot her, and next morning at breakfast Duke come running in and says come on out and look what happened. So we went out there, and there in the cage with her was the prettiest he mountain-lion you ever seen in your life. He was big, probably weighed a hundred and fifty pounds, and his coat was a pearl gray so glossy it looked like a pair of new gloves, and he had a spot of white on his throat. Sometimes they have white.

"He come down from the hills when he heard her call last night," says Duke, "and he got in there somehow. Ain't it funny? When they hear that note nothing can stop them."

"Yeah," I says. "It's love."

"That's it," says Duke. "Well, we'll be having some little ones soon. Cheaper'n buying them."

After he had went off to town to buy the stuff for the day, Lura sat down to the table with me. "Nice of you," I says, "to let Romeo in last night."

"Romeo?" she says.

"Yes, Romeo. That's going to be papa of twins soon, out in the lion cage."

"Oh," she says, "didn't he get in there himself?"

"He did not. If she couldn't get out, how could he get in?"

All she give me at that time was a dead pan. Didn't know nothing about it at all. Fact of the matter, she made me a little sore. But after she brung me my second cup of coffee she kind of smiled. "Well?" she says. "You wouldn't keep two loving hearts apart, would you?"

So things was, like you might say, a little gritty, but they got a whole lot worse when Duke come home with Rajah, the tiger. Because by that time, he had told so many lies that he begun to believe them hisself, and put on all the airs of a big animal-trainer. When people come out on Sundays, he would take a black-snake whip and go in with the mountain-lions and wildcats, and snap it at them, and they would snarl and yowl, and Duke acted like he was doing something. Before he went in, he would let the people see him strapping on a big six-shooter, and Lura got sorer by the week.

For one thing, he looked so silly. She couldn't see nothing to going in with the cats, and specially couldn't see no sense in going in with a whip, a six-shooter, and a ten-gallon hat like them cow people wears. And for another thing, it was bad for business. In the beginning, when Lura would take the customers' kids out and make out the cat had their finger, they loved it, and they loved it still more when the little mountain-lions come and they had spots and would push up their ears to be scratched. But when Duke started that stuff with the whip it scared them to death, and even the fathers and mothers was nervous, because there was the gun and they didn't know what would happen next. So business begun to fall off.

And then one afternoon he put down a couple of drinks and figured it was time for him to go in there with Rajah. Now it had took Lura one minute to tame Rajah. She was in there sweeping out his cage one morning when Duke was away, and when he started sliding around on his belly he got a bucket of water in the face, and that was that. From then on he was her cat. But what happened when Duke tried to tame him was awful. The first I knew what he was up to was when he made a speech to the people from the mountain-lion cage telling them not to go away yet, there was more to come. And when he come out he headed over to the tiger.

"What's the big idea?" I says. "What you up to now?"

"I'm going in with that tiger," he says. "It's got to be done, and I might as well do it now."

"Why has it got to be done?" I says.

He looked at me like as though he pitied me.

"I guess there's a few things about cats you don't know yet," he says. "You got a tiger on your hands, you got to let him know who's boss, that's all."

"Yeah?" I says. "And who *is* boss?"

"You see that?" he says, and cocks his finger at his face.

"See what?" I says.

"The human eye," he says. "The human eye, that's all. A cat's afraid of it. And if you know your business, you'll keep him afraid of it. That's all I'll use, the human eye. But of course, just for protection, I've got these too."

"Listen, sweetheart," I says to him. "If you give me a choice between the human eye and a Bengal tiger, which one *I* got the most fear of, you're going to see a guy getting a shiner every time. If I was you, I'd lay off that cat."

He didn't say nothing: hitched up his holster, and went in. He didn't even get a chance to unlimber his whip. That tiger, soon as he saw him, begun to move around in a way that made your blood run cold. He didn't make for Duke first, you understand. He slid over, and in a second he was between Duke and the gate. That's one thing about a tiger you better not forget if you ever meet one. He can't work examples in arithmetic, but when it comes to the kind of brains that mean meat, he's the brightest boy in the class and then some. He's born knowing more about cutting off a retreat than you'll ever know, and his legs do it for him, just automatic, so his jaws will be free for the main business of the meeting.

Duke backed away, and his face was awful to see. He was straining every muscle to keep his mouth from sliding down in his collar. His left hand fingered the whip a little, and his right pawed around, like he had some idea of drawing the gun. But the tiger didn't give him time to make up his mind what his idea was, if any.

He would slide a few feet on his belly, then get up and trot a step or two, then slide on his belly again. He didn't make no noise, you understand. He wasn't telling Duke, Please go away: he meant to kill him, and a killer don't generally make no more fuss than he has to. So for a few seconds you could even hear Duke's feet sliding over the floor. But all of a sudden a kid begun to whimper, and I come to my senses. I run around to the back of the cage, because that was where the tiger was crowding him, and I yelled at him.

"Duke!" I says. "In his kennel! Quick!"

He didn't seem to hear me. He was still backing, and the tiger was still coming. A woman screamed. The tiger's head went down, he crouched on the ground, and tightened every muscle. I knew what that meant. Everybody knew what it meant, and specially Duke knew what it meant. He made a funny sound in his throat, turned, and ran.

That was when the tiger sprung. Duke had no idea where he was going, but when he turned he fell through the trap door and I snapped it down. The tiger hit it so hard I thought it would split. One of Duke's legs was out, and the tiger was on it in a flash, but all he got on that grab was the sole of Duke's shoe. Duke got his leg in somehow and I jammed the door down tight.

It was a sweet time at supper that night. Lura didn't see this here, because she was busy in the lunchroom when it happened, but them people had talked on their way out, and she knowed all about it. What she was plenty. And Duke, what do you think he done? He passed it off like it wasn't nothing at all. "Just one of them things you got to expect," he says. And then he let on he knowed what he was doing all the time, and the only lucky part of it was that he didn't have to shoot a valuable animal like Rajah was. "Keep cool, that's the main thing," he says. "A thing like that can happen now and then, but never let a animal see you excited."

I heard him, and I couldn't believe my ears, but when I looked at Lura I jumped. I think I told you she wasn't hard to look at. She was a kind of medium size, with a shape that would make a guy leave his happy home, sunburned all over, and high cheekbones that give her eyes a funny slant. But her eyes was narrowed down to slits, looking at Duke, and they shot green where the light hit them, and it come over me all of a sudden that she looked so much like Rajah, when he was closing in on Duke in the afternoon, that she could have been his twin sister.

Next off, Duke got it in his head he was such a big cat man now that he had to go up in the hills and do some trapping. Bring in his own stuff, he called it.

I didn't pay much attention to it at the time. Of course, he never brought in no stuff, except a couple of raccoons that he probably bought down the road for $2, but Duke was the kind of a guy that every once in a while has to sit on a rock and fish, so when he loaded up the flivver and blew, it wasn't nothing you would get excited about. Maybe I didn't really care what he was up to, because it was pretty nice, running the place with Lura with him out of the way, and I didn't ask no questions. But it was more to it than cats or 'coons or fish, and Lura knowed it, even if I didn't.

Anyhow, it was while he was away on one of them trips of his that Wild Bill Smith the Texas Tornado showed up. Bill was a snake-doctor. He had a truck, with his picture painted on it, and two or three boxes of old rattlesnakes with their teeth pulled out, and he sold snake-oil that would cure what ailed you, and a Indian herb medicine that would do the same. He was a fake, but he was big and brown and had white teeth, and I guess he really wasn't no bad guy. The first I seen of him was when he drove up in his truck, and told me to gas him up and look at his tires. He had a bum differential that made a funny rattle, but he said never mind and went over to the lunchroom.

He was there a long time, and I thought I better let him know his car was ready. When I went over there, he was setting on a stool with a sheepish look on his face, rubbing his hand. He had a snake ring on one finger, with two red eyes, and on the back of his hand was red streaks. I knew what that meant. He had started something and Lura had fixed him. She had a pretty arm, but a grip like iron, that she said come from milking cows when she was a kid. What she done when a guy got fresh was take hold of his hand and squeeze it so the bones cracked, and he generally changed his mind.

She handed him his check without a word, and I told him what he owed on the car, and he paid up and left.

"So you settled his hash, hey?" I says to her.

"If there's one thing gets on my nerves," she says, "it's a man that starts something the minute he gets in the door."

"Why didn't you yell for me?"

"Oh, I didn't need no help."

But the next day he was back, and after I filled up his car I went over to see how he was behaving. He was setting at one of the tables this time, and Lura was standing beside him. I saw her jerk her hand away quick, and he give me the bright grin a man has when he's got something he wants to cover up. He was all teeth.

"Nice day," he says. "Great weather you have in this country."

"So I hear," I says. "Your car's ready."

"What I owe you?" he says.

"Dollar twenty."

He counted it out and left.

"Listen," says Lura: "we weren't doing anything when you come in. He was just reading my hand. He's a snake doctor, and knows about the zodiac."

"Oh, wasn't we?" I says. "Well, wasn't we nice!"

"What's it to you?" she says.

"Nothing," I snapped at her. I was pretty sore.

"He says I was born under the sign of Yin," she says. You would of thought it was a piece of news fit to put in the paper.

"And who is Yin?" I says.

"It's Chinese for tiger," she says.

"Then bite yourself off a piece of raw meat," I says, and slammed out of there. We didn't have no nice time running the joint *that* day.

Next morning he was back. I kept away from the lunchroom, but I took a stroll, and seen them back there with the tiger. We had hauled a tree in there by that time, for Rajah to sharpen his claws on, and she was setting on that. The tiger had his head in her lap, and Wild Bill was looking through the wire. He couldn't even draw his breath. I didn't go near enough to hear what they was saying. I went back to the car and begin blowing the horn.

He was back quite a few times after that, in between while Duke was away. Then one night I heard a truck drive up. I knowed that truck by its rattle. And it was daylight before I heard it go away.

Couple weeks after that, Duke comes running over to me at the filling-station. "Shake hands with me," he says. "I'm going to be a father."

"Gee," I says, "that's great!"

But I took good care he wasn't around when I mentioned it to Lura.

"Congratulations," I says. "Letting Romeos into the place seems to be about the best thing you do."

"What do you mean?" she says.

"Nothing," I says. "Only I heard him drive up that night. Look like to me the moon was under the sign of Cupid. Well, it's nice if you can get away with it."

"Oh," she says.

"Yeah," I says. "A fine double cross you thought up. I didn't know they tried that any more."

She set and looked at me, and then her mouth begin to twitch and her eyes filled with tears. She tried to snuffle them up but it didn't work. "It's not any double cross," she says. "That night, I never went out there. And I never let anybody in. I was supposed to go away with him that night, but —"

She broke off and begin to cry. I took her in my arms. "But then you found this out?" I says. "Is that it?" She nodded her head. It's awful to have a pretty woman in your arms that's crying over somebody else.

From then on, it was terrible. Lura would go along two or three days pretty nice, trying to like Duke again on account of the baby coming, but then would come a day when she looked like some kind of a hex, with her eyes all sunk in so you could hardly see them at all, and not a word out of her.

Them bad days, anyhow when Duke wasn't around, she would spend with the tiger. She would set and watch him sleep, or maybe play with him, and he seemed to like it as much as she did. He was young when we got him, and mangy and thin, so you could see his slats. But now he was about six year old, and had been fed good, so he had got his growth and his coat was nice, and I think he was the biggest tiger I ever seen. A tiger, when he is really big, is a lot bigger than a lion, and sometimes when Rajah would be rubbing around Lura, he looked more like a mule than a cat.

His shoulders come up above her waist, and his head was so big it would cover both her legs when he put it in her lap. When his tail would go sliding past her it looked like some kind of a constrictor snake. His teeth were something to make you lie awake nights. A tiger has the biggest teeth of any cat, and Rajah's must have been four inches long, curved like a cavalry sword, and ivory white. They were the most murderous-looking fangs I ever set eyes on.

When Lura went to the hospital it was a hurry call, and she didn't even have time to get her clothes together. Next day Duke had to pack her bag, and he was strutting around, because it was a boy, and Lura had named him Ron. But when he come out with the bag, he didn't have much of a strut.

"Look what I found," he says to me, and fishes something out of his pocket. It was the snake ring.

"Well?" I says. "They sell them in any dime store."

"H'm," he says, and kind of weighed the ring in his hand. That afternoon, when he come back, he says, "Ten-cent store, hey? I took it to a jeweler today, and he offered me two hundred dollars for it."

"You ought to sold it," I says. "Maybe save you bad luck."

Duke went away again right after Lura come back, and for a little while things was all right. She was crazy about the little boy, and I thought he was pretty cute myself, and we got along fine. But then Duke come back and at lunch one day he made a crack about the ring. Lura didn't say nothing, but he kept at it, and pretty soon she wheeled on him.

"All right," she says. "There was another man around here, and I loved him. He give me that ring, and it meant that he and I belonged to each other. But I didn't go with him, and you know why I didn't. For Ron's sake. I'ved tried to love you again, and maybe I can yet. God knows. A woman can do some funny things if she tries. But that's where we're at now. That's right where we're at. And if you don't like it, you better say what you're going to do."

"When was this?" says Duke.

"It was quite a while ago. I told you I give him up, and I give him up for keeps."

"It was just before you knowed about Ron, wasn't it?" he says.

"Hey," I cut in. "That's no way to talk."

"Just what I thought," he says, not paying no attention to me. "Ron. That's a funny name for a kid. I thought it was funny, right off when I heard it. Ron. Ron. That's a laugh, ain't it?"

"That's a lie," she says. "That's a lie, every bit of it. And it's not the only lie you've been getting away with around here. Or think you have. Trapping up in the hills, hey? And what do you trap?"

But she looked at me, and choked it back. I begun to see that the cats wasn't the only things that had been gumming it up.

"All right," she wound up. "Say what you're gong to do. Go on. Say it!"

But he didn't.

"Ron," he cackles, "that's a hot one," and walks out.

Next day was Saturday, and he acted funny all day. He wouldn't speak to me or Lura, and once or twice I heard him mumbling to himself. Right after supper he says to me, "How are we on oil?"

"All right," I says. "The truck was around yesterday."

"You better drive in and get some," he says. "I don't think we got enough."

"Enough?" I says. "We got enough for two weeks."

"Tomorrow is Sunday," he says, "and there'll be a big call for it. Bring out a hundred gallon and tell them to put it on the account."

By that time, I would give in to one of his nutty ideas rather than have an argument with him, and besides, I never tumbled that he was up to anything. So I wasn't there for what happened next, but I got it out of Lura later, so here is how it was:

Lura didn't pay much attention to the argument about the oil, but washed up the supper dishes, and then went in the bedroom to make sure everything was all right with the baby. When she come out she left the door open, so she could hear if he cried. The bedroom was off the sitting-room, because these here California houses don't have but one floor, and all the rooms connect. Then she lit the fire, because it was cool, and sat there watching it burn. Duke come in, walked around, and then went out back. "Close the door," she says to him. "I'll be right back," he says.

So she sat looking at the fire, she didn't know how long, maybe five minutes, maybe ten minutes. But pretty soon she felt the house shake. She thought maybe it was a earthquake, and looked at the pictures, but they was all hanging straight. Then she felt the house shake again. She listened, but it wasn't no truck outside that would cause it, and it wouldn't be no State road blasting or nothing like that at that time of night. Then she felt it shake again, and this time it shook in a regular movement, one, two, three, four, like that. And then all of a sudden she knew what it was, why Duke had acted so funny all day, why he had sent me off for the gas, why he had left the door open, and all the rest of it. There was five hundred pounds of cat walking through the house, and Duke had turned him loose to kill her.

She turned around, and Rajah was looking at her, not five foot away. She didn't do nothing for a minute, just set there thinking what a boob Duke was to figure on the tiger doing his dirty work for him, when all the time she could handle him easy as a kitten, only Duke didn't know it. Then she spoke. She expected Rajah to come and put his head in her lap, but he didn't. He stood there and growled, and his ears flattened back. That scared her, and she thought of the baby. I told you a tiger has that kind of brains. It no sooner went through her head about the baby than Rajah knowed she wanted to get to that door, and he was over there before she could get out of the chair.

He was snarling in a regular roar now, but he hadn't got a whiff of the baby yet, and he was still facing Lura. She could see he meant business. She reached in the fireplace, grabbed a stick that was burning bright, and walked him down with it. A tiger is afraid of fire, and she shoved it right in his eyes. He backed past the door, and she slid in the bedroom. But he was right after her, and she had to hold the stick at him with one hand and grab the baby with the other.

But she couldn't get out. He had her cornered, and he was kicking up such a awful fuss she knowed the stick wouldn't stop him long. So she dropped it, grabbed up the baby's covers, and threw them at his head. They went wild, but they saved her just the same. A tiger, if you throw something at him with a human smell, will generally jump on it and bite at it before he does anything else, and that's what he done now. He jumped so hard the rug went out from under him, and while he was scrambling to his feet she shot past him with the baby and pulled the door shut after her.

She run in my room, got a blanket, wrapped the baby in it, and run out to the electric icebox. It was the only thing around the place that was steel. Soon as she opened the door she knowed why she couldn't do nothing with Rajah. His meat was in there, Duke hadn't fed him. She pulled the meat out, shoved the baby in, cut off the current, and closed the door. Then she picked up the meat and went around outside of the house to the window of the bedroom. She could see Rajah in there, biting at the top of the door, where a crack of light showed through. He reached to the ceiling. She took a grip on the meat and drove at the screen with it. It gave way, and the meat went through. He was on it before it hit the floor.

Next thing was to give him time to eat. She figured she could handle him once he got something in his belly. She went back to the sitting-room. And in there, kind of peering around, was Duke. He had his gun strapped on, and one look at his face was all she needed to know she hadn't made no mistake about why the tiger was loose.

"Oh," he says, kind of foolish, and then walked back and closed the door. "I meant to come back sooner, but I couldn't help looking at the night. You got no idea how beautiful it is. Stars is bright as anything."

"Yeah," she says. "I noticed."

"Beautiful," he says. "Beautiful."

"Was you expecting burglars or something?" she says, looking at the gun.

"Oh, that," he says. "No. Cats been kicking up a fuss. I put it on, case I have to go back there. Always like to have it handy."

"The tiger," she says. "I thought I heard him, myself."

"Loud," says Duke. "Awful loud."

He waited. She waited. She wasn't going to give him the satisfaction of opening up first. But just then there come a growl from the bedroom, and the sound of bones cracking. A tiger acts awful sore when he eats. "What's that?" says Duke.

"I wonder," says Lura. She was hell-bent on making him spill it first.

They both looked at each other, and then there was more growls, and more sound of cracking bones. "You better go in there," says Duke, soft and easy, with the sweat standing out on his forehead and his eyes shining bright as marbles. "Something might be happening to Ron."

"Do you know what I think it is?" says Lura.

"What's that?" says Duke. His breath was whistling through his nose like it always done when he got excited.

"I think it's that tiger you sent in here to kill me," says Lura. "So you could bring in that woman you been running around with for over a year. That redhead that raises rabbit fryers on the Ventura road. That cat you been trapping!"

"And stead of getting you he got Ron," says Duke. "Little Ron! Oh my, ain't that tough? Go in there, why don't you? Ain't you got no mother love? Why don't you call up his pappy, get him in there? What's the matter? Is he afraid of a cat?"

Lura laughed at him. "All right," she says. "Now you go." With that she took hold of him. He tried to draw the gun, but she crumpled up his hand like a piece of wet paper and the gun fell on the floor. She bent him back on the table and beat his face in for him. Then she picked him up, dragged him to the front door, and threw him out. He run off a little ways. She come back and saw the gun. She picked it up, went to the door again, and threw it after him. "And take that peashooter with you," she says.

That was where she made her big mistake. When she turned to go back in the house, he shot, and that was the last she knew for a while.

Now, for what happened next, it wasn't nobody there, only Duke and the tiger, but after them State cops got done fitting it all together, combing the ruins and all, it wasn't no trouble to tell how it was, anyway most of it, and here's how they figured it out:

Soon as Duke seen Lura fall, right there in front of the house, he knowed he was up against it. So the first thing he done was to run to where she was and put the gun in her hand, to make it look like she had shot herself. That was where he made *his* big mistake, because if he had kept the gun he might of had a chance. Then he went inside to telephone, and what he said was, soon as he got hold of the State police:

"For God's sake come out here quick. My wife has went crazy and throwed the baby to the tiger and shot herself and I'm all alone in the house with him and — *Oh, my God, here he comes!*"

Now, that last was something he didn't figure on saying. So far as he knowed, the tiger was in the room, having a nice meal off his son, so everything was hotsy-totsy. But what he didn't know was that that piece of burning firewood that Lura had dropped had set the room on fire and on account of that the tiger had got out. How did he get out? We never did quite figure that out. But this is how I figure it, and one man's guess is good as another's:

The fire started near the window, we knew that much. That was where Lura dropped the stick, right next to the cradle, and that was where a guy coming down the road in a car first seen the flames. And what I think is that soon as the tiger got his eye off the meat and seen the fire, he begun to scramble away from it, just wild. And when a wild tiger hits a beaverboard wall, he goes through, that's all. While Duke was telephoning, Rajah come through the wall like a clown through a hoop, and the first thing he seen was Duke, at the telephone, and Duke wasn't no friend, not to Rajah he wasn't.

Anyway, that's how things was when I got there, with the oil. The State cops was a little ahead of me, and I met the ambulance with Lura in it, coming down the road seventy mile an hour, but just figured there had been a crash up the road, and didn't know nothing about it having Lura in it. And when I drove up, there was plenty to look at all right. The house was in flames, and the police was trying to get in, but couldn't get nowheres near it on account of the heat, and about a hundred cars parked all around, with people looking, and a gasoline pumper cruising up and down the road, trying to find a water connection somewheres they could screw their hose to.

But inside the house was the terrible part. You could hear Duke screaming, and in between Duke was the tiger. And both of them was screams of fear, but I think the tiger was worse. It is a awful thing to hear a animal letting out a sound like that. It kept up about five minutes after I got there, and then all of a sudden you couldn't hear nothing but the tiger. And then in a minute that stopped.

There was nothing to do about the fire. In a half hour the whole place was gone, and they was combing the ruins for Duke. Well, they found him. And in his head was four holes, two on each side, deep. We measured them fangs of the tiger. They just fit.

Soon as I could I run to the hospital. They had got the bullet out by that time, and Lura was laying in bed all bandaged around the head, but there was a guard over her, on account of what Duke said over the telephone. He was a State cop. I sat down with him, and he didn't like it none. Neither did I. I knowed there was something funny about it, but what broke your heart was Lura, coming out of the ether. She would groan and mutter and try to say something so hard it would make your head ache. After a while I got up and went in the hall. But then I see the State cop shoot out of the room and line down the hall as fast as he could go. At last she had said it. The baby was in the electric icebox. They found him there, still asleep and just about ready for his milk. The fire had blacked up the outside, but inside it was as cool and nice as a new bathtub.

Well, that was about all. They cleared Lura, soon as she told her story, and the baby in the icebox proved it. Soon as she got out of the hospital she got a offer from the movies, but stead of taking it she come out to the place and her and I run it for a while, anyway the filling-station end, sleeping in the shacks and getting along nice. But one night I heard a rattle from a bum differential, and I never even bothered to show up for breakfast the next morning.

I often wish I had. Maybe she left me a note.

1933

JOHN STEINBECK

....

The Murder

THIS happened a number of years ago in Monterey County, in central
California. The Cañon del Castillo is one of those valleys in the Santa
Lucia range which lie between its many spurs and ridges. From the
main Cañon del Castillo a number of little arroyos cut back into the
mountains, oak-wooded canyons, heavily brushed with poison oak and
sage. At the head of the canyon there stands a tremendous stone castle,
buttressed and towered like those strongholds the Crusaders put up in
the path of their conquests. Only a close visit to the castle shows it to be
a strange accident of time and water and erosion working on soft,
stratified sandstone. In the distance the ruined battlements, the gates,
the towers, even the arrow slits require little imagination to make out.

Below the castle, on the nearly level floor of the canyon, stand an old
ranch house, a weathered and mossy barn and a warped feeding shed
for cattle. The house is empty and deserted; the doors, swinging on
rusted hinges, squeal and bang on nights when the wind courses down
from the castle. Not many people visit the house. Sometimes a crowd of
boys tramp through the rooms, peering into empty closets and loudly
defying the ghosts they deny.

Jim Moore, who owns the land, does not like to have people about
the house. He rides up from his new house, farther down the valley, and
chases the boys away. He has put "No Trespassing" signs on his fences to
keep curious and morbid people out. Sometimes he thinks of burning
the old house down, but then a strange and powerful relation with the
swinging doors, the blind and desolate windows forbids the destruction. If he should burn the house he would destroy a great and important piece of his life. He knows that when he goes to town with his

plump and still pretty wife, people turn and look at his retreating back with awe and some admiration.

Jim Moore was born in the old house and grew up in it. He knew every grained and weathered board of the barn, every smooth, worn manger rack. His mother and father were both dead when he was thirty. He celebrated his majority by raising a beard. He sold the pigs and decided never to have any more. At last he bought a fine Guernsey bull to improve his stock, and he began to go to Monterey on Saturday nights, to get drunk and to talk with the noisy girls of the Three Star.

Within a year Jim Moore married Jelka Šepić, a Jugoslav girl, daughter of a heavy and patient farmer of Pine Canyon. Jim was not proud of her foreign family, of her many brothers and sisters and cousins, but he delighted in her beauty. Jelka had eyes as large and questioning as a doe's eyes. Her nose was thin and sharply faceted, and her lips were deep and soft. Jelka's skin always startled Jim, for between night and night he forgot how beautiful it was. She was so smooth and quiet and gentle, such a good housekeeper, that Jim often thought with disgust of her father's advice on the wedding day. The old man, bleary and bloated with festival beer, elbowed Jim in the ribs and grinned suggestively, so that his little dark eyes almost disappeared behind puffed and wrinkled lids.

"Don't be big fool, now," he said. "Jelka is Slav girl. He's not like American girl. If he is bad, beat him. If he's good too long, beat him too. I beat his mama. Papa beat my mama. Slav girl! He's not like a man that don't beat hell out of him."

"I wouldn't beat Jelka," Jim said.

The father giggled and nudged him again with his elbow. "Don't be big fool," he warned. "Sometime you see." He rolled back to the beer barrel.

Jim found soon enough that Jelka was not like American girls. She was very quiet. She never spoke first, but only answered his questions, and then with soft short replies. She learned her husband as she learned passages of Scripture. After they had been married a while, Jim never wanted for any habitual thing in the house but Jelka had it ready for him before he could ask. She was a fine wife, but there was no companionship in her. She never talked. Her great eyes followed him, and when he smiled, sometimes she smiled too, a distant and covered smile. Her knitting and mending and sewing were interminable. There she sat, watching her wise hands, and she seemed to regard with wonder and pride the little white hands that could do such nice and useful things. She was so much like an animal that sometimes Jim patted her head and neck under the same impulse that made him stroke a horse.

In the house Jelka was remarkable. No matter what time Jim came in from the hot dry range or from the bottom farm land, his dinner was exactly, steamingly ready for him. She watched while he ate, and pushed the dishes close when he needed them, and filled his cup when it was empty.

Early in the marriage he told her things that happened on the farm, but she smiled at him as a foreigner does who wishes to be agreeable even though he doesn't understand.

"The stallion cut himself on the barbed wire," he said.

And she replied, "Yes," with a downward inflection that held neither question nor interest.

He realized before long that he could not get in touch with her in any way. If she had a life apart, it was so remote as to be beyond his reach. The barrier in her eyes was not one that could be removed, for it was neither hostile nor intentional.

At night he stroked her straight black hair and her unbelievably smooth golden shoulders, and she whimpered a little with pleasure. Only in the climax of his embrace did she seem to have a life apart and fierce and passionate. And then immediately she lapsed into the alert and painfully dutiful wife.

"Why don't you ever talk to me?" he demanded. "Don't you want to talk to me?"

"Yes," she said. "What do you want me to say?" She spoke the language of his race out of a mind that was foreign to his race.

When a year had passed, Jim began to crave the company of women, the chattery exchange of small talk, the shrill pleasant insults, the shame-sharpened vulgarity. He began to go again to town, to drink and to play with the noisy girls of the Three Star. They liked him there for his firm, controlled face and for his readiness to laugh.

"Where's your wife?" they demanded.

"Home in the barn," he responded. It was a never failing joke.

Saturday afternoons he saddled a horse and put a rifle in the scabbard in case he should see a deer. Always he asked, "You don't mind staying alone?"

"No. I don't mind."

And once he asked, "Suppose some one should come?"

Her eyes sharpened for a moment, and then she smiled. "I would send them away," she said.

"I'll be back about noon tomorrow. It's too far to ride in the night." He felt that she knew where he was going, but she never protested nor gave any sign of disapproval. "You should have a baby," he said.

Her face lighted up. "Sometime God will be good," she said eagerly.

He was sorry for her loneliness. If only she visited with the other women of the canyon she would be less lonely, but she had no gift for visiting. Once every month or so she put horses to the buckboard and went to spend an afternoon with her mother, and with the brood of brothers and sisters and cousins who lived in her father's house.

"A fine time you'll have," Jim said to her. "You'll gabble your crazy language like ducks for a whole afternoon. You'll giggle with that big grown cousin of yours with the embarrassed face. If I could find any fault with you, I'd call you a damn foreigner." He remembered how she blessed the bread with the sign of the cross before she put it in the oven, how she knelt at the bedside every night, how she had a holy picture tacked to the wall in the closet.

On Saturday of a hot dusty June, Jim cut hay in the farm flat. The day was long. It was after six o'clock when the mower tumbled the last band of oats. He drove the clanking machine up into the barnyard and backed it into the implement shed, and there he unhitched the horses and turned them out to graze on the hills over Sunday. When he entered the kitchen Jelka was just putting his dinner on the table. He washed his hands and face, and sat down to eat.

"I'm tired," he said, "but I think I'll go to Monterey anyway. There'll be a full moon."

Her soft eyes smiled.

"I'll tell you what I'll do," he said. "If you would like to go, I'll hitch up a rig and take you with me."

She smiled again and shook her head. "No, the stores would be closed. I would rather stay here."

"Well all right, I'll saddle a horse then. I didn't think I was going. The stock's all turned out. Maybe I can catch a horse easy. Sure you don't want to go?"

"If it was early, and I could go to the stores — but it will be ten o'clock when you get there."

"Oh, no — well, anyway, on horseback I'll make it a little after nine."

Her mouth smiled to itself, but her eyes watched him for the development of a wish. Perhaps because he was tired from the long day's work, he demanded, "What are you thinking about?"

"Thinking about? I remember, you used to ask that nearly every day when we were first married."

"But what are you?" he insisted irritably.

"Oh — I'm thinking about the eggs under the black hen." She got up and went to the big calendar on the wall. "They will hatch tomorrow or maybe Monday."

It was almost dusk when he had finished shaving and putting on his blue serge suit and his new boots. Jelka had the dishes washed and put away. As Jim went through the kitchen he saw that she had taken the lamp to the table near the window, and that she sat beside it knitting a brown wool sock.

"Why do you sit there tonight?" he asked. "You always sit over here. You do funny things sometimes."

Her eyes arose slowly from her flying hands. "The moon," she said quietly. "You said it would be full tonight. I want to see the moon rise."

"But you're silly. You can't see it from that window. I thought you knew direction better than that."

She smiled remotely. "I will look out of the bedroom window then."

Jim put on his black hat and went out. Walking through the dark empty barn, he took a halter from the rack. On the grassy sidehill he whistled high and shrill. The horses stopped feeding and moved slowly in toward him, and stopped twenty feet away. Carefully he approached his bay gelding and moved his hand from its rump along its side and up and over its neck. The halterstrap clicked in its buckle. Jim turned and led the horse back to the barn. He threw his saddle on and cinched it tight, put his silver-bound bridle over the stiff ears, buckled the throat latch, knotted the tie-rope about the gelding's neck and fastened the neat coil-end to the saddle string. Then he slipped the halter and led the horse to the house. A radiant crown of soft red light lay over the eastern hills. The full moon would rise before the valley had completely lost the daylight.

In the kitchen Jelka still knitted by the window. Jim strode to the corner of the room and took up his 30-30 carbine. As he rammed shells into the magazine, he said, "The moon glow is on the hills. If you are going to see it rise, you better go outside now. It's going to be a good red one at rising."

"In a moment," she replied, "when I come to the end here." He went to her and patted her sleek head.

"Good night. I'll probably be back by noon tomorrow." Her dusty black eyes followed him out the door.

Jim thrust the rifle into his saddle-scabbard, and mounted and swung his horse down the canyon. On his right, from behind the blackening hills, the great red moon slid rapidly up. The double light of the day's last afterglow and the rising moon thickened the outlines of the trees and gave a mysterious new perspective to the hills. The dusty oaks shimmered and glowed, and the shade under them was black as velvet. A huge, long-legged shadow of a horse and half a man rode to the left and slightly ahead of Jim. From the ranches near and distant came the sound of dogs tuning up for a night of song. And the roosters crowed, thinking a new dawn had come too quickly. Jim lifted the gelding to a trot. The spattering hoofsteps echoed back from the castle behind him. He thought of blonde May at the Three Star in Monterey. "I'll be late. Maybe some one else'll have her," he thought. The moon was clear of the hills now.

Jim had gone a mile when he heard the hoofbeats of a horse coming toward him. A horseman cantered up and pulled to a stop. "That you, Jim?"

"Yes. Oh, hello, George."

"I was just riding up to your place. I want to tell you — you know the springhead at the upper end of my land?"

"Yes. I know."

"Well, I was up there this afternoon. I found a dead campfire and a calf's head and feet. The skin was in the fire, half burned, but I pulled it out and it had your brand."

"The hell," said Jim. "How old was the fire?"

"The ground was still warm in the ashes. Last night, I guess. Look, Jim, I can't go up with you. I've got to go to town, but I thought I'd tell you, so you could take a look around."

Jim asked quietly, "Any idea how many men?"

"No. I didn't look close."

"Well, I guess I better go up and look. I was going to town too. But if there are thieves working, I don't want to lose any more stock. I'll cut up through your land if you don't mind, George."

"I'd go with you, but I've got to go to town. You got a gun with you?"

"Oh yes, sure. Here under my leg. Thanks for telling me."

"That's all right. Cut through any place you want. Good night." The neighbor turned his horse and cantered back in the direction from which he had come.

For a few moments Jim sat in the moonlight, looking down at his stilted shadow. He pulled his rifle from its scabbard, levered a shell into the chamber, and held the gun across the pommel of his saddle. He turned left from the road, went up the little ridge, through the oak grove, over the grassy hog-back and down the other side into the next canyon.

In half an hour he had found the deserted camp. He turned over the heavy, leathery calf's head and felt its dusty tongue to judge by the dryness how long it had been dead. He lighted a match and looked at his brand on the half-burned hide. At last he mounted his horse again, rode over the bald grassy hills and crossed into his own land.

A warm summer wind was blowing on the hilltops. The moon, as it quartered up the sky, lost its redness and turned the color of strong tea. Among the hills the coyotes were singing, and the dogs at the ranch houses below joined them with broken-hearted howling. The dark green oaks below and the yellow summer grass showed their colors in the moonlight.

Jim followed the sound of the cowbells to his herd, and found them eating quietly, and a few deer feeding with them. He listened long for the sound of hoofbeats or the voices of men on the wind.

It was after eleven when he turned his horse toward home. He rounded the west tower of the sandstone castle, rode through the shadow and out into the moonlight again. Below, the roofs of his barn and house shone dully. The bedroom window cast back a streak of reflection.

The feeding horses lifted their heads as Jim came down through the pasture. Their eyes glinted redly when they turned their heads.

Jim had almost reached the corral fence — he heard a horse stamping in the barn. His hand jerked the gelding down. He listened. It came again, the stamping from the barn. Jim lifted his rifle and dismounted silently. He turned his horse loose and crept toward the barn.

In the blackness he could hear the grinding of the horse's teeth as it chewed hay. He moved along the barn until he came to the occupied stall. After a moment of listening he scratched a match on the butt of his rifle. A saddled and bridled horse was tied in the stall. The bit was slipped under the chin and the cinch loosened. The horse stopped eating and turned its head toward the light.

Jim blew out the match and walked quickly out of the barn. He sat on the edge of the horse trough and looked into the water. His thoughts came so slowly that he put them into words and said them under his breath.

"Shall I look through the window? No. My head would throw a shadow in the room."

He regarded the rifle in his hand. Where it had been rubbed and handled, the black gun-finish had worn off, leaving the metal silvery.

At last he stood up with decision and moved toward the house. At the steps, an extended foot tried each board tenderly before he put his weight on it. The three ranch dogs came out from under the house and shook themselves, stretched and sniffed, wagged their tails and went back to bed.

The kitchen was dark, but Jim knew where every piece of furniture was. He put out his hand and touched the corner of the table, a chair-back, the towel hanger, as he went along. He crossed the room so silently that even he could hear only his breath and the whisper of his trousers legs together, and the beating of his watch in his pocket. The bedroom door stood open and spilled a patch of moonlight on the kitchen floor. Jim reached the door at last and peered through.

The moonlight lay on the white bed. Jim saw Jelka lying on her back, one soft bare arm flung across her forehead and eyes. He could not see who the man was, for his head was turned away. Jim watched, holding his breath. Then Jelka twitched in her sleep and the man rolled his head and sighed — Jelka's cousin, her grown, embarrassed cousin.

Jim turned and quickly stole back across the kitchen and down the back steps. He walked up the yard to the water trough again, and sat down on the edge of it. The moon was white as chalk, and it swam in the water, and lighted the straws and barley dropped by the horses' mouths. Jim could see the mosquito wigglers, tumbling up and down, end over end, in the water, and he could see a newt lying in the sun moss in the bottom of the trough.

He cried a few dry, hard, smothered sobs, and wondered why, for his thought was of the grassed hilltops and of the lonely summer wind whisking along.

His thought turned to the way his mother used to hold a bucket to catch the throat blood when his father killed a pig. She stood as far away as possible and held the bucket at arm's length to keep her clothes from getting spattered.

Jim dipped his hand into the trough and stirred the moon to broken, swirling streams of light. He wetted his forehead with his damp hands and stood up. This time he did not move so quietly, but he crossed the kitchen on tiptoe and stood in the bedroom door. Jelka moved her arm and opened her eyes a little. Then the eyes sprang wide, then they glistened with moisture. Jim looked into her eyes; his face was blank of expression. A little drop ran out of Jelka's nose and lodged in the hollow of her upper lip. She stared back at him.

Jim cocked the rifle. The steel click sounded through the house. The man on the bed stirred uneasily in his sleep. Jim's hands were quivering. He raised the gun to his shoulder and held it tightly to keep from shaking. Over the sights he saw the little white square between the man's brows and hair. The front sight wavered a moment and then came to rest.

The gun crash tore the air. Jim, still looking down the barrel, saw the whole bed jolt under the blow. A small, black, bloodless hole was in the man's forehead. But behind, the hollow-point bullet took brain and bone and splashed them on the pillow.

Jelka's cousin gurgled in his throat. His hands came crawling out from under the covers like big white spiders, and they walked for a moment, then shuddered and fell quiet.

Jim looked slowly back at Jelka. Her nose was running. Her eyes had moved from him to the end of the rifle. She whined softly, like a cold puppy.

Jim turned in panic. His boot-heels beat on the kitchen floor, but outside he moved slowly toward the watering trough again. There was a taste of salt in his throat, and his heart heaved painfully. He pulled his hat off and dipped his head into the water, then he leaned over and vomited on the ground. In the house he could hear Jelka moving about. She whimpered like a puppy. Jim straightened up, weak and dizzy.

He walked tiredly through the corral and into the pasture. His saddled horse came at his whistle. Automatically he tightened the cinch, mounted and rode away, down the road to the valley. The squat black shadow traveled under him. The moon sailed high and white. The uneasy dogs barked monotonously.

At daybreak a buckboard and pair trotted up to the ranch yard, scattering the chickens. A deputy sheriff and a coroner sat in the seat. Jim Moore half reclined against his saddle in the wagon-box. His tired gelding followed behind. The deputy sheriff set the brake and wrapped the lines around it. The men dismounted.

Jim asked, "Do I have to go in? I'm too tired and wrought up to see it now."

The coroner pulled his lip and studied. "Oh, I guess not. We'll tend to things and look around."

Jim sauntered away toward the watering trough. "Say," he called, "kind of clean up a little, will you? You know."

The men went on into the house.

In a few minutes they emerged, carrying the stiffened body between them. It was wrapped up in a comforter. They eased it up into the wagon-box. Jim walked back toward them. "Do I have to go in with you now?"

"Where's your wife, Mr. Moore?" the deputy sheriff demanded.

"I don't know," he said wearily. "She's somewhere around."

"You're sure you didn't kill her too?"

"No. I didn't touch her. I'll find her and bring her in this afternoon. That is, if you don't want me to go in with you now."

"We've got your statement," the coroner said. "And by God, we've got eyes, haven't we, Will? Of course there's a technical charge of murder against you, but it'll be dismissed. Always is in this part of the country. Go kind of light on your wife, Mr. Moore."

"I won't hurt her," said Jim.

He stood and watched the buckboard jolt away. He kicked his feet reluctantly in the dust. The hot June sun showed its face over the hills and flashed viciously on the bedroom window.

Jim went slowly into the house, and brought out a nine-foot, loaded bull whip. He crossed the yard and walked into the barn. And as he climbed the ladder to the hayloft, he heard the high, puppy whimpering start.

When Jim came out of the barn again, he carried Jelka over his shoulder. By the watering trough he set her tenderly on the ground. Her hair was littered with bits of hay. The back of her shirtwaist was streaked with blood.

Jim wetted his bandana at the pipe and washed her bitten lips, and washed her face and brushed back her hair. Her dusty black eyes followed every move he made.

"You hurt me," she said. "You hurt me bad."

He nodded gravely. "Bad as I could without killing you."

The sun shone hotly on the ground. A few blowflies buzzed about, looking for the blood.

Jelka's thickened lips tried to smile. "Did you have any breakfast at all?"

"No," he said. "None at all."

"Well, then I'll fry you up some eggs." She struggled painfully to her feet.

"Let me help you," he said. "I'll help you get your waist off. It's drying stuck to your back. It'll hurt."

"No. I'll do it myself." Her voice had a peculiar resonance in it. Her dark eyes dwelt warmly on him for a moment, and then she turned and limped into the house.

Jim waited, sitting on the edge of the watering trough. He saw the smoke start up out of the chimney and sail straight up into the air. In a very few moments Jelka called him from the kitchen door.

"Come, Jim. Your breakfast."

Four fried eggs and four thick slices of bacon lay on a warmed plate for him. "The coffee will be ready in a minute," she said.

"Won't you eat?"

"No. Not now. My mouth's too sore."

He ate his eggs hungrily and then looked up at her. Her black hair was combed smooth. She had on a fresh white shirtwaist. "We're going to town this afternoon," he said. "I'm going to order lumber. We'll build a new house farther down the canyon."

Her eyes darted to the closed bedroom door and then back to him. "Yes," she said. "That will be good." And then, after a moment, "Will you whip me any more — for this?"

"No, not any more, for this."

Her eyes smiled. She sat down on a chair beside him, and Jim put out his hand and stroked her hair, and the back of her neck.

1934

DAMON RUNYON

··

Sense of Humor

ONE NIGHT I am standing in front of Mindy's restaurant on Broadway, thinking of practically nothing whatever, when all of a sudden I feel a very terrible pain in my left foot.

In fact, this pain is so very terrible that it causes me to leap up and down like a bullfrog, and to let out loud cries of agony, and to speak some very profane language, which is by no means my custom, although of course I recognize the pain as coming from a hot foot, because I often experience this pain before.

Furthermore, I know Joe the Joker must be in the neighborhood, as Joe the Joker has the most wonderful sense of humor of anybody in this town, and is always around giving people the hot foot, and gives it to me more times than I can remember. In fact, I hear Joe the Joker invents the hot foot, and it finally becomes a very popular idea all over the country.

The way you give a hot foot is to sneak up behind some guy who is standing around thinking of not much, and stick a paper match in his shoe between the sole and the upper along about where his little toe ought to be, and then light the match. By and by the guy will feel a terrible pain in his foot, and will start stamping around, and hollering, and carrying on generally, and it is always a most comical sight and a wonderful laugh to one and all to see him suffer.

No one in the world can give a hot foot as good as Joe the Joker, because it takes a guy who can sneak up very quiet on the guy who is to get the hot foot, and Joe can sneak up so quiet many guys on Broadway are willing to lay you odds that he can give a mouse a hot foot if you can find a mouse that wears shoes. Furthermore, Joe the Joker can take plenty of care of himself in case the guy who gets the hot foot feels like taking the matter up, which sometimes happens, especially with guys who get their shoes made to order at forty bobs per copy and do not care to have holes burned in these shoes.

But Joe does not care what kind of shoes the guys are wearing when he feels like giving out hot foots, and furthermore, he does not care who the guys are, although many citizens think he makes a mistake the time he gives a hot foot to Frankie Ferocious. In fact, many citizens are greatly horrified by this action, and go around saying no good will come of it.

This Frankie Ferocious comes from over in Brooklyn, where he is considered a rising citizen in many respects, and by no means a guy to give hot foots to, especially as Frankie Ferocious has no sense of humor whatever. In fact, he is always very solemn, and nobody ever sees him laugh, and he certainly does not laugh when Joe the Joker gives him a hot foot one day on Broadway when Frankie Ferocious is standing talking over a business matter with some guys from the Bronx.

He only scowls at Joe, and says something in Italian, and while I do not understand Italian, it sounds so unpleasant that I guarantee I will leave town inside of the next two hours if he says it to me.

Of course Frankie Ferocious's name is not really Ferocious, but something in Italian like Feroccio, and I hear he originally comes from Sicily, although he lives in Brooklyn for quite some years, and from a modest beginning he builds himself up until he is a very large operator in merchandise of one kind and another, especially alcohol. He is a big guy of maybe thirty-odd, and he has hair blacker than a yard up a chimney, and black eyes, and black eyebrows, and a slow way of looking at people.

Nobody knows a whole lot about Frankie Ferocious, because he never has much to say, and he takes his time saying it, but everybody gives him plenty of room when he comes around, as there are rumors that Frankie never likes to be crowded. As far as I am concerned, I do not care for any part of Frankie Ferocious, because his slow way of looking at people always makes me nervous, and I am always sorry Joe the Joker gives him a hot foot, because I figure Frankie Ferocious is bound to consider it a most disrespectful action, and hold it against everybody that lives on the Island of Manhattan.

But Joe the Joker only laughs when anybody tells him he is out of line in giving Frankie the hot foot, and says it is not his fault if Frankie has no sense of humor. Furthermore, Joe says he will not only give Frankie another hot foot if he gets a chance, but that he will give hot foots to the Prince of Wales or Mussolini, if he catches them in the right spot, although Regret, the horse player, states that Joe can have twenty to one any time that he will not give Mussolini any hot foots and get away with it.

Anyway, just as I suspect, there is Joe the Joker watching me when I feel the hot foot, and he is laughing very heartily, and furthermore, a large number of other citizens are also laughing heartily, because Joe the Joker never sees any fun in giving people the hot foot unless others are present to enjoy the joke.

Well, naturally when I see who it is gives me the hot foot I join in the laughter, and go over and shake hands with Joe, and when I shake hands with him there is more laughter, because it seems Joe has a hunk of Limburger cheese in his duke, and what I shake hands with is this Limburger. Furthermore, it is some of Mindy's Limburger cheese, and everybody knows Mindy's Limburger is very squashy, and also very loud.

Of course I laugh at this, too, although to tell the truth I will laugh much more heartily if Joe the Joker drops dead in front of me, because I do not like to be made the subject of laughter on Broadway. But my laugh is really quite hearty when Joe takes the rest of the cheese that is not on my fingers and smears it on the steering wheels of some automobiles parked in front of Mindy's, because I get to thinking of what the drivers will say when they start steering their cars.

Then I get to talking to Joe the Joker, and I ask him how things are up in Harlem, where Joe and his younger brother, Freddy, and several other guys have a small organization operating in beer, and Joe says things are as good as can be expected considering business conditions. Then I ask him how Rosa is getting along, this Rosa being Joe the Joker's ever-loving wife, and a personal friend of mine, as I know her when she is Rosa Midnight and is singing in the old Hot Box before Joe hauls off and marries her.

Well, at this question Joe the Joker starts laughing, and I can see that something appeals to his sense of humor, and finally he speaks as follows:

"Why," he says, "do you not hear the news about Rosa? She takes the wind on me a couple of months ago for my friend Frankie Ferocious, and is living in an apartment over in Brooklyn, right near his house, although," Joe says, "of course you understand I am telling you this only to answer your question, and not to holler copper on Rosa."

Then he lets out another large ha-ha, and in fact Joe the Joker keeps laughing until I am afraid he will injure himself internally. Personally, I do not see anything comical in a guy's ever-loving wife taking the wind on him for a guy like Frankie Ferocious, so when Joe the Joker quiets down a bit I ask him what is funny about the proposition.

"Why," Joe says, "I have to laugh every time I think of how the big greaseball is going to feel when he finds out how expensive Rosa is. I do not know how many things Frankie Ferocious has running for him in Brooklyn," Joe says, "but he better try to move himself in on the mint if he wishes to keep Rosa going."

Then he laughs again, and I consider it wonderful the way Joe is able to keep his sense of humor even in such a situation as this, although up to this time I always think Joe is very daffy indeed about Rosa, who is a little doll, weighing maybe ninety pounds with her hat on and quite cute.

Now I judge from what Joe the Joker tells me that Frankie Ferocious knows Rosa before Joe marries her and is always pitching to her when she is singing in the Hot Box, and even after she is Joe's ever-loving wife, Frankie occasionally calls her up, especially when he commences to be a rising citizen of Brooklyn, although of course Joe does not learn about these calls until later. And about the time Frankie Ferocious commences to be a rising citizen of Brooklyn, things begin breaking a little tough for Joe the Joker, what with the depression and all, and he has to economize on Rosa in spots, and if there is one thing Rosa cannot stand it is being economized on.

Along about now, Joe the Joker gives Frankie Ferocious the hot foot, and just as many citizens state at the time, it is a mistake, for Frankie starts calling Rosa up more than somewhat, and speaking of what a nice place Brooklyn is to live in — which it is, at that — and between these boosts for Brooklyn and Joe the Joker's economy, Rosa hauls off and takes the subway to Borough Hall, leaving Joe a note telling him that if he does not like it he knows what he can do.

"Well, Joe," I say, after listening to his story, "I always hate to hear of these little domestic difficulties among my friends, but maybe this is all for the best. Still, I feel sorry for you, if it will do you any good," I say.

"Do not feel sorry for me," Joe says. "If you wish to feel sorry for anybody, feel sorry for Frankie Ferocious, and," he says, "if you can spare a little more sorrow, give it to Rosa."

And Joe the Joker laughs very hearty again and starts telling me about a little scatter that he has up in Harlem where he keeps a chair fixed up with electric wires so he can give anybody that sits down in it a nice jolt, which sounds very humorous to me, at that, especially when Joe tells me how they turn on too much juice one night and almost kill Commodore Jake.

Finally Joe says he has to get back to Harlem, but first he goes to the telephone in the corner cigar store and calls up Mindy's and imitates a doll's voice, and tells Mindy he is Peggy Joyce, or somebody, and orders fifty dozen sandwiches sent up at once to an apartment in West Seventy-second Street for a birthday party, although of course there is no such number as he gives, and nobody there will wish fifty dozen sandwiches if there is such a number.

Then Joe gets in his car and starts off, and while he is waiting for the traffic lights at Fiftieth Street, I see citizens on the sidewalks making sudden leaps, and looking around very fierce, and I know Joe the Joker is plugging them with pellets made out of tin foil, which he fires from a rubber band hooked between his thumb and forefinger.

Joe the Joker is very expert with this proposition, and it is very funny to see the citizens jump, although once or twice in his life Joe makes a miscue and knocks out somebody's eye. But it is all in fun, and shows you what a wonderful sense of humor Joe has.

Well, a few days later I see by the papers where a couple of Harlem guys Joe the Joker is mobbed up with are found done up in sacks over in Brooklyn, very dead indeed, and the coppers say it is because they are trying to move in on certain business enterprises that belong to nobody but Frankie Ferocious. But of course the coppers do not say Frankie Ferocious puts these guys in the sacks, because in the first place Frankie will report them to Headquarters if the coppers say such a thing about him, and in the second place putting guys in sacks is strictly a St. Louis idea and to have a guy put in a sack properly you have to send to St. Louis for experts in this matter.

Now, putting a guy in a sack is not as easy as it sounds, and in fact it takes quite a lot of practice and experience. To put a guy in a sack properly, you first have to put him to sleep, because naturally no guy is going to walk into a sack wide awake unless he is a plumb sucker. Some people claim the best way to put a guy to sleep is to give him a sleeping powder of some kind in a drink, but the real experts just tap the guy on the noggin with a blackjack, which saves the expense of buying the drink.

Anyway, after the guy is asleep, you double him up like a pocketknife, and tie a cord or a wire around his neck and under his knees. Then you put him in a gunny sack, and leave him some place, and by and by when the guy wakes up and finds himself in the sack, naturally he wants to get out and the first thing he does is to try to straighten out his knees. This pulls the cord around his neck up so tight that after a while the guy is all out of breath.

So then when somebody comes along and opens the sack they find the guy dead, and nobody is responsible for this unfortunate situation, because after all the guy really commits suicide, because if he does not try to straighten out his knees he may live to a ripe old age, if he recovers from the tap on the noggin.

Well, a couple of days later I see by the papers where three Brooklyn citizens are scragged as they are walking peaceably along Clinton Street, the scragging being done by some parties in an automobile who seem to have a machine gun, and the papers state that the citizens are friends of Frankie Ferocious, and that it is rumored the parties with the machine gun are from Harlem.

I judge by this that there is some trouble in Brooklyn, especially as about a week after the citizens are scragged in Clinton Street, another Harlem guy is found done up in a sack like a Virginia ham near Prospect Park, and now who is it but Joe the Joker's brother, Freddy, and I know Joe is going to be greatly displeased by this.

By and by it gets so nobody in Brooklyn will open as much as a sack of potatoes without first calling in the gendarmes, for fear a pair of No. 8 shoes will jump out at them.

Now one night I see Joe the Joker, and this time he is all alone, and I wish to say I am willing to leave him all alone, because something tells me he is hotter than a stove. But he grabs me as I am going past, so naturally I stop to talk to him, and the first thing I say is how sorry I am about his brother.

"Well," Joe the Joker says, "Freddy is always a kind of a sap. Rosa calls him up and asks him to come over to Brooklyn to see her. She wishes to talk to Freddy about getting me to give her a divorce," Joe says, "so she can marry Frankie Ferocious, I suppose. Anyway," he says, "Freddy tells Commodore Jake why he is going to see her. Freddy always likes Rosa, and thinks maybe he can patch it up between us. So," Joe says, "he winds up in a sack. They get him after he leaves her apartment. I do not claim Rosa will ask him to come over if she has any idea he will be sacked," Joe says, "but," he says, "she is responsible. She is a bad-luck doll."

Then he starts to laugh, and at first I am greatly horrified, thinking it is because something about Freddy being sacked strikes his sense of humor, when he says to me like this:

"Say," he says, "I am going to play a wonderful joke on Frankie Ferocious."

"Well, Joe," I say, "you are not asking me for advice, but I am going to give you some free gratis, and for nothing. Do not play any jokes on Frankie Ferocious, as I hear he has no more sense of humor than a nanny goat. I hear Frankie Ferocious will not laugh if you have Al Jolson, Eddie Cantor, Ed Wynn and Joe Cook telling him jokes all at once. In fact," I say, "I hear he is a tough audience."

"Oh," Joe the Joker says, "he must have some sense of humor somewhere to stand for Rosa. I hear he is daffy about her. In fact, I understand she is the only person in the world he really likes, and trusts. But I must play a joke on him. I am going to have myself delivered to Frankie Ferocious in a sack."

Well, of course I have to laugh at this myself, and Joe the Joker laughs with me. Personally, I am laughing just at the idea of anybody having themselves delivered to Frankie Ferocious in a sack, and especially Joe the Joker, but of course I have no idea Joe really means what he says.

"Listen," Joe says, finally. "A guy from St. Louis who is a friend of mine is doing most of the sacking for Frankie Ferocious. His name is Ropes McGonnigle. In fact," Joe says, "he is a very dear old pal of mine, and he has a wonderful sense of humor like me. Ropes McGonnigle has nothing whatever to do with sacking Freddy," Joe says, "and he is very indignant about it since he finds out Freddy is my brother, so he is anxious to help me play a joke on Frankie.

"Only last night," Joe says, "Frankie Ferocious sends for Ropes and tells him he will appreciate it as a special favor if Ropes will bring me to him in a sack. I suppose," Joe says, "that Frankie Ferocious hears from Rosa what Freddy is bound to tell her about my ideas on divorce. I have very strict ideas on divorce," Joe says, "especially where Rosa is concerned. I will see her in what's-this before I ever do her and Frankie Ferocious such a favor as giving her a divorce.

"Anyway," Joe the Joker says, "Ropes tells me about Frankie Ferocious propositioning him, so I send Ropes back to Frankie Ferocious to tell him he knows I am to be in Brooklyn tomorrow night, and furthermore, Ropes tells Frankie that he will have me in a sack in no time. And so he will," Joe says.

"Well," I say, "personally, I see no percentage in being delivered to Frankie Ferocious in a sack, because as near as I can make out from what I read in the papers, there is no future for a guy in a sack that goes to Frankie Ferocious. What I cannot figure out," I say, "is where the joke on Frankie comes in."

"Why," Joe the Joker says, "the joke is, I will not be asleep in the sack, and my hands will not be tied, and in each of my hands I will have a John Roscoe, so when the sack is delivered to Frankie Ferocious and I pop out blasting away, can you not imagine his astonishment?"

Well, I can imagine this, all right. In fact, when I get to thinking of the look of surprise that is bound to come to Frankie Ferocious's face when Joe the Joker comes out of the sack I have to laugh, and Joe the Joker laughs right along with me.

"Of course," Joe says, "Ropes McGonnigle will be there to start blasting with me, in case Frankie Ferocious happens to have any company."

Then Joe the Joker goes on up the street, leaving me still laughing from thinking of how amazed Frankie Ferocious will be when Joe bounces out of the sack and starts throwing slugs around and about. I do not hear of Joe from that time to this, but I hear the rest of the story from very reliable parties.

It seems that Ropes McGonnigle does not deliver the sack himself, after all, but sends it by an expressman to Frankie Ferocious's home. Frankie Ferocious receives many sacks such as this in his time, because it seems that it is a sort of passion with him to personally view the contents of the sacks and check up on them before they are distributed about the city, and of course Ropes McGonnigle knows about this passion from doing so much sacking for Frankie.

When the expressman takes the sack into Frankie's house, Frankie personally lugs it down into his basement, and there he outs with a big John Roscoe and fires six shots into the sack, because it seems Ropes McGonnigle tips him off to Joe the Joker's plan to pop out of the sack and start blasting.

I hear Frankie Ferocious has a very strange expression on his pan and is laughing the only laugh anybody ever hears from him when the gendarmes break in and put the arm on him for murder, because it seems that when Ropes McGonnigle tells Frankie of Joe the Joker's plan, Frankie tells Ropes what he is going to do with his own hands before opening the sack. Naturally, Ropes speaks to Joe the Joker of Frankie's idea about filling the sack full of slugs, and Joe's sense of humor comes right out again.

So, bound and gagged, but otherwise as right as rain in the sack that is delivered to Frankie Ferocious, is by no means Joe the Joker, but Rosa.

1938

PEARL S. BUCK

....

Ransom

THE BEETHOVEN SYMPHONY stopped abruptly. A clear metallic voice broke across the melody of the third movement.

"Press radio news. The body of Jimmie Lane, kidnaped son of Mr. Headley Lane, has been found on the bank of the Hudson River near his home this afternoon. This ends the search of —"

"Kent, turn it off, please!" Allin exclaimed.

Kent Crothers hesitated a second. Then he turned off the radio.

In the silence Allin sat biting her lower lip. "That poor mother!" she exclaimed. "All these days — not giving up hope."

"I suppose it is better to know something definite," he said quietly, "even though it is the worst."

Perhaps this would be a good time to talk with her, to warn her that she was letting this kidnaping business grow into an obsession. After all, children did grow up in the United States, even in well-to-do families like theirs. The trouble was that they were not quite rich enough and still too rich — not rich enough to hire guards for their children, but rich enough, because his father owned the paper mill, to make them known in the neighborhood, at least.

The thing was to take it for granted that they did not belong to the millionaire class and therefore were not prize for kidnapers. They should do this for Bruce's sake. He would be starting to school next autumn. Bruce would have to walk back and forth on the streets like millions of other American children. Kent wouldn't have his son driven three blocks, even by Peter the outdoor man; it would do him more harm than . . . after all, it was a democracy they lived in, and Bruce had to grow up with the crowd.

"I'll go and see that the children are covered," Allin said. "Betsy throws off the covers whenever she can."

Kent knew that she simply wanted to make sure they were there. But he rose with her, lighting his pipe, thinking how to begin. They walked up the stairs together, their fingers interlaced. Softly she opened the nursery door. It was ridiculous how even he was being affected by her fears. Whenever the door opened his heart stood cold for a second, until he saw the two beds, each with a little head on the pillow.

They were there now, of course. He stood beside Bruce's bed and looked down at his son. Handsome little devil. He was sleeping so soundly that when his mother leaned over him he did not move. His black hair was a tousle; his red lips pouted. He was dark, but he had Allin's blue eyes.

They did not speak. Allin drew the cover gently over his outflung arm, and they stood a moment longer, hand in hand, gazing at the child. Then Allin looked up at Kent and smiled, and he kissed her. He put his arm about her shoulder, and they went to Betsy's bed.

Here was his secret obsession. He could say firmly that Bruce must take his chances with the other children, because a boy had to learn to be brave. But this baby — such a tiny feminine creature, his little daughter. She had Allin's auburn coloring, but by some miracle she had his dark eyes, so that when he looked into them he seemed to be looking into himself.

She was breathing now, a little unevenly, through her tiny nose.

"How's her cold?" he whispered.

"It doesn't seem worse," Allin whispered back. "I put stuff on her chest."

He was always angry when anything happened to this baby. He didn't trust her nurse, Mollie, too much. She was good-hearted, maybe, but easygoing.

The baby stirred and opened her eyes. She blinked, smiled and put up her arms to him.

"Don't pick her up, darling," Allin counseled. "She'll only want it every time."

So he did not take her. Instead, he put her arms down, one and then the other, playfully, under the cover.

"Go to sleep-bye, honey," he said. And she lay, sleepily smiling. She was a good little thing.

"Come — let's put out the light," Allin whispered. They tiptoed out and went back to the living room.

Kent sat down, puffed on his pipe, his mind full of what he wanted to say to Allin. It was essential to their life to believe that nothing could happen to their children.

"Kidnaping's like lightning," he began abruptly. "It happens, of course — once in a million. What you have to remember is all the rest of the children who are perfectly safe."

She had sat down on the ottoman before the fire, but she turned to him when he said this. "What would you do, honestly, Kent, if some night when we went upstairs —"

"Nonsense!" he broke in. "That's what I've been trying to tell you. It's so unlikely as to be — it's these damned newspapers! When a thing happens in one part of the country, every little hamlet hears of it."

"Jane Eliot told me there are three times as many kidnapings as ever get into the newspapers," Allin said.

"Jane's a newspaperwoman," Kent said. "You mustn't let her sense of drama —"

"Still, she's been on a lot of kidnaping cases," Allin replied. "She was telling me about the Wyeth case —"

This was the time to speak, now when all Allin's secret anxiety was quivering in her voice. Kent took her hand and fondled it as he spoke. He must remember how deeply she felt everything, and this thing had haunted her before Bruce was born. He had not even thought of it until one night in the darkness she had asked him the same question, "What would we do, Kent, if —" Only then he had not known what she meant.

"If what?" he had asked.

"If our baby were ever kidnaped."

He had answered what he had felt then and believed now to be true. "Why worry about what will never happen?" he had said. Nevertheless, he had followed all the cases since Bruce was born.

He kissed her palm now. "I can't bear having you afraid," he said. "It isn't necessary, you know, darling. We can't live under the shadow of this thing," he went on. "We have to come to some rational position on it."

"That's what I want, Kent. I'd be glad not to be afraid — if I knew how."

"After all," he went on again, "most people bring up their families without thinking about it."

"Most mothers think of it," she said. "Most of the women I know have said something about it to me — some time or other — enough to make me know they think about it all the time."

"You'd be better off not talking about it," he said.

But she said, "We keep wondering what we would do, Kent."

"That's just it!" he exclaimed. "That's why I think if we decided now what we would do — always bearing in mind that it's only the remotest possibility —"

"What *would* we do, Kent?" she asked.

He answered half playfully, "Promise to remember it's as remote as — an airplane attack on our home?"

She nodded.

"I've always thought that if one of the children were kidnaped I'd simply turn the whole thing over to the police at once."

"What police?" she asked instantly. "Gossipy old Mike O'Brien, who'd tell the newspapers the first thing? It's fatal to let it get into the papers, Jane says."

"Well, the Federal police, then — the G-men."

"How does one get in touch with them?"

He had to confess he did not know. "I'll find out," he promised. "Anyway, it's the principle, darling, that we want to determine. Once we know what we'll do, we can put it out of our minds. No ransom, Allin — that I feel sure about. As long as we keep on paying ransoms, we're going to have kidnapings. Somebody has to be strong enough to take the stand. Then maybe other people will see what they ought to do."

But she did not look convinced. When she spoke, her voice was low and full of dread. "The thing is, Kent, if we decided not to pay ransom, we just couldn't stick to it — not really, I mean. Suppose it were Bruce — suppose he had a cold and it was winter — and he was taken out of his warm bed in his pajamas, we'd do anything. You know we would!" She rushed on. "We wouldn't care about other children, Kent. We would only be thinking of our own little Bruce — and no one else. How to get him back again, at whatever cost."

"Hush, darling," he said. "If you're going to be like this we can't talk about it, after all."

"No, Kent, please. I do want to talk. I want to know what we ought to do. If only I could be not afraid!" she whispered.

"Come here by me," he said. He drew her to the couch beside him. "First of all, you know I love the children as well as you do, don't you?"

She nodded, and he went on, "Then, darling, I'd do anything I thought would be best for our children, wouldn't I?"

"You'd do the best you knew, Kent. The question is, do any of us know what to do?"

"I do know," he said gravely, "that until we make the giving and taking of ransoms unlawful we shall have kidnapers. And until somebody begins it, it will never be done. That's the law of democratic government. The people have to begin action before government takes a stand."

"What if they said not to tell the police?" she asked.

Her concreteness confounded him. It was not as if the thing could happen!

"It all depends," he retorted, "on whether you want to give in to rascals or stand on your principle."

"But if it were our own child?" she persisted. "Be honest, Kent. Please don't retire into principles."

"I am trying to be honest," he said slowly. "I think I would stick by principle and trust somehow to think of some way —" He looked waveringly into her unbelieving eyes.

"Try to remember exactly what happened!" he was shouting at the silly nurse. "Where did you leave her?"

Allin was quieter than he, but Allin's voice on the telephone half an hour ago had been like a scream: "Kent, we can't find Betsy!"

He had been in the mill directors' meeting, but he'd risen instantly. "Sorry," he'd said sharply. "I have to leave at once."

"Nothing serious, Kent?" His father's white eyebrows had lifted.

"I think not," he'd answered. He had sense enough not to say what Allin had screamed. "I'll let you know if it is."

He had leaped into his car and driven home like a crazy man. He'd drawn up in a spray of gravel at his own gate. Allin was there, and Mollie, the silly nurse. Mollie was sobbing.

"We was at the gate, sir, watchin' for Brucie to come home from school, like we do every day, and I put 'er down — she's heavy to carry — while I went in to get a clean hankie to wipe her little hands. She'd stepped into a puddle from the rain this morning. When I came back, she wasn't there. I ran around the shrubs, sir, lookin' — and then I screamed for the madam."

"Kent, I've combed the place," Allin whispered.

"The gate!" he gasped.

"It was shut, and the bar across," Mollie wailed. "I'd sense enough to see to that before I went in."

"How long were you gone?" he shouted at her.

"I don't know, sir," Mollie sobbed. "It didn't seem a minute!"

He rushed into the yard. "Betsy, Betsy!" he cried. "Come to Daddy! Here's Daddy!" He stooped under the big lilac bushes. "Have you looked in the garage?" he demanded of Allin.

"Peter's been through it twice," she answered.

"I'll see for myself," he said. "Go into the house, Allin. She may have got inside, somehow."

He tore into the garage. Peter crawled out from under the small car.

"She ain't hyah, suh," he whispered. "Ah done looked ev'ywheah."

But Kent looked again, Peter following him like a dog. In the back of his mind was a telephone number, National 7117. He had found out about that number the year before, after he and Allin had talked that evening. Only he wouldn't call yet. Betsy was sure to be somewhere.

The gate clicked, and he rushed out. But it was only Bruce.

"Why, what's the matter with you, Daddy?" Bruce asked.

Kent swallowed — no use scaring Bruce. "Bruce, did you — you didn't see Betsy on the way home, did you?"

"No, Daddy. I didn't see anybody except Mike to help me across the square 'cause there was a notomobile."

"Wha' dat?" Peter was pointing at something. It was a bit of white paper, held down by a stone.

As well as he knew anything, Kent knew what it was. He had read that note a dozen times in the newspaper accounts. He stooped and picked it up. There it was — the scrawled handwriting.

"We been waiting this chanse." The handwriting was there, illiterate, disguised. "Fifty grand is the price. Your dads got it if you aint. Youll hear where to put it. If you tell the police we kill the kid."

"Daddy, what's —" Bruce began.

"Bring him indoors," he ordered Peter.

Where was Allin? He had to — he had promised her it would not happen! The telephone number was — but —

"Allin!" he shouted.

He heard her running down from the attic.

"Allin!" he gasped. She was there, white and piteous with terror — and so helpless. God, they were both so helpless! He had to have help; he had to know what to do. But had not he — he had decided long ago what he must do, because what did he know about crooks and kidnapers? People gave the ransom and lost their children, too. He had to have advice he could trust.

"I'm going to call National 7117!" he blurted at her.

"No, Kent — wait!" she cried.

"I've got to," he insisted. Before she could move, he ran to the telephone and took up the receiver. "I want National 7117!" he shouted.

Her face went white. He held out his hand with the crumpled note. She read it and snatched at the receiver.

"No, Kent — wait. We don't know. Wait and see what they say!"

But a calm voice was already speaking at the other end of the wire: "This is National 7117." And Kent was shouting hoarsely, "I want to report a kidnaping. It's our baby girl. Kent Crothers, 134 Eastwood Avenue, Greenvale, New York."

He listened while the voice was telling him to do nothing, to wait until tomorrow, and then at a certain village inn, fifty miles away, to meet a certain man who would wear a plain gray suit.

And all the time Allin was whispering, "They'll kill her — they'll kill her, Kent."

"They won't know," he whispered back. "Nobody will know." When he put the receiver down he cried at her angrily, "They won't tell anybody — those fellows in Washington! Besides, I've got to have help, I tell you!"

She stood staring at him with horrified eyes. "They'll kill her," she repeated.

He wanted to get somewhere to weep, only men could not weep. But Allin was not weeping, either. Then suddenly they flung their arms about each other, and together broke into silent terrible tears.

He was not used to waiting, but he had to wait. And he had to help Allin wait. Men were supposed to be stronger.

At first it had been a comfort to have the directions to follow. First, everybody in the house — that was easy: simply the cook Sarah, the maid Rose, and Mollie and Peter. They of course were beyond blame, except Mollie. Perhaps Mollie was more than just a fool. They all had to be told they were to say absolutely nothing.

"Get everybody together in the dining room," Kent had told Allin. He had gone into the dining room.

"Daddy!" He saw Bruce's terrified figure in the doorway. "What's the matter? Where's Betsy?"

"We can't find her, son," Kent said, trying to make his voice calm. "Of course we will, but just now nobody must know she isn't here."

"Shall I go out in the yard?" Bruce asked. "Maybe I could find her."

"No," Kent said sharply. "I'd rather you went upstairs to your own room. I'll be up — in a minute."

The servants were coming in, Allin behind them.

"I'll go with Bruce," she said.

She was so still and so controlled, but he could tell by the quiver about her lips that she was only waiting for him.

"I'll be up in a very few minutes," he promised her. He stood until she had gone, Bruce's hand in hers. Then he turned to the four waiting figures. Mollie was still crying. He could tell by their faces that they all knew about the note.

"I see you know what has happened," he said. Strange how all these familiar faces looked sinister to him! Peter and Sarah had been in his mother's household. They had known him for years. And Rose was Sarah's niece. But they all looked hostile, or he imagined they did. "And I want not one word said of this to anyone in the town," he said harshly. "Remember, Betsy's life depends on no one outside knowing."

He paused, setting his jaws. He would not have believed he could cry as easily as a woman, but he could.

He cleared his throat. "Her life depends on how we behave now — in the next few hours." Mollie's sobbing burst out into wails. He rose. "That's all," he said. "We must simply wait."

The telephone rang, and he hurried to it. There was no way of knowing how the next message would come. But it was his father's peremptory voice: "Anything wrong over there, Kent?"

He knew now it would never do for his father to know what had happened. His father could keep nothing to himself.

"Everything is all right, Dad," he answered. "Allin's not feeling very well, that's all."

"Have you had the doctor?" his father shouted.

"We will if it is necessary, Dad," he answered and put up the receiver abruptly. He could not go on with that.

He thought of Bruce and went to find him. He was eating his supper in the nursery, and Allin was with him. She had told Mollie to stay downstairs. She could not bear to see the girl any more than he could.

But the nursery was unbearable, too. This was the time when Betsy, fresh from her bath . . .

"I'm — I'll be downstairs in the library," he told Allin hurriedly, and she nodded.

In the library the silence was torture. There was nothing to do but wait.

And all the time who knew what was happening to the child? Tomorrow, the man had said an hour ago. Wait, he had said. But what about tonight? In what sort of place would the child be sleeping?

Kent leaped to his feet. Something had to be done. He would have a look around the yard. There might be another letter.

He went out into the early autumn twilight. He had to hold himself together to keep from breaking into foolish shouts and curses. It was the agony of not being able to do anything. Then he controlled himself. The thing was to go on following a rational plan. He had come out to see if he could find anything.

He searched every inch of the yard. There was no message of any sort.

Then in the gathering darkness he saw a man at the gate. "Mist' Crothers!" It was Peter's voice. "Fo' God, Mist' Crothers, Ah don' know why they should pick on mah ole 'ooman. When Ah come home fo' suppah, she give it to me — she cain't read, so she don' know what wuz in it. Ah run all de way."

Kent snatched a paper from Peter's shaking hand and ran to the house. In the lighted hall he read:

> Get the dough ready all banknotes dont mark any or well get the other kid too. Dont try double-crossing us. You cant get away with nothing. Put it in a box by the dead oak at the mill creek. You know where. At twelve o'clock tomorrow night.

He knew where, indeed. He had fished there from the time he was a little boy. The lightning had struck that oak tree one summer when he had been only a hundred yards away, standing in the doorway of the mill during a thunderstorm. How did they know he knew?

He turned on Peter. "Who brought this?" he demanded.

"Ah don' know, suh," Peter stammered. "She couldn't tell me nothin' 'cep'n' it wuz a white man. He chuck it at 'er and say, 'Give it to yo' ole man.' So she give it to me, and Ah come a-runnin'."

Kent stared at Peter, trying to ferret into that dark brain. Was Peter being used by someone; bribed, perhaps, to take a part? Did he know anything?

"If I thought you knew anything about Betsy, I'd kill you myself," he said.

"Fo' God, Ah don', Mist' Crothers — you know me, suh! Ah done gyardened for yo' since yo' and Miss Allin got mah'ied. 'Sides, whut Ah want in such devilment? Ah got all Ah want — mah house and a sal'ry. Ah don' want nuthin'."

It was all true, of course. The thing was, you suspected everybody.

"You tell Flossie to tell no one," he commanded Peter.

"Ah done tole 'er," Peter replied fervently. "Ah tole 'er Ah'd split 'er open if she tole anybody 'bout dat white man."

"Get along, then," said Kent. "And remember what I told you."

"Yassuh," Peter replied.

"Of course we'll pay the ransom!" Allin was insisting.

They were in their own room, the door open into the narrow passage, and beyond that the door into the nursery was open, too. They sat where, in the shadowy light of a night lamp, they could see Bruce's dark head on the pillow. Impossible, of course, to sleep. Sarah had sent up some cold chicken and they had eaten it here, and later Kent had made Allin take a hot bath and get into a warm robe and lie down on the chaise longue. He did not undress. Someone might call.

"I'll have to see what the man says tomorrow," he answered.

Terrifying to think how he was pinning everything on that fellow tomorrow — a man whose name, even, he did not know. All he knew was he'd wear a plain gray suit and he'd have a blue handkerchief in his pocket. That was all he had to save Betsy's life. No, that wasn't true. Behind that one man were hundreds of others, alert, strong, and ready to help him.

"We've got to pay it," Allin was saying hysterically. "What's money now?"

"Allin!" he cried. "You don't think I'm trying to save the money, in God's name!"

"We have about twenty thousand, haven't we, in the bank?" she said hurriedly. "Your father would have the rest, though, and we could give him the securities. It isn't as if we didn't have it."

"Allin, you're being absurd! The thing is to know how to —"

But she flew at him fiercely. "The thing is to save Betsy — that's all; there's nothing else — absolutely nothing. I don't care if it takes everything your father has."

"Allin, be quiet!" he shouted at her. "Do you mean my father would begrudge anything — ?"

"You're afraid of him, Kent," she retorted. "Well, I'm not! If you don't go to him, I will."

They were quarreling now, like two insane people. They were both stretched beyond normal reason.

Suddenly Allin was sobbing. "I can't forget what you said that night," she cried. "All that standing on principle! Oh, Kent, she's with strangers, horrible people, crying her little heart out; perhaps they're even — hurting her, trying to make her keep quiet. Oh, Kent, Kent!"

He took her in his arms. They must not draw apart now. He must think of her.

"I'll do anything, darling," he said. "The first thing in the morning I'll get hold of Dad and have the money ready."

"If they could only *know* it," she said.

"I could put something in the paper, perhaps," he said. "I believe I could word something that no one else would understand."

"Let's try, Kent!"

He took a pencil and envelope from his pocket and wrote. "How's this?" he asked. "Fifty agreed by dead oak at twelve."

"I can't see how it could do any harm," she said eagerly. "And if they see it, they'll understand we're willing to do anything."

"I'll go around to the newspaper office and pay for this in cash," he said. "Then I won't have to give names."

"Yes, yes!" she urged him. "It's something more than just sitting here!"

He drove through the darkness the two miles to the small town and parked in front of the ramshackle newspaper office. A red-eyed night clerk took his advertisement and read it off.

"This is a funny one," he said. "We get some, now and then. That'll be a dollar, Mr. —"

Kent did not answer. He put a dollar bill on the desk.

"I don't know what I've done, even so," he groaned to himself.

He drove back quietly through the intense darkness. The storm had not yet come, and the air was strangely silent. He kept his motor at its most noiseless, expecting somehow to hear through the sleeping still-ness Betsy's voice, crying.

They scarcely slept, and yet when they looked at each other the next morning the miracle was that they had slept at all. But he had made Allin go to bed at last, and then, still dressed, he had lain down on his own bed near her. It was Bruce who waked them. He stood hesitatingly between their beds. They heard his voice.

"Betsy hasn't come back yet, Mommie."

The name waked them. And they looked at each other.

"How could we!" Allin whispered.

"It may be a long pull, dearest," he said, trying to be steady. He got up, feeling exhausted.

"Will she come back today?" Bruce asked.

"I think so, son."

At least it was Saturday, and Bruce need not go to school today.

"I'm going to get her tonight," Kent said after a moment.

Instantly he felt better. They must not give up hope — not by a great deal. There was too much to do: his father to see and the money to get. Secretly, he still reserved his own judgment about the ransom. If the man in gray was against it, he would tell Allin nothing — he simply would not give it. The responsibility would be his.

"You and Mommie will have to get Betsy's things ready for her to-night," he said cheerfully. He would take a bath and get into a fresh suit. He had to have all his wits about him today, every moment — listen to everybody, and use his own judgment finally. In an emergency, one person had to act.

He paused at the sight of himself in the mirror. Would he be able to keep it from Allin if he made a mistake? Suppose they never got Betsy back. Suppose she just — disappeared. Or suppose they found her little body somewhere.

This was the way all those other parents had felt — this sickness and faintness. If he did not pay the ransom and *that* happened, would he be able *not* to tell Allin — or to tell her it was his fault? Both were impossible.

"I'll just have to go on from one thing to the next," he decided.

The chief thing was to try to be hopeful. He dressed and went back into the bedroom. Bruce had come in to dress in their room. But Allin was still in bed, lying against the pillows, white and exhausted.

He bent over her and kissed her. "I'll send your breakfast up," he said. "I'm going to see Father first. If any message comes through, I'll be there — then at the bank."

She nodded, glanced up at him and closed her eyes. He stood looking down into her tortured face. Every nerve in it was quivering under the set stillness.

"Can't break yet," he said sharply. "The crisis is ahead."

"I know," she whispered. Then she sat up. "I can't lie here!" she exclaimed. "It's like lying on a bed of swords, being tortured. I'll be down, Kent — Bruce and I."

She flew into the bathroom. He heard the shower turned on instantly and strongly. But he could wait for no one.

"Come down with Mother, son," he said. And he went on alone.

"If you could let me have thirty thousand today," he said to his father, "I can give it back as soon as I sell some stock."

"I don't care when I get it back," his father said irritably. "Good God, Kent, it's not that. It's just that I — it's none of my business, of course, but thirty thousand in cold cash! I'd like to ask what on earth you've been doing, but I won't."

Kent had made up his mind at the breakfast table when he picked up the paper that if he could keep the thing out of the papers, he would keep it from his father and mother. He'd turned to the personals. There it was, his answer to those scoundrels. Well, he wouldn't stick to it unless it were best for Betsy. Meanwhile, silence!

To Rose, bringing in the toast, he'd said sharply, "Tell everybody to come in now before your mistress comes down."

They had filed in, subdued and drooping, looking at him with frightened eyes.

"Oh, sir!" Mollie had cried hysterically.

"Please!" he'd exclaimed, glancing at her. Maybe the man in gray ought to see her. But last night he had distrusted Peter. This morning Peter looked like a faithful old dog, and as incapable of evil.

"I only want to thank you for obeying me so far," he'd said wearily. "If we can keep our trouble out of the papers, perhaps we can get Betsy back. At least, it's the only hope. If you succeed in letting no one know until we know — the end, I shall give each of you a hundred dollars as a token of my gratitude."

"Thank you, sir," Sarah and Rose had said. Mollie only sobbed. Peter was murmuring, "Ah don' wan' no hundred dollahs, Mist' Crothers. All Ah wan' is dat little chile back."

How could Peter be distrusted? Kent had wrung his hand. "That's all I want, too, Peter," he'd said fervently.

Strange how shaky and emotional he had felt!

Now, under his father's penetrating eyes, he held himself calm. "I know it sounds outrageous, Father," he admitted, "but I simply ask you to trust me for a few days."

"You're not speculating, I hope. It's no time for that. The market's crazy."

It was, Kent thought grimly, the wildest kind of speculation — with his own child's life.

"It's not ordinary speculation, certainly," he said. "I can manage through the bank, Dad," he said. "Never mind. I'll mortgage the house."

"Oh, nonsense!" his father retorted. He had his checkbook out and was writing. "I'm not going to have it get around that my son had to go mortgaging his place."

"Thanks," Kent said briefly.

Now for the bank!

Step by step the day went. It was amazing how quickly the hours passed. It was noon before he knew it, and in an hour he must start for the inn. He went home and found Allin on the front porch in the sunshine. She had a book in her hand, and Bruce was playing with his red truck out in the yard. Anyone passing would never dream there was tragedy here.

"Do you have it?" she asked him.

He touched his breast pocket. "All ready," he answered.

They sat through a silent meal, listening to Bruce's chatter. Allin ate nothing and he very little, but he was grateful to her for being there, for keeping the outward shape of the day usual.

"Good sport!" he said to her across the table in the midst of Bruce's conversation. She smiled faintly. "Thank you, no more coffee," he said to Rose. "I must be going, Allin."

"Yes," she said, and added, "I wish it were I — instead of waiting."

"I know," he replied, and kissed her.

Yesterday, waiting had seemed intolerable to him, too. But now that he was going toward the hour for which he had been waiting, he clung to the hopefulness of uncertainty.

He drove alone to the inn. The well-paved roads, the tended fields and comfortable farmhouses were not different from the landscape any day. He would have said, only yesterday, that it was impossible that underneath all this peace and plenty there could be men so evil as to take a child out of its home, away from its parents, for money.

There was, he pondered, driving steadily west, no other possible reason. He had no enemies; none, that is, whom he knew. There were always discontented people, of course, who hated anyone who seemed successful. There was, of course, too, the chance that his father had enemies — he was ruthless with idle workers.

"I can't blame a man if he is born a fool," Kent had heard his father maintain stoutly, "but I can blame even a fool for being lazy." It might be one of these. If only it were not some perverted mind!

He drove into the yard of the inn and parked his car. His heart was thudding in his breast, but he said casually to the woman at the door, "Have you a bar?"

"To the right," she answered quickly. It was Saturday afternoon, and business was good. She did not even look at him as he sauntered away.

The moment he entered the door of the bar he saw the man. He stood at the end of the bar, small, inconspicuous, in a gray suit and a blue-striped shirt. He wore a solid blue tie, and in his pocket was the blue handkerchief. Kent walked slowly to his side.

"Whisky and soda, please," he ordered the bartender. The room was full of people at tables, drinking and talking noisily. He turned to the man in gray and smiled. "Rather unusual to find a bar like this in a village inn," he said.

"Yes, it is," the little man agreed. He had a kind, brisk voice, and he was drinking a tall glass of something clear, which he finished. "Give me another of the same," he remarked to the bartender. "London Washerwoman's Treat, it's called," he explained to Kent.

It was hard to imagine that this small hatchet-faced man had any importance.

"Going my way?" Kent asked suddenly.

"If you'll give me a lift," the little man replied.

Kent's heart subsided. The man knew him, then. He nodded. They paid for their drinks and went out to the car.

"Drive due north into a country road," the little man said with sudden sharpness. All his dreaminess was gone. He sat beside Kent, his arms folded. "Please tell me exactly what's happened, Mr. Crothers."

And Kent, driving along, told him.

He was grateful for the man's coldness; for the distrust of everything and everybody. He was like a lean hound in a life-and-death chase. Because of his coldness, Kent could talk without fear of breaking.

"I don't know your name," Kent said.

"Don't matter," said the man. "I'm detailed for the job."

"As I was saying," Kent went on, "we have no enemies — at least, none I know."

"Fellow always has enemies," the little man murmured.

"It hardly seems likely a gangster would —" Kent began again.

"No, gangsters don't kidnap children," the little man told him. "Adults, yes. But they don't monkey with kids. It's too dangerous, for one thing. Kidnaping children's the most dangerous job there is in crime, and the smart ones know it. It's always some little fellow does it — him and a couple of friends, maybe."

"Why dangerous?" Kent demanded.

"Always get caught," the little man said, shrugging. "Always!"

There was something so reassuring about this strange sharp creature that Kent said abruptly, "My wife wants to pay the ransom. I suppose you think that's wrong, don't you?"

"Perfectly *right*," the man said. "Absolutely! We aren't magicians, Mr. Crothers. We got to get in touch somehow. The only two cases I ever knew where nothing was solved was where the parents wouldn't pay. So we couldn't get a clue."

Kent set his lips. "Children killed?"

"Who knows?" the little man said, shrugging again. "Anyway, one of them was. And the other never came back."

There might be comfort, then, in death, Kent thought. He had infinitely rather hold Betsy's dead body in his arms than never know . . .

"Tell me what to do, and I'll do it," he said.

The little man lighted a cigarette. "Go on just as though you'd never told us. Go on and pay your ransom. Make a note of the numbers of the notes, of course — no matter what that letter says. How's he going to know? But pay it over — and do what he says next. You can call me up here." He took a paper out of his coat pocket and put it in Kent's pocket. "I maybe ought to tell you, though, we'll tap your telephone wire."

"Do anything you like," Kent said.

"That's all I need!" the man exclaimed. "That's our orders — to do what the parents want. You're a sensible one. Fellow I knew once walked around with a shotgun to keep off the police. Said he'd handle things himself."

"Did he get his child back?"

"Nope — paid the ransom, too. Paying the ransom's all right — that's the way we get 'em. But he went roarin' around the neighborhood trying to be his own law. We didn't get a chance."

Kent thought of one more thing. "I don't want anything spared — money or trouble. I'll pay anything, of course."

"Oh, sure," the man said. "Well, I guess that'll be all. You might let me off near the inn. I'll go in and get another drink."

He lapsed into dreaminess again, and in silence Kent drove back to the village.

"All right," the little man said. "So long. Good luck to you." He leaped out and disappeared into the bar.

And Kent, driving home through the early sunset, thought how little there was to tell Allin — really nothing at all, except that he liked and trusted the man in gray. No, it was much more than that: the fellow stood for something far greater than himself — he stood for all the power of the government organized against crimes like this. That was the comfort of the thing. Behind that man was the nation's police, all for him, Kent Crothers, helping him find his child.

When he reached home, Allin was in the hall waiting.

"He really said nothing, darling," Kent said, kissing her, "except you were right about the ransom. We have to pay that. Still, he was extraordinary. Somehow I feel — if she's still alive, we'll get her back. He's that sort of fellow." He did not let her break, though he felt her trembling against him. He said very practically, "We must check these banknotes, Allin."

And then, when they were checking them upstairs in their bedroom with doors locked, he kept insisting that what they were doing was right.

At a quarter to twelve he was bumping down the rutted road to the forks. He knew every turn the road made, having traveled it on foot from the time he was a little boy. But that boy out on holiday had nothing to do with himself as he was tonight, an anxious, harried man.

He drew up beneath the dead oak and took the cardboard box in which he and Allin had packed the money and stepped out of the car. There was not a sound in the dark night, yet he knew that somewhere not far away were the men who had his child.

He listened, suddenly swept again with the conviction he had had the night before, that she would cry out. She might even be this moment in the old mill. But there was not a sound. He stooped and put the box at the root of the tree.

And as he did this, he stumbled over a string raised from the ground above a foot. What was this? He followed it with his hands. It encircled the tree — a common piece of twine. Then it went under a stone, and under the stone was a piece of paper. He seized it, snapped on his cigarette lighter, read the clumsy printing.

If everything turns out like we told you to do, go to your hired mans house at twelve tomorrow night for the kid. If you double-cross us you get it back dead.

He snapped off the light. He'd get her back dead! It all depended on what he did. And what he did, he would have to do alone. He would not go home to Allin until he had decided every step.

He drove steadily away. If he did not call the man in gray, Betsy might be at Peter's alive. If he called, and they did not find out, she might be alive anyway. But if the man fumbled and they did find out, she would be dead.

He knew what Allin would say: "Just so we get her home, Kent, nothing else! People have to think for themselves, first." Yes, she was right. He would keep quiet; anyway, he would give the kidnapers a chance. If she were safe and alive, that would be justification for anything. If she were dead . . .

Then he remembered that there was something courageous and reassuring about that little man. Only he had seemed to know what to do. And anyway, what about those parents who had tried to manage it all themselves? Their children had never come back, either. No, he had better do what he knew he ought to do.

He tramped into the house. Allin was lying upstairs on her bed, her eyes closed.

"Darling," he said gently. Instantly she opened her eyes and sat up. He handed her the paper and sat down on her bed. She lifted miserable eyes to him.

"Twenty-four more hours!" she whispered. "I can't do it, Kent."

"Yes, you can," he said harshly. "You'll do it because you damned well have to." He thought, She can't break now, if I have to whip her! "We've got to wait," he went on. "Is there anything else we can do? Tell Mike O'Brien? Let the newspapers get it and ruin everything?"

She shook her head. "No," she said.

He got up. He longed to take her in his arms, but he did not dare. If this was ever over, he would tell her what he thought of her — how wonderful she was; how brave and game — but he could not now. It was better for them both to stay away from that edge of breaking.

"Get up," he said. "Let's have something to eat. I haven't really eaten all day."

It would be good for her to get up and busy herself. She had not eaten either.

"All right, Kent," she said. "I'll wash my face in cold water and be down."

"I'll be waiting," he replied.

This gave him the moment he had made up his mind he would use — damned if he wouldn't use it! The scoundrels had his money now, and he would take the chance on that queer fellow. He called the number the man had put into his pocket. And almost instantly he heard the fellow's drawl.

"Hello?" the man said.

"This is Kent Crothers," he answered. "I've had that invitation!"

"Yes?" The voice was suddenly alert.

"Twelve tomorrow!"

"Yes? Where? Midnight, of course. They always make it midnight."

"My gardener's house."

"Okay, Mr. Crothers. Go right ahead as if you hadn't told us." The phone clicked.

Kent listened, but there was nothing more. Everything seemed exactly the same, but nothing was the same. This very telephone wire was cut somewhere, by someone. Someone was listening to every word anyone spoke to and from his house. It was sinister and yet reassuring — sinister if you were the criminal.

He heard Allin's step on the stair and went out to meet her. "I have a hunch," he told her, smiling.

"What?" She tried to smile back.

He drew her toward the dining room. "We're going to win," he said.

Within himself he added, If she were still alive, that little heart of his life. Then he put the memory of Betsy's face away from him resolutely.

"I'm going to eat," he declared. "And so must you. We'll beat them tomorrow."

But tomorrow very nearly beat them. Time stood still — there was no making it pass. They filled it full of a score of odd jobs about the house. Lucky for them it was Sunday; luckier that Kent's mother had a cold and telephoned that she and Kent's father would not be over for their usual visit.

They stayed together, a little band of three. By midafternoon Kent had cleaned up everything — a year's odd jobs — and there were hours to go.

They played games with Bruce, and at last it was his suppertime and they put him to bed. Then they sat upstairs in their bedroom again, near the nursery, each with a book.

Sometime, after these hours were over, he would have to think about a lot of things again. But everything had to wait now, until this life ended at midnight. Beyond that no thought could reach.

At eleven he rose. "I'm going now," he said, and stooped to kiss her. She clung to him, and then in an instant they drew apart. In strong accord they knew it was not yet time to give way.

He ran the car as noiselessly as he could and left it at the end of the street, six blocks away. Then he walked past the few tumble-down bungalows, past two empty lots, to Peter's rickety gate. There was no light in the house. He went to the door and knocked softly. He heard Peter's mumble: "Who dat?"

"Let me in, Peter," he called in a low voice. The door opened. "It's I, Peter — Kent Crothers. Let me in. Peter, they're bringing the baby here."

"To mah house? Lemme git de light on."

"No, Peter, no light. I'll just sit down here in the darkness, like this. Only don't lock the door, see? I'll sit by the door. Where's a chair? That's it." He was trembling so that he stumbled into the chair Peter pushed forward.

"Mist' Crothers, suh, will yo' have a drink? Ah got some corn likker."

"Thanks, Peter."

He heard Peter's footsteps shuffling away, and in a moment a tin cup was thrust into his hand. He drank the reeking stuff down. It burned him like indrawn flame, but he felt steadier for it.

"Ain't a thing Ah can do, Mist' Crothers?" Peter's whisper came ghostly out of the darkness.

"Not a thing. Just wait."

"Ah'll wait here, then. Mah ole 'ooman's asleep. Ah'll jest git thrashin' round if Ah go back to bed."

"Yes, only we mustn't talk," Kent whispered back.

"Nosuh."

This was the supremest agony of waiting in all the long agony that this day had been. To sit perfectly still, straining to hear, knowing nothing, wondering . . .

Suppose something went wrong with the man in gray, and they fumbled, and frightened the man who brought Betsy back. Suppose he just sat here waiting and waiting until dawn came. And at home Allin was waiting.

The long day had been nothing to this. He sat reviewing all his life, pondering on the horror of this monstrous situation in which he and

Allin now were. A free country, was it? No one was free when his lips were locked against crime, because he dared not speak lest his child be murdered. If Betsy were dead, if they didn't bring her back, he'd never tell Allin he had telephoned the man in gray. He was still glad he had done it. After all, were respectable men and women to be at the mercy of — but if Betsy were dead, he'd wish he had killed himself before he had anything to do with the fellow!

He sat, his hands interlocked so tightly he felt them grow cold and bloodless and stinging, but he could not move. Someone came down the street roaring out a song.

"Thass a drunk man," Peter whispered.

Kent did not answer. The street grew still again.

And then in the darkness — hours after midnight, it seemed to him — he heard a car come up to the gate and stop. The gate creaked open and then shut, and the car drove away.

"Guide me down the steps," he told Peter.

It was the blackest night he had ever seen. But the stars were shining when he stepped out. Peter pulled him along the path. Then, by the gate, Peter stooped.

"She's here," he said.

And Kent, wavering and dizzy, felt her in his arms again, limp and heavy. "She's warm," he muttered. "That's something."

He carried her into the house, and Peter lighted a candle and held it up. It was she — his little Betsy, her white dress filthy and a man's sweater drawn over her. She was breathing heavily.

"Look lak she done got a dose of sumpin," Peter muttered.

"I must get her home," Kent whispered frantically. "Help me to the car, Peter."

"Yassuh," Peter said, and blew out the candle.

They walked silently down the street, Peter's hand on Kent's arm. When he got Betsy home, he — he —

"Want I should drive you?" Peter was asking him.

"I — maybe you'd better," he replied.

He climbed into the seat with her. She was so fearfully limp. Thank God he could hear her breathing! In a few minutes he would put Betsy into her mother's arms.

"Don't stay, Peter," he said.

"Nosuh," Peter answered.

Allin was at the door, waiting. She opened it and without a word reached for the child. He closed the door behind them.

Then he felt himself grow sick. "I was going to tell you," he gasped, "I didn't know whether to tell you —" He swayed and felt himself fall upon the floor.

Allin was a miracle; Allin was wonderful, a rock of a woman. This tender thing who had endured the torture of these days was at his bedside when he woke next day, smiling, and only a little pale.

"The doctor says you're not to go to work, darling," she told him.

"The doctor?" he repeated.

"I had him last night for both of you — you and Betsy. He won't tell anyone."

"I've been crazy," he said, dazed. "Where is she? How —"

"She's going to be all right," Allin said.

"No, but — you're not telling me!"

"Come in here and see," she replied.

He got up, staggering a little. Funny how his legs had collapsed under him last night! His withers still felt all unstrung.

They went into the nursery. There in her bed she lay, his beloved child. She was more naturally asleep now, and her face bore no other mark than pallor.

"She won't even remember it," Allin said. "I'm glad it wasn't Bruce."

He did not answer. He couldn't think — nothing had to be thought about now.

"Come back to bed, Kent," Allin was saying. "I'm going to bring your breakfast up. Bruce is having his downstairs."

He climbed back into bed, shamefaced at his weakness. "I'll be all right after a little coffee. I'll get up then, maybe."

But his bed felt wonderfully good. He lay back, profoundly grateful to it — to everything. But as long as he lived he would wake up to sweat in the night with memory.

The telephone by his bed rang, and he picked it up. "Hello?" he called.

"Hello, Mr. Crothers," a voice answered. It was the voice of the man in gray. "Say, was the little girl hurt?"

"No!" Kent cried. "She's all right!"

"Fine. Well, I just wanted to tell you we caught the fellow last night."

"You *did!*" Kent leaped up. "No! Why, that's — that's extraordinary."

"We had a cordon around the place for blocks and got him. You'll get your money back, too."

"That — it doesn't seem to matter. Who was he?"

"Fellow named Harry Brown — a young chap in a drugstore."

"I never heard of him!"

"No, he says you don't know him — but his dad went to school with yours, and he's heard a lot of talk about you. His dad's a poor stick, I guess, and got jealous of yours. That's about it, probably. Fellow says he figured you sort of owed him something. Crazy, of course.

"Well, it was an easy case — he wasn't smart, and scared to death, besides. You were sensible about it. Most people ruin their chances with their own fuss. So long, Mr. Crothers. Mighty glad."

The telephone clicked. That was all. Everything was incredible, impossible. Kent gazed around the familiar room. Had this all happened? It had happened, and it was over. This was one of those cases of kidnaping that went on in this mad country, unheard of until they were all over and the criminals arrested.

When he went downstairs he would give the servants their hundred dollars apiece. Mollie had had nothing to do with it, after all. The mystery had dissolved like a mist at morning.

Allin was at the door with her tray. Behind her came Bruce, ready for school. She said, so casually Kent could hardly catch the tremor underneath her voice, "What would you say, darling, if we let Peter walk to school with Bruce today?"

Her eyes pleaded with him: "No? Oughtn't we to? What shall we do?"

Then he thought of something else that indomitable man in gray had said, that man whose name he would never know, one among all those other men trying to keep the law for the nation. "We're a lawless people," the little man had said that day in the car. "If we made a law against paying ransoms, nobody would obey it any more than they did Prohibition. No, when the Americans don't like a law, they break it. And so we still have kidnapers. It's the price you pay for a democracy."

Yes, it was the price. Everybody paid — he and Allin; the child they had so nearly lost; that boy locked up in prison.

"Bruce has to live in his own country," he said. "I guess you can go alone, can't you son?"

"Course I can," Bruce said sturdily.

1938

RAYMOND CHANDLER

....

Red Wind

I

THERE WAS a desert wind blowing that night. It was one of those hot
dry Santa Anas that come down through the mountain passes and curl
your hair and make your nerves jump and your skin itch. On nights like
that every booze party ends in a fight. Meek little wives feel the edge of
the carving knife and study their husbands' necks. Anything can happen. You can even get a full glass of beer at a cocktail lounge.

I was getting one in a flossy new place across the street from the
apartment house where I lived. It had been open about a week and it
wasn't doing any business. The kid behind the bar was in his early twenties and looked as if he had never had a drink in his life.

There was only one other customer, a souse on a bar stool with his
back to the door. He had a pile of dimes stacked neatly in front of him,
about two dollars' worth. He was drinking straight rye in small glasses
and he was all by himself in a world of his own.

I sat farther along the bar and got my glass of beer and said: "You
sure cut the clouds off them, buddy. I will say that for you."

"We just opened up," the kid said. "We got to build up trade. Been in
before, haven't you, mister?"

"Uh-huh."

"Live around here?"

"In the Berglund Apartments across the street," I said. "And the name
is John Dalmas."

"Thanks, mister. Mine's Lew Petrolle." He leaned close to me across
the polished dark bar. "Know that guy?"

"No."

"He ought to go home, kind of. I ought to call a taxi and send him home. He's doing his next week's drinking too soon."

"A night like this," I said. "Let him alone."

"It's not good for him," the kid said, scowling at me.

"Rye!" the drunk croaked, without looking up. He snapped his fingers so as not to disturb his piles of dimes by banging on the bar.

The kid looked at me and shrugged. "Should I?"

"Whose stomach is it? Not mine."

The kid poured him another straight rye and I think he doctored it with water down behind the bar because when he came up with it he looked as guilty as if he'd kicked his grandmother. The drunk paid no attention. He lifted two dimes off his pile with the exact care of a crack surgeon operating on a brain tumor.

The kid came back and put more beer in my glass. Outside the wind howled. Every once in a while it blew the stained-glass swing-door open a few inches. It was a heavy door.

The kid said: "I don't like drunks in the first place and in the second place I don't like them getting drunk in here, and in the third place I don't like them in the first place."

"Warner Brothers could use that," I said.

"They did."

Just then we had another customer. A car squeaked to a stop outside and the swinging door came open. A fellow came in who looked a little in a hurry. He held the door and ranged the place quickly with flat, shiny, dark eyes. He was well set up, dark, good-looking in a narrow-faced, tight-lipped way. His clothes were dark and a white handkerchief peeped coyly from his pocket and he looked cool as well as under a tension of some sort. I guessed it was the hot wind. I felt a bit the same myself only not cool.

He looked at the drunk's back. The drunk was playing checkers with his empty glasses. The new customer looked at me, then he looked along the line of half-booths at the other side of the place. They were all empty. He came on in — down past where the drunk sat swaying and muttering to himself — and spoke to the bar kid.

"Seen a lady in here, buddy? Tall, pretty, brown hair, in a print bolero jacket over a blue crepe silk dress. Wearing a wide-brimmed straw hat with a velvet band." He had a tight voice I didn't like.

"No, sir. Nobody like that's been in," the bar kid said.

"Thanks. Straight Scotch. Make it fast, will you?"

The kid gave it to him and the fellow paid and put the drink down in a gulp and started to go out. He took three or four steps and stopped, facing the drunk. The drunk was grinning. He swept a gun from somewhere so fast that it was just a blur coming out. He held it steady and he didn't look any drunker than I was. The tall dark guy stood quite still and then his head jerked back a little and then he was still again.

A car tore by outside. The drunk's gun was a .22 target automatic, with a large front sight. It made a couple of hard snaps and a little smoke curled — very little.

"So long, Waldo," the drunk said.

Then he put the gun on the barman and me.

The dark guy took a week to fall down. He stumbled, caught himself, waved one arm, stumbled again. His hat fell off, and then he hit the floor with his face. After he hit it he might have been poured concrete for all the fuss he made.

The drunk slid down off the stool and scooped his dimes into a pocket and slid towards the door. He turned sideways, holding the gun across his body. I didn't have a gun. I hadn't thought I needed one to buy a glass of beer. The kid behind the bar didn't move or make the slightest sound.

The drunk felt the door lightly with his shoulder, keeping his eyes on us, then pushed through it backwards. When it was wide a hard gust of air slammed in and lifted the hair of the man on the floor. The drunk said: "Poor Waldo. I bet I made his nose bleed."

The door swung shut. I started to rush it — from long practice in doing the wrong thing. In this case it didn't matter. The car outside let out a roar and when I got onto the sidewalk it was flicking a red smear of tail-light around the nearby corner. I got its license number the way I got my first million.

There were people and cars up and down the block as usual. Nobody acted as if a gun had gone off. The wind was making enough noise to make the hard quick rap of .22 ammunition sound like a slammed door, even if anyone heard it. I went back into the cocktail bar.

The kid hadn't moved, even yet. He just stood with his hands flat on the bar, leaning over a little and looking down at the dark guy's back. The dark guy hadn't moved either. I bent down and felt his neck artery. He wouldn't move — ever.

The kid's face had as much expression as a cut of round steak and was about the same color. His eyes were more angry than shocked.

I lit a cigarette and blew smoke at the ceiling and said shortly: "Get on the phone."

"Maybe he's not dead," the kid said.

"When they use a .22 that means they don't make mistakes. Where's the phone?"

"I don't have one. I got enough expenses without that. Boy, can I kick eight hundred bucks in the face!"

"You own this place?"

"I did till this happened."

He pulled his white coat off and his apron and came around the inner end of the bar. "I'm locking the door," he said, taking keys out.

He went out, swung the door to and jiggled the lock from the outside until the bolt clicked into place. I bent down and rolled Waldo over. At first I couldn't even see where the shots went in. Then I could. A couple of tiny holes in his coat, over his heart. There was a little blood on his shirt.

The drunk was everything you could ask — as a killer.

The prowl-car boys came in about eight minutes. The kid, Lew Petrolle, was back behind the bar by then. He had his white coat on again and he was counting the money in the register and putting it in his pocket and making notes in a little book.

I sat at the edge of one of the half-booths and smoked cigarettes and watched Waldo's face get deader and deader. I wondered who the girl in the print coat was, why Waldo had left the engine of his car running outside, why he was in a hurry, whether the drunk had been waiting for him or just happened to be there.

The prowl-car boys came in perspiring. They were the usual large size and one of them had a flower stuck under his cap and his cap on a bit crooked. When he saw the dead man he got rid of the flower and leaned down to feel Waldo's pulse.

"Seems to be dead," he said, and rolled him around a little more. "Oh yeah, I see where they went in. Nice clean work. You two see him get it?"

I said yes. The kid behind the bar said nothing. I told them about it, that the killer seemed to have left in Waldo's car.

The cop yanked Waldo's wallet out, went through it rapidly and whistled. "Plenty jack and no driver's license." He put the wallet away. "O.K., we didn't touch him, see? Just a chance we could find did he have a car and put it on the air."

"The hell you didn't touch him," Lew Petrolle said.

The cop gave him one of these looks. "O.K., pal," he said softly. "We touched him."

The kid picked up a clean highball glass and began to polish it. He polished it all the rest of the time we were there.

In another minute a homicide fast-wagon sirened up and screeched to a stop outside the door and four men came in, two dicks, a photographer and a laboratory man. I didn't know either of the dicks. You can be in the detecting business a long time and not know all the men on a big city force.

One of them was a short, smooth, dark, quiet, smiling man, with curly black hair and soft intelligent eyes. The other was big, rawboned, long-jawed, with a veined nose and glassy eyes. He looked like a heavy drinker. He looked tough, but he looked as if he thought he was a little tougher than he was. He shooed me into the last booth against the wall and his partner got the kid up front and the bluecoats went out. The fingerprint man and photographer set about their work.

A medical examiner came, stayed just long enough to get sore because there was no phone for him to call the morgue wagon.

The short dick emptied Waldo's pockets and then emptied his wallet and dumped everything into a large handkerchief on a booth table. I saw a lot of currency, keys, cigarettes, another handkerchief, very little else.

The big dick pushed me back into the end of the half-booth. "Give," he said. "I'm Copernik, Detective-Lieutenant."

I put my wallet in front of him. He looked at it, went through it, tossed it back, made a note in a book.

"John Dalmas, huh? A shamus. You here on business?"

"Drinking business," I said. "I live just across the street in the Berglund."

"Know this kid up front?"

"I've been in here once since he opened up."

"See anything funny about him now?"

"No."

"Takes it too light for a young fellow, don't he? Never mind answering. Just tell the story."

I told it — three times. Once for him to get the outline, once for him to get the details and once for him to see if I had it too pat. At the end he said: "This dame interests me. And the killer called the guy Waldo, yet didn't seem to be anyways sure he would be in. I mean, if Waldo wasn't sure the dame would be here, nobody could be sure Waldo would be here."

"That's pretty deep," I said.

He studied me. I wasn't smiling. "Sounds like a grudge job, don't it? Don't sound planned. No getaway except by accident. A guy don't leave his car unlocked much in this town. And the killer works in front of two good witnesses. I don't like that."

"I don't like being a witness," I said. "The pay's too low."

He grinned. His teeth had a freckled look. "Was the killer drunk really?"

"With that shooting? No."

"Me too. Well, it's a simple job. The guy will have a record and he's left plenty prints. Even if we don't have his mug here we'll make him in hours. He had something on Waldo, but he wasn't meeting Waldo tonight. Waldo just dropped in to ask about a dame he had a date with and had missed connections on. It's a hot night and this wind would kill a girl's face. She'd be apt to drop in somewhere to wait. So the killer feeds Waldo two in the right place and scrams and don't worry about you boys at all. It's that simple."

"Yeah," I said.

"It's so simple it stinks," Copernik said.

He took his felt hat off and tousled up his ratty blond hair and leaned his head on his hands. He had a long mean horse face. He got a handkerchief out and mopped it, and the back of his neck and the back of his hands. He got a comb out and combed his hair — he looked worse with it combed — and put his hat back on.

"I was just thinking," I said.

"Yeah? What?"

"This Waldo knew just how the girl was dressed. So he must already have been with her tonight."

"So what? Maybe he had to go to the can. And when he came back she's gone. Maybe she changed her mind about him."

"That's right," I said.

But that wasn't what I was thinking at all. I was thinking that Waldo had described the girl's clothes in a way the ordinary man wouldn't know how to describe them. Printed bolero jacket over blue crepe silk dress. I didn't even know what a bolero jacket was. And I might have said blue dress or even blue silk dress, but never blue crepe silk dress.

After a while two men came with a basket. Lew Petrolle was still polishing his glass and talking to the short dark dick.

We all went down to headquarters.

Lew Petrolle was all right when they checked on him. His father had a grape ranch near Antioch in Contra Costa County. He had given Lew a thousand dollars to go into business and Lew had opened the cocktail bar, neon sign and all, on eight hundred flat.

They let him go and told him to keep the bar closed until they were sure they didn't want to do any more printing. He shook hands all around and grinned and said he guessed the killing would be good for business after all, because nobody believed a newspaper account of any-thing and people would come to him for the story and buy drinks while he was telling it.

"There's a guy won't ever do any worrying," Copernik said, when he was gone. "Over anybody else."

"Poor Waldo," I said. "The prints any good?"

"Kind of smudged," Copernik said sourly. "But we'll get a classifica-tion and teletype it to Washington some time tonight. If it don't click, you'll be in for a day on the steel picture-racks downstairs."

I shook hands with him and his partner, whose name was Ybarra, and left. They didn't know who Waldo was yet either. Nothing in his pockets told.

II

I got back to my street about 9 P.M. I looked up and down the block be-fore I went into the Berglund. The cocktail bar was farther down on the other side, dark, with a nose or two against the glass, but no real crowd. People had seen the law and the morgue wagon, but they didn't know what had happened. Except the boys playing pinball games in the drug-store on the corner. They know everything, except how to hold a job.

The wind was still blowing, oven-hot, swirling dust and torn paper up against the walls.

I went into the lobby of the apartment house and rode the automatic elevator up to the fourth floor. I unwound the doors and stepped out and there was a tall girl standing there waiting for the car.

She had brown wavy hair under a wide-brimmed straw hat with a velvet band and loose bow. She had wide blue eyes and eyelashes that didn't quite reach her chin. She wore a blue dress that might have been crepe silk, simple in lines but not missing any curves. Over it she wore what might have been a print bolero jacket.

I said: "Is that a bolero jacket?"

She gave me a distant glance and made a motion as if to brush a cob-web out of the way.

"Yes. Would you mind — I'm rather in a hurry. I'd like —"

I didn't move. I blocked her off from the elevator. We stared at each other and she flushed very slowly.

"Better not go out on the street in those clothes," I said.

"Why, how dare you —"

The elevator clanked and started down again. I didn't know what she was going to say. Her voice lacked the edgy twang of a beer-parlor frill. It had a soft light sound, like spring rain.

"It's not a make," I said. "You're in trouble. If they come to this floor in the elevator, you have just that much time to get off the hall. First take off the hat and jacket — and snap it up!"

She didn't move. Her face seemed to whiten a little behind the not-too-heavy make-up.

"Cops," I said, "are looking for you. In those clothes. Give me the chance and I'll tell you why."

She turned her head swiftly and looked back along the corridor. With her looks I didn't blame her for trying one more bluff.

"You're impertinent, whoever you are. I'm Mrs. Leroy in Apartment Thirty-one. I can assure you —"

"That you're on the wrong floor," I said. "This is the fourth." The elevator had stopped down below. The sound of doors being wrenched open came up the shaft.

"Off!" I rapped. "Now!"

She switched her hat off and slipped out of the bolero jacket, fast. I grabbed them and wadded them into a mess under my arm. I took her elbow and turned her and we were going down the hall.

"I live in Forty-two. The front one across from yours, just a floor up. Take your choice. Once again — I'm not on the make."

She smoothed her hair with that quick gesture, like a bird preening itself. Ten thousand years of practice behind it.

"Mine," she said, and tucked her bag under her arm and strode down the hall fast. The elevator stopped at the floor below. She stopped when it stopped. She turned and faced me.

"The stairs are back by the elevator shaft," I said gently.

"I don't have an apartment," she said.

"I didn't think you had."

"Are they searching for me?"

"Yes, but they won't start gouging the block stone by stone before tomorrow. And then only if they don't make Waldo."

She stared at me. "Waldo?"

"Oh, you don't know Waldo," I said.

She shook her head slowly. The elevator started down in the shaft again. Panic flicked in her blue eyes like a ripple on water.

"No," she said breathlessly, "but take me out of this hall."

We were almost at my door. I jammed the key in and shook the lock around and heaved the door inward. I reached in far enough to switch lights on. She went in past me like a wave. Sandalwood floated on the air, very faint.

I shut the door, threw my hat into a chair and watched her stroll over to a card table on which I had a chess problem set out that I couldn't solve. Once inside, with the door locked, her panic had left her.

"So you're a chess-player," she said, in that guarded tone, as if she had come to look at my etchings. I wished she had.

We both stood still then and listened to the distant clang of elevator doors and then steps — going the other way.

I grinned, but with strain, not pleasure, went out into the kitchenette and started to fumble with a couple of glasses and then realized I still had her hat and bolero jacket under my arm. I went into the dressing-room behind the wall bed and stuffed them into a drawer, went back out to the kitchenette, dug out some extra fine Scotch and made a couple of highballs.

When I went in with the drinks she had a gun in her hand. It was a small automatic with a pearl grip. It jumped up at me and her eyes were full of horror.

I stopped, with a glass in each hand, and said: "Maybe this hot wind has got you crazy too. I'm a private detective. I'll prove it if you let me."

She nodded slightly and her face was white. I went over slowly and put a glass down beside her, and went back and set mine down and got a card out that had no bent corners. She was sitting down, smoothing one blue knee with her left hand, and holding the gun on the other. I put the card down beside her drink and sat with mine.

"Never let a guy get that close to you," I said. "Not if you mean business. And your safety catch is on."

She flashed her eyes down, shivered, and put the gun back in her bag. She drank half the drink without stopping, put the glass down hard and picked the card up.

"I don't give many people that liquor," I said. "I can't afford to."

Her lips curled. "I supposed you would want money."

"Huh?"

She didn't say anything. Her hand was close to her bag again.

"Don't forget the safety catch," I said. Her hand stopped. I went on: "This fellow I called Waldo is quite tall, say five-eleven, slim, dark, brown eyes with a lot of glitter. Nose and mouth too thin. Dark suit, white handkerchief showing, and in a hurry to find you. Am I getting anywhere?"

She took her glass again. "So that's Waldo," she said. "Well, what about him?" Her voice seemed to have a slight liquor edge now.

"Well, a funny thing. There's a cocktail bar across the street . . . Say, where have you been all evening?"

"Sitting in my car," she said coldly, "most of the time."

"Didn't you see a fuss across the street up the block?"

Her eyes tried to say no and missed. Her lips said: "I knew there was some kind of disturbance. I saw policemen and red searchlights. I supposed someone had been hurt."

"Someone was. And this Waldo was looking for you before that. In the cocktail bar. He described you and your clothes."

Her eyes were set like rivets now and had the same amount of expression. Her mouth began to tremble and kept on trembling.

"I was in there," I said, "talking to the kid that runs it. There was nobody in there but a drunk on a stool and the kid and myself. The drunk wasn't paying any attention to anything. Then Waldo came in and asked about you and we said no, we hadn't seen you and he started to leave."

I sipped my drink. I like an effect as well as the next fellow. Her eyes ate me.

"Just started to leave. Then this drunk that wasn't paying any attention to anyone called him Waldo and took a gun out. He shot him twice —" I snapped my fingers twice — "like that. Dead."

She fooled me. She laughed in my face. "So my husband hired you to spy on me," she said. "I might have known the whole thing was an act. You and your Waldo."

I gawked at her.

"I never thought of him as jealous," she snapped. "Not of a man who had been our chauffeur anyhow. A little about Stan, of course — that's natural. But Joseph Choate —"

I made motions in the air. "Lady, one of us has this book open at the wrong page," I grunted. "I don't know anybody named Stan or Joseph Choate. So help me, I didn't even know you had a chauffeur. People around here don't run to them. As for husbands — yeah, we do have a husband once in a while. Not often enough."

She shook her head slowly and her hand stayed near her bag and her blue eyes had glitters in them.

"Not good enough, Mr. Dalmas. No, not nearly good enough. I know you private detectives. You're all rotten. You tricked me into your apartment, if it is your apartment. More likely it's the apartment of some horrible man who will swear anything for a few dollars. Now you're trying to scare me. So you can blackmail me — as well as get money from my husband. All right," she said breathlessly, "how much do I have to pay?"

I put my empty glass aside and leaned back. "Pardon me if I light a cigarette," I said. "My nerves are frayed."

I lit it while she watched me grimly, no fear — or not enough fear for any real guilt to be under it. "So Joseph Choate is his name," I said. "The guy that killed him in the cocktail bar called him Waldo."

She smiled a bit disgustedly, but almost tolerantly. "Don't stall. How much?"

"Why were you trying to meet this Joseph Choate?"

"I was going to buy something he stole from me, of course. Something that's valuable in the ordinary way too. Almost fifteen thousand dollars. The man I loved gave it to me. He's dead. There! He's dead! He died in a burning plane. Now, go back and tell my husband that, you slimy little rat!"

"Hey, I weigh a hundred and ninety stripped," I yelled.

"You're still slimy," she yelled back. "And don't bother about telling my husband. I'll tell him myself. He probably knows anyway."

I grinned. "That's smart. Just what was I supposed to find out?"

She grabbed her glass and finished what was left of her drink. "So he thinks I'm meeting Joseph," she sneered. "Well, I was. But not to make love. Not with a chauffeur. Not with a bum I picked off the front step and gave a job to. I don't have to dig down that far, if I want to play around."

"Lady," I said, "you don't indeed."

"Now I'm going," she said. "You just try and stop me." She snatched the pearl-handled gun out of her bag.

I grinned and kept on grinning. I didn't move.

"Why you nasty little string of nothing," she stormed. "How do I know you're a private detective at all? You might be a crook. This card you gave me doesn't mean anything. Anybody can have cards printed."

"Sure," I said. "And I suppose I'm smart enough to live here two years because you were going to move in today so I could blackmail you for not meeting a man named Joseph Choate who was bumped off across the street under the name of Waldo. Have you got the money to buy this something that cost fifteen grand?"

"Oh! You think you'll hold me up, I suppose!"

"Oh!" I mimicked her, "I'm a stick-up artist now, am I? Lady, will you please either put that gun away or take the safety catch off? It hurts my professional feelings to see a nice gun made a monkey of that way."

"You're a full portion of what I don't like," she said. "Get out of my way."

I didn't move. She didn't move. We were both sitting down — and not even close to each other.

"Let me in on one secret before you go," I pleaded. "What in hell did you take the apartment down on the floor below for? Just to meet a guy down on the street?"

"Stop being silly," she snapped. "I didn't. I lied. It's his apartment."

"Joseph Choate's?"

She nodded sharply.

"Does my description of Waldo sound like Joseph Choate?"

She nodded sharply again.

"All right. That's one fact learned at last. Don't you realize Waldo described your clothes before he was shot — when he was looking for you — that the description was passed on to the police — that the police don't know who Waldo is — and are looking for somebody in those clothes to help tell them? Don't you get that much?"

The gun suddenly started to shake in her hand. She looked down at it, sort of vacantly, slowly put it back in her bag.

"I'm a fool," she whispered, "to be even talking to you." She stared at me for a long time, then pulled in a deep breath. "He told me where he was staying. He didn't seem afraid. I guess blackmailers are like that. He was to meet me on the street, but I was late. It was full of police when I got here. So I went back and sat in my car for a while. Then I came up to Joseph's apartment and knocked. Then I went back to my car and waited again. I came up here three times in all. The last time I walked up a flight to take the elevator. I had already been seen twice on the third floor. I met you. That's all."

"You said something about a husband," I grunted. "Where is he?"

"He's at a meeting."

"Oh, a meeting," I said nastily.

"My husband's a very important man. He has lots of meetings. He's a hydro-electric engineer. He's been all over the world. I'd have you know —"

"Skip it," I said. "I'll take him to lunch some day and have him tell me himself. Whatever Joseph had on you is dead stock now. Like Joseph."

She believed it at last. I hadn't thought she ever would somehow. "He's really dead?" she whispered. "Really?"

"He's dead," I said. "Dead, dead, dead. Lady, he's dead."

Her face fell apart like a bride's piecrust. Her mouth wasn't large, but I could have got my fist into it at that moment. In the silence the elevator stopped at my floor.

"Scream," I rapped, "and I'll give you two black eyes."

It didn't sound nice, but it worked. It jarred her out of it. Her mouth shut like a trap.

I heard steps coming down the hall. We all have hunches. I put my finger to my lips. She didn't move now. Her face had a frozen look. Her big blue eyes were as black as the shadows below them. The hot wind boomed against the shut windows. Windows have to be shut when a Santa Ana blows, heat or no heat.

The steps that came down the hall were the casual ordinary steps of one man. But they stopped outside my door, and somebody knocked.

I pointed to the dressing-room behind the wall bed. She stood up without a sound, her bag clenched against her side. I pointed again, to her glass. She lifted it swiftly, slid across the carpet, through the door, drew the door quietly shut after her.

I didn't know just what I was going to all this trouble for.

The knocking sounded again. The backs of my hands were wet. I creaked my chair and stood up and made a loud yawning sound. Then I went over and opened the door — without a gun. That was a mistake.

III

I didn't know him at first. Perhaps for the opposite reason Waldo hadn't seemed to know him. He'd had a hat on all the time over at the cocktail bar and he didn't have one on now. His hair ended completely and exactly where his hat would start. Above that line was hard white sweatless skin almost as glaring as scar tissue. He wasn't just twenty years older. He was a different man.

But I knew the gun he was holding, the .22 target automatic with the big front sight. And I knew his eyes. Bright, brittle, shallow eyes like the eyes of a lizard.

He was alone. He put the gun against my face very lightly and said between his teeth: "Yeah, me. Let's go on in."

I backed in just far enough and stopped. Just the way he would want me to, so he could shut the door without moving much. I knew from his eyes that he would want me to do just that.

I wasn't scared. I was paralyzed.

When he had the door shut he backed me some more, slowly, until there was something against the back of my legs. His eyes looked into mine.

"That's a card table," he said. "Some goon here plays chess. You?"

I swallowed. "I don't exactly play it. I just fool around."

"That means two," he said with a kind of hoarse softness, as if some cop had hit him across the windpipe with a blackjack once, in a third-degree session.

"It's a problem," I said. "Not a game. Look at the pieces."

"I wouldn't know."

"Well, I'm alone," I said, and my voice shook just enough.

"It don't make any difference," he said. "I'm washed up anyway. Some nose puts the but on me tomorrow, next week, what the hell? I just didn't like your map, pal. And that smug-faced pansy in the barcoat that played left tackle for Fordham or something. To hell with guys like you guys."

I didn't speak or move. The big front sight raked my cheek lightly, almost caressingly. The man smiled.

"It's kind of good business too," he said. "Just in case. An old con like me don't make good prints — not even when he's lit. And if I don't make good prints all I got against me is two witnesses. The hell with it. You're slammin' off, pal. I guess you know that."

"What did Waldo do to you?" I tried to make it sound as if I wanted to know, instead of just not wanting to shake too hard.

"Stooled on a bank job in Michigan and got me four years. Got himself a nolle prosse. Four years in Michigan ain't no summer cruise. They make you be good in them lifer states."

"How'd you know he'd come in there?" I croaked.

"I didn't. Oh yeah, I was lookin' for him. I was wanting to see him all right. I got a flash of him on the street night before last but I lost him. Up to then I wasn't lookin' for him. Then I was. A cute guy, Waldo. How is he?"

"Dead," I said.

"I'm still good," he chuckled. "Drunk or sober. Well, that don't make no doughnuts for me now. They make me downtown yet?"

I didn't answer him quick enough. He jabbed the gun into my throat and I choked and almost grabbed for it by instinct.

"Naw," he cautioned me softly. "Naw. You ain't that dumb."

I put my hands back, down at my sides, open, the palms towards him. He would want them that way. He hadn't touched me, except with the gun. He didn't seem to care whether I might have one too. He wouldn't — if he just meant the one thing.

He didn't seem to care very much about anything, coming back on that block. Perhaps the hot wind did something to him. It was booming against my shut windows like the surf under a pier.

"They got prints," I said. "I don't know how good."

"They'll be good enough — but not for teletype work. Take 'em airmail time to Washington and back to check 'em right. Tell me why I come here, pal."

"You heard the kid and me talking in the bar. I told him my name, where I lived."

"That's how, pal. I said why." He smiled at me. It was a lousy smile to be the last one you might see.

"Skip it," I said. "The hangman won't ask you to guess why he's there."

"Say, you're tough at that. After you, I visit that kid. I tailed him home from headquarters, but I figure you're the guy to put the bee on first. I tail him home from the city hall, in the rent car Waldo had. From headquarters, pal. Them funny dicks. You can sit in their laps and they don't know you. Start runnin' for a street car and they open up with machine guns and bump two pedestrians, a hacker asleep in his cab, and an old scrubwoman on the second floor workin' a mop. And they miss the guy they're after. Them funny lousy dicks."

He twisted the gun muzzle in my neck. His eyes looked madder than before.

"I got time," he said. "Waldo's rent car don't get a report right away. And they don't make Waldo very soon. I know Waldo. Smart he was. A smooth boy, Waldo."

"I'm going to vomit," I said, "if you don't take that gun out of my throat."

He smiled and moved the gun down to my heart. "This about right? Say when."

I must have spoken louder than I meant to. The door of the dressing-room by the wall bed showed a crack of darkness. Then an inch. Then four inches. I saw eyes, but I didn't look at them. I stared hard into the baldheaded man's eyes. Very hard. I didn't want him to take his eyes off mine.

"Scared?" he asked softly.

I leaned against his gun and began to shake. I thought he would enjoy seeing me shake. The girl came out through the door. She had her gun in her hand again. I was sorry as hell for her. She'd try to make the door — or scream. Either way it would be curtains — for both of us.

"Well, don't take all night about it," I bleated. My voice sounded far away, like a voice on a radio on the other side of a street.

"I like this, pal," he smiled. "I'm like that."

The girl floated in the air, somewhere behind him. Nothing was ever more soundless than the way she moved. It wouldn't do any good, though. He wouldn't fool around with her at all. I had known him all my life but I had been looking into his eyes for only five minutes.

"Suppose I yell," I said.

"Yeah. Suppose you yell. Go ahead and yell," he said, with his killer's smile.

She didn't go near the door. She was right behind him.

"Well — here's where I yell," I said.

As if that was the cue she jabbed the little gun hard into his short ribs, without a single sound.

He had to react. It was like a knee reflex. His mouth snapped open and both his arms jumped out from his sides and he arched his back just a little. The gun was pointing at my right eye.

I sank and kneed him with all my strength, in the groin.

His chin came down and I hit it. I hit it as if I was driving the last spike on the first transcontinental railroad. I can still feel it when I flex my knuckles.

His gun raked the side of my face but it didn't go off. He was already limp. He writhed down gasping his left side against the floor. I kicked his right shoulder — hard. The gun jumped away from him, skidded on the carpet, under a chair. I heard the chessmen tinkling on the floor behind me somewhere.

The girl stood over him, looking down. Then her wide dark horrified eyes came up and fastened on mine.

"That buys me," I said. "Anything I have is yours — now and forever."

She didn't hear me. Her eyes were strained open so hard that the whites showed under the vivid blue iris. She backed quickly to the door with her little gun up, felt behind her for the knob and twisted it. She pulled the door open and slipped out.

The door shut.

She was bareheaded and without her bolero jacket.

She had only the gun, and the safety catch on that was still set so that she couldn't fire it.

It was silent in the room then, in spite of the wind. Then I heard him gasping on the floor. His face had a greenish pallor. I moved behind him and pawed him for more guns, and didn't find any. I got a pair of store cuffs out of my desk and pulled his arms in front of him and snapped them on his wrists. They would hold if he didn't shake them too hard.

His eyes measured me for a coffin, in spite of their suffering. He lay in the middle of the floor, still on his left side, a twisted, wizened, bald-headed little guy with drawn-back lips and teeth spotted with cheap silver fillings. His mouth looked like a black pit and his breath came in little waves, choked, stopped, came on again, limping.

"I'm sorry, guy," I grunted. "What could I do?"

That — to this sort of killer.

I went into the dressing-room and opened the drawer of the chest. Her hat and jacket lay there on my shirts. I put them underneath, at the back, and smoothed the shirts over them. Then I went out to the kitchenette and poured a stiff jolt of whiskey and put it down and stood a moment listening to the hot wind howl against the window glass. A garage door banged, and a power-line wire with too much play between the insulators thumped the side of the building with a sound like somebody beating a carpet.

The drink worked on me. I went back into the living-room and opened a window. The guy on the floor hadn't smelled her sandalwood, but somebody else might.

I shut the window again, wiped the palms of my hands and used the phone to dial headquarters.

Copernik was still there. His smart-aleck voice said: "Yeah? Dalmas? Don't tell me. I bet you got an idea."

"Make that killer yet?"

"We're not saying, Dalmas. Sorry as all hell and so on. You know how it is."

"O.K. I don't care who he is. Just come and get him off the floor of my apartment."

"Holy —" Then his voice hushed and went down low. "Wait a minute, now. Wait a minute." A long way off I seemed to hear a door shut. Then his voice again. "Shoot," he said softly.

"Handcuffed," I said. "All yours. I had to knee him, but he'll be all right. He came here to eliminate a witness."

Another pause. The voice was full of honey. "Now listen, boy, who else is in this with you?"

"Who else? Nobody. Just me."

"Keep it that way, boy. All quiet. O.K.?"

"Think I want all the bums in the neighborhood in here sightseeing?"

"Take it easy, boy. Easy. Just sit tight and sit still. I'm practically there. No touch nothing. Get me?"

"Yeah." I gave him the address and apartment number again to save him time.

I could see his big bony face glisten. I got the .22 target gun from under the chair and sat holding it until feet hit the hallway outside my door and knuckles did a quiet tattoo on the door panel.

Copernik was alone. He filled the doorway quickly, pushed me back into the room with a tight grin and shut the door. He stood with his back to it, his hand under the left side of his coat. A big hard bony man with flat cruel eyes.

He lowered them slowly and looked at the man on the floor. The lad's neck was twitching a little. His eyes moved in short stabs — sick eyes.

"Sure it's the guy?" Copernik's voice was hoarse.

"Positive. Where's Ybarra?"

"Oh, he was busy." He didn't look at me when he said that. "Those your cuffs?"

"Yeah."

"Key."

I tossed it to him. He went down swiftly on one knee beside the killer and took my cuffs off his wrists, tossed them to one side. He got his own off his hip, twisted the bald man's hands behind him and snapped the cuffs on.

"All right, you —" the killer said tonelessly.

Copernik grinned and balled his fist and hit the handcuffed man in the mouth a terrific blow. His head snapped back almost enough to break his neck. Blood dribbled from the lower corner of his mouth.

"Get a towel," Copernik ordered.

I got a hand towel and gave it to him. He stuffed it between the handcuffed man's teeth, viciously, stood up and rubbed his bony fingers through his ratty blond hair.

"All right. Tell it."

I told it — leaving the girl out completely. It sounded a little funny. Copernik watched me, said nothing. He rubbed the side of his veined nose. Then he got his comb out and worked on his hair just as he had done earlier in the evening, in the cocktail bar.

I went over and gave him the gun. He looked at it casually, dropped it into his side pocket. His eyes had something in them and his face moved in a hard bright grin.

I bent down and began picking up my chessmen and dropping them into the box. I put the box on the mantel, straightened out a leg of the card table, played around for a while. All the time Copernik watched me. I wanted him to think something out.

At last he came out with it. "This guy uses a twenty-two," he said. "He uses it because he's good enough to get by with that much gun. That mean's he's good. He knocks at your door, pokes that gat in your belly, walks you back into the room, says he's here to close your mouth for keeps — and yet you take him. You not having any gun. You take him alone. You're kind of good yourself, pal."

"Listen," I said, and looked at the floor. I picked up another chessman and twisted it between my fingers. "I was doing a chess problem," I said. "Trying to forget things."

"You got something on your mind, pal," Copernik said softly. "You wouldn't try to fool an old copper, would you, boy?"

"It's a swell pinch and I'm giving it to you," I said. "What the hell more do you want?"

The man on the floor made a vague sound behind the towel. His bald head glistened with sweat.

"What's the matter, pal? You been up to something?" Copernik almost whispered.

I looked at him quickly, looked away again. "All right," I said. "You know damn well I couldn't take him alone. He had the gun on me and he shoots where he looks."

Copernik closed one eye and squinted at me amiably with the other. "Go on, pal. I kind of thought of that too."

I shuffled around a little more, to make it look good. I said slowly: "There was a kid here who pulled a job over in Boyle Heights, a heist job, and didn't take. A two-bit service station stickup. I know his family. He's not really bad. He was here trying to beg train money off me. When the knock came he sneaked in — there."

I pointed at the wall bed and the door beside. Copernik's head swiveled slowly, swiveled back. His eyes winked again. "And this kid had a gun," he said.

I nodded. "And he got behind him. That takes guts, Copernik. You've got to give the kid a break. You've got to let him stay out of it."

"Tag out for this kid?" Copernik asked softly.

"Not yet, he says. He's scared there will be."

Copernik smiled. "I'm a homicide man," he said. "What you have done, pal?"

I pointed down at the gagged and handcuffed man on the floor. "You took him, didn't you?" I said gently.

Copernik kept on smiling. A big whitish tongue came out and massaged his thick lower lip. "How'd I do it?" he whispered.

"Get the slugs out of Waldo?"

"Sure. Long twenty-twos. One smashed on a rib, one good."

"You're a careful guy. You don't miss any angles. You know anything about me. You dropped in on me to see what guns I had."

Copernik got up and went down on one knee again beside the killer. "Can you hear me, guy?" he asked with his face close to the face of the man on the floor.

The man made some vague sound. Copernik stood up and yawned. "Who the hell cares what he says? Go on, pal."

"You wouldn't expect to find I had anything, but you wanted to look around my place. And while you were mousing around in there" — I pointed to the dressing-room — "and me not saying anything, being a little sore, maybe, a knock came on the door. So he came in. So after a while you sneaked out and took him."

"Ah." Copernik grinned widely, with as many teeth as a horse. "You're on, pal. I socked him and I kneed him and I took him. You didn't have no gun and the guy swiveled on me pretty sharp and I left-hooked him down the backstairs, O.K.?"

"O.K.," I said.

"You'll tell it like that downtown?"

"Yeah," I said.

"I'll protect you, pal. Treat me right and I'll always play ball. Forget about that kid. Let me know if he needs a break."

He came over and held out his hand. I shook it. It was as clammy as a dead fish. Clammy hands and the people who own them make me sick.

"There's just one thing," I said. "This partner of yours — Ybarra. Won't he be a bit sore you didn't bring him along on this?"

Copernik tousled his hair and wiped his hatband with a large yellowish silk handkerchief.

"That guinea?" he sneered. "To hell with him!" He came close to me and breathed in my face. "No mistakes, pal — about that story of ours."

His breath was bad. It would be.

IV

There were just five of us in the chief-of-detective's office when Copernik laid it before them. A stenographer, the chief, Copernik, myself, Ybarra. Ybarra sat on a chair tilted against the side wall. His hat was down over his eyes but their softness loomed underneath, and the small still smile hung at the corners of the cleancut Latin lips. He didn't look directly at Copernik. Copernik didn't look at him at all.

Outside in the corridor there had been photos of Copernik shaking hands with me, Copernik with his hat on straight and his gun in his hand and a stern, purposeful look on his face.

They said they knew who Waldo was, but they wouldn't tell me. I didn't believe they knew, because the chief-of-detectives had a morgue photo of Waldo on his desk. A beautiful job, his hair combed, his tie straight, the light hitting his eyes just right to make them glisten. Nobody would have known it was a photo of a dead man with two bullet holes in his heart. He looked like a dance-hall sheik making up his mind whether to take the blonde or the redhead.

It was about midnight when I got home. The apartment-door was locked and while I was fumbling for my keys a low voice spoke to me out of the darkness.

All it said was: "Please!" but I knew it. I turned and looked at a dark Cadillac coupe parked just off the loading zone. It had no lights. Light from the street touched the brightness of a woman's eyes.

I went over there. "You're a darn fool," I said.

She said: "Get in."

I climbed in and she started the car and drove it a block and a half along Franklin and turned down Kingsley Drive. The hot wind still burned and blustered. A radio lilted from an open, sheltered, side window of an apartment house. There were a lot of parked cars but she found a vacant space behind a small brand-new Packard cabriolet that had the dealer's sticker on the windshield glass. After she'd jockeyed us up to the curb she leaned back in the corner with her gloved hands on the wheel.

She was all in black now, or dark brown, with a small foolish hat. I smelled the sandalwood in her perfume.

"I wasn't very nice to you, was I?" she said.

"All you did was save my life."

"What happened?"

"I called the law and fed a few lies to a cop I don't like and gave him all the credit for the pinch and that was that. That guy you took away from me was the man who killed Waldo."

"You mean — you didn't tell them about me?"

"Lady," I said again, "all you did was save my life. What else do you want done? I'm ready, willing, and I'll try to be able."

She didn't say anything, or move.

"Nobody learned who you are from me," I said. "Incidentally, I don't know myself."

"I'm Mrs. Frank C. Barsaly, Two-twelve Fremont Place. Olympia Two-four-five-nine-six. Is that what you wanted?"

"Thanks," I mumbled, and rolled a dry unlit cigarette around in my fingers. "Why did you come back?" Then I snapped the fingers of my left hand. "The hat and jacket," I said. "I'll go up and get them."

"It's more than that," she said. "I want my pearls."

I might have jumped a little. It seemed as if there had been enough without pearls.

A car tore by down the street going twice as fast as it should. A thin bitter cloud of dust lifted in the street lights and whirled and vanished. The girl ran the window up quickly against it.

"All right," I said. "Tell me about the pearls. We have had a murder and a mystery woman and a mad killer and a heroic rescue and a police detective framed into making a false report. Now we will have pearls. All right — feed it to me."

"I was to buy them for five thousand dollars. From the man you call Waldo and I call Joseph Choate. He should have had them."

"No pearls," I said. "I saw what came out of his pockets. A lot of money but no pearls."

"Could they be hidden in his apartment?"

"Yes," I said. "So far as I know he could have had them hidden anywhere in California except in his pockets. How's Mr. Barsaly this hot night?"

"He's still downtown at his meeting. Otherwise I couldn't have come."

"Well, you could have brought him," I said. "He could have sat in the rumble seat."

"Oh, I don't know," she said. "Frank weighs two hundred pounds and he's pretty solid. I don't think he would like to sit in the rumble seat, Mr. Dalmas."

"What the hell are we talking about, anyway?"

She didn't answer. Her gloved hands tapped lightly, provokingly on the rim of the slender wheel. I threw the unlit cigarette out the window, turned a little and took hold of her.

I was shaking when I let go of her. She pulled as far away from me as she could against the side of the car and rubbed the back of her glove against her mouth. I sat quite still.

We didn't speak for some time. Then she said very slowly: "I meant you to do that. But I wasn't always that way. It's only been since Stan Phillips was killed in his plane. If it hadn't been for that, I'd be Mrs. Phillips now. Stan gave me the pearls. They cost fifteen thousand dollars, he said once. White pearls, forty-one of them, the largest about a third of an inch across. I don't know how many grains. I never had them appraised or showed them to a jeweler, so I don't know those things. But I loved them on Stan's account. I loved Stan. The way you do just the one time. Can you understand?"

"What's your first name?" I asked.

"Lola."

"Go on talking, Lola." I got another dry cigarette out of my pocket and fumbled it between my fingers just to give them something to do.

"They had a simple silver clasp in the shape of a two-bladed propeller. There was one small diamond where the boss would be. That was because I told Frank they were store pearls I had bought myself. He didn't know the difference. It's not so easy to tell, I dare say. You see — Frank is pretty jealous."

In the darkness she came closer to me and her side touched my side. But I didn't move this time. The wind howled and the trees shook. I kept on rolling the cigarette around in my fingers.

"I suppose you've read that story," she said. "About the wife and the real pearls and her telling her husband —"

"I've read it," I said.

"I hired Joseph. My husband was in Argentina at the time. I was pretty lonely."

"*You* should be lonely," I said.

"Joseph and I went driving a good deal. Sometimes we had a drink or two together. But that's all. I don't go around —"

"You told him about the pearls," I snarled. "And when your two hundred pounds of beef came back from Argentina and kicked him out — he took the pearls, because he knew they were real. And then offered them back to you for five grand."

"Yes," she said simply. "Of course I didn't want to go to the police. And of course in the circumstance Joseph wasn't afraid of my knowing where he lived."

"Poor Waldo," I said. "I feel kind of sorry for him. It was a hell of a time to run into an old friend that had a down on you."

I struck a match on my shoe sole and lit the cigarette. The tobacco was so dry from the hot wind that it burned like grass. The girl sat quietly beside me, her hands on the wheel again.

"Hell with women — these fliers," I said. "And you're still in love with him, or think you are. Where did you keep the pearls?"

"In a Russian malachite jewelry box on my dressing-table. With some other costume jewelry. I had to, if I ever wanted to wear them."

"And they were worth fifteen grand. And you think Joseph might have hidden them in his apartment. Thirty-one, wasn't it?"

"Yes," she said. "I guess it's a lot to ask."

I opened the door and got out of the car. "I've been paid," I said. "I'll go look. The doors in my apartment house are not very obstinate. The cops will find out where Waldo lived when they publish his photo, but not tonight, I guess."

"It's awfully sweet of you," she said. "Shall I wait here?"

I stood with a foot on the running-board, leaning in, looking at her. I didn't answer her question. I just stood there looking in at the shine of her eyes. Then I shut the car door and walked up the street towards Franklin.

Even with the wind shriveling my face I could still smell the sandalwood in her hair. And feel her lips.

I unlocked the Berglund door, walked through the silent lobby to the elevator, and rode up to 3. Then I soft-footed along the silent corridor and peered down at the sill of Apartment 31. No light. I rapped — the old light, confidential tattoo of the bootlegger with the big smile and the extra-deep hip pockets. No answer. I took the piece of thick hard celluloid that pretended to be a window over the driver's license in my wallet, and eased it between the lock and the jamb, leaning hard on the knob, pushing it toward the hinges. The edge of the celluloid caught the slope of the spring lock and snapped it back with a small brittle sound, like an icicle breaking. The door yielded and I went into near darkness. Street light filtered in and touched a high spot here and there.

I shut the door and snapped the light on and just stood. There was a queer smell in the air. I made it in a moment — the smell of dark-cured tobacco. I prowled over to a smoking-stand by the window and looked down at four brown butts — Mexican or South American cigarettes.

Upstairs, on my floor, feet hit the carpet and somebody went into a bathroom. I heard the toilet flush. I went into the bathroom of Apartment 31. A little rubbish, nothing, no place to hide anything. The kitchenette was a longer job, but I only half searched. I knew there were no pearls in that apartment. I knew Waldo had been on his way out and that he was in a hurry and that something was riding him when he turned and took two bullets from an old friend.

I went back to the living-room and swung the wall bed and looked past its mirror side into the dressing-room for signs of still current occupancy. Swinging the bed farther I was no longer looking for pearls. I was looking at a man.

He was small, middle-aged, iron-gray at the temples, with a very dark skin, dressed in a fawn-colored suit with a wine-colored tie. His neat little brown hands hung limply by his sides. His small feet, in pointed polished shoes, pointed almost at the floor.

He was hanging by a belt around his neck from the metal top of the bed. His tongue stuck out farther than I thought it possible for a tongue to stick out.

He swung a little and I didn't like that, so I pulled the bed down and he nestled quietly between the two clamped pillows. I didn't touch him yet. I didn't have to touch him to know that he would be cold as ice.

I went around him into the dressing-room and used my handkerchief on drawer-knobs. The place was stripped clean except for the light litter of a man living alone.

I came out of there and began on the man. No wallet. Waldo would have taken that and ditched it. A flat box of cigarettes, half full, stamped in gold: "Louis Tapia y Cia, Calle de Paysand, 19, Montevideo." Matches from the Spezzia Club. An under-arm holster of dark grained leather and in it a 9 millimeter Mauser.

The Mauser made him a professional, so I didn't feel so badly. But not a very good professional, or bare hands would not have finished him, with the Mauser — a gun you can blast through a wall with — undrawn in his shoulder holster.

I made a little sense of it, not much. Four of the brown cigarettes had been smoked, so there had been either waiting or discussion. Somewhere along the line Waldo had got the little man by the throat and held him in just the right way to make him pass out in a matter of seconds. The Mauser had been less useful to him than a toothpick. Then Waldo had hung him up by the strap, probably dead already. That would account for haste, for cleaning out the apartment, for Waldo's anxiety about the girl. It would account for the car left unlocked outside the cocktail bar.

That is, it would account for these things if Waldo had killed him, if this was really Waldo's apartment — if I wasn't just being kidded.

I examined some more pockets. In the left trouser one I found a gold penknife, some silver. In the left hip pocket a handkerchief, folded, scented. On the right hip another, unfolded but clean. In the right leg pocket four or five tissue handkerchiefs. A clean little guy. He didn't like to blow his nose on his handkerchief. Under these there was a small new keytainer holding four new keys — car keys. Stamped in gold on the keytainer was: Compliments of R. K. Vogelsang, Inc. "The Packard House."

I put everything as I had found it, swung the bed back, used my handkerchief on knobs and other projections, and flat surfaces, killed the light and poked my nose out the door. The hall was empty. I went down to the street and around the corner to Kingsley Drive. The Cadillac hadn't moved.

I opened the car door and leaned on it. She didn't seem to have moved, either. It was hard to see any expression on her face. Hard to see anything but her eyes and chin, but not hard to smell the sandalwood.

"That perfume," I said, "would drive a deacon nuts . . . no pearls."

"Well — thanks for trying," she said in a low, soft, vibrant voice. "I guess I can stand it. Shall I . . . Do we . . . Or . . . ?"

"You go on home now," I said. "And whatever happens you never saw me before. Whatever happens. Just as you may never see me again."

"I'd hate —"

"Good luck, Lola." I shut the car door and stepped back.

The lights blazed on, the motor turned over. Against the wind at the corner the big coupe made a slow contemptuous turn and was gone. I stood there by the vacant space at the curb where it had been.

It was quite dark there now. Windows had become blanks in the apartment where the radio sounded. I stood looking at the back of a Packard cabriolet which seemed to be brand new. I had seen it before — before I went upstairs, in the same place, in front of Lola's car. Parked, dark, silent, with a blue sticker pasted to the right-hand corner of the shiny windshield.

And in my mind I was looking at something else, a set of brand-new car keys in a keytainer stamped, "The Packard House," upstairs, in a dead man's pocket.

I went up to the front of the cabriolet and put a small pocket flash on the blue slip. It was the same dealer all right. Written in ink below his name and slogan was a name and address — Eugenie Kolchenko, 5315 Arvieda Street, West Los Angeles.

It was crazy. I went back up to Apartment 31, jimmied the door as I had done before, stepped in behind the wall bed and took the keytainer from the trousers pocket of the neat brown dangling corpse. I was back down on the street beside the cabriolet in five minutes. The keys fitted.

V

It was a small house, near a canyon rim out beyond Sawtelle, with a circle of writhing eucalyptus trees in front of it. Beyond that, on the other side of the street, one of those parties was going on where they come out and smash bottles on the sidewalk with a whoop like Yale making a touchdown against Princeton.

There was a wire fence at my number and some rose-trees, and a flagged walk and a garage that was wide open and had no car in it. There was no car in front of the house either. I rang the bell. There was a long wait, then the door opened rather suddenly.

I wasn't the man she had been expecting. I could see it in her glittering kohl-rimmed eyes. Then I couldn't see anything in them. She just stood and looked at me, a long, lean, hungry brunette, with rouged cheekbones, thick black hair parted in the middle, a mouth made for three-decker sandwiches, coral-and-gold pajamas, sandals — and gilded toenails. Under her ear lobes a couple of miniature temple bells gonged lightly in the breeze. She made a slow disdainful motion with a cigarette in a holder as long as a baseball bat.

"We-el, what ees it, little man? You want sometheeng? You are lost from the bee-ootiful party across the street, hein?"

"Ha, ha," I said. "Quite a party, isn't it? No. I just brought your car home. Lost it, didn't you?"

Across the street somebody had delirium tremens in the front yard and a mixed quartet tore what was left of the night into small strips and did what they could to make the strips miserable. While this was going on the exotic brunette didn't move more than one eyelash.

She wasn't beautiful, she wasn't even pretty, but she looked as if things would happen where she was.

"You have said what?" she got out, at last, in a voice as silky as a burnt crust of toast.

"Your car." I pointed over my shoulder and kept my eyes on her. She was the type that uses a knife.

The long cigarette holder dropped very slowly to her side and the cigarette fell out of it. I stamped it out, and that put me in the hall. She backed away from me and I shut the door.

The hall was like the long hall of a railroad flat. Lamps glowed pinkly in iron brackets. There was a bead curtain at the end, a tiger skin on the floor. The place went with her.

"You're Miss Kolchenko?" I asked, not getting any more action.

"Ye-es. I am Mees Kolchenko. What thee 'ell you want?"

She was looking at me now as if I had come to wash the windows, but at an inconvenient time.

I got a card out with my left hand, held it out to her. She read it in my hand, moving her head just enough. "A detective?" she breathed.

"Yeah."

She said something in a spitting language. Then in English: "Come in! Thees damn wind dry up my skeen like so much teessue paper."

"We're in," I said. "I just shut the door. Snap out of it, Nazimova. Who was he? The little guy?"

Beyond the bead curtain a man coughed. She jumped as if she had been stuck with an oyster fork. Then she tried to smile. It wasn't very successful.

"A reward," she said softly. "You weel wait 'ere? Ten dollars it is fair to pay, no?"

"No," I said.

I reached a finger towards her slowly and added: "He's dead."

She jumped about three feet and let out a yell.

A chair creaked harshly. Feet pounded beyond the bead curtain, a large hand plunged into view and snatched it aside, and a big hard-looking blond man was with us. He had a purple robe over his pajamas.

His right hand held something in his robe pocket. He stood quite still as soon as he was through the curtain, his feet planted solidly, his jaw out, his colorless eyes like gray ice. He looked like a man who would be hard to take out on an off-tackle play.

"What's the matter, honey?" He had a solid, burring voice, with just the right sappy tone to belong to a guy who would go for a woman with gilded toenails.

"I came about Miss Kolchenko's car," I said.

"Well, you could take your hat off," he said. "Just for a light workout."

I took it off and apologized.

"O.K.," he said, and kept his right hand shoved down hard in the purple pocket. "So you came about Miss Kolchenko's car. Take it from there."

I pushed past the woman and went closer to him. She shrank back against the wall and flattened her palms against it. Camille in a high-school play. The long holder lay empty at her toes.

When I was six feet from the big man he said easily: "I can hear you from there. Just take it easy. I've got a gun in this pocket and I've had to learn to use one. Now about the car?"

"The man who borrowed it couldn't bring it," I said, and pushed the card I was still holding towards his face. He barely glanced at it. He looked back at me.

"So what?" he said.

"Are you always this tough?" I asked, "or only when you have your pajamas on?"

"So why couldn't he bring it himself?" he asked. "And skip the mushy talk."

The dark woman made a stuffed sound at my elbow.

"It's all right, honeybunch," the man said. "I'll handle this. Go on in."

She slid past both of us and flicked through the bead curtain.

I waited a little while. The big man didn't move a muscle. He didn't look any more bothered than a toad in the sun.

"He couldn't bring it because somebody bumped him off," I said. "Let's see you handle that."

"Yeah?" he said. "Did you bring him with you to prove it?"

"No," I said. "But if you put your tie and crush hat on, I'll take you down and show you."

"Who the hell did you say you were, now?"

"I didn't say. I thought maybe you could read." I held the card at him some more.

"Oh, that's right," he said. "John Dalmas, Private Investigator. Well, well. So I should go with you to look at who, why?"

"Maybe he stole the car," I said.

The big man nodded. "That's a thought. Maybe he did. Who?"

"The little brown guy who had the keys to it in his pocket, and had it parked around the corner from the Berglund Apartments."

He thought that over, without any apparent embarrassment. "You've got something there," he said. "Not much. But a little. I guess this must be the night of the Police Smoker. So you're doing all their work for them."

"Huh?"

"The card says private detective to me," he said. "Have you got some cops outside that were too shy to come in?"

"No, I'm alone."

He grinned. The grin showed white ridges in his tanned skin. "So you find somebody dead and take some keys and find a car and come riding out here — all alone. No cops. Am I right?"

"Correct."

He sighed. "Let's go inside," he said. He yanked the bead curtain aside and made an opening for me to go through. "It might be you have an idea I ought to hear."

I went past him and he turned, keeping his heavy pocket towards me. I hadn't noticed until I got quite close that there were beads of sweat on his face. It might have been the hot wind, but I didn't think so.

We were in the living-room of the house.

We sat down and looked at each other across a dark floor, on which a few Navajo rugs and a few dark Turkish rugs made a decorating combination with some well-used over-stuffed furniture. There was a fireplace, a small baby grand, a Chinese screen, a tall Chinese lantern on a teakwood pedestal, and gold net curtains against lattice windows. The windows to the south were open. A fruit tree with a white-washed trunk whipped about outside the screen, adding its bit to the noise from across the street.

The big man eased back into a brocaded chair and put his slippered feet on a footstool. He kept his right hand where it had been since I met him — on his gun.

The brunette hung around in the shadows and a bottle gurgled and her temple bells gonged in her ears.

"It's all right, honeybunch," the man said. "It's all under control.

Somebody bumped somebody off and this lad thinks we're interested.
Just sit down and relax."

The girl tilted her head and poured half a tumbler of whisky down
her throat. She sighed, said, "Goddam," in a casual voice, and curled up
on a davenport. It took all of the davenport. She had plenty of legs. Her
gilded toenails winked at me from the shadowy corner where she kept
herself quiet from then on.

I got a cigarette out without being shot at, lit it and went into my
story. It wasn't all true, but some of it was. I told them about the
Berglund Apartments and that I had lived there and that Waldo was living there in Apartment 31 on the floor below mine and that I had been
keeping an eye on him for business reasons.

"Waldo what?" the blond man put in. "And what business reasons?"

"Mister," I said, "have you no secrets?" He reddened slightly.

I told him about the cocktail lounge across the street from the Berglund and what had happened there. I didn't tell him about the printed
bolero jacket or the girl who had worn it. I left her out of the story altogether.

"It was an undercover job — from my angle," I said. "If you know
what I mean." He reddened again, bit his teeth. I went on: "I got back
from the city hall without telling anybody I knew Waldo. In due time,
when I decided they couldn't find out where he lived that night, I took
the liberty of examining his apartment."

"Looking for what?" the big man said thickly.

"For some letters. I might mention in passing there was nothing
there at all — except a dead man. Strangled and hanging by a belt to the
top of the wall bed — well out of sight. A small man, about forty-five,
Mexican or South American, well-dressed in a fawn-colored —"

"That's enough," the big man said. "I'll bite, Dalmas. Was it a blackmail job you were on?"

"Yeah. The funny part was this little brown man had plenty of gun
under his arm."

"He wouldn't have five hundred bucks in twenties in his pocket, of
course? Or are you saying?"

"He wouldn't. But Waldo had over seven hundred in currency when
he was killed in the cocktail bar."

"Looks like I underrated this Waldo," the big man said calmly. "He
took my guy and his payoff money, gun and all. Waldo have a gun?"

"Not on him."

"Get us a drink, honeybunch," the big man said. "Yes, I certainly did sell this Waldo person shorter than a bargain-counter shirt."

The brunette unwound her legs and made two drinks with soda and ice. She took herself another gill without trimmings, wound herself back on the davenport. Her big glittering black eyes watched me solemnly.

"Well, here's how," the big man said, lifting his glass in salute. "I haven't murdered anybody, but I've got a divorce suit on my hands from now on. You haven't murdered anybody, the way you tell it, but you laid an egg down at police headquarters. What the hell! Life's a lot of trouble, anyway you look at it. I've still got honeybunch, here. She's a white Russian I met in Shanghai. She's safe as a vault and she looks as if she would cut your throat for a nickel. That's what I like about her. You get the glamour without the risk."

"You talk damn foolish," the girl spat at him.

"You look O.K. to me," the big man went on ignoring her. "That is, for a keyhole peeper. Is there an out?"

"Yeah. But it will cost a little money."

"I expected that. How much?"

"Say another five hundred."

"Goddam, thees hot wind make me dry like the ashes of love," the Russian girl said bitterly.

"Five hundred might do," the blond man said. "What do I get for it?"

"If I swing it — you get left out of the story. If I don't — you don't pay."

He thought it over. His face looked lined and tired now. The small beads of sweat twinkled in his short blond hair.

"This murder will make you talk," he grumbled. "The second one, I mean. And I don't have what I was going to buy. And if it's a hush, I'd rather buy it direct."

"Who was the little brown man?" I asked.

"Name's Leon Valesanos, a Uruguayan. Another of my importations. I'm in a business that takes me a lot of places. He was working in the Spezzia Club in Chiseltown — you know, the strip of Sunset next to Beverly Hills. Working on roulette, I think. I gave him the five hundred to go down to this — this Waldo — and buy back some bills for stuff Miss Kolchenko had charged to my account and delivered here. That wasn't bright, was it? I had them in my brief case and this Waldo got a chance to steal them. What's your hunch about what happened?"

I sipped my drink and looked at him down my nose. "Your Uruguayan pal probably talked cut and Waldo didn't listen good. Then the little guy thought maybe that Mauser might help his argument — and Waldo was too quick for him. I wouldn't say Waldo was a killer — not by intention. A blackmailer seldom is. Maybe he lost his temper and maybe he just held on to the little guy's neck too long. Then he had to take it on the lam. But he had another date, with more money coming up. And he worked the neighborhood looking for the party. And accidentally he ran into a pal who was hostile enough and drunk enough to blow him down."

"There's a hell of a lot of coincidence in all this business," the big man said.

"It's the hot wind," I grinned. "Everybody's screwy tonight."

"For the five hundred you guarantee nothing? If I don't get my cover-up, you don't get your dough. Is that it?"

"That's it," I said, smiling at him.

"Screwy is right," he said, and drained his highball. "I'm taking you up on it."

"There are just two things," I said softly, leaning forward in my chair. "Waldo had a getaway car parked outside the cocktail bar where he was killed, unlocked with the motor running. The killer took it. There's always the chance of a kickback from that direction. You see, all Waldo's stuff must have been in that car."

"Including my bills and your letters."

"Yeah. But the police are reasonable about things like that — unless you're good for a lot of publicity. If you're not, I think I can eat some stale dog downtown and get by. If you are — that's the second thing. What did you say your name was?"

The answer was a long time coming. When it came I didn't get as much kick out of it as I thought I would. All at once it was too logical.

"Frank C. Barsaly," he said.

After a while the Russian girl called me a taxi. When I left the party across the street was still doing all that a party could do. I noticed the walls of the house were still standing. That seemed a pity.

VI

When I unlocked the glass entrance door of the Berglund I smelled policeman. I looked at my wrist watch. It was nearly 3 A.M. In the dark corner of the lobby a man dozed in a chair with a newspaper over his face. Large feet stretched out before him. A corner of the paper lifted an inch, dropped again. The man made no other movement.

I went on along the hall to the elevator and rode up to my floor. I soft-footed along the hallway, unlocked my door, pushed it wide and reached in for the light-switch.

A chain-switch tinkled and light glared from a standing-lamp by the easy chair, beyond the card table on which my chessmen were still scattered.

Copernik sat there with a stiff unpleasant grin on his face. The short dark man, Ybarra, sat across the room from him, on my left, silent, half-smiling as usual.

Copernik showed more of his big yellow horse teeth and said: "Hi. Long time no see. Been out with the girls?"

I shut the door and took my hat off and wiped the back of my neck slowly, over and over again. Copernik went on grinning. Ybarra looked at nothing with his soft dark eyes.

"Take a seat, pal," Copernik drawled. "Make yourself to home. We got pow-wow to make. Boy, do I hate this night sleuthing. Did you know you were all out of hooch?"

"I could have guessed it," I said. I leaned against the wall.

Copernik kept on grinning. "I always did hate private dicks," he said, "but I never had a chance to twist one like I got tonight."

He reached down lazily beside his chair and picked up a printed bolero jacket, tossed it on the card table. He reached down again and put a wide-brimmed hat beside it.

"I bet you look cuter than all hell with these on," he said.

I took hold of a straight chair, twisted it around and straddled it, leaned my folded arms on the chair and looked at Copernik.

He got up very slowly — with an elaborate slowness, walked across the room and stood in front of me smoothing his coat down. Then he lifted his open right hand and hit me across the face with it — hard. It stung but I didn't move.

Ybarra looked at the wall, looked at the floor, looked at nothing.

"Shame on you, pal," Copernik said lazily. "The way you was taking care of this nice exclusive merchandise. Wadded down behind your old shirts. You punk peepers always did make me sick."

He stood there over me for a moment. I didn't move or speak. I looked into his glazed drinker's eyes. He doubled a fist at his side, then shrugged and turned and went back to the chair.

"O.K.," he said. "The rest will keep. Where did you get these things?"

"They belong to a lady."

"Do tell. They belong to a lady. Ain't you the lighthearted — ! I'll tell you what lady they belong to. They belong to the lady a guy named Waldo asked about in a bar across the street — about two minutes before he got shot kind of dead. Or would that have slipped your mind?"

I didn't say anything.

"You was curious about her yourself," Copernik sneered on. "But you were smart, pal. You fooled me."

"That wouldn't make me smart," I said.

His face twisted suddenly and he started to get up. Ybarra laughed, suddenly and softly, almost under his breath. Copernik's eyes swung on him, hung there. Then he faced me again, blank-eyed.

"The guinea likes you," he said. "He thinks you're good."

The smile left Ybarra's face, but no expression took its place. No expression at all.

Copernik said: "You knew who the dame was all the time. You knew who Waldo was and where he lived. Right across the hall a floor below you. You knew this Waldo person had bumped a guy off and started to lam; only this broad came into his plans somewhere and he was anxious to meet up with her before he went away. Only he never got the chance. A heist guy from back East named Al Tessilore took care of that by taking care of Waldo. So you met the gal and hid her clothes and sent her on her way and kept your trap glued. That's the way guys like you make your beans. Am I right?"

"Yeah," I said. "Except that I only knew these things very recently. Who was Waldo?"

Copernik bared his teeth at me. Red spots burned high on his sallow cheeks. Ybarra, looking down at the floor, said very softly: "Waldo Ratigan. We got him from Washington by teletype. He was a two-bit porch-climber with a few small terms on him. He drove a car in a bank stickup job in Detroit. He turned the gang in later and got a nolle prosse. One of the gang was this Al Tessilore. He hasn't talked a word, but we think the meeting across the street was purely accidental."

Ybarra spoke in the soft quiet modulated voice of a man for whom sounds have a meaning. I said: "Thanks, Ybarra. Can I smoke — or would Copernik kick it out of my mouth?"

Ybarra smiled suddenly. "You may smoke, sure," he said.

"The guinea likes you all right," Copernik jeered. "You never know what a guinea will like, do you?"

I lit a cigarette. Ybarra looked at Copernik and said very softly, "The word guinea — you overwork it. I don't like it so well applied to me."

"The hell with what you like, guinea."

Ybarra smiled a little more. "You are making a mistake," he said. He took a pocket nailfile out and began to use it, looking down.

Copernik blared: "I smelled something rotten on you from the start, Dalmas. So when we make these two mugs, Ybarra and me think we'll drift over and dabble a few more words with you. I bring one of Waldo's morgue photos — nice work, the light just right in his eyes, his tie all straight and a white handkerchief showing just right in his pocket. Nice work. So on the way up, just as a matter of routine, we rout out the manager here and let him lamp it. And he knows the guy. He's here as A. B. Hummel, Apartment Thirty-one. So we go in there and find a stiff. Then we go round and round with that. Nobody knows him yet, but he's got some swell finger bruises under that strap and I hear they fit Waldo's fingers very nicely."

"That's something," I said. "I thought maybe I murdered him."

Copernik stared at me for a long time. His face had stopped grinning and was just a hard brutal face now. "Yeah. We got something else even," he said. "We got Waldo's getaway car — and what Waldo had in it to take with him."

I blew cigarette smoke jerkily. The wind pounded the shut windows. The air in the room was foul.

"Oh we're bright boys," Copernik sneered. "We never figured you with that much guts. Take a look at this."

He plunged his bony hand into his coat pocket and drew something up slowly over the edge of the card table, drew it along the green top and left it there stretched out, gleaming. A string of white pearls with a clasp like a two-bladed propeller. They shimmered softly in the thick smoky air.

Lola Barsaly's pearls. The pearls the flier had given her. The guy who was dead, the guy she still loved.

I stared at them, but I didn't move. After a long moment, Copernik said almost gravely: "Nice, ain't they? Would you feel like telling us a story about now, Mis-ter Dalmas?"

I stood up and pushed the chair from under me, walked slowly across the room and stood looking down at the pearls. The largest was perhaps a third of an inch across. They were pure white, iridescent, with a mellow softness. I lifted them slowly off the card table from beside her clothes. They felt heavy, smooth, fine.

"Nice," I said. "A lot of the trouble was about these. Yeah, I'll talk now. They must be worth a lot of money."

Ybarra laughed behind me. It was a very gentle laugh. "About a hundred dollars," he said. "They're good phonies — but they're phoney."

I lifted the pearls again. Copernik's glassy eyes gloated at me. "How do you tell?" I asked.

"I know pearls," Ybarra said. "These are good stuff, the kind women very often have made on purpose, as a kind of insurance. But they are slick like glass. Real pearls are gritty between the edges of the teeth. Try."

I put two or three of them between my teeth and moved my teeth back and forth, then sideways. Not quite biting them. The beads were hard and slick.

"Yes. They are very good," Ybarra said. "Seven even have little waves and flat spots, as real pearls might have."

"Would they cost fifteen grand — if they were real?" I asked.

"Si. Probably. That's hard to say. It depends on a lot of things."

"This Waldo wasn't so bad," I said.

Copernik stood up quickly, but I didn't see him swing. I was still looking down at the pearls. His fist caught me on the side of the face, against the molars. I tasted blood at once. I staggered back and made it look like a worse blow than it was.

"Sit down and talk, you — !" Copernik almost whispered.

I sat down and used a handkerchief to pat my cheek. I licked at the cut inside my mouth. Then I got up again and went over and picked up the cigarette he had knocked out of my mouth. I crushed it out in a tray and sat down again.

Ybarra filed at his nails and held one up against the lamp. There were beads of sweat on Copernik's eyebrows, at the inner ends.

"You found the beads in Waldo's car," I said, looking at Ybarra. "Find any papers?"

He shook his head without looking up.

"I'd believe *you*," I said. "Here it is. I never saw Waldo until he stepped into the cocktail bar tonight and asked about the girl. I knew nothing I didn't tell. When I got home and stepped out of the elevator this girl, in the printed bolero jacket and the wide hat and the blue silk crepe dress — all as he had described them — was waiting for the elevator, here, on my floor. And she looked like a nice girl."

Copernik laughed jeeringly. It didn't make any difference to me. I had him cold. All he had to do was know that. He was going to know it now, very soon.

"I knew what she was up against as a police witness," I said. "And I suspected there was something else to it. But I didn't suspect for a minute that there was anything wrong with her. She was just a nice girl in a jam — and she didn't even know she was in a jam. I got her in here. She pulled a gun on me. But she didn't mean to use it."

Copernik sat up very suddenly and he began to lick his lips. His face had a stony look now. A look like wet gray stone. He didn't make a sound.

"Waldo had been her chauffeur," I went on. "His name then was Joseph Choate. Her name is Mrs. Frank C. Barsaly. Her husband is a big hydro-electric engineer. Some guy gave her the pearls once and she told her husband they were just store pearls. Waldo got wise somehow there was a romance behind them and when Barsaly come home from South America and fired him, because he was too good-looking, he lifted the pearls."

Ybarra lifted his head suddenly and his teeth flashed. "You mean he didn't know they were phony?"

"I thought he fenced the real ones and had imitations fixed up," I said.

Ybarra nodded. "It's possible."

"He lifted something else," I said. "Some stuff from Barsaly's briefcase that showed he was keeping a woman — out in Brentwood. He was blackmailing wife and husband both, without either knowing about the other. Get it so far?"

"I get it," Copernik said harshly, between his tight lips. His face was still wet gray stone. "Get the hell on with it."

"Waldo wasn't afraid of them," I said. "He didn't conceal where he lived. That was foolish, but it saved a lot of finagling, if he was willing to risk it. The girl came down here tonight with five grand to buy back her pearls. She never met Waldo. She came up here to look for him and walked up a floor before she went back down. A woman's idea of being cagey. So I met her. So I brought her in here. So she was in that dressing-room when Al Tessilore visited me to rub out a witness." I pointed to the dressing-room door. "So she came out with her little gun and stuck it in his back and saved my life," I said.

Copernik didn't move. There was something horrible in his face now. Ybarra slipped his nailfile into a small leather case and slowly tucked it into his pocket.

"Is that all?" he asked gently.

I nodded. "Except that she told me where Waldo's apartment was and I went in there and looked for the pearls. I found the dead man. In his pocket I found new car keys in a case from a Packard agency. And down on the street I found the Packard and took it to where it came from. Barsaly's kept woman. Barsaly had sent a friend from the Spezzia Club down to buy something and he had tried to buy it with his gun instead of the money Barsaly gave him. And Waldo beat him to the punch."

"Is that all?" Ybarra asked softly.

"That's all," I said, licking the torn place on the inside of my cheek.

Ybarra said slowly: "What do you want?"

Copernik's face convulsed and he slapped his long hard thigh. "This guy is good," he jeered. "He falls for a stray broad and breaks every law in the book and you ask him what docs he want? I'll give him what he wants, guinea!"

Ybarra turned his head slowly and looked at him. "I don't think you will," he said. "I think you'll give him a clean bill of health and anything else he wants. He's giving you a lesson in police work."

Copernik didn't move or make a sound for a long minute. None of us moved. Then Copernik leaned forward and his coat fell open. The butt of his service gun looked out of its underarm holster.

"So what do you want?" he asked me.

"What's on the card table there. The jacket and hat and the phony pearls. And some names kept away from the papers. Is that too much?"

"Yeah — it's too much," Copernik said almost gently. He swayed sideways and his gun jumped neatly into his hand. He rested his forearm on his thigh and pointed the gun at my stomach.

"I like better that you get a slug in the guts resisting arrest," he said. "I like that better, because of a report I made out on Al Tessilore's arrest and how I made the pinch. Because of some photos of me that are in the morning sheets going out about now. I like it better that you don't live long enough to laugh about that, baby."

My mouth felt suddenly hot and dry. Far off I heard the wind booming. It seemed like the sound of guns.

Ybarra moved his feet on the floor and said coldly: "You've got a couple of cases all solved, policeman. All you do for it is leave some junk here and keep some names from the papers. Which means from the D.A. If he gets them anyway, too bad for you."

Copernik said: "I like the other way." The blue gun in his hand was like a rock. "And God help you, if you don't back me up on it."

Ybarra said: "If the woman is brought out into the open, you'll be a liar on a police report and a chiseler on your own partner. In a week they won't even speak your name at headquarters. The taste of it would make them sick."

The hammer clicked back on Copernik's gun and I watched his big bony finger slide in farther around the trigger. The back of my neck was as wet as a dog's nose.

Ybarra stood up. The gun jumped at him. He said: "We'll see how yellow a guinea is. I'm telling you to put that gun up, Sam."

He started to move. He moved four even steps. Copernik was a man without a breath of movement, a stone man.

Ybarra took one more step and quite suddenly the gun began to shake.

Ybarra said evenly: "Put it up, Sam. If you keep your head everything lies the way it is. If you don't — you're gone."

He took one more step. Copernik's mouth opened wide and made a gasping sound and then he sagged in the chair as if he had been hit on the head. His eyelids drooped.

Ybarra jerked the gun out of his hand with a movement so quick it was no movement at all. He stepped back quickly, held the gun low at his side.

"It's the hot wind, Sam. Let's forget it," he said in the same even, almost dainty voice.

Copernik's shoulders sagged lower and he put his face in his hands. "O.K.," he said between his fingers.

Ybarra went softly across the room and opened the door. He looked at me with lazy, half-closed eyes. "I'd do a lot for a woman who saved my life, too," he said. "I'm eating this dish, but as a cop you can't expect me to like it."

I said: "The little man in the bed is called Leon Valesanos. He was a croupier at the Spezzia Club."

"Thanks," Ybarra said. "Let's go, Sam."

Copernik got up heavily and walked across the room and out of the open door and out of my sight. Ybarra stepped through the door after him and started to close it.

I said: "Wait a minute."

He turned his head slowly, his left hand on the door, the blue gun hanging down close to his right side.

"I'm not in this for money," I said. "The Barsalys live at Two-twelve Fremont Place. You can take the pearls to her. If Barsaly's name stays out of the paper, I get five C's. It goes to the Police Fund. I'm not so damn smart as you think. It just happened that way — and you had a heel for a partner."

Ybarra looked across the room at the pearls on the card table. His eyes glistened. "You take them," he said. "The five hundred's O.K. I think the fund has it coming."

He shut the door quietly and in a moment I heard the elevator doors clang.

VII

I opened a window and stuck my head out into the wind and watched the squad car tool off down the block. The wind blew in hard and I let it blow. A picture fell off the wall and two chessmen rolled off the card table. The material of Lola Barsaly's bolero jacket lifted and shook.

I went out to the kitchenette and drank some Scotch and went back into the living-room and called her — late as it was.

She answered the phone herself, very quickly, with no sleep in her voice.

"Dalmas," I said. "O.K. your end?"

"Yes. . . . yes," she said. "I'm alone."

"I found something," I said. "Or rather the police did. But your dark boy gypped you. I have a string of pearls. They're not real. He sold the real ones, I guess, and made you up a string of ringers, with your clasp."

She was silent for a long time. Then, a little faintly: "The police found them?"

"In Waldo's car. But they're not telling. We have a deal. Look at the papers in the morning and you'll be able to figure out why."

"There doesn't seem to be anything more to say," she said. "Can I have the clasp?"

"Yes. Can you meet me tomorrow at four in the Club Esquire bar?"

"You're rather sweet," she said in a dragged out voice. "I can. Frank is still at his meeting."

"Those meetings — they take it out of a guy," I said. We said goodbye.

I called a West Los Angeles number. He was still there, with the Russian girl.

"You can send me a check for five hundred in the morning," I told him. "Made out to the Police Fund, if you want to. Because that's where it's going."

Copernik made the third page of the morning papers with two photos and a nice half-column. The little brown man in Apartment 31 didn't make the paper at all. The Apartment House Association has a good lobby too.

I went out after breakfast and the wind was all gone. It was soft, cool, a little foggy. The sky was close and comfortable and gray. I rode down to the boulevard and picked out the best jewelry store on it and laid a string of pearls on a black velvet mat under a daylight-blue lamp. A man in a wing collar and striped trousers looked down at them languidly.

"How good?" I asked.

"I'm sorry, sir. We don't make appraisals. I can give you the name of an appraiser."

"Don't kid me," I said. "They're Dutch."

He focussed the light a little and leaned down and toyed with a few inches of the string.

"I want a string just like them, fitted to that clasp, and in a hurry," I added.

"How, like them?" He didn't look up. "And they're not Dutch. They're Bohemian."

"O.K., can you duplicate them?"

He shook his head and pushed the velvet pad away as if it soiled him. "In three months, perhaps. We don't blow glass like that in this country. If you wanted them matched — three months at least. And this house would not do that sort of thing at all."

"It must be swell to be that snooty," I said. I put a card under his black sleeve. "Give me a name that will — and not in three months — and maybe not exactly like them."

He shrugged, went away with the card, came back in five minutes and handed it back to me. There was something written on the back.

The old Levantine had a shop on Melrose, a junk shop with everything in the window from a folding baby carriage to a French horn, from a mother-of-pearl lorgnette in a faded plush case to one of those .44 Special Single Action Six-shooters they still make for Western peace officers whose grandfathers were tough.

The old Levantine wore a skull cap and two pairs of glasses and a full beard. He studied my pearls, shook his head sadly, and said: "For twenty dollars, almost so good. Not so good, you understand. Not so good glass."

"How like will they look?"

He spread his firm strong hands. "I am telling you the truth," he said. "They would not fool a baby."

"Make them up," I said. "With this clasp. And I want the others back too, of course."

"Yah. Two o'clock," he said.

Leon Valesanos, the little brown man from Uruguay, made the afternoon papers. He had been found hanging in an unnamed apartment. The police were investigating.

At four o'clock I walked into the long cool bar of the Club Esquire and prowled along the row of booths until I found one where a woman sat alone. She wore a hat like a shallow soup plate with a very wide edge, a brown tailor-made suit with a severe mannish shirt and tie.

I sat down beside her and slipped a parcel along the seat. "You don't open that," I said. "In fact you can slip it into the incinerator as is, if you want to."

She looked at me with dark tired eyes. Her fingers twisted a thin glass that smelled of peppermint. "Thanks." Her face was very pale.

I ordered a highball and the waiter went away. "Read the papers?"

"Yes."

"You understand now about this fellow Copernik who stole your act? That's why they won't change the story or bring you into it."

"It doesn't matter now," she said. "Thank you, all the same. Please — please, show them to me."

I pulled a string of pearls out of the loosely wrapped tissue paper in my pocket and slid them across to her. The silver propeller clasp winked in the light of the wall bracket. The little diamond winked. The pearls were as dull as white soap. They didn't even match in size.

"You were right," she said tonelessly. "They are not my pearls."

The waiter came with my drink and she put her bag on them deftly. When he was gone she fingered them slowly once more, dropped them into the bag and gave me a dry mirthless smile.

"As you said — I'll keep the clasp."

I said slowly: "You don't know anything about me. You saved my life last night and we had a moment, but it was just a moment. You still don't know anything about me. There's a detective downtown named

Ybarra, a Mexican of the nice sort, who was on the job when the pearls were found in Waldo's suitcase. That's in case you would like to make sure —"

She said: "Don't be silly. It's all finished. It was a memory. I'm too young to nurse memories. It may be all for the best. I loved Stan Phillips — but he's gone — long gone."

I stared at her, didn't say anything.

She added quietly: "This morning my husband told me something I hadn't known. We are to separate. So I have very little to laugh about to-day."

"I'm sorry," I said lamely. "There's nothing to say. I may see you sometime. Maybe not. I don't move much in your circle. Good luck."

I stood up. We looked at each other for a moment. "You haven't touched your drink," she said.

"You drink it. That peppermint stuff will just make you sick."

I stood there a moment with a hand hard on the table.

"If anybody ever bothers you," I said, "let me know."

I went out of the bar without looking back at her, got into my car and drove west on Sunset and down all the way to the Coast Highway. Everywhere along the way gardens were full of withered and blackened leaves and flowers which the hot wind had burned.

But the ocean looked cool and languid and just the same as ever. I drove on almost to Malibu and then parked and went and sat on a big rock that was inside somebody's wire fence. It was about half-tide and coming in. The air smelled of kelp. I watched the water for a while and then I pulled a string of Bohemian glass imitation pearls out of my pocket and cut the knot at one end and slipped the pearls off one by one.

When I had them all loose in my left hand I held them like that for a while and thought. There wasn't really anything to think about. I was sure.

"To the memory of Mr. Stan Phillips," I said loud. "Just another four-flusher."

I flipped her pearls out into the water one by one, at the floating sea-gulls.

They made little splashes and the seagulls rose off the water and swooped at the splashes.

1942

JAMES THURBER

....

The Catbird Seat

MR. MARTIN bought the pack of Camels on Monday night in the most crowded cigar store on Broadway. It was theater time and seven or eight men were buying cigarettes. The clerk didn't even glance at Mr. Martin, who put the pack in his overcoat pocket and went out. If any of the staff at F & S had seen him buy the cigarettes, they would have been astonished, for it was generally known that Mr. Martin did not smoke, and never had. No one saw him.

It was just a week to the day since Mr. Martin had decided to rub out Mrs. Ulgine Barrows. The term "rub out" pleased him because it suggested nothing more than the correction of an error — in this case an error of Mr. Fitweiler. Mr. Martin had spent each night of the past week working out his plan and examining it. As he walked home now he went over it again. For the hundredth time he resented the element of imprecision, the margin of guesswork that entered into the business. The project as he had worked it out was casual and bold, the risks were considerable. Something might go wrong anywhere along the line. And therein lay the cunning of his scheme. No one would ever see in it the cautious, painstaking hand of Erwin Martin, head of the filing department at F & S, of whom Mr. Fitweiler had once said, "Man is fallible but Martin isn't." No one would see his hand, that is, unless it were caught in the act.

Sitting in his apartment, drinking a glass of milk, Mr. Martin reviewed his case against Mrs. Ulgine Barrows, as he had every night for seven nights. He began at the beginning. Her quacking voice and braying laugh had first profaned the halls of F & S on March 7, 1941 (Mr. Martin had a head for dates). Old Roberts, the personnel chief, had introduced her as the newly appointed special adviser to the president of the firm, Mr. Fitweiler. The woman had appalled Mr. Martin instantly, but he hadn't shown it. He had given her his dry hand, a look of studious concentration, and a faint smile. "Well," she had said, looking at the papers on his desk, "are you lifting the oxcart out of the ditch?" As Mr. Martin recalled that moment, over his milk, he squirmed slightly. He must keep his mind on her crimes as a special adviser, not on her peccadillos as a personality. This he found difficult to do, in spite of entering an objection and sustaining it. The faults of the woman as a woman kept chattering on in his mind like an unruly witness. She had, for almost two years now, baited him. In the halls, in the elevator, even in his own office, into which she romped now and then like a circus horse, she was constantly shouting these silly questions at him. "Are you lifting the oxcart out of the ditch? Are you tearing up the pea patch? Are you hollering down the rain barrel? Are you scraping around the bottom of the pickle barrel? Are you sitting in the catbird seat?"

It was Joey Hart, one of Mr. Martin's two assistants, who had explained what the gibberish meant. "She must be a Dodger fan," he had said. "Red Barber announces the Dodger games over the radio and he uses those expressions — picked 'em up down South." Joey had gone on to explain one or two. "Tearing up the pea patch" meant going on a rampage; "sitting in the catbird seat" meant sitting pretty, like a batter with three balls and no strikes on him. Mr. Martin dismissed all this with an effort. It had been annoying, it had driven him near to distraction, but he was too solid a man to be moved to murder by anything so childish. It was fortunate, he reflected as he passed on to the important charges against Mrs. Barrows, that he had stood up under it so well. He had maintained always an outward appearance of polite tolerance. "Why, I even believe you like the woman," Miss Paird, his other assistant, had once said to him. He had simply smiled.

A gavel rapped in Mr. Martin's mind and the case proper was resumed. Mrs. Ulgine Barrows stood charged with willful, blatant, and persistent attempts to destroy the efficiency and system of F & S. It was competent, material, and relevant to review her advent and rise to power. Mr. Martin had got the story from Miss Paird, who seemed always able to find things out. According to her, Mrs. Barrows had met Mr. Fitweiler at a party, where she had rescued him from the embraces of a powerfully built drunken man who had mistaken the president of F & S for a famous retired Middle Western football coach. She had led him to a sofa and somehow worked upon him a monstrous magic. The aging gentleman had jumped to the conclusion there and then that this was a woman of singular attainments, equipped to bring out the best in him and in the firm. A week later he had introduced her into F & S as his special adviser. On that day confusion got its foot in the door. After Miss Tyson, Mr. Brundage, and Mr. Bartlett had been fired and Mr. Munson had taken his hat and stalked out, mailing in his resignation later, old Roberts had been emboldened to speak to Mr. Fitweiler. He mentioned that Mr. Munson's department had been "a little disrupted" and hadn't they perhaps better resume the old system there? Mr. Fitweiler had said certainly not. He had the greatest faith in Mrs. Barrows's ideas. "They require a little seasoning, a little seasoning, is all," he had added. Mr. Roberts had given it up. Mr. Martin reviewed in detail all the changes wrought by Mrs. Barrows. She had begun chipping at the cornices of the firm's edifice and now she was swinging at the foundation stones with a pickaxe.

Mr. Martin came now, in his summing up, to the afternoon of Monday, November 2, 1942 — just one week ago. On that day, at 3 P.M., Mrs. Barrows had bounced into his office. "Boo!" she had yelled. "Are you scraping around the bottom of the pickle barrel?" Mr. Martin had looked at her from under his green eyeshade, saying nothing. She had begun to wander about the office, taking it in with her great, popping eyes. "Do you really need *all* these filing cabinets?" she had demanded suddenly. Mr. Martin's heart had jumped. "Each of these files," he had said, keeping his voice even, "plays an indispensable part in the system of F & S." She had brayed at him, "Well, don't tear up the pea patch!" and gone to the door. From there she had bawled, "But you sure have got a lot of fine scrap in here!" Mr. Martin could no longer doubt that the finger was on his beloved department. Her pickaxe was on the upswing, poised for the first blow. It had not come yet; he had received no blue memo from the enchanted Mr. Fitweiler bearing nonsensical instructions deriving from the obscene woman. But there was no doubt in Mr. Martin's mind that one would be forthcoming. He must act quickly. Already a precious week had gone by. Mr. Martin stood up in his living room, still holding his milk glass. "Gentlemen of the jury," he said to himself, "I demand the death penalty for this horrible person."

The next day Mr. Martin followed his routine, as usual. He polished his glasses more often and once sharpened an already sharp pencil, but not even Miss Paird noticed. Only once did he catch sight of his victim; she swept past him in the hall with a patronizing "Hi!" At five-thirty he walked home, as usual, and had a glass of milk, as usual. He had never drunk anything stronger in his life — unless you could count ginger ale. The late Sam Schlosser, the S of F & S, had praised Mr. Martin at a staff meeting several years before for his temperate habits. "Our most efficient worker neither drinks nor smokes," he had said. "The results speak for themselves." Mr. Fitweiler had sat by, nodding approval.

Mr. Martin was still thinking about that red-letter day as he walked over to the Schrafft's on Fifth Avenue near Forty-sixth Street. He got there, as he always did, at eight o'clock. He finished his dinner and the financial page of the *Sun* at a quarter to nine, as he always did. It was his custom after dinner to take a walk. This time he walked down Fifth Avenue at a casual pace. His gloved hands felt moist and warm, his forehead cold. He transferred the Camels from his overcoat to a jacket pocket. He wondered, as he did so, if they did not represent an unnecessary note of strain. Mrs. Barrows smoked only Luckies. It was his idea to puff a few puffs on a Camel (after the rubbing-out), stub it out in the ashtray holding her lipstick-stained Luckies, and thus drag a small red herring across the trail. Perhaps it was not a good idea. It would take time. He might even choke, too loudly.

Mr. Martin had never seen the house on West Twelfth Street where Mrs. Barrows lived, but he had a clear enough picture of it. Fortunately, she had bragged to everybody about her ducky first-floor apartment in the perfectly darling three-story red-brick. There would be no doorman or other attendants; just the tenants of the second and third floors. As he walked along, Mr. Martin realized that he would get there before nine-thirty. He had considered walking north on Fifth Avenue from Schrafft's to a point from which it would take him until ten o'clock to reach the house. At that hour people were less likely to be coming in or going out. But the procedure would have made an awkward loop in the straight thread of his casualness, and he had abandoned it. It was impossible to figure when people would be entering or leaving the house, anyway. There was a great risk at any hour. If he ran into anybody, he would simply have to place the rubbing-out of Ulgine Barrows in the inactive file forever. The same thing would hold true if there were someone in her apartment. In that case he would just say that he had been passing by, recognized her charming house and thought to drop in.

It was eighteen minutes after nine when Mr. Martin turned into Twelfth Street. A man passed him, and a man and a woman talking. There was no one within fifty paces when he came to the house, halfway down the block. He was up the steps and in the small vestibule in no time, pressing the bell under the card that said "Mrs. Ulgine Barrows." When the clicking in the lock started, he jumped forward against the door. He got inside fast, closing the door behind him. A bulb in a lantern hung from the hall ceiling on a chain seemed to have a monstrously bright light. There was nobody on the stair, which went up ahead of him along the left wall. A door opened down the hall in the wall on the right. He went toward it swiftly, on tiptoe.

"Well, for God's sake, look who's here!" bawled Mrs. Barrows, and her braying laugh rang out like the report of a shotgun. He rushed past her like a football tackle, bumping her. "Hey, quit shoving!" she said, closing the door behind them. They were in her living room, which seemed to Mr. Martin to be lighted by a hundred lamps. "What's after you?" she said. "You're as jumpy as a goat." He found he was unable to speak. His heart was wheezing in his throat. "I — yes," he finally brought out. She was jabbering and laughing as she started to help him off with his coat. "No, no," he said. "I'll put it here." He took it off and put it on a chair near the door. "Your hat and gloves, too," she said. "You're in a lady's house." He put his hat on top of the coat. Mrs. Barrows seemed larger than he had thought. He kept his gloves on. "I was passing by," he said. "I recognized — is there anyone here?" She laughed louder than ever. "No," she said, "we're all alone. You're as white as a sheet, you funny man. Whatever *has* come over you? I'll mix you a toddy." She started toward a door across the room. "Scotch-and-soda be all right? But say, you don't drink, do you?" She turned and gave him her amused look. Mr. Martin pulled himself together. "Scotch-and-soda will be all right," he heard himself say. He could hear her laughing in the kitchen.

Mr. Martin looked quickly around the living room for the weapon. He had counted on finding one there. There were andirons and a poker and something in a corner that looked like an Indian club. None of them would do. It couldn't be that way. He began to pace around. He came to a desk. On it lay a metal paper knife with an ornate handle. Would it be sharp enough? He reached for it and knocked over a small brass jar. Stamps spilled out of it and it fell to the floor with a clatter. "Hey," Mrs. Barrows yelled from the kitchen, "are you tearing up the pea patch?" Mr. Martin gave a strange laugh. Picking up the knife, he tried its point against his left wrist. It was blunt. It wouldn't do.

* * *

When Mrs. Barrows reappeared, carrying two highballs, Mr. Martin, standing there with his gloves on, became acutely conscious of the fantasy he had wrought. Cigarettes in his pocket, a drink prepared for him — it was all too grossly improbable. It was more than that; it was impossible. Somewhere in the back of his mind a vague idea stirred, sprouted. "For heaven's sake, take off those gloves," said Mrs. Barrows. "I always wear them in the house," said Mr. Martin. The idea began to bloom, strange and wonderful. She put the glasses on a coffee table in front of a sofa and sat on the sofa. "Come over here, you odd little man," she said. Mr. Martin went over and sat beside her. It was difficult getting a cigarette out of the pack of Camels, but he managed it. She held a match for him, laughing. "Well," she said, handing him his drink, "this is perfectly marvelous. You with a drink and a cigarette."

Mr. Martin puffed, not too awkwardly, and took a gulp of the highball. "I drink and smoke all the time," he said. He clinked his glass against hers. "Here's nuts to that old windbag, Fitweiler," he said, and gulped again. The stuff tasted awful, but he made no grimace. "Really, Mr. Martin," she said, her voice and posture changing, "you are insulting our employer." Mrs. Barrows was now all special adviser to the president. "I am preparing a bomb," said Mr. Martin, "which will blow the old goat higher than hell." He had only had a little of the drink, which was not strong. It couldn't be that. "Do you take dope or something?" Mrs. Barrows asked coldly. "Heroin," said Mr. Martin. "I'll be coked to the gills when I bump that old buzzard off." "Mr. Martin!" she shouted, getting to her feet. "That will be all of that. You must go at once." Mr. Martin took another swallow of his drink. He tapped his cigarette out in the ashtray and put the pack of Camels on the coffee table. Then he got up. She stood glaring at him. He walked over and put on his hat and coat. "Not a word about this," he said, and laid an index finger against his lips. All Mrs. Barrows could bring out was "Really!" Mr. Martin put his hand on the doorknob. "I'm sitting in the catbird seat," he said. He stuck his tongue out at her and left. Nobody saw him go.

Mr. Martin got to his apartment, walking, well before eleven. No one saw him go in. He had two glasses of milk after brushing his teeth, and he felt elated. It wasn't tipsiness, because he hadn't been tipsy. Anyway, the walk had worn off all effects of the whisky. He got in bed and read a magazine for a while. He was asleep before midnight.

*   *   *

Mr. Martin got to the office at eight-thirty the next morning, as usual. At a quarter to nine, Ulgine Barrows, who had never before arrived at work before ten, swept into his office. "I'm reporting to Mr. Fitweiler now!" she shouted. "If he turns you over to the police, it's no more than you deserve!" Mr. Martin gave her a look of shocked surprise. "I beg your pardon?" he said. Mrs. Barrows snorted and bounced out of the room, leaving Miss Paird and Joey Hart staring after her. "What's the matter with that old devil now?" asked Miss Paird. "I have no idea," said Mr. Martin, resuming his work. The other two looked at him and then at each other. Miss Paird got up and went out. She walked slowly past the closed door of Mr. Fitweiler's office. Mrs. Barrows was yelling inside, but she was not braying. Miss Paird could not hear what the woman was saying. She went back to her desk.

Forty-five minutes later, Mrs. Barrows left the president's office and went into her own, shutting the door. It wasn't until half an hour later that Mr. Fitweiler sent for Mr. Martin. The head of the filing department, neat, quiet, attentive, stood in front of the old man's desk. Mr. Fitweiler was pale and nervous. He took his glasses off and twiddled them. He made a small, bruffing sound in his throat. "Martin," he said, "you have been with us more than twenty years." "Twenty-two, sir," said Mr. Martin. "In that time," pursued the president, "your work and your — uh — manner have been exemplary." "I trust so, sir," said Mr. Martin. "I have understood, Mr. Martin," said Mr. Fitweiler, "that you have never taken a drink or smoked." "That is correct, sir," said Mr. Martin. "Ah, yes." Mr. Fitweiler polished his glasses. "You may describe what you did after leaving the office yesterday, Martin," he said. Mr. Martin allowed less than a second for his bewildered pause. "Certainly, sir," he said. "I walked home. Then I went to Schrafft's for dinner. Afterwards I walked home again. I went to bed early, sir, and read a magazine for a while. I was asleep before eleven." "Ah, yes," said Mr. Fitweiler again. He was silent for a moment, searching for the proper words to say to the head of the filing department. "Mrs. Barrows," he said finally, "Mrs. Barrows has worked hard, Martin, very hard. It grieves me to report that she has suffered a severe breakdown. It has taken the form of a persecution complex accompanied by distressing hallucinations." "I am very sorry, sir," said Mr. Martin. "Mrs. Barrows is under the delusion," continued Mr. Fitweiler, "that you visited her last evening and behaved yourself in an — uh — unseemly manner." He raised his hand to silence Mr. Martin's little pained outcry. "It is the nature of these psychological diseases," Mr. Fitweiler said, "to fix upon the least likely and most innocent party as the — uh — source of persecution. These matters are not for the lay mind to grasp, Martin. I've just had my psychiatrist, Dr. Fitch, on the phone. He would not, of course, commit himself, but he made enough generalizations to substantiate my suspicions. I suggested to Mrs. Barrows when she had completed her — uh — story to me this morning, that she visit Dr. Fitch, for I suspected a condition at once. She flew, I regret to say, into a rage, and demanded — uh — requested that I call you on the carpet. You may not know, Martin, but Mrs. Barrows had planned a reorganization of your department — subject to my approval, of course, subject to my approval. This brought you, rather than anyone else, to her mind — but again that is a phenomenon for Dr. Fitch and not for us. So, Martin, I am afraid Mrs. Barrows' usefulness here is at an end."

"I am dreadfully sorry, sir," said Mr. Martin.

It was at this point that the door to the office blew open with the suddenness of a gas-main explosion and Mrs. Barrows catapulted through it. "Is the little rat denying it?" she screamed. "He can't get away with that!" Mr. Martin got up and moved discreetly to a point beside Mr. Fitweiler's chair. "You drank and smoked at my apartment," she bawled at Mr. Martin, "and you know it! You called Mr. Fitweiler an old windbag and said you were going to blow him up when you got coked to the gills on your heroin!" She stopped yelling to catch her breath and a new glint came into her popping eyes. "If you weren't such a drab, ordinary little man," she said, "I'd think you'd planned it all. Sticking your tongue out, saying you were sitting in the catbird seat, because you thought no one would believe me when I told it! My God, it's really too perfect!" She brayed loudly and hysterically, and the fury was on her again. She glared at Mr. Fitweiler. "Can't you see how he has tricked us, you old fool? Can't you see his little game?" But Mr. Fitweiler had been surreptitiously pressing all the buttons under the top of his desk and employees of F & S began pouring into the room. "Stockton," said Mr. Fitweiler, "you and Fishbein will take Mrs. Barrows to her home. Mrs. Powell, you will go with them." Stockton, who had played a little football in high school, blocked Mrs. Barrows as she made for Mr. Martin. It took him and Fishbein together to force her out of the door into the hall, crowded with stenographers and office boys. She was still screaming imprecations at Mr. Martin, tangled and contradictory imprecations. The hubbub finally died out down the corridor.

"I regret that this has happened," said Mr. Fitweiler. "I shall ask you to dismiss it from your mind, Martin." "Yes, sir," said Mr. Martin, anticipating his chief's "That will be all" by moving to the door. "I will dismiss it." He went out and shut the door, and his step was light and quick in the hall. When he entered his department he had slowed down to his customary gait, and he walked quietly across the room to the W 20 file, wearing a look of studious concentration.

1942

CORNELL WOOLRICH

Rear Window

I DIDN'T KNOW their names. I'd never heard their voices. I didn't even know them by sight, strictly speaking, for their faces were too small to fill in with identifiable features at that distance. Yet I could have constructed a timetable of their comings and goings, their daily habits and activities. They were the rear-window dwellers around me.

Sure, I suppose it *was* a little bit like prying, could even have been mistaken for the fevered concentration of a Peeping Tom. That wasn't my fault, that wasn't the idea. The idea was, my movements were strictly limited just around this time. I could get from the window to the bed, and from the bed to the window, and that was all. The bay window was about the best feature my rear bedroom had in the warm weather. It was unscreened, so I had to sit with the light out or I would have had every insect in the vicinity in on me. I couldn't sleep, because I was used to getting plenty of exercise. I'd never acquired the habit of reading books to ward off boredom, so I hadn't that to turn to. Well, what should I do, sit there with my eyes tightly shuttered?

Just to pick a few at random: Straight over, and the windows square, there was a young jitter-couple, kids in their teens, only just married. It would have killed them to stay home one night. They were always in such a hurry to go, wherever it was they went, they never remembered to turn out the lights. I don't think it missed once in all the time I was watching. But they never forgot altogether, either. I was to learn to call this delayed action, as you will see. He'd always come skittering madly back in about five minutes, probably from all the way down in the street, and rush around killing the switches. Then fall over something in the dark on his way out. They gave me an inward chuckle, those two.

The next house down, the windows already narrowed a little with perspective. There was a certain light in that one that always went out each night too. Something about it, it used to make me a little sad. There was a woman living there with her child, a young widow I suppose. I'd see her put the child to bed, and then bend over and kiss her in a wistful sort of way. She'd shade the light off her and sit there painting her eyes and mouth. Then she'd go out. She'd never come back till the night was nearly spent. Once I was still up, and I looked and she was sitting there motionless with her head buried in her arms. Something about it, it used to make me a little sad.

The third one down no longer offered any insight, the windows were just slits like in a medieval battlement, due to foreshortening. That brings us around to the one on the end. In that one, frontal vision came back full-depth again, since it stood at right angles to the rest, my own included, sealing up the inner hollow all these houses backed on. I could see into it, from the rounded projection of my bay window, as freely as into a doll house with its rear wall sliced away. And scaled down to about the same size.

It was a flat building. Unlike all the rest it had been constructed originally as such, not just cut up into furnished rooms. It topped them by two stories and had rear fire escapes, to show for this distinction. But it was old, evidently hadn't shown a profit. It was in the process of being modernized. Instead of clearing the entire building while the work was going on, they were doing it a flat at a time, in order to lose as little rental income as possible. Of the six rearward flats it offered to view, the topmost one had already been completed, but not yet rented. They were working on the fifth-floor one now, disturbing the peace of everyone all up and down the "inside" of the block with their hammering and sawing.

I felt sorry for the couple in the flat below. I used to wonder how they stood it with that bedlam going on above their heads. To make it worse the wife was in chronic poor health, too; I could tell that even at a distance by the listless way she moved about over there, and remained in her bathrobe without dressing. Sometimes I'd see her sitting by the window, holding her head. I used to wonder why he didn't have a doctor in to look her over, but maybe they couldn't afford it. He seemed to be out of work. Often their bedroom light was on late at night behind the drawn shade, as though she were unwell and he was sitting up with her. And one night in particular he must have had to sit up with her all night, it remained on until nearly daybreak. Not that I sat watching all that time. But the light was still burning at three in the morning, when I finally transferred from chair to bed to see if I could get a little sleep myself. And when I failed to, and hopscotched back again around dawn, it was still peering wanly out behind the tan shade.

Moments later, with the first brightening of day, it suddenly dimmed around the edges of the shade, and then shortly afterward, not that one, but a shade in one of the other rooms — for all of them alike had been down — went up, and I saw him standing there looking out.

He was holding a cigarette in his hand. I couldn't see it, but I could tell it was that by the quick, nervous little jerks with which he kept putting his hand to his mouth, and the haze I saw rising around his head. Worried about her, I guess. I didn't blame him for that. Any husband would have been. She must have only just dropped off to sleep, after night-long suffering. And then in another hour or so, at the most, that sawing of wood and clattering of buckets was going to start in over them again. Well, it wasn't any of my business, I said to myself, but he really ought to get her out of there. If I had an ill wife on my hands....

He was leaning slightly out, maybe an inch past the window frame, carefully scanning the back faces of all the houses abutting on the hollow square that lay before him. You can tell, even at a distance, when a person is looking fixedly. There's something about the way the head is held. And yet his scrutiny wasn't held fixedly to any one point, it was a slow, sweeping one, moving along the houses on the opposite side from me first. When it got to the end of them, I knew it would cross over to my side and come back along there. Before it did, I withdrew several yards inside my room, to let it go safely by. I didn't want him to think I was sitting there prying into his affairs. There was still enough blue night-shade in my room to keep my slight withdrawal from catching his eye.

When I returned to my original position a moment or two later, he was gone. He had raised two more of the shades. The bedroom one was still down. I wondered vaguely why he had given that peculiar, comprehensive, semicircular stare at all the rear windows around him. There wasn't anyone at any of them, at such an hour. It wasn't important, of course. It was just a little oddity, it failed to blend in with his being worried or disturbed about his wife. When you're worried or disturbed, that's an internal preoccupation, you stare vacantly at nothing at all. When you stare around you in a great sweeping arc at windows, that betrays external preoccupation, outward interest. One doesn't quite jibe with the other. To call such a discrepancy trifling is to add to its importance. Only someone like me, stewing in a vacuum of total idleness, would have noticed it at all.

The flat remained lifeless after that, as far as could be judged by its windows. He must have either gone out or gone to bed himself. Three of the shades remained at normal height, the one masking the bedroom remained down. Sam, my day houseman, came in not long after with my eggs and morning paper, and I had that to kill time with for awhile. I stopped thinking about other people's windows and staring at them.

The sun slanted down on one side of the hollow oblong all morning long, then it shifted over to the other side for the afternoon. Then it started to slip off both alike, and it was evening again — another day gone.

The lights started to come on around the quadrangle. Here and there a wall played back, like a sounding board, a snatch of radio program that was coming in too loud. If you listened carefully you could hear an occasional click of dishes mixed in, faint, far off. The chain of little habits that were their lives unreeled themselves. They were all bound in them tighter than the tightest straitjacket any jailer ever devised, though they all thought themselves free. The jitterbugs made their nightly dash for the great open spaces, forgot their lights, he came careening back, thumbed them out, and their place was dark until the early morning hours. The woman put her child to bed, leaned mournfully over its cot, then sat down with heavy despair to redden her mouth.

In the fourth floor flat at right angles to the long, interior "street" the three shades had remained up, and the fourth shade had remained at full length, all day long. I hadn't been conscious of that because I hadn't particularly been looking at it, or thinking of it, until now. My eyes may have rested on those windows at times, during the day, but my thoughts had been elsewhere. It was only when a light suddenly went up in the end room behind one of the raised shades, which was their kitchen, that I realized that the shades had been untouched like that all day. That also brought something else to my mind that hadn't been in it until now: I hadn't seen the woman all day. I hadn't seen any sign of life within those windows until now.

He'd come in from outside. The entrance was at the opposite side of their kitchen, away from the window. He'd left his hat on, so I knew he'd just come in from the outside.

He didn't remove his hat. As though there was no one there to remove it for any more. Instead, he pushed it farther to the back of his head by pronging a hand to the roots of his hair. That gesture didn't denote removal of perspiration, I knew. To do that a person makes a sidewise sweep — this was up over his forehead. It indicated some sort of harassment or uncertainty. Besides, if he'd been suffering from excess warmth, the first thing he would have done would be to take off his hat altogether.

She didn't come out to greet him. The first link, of the so-strong chain of habits, of custom, that binds us all, had snapped wide open.

She must be so ill she had remained in bed, in the room behind the lowered shade, all day. I watched. He remained where he was, two rooms away from there. Expectancy became surprise, surprise incomprehension. Funny, I thought, that he doesn't go in to her. Or at least go as far as the doorway, look in to see how she is.

Maybe she was asleep, and he didn't want to disturb her. Then immediately: but how can he know for sure that she's asleep, without at least looking in at her? He just came in himself.

He came forward and stood there by the window, as he had at dawn. Sam had carried out my tray quite some time before, and my lights were out. I held my ground. I knew he couldn't see me within the darkness of the bay window. He stood there motionless for several minutes. And now his attitude was the proper one for inner preoccupation. He stood there looking downward at nothing, lost in thought.

He's worried about her, I said to myself, as any man would be. It's the most natural thing in the world. Funny, though, he should leave her in the dark like that, without going near her. If he's worried, then why didn't he at least look in on her on returning? Here was another of those trivial discrepancies, between inward motivation and outward indication. And just as I was thinking that, the original one, that I had noted at daybreak, repeated itself. His head went up with renewed alertness, and I could see it start to give that slow circular sweep of interrogation around the panorama of rearward windows again. True, the light was behind him this time, but there was enough of it falling on him to show me the microscopic but continuous shift of direction his head made in the process. I remained carefully immobile until the distant glance had passed me safely by. Motion attracts.

Why is he so interested in other people's windows, I wondered detachedly. And of course an effective brake to dwell on that thought too lingeringly clamped down almost at once: Look who's talking. What about you yourself?

An important difference escaped me. I wasn't worried about anything. He, presumably, was.

Down came the shades again. The lights stayed on behind their beige opaqueness. But behind the one that had remained down all along, the room remained dark.

Time went by. Hard to say how much — a quarter of an hour, twenty minutes. A cricket chirped in one of the back yards. Sam came in to see if I wanted anything before he went home for the night. I told him no, I didn't — it was all right, run along. He stood there for a minute, head down. Then I saw him shake it slightly, as if at something he didn't like. "What's the matter?" I asked.

"You know what that means? My old mammy told it to me, and she never told me a lie in her life. I never once seen it to miss, either."

"What, the cricket?"

"Any time you hear one of them things, that's a sign of death — someplace close around."

I swept the back of my hand at him. "Well, it isn't in here, so don't let it worry you."

He went out, muttering stubbornly: "It's somewhere close by, though. Somewhere not very far off. Got to be."

The door closed after him, and I stayed there alone in the dark.

It was a stifling night, much closer than the one before. I could hardly get a breath of air even by the open window at which I sat. I wondered how he — that unknown over there — could stand it behind those drawn shades.

Then suddenly, just as idle speculation about this whole matter was about to alight on some fixed point in my mind, crystallize into something like suspicion, up came the shades again, and off it flitted, as formless as ever and without having had a chance to come to rest on anything.

He was in the middle windows, the living room. He'd taken off his coat and shirt, was bare-armed in his undershirt. He hadn't been able to stand it himself, I guess — the sultriness.

I couldn't make out what he was doing at first. He seemed to be busy in a perpendicular, up-and-down way rather than lengthwise. He remained in one place, but he kept dipping down out of sight and then straightening up into view again, at irregular intervals. It was almost like some sort of calisthenic exercise, except that the dips and rises weren't evenly timed enough for that. Sometimes he'd stay down a long time, sometimes he'd bob right up again, sometimes he'd go down two or three times in rapid succession. There was some sort of a widespread black V railing him off from the window. Whatever it was, there was just a sliver of it showing above the upward inclination to which the window still deflected my line of vision. All it did was strike off the bottom of his undershirt, to the extent of a sixteenth of an inch maybe. But I haven't seen it there at other times, and I couldn't tell what it was.

Suddenly he left it for the first time since the shades had gone up, came out around it to the outside, stooped down into another part of the room, and straightened again with an armful of what looked like varicolored pennants at the distance at which I was. He went back behind the V and allowed them to fall across the top of it for a moment, and stay that way. He made one of his dips down out of sight and stayed that way a good while.

The "pennants" slung across the V kept changing color right in front of my eyes. I have very good sight. One moment they were white, the next red, the next blue.

Then I got it. They were a woman's dresses, and he was pulling them down to him one by one, taking the topmost one each time. Suddenly they were all gone, the V was black and bare again, and his torso had reappeared. I knew what it was now, and what he was doing. The dresses had told me. He confirmed it for me. He spread his arms to the ends of the V, I could see him heave and hitch, as if exerting pressure, and suddenly the V had folded up, become a cubed wedge. Then he made rolling motions with his whole upper body, and the wedge disappeared off to one side.

He'd been packing a trunk, packing his wife's things into a large upright trunk.

He reappeared at the kitchen window presently, stood still for a moment. I saw him draw his arm across his forehead, not once but several times, and then whip the end of it off into space. Sure, it was hot work for such a night. Then he reached up along the wall and took something down. Since it was the kitchen he was in, my imagination had to supply a cabinet and a bottle.

I could see the two or three quick passes his hand made to his mouth after that. I said to myself tolerantly: That's what nine men out of ten would do after packing a trunk — take a good stiff drink. And if the tenth didn't, it would only be because he didn't have any liquor at hand.

Then he came closer to the window again, and standing edgewise to the side of it, so that only a thin paring of his head and shoulder showed, peered watchfully out into the dark quadrilateral, along the line of windows, most of them unlighted by now, once more. He always started on the left-hand side, the side opposite mine, and made his circuit of inspection from there on around.

That was the second time in one evening I'd seen him do that. And once at daybreak, made three times altogether. I smiled mentally. You'd almost think he felt guilty about something. It was probably nothing, just an odd little habit, a quirk, that he didn't know he had himself. I had them myself, everyone does.

He withdrew into the room, and it blacked out. His figure passed into the one that was still lighted next to it, the living room. That blacked next. It didn't surprise me that the third room, the bedroom with the drawn shade, didn't light up on his entering there. He wouldn't want to disturb her, of course — particularly if she was going away tomorrow for her health, as his packing of her trunk showed. She needed all the rest she could get, before making the trip. Simple enough for him to slip into bed in the dark.

It did surprise me, though, when a match-flare winked some time later, to have it still come from the darkened living room. He must be lying down in there, trying to sleep on a sofa or something for the night. He hadn't gone near the bedroom at all, was staying out of it altogether. That puzzled me, frankly. That was carrying solicitude almost too far.

Ten minutes or so later, there was another matchwink, still from that same living room window. He couldn't sleep.

The night brooded down on both of us alike, the curiosity-monger in the bay window, the chain-smoker in the fourth-floor flat, without giving any answer. The only sound was that interminable cricket.

I was back at the window again with the first sun of morning. Not because of him. My mattress was like a bed of hot coals. Sam found me there when he came in to get things ready for me. "You're going to be a wreck, Mr. Jeff," was all he said.

First, for awhile, there was no sign of life over there. Then suddenly I saw his head bob up from somewhere down out of sight in the living room, so I knew I'd been right; he'd spent the night on a sofa or easy chair in there. Now, of course, he'd look in at her, to see how she was, find out if she felt any better. That was only common ordinary humanity. He hadn't been near her, so far as I could make out, since two nights before.

He didn't. He dressed, and he went in the opposite direction, into the kitchen, and wolfed something in there, standing up and using both hands. Then he suddenly turned and moved off side, in the direction in which I knew the flat-entrance to be, as if he had just heard some summons, like the doorbell.

Sure enough, in a moment he came back, and there were two men with him in leather aprons. Expressmen. I saw him standing by while they laboriously maneuvered that cubed black wedge out between them, in the direction they'd just come from. He did more than just stand by. He practically hovered over them, kept shifting from side to side, he was so anxious to see that it was done right.

Then he came back alone, and I saw him swipe his arm across his head, as though it was he, not they, who was all heated up from the effort.

So he was forwarding her trunk, to wherever it was she was going. That was all.

He reached up along the wall again and took something down. He was taking another drink. Two. Three. I said to myself, a little at a loss: Yes, but he hasn't just packed a trunk this time. That trunk has been standing packed and ready since last night. Where does the hard work come in? The sweat and the need for a bracer?

Now, at last, after all those hours, he finally did go in to her. I saw his form pass through the living room and go beyond, into the bedroom. Up went the shade, that had been down all this time. Then he turned his head and looked around behind him. In a certain way, a way that was unmistakable, even from where I was. Not in one certain direction, as one looks at a person. But from side to side, and up and down, and all around, as one looks at — *an empty room.*

He stepped back, bent a little, gave a fling of his arms, and an unoccupied mattress and bedding upended over the foot of a bed, stayed that way, emptily curved. A second one followed a moment later.

She wasn't in there.

They use the expression "delayed action." I found out then what it meant. For two days a sort of formless uneasiness, a disembodied suspicion, I don't know what to call it, had been flitting and volplaning around in my mind, like an insect looking for a landing place. More than once, just as it had been ready to settle, some slight thing, some slight reassuring thing, such as the raising of the shades after they had been down unnaturally long, had been enough to keep it winging aimlessly, prevent it from staying still long enough for me to recognize it. The point of contact had been there all along, waiting to receive it. Now, for some reason, within a split second after he tossed over the empty mattresses, it landed — *zoom!* And the point of contact expanded — or exploded, whatever you care to call it — into a certainty of murder.

In other words, the rational part of my mind was far behind the instinctive, subconscious part. Delayed action. Now the one had caught up to the other. The thought-message that sparked from the synchronization was: He's done something to her!

I looked down and my hand was bunching the goods over my knee-cap, it was knotted so tight. I forced it to open. I said to myself, steadyingly: Now wait a minute, be careful, go slow. You've seen nothing. You know nothing. You only have the negative proof that you don't see her any more.

Sam was standing there looking over at me from the pantryway. He said accusingly: "You ain't touched a thing. And your face looks like a sheet."

It felt like one. It had that needling feeling, when the blood has left it involuntarily. It was more to get him out of the way and give myself some elbow room for undisturbed thinking, than anything else, that I said: "Sam, what's the street address of that building down there? Don't stick your head too far out and gape at it."

"Somep'n or other Benedict Avenue." He scratched his neck helpfully.

"I know that. Chase around the corner a minute and get me the exact number on it, will you?"

"Why you want to know that for?" he asked as he turned to go.

"None of your business," I said with the good-natured firmness that was all that was necessary to take care of that once and for all. I called after him just as he was closing the door: "And while you're about it, step into the entrance and see if you can tell from the mailboxes who has the fourth-floor rear. Don't get me the wrong one now. And try not to let anyone catch you at it."

He went out mumbling something that sounded like, "When a man ain't got nothing to do but just sit all day, he sure can think up the blamest things —" The door closed and I settled down to some good constructive thinking.

I said to myself: What are you really building up this monstrous supposition on? Let's see what you've got. Only that there were several little things wrong with the mechanism, the chain-belt, of their recurrent daily habits over there. 1. The lights were on all night the first night. 2. He came in later than usual the second night. 3. He left his hat on. 4. She didn't come out to greet him — she hasn't appeared since the evening before the lights were on all night. 5. He took a drink after he finished packing her trunk. But he took three stiff drinks the next morning, immediately after her trunk went out. 6. He was inwardly disturbed and worried, yet superimposed upon this was an unnatural external concern about the surrounding rear windows that was off-key. 7. He slept in the living room, didn't go near the bedroom, during the night before the departure of the trunk.

Very well. If she had been ill that first night, and he had sent her away for her health, that automatically canceled out points 1, 2, 3, 4. It left points 5 and 6 totally unimportant and unincriminating. But when it came up against 7, I hit a stumbling block.

If she went away immediately after being ill that first night, why didn't he want to sleep in their bedroom *last night?* Sentiment? Hardly. Two perfectly good beds in one room, only a sofa or uncomfortable easy chair in the other. Why should he stay out of there if she was already gone? Just because he missed her, was lonely? A grown man doesn't act that way. All right, then she was still in there.

Sam came back parenthetically at this point and said: "That house is Number 525 Benedict Avenue. The fourth-floor rear, it got the name of Mr. and Mrs. Lars Thorwald up."

"Sh-h," I silenced, and motioned him backhand out of my ken.

"First he wants it, then he don't," he grumbled philosophically, and retired to his duties.

I went ahead digging at it. But if she was still in there, in that bedroom last night, then she couldn't have gone away to the country, because I never saw her leave today. She could have left without my seeing her in the early hours of yesterday morning. I'd missed a few hours, been asleep. But this morning I had been up before he was himself, I only saw his head rear up from the sofa after I'd been at the window for some time.

To go at all she would have had to go yesterday morning. Then why had he left the bedroom shade down, left the mattresses undisturbed, until today? Above all, why had he stayed out of that room last night? That was evidence that she hadn't gone, was still in there. Then today, immediately after the trunk had been dispatched, he went in, pulled up the shade, tossed over the mattresses, and showed that she hadn't been in there. The thing was like a crazy spiral.

No, it wasn't either. *Immediately after the trunk had been dispatched —* The trunk.

That did it.

I looked around to make sure the door was safely closed between Sam and me. My hand hovered uncertainly over the telephone dial a minute. Boyne, he'd be the one to tell about it. He was on Homicide. He had been, anyway, when I'd last seen him. I didn't want to get a flock of strange dicks and cops into my hair. I didn't want to be involved any more than I had to. Or at all, if possible.

They switched my call to the right place after a couple of wrong tries, and I got him finally.

"Look, Boyne? This is Hal Jeffries —"

"Well, where've you been the last sixty-two years?" he started to enthuse.

"We can take that up later. What I want you to do now is take down a name and address. Ready? Lars Thorwald. Five twenty-five Benedict Avenue. Fourth-floor rear. Got it?"

"Fourth-floor rear. Got it. What's it for?"

"Investigation. I've got a firm belief you'll uncover a murder there if you start digging at it. Don't call on me for anything more than that — just a conviction. There's been a man and wife living there until now. Now there's just the man. Her trunk went out early this morning. If you can find someone who saw *her* leave herself —"

Marshaled aloud like that and conveyed to somebody else, a lieutenant of detectives above all, it did sound flimsy, even to me. He said hesitantly, "Well, but —" Then he accepted it as was. Because I was the source. I even left my window out of it completely. I could do that with him and get away with it because he'd known me years, he didn't question my reliability. I didn't want my room all cluttered up with dicks and cops taking turns nosing out of the window in this hot weather. Let them tackle it from the front.

"Well, we'll see what we see," he said. "I'll keep you posted."

I hung up and sat back to watch and wait events. I had a grandstand seat. Or rather a grandstand seat in reverse. I could only see from behind the scenes, but not from the front. I couldn't watch Boyne go to work. I could only see the results, when and if there were any.

Nothing happened for the next few hours. The police work that I knew must be going on was as invisible as police work should be. The figure in the fourth-floor windows over there remained in sight, alone and undisturbed. He didn't go out. He was restless, roamed from room to room without staying in one place very long, but he stayed in. Once I saw him eating again — sitting down this time — and once he shaved, and once he even tried to read the paper, but he didn't stay with it long.

Little unseen wheels were in motion around him. Small and harmless as yet, preliminaries. If he knew, I wondered to myself, would he remain there quiescent like that, or would he try to bolt out and flee? That mightn't depend so much upon his guilt as upon his sense of immunity, his feeling that he could outwit them. Of his guilt I myself was already convinced, or I wouldn't have taken the step I had.

At three my phone rang. Boyne calling back. "Jeffries? Well, I don't know. Can't you give me a little more than just a bald statement like that?"

"Why?" I fenced. "Why do I have to?"

"I've had a man over there making inquiries. I've just had his report. The building superintendent and several of the neighbors all agree she left for the country, to try and regain her health, early yesterday morning."

"Wait a minute. Did any of them *see* her leave, according to your man?"

"No."

"Then all you've gotten is a second-hand version of an unsupported statement by him. Not an eyewitness account."

"He was met returning from the depot, after he'd bought her ticket and seen her off on the train."

"That's still an unsupported statement, once removed."

"I've sent a man down there to the station to try and check with the ticket agent if possible. After all, he should have been fairly conspicuous at that early hour. And we're keeping him under observation, of course, in the meantime, watching all his movements. The first chance we get we're going to jump in and search the place."

I had a feeling that they wouldn't find anything, even if they did.

"Don't expect anything more from me. I've dropped it in your lap. I've given you all I have to give. A name, an address, and an opinion."

"Yes, and I've always valued your opinion highly before now, Jeff —"

"But now you don't, that it?"

"Not at all. The thing is, we haven't turned up anything that seems to bear out your impression so far."

"You haven't gotten very far along, so far."

He went back to his previous cliché. "Well, we'll see what we see. Let you know later."

Another hour or so went by, and sunset came on. I saw him start to get ready to go out, over there. He put on his hat, put his hand in his pocket and stood still looking at it for a minute. Counting change, I guess. It gave me a peculiar sense of suppressed excitement, knowing they were going to come in the minute he left. I thought grimly, as I saw him take a last look around: If you've got anything to hide, brother, now's the time to hide it.

He left. A breath-holding interval of misleading emptiness descended on the flat. A three-alarm fire couldn't have pulled my eyes off those windows. Suddenly the door by which he had just left parted slightly and two men insinuated themselves, one behind the other. There they were now. They closed it behind them, separated at once, and got busy. One took the bedroom, one the kitchen, and they started to work their way toward one another again from those extremes of the flat. They were thorough. I could see them going over everything from top to bottom. They took the living room together. One cased one side, the other man the other.

They'd already finished before the warning caught them. I could tell that by the way they straightened up and stood facing one another frustratedly for a minute. Then both their heads turned sharply, as at a tip-off by doorbell that he was coming back. They got out fast.

I wasn't unduly disheartened, I'd expected that. My own feeling all along had been that they wouldn't find anything incriminating around. The trunk had gone.

He came in with a mountainous brown-paper bag sitting in the curve of one arm. I watched him closely to see if he'd discover that someone had been there in his absence. Apparently he didn't. They'd been adroit about it.

He stayed in the rest of the night. Sat tight, safe and sound. He did some desultory drinking, I could see him sitting there by the window and his hand would hoist every once in a while, but not to excess. Apparently everything was under control, the tension had eased, now that — the trunk was out.

Watching him across the night, I speculated: Why doesn't he get out? If I'm right about him, and I am, why does he stick around — after it? That brought its own answer: Because he doesn't know anyone's on to him yet. He doesn't think there's any hurry. To go too soon, right after she has, would be more dangerous than to stay awhile.

The night wore on. I sat there waiting for Boyne's call. It came later than I thought it would. I picked the phone up in the dark. He was getting ready to go to bed, over there, now. He'd risen from where he'd been sitting drinking in the kitchen, and put the light out. He went into the living room, lit that. He started to pull his shirttail up out of his belt.

Boyne's voice was in my ear as my eyes were on him, over there. Three-cornered arrangement.

"Hello, Jeff? Listen, absolutely nothing. We searched the place while he was out —"

I nearly said, "I know you did, I saw it," but checked myself in time.

"— and didn't turn up a thing. But —" He stopped as though this was going to be important. I waited impatiently for him to go ahead.

"Downstairs in his letter box we found a post card waiting for him. We fished it up out of the slot with bent pins —"

"And?"

"And it was from his wife, written only yesterday from some farm up-country. Here's the message we copied: 'Arrived O.K. Already feeling a little better. Love, Anna.'"

I said, faintly but stubbornly: "You say, written only yesterday. Have you proof of that? What was the postmark-date on it?"

He made a disgusted sound down in his tonsils. At me, not it. "The postmark was blurred. A corner of it got wet, and the ink smudged."

"All of it blurred?"

"The year-date," he admitted. "The hour and the month came out O.K. August. And seven thirty P.M., it was mailed at."

This time I made the disgusted sound, in my larynx. "August, seven thirty P.M. — 1937 or 1939 or 1942. You have no proof how it got into that mail box, whether it came from a letter carrier's pouch or from the back of some bureau drawer!"

"Give up, Jeff," he said. "There's such a thing as going too far."

I don't know what I would have said. That is, if I hadn't happened to have my eyes on the Thorwald flat living room windows just then. Probably very little. The post card *had* shaken me, whether I admitted it or not. But I was looking over there. The light had gone out as soon as he'd taken his shirt off. But the bedroom didn't light up. A match-flare winked from the living room, low down, as from an easy chair or sofa. With two unused beds in the bedroom, he was *still staying out of there.*

"Boyne," I said in a glassy voice, "I don't care what post cards from the other world you've turned up, I say that man has done away with his wife! Trace that trunk he shipped out. Open it up when you've located it — and I think you'll find her!"

And I hung up without waiting to hear what he was going to do about it. He didn't ring back, so I suspected he was going to give my suggestion a spin after all, in spite of his loudly proclaimed skepticism.

I stayed there by the window all night, keeping a sort of death-watch. There were two more match-flares after the first, at about half-hour intervals. Nothing more after that. So possibly he was asleep over there. Possibly not. I had to sleep some myself, and I finally succumbed in the flaming light of the early sun. Anything that he was going to do, he would have done under cover of darkness and not waited for broad daylight. There wouldn't be anything much to watch, for a while now. And what was there that he needed to do any more, anyway? Nothing, just sit tight and let a little disarming time slip by.

It seemed like five minutes later that Sam came over and touched me, but it was already high noon. I said irritably: "Didn't you lamp that note I pinned up, for you to let me sleep?"

He said: "Yeah, but it's your old friend Inspector Boyne. I figured you'd sure want to —"

It was a personal visit this time. Boyne came into the room behind him without waiting, and without much cordiality.

I said to get rid of Sam: "Go inside and smack a couple of eggs together."

Boyne began in a galvanized-iron voice: "Jeff, what do you mean by doing anything like this to me? I've made a fool out of myself thanks to you. Sending my men out right and left on wild-goose chases. Thank God, I didn't put my foot in it any worse than I did, and have this guy picked up and brought in for questioning."

"Oh, then you don't think that's necessary?" I suggested, dryly.

The look he gave me took care of that. "I'm not alone in the department, you know. There are men over me I'm accountable to for my actions. That looks great, don't it, sending one of my fellows one-half-a-day's train ride up into the sticks to some God-forsaken whistle-stop or other at departmental expense —"

"Then you located the trunk?"

"We traced it through the express agency," he said flintily.

"And you opened it?"

"We did better than that. We got in touch with the various farmhouses in the immediate locality, and Mrs. Thorwald came down to the junction in a produce-truck from one of them and opened it for him herself, with her own keys!"

Very few men have ever gotten a look from an old friend such as I got from him. At the door he said, stiff as a rifle barrel: "Just let's forget all about it, shall we? That's about the kindest thing either one of us can do

for the other. You're not yourself, and I'm out a little of my own pocket
money, time and temper. Let's let it go at that. If you want to telephone
me in future I'll be glad to give you my home number."

The door went *whopp!* behind him.

For about ten minutes after he stormed out my numbed mind was in
a sort of straitjacket. Then it started to wriggle its way free. The hell
with the police. I can't prove it to them, maybe, but I can prove it to myself, one way or the other, once and for all. Either I'm wrong or I'm
right. He's got his armor on against them. But his back is naked and un-
protected against me.

I called Sam in. "Whatever became of that spyglass we used to have,
when we were bumming around on that cabin-cruiser that season?"

He found it some place downstairs and came in with it, blowing on it
and rubbing it along his sleeve. I let it lie idle in my lap first. I took a
piece of paper and a pencil and wrote six words on it: *What have you
done with her?*

I sealed it in an envelope and left the envelope blank. I said to Sam:
"Now here's what I want you to do, and I want you to be slick about it.
You take this, go in that building 525, climb the stairs to the fourth-floor
rear, and ease it under the door. You're fast, at least you used to be. Let's
see if you're fast enough to keep from being caught at it. Then when you
get safely down again, give the outside doorbell a little poke, to attract
attention."

His mouth started to open.

"And don't ask me any questions, you understand? I'm not fooling."

He went, and I got the spyglass ready.

I got him in the right focus after a minute or two. A face leaped up,
and I was really seeing him for the first time. Dark-haired, but unmistakable Scandinavian ancestry. Looked like a sinewy customer, although
he didn't run to much bulk.

About five minutes went by. His head turned sharply, profilewards.
That was the bell-poke, right there. The note must be in already.

He gave me the back of his head as he went back toward the flat-
door. The lens could follow him all the way to the rear, where my unaided eyes hadn't been able to before.

He opened the door first, missed seeing it, looked out on a level. He
closed it. Then dipped, straightened up. He had it. I could see him turning it this way and that.

He shifted in, away from the door, nearer the window. He thought
danger lay near the door, safety away from it. He didn't know it was the

other way around, the deeper into his own rooms he retreated the greater the danger.

He'd torn it open, he was reading it. God, how I watched his expression. My eyes clung to it like leeches. There was a sudden widening, a pulling — the whole skin of his face seemed to stretch back behind the ears, narrowing his eyes to Mongoloids. Shock. Panic. His hand pushed out and found the wall, and he braced himself with it. Then he went back toward the door again slowly. I could see him creeping up on it, stalking it as though it were something alive. He opened it so slenderly you couldn't see it at all, peered fearfully through the crack. Then he closed it, and he came back, zigzag, off balance from sheer reflex dismay. He toppled into a chair and snatched up a drink. Out of the bottle neck itself this time. And even while he was holding it to his lips, his head was turned looking over his shoulder at the door that had suddenly thrown his secret in his face.

I put the glass down.

Guilty! Guilty as all hell, and the police be damned!

My hand started toward the phone, came back again. What was the use? They wouldn't listen now any more than they had before. "You should have seen his face, etc." And I could hear Boyne's answer: "Anyone gets a jolt from an anonymous letter, true or false. You would yourself." They had a real live Mrs. Thorwald to show me — or thought they had. I'd have to show them the dead one, to prove that they both weren't one and the same. I, from my window, had to show them a body.

Well, he'd have to show me first.

It took hours before I got it. I kept pegging away at it, pegging away at it, while the afternoon wore away. Meanwhile he was pacing back and forth there like a caged panther. Two minds with but one thought, turned inside-out in my case. How to keep it hidden, how to see that it wasn't kept hidden.

I was afraid he might try to light out, but if he intended doing that he was going to wait until after dark, apparently, so I had a little time yet. Possibly he didn't want to himself, unless he was driven to it — still felt that it was more dangerous than to stay.

The customary sights and sounds around me went on unnoticed, while the main stream of my thoughts pounded like a torrent against that one obstacle stubbornly damming them up: how to get him to give the location away to me, so that I could give it away in turn to the police.

I was dimly conscious, I remember, of the landlord or somebody bringing in a prospective tenant to look at the sixth-floor apartment, the one that had already been finished. This was two over Thorwald's; they were still at work on the in-between one. At one point an odd little bit of synchronization, completely accidental of course, cropped up. Landlord and tenant both happened to be near the living room windows on the sixth at the same moment that Thorwald was near those on the fourth. Both parties moved onward simultaneously into the kitchen from there, and, passing the blind spot of the wall, appeared next at the kitchen windows. It was uncanny, they were almost like precision-strollers or puppets manipulated on one and the same string. It probably wouldn't have happened again just like that in another fifty years. Immediately afterwards they digressed, never to repeat themselves like that again.

The thing was, something about it had disturbed me. There had been some slight flaw or hitch to mar its smoothness. I tried for a moment or two to figure out what it had been, and couldn't. The landlord and tenant had gone now, and only Thorwald was in sight. My unaided memory wasn't enough to recapture it for me. My eyesight might have if it had been repeated, but it wasn't.

It sank into my subconscious, to ferment there like yeast, while I went back to the main problem at hand.

I got it finally. It was well after dark, but I finally hit on a way. It mightn't work, it was cumbersome and roundabout, but it was the only way I could think of. An alarmed turn of the head, a quick precautionary step in one certain direction, was all I needed. And to get this brief, flickering, transitory give-away, I needed two phone calls and an absence of about half an hour on his part between them.

I leafed a directory by matchlight until I'd found what I wanted: *Thorwald, Lars. 525 Bndct. . . . S Wansea 5-2114.*

I blew out the match, picked up the phone in the dark. It was like television. I could see to the other end of my call, only not along the wire but by a direct channel of vision from window to window.

He said "Hullo?" gruffly.

I thought: How strange this is. I've been accusing him of murder for three days straight, and only now I'm hearing his voice for the first time.

I didn't try to disguise my own voice. After all, he'd never see me and I'd never see him. I said: "You got my note?"

He said guardedly: "Who is this?"

"Just somebody who happens to know."

He said craftily: "Know what?"

"Know what you know. You and I, we're the only ones."

He controlled himself well. I didn't hear a sound. But he didn't know he was open another way too. I had the glass balanced there at proper height on two large books on the sill. Through the window I saw him pull open the collar of his shirt as though its stricture was intolerable. Then he backed his hand over his eyes like you do when there's a light blinding you.

His voice came back firmly. "I don't know what you're talking about."

"Business, that's what I'm talking about. It should be worth something to me, shouldn't it? To keep it from going any further." I wanted to keep him from catching on that it was the windows. I still needed them, I needed them now more than ever. "You weren't very careful about your door the other night. Or maybe the draft swung it open a little."

That hit him where he lived. Even the stomach-heave reached me over the wire. "You didn't see anything. There wasn't anything to see."

"That's up to you. Why should I go to the police?" I coughed a little. "If it would pay me not to."

"Oh," he said. And there was relief of a sort in it. "D'you want to — see me? Is that it?"

"That would be the best way, wouldn't it? How much can you bring with you for now?"

"I've only got about seventy dollars around here."

"All right, then we can arrange the rest for later. Do you know where Lakeside Park is? I'm near there now. Suppose we make it there." That was about thirty minutes away. Fifteen there and fifteen back. "There's a little pavilion as you go in."

"How many of you are there?" he asked cautiously.

"Just me. It pays to keep things to yourself. That way you don't have to divvy up."

He seemed to like that too. "I'll take a run out," he said, "just to see what it's all about."

I watched him more closely than ever, after he'd hung up. He flitted straight through to the end room, the bedroom, that he didn't go near any more. He disappeared into a clothes-closet in there, stayed a minute, came out again. He must have taken something out of a hidden cranny or niche in there that even the dicks had missed. I could tell by the piston-like motion of his hand, just before it disappeared inside his coat, what it was. A gun.

It's a good thing, I thought, I'm not out there in Lakeside Park waiting for my seventy dollars.

The place blacked and he was on his way.

I called Sam in. "I want you to do something for me that's a little risky. In fact, damn risky. You might break a leg, or you might get shot, or you might even get pinched. We've been together ten years, and I wouldn't ask you anything like that if I could do it myself. But I can't, and it's got to be done." Then I told him. "Go out the back way, cross the back yard fences, and see if you can get into that fourth-floor flat up the fire escape. He's left one of the windows down a little from the top."

"What do you want me to look for?"

"Nothing." The police had been there already, so what was the good of that? "There are three rooms over there. I want you to disturb everything just a little bit, in all three, to show someone's been in there. Turn up the edge of each rug a little, shift every chair and table around a little, leave the closet doors standing out. Don't pass up a thing. Here, keep your eyes on this." I took off my own wrist watch, strapped it on him. "You've got twenty-five minutes, starting from now. If you stay within those twenty-five minutes, nothing will happen to you. When you see they're up, don't wait any longer, get out and get out fast."

"Climb back down?"

"No." He wouldn't remember, in his excitement, if he'd left the windows up or not. And I didn't want him to connect danger with the back of his place, but with the front. I wanted to keep my own window out of it. "Latch the window down tight, let yourself out the door, and beat it out of the building the front way, for your life!"

"I'm just an easy mark for you," he said ruefully, but he went.

He came out through our own basement door below me, and scrambled over the fences. If anyone had challenged him from one of the surrounding windows, I was going to backstop for him, explain I'd sent him down to look for something. But no one did. He made it pretty good for anyone his age. He isn't so young any more. Even the fire escape backing the flat, which was drawn up short, he managed to contact by standing up on something. He got in, lit the light, looked over at me. I motioned him to go ahead, not weaken.

I watched him at it. There wasn't any way I could protect him, now that he was in there. Even Thorwald would be within his rights in shooting him down — this was break and entry. I had to stay in back behind the scenes, like I had been all along. I couldn't get out in front of him as a lookout and shield him. Even the dicks had had a lookout posted.

He must have been tense, doing it. I was twice as tense, watching him do it. The twenty-five minutes took fifty to go by. Finally he came over to the window, latched it fast. The lights went, and he was out. He'd made it. I blew out a bellyful of breath that was twenty-five minutes old.

I heard him keying the street door, and when he came up I said warningly: "Leave the light out in here. Go and build yourself a great big two-story whisky punch; you're as close to white as you'll ever be."

Thorwald came back twenty-nine minutes after he'd left for Lakeside Park. A pretty slim margin to hang a man's life on. So now for the finale of the long-winded business, and here was hoping. I got my second phone call in before he had time to notice anything amiss. It was tricky timing but I'd been sitting there with the receiver ready in my hand, dialing the number over and over, then killing it each time. He came in on the 2 of 5-2114, and I saved that much time. The ring started before his hand came away from the light switch.

This was the one that was going to tell the story.

"You were supposed to bring money, not a gun; that's why I didn't show up." I saw the jolt that threw him. The window still had to stay out of it. "I saw you tap the inside of your coat, where you had it, as you came out on the street." Maybe he hadn't, but he wouldn't remember by now whether he had or not. You usually do when you're packing a gun and aren't an habitual carrier.

"Too bad you had your trip out and back for nothing. I didn't waste my time while you were gone, though. I know more now than I knew before." This was the important part. I had the glass up and I was practically fluoroscoping him. "I've found out where — it is. You know what I mean. I know now where you've got — it. I was there while you were out."

Not a word. Just quick breathing.

"Don't you believe me? Look around. Put the receiver down and take a look for yourself. I found it."

He put it down, moved as far as the living room entrance, and touched off the lights. He just looked around him once, in a sweeping, all-embracing stare, that didn't come to a head on any one fixed point, didn't center at all.

He was smiling grimly when he came back to the phone. All he said, softly and with malignant satisfaction, was: "You're a liar."

Then I saw him lay the receiver down and take his hand off it. I hung up at my end.

The test had failed. And yet it hadn't. He hadn't given the location away as I'd hoped he would. And yet that "You're a liar" was a tacit admission that it was there to be found, somewhere around him, somewhere on those premises. In such a good place that he didn't have to worry about it, didn't even have to look to make sure.

So there was a kind of sterile victory in my defeat. But it wasn't worth a damn to me.

He was standing there with his back to me, and I couldn't see what he was doing. I knew the phone was somewhere in front of him, but I thought he was just standing there pensive behind it. His head was slightly lowered, that was all. I'd hung up at my end. I didn't even see his elbow move. And if his index finger did, I couldn't see it.

He stood like that a moment or two, then finally he moved aside. The lights went out over there; I lost him. He was careful not even to strike matches, like he sometimes did in the dark.

My mind no longer distracted by having him to look at, I turned to trying to recapture something else — that troublesome little hitch in synchronization that had occurred this afternoon, when the renting agent and he both moved simultaneously from one window to the next. The closest I could get was this: it was like when you're looking at someone through a pane of imperfect glass, and a flaw in the glass distorts the symmetry of the reflected image for a second, until it has gone on past that point. Yet that wouldn't do, that was not it. The windows had been open and there had been no glass between. And I hadn't been using the lens at the time.

My phone rang. Boyne, I supposed. It wouldn't be anyone else at this hour. Maybe, after reflecting on the way he'd jumped all over me — I said "Hello" unguardedly, in my own normal voice.

There wasn't any answer.

I said: "Hello? Hello? Hello?" I kept giving away samples of my voice.

There wasn't a sound from first to last.

I hung up finally. It was still dark over there, I noticed.

Sam looked in to check out. He was a bit thick-tongued from his restorative drink. He said something about "Awri' if I go now?" I half heard him. I was trying to figure out another way of trapping *him* over there into giving away the right spot. I motioned my consent absently.

He went a little unsteadily down the stairs to the ground floor and after a delaying moment or two I heard the street door close after him. Poor Sam, he wasn't much used to liquor.

I was left alone in the house, one chair the limit of my freedom of movement.

Suddenly a light went on over there again, just momentarily, to go right out again afterwards. He must have needed it for something, to locate something that he had already been looking for and found he wasn't able to put his hands on readily without it. He found it, whatever it was, almost immediately, and moved back at once to put the lights out again. As he turned to do so, I saw him give a glance out the window. He didn't come to the window to do it, he just shot it out in passing.

Something about it struck me as different from any of the others I'd seen him give in all the time I'd been watching him. If you can qualify such an elusive thing as a glance, I would have termed it a glance with a purpose. It was certainly anything but vacant or random, it had a bright spark of fixity in it. It wasn't one of those precautionary sweeps I'd seen him give, either. It hadn't started over on the other side and worked its way around to my side, the right. It had hit dead-center at my bay window, for just a split second while it lasted, and then was gone again. And the lights were gone and he was gone.

Sometimes your senses take things in without your mind translating them into their proper meaning. My eyes saw that look. My mind refused to smelter it properly. "It was meaningless," I thought. "An unintentional bull's-eye, that just happened to hit square over here, as he went toward the lights on his way out."

Delayed action. A wordless ring of the phone. To test a voice? A period of bated darkness following that, in which two could have played at the same game — stalking one another's window-squares, unseen. A last-moment flicker of the lights, that was bad strategy but unavoidable. A parting glance, radioactive with malignant intention. All these things sank in without fusing. My eyes did their job, it was my mind that didn't — or at least took its time about it.

Seconds went by in packages of sixty. It was very still around the familiar quadrangle formed by the back of the houses. Sort of a breathless stillness. And then a sound came into it, starting up from nowhere, nothing. The unmistakable, spaced clicking a cricket makes in the silence of the night. I thought of Sam's superstition about them, that he claimed had never failed to fulfill itself yet. If that was the case, it looked bad for somebody in one of these slumbering houses around here —

Sam had been gone only about ten minutes. And now he was back again, he must have forgotten something. That drink was responsible. Maybe his hat, or maybe even the key to his own quarters uptown. He knew I couldn't come down and let him in, and he was trying to be quiet about it, thinking perhaps I'd dozed off. All I could hear was this faint jiggling down at the lock of the front door. It was one of those old-fashioned stoop houses, with an outer pair of storm doors that were allowed to swing free all night, and then a small vestibule, and then the inner door, worked by a simple iron key. The liquor had made his hand a little unreliable, although he'd had this difficulty once or twice before, even without it. A match would have helped him find the keyhole quicker, but then, Sam doesn't smoke. I knew he wasn't likely to have one on him.

The sound had stopped now. He must have given up, gone away again, decided to let whatever it was go until tomorrow. He hadn't gotten in, because I knew his noisy way of letting doors coast shut by themselves too well, and there hadn't been any sound of that sort, that loose slap he always made.

Then suddenly it exploded. Why at this particular moment, I don't know. That was some mystery of the inner workings of my own mind. It flashed like waiting gunpowder which a spark has finally reached along a slow train. Drove all thoughts of Sam, and the front door, and this and that completely out of my head. It had been waiting there since midafternoon today, and only now — More of that delayed action. Damn that delayed action.

The renting agent and Thorwald had both started even from the living room window. An intervening gap of blind wall, and both had reappeared at the kitchen window, still one above the other. But some sort of a hitch or flaw or jump had taken place, right there, that bothered me. The eye is a reliable surveyor. There wasn't anything the matter with their timing, it was with their parallel-ness, or whatever the word is. The hitch had been vertical, not horizontal. There had been an upward "jump."

Now I had it, now I knew. And it couldn't wait. It was too good. They wanted a body? Now I had one for them.

Sore or not, Boyne would *have* to listen to me now. I didn't waste any time, I dialed his precinct-house then and there in the dark, working the slots in my lap by memory alone. They didn't make much noise going around, just a light click. Not even as distinct as that cricket out there —

"He went home long ago," the desk sergeant said.

This couldn't wait. "All right, give me his home phone number."

He took a minute, came back again. "Trafalgar," he said. Then nothing more.

"Well? Trafalgar what?" Not a sound.

"Hello? Hello?" I tapped it. "Operator, I've been cut off. Give me that party again." I couldn't get her either.

I hadn't been cut off. My wire had been cut. That had been too sudden, right in the middle of — And to be cut like that it would have to be done somewhere right here inside the house with me. Outside it went underground.

Delayed action. This time final, fatal, altogether too late. A voiceless ring of the phone. A direction-finder of a look from over there. "Sam" seemingly trying to get back in a while ago.

Suddenly, death was somewhere inside the house here with me. And I couldn't move, I couldn't get up out of this chair. Even if I had gotten through to Boyne just now, that would have been too late. There wasn't time enough now for one of those camera-finishes in this. I could have shouted out the window to that gallery of sleeping rear-window neighbors around me, I supposed. It would have brought them to the windows. It couldn't have brought them over here in time. By the time they had even figured which particular house it was coming from, it would stop again, be over with. I didn't open my mouth. Not because I was brave, but because it was so obviously useless.

He'd be up in a minute. He must be on the stairs now, although I couldn't hear him. Not even a creak. A creak would have been a relief, would have placed him. This was like being shut up in the dark with the silence of a gliding, coiling cobra somewhere around you.

There wasn't a weapon in the place with me. There were books there on the wall, in the dark, within reach. Me, who never read. The former owner's books. There was a bust of Rousseau or Montesquieu, I'd never been able to decide which, one of those gents with flowing manes, topping them. It was a monstrosity, bisque clay, but it too dated from before my occupancy.

I arched my middle upward from the chair seat and clawed desperately up at it. Twice my fingertips slipped off it, then at the third raking I got it to teeter, and the fourth brought it down into my lap, pushing me down into the chair. There was a steamer rug under me. I didn't need it around me in this weather, I'd been using it to soften the seat of the chair. I tugged it out from under and mantled it around me like an Indian brave's blanket. Then I squirmed far down in the chair, let my head and one shoulder dangle out over the arm, on the side next to the wall. I hoisted the bust to my other, upward shoulder, balanced it there precariously for a second head, blanket tucked around its ears. From the back, in the dark, it would look — I hoped —

I proceeded to breathe adenoidally, like someone in heavy upright sleep. It wasn't hard. My own breath was coming nearly that labored anyway, from tension.

He was good with knobs and hinges and things. I never heard the door open, and this one, unlike the one downstairs, was right behind me. A little eddy of air puffed through the dark at me. I could feel it because my scalp, the real one, was all wet at the roots of the hair right then.

If it was going to be a knife or head-blow, the dodge might give me a second chance, that was the most I could hope for, I knew. My arms and shoulders are hefty. I'd bring him down on me in a bear-hug after the first slash or drive, and break his neck or collarbone against me. If it was going to be a gun, he'd get me anyway in the end. A difference of a few seconds. He had a gun, I knew, that he was going to use on me in the open, over at Lakeside Park. I was hoping that here, indoors, in order to make his own escape more practicable —

Time was up.

The flash of the shot lit up the room for a second, it was so dark. Or at least the corners of it, like flickering, weak lightning. The bust bounced on my shoulder and disintegrated into chunks.

I thought he was jumping up and down on the floor for a minute with frustrated rage. Then when I saw him dart by me and lean over the window sill to look for a way out, the sound transferred itself rearwards and downwards, became a pummeling with hoof and hip at the street door. The camera-finish after all. But he still could have killed me five times.

I flung my body down into the narrow crevice between chair arm and wall, but my legs were still up, and so was my head and that one shoulder.

He whirled, fired at me so close that it was like looking at sunrise in the face. I didn't feel it, so — it hadn't hit.

"You —" I heard him grunt to himself. I think it was the last thing he said. The rest of his life was all action, not verbal.

He flung over the sill on one arm and dropped into the yard. Two-story drop. He made it because he missed the cement, landed on the sod-strip in the middle. I jacked myself up over the chair arm and flung myself bodily forward at the window, neatly hitting it chin first.

He went all right. When life depends on it, you go. He took the first fence, rolled over that bellywards. He went over the second like a cat, hands and feet pointed together in a spring. Then he was back in the rear yard of his own building. He got up on something, just about like Sam had — The rest was all footwork, with quick little corkscrew twists at each landing stage. Sam had latched his windows down when he was over there, but he'd reopened one of them for ventilation on his return. His whole life depended now on that casual, unthinking little act —

Second, third. He was up to his own windows. He'd made it. Something went wrong. He veered out away from them in another pretzel-twist, flashed up toward the fifth, the one above. Something sparked in the darkness of one of his own windows where he'd been just now, and a shot thudded heavily out around the quadrangle enclosure like a big bass drum.

He passed the fifth, the sixth, got to the roof. He'd made it a second time. Gee, he loved life! The guys in his own windows couldn't get him, he was over them in a straight line and there was too much fire escape interlacing in the way.

I was too busy watching him to watch what was going on around me. Suddenly Boyne was next to me, sighting. I heard him mutter: "I almost hate to do this, he's got to fall so far."

He was balanced on the roof parapet up there, with a star right over his head. An unlucky star. He stayed a minute too long, trying to kill before he was killed. Or maybe he was killed, and knew it.

A shot cracked, high up against the sky, the window pane flew apart all over the two of us, and one of the books snapped right behind me.

Boyne didn't say anything more about hating to do it. My face was pressing outward against his arm. The recoil of his elbow jarred my teeth. I blew a clearing through the smoke to watch him go.

It was pretty horrible. He took a minute to show anything, standing up there on the parapet. Then he let his gun go, as if to say: "I won't need this any more." Then he went after it. He missed the fire escape entirely, came all the way down on the outside. He landed so far out he hit one of the projecting planks, down there out of sight. It bounced his body up, like a springboard. Then it landed again — for good. And that was all.

I said to Boyne: "I got it. I got it finally. The fifth-floor flat, the one over his, that they're still working on. The cement kitchen floor, raised above the level of the other rooms. They wanted to comply with the fire laws and also obtain a dropped living room effect, as cheaply as possible. Dig it up —"

He went right over then and there, down through the basement and over the fences, to save time. The electricity wasn't turned on yet in that one, they had to use their torches. It didn't take them long at that, once they'd got started. In about half an hour he came to the window and wigwagged over for my benefit. It meant yes.

He didn't come over until nearly eight in the morning; after they'd tidied up and taken them away. Both away, the hot dead and the cold dead. He said: "Jeff, I take it all back. That damn fool that I sent up there about the trunk — well, it wasn't his fault, in a way. I'm to blame. He didn't have orders to check on the woman's description, only on the contents of the trunk. He came back and touched on it in a general way. I go home and I'm in bed already, and suddenly pop! into my brain — one of the tenants I questioned two whole days ago had given us a few details and they didn't tally with his on several important points. Talk about being slow to catch on!"

"I've had that all the way through this damn thing," I admitted ruefully. "I called it delayed action. It nearly killed me."

"I'm a police officer and you're not."

"That how you happened to shine at the right time?"

"Sure. We came over to pick him up for questioning. I left them planted there when we saw he wasn't in, and came on over here by myself to square it up with you while we were waiting. How did you happen to hit on that cement floor?"

I told him about the freak synchronization. "The renting agent showed up taller at the kitchen window in proportion to Thorwald, than he had been a moment before when both were at the living room windows together. It was no secret that they were putting in cement floors, topped by a cork composition, and raising them considerably. But it took on new meaning. Since the top floor one has been finished for some time, it had to be the fifth. Here's the way I have it lined up, just in theory. She's been in ill health for years, and he's been out of work, and he got sick of that and of her both. Met this other —"

"She'll be here later today, they're bringing her down under arrest."

"He probably insured her for all he could get, and then started to poison her slowly, trying not to leave any trace. I imagine — and remember, this is pure conjecture — she caught him at it that night the light was on all night. Caught on in some way, or caught him in the act. He lost his head, and did the very thing he had wanted all along to avoid doing. Killed her by violence — strangulation or a blow. The rest had to be hastily improvised. He got a better break than he deserved at that. He thought of the apartment upstairs, went up and looked around. They'd just finished laying the floor, the cement hadn't hardened yet, and the materials were still around. He gouged a trough out of it just wide enough to take her body, put her in it, mixed fresh cement and recemented over her, possibly raising the general level of the floor an inch or two so that she'd be safely covered. A permanent, odorless coffin. Next day the workmen came back, laid down the cork surfacing on top of it without noticing anything, I suppose he'd used one of their own trowels to smooth it. Then he sent his accessory upstate fast, near where his wife had been several summers before, but to a different farmhouse where she wouldn't be recognized, along with the trunk keys. Sent the trunk up after her, and dropped himself an already used post card into his mailbox, with the year-date blurred. In a week or two she would have probably committed 'suicide' up there as Mrs. Anna Thorwald. Despondency due to ill health. Written him a farewell note and left her clothes beside some body of deep water. It was risky, but they might have succeeded in collecting the insurance at that."

By nine Boyne and the rest had gone. I was still sitting there in the chair, too keyed up to sleep. Sam came in and said: "Here's Doc Preston."

He showed up rubbing his hands, in that way he has. "Guess we can take that cast off your leg now. You must be tired of sitting there all day doing nothing."

WILLIAM FAULKNER

···

An Error in Chemistry

IT WAS JOEL FLINT HIMSELF who telephoned the sheriff that he had killed his wife. And when the sheriff and his deputy reached the scene, drove the twenty-odd miles into the remote back-country region where old Wesley Pritchel lived, Joel Flint himself met them at the door and asked them in. He was the foreigner, the outlander, the Yankee who had come into our county two years ago as the operator of a pitch — a lighted booth where a roulette wheel spun against a bank of nickel-plated pistols and razors and watches and harmonicas, in a traveling street carnival — and who when the carnival departed had remained, and two months later was married to Pritchel's only living child: the dim-witted spinster of almost forty who until then had shared her irascible and violent-tempered father's almost hermit-existence on the good though small farm which he owned.

But even after the marriage, old Pritchel still seemed to draw the line against his son-in-law. He built a new small house for them two miles from his own, where the daughter was presently raising chickens for the market. According to rumor old Pritchel, who hardly ever went any-where anyway, had never once entered the new house, so that he saw even this last remaining child only once a week. This would be when she and her husband would drive each Sunday in the second-hand truck in which the son-in-law marketed the chickens, to take Sunday dinner with old Pritchel in the old house where Pritchel now did his own cooking and housework. In fact, the neighbors said the only reason he allowed the son-in-law to enter his house even then was so that his daughter could prepare him a decent hot meal once a week.

So for the next two years, occasionally in Jefferson, the county seat, but more frequently in the little crossroads hamlet near his home, the son-in-law would be seen and heard too. He was a man in the middle forties, neither short nor tall nor thin nor stout (in fact, he and his father-in-law could easily have cast that same shadow which later for a short time they did), with a cold, contemptuous intelligent face and a voice lazy with anecdote of the teeming outland which his listeners had never seen — a dweller among the cities, though never from his own accounting long resident in any one of them, who within the first three months of his residence among them had impressed upon the people whose way of life he had assumed, one definite personal habit by which he presently became known throughout the whole county, even by men who had never seen him. This was a harsh and contemptuous derogation, sometimes without even provocation or reason or opportunity, of our local southern custom of drinking whiskey by mixing sugar and water with it. He called it effeminacy, a pap for children, himself drinking even our harsh, violent, illicit and unaged homemade corn whiskey without even a sip of water to follow it.

Then on this last Sunday morning he telephoned the sheriff that he had killed his wife and met the officers at his father-in-law's door and said: "I have already carried her into the house. So you won't need to waste breath telling me I shouldn't have touched her until you got here."

"I reckon it was all right to take her up out of the dirt," the sheriff said. "It was an accident, I believe you said."

"Then you believe wrong," Flint said. "I said I killed her."

And that was all.

The sheriff brought him to Jefferson and locked him in a cell in the jail. And that evening after supper the sheriff came through the side door into the study where Uncle Gavin was supervising me in the drawing of a brief. Uncle Gavin was only county, not District, attorney. But he and the sheriff, who had been sheriff off and on even longer that Uncle Gavin had been county attorney, had been friends all that while. I mean friends in the sense that two men who play chess together are friends, even though sometimes their aims are diametrically opposed. I heard them discuss it once.

"I'm interested in truth," the sheriff said.

"So am I," Uncle Gavin said. "It's so rare. But I am more interested in justice and human beings."

"Ain't truth and justice the same thing?" the sheriff said.

"Since when?" Uncle Gavin said. "In my time I have seen truth that was anything under the sun but just, and I have seen justice using tools and instruments I wouldn't want to touch with a ten-foot fence rail."

The sheriff told us about the killing, standing, looming above the table lamp — a big man with little hard eyes, talking down at Uncle Gavin's wild shock of prematurely white hair and his quick thin face, while Uncle Gavin sat on the back of his neck practically, his legs crossed on the desk, chewing the bit of his corncob pipe and spinning and unspinning around his finger his watch chain weighted with the Phi Beta Kappa key he got at Harvard.

"Why?" Uncle Gavin said.

"I asked him that, myself," the sheriff said. "He said, 'Why do men ever kill their wives? Call it for the insurance.'"

"That's wrong," Uncle Gavin said. "It's women who murder their spouses for immediate personal gain — insurance policies, or at what they believe is the instigation or promise of another man. Men murder their wives from hatred or rage or despair, or to keep them from talking since not even bribery not even simple absence can bridle a woman's tongue."

"Correct," the sheriff said. He blinked his little eyes at Uncle Gavin. "It's like he *wanted* to be locked up in jail. Not like he was submitting to arrest because he had killed his wife, but like he had killed her so that he would be locked up, arrested. Guarded."

"Why?" Uncle Gavin said.

"Correct too," the sheriff said. "When a man deliberately locks doors behind himself, it's because he's afraid. And a man who would voluntarily have himself locked up on suspicion of murder . . ." He batted his hard little eyes at Uncle Gavin for a good ten seconds while Uncle Gavin looked just as hard back at him. "Because he wasn't afraid. Not then nor at any time. Now and then you meet a man that ain't ever been afraid, not even of himself. He's one."

"If that's what he wanted you to do," Uncle Gavin said, "why did you do it?"

"You think I should have waited a while?"

They looked at one another a while. Uncle Gavin wasn't spinning the watch chain now. "All right," he said. "Old Man Pritchel —"

"I was coming to that," the sheriff said. "Nothing."

"Nothing?" Uncle Gavin said. "You didn't even see him?" And the sheriff told that too — how as he and the deputy and Flint stood on the gallery, they suddenly saw the old man looking out at them through a window — a face rigid, furious, glaring at them through the glass for a second and then withdrawn, vanished, leaving an impression of furious exultation and raging triumph, and something else. . . .

"Fear?" the sheriff said. "No. I tell you, he wasn't afraid — Oh," he said. "You mean Pritchel." This time he looked at Uncle Gavin so long that at last Uncle Gavin said:

"All right. Go on." And the sheriff told that too: how they entered the house, the hall, and he stopped and knocked at the locked door of the room where they had seen the face and he even called old Pritchel's name and still got no answer. And how they went on and found Mrs. Flint on a bed in the back room with the shotgun wound in her neck, and Flint's battered truck drawn up beside the back steps as if they had just got out of it.

"There were three dead squirrels in the truck," the sheriff said. "I'd say they had been shot since daylight" — and the blood on the steps, and on the ground between the steps and the truck, as if she had been shot from inside the truck, and the gun itself, still containing the spent shell, standing just inside the hall door as a man would put it down when he entered the house. And how the sheriff went back up to the hall and knocked again at the locked door —

"Locked where?" Uncle Gavin said.

"On the inside," the sheriff said — and shouted against the door's blank surface that he would break the door in if Mr. Pritchel didn't answer and open it, and how this time the harsh furious old voice answered, shouting:

"Get out of my house! Take that murderer and get out of my house."

"You will have to make a statement," the sheriff answered.

"I'll make my statement when the time comes for it!" the old man shouted. "Get out of my house, all of you!" And how he (the sheriff) sent the deputy in the car to fetch the nearest neighbor, and he and Flint waited until the deputy came back with a man and his wife. Then they brought Flint on to town and locked him up and the sheriff telephoned back to old Pritchel's house and the neighbor answered and told him how the old man was still locked in the room, refusing to come out or even to answer save to order them all (several other neighbors had arrived by now, word of the tragedy having spread) to leave. But some of them would stay in the house, no matter what the seemingly crazed old man said or did, and the funeral would be tomorrow.

"And that's all?" Uncle Gavin said.

"That's all," the sheriff said. "Because it's too late now."

"For instance?" Uncle Gavin said.

"The wrong one is dead."

"That happens," Uncle Gavin said.

"For instance?"

"That clay-pit business."

"What clay-pit business?" Because the whole county knew about old Pritchel's clay pit. It was a formation of malleable clay right in the middle of his farm, of which people in the adjacent countryside made quite serviceable though crude pottery — those times they could mange to dig that much of it up before Mr. Pritchel saw them and drove them off. For generations, Indian and even aboriginal relics — flint arrowheads, axes and dishes and skulls and thighbones and pipes — had been excavated from it by random boys, and a few years ago a party of archeologists from the State University had dug into it until Old Man Pritchel got there, this time with a shotgun. But everybody knew this; this was not what the sheriff was telling, and now Uncle Gavin was sitting erect in the chair and his feet were on the floor now.

"I hadn't heard about this," Uncle Gavin said.

"It's common knowledge out there," the sheriff said. "In fact, you might call it the local outdoor sport. It began about six weeks ago. They are three northern men. They're trying to buy the whole farm from old Pritchel to get the pit and manufacture some kind of road material out of the clay, I understand. The folks out there are still watching them try to buy it. Apparently the northerners are the only folks in the county that don't know yet old Pritchel ain't got any notion of selling even the clay to them, let alone the farm."

"They've made him an offer, of course."

"Probably a good one. It runs all the way from two hundred and fifty dollars to two hundred and fifty thousand, depending on who's telling it. Them northerners just don't know how to handle him. If they would just set and convince him that everybody in the county is hoping he won't sell it to them, they could probably buy it before supper tonight." He stared at Uncle Gavin, batting his eyes again. "So the wrong one is dead, you see. If it was that clay pit, he's no nearer to it than he was yesterday. He's worse off than he was yesterday. Then there wasn't anything between him and his pa-in-law's money but whatever private wishes and hopes and feelings that dim-witted girl might have had. Now there's a penitentiary wall, and likely a rope. It don't make sense. If he was afraid of a possible witness, he not only destroyed the witness before there was anything to be witnessed but also before there was any witness to be destroyed. He set up a signboard saying 'Watch me and mark me,' not just to this county and this state but to all folks everywhere who believe the Book where it says *Thou Shalt Not Kill* — and then went and got himself locked up in the very place created to punish him for this crime and restrain him from the next one. Something went wrong."

"I hope so," Uncle Gavin said.

"You hope so?"

"Yes. That something went wrong in what has already happened, rather than what has already happened is not finished yet."

"How not finished yet?" the sheriff said. "How can he finish whatever it is he aims to finish? Ain't he already locked up in jail, with the only man in the county who might make bond to free him being the father of the woman he as good as confessed he murdered?"

"It looks that way," Uncle Gavin said. "Was there an insurance policy?"

"I don't know," the sheriff said. "I'll find that out tomorrow. But that ain't what I want to know. I want to know why he *wanted* to be locked up in jail. Because I tell you he wasn't afraid, then nor at any other time. You already guessed who it was out there that was afraid."

But we were not to learn that answer yet. And there was an insurance policy. But by the time we learned about that, something else had happened which sent everything else temporarily out of mind. At daylight the next morning, when the jailer went and looked into Flint's cell, it was empty. He had not broken out. He had walked out, out of the cell, out of the jail, out of the town and apparently out of the county — no trace, no sign, no man who had seen him or seen anyone who might have been him. It was not yet sunup when I let the sheriff in at the side study door; Uncle Gavin was already sitting up in bed when we reached his bedroom.

"Old Man Pritchel!" Uncle Gavin said. "Only we are already too late."

"What's the matter with you?" the sheriff said. "I told you last night he was already too late the second he pulled the wrong trigger. Besides, just to be in position to ease your mind, I've already telephoned out there. Been a dozen folks in the house all night, sitting up with the — with Mrs. Flint, and old Pritchel's still locked in his room and all right too. They heard him bumping and blundering around in there just before daylight, and so somebody knocked on the door and kept on knocking and calling him until he finally opened the door wide enough to give them all a good cussing and order them again to get out of his house and stay out. Then he locked the door again. Old fellow's been hit pretty hard, I reckon. He must have seen it when it happened, and at his age, and having already druv the whole human race away from his house except that half-wit girl, until at last even she up and left him, even at any cost. I reckon it ain't any wonder she married even a man like Flint. What is it the Book says? 'Who lives by the sword, so shall he die?' — the sword in old Pritchel's case being whatever it was he decided he preferred in place of human beings, while he was still young and hale and strong and didn't need them. But to keep your mind easy, I sent Bryan Ewell out there thirty minutes ago and told him not to let that locked door — or old Pritchel himself, if he comes out of it — out of his sight until I told him to, and I sent Ben Berry and some others out to Flint's house and told Ben to telephone me. And I'll call you when I hear anything. Which won't be anything, because that fellow's gone. He got caught yesterday because he made a mistake, and the fellow that can walk out of that jail like he did ain't going to make two mistakes within five hundred miles of Jefferson or Mississippi either."

"Mistake?" Uncle Gavin said. "He just told us this morning why he wanted to be put in jail."

"And why was that?"

"So he could escape from it."

"And why get out again, when he was already out and could have stayed out by just running instead of telephoning me he had committed a murder?"

"I don't know," Uncle Gavin said. "Are you sure Old Man Pritchel —"

"Didn't I just tell you folks saw and talked to him through that half-opened door this morning? And Bryan Ewell probably sitting in a chair tilted against that door right this minute — or he better be. I'll telephone you if I hear anything. But I've already told you that too — that it won't be nothing."

He telephoned an hour later. He had just talked to the deputy who had searched Flint's house, reporting only that Flint had been there sometime in the night — the back door open, an oil lamp shattered on the floor where Flint had apparently knocked it while fumbling in the dark, since the deputy found, behind a big, open, hurriedly ransacked trunk, a twisted spill of paper which Flint had obviously used to light his search of the trunk — a scrap of paper torn from a billboard —

"A what?" Uncle Gavin said.

"That's what I said," the sheriff said. "And Ben says, 'All right, then send somebody else out here, if my reading ain't good enough to suit you. It was a scrap of paper which was evidently tore from the corner of a billboard because it says on the scrap in English that even I can read —' and I says, 'Tell me exactly what it is you're holding in your hand.' And he did. It's a page, from a magazine or a small paper named *Billboard* or maybe *The Billboard*. There's some more printing on it but Ben can't read it because he lost his spectacles back in the woods while he was surrounding the house to catch Flint doing whatever it was he expected to catch him doing — cooking breakfast, maybe. Do you know what it is?"

"Yes," Uncle Gavin said.

"Do you know what it means, what it was doing there?"

"Yes," Uncle Gavin said. "Buy why?"

"Well, I can't tell you. And he never will. Because he's gone, Gavin. Oh, we'll catch him — somebody will, I mean, someday, somewhere. But it won't be here, and it won't be for this. It's like that poor, harmless, half-witted girl wasn't important enough for even that justice you claim you prefer above truth, to avenge her."

And that did seem to be all of it. Mrs. Flint was buried that afternoon. The old man was still locked up in his room during the funeral, and even after they departed with the coffin for the churchyard, leaving in the house only the deputy in his tilted chair outside the locked door, and two neighbor women who remained to cook a hot meal for old Pritchel, finally prevailing on him to open the door long enough to take the tray from them. And he thanked them for it, clumsily and gruffly, thanking them for their kindness during all the last twenty-four hours. One of the women was moved enough to offer to return tomorrow and cook another meal for him, whereupon his old-time acerbity and choler returned and the kind-hearted woman was even regretting that she had made the offer at all when the harsh, cracked old voice from inside the half-closed door added: "I don't need no help. I ain't had no darter nohow in two years," and the door slammed in their faces and the bolt shot home.

Then the two women left, and there was only the deputy sitting in his tilted chair beside the door. He was back in town the next morning, telling how the old man had snatched the door suddenly open and kicked the chair out from beneath the dozing deputy before he could move and ordered him off the place with violent curses, and how as he (the deputy) peered at the house from around the corner of the barn a short

time later, the shotgun blared from the kitchen window and the charge
of squirrel shot slammed into the stable wall not a yard above his head.
The sheriff telephoned that to Uncle Gavin too:

"So he's out there alone again. And since that's what he seems to
want, it's all right with me. Sure I feel sorry for him. I feel sorry for anybody that has to live with a disposition like his. Old and alone, to have
all this happen to him. It's like being snatched up by a tornado and
whirled and slung and then slammed right back down where you
started from, without even the benefit and pleasure of having taken a
trip. What was it I said yesterday about living by the sword?"

"I don't remember," Uncle Gavin said. "You said a lot yesterday."

"And a lot of it was right. I said it was finished yesterday. And it is.
That fellow will trip himself again someday, but it won't be here."

Only it was more than that. It was as if Flint had never been here at
all — no mark, no scar to show that he had even been in the jail cell.
The meager group of people who pitied but did not mourn, departing,
separating, from the raw grave of the woman who had had little enough
hold on our lives at best, whom a few of us had known without ever
having seen her and some of us had seen without ever knowing her. . . .
The childless old man whom most of us had never seen at all, once
more alone in the house where, as he said himself, there had been no
child anyway in two years. . . .

"As though none of it had ever happened." Uncle Gavin said. "As if
Flint had not only never been in that cell but had never existed at all.
That triumvirate of murder, victim, and bereaved — not three flesh-
and-blood people but just an illusion, a shadow-play on a sheet — not
only neither men nor women nor young nor old but just three labels
which cast two shadows for the simple and only reason that it requires
a minimum of two in order to postulate the verities of injustice and
grief. That's it. They have never cast but two shadows, even though they
did bear three labels, names. It was as though only by dying did that
poor woman ever gain enough substance and reality even to cast a
shadow."

"But somebody killed her," I said.

"Yes," Uncle Gavin said. "Somebody killed her."

That was at noon. About five that afternoon I answered the telephone. It was the sheriff. "Is your uncle there?" he said. "Tell him to
wait. I'm coming right over." He had a stranger with him — a city man,
in neat city clothes.

"This is Mr. Workman," the sheriff said. "The adjustor. There was an insurance policy. For five hundred, taken out seventeen months ago. Hardly enough to murder anybody for."

"If it ever was a murder," the adjustor said. His voice was cold too, cold yet at the same time at a sort of seething boil. "That policy will be paid at once, without question or any further investigation. And I'll tell you something else you people here don't seem to know yet. That old man is crazy. It was not the man Flint who should have been brought to town and locked up."

Only it was the sheriff who told that too: how yesterday afternoon the insurance company's Memphis office had received a telegram, signed with Old Man Pritchel's name, notifying them of the insured's death, and the adjustor arrived at Old Man Pritchel's house about two o'clock this afternoon and within thirty minutes had extracted from Old Man Pritchel himself the truth about his daughter's death: the facts of it which the physical evidence — the truck and the three dead squirrels and the blood on the steps and on the ground — supported. This was that while the daughter was cooking dinner, Pritchel and Flint had driven the truck down to Pritchel's woods lot to shoot squirrels for supper — "And that's correct," the sheriff said. "I asked. They did that every Sunday morning. Pritchel wouldn't let anybody but Flint shoot his squirrels, and he wouldn't even let Flint shoot them unless he was along" — and they shot the three squirrels and Flint drove the truck back to the house and up beside the back steps and the woman came out to take the squirrels and Flint opened the door and picked up the gun to get out of the truck and stumbled, caught his heel on the edge of the running board and flinging up the hand carrying the gun to break his fall, so that the muzzle of the gun was pointing right at his wife's head when it went off. And Old Man Pritchel not only denied having sent the wire, he violently and profanely repudiated any and all implication or suggestion that he even knew the policy existed at all. He denied to the very last that the shooting had been any part of an accident. He tried to revoke his own testimony as to what had happened when the daughter came out to get the dead squirrels and the gun went off, repudiating his own story when he realized that he had cleared his son-in-law of murder, snatching the paper from the adjustor's hand, which he apparently believed was the policy itself, and attempting to tear it up and destroy it before the adjustor could stop him.

"Why?" Uncle Gavin said.

"Why not?" the sheriff said. "We had let Flint get away; Mr. Pritchel knew he was loose somewhere in the world. Do you reckon he aimed to let the man that killed his daughter get paid for it?"

"Maybe," Uncle Gavin said. "But I don't think so. I don't think he is worried about that at all. I think Mr. Pritchel knows that Joel Flint is not going to collect that policy or any other prize. Maybe he knew a little country jail like ours wasn't going to hold a wide-traveled ex-carnival man, and he expected Flint to come back out there and this time he was ready for him. And I think that as soon as people stop worrying him, he will send you word to come out there, and he will tell you so."

"Hah," the adjustor said. "Then they must have stopped worrying him. Listen to this. When I got there this afternoon, there were three men in the parlor with him. They had a certified check. It was a big check. They were buying his farm from him — lock, stock and barrel — and I didn't know land in this country was worth that much either, incidentally. He had the deed all drawn and signed, but when I told them who I was, they agreed to wait until I could get back to town here and tell somebody — the sheriff, probably. And I left, and that old lunatic was still standing in the door, shaking that deed at me and croaking: 'Tell the sheriff, damn you! Get a lawyer, too! Get that lawyer Gavin. I hear tell he claims to be pretty slick!'"

"We thank you," the sheriff said. He spoke and moved with that deliberate, slightly florid, old-fashioned courtesy which only big men can wear, except that his was constant; this was the first time I ever saw him quit anyone shortly, even when he would see them again tomorrow. He didn't even look at the adjustor again. "My car's outside," he told Uncle Gavin.

So just before sunset we drove up to the neat picket fence enclosing Old Man Pritchel's neat, bare little yard and neat, tight little house, in front of which stood the big, dust-covered car with its city license plates and Flint's battered truck with a strange Negro youth at the wheel — strange because Old Man Pritchel had never had a servant of any sort save his daughter.

"He's leaving too," Uncle Gavin said.

"That's his right," the sheriff said. We mounted the steps. But before we reached the door, Old Man Pritchel was already shouting for us to come in — the harsh, cracked old man's voice shouting at us from beyond the hall, beyond the door to the dining room where a tremendous old-fashioned telescope bag, strapped and bulging, sat on a chair and the three northerners in dusty khaki stood watching the door and Old

Man Pritchel himself sat at the table. And I saw for the first time (Uncle Gavin told me he had seen him only twice) the uncombed thatch of white hair, a fierce tangle of eyebrows above steel-framed spectacles, a jut of untrimmed mustache and a scrabble of beard stained with chewing tobacco to the color of dirty cotton.

"Come in," he said. "That lawyer Gavin, heh?"

"Yes, Mr. Pritchel," the sheriff said.

"Hehm," the old man barked. "Well, Hub," he said. "Can I sell my land, or can't I?"

"Of course, Mr. Pritchel," the sheriff said. "We hadn't heard you aimed to."

"Heh," the old man said. "Maybe this changed my mind." The check and the folded deed both lay on the table in front of him. He pushed the check toward the sheriff. He didn't look at Uncle Gavin again; he just said: "You, too." Uncle Gavin and the sheriff moved to the table and stood looking down at the check. Neither of them touched it. I could see their faces. There was nothing in them. "Well?" Mr. Pritchel said.

"It's a good price," the sheriff said.

This time the old man said "Hah!" short and harsh. He unfolded the deed and spun it to face, not the sheriff but Uncle Gavin. "Well?" he said. "You, lawyer?"

"It's all right, Mr. Pritchel," Uncle Gavin said. The old man sat back, both hands on the table before him, his head tilted back as he looked up at the sheriff.

"Well?" he said. "Fish, or cut bait."

"It's your land," the sheriff said. "What you do with it is no man's business else."

"Hah," Mr. Pritchel said. He didn't move. "All right, gentlemen." He didn't move at all; one of the strangers came forward and took up the deed. "I'll be out of the house in thirty minutes. You can take possession then, or you will find the key under the mat tomorrow morning." I don't believe he even looked after them as they went out, though I couldn't be sure because of the glare of his spectacles. Then I knew that he was looking at the sheriff, had been looking at him for a minute or more, and then I saw that he was trembling, jerking and shaking as the old tremble, although his hands on the table were as motionless as two lumps of the clay would have been.

"So you let him get away," he said.

"That's right," the sheriff said. "But you wait, Mr. Pritchel. We'll catch him."

"When?" the old man said. "Two years? Five years? Ten years? I am seventy-four years old; buried my wife and four children. Where will I be in ten years?"

"Here, I hope," the sheriff said.

"Here?" the old man said. "Didn't you just hear me tell that fellow he could have this house in thirty minutes? I own a automobile truck now; I got money to spend now, and something to spend it for."

"Spend it for what?" the sheriff said. "That check? Even this boy here would have to start early and run late to get shut of that much money in ten years."

"Spend it running down the man that killed my Ellie!" He rose suddenly, thrusting his chair back. He staggered, but when the sheriff stepped quickly toward him, he flung his arm out and seemed actually to strike the sheriff back a pace. "Let be," he said, panting. Then he said, harsh and loud in his cracked shaking voice: "Get out of here? Get out of my house all of you!" But the sheriff didn't move, nor did we, and after a moment the old man stopped trembling. But he was still holding to the table edge. But his voice was quiet. "Hand me my whiskey. On the sideboard. And three glasses." The sheriff fetched them — an old-fashioned cut-glass decanter and three heavy tumblers — and set them before him. And when he spoke this time, his voice was almost gentle and I knew what the woman had felt that evening when she offered to come back tomorrow and cook another meal for him: "You'll have to excuse me. I'm tired. I've had a heap of trouble lately, and I reckon I'm wore out. Maybe a change is what I need."

"But not tonight, Mr. Pritchel," the sheriff said.

And then again, as when the woman had offered to come back and cook, he ruined it. "Maybe I won't start tonight," he said. "And then maybe again I will. But you folks want to get on back to town, so we'll just drink to goodbye and better days." He unstoppered the decanter and poured whiskey into the three tumblers and set the decanter down and looked about the table. "You, boy," he said, "hand me the water bucket. It's on the back gallery shelf." Then, as I turned and started toward the door, I saw him reach up and take up the sugar bowl and plunge the spoon into the sugar and then I stopped too. And I remember Uncle Gavin's and the sheriff's faces and I could not believe my eyes either as he put the spoonful of sugar into the raw whiskey and started to stir it. Because I had not only watched Uncle Gavin, and the sheriff when he would come to play chess with Uncle Gavin, but Uncle Gavin's father too who was my grandfather, and my own father before he died, and all the other men who would come to Grandfather's house who drank cold toddies as we call them, and even I knew that to make a cold toddy you do not put the sugar into the whiskey because sugar will not dissolve in raw whiskey but only lies in a little intact swirl like sand at the bottom of the glass; that you first put the water into the glass and dissolve the sugar into the water, in a ritual almost; then you add the whiskey, and that anyone like Old Man Pritchel who must have been watching men make cold toddies for nearly seventy years and had been making and drinking them himself for at least fifty-three, would know this too. And I remember how the man we had thought was Old Man Pritchel realized too late what he was doing and jerked his head up just as Uncle Gavin sprang toward him, and swung his arm back and hurled the glass at Uncle Gavin's head, and the thud of the flung glass against the wall and the dark splash it made and the crash of the table as it went over and the raw stink of the spilled whiskey from the decanter and Uncle Gavin shouting at the sheriff: "Grab him, Hub! Grab him!"

Then we were all three on him. I remember the savage strength and speed of the body which was no old man's body; I saw him duck beneath the sheriff's arm and the entire wig came off; I seemed to see his whole face wrenching itself furiously free from beneath the makeup which bore the painted wrinkles and the false eyebrows. When the sheriff snatched the beard and mustache off, the flesh seemed to come with it, springing quick and pink and then crimson, as though in that last desperate cast he had had to beard, disguise, not his face so much as the very blood which he had spilled.

It took us only thirty minutes to find old Mr. Pritchel's body. It was under the feed room in the stable, in a shallow and hurried trench, scarcely covered from sight. His hair had not only been dyed, it had been trimmed, the eyebrows trimmed and dyed too, and the mustache and beard shaved off. He was wearing the identical garments which Flint had worn to the jail and he had been struck at least one crushing blow on the face, apparently with the flat of the same axe which had split his skull from behind, so that his features were almost unrecognizable and, after another two or three weeks underground, would perhaps have been even unidentifiable as those of the old man. And pillowed carefully beneath the head was a big ledger almost six inches thick and weighing almost twenty pounds and filled with the carefully pasted clippings which covered twenty years and more. It was the record and tale of the gift, the talent, which at the last he had misapplied and betrayed and which had then turned and destroyed him. It was all there: inception, course, peak, and then decline — the handbills, the theater programs, the news clippings, and even one actual ten-foot poster:

SIGNOR CANOVA
Master of Illusion
He Disappears While You Watch Him
Management offers One Thousand Dollars in Cash
To Any Man or Woman or Child Who . . .

Last of all was the final clipping, from our Memphis-printed daily paper, under the Jefferson date line, which was news and not press-agentry. This was the account of that last gamble in which he had cast his gift and his life against money, wealth, and lost — the clipped fragment of newssheet which recorded the end not of one life but of three, though even here two of them cast but one shadow: not only that of the harmless dim-witted woman but of Joel Flint and Signor Canova too, with scattered among them and marking the date of that death too, the cautiously worded advertisements in *Variety* and *Billboard,* using the new changed name and no takers probably, since Signor Canova the Great was already dead then and already serving his purgatory in this circus for six months and that circus for eight — bandsman, ringman, Bornean wild man, down to the last stage where he touched bottom: the traveling from country town to country town with a roulette wheel wired against imitation watches and pistols which would not shoot, until one day instinct perhaps showed him one more chance to use the gift again.

"And lost this time for good," the sheriff said. We were in the study again. Beyond the open side door fireflies winked and drifted across the summer night and the crickets and tree frogs cheeped and whirred. "It was that insurance policy. If that adjustor hadn't come to town and sent us back out there in time to watch him try to dissolve sugar in raw whiskey, he would have collected that check and taken that truck and got clean away. Instead, he sends for the adjustor, then he practically dares you and me to come out there and see past that wig and paint —"

"You said something the other day about his destroying his witness too soon," Uncle Gavin said. "She wasn't his witness. The witness he destroyed was the one we were supposed to find under that feed room."

"Witness to what?" the sheriff said. "To the fact that Joel Flint no longer existed?"

"Partly. But mostly to the first crime, the old one: the one in which Signor Canova died. He intended for that witness to be found. That's why he didn't bury it, hide it better and deeper. As soon as somebody found it, he would be at once and forever not only rich but free, free not only of Signor Canova who had betrayed him by dying eight years ago, but of Joel Flint too. Even if we had found it before he had a chance to leave, what would he have said?"

"He ought to have battered the face a little more," the sheriff said.

"I doubt it," Uncle Gavin said. "What would he have said?"

"All right," the sheriff said. "What?"

"'Yes, I killed him. He murdered my daughter.' And what would you have said, being, as you are, the Law?"

"Nothing," the sheriff said after a time.

"Nothing," Uncle Gavin said. A dog was barking somewhere, not a big dog, and then a screech owl flew into the mulberry tree in the back yard and began to cry, plaintive and tremulous, and all the little furred creatures would be moving now — the field mice, the possums and rabbits and foxes and the legless vertebrates — creeping or scurrying about the dark land which beneath the rainless summer stars was just dark: not desolate. "That's one reason he did it," Uncle Gavin said.

"One reason?" the sheriff said. "What's the other?"

"The other is the real one. It had nothing to do with the money; he probably could not have helped obeying it if he had wanted to. That gift he had. His first regret right now is probably not that he was caught, but that he was caught too soon, before the body was found and he had the chance to identify it as his own; before Signor Canova had had time to toss his gleaming top hat vanishing behind him and bow to the amazed and stormlike staccato of adulant palms and turn and stride once or twice and then himself vanish from the pacing spotlight — gone, to be seen no more. Think what he did: he convicted himself of murder when he could very likely have escaped by flight; he acquitted himself of it after he was already free again. Then he dared you and me to come out there and actually be his witnesses and guarantors in the consummation of the very act which he knew we had been trying to prevent. What else could the possession of such a gift as his have engendered, and the successful practising of it have increased, but a supreme contempt for mankind? You told me yourself that he had never been afraid in his life."

"Yes," the sheriff said. "The Book itself says somewhere, *Know thyself.* Ain't there another book somewhere that says, *Man, fear thyself, thine arrogance and vanity and pride?* You ought to know; you claim to be a book man. Didn't you tell me that's what that luck charm on your watch chain means? What book is that in?"

"It's in all of them," Uncle Gavin said. "The good ones, I mean. It's said in a lot of different ways, but it's there."

1947

HARRY KEMELMAN

....

The Nine Mile Walk

I HAD MADE AN ASS OF MYSELF in a speech I had given at the Good Government Association dinner, and Nicky Welt had cornered me at breakfast at the Blue Moon, where we both ate occasionally, for the pleasure of rubbing it in. I had made the mistake of departing from my prepared speech to criticize a statement my predecessor in the office of county attorney had made to the press. I had drawn a number of inferences from his statement and had thus left myself open to a rebuttal, which he had promptly made and which had the effect of making me appear intellectually dishonest. I was new to this political game, having but a few months before left the law school faculty to become the Reform party candidate for county attorney. I said as much in extenuation, but Nicholas Welt, who could never drop his pedagogical manner (he was Snowdon Professor of English Language and Literature), replied in much the same tone that he would dismiss a request from a sophomore for an extension on a term paper, "That's no excuse."

Although he is only two or three years older than I, in his late forties, he always treats me like a schoolmaster hectoring a stupid pupil. And I, perhaps because he looks so much older with his white hair and lined, gnome-like face, suffer it.

"They were perfectly logical inferences," I pleaded.

"My dear boy," he purred, "although human intercourse is well-nigh impossible without inference, most inferences are usually wrong. The percentage of error is particularly high in the legal profession, where the intention is not to discover what the speaker wishes to convey, but rather what he wishes to conceal."

I picked up my check and eased out from behind the table.

"I suppose you are referring to cross-examination of witnesses in court. Well, there's always an opposing counsel who will object if the inference is illogical."

"Who said anything about logic?" he retorted. "An inference can be logical and still not be true."

He followed me down the aisle to the cashier's booth. I paid my check and waited impatiently while he searched in an old-fashioned change purse, fishing out coins one by one and placing them on the counter beside his check, only to discover that the total was insufficient. He slid them back into his purse and with a tiny sigh extracted a bill from another compartment of the purse and handed it to the cashier.

"Give me any sentence of ten or twelve words," he said, "and I'll build you a logical chain of inferences that you never dreamed of when you framed the sentence."

Other customers were coming in, and since the space in front of the cashier's booth was small, I decided to wait outside until Nicky completed his transaction with the cashier. I remember being mildly amused at the idea that he probably thought I was still at his elbow and was going right ahead with his discourse.

When he joined me on the sidewalk I said, "A nine mile walk is no joke, especially in the rain."

"No, I shouldn't think it would be," he agreed absently. Then he stopped in his stride and looked at me sharply. "What the devil are you talking about?"

"It's a sentence and it has eleven words," I insisted. And I repeated the sentence, ticking off the words on my fingers.

"What about it?"

"You said that given a sentence of ten or twelve words —"

"Oh, yes." He looked at me suspiciously. "Where did you get it?"

"It just popped into my head. Come on now, build your inferences."

"You're serious about this?" he asked, his little blue eyes glittering with amusement. "You really want me to?"

It was just like him to issue a challenge and then to appear amused when I accepted it. And it made me angry.

"Put up or shut up," I said.

"All right," he said mildly. "No need to be huffy. I'll play. Hm-m, let me see, how did the sentence go? 'A nine mile walk is no joke, especially in the rain.' Not much to go on there."

"It's more than ten words," I rejoined.

"Very well." His voice became crisp as he mentally squared off to the problem. "First inference: the speaker is aggrieved."

"I'll grant that," I said, "although it hardly seems to be an inference. It's really implicit in the statement."

He nodded impatiently. "Next inference: the rain was unforeseen, otherwise he would have said, 'A nine mile walk in the rain is a joke,' instead of using the 'especially' phrase as an afterthought."

"I'll allow that," I said, "although it's pretty obvious."

"First inferences should be obvious," said Nicky tartly.

I let it go at that. He seemed to be floundering and I didn't want to rub it in.

"Next inference: the speaker is not an athlete or an outdoorsman."

"You'll have to explain that one," I said.

"It's the 'especially' phrase again," he said. "The speaker does not say that a nine mile walk in the rain is no joke, but merely the walk — just the distance, mind you — is no joke. Now, nine miles is not such a terribly long distance. You walk more than half that in eighteen holes of golf — and golf is an old man's game," he added slyly. *I* play golf.

"Well, that would be all right under ordinary circumstances," I said, "but there are other possibilities. The speaker might be a soldier in the jungle, in which case nine miles would be a pretty good hike, rain or no rain."

"Yes," and Nicky was sarcastic, "and the speaker might be one-legged. For that matter, the speaker might be a graduate student writing a Ph.D. thesis on humor and starting by listing all the things that are not funny. See here, I'll have to make a couple of assumptions before I continue."

"How do you mean?" I asked, suspiciously.

"Remember, I'm taking this sentence *in vacuo,* as it were. I don't know who said it or what the occasion was. Normally a sentence belongs in the framework of a situation."

"I see. What assumptions do you want to make?"

"For one thing, I want to assume that the intention was not frivolous, that the speaker is referring to a walk that was actually taken, and that the purpose of the walk was not to win a bet or something of that sort."

"That seems reasonable enough," I said.

"And I also want to assume that the locale of the walk is here."

"You mean here in Fairfield?"

"Not necessarily. I mean in this general section of the country."

"Fair enough."

"Then, if you grant those assumptions, you'll have to accept my last inference that the speaker is no athlete or outdoorsman."

"Well, all right, go on."

"Then my next inference is that the walk was taken very late at night or very early in the morning — say, between midnight and five or six in the morning."

"How do you figure that one?" I asked.

"Consider the distance, nine miles. We're in a fairly well-populated section. Take any road and you'll find a community of some sort in less than nine miles. Hadley is five miles away, Hadley Falls is seven and a half, Goreton is eleven, but East Goreton is only eight and you strike East Goreton before you come to Goreton. There is a local train service along the Goreton road and bus service along the others. All the highways are pretty well traveled. Would anyone have to walk nine miles in a rain unless it were late at night when no buses or trains were running and when the few automobiles that were out would hesitate to pick up a stranger on the highway?"

"He might not have wanted to be seen," I suggested.

Nicky smiled pityingly. "You think he would be less noticeable trudging along the highway than he would be riding in a public conveyance where everyone is usually absorbed in his newspaper?"

"Well, I won't press the point," I said brusquely.

"Then try this one: he was walking toward a town rather than away from one."

I nodded. "It is more likely, I suppose. If he were in a town, he could probably arrange for some sort of transportation. Is that the basis for your inference?"

"Partly that," said Nicky, "but there is also an inference to be drawn from the distance. Remember, it's a *nine* mile walk and nine is one of the exact numbers."

"I'm afraid I don't understand."

That exasperated schoolteacher-look appeared on Nicky's face again. "Suppose you say, 'I took a ten mile walk' or 'a hundred mile drive'; I would assume that you actually walked anywhere from eight to a dozen miles, or that you rode between ninety and a hundred and ten miles. In other words, *ten* and *hundred* are round numbers. You might have walked *exactly* ten miles or just as likely you might have walked *approximately* ten miles. But when you speak of walking *nine* miles, I have a right to assume that you have named an exact figure. Now, we are far more likely to know the distance of the city from a given point than we are to know the distance of a given point from the city. That is, ask anyone in the city how far out Farmer Brown lives, and if he knows him, he will say, 'Three or four miles.' But ask Farmer Brown how far he lives from the city and he will tell you, 'Three and six-tenths miles — measured it on my speedometer many a time.'"

"It's weak, Nicky," I said.

"But in conjunction with your own suggestion that he could have arranged transportation if he had been in a city —"

"Yes, that would do it," I said. "I'll pass it. Any more?"

"I've just begun to hit my stride," he boasted. "My next inference is that he was going to a definite destination and that he had to be there at a particular time. It was not a case of going off to get help because his car broke down or his wife was going to have a baby or somebody was trying to break into his house."

"Oh, come now," I said, "the car breaking down is really the most likely situation. He could have known the exact distance from having checked the mileage just as he was leaving the town."

Nicky shook his head. "Rather than walk nine miles in the rain, he would have curled up on the backseat and gone to sleep, or at least stayed by his car and tried to flag another motorist. Remember, it's nine miles. What would be the least it would take him to hike it?"

"Four hours," I offered.

He nodded. "Certainly no less, considering the rain. We've agreed that it happened very late at night or very early in the morning. Suppose he had his breakdown at one o'clock in the morning. It would be five o'clock before he would arrive. That's daybreak. You begin to see a lot of cars on the road. The buses start just a little later. In fact, the first buses hit Fairfield around five-thirty. Besides, if he were going for help, he would not have to go all the way to town — only as far as the nearest telephone. No, he had a definite appointment, and it was in a town, and it was for some time before five-thirty."

"Then why couldn't he have got there earlier and waited?" I asked. "He could have taken the last bus, arrived around one o'clock, and waited until his appointment. He walks nine miles in the rain instead, and you said he was no athlete."

We had arrived at the Municipal Building, where my office is. Normally, any arguments begun at the Blue Moon ended at the entrance to the Municipal Building. But I was interested in Nicky's demonstration and I suggested that he come up for a few minutes.

When we were seated I said, "How about it, Nicky, why couldn't he have arrived early and waited?"

"He could have," Nicky retorted. "But since he did not, we must assume that he was either detained until after the last bus left, or that he had to wait where he was for a signal of some sort, perhaps a telephone call."

"Then according to you, he had an appointment some time between midnight and five-thirty —"

"We can draw it much finer than that. Remember, it takes him four hours to walk the distance. The last bus stops at twelve-thirty A.M. If he doesn't take that, but starts at the same time, he won't arrive at his destination until four-thirty. On the other hand, if he takes the first bus in the morning, he will arrive around five-thirty. That would mean that his appointment was for some time between four-thirty and five-thirty."

"You mean that if his appointment was earlier than four-thirty, he would have taken the last night bus, and if it was later than five-thirty, he would have taken the first morning bus?"

"Precisely. And another thing: if he was waiting for a signal or a phone call, it must have come not much later than one o'clock."

"Yes, I see that," I said. "If his appointment is around five o'clock and it takes him four hours to walk the distance, he'd have to start around one."

He nodded, silent and thoughtful. For some queer reason I could not explain, I did not feel like interrupting his thoughts. On the wall was a large map of the county and I walked over to it and began to study it.

"You're right, Nicky," I remarked over my shoulder, "there's no place as far as nine miles away from Fairfield that doesn't hit another town first. Fairfield is right in the middle of a bunch of smaller towns."

He joined me at the map. "It doesn't have to be Fairfield, you know," he said quietly. "It was probably one of the outlying towns he had to reach. Try Hadley."

"Why Hadley? What would anyone want in Hadley at five o'clock in the morning?"

"The Washington Flyer stops there to take on water about that time," he said quietly.

"That's right, too," I said. "I've heard that train many a night when I couldn't sleep. I'd hear it pulling in and then a minute or two later I'd hear the clock on the Methodist Church banging out five." I went back to my desk for a timetable. "The Flyer leaves Washington at twelve forty-seven A.M. and gets into Boston at eight A.M."

Nicky was still at the map measuring distances with a pencil.

"Exactly nine miles from Hadley is the Old Sumter Inn," he announced.

"Old Sumter Inn," I echoed. "But that upsets the whole theory. You can arrange for transportation there as easily as you can in a town."

He shook his head. "The cars are kept in an enclosure and you have to get an attendant to check you through the gate. The attendant would remember anyone taking out his car at a strange hour. It's a pretty conservative place. He could have waited in his room until he got a call from Washington about someone on the Flyer — maybe the number of the car and the berth. Then he could just slip out of the hotel and walk to Hadley."

I stared at him, hypnotized.

"It wouldn't be difficult to slip aboard while the train was taking on water, and then if he knew the car number and the berth —"

"Nicky," I said portentously, "as the Reform District Attorney who campaigned on an economy program, I am going to waste the taxpayers' money and call Boston long distance. It's ridiculous, it's insane — but I'm going to do it!"

His little blue eyes glittered and he moistened his lips with the tip of his tongue.

"Go ahead," he said hoarsely.

I replaced the telephone in its cradle.

"Nicky," I said, "this is probably the most remarkable coincidence in the history of criminal investigation: *a man was found murdered in his berth on last night's twelve-forty-seven from Washington!* He'd been dead about three hours, which would make it exactly right for Hadley."

"I thought it was something like that," said Nicky. "But you're wrong about its being a coincidence. It can't be. Where did you get that sentence?"

"It was just a sentence. It simply popped into my head."

"It couldn't have! It's not the sort of sentence that pops into one's head. If you had taught composition as long as I have, you'd know that when you ask someone for a sentence of ten words or so, you get an ordinary statement such as 'I like milk' — with the other words made up by a modifying clause like, 'because it is good for my health.' The sentence you offered related to a *particular situation*."

"But I tell you I talked to no one this morning. And I was alone with you at the Blue Moon."

"You weren't with me all the time I paid my check," he said sharply. "Did you meet anyone while you were waiting on the sidewalk for me to come out of the Blue Moon?"

I shook my head. "I was outside for less than a minute before you joined me. You see, a couple of men came in while you were digging out your change and one of them bumped me, so I thought I'd wait —"

"Did you ever see them before?"

"Who?"

"The two men who came in," he said, the note of exasperation creeping into his voice again.

"Why no — they weren't anyone I knew."

"Were they talking?"

"I guess so. Yes, they were. Quite absorbed in their conversation, as a matter of fact — otherwise, they would have noticed me and I would not have been bumped."

"Not many strangers come into the Blue Moon," he remarked.

"Do you think it was they?" I asked eagerly. "I think I'd know them again if I saw them."

Nicky's eyes narrowed. "It's possible. There had to be two — one to trail the victim in Washington and ascertain his berth number, the other to wait here and do the job. The Washington man would be likely to come down here afterward. If there was theft as well as murder, it would be to divide the spoils. If it was just murder, he would probably have to come down to pay off his confederate."

I reached for the telephone.

"We've been gone less than half an hour," Nicky went on. "They were just coming in and service is slow at the Blue Moon. The one who walked all the way to Hadley must certainly be hungry and the other probably drove all night from Washington."

"Call me immediately if you make an arrest," I said into the phone and hung up.

Neither of us spoke a word while we waited. We paced the floor, avoiding each other almost as though we had done something we were ashamed of.

The telephone rang at last. I picked it up and listened. Then I said, "Okay," and turned to Nicky.

"One of them tried to escape through the kitchen but Winn had someone stationed at the back and they got him."

"That would seem to prove it," said Nicky with a frosty little smile.

I nodded agreement.

He glanced at his watch. "Gracious," he exclaimed, "I wanted to make an early start on my work this morning, and here I've already wasted all this time talking with you."

I let him get to the door. "Oh, Nicky," I called, "what was it you set out to prove?"

"That a chain of inferences could be logical and still not be true," he said.

"Oh."

"What are you laughing at?" he asked snappishly. And then he laughed too.

1947

ELLERY QUEEN

The Adventure of the President's Half Disme

THOSE FEW CURIOUS MEN who have chosen to turn off the humdrum highway to hunt for their pleasure along the back trails expect — indeed, they look confidently forward to — many strange encounters; and it is the dull stalk which does not turn up at least a hippogriff. But it remained for Ellery Queen to experience the ultimate excitement. On one of his prowls he collided with a President of the United States.

This would have been joy enough if it had occurred as you might imagine: by chance, on a dark night, in some back street of Washington, D.C., with Secret Service men closing in on the delighted Mr. Queen to question his motives by way of his pockets while a large black bullet-proof limousine rushed up to spirit the President away. But mere imagination fails in this instance. What is required is the power of fancy, for the truth is fantastic. Ellery's encounter with the President of the United States took place, not on a dark night, but in the unromantic light of several days (although the night played its rôle, too). Nor was it by chance: the meeting was arranged by a farmer's daughter. And it was not in Washington, D.C., for this President presided over the affairs of the nation from a different city altogether. Not that the meeting took place in that city, either; it did not take place in a city at all, but on a farm some miles south of Philadelphia. Oddest of all, there was no limousine to spirit the Chief Executive away, for while the President was a man of great wealth, he was still too poor to possess an automobile and, what is more, not all the resources of his Government — indeed, not all the riches of the world — could have provided one for him.

There are even more curious facts to this jewel of paradox. This was an encounter in the purest sense, and yet, physically, it did not occur at all. The President in question was dead. And while there are those who would not blink at a rubbing of shoulders or a clasping of hands even though one of the parties was in his grave, and to such persons the thought might occur that the meeting took place on a psychic plane — alas, Ellery Queen is not of their company. He does not believe in ghosts, consequently he never encounters them. So he did not collide with the President's shade, either.

And yet their meeting was as palpable as, say, the meeting between two chess masters, one in Moscow and the other in New York, who never leave their respective armchairs and still play a game to a decision. It is even more wonderful than that, for while the chess players merely annihilate space, Ellery and the father of both their countries annihilated time — a century and a half of it.

In fine, this is the story of how Ellery Queen matched wits with George Washington.

Those who are finicky about their fashions complain that the arms of coincidence are too long; but in this case the designer might say that He cut to measure. Or, to put it another way, an event often brews its own mood. Whatever the cause — whether coincidental or incidental — the fact is The Adventure of the President's Half Disme, which was to concern itself with the events surrounding President Washington's fifty-ninth birthday, actually first engrossed Ellery on February the nineteenth and culminated three days later.

Ellery was in his study that morning of the nineteenth of February, wrestling with several reluctant victims of violence, none of them quite flesh and blood, since his novel was still in the planning stage. So he was annoyed when Nikki came in with a card.

"James Ezekiel Patch," growled the great man; he was never in his best humor during the planning stage. "I don't know any James Ezekiel Patch, Nikki. Toss the fellow out and get back to transcribing those notes on Possible Motives —"

"Why, Ellery," said Nikki. "This isn't like you at all."

"What isn't like me?"

"To renege on an appointment."

"Appointment? Does this Patch character claim — ?"

"He doesn't merely claim it. He proves it."

"Someone's balmy," snarled Mr. Queen; and he strode into the living room to contend with James Ezekiel Patch. This, he perceived as soon as

James Ezekiel Patch rose from the Queen fireside chair, was likely to be a heroic project. Mr. Patch, notwithstanding his mild, even studious, eyes, seemed to rise indefinitely; he was a large, a very large, man.

"Now what's all this, what's all this?" demanded Ellery fiercely; for after all Nikki was there.

"That's what I'd like to know," said the large man amiably. "What did you want with me, Mr. Queen?"

"What did I want with you! What did you want with me?"

"I find this very strange, Mr. Queen."

"Now see here, Mr. Patch, I happen to be extremely busy this morning —"

"So am I." Mr. Patch's large thick neck was reddening and his tone was no longer amiable. Ellery took a cautious step backward as his visitor lumbered forward to thrust a slip of yellow paper under his nose. "Did you send me this wire, or didn't you?"

Ellery considered it tactfully expedient to take the telegram, although for strategic reasons he did so with a bellicose scowl.

IMPERATIVE YOU CALL AT MY HOME TOMORROW FEBRUARY NINE-
TEEN PROMPTLY TEN A.M. SIGNED ELLERY QUEEN

"Well, sir?" thundered Mr. Patch. "Do you have something on Washington for me, or don't you?"

"Washington?" said Ellery absently, studying the telegram.

"*George* Washington, Mr. Queen! I'm Patch the antiquarian. I *collect* Washington. I'm an *authority* on Washington! I have a large fortune and I spend it all on Washington! I'd never have wasted my time this morning if your name hadn't been signed to this wire! This is my busiest week of the year. I have engagements to speak on Washington —"

"Desist, Mr. Patch," said Ellery. "This is either a practical joke, or —"

"The Baroness Tchek," announced Nikki clearly. "With another telegram." And then she added: "And Professor John Cecil Shaw ditto."

The three telegrams were identical.

"Of course, I didn't send them," said Ellery thoughtfully, regarding his three visitors. Baroness Tchek was a short powerful woman, resembling a dumpling with gray hair; an angry dumpling. Professor Shaw was lank and long-jawed, wearing a sack suit which hung in some places and failed in its purpose by inches at the extremities. Along with Mr. Patch, they constituted as deliciously queer a trio as had ever congregated in the Queen apartment. Their host suddenly determined not to let go of them. "On the other hand, someone obviously did, using my name. . . ."

"Then there's nothing more to be said," snapped the Baroness, snapping her bag for emphasis.

"I should think there's a great deal more to be said," began Professor Shaw in a troubled way. "Wasting people's time this way —"

"It's not going to waste any more of *my* time," growled the large Mr. Patch. "Washington's Birthday only three days off — !"

"Exactly," smiled Ellery. "Won't you all sit down? There's more in this than meets the eye. . . . Baroness Tchek, if I'm not mistaken, you're the one who brought that fabulous collection of rare coins into the United States just before Hitler invaded Czechoslovakia? You're in the rare-coin business in New York now?"

"Unfortunately," said the Baroness coldly, "one must eat."

"And you, sir? I seem to know you."

"Rare books," said the Professor in the same troubled way.

"Of course. John Cecil Shaw, the rare-book collector. We've met at Mim's and other places. I abandon my first theory. There's a pattern here, distinctly unhumorous. An antiquarian, a coin dealer, and a collector of rare books — Nikki? Whom have you out there this time?"

"If this one collects anything," muttered Nikki into her employer's ear, "I'll bet it's things with two legs and hair on their chests. A darned pretty girl —"

"Named Martha Clarke," said a cool voice; and Ellery turned to find himself regarding one of the most satisfying sights in the world.

"Ah. I take it, Miss Clarke, you also received one of these wires signed with my name?"

"Oh, no," said the pretty girl. "I'm the one who sent them."

There was something about the comely Miss Clarke which inspired, if not confidence, at least an openness of mind. Perhaps it was the self-possessed manner in which she sat all of them, including Ellery, down in Ellery's living room while she waited on the hearth-rug, like a conductor on the podium, for them to settle down in their chairs. And it was the measure of Miss Clarke's assurance that none of them was indignant, only curious.

"I'll make it snappy," said Martha Clarke briskly. "I did what I did the way I did because, first I had to make sure I could see Mr. Patch, Baroness Tchek, and Professor Shaw today. Second, because I may need a detective before I'm through. . . . Third," she added, almost absently, "because I'm pretty desperate.

"My name is Martha Clarke. My father Tobias is a farmer. Our farm lies just south of Philadelphia, it was built by a Clarke in 1761, and it's been in our family ever since. I won't go gooey on you. We're broke and there's a mortgage. Unless papa and I can raise six thousand dollars in the next couple of weeks we lose the old homestead."

Professor Shaw looked vague. But the Baroness said, "Deplorable, Miss Clarke. Now, if I'm to run my auction this afternoon —"

And James Ezekiel Patch grumbled, "If it's money you want, young woman —"

"Certainly it's money I want. But I have something to sell."

"Ah!" said the Baroness.

"Oh?" said the Professor.

"Hm," said the antiquarian.

Mr. Queen said nothing, and Miss Porter jealously chewed the end of her pencil.

"The other day while I was cleaning out the attic, I found an old book."

"Well, now," said Professor Shaw indulgently. "An old book, eh?"

"It's called *The Diary of Simeon Clarke.* Simeon Clarke was papa's great-great-great-something or other. His *Diary* was privately printed in 1792 in Philadelphia, Professor, by a second cousin of his, Jonathan, who was in the printing business there."

"Jonathan Clarke. *The Diary of Simeon Clarke*," mumbled the cadaverous book collector. "I don't believe I know either, Miss Clarke. Have you . . . ?"

Martha Clarke carefully unclasped a large manila envelope and drew forth a single yellowed sheet of badly printed paper. "The title page was loose, so I brought it along."

Professor Shaw silently examined Miss Clarke's exhibit, and Ellery got up to squint at it. "Of course," said the Professor after a long scrutiny, in which he held the sheet up to the light, peered apparently at individual characters, and performed other mysterious rites, "mere age doesn't connote rarity, nor does rarity of itself constitute value. And while this page looks genuine for the purported period and is rare enough to be unknown to me, still. . . ."

"Suppose I told you," said Miss Martha Clarke, "that the chief purpose of the *Diary* — which I have at home — is to tell the story of how George Washington visited Simeon Clarke's farm in the winter of 1791 —"

"Clarke's farm? 1791?" exclaimed James Ezekiel Patch. "Preposterous. There's no record of —"

"And of what George Washington buried there," the farmer's daughter concluded.

By executive order, the Queen telephone was taken off its hook, the door was bolted, the shades were drawn, and the long interrogation began. By the middle of the afternoon, the unknown chapter in the life of the Father of His Country was fairly sketched.

Early on an icy gray February morning in 1791, Farmer Clarke had looked up from the fence he was mending to observe a splendid cortege galloping down on him from the direction of the City of Philadelphia. Outriders thundered in the van, followed by a considerable company of gentlemen on horse-back and several great coaches-and-six driven by liveried Negroes. To Simeon Clarke's astonishment, the entire equipage stopped before his farmhouse. He began to run. He could hear the creak of springs and the snorting of sleek and sweating horses. Gentlemen and lackeys were leaping to the frozen ground and, by the time Simeon had reached the farmhouse, all were elbowing about the first coach, a magnificent affair bearing a coat of arms. Craning, the farmer saw within the coach a very large, great nosed gentleman clad in a black velvet suit and a black cloak faced with gold; there was a cocked hat on his wigged head and a great sword in a white leather scabbard at his side. This personage was on one knee, leaning with an expression of considerable anxiety over a chubby lady of middle age, swathed in furs, who was half-sitting, half-lying on the upholstered seat, her eyes closed and her cheeks waxen under the rouge. Another gentleman, soberly attired, was stooping over the lady, his fingers on one pale wrist.

"I fear," he was saying with great gravity to the kneeling man, "that it would be imprudent to proceed another yard in this weather, Your Excellency. Lady Washington requires physicking and a warm bed immediately."

Lady Washington! Then the large, richly dressed gentleman was the President! Simeon Clarke pushed excitedly through the throng.

"Your Mightiness! Sir!" he cried. "I am Simeon Clarke. This is my farm. We have warm beds, Sarah and I!"

The President considered Simeon briefly. "I thank you, Farmer Clarke. No, no, Dr. Craik. I shall assist Lady Washington myself."

And George Washington carried Martha Washington into the little Pennsylvania farmhouse of Simeon and Sarah Clarke. An aide informed the Clarkes that President Washington had been on his way to Virginia to celebrate his fifty-ninth birthday in the privacy of Mount Vernon.

Instead, he passed his birthday on the Clarke farm, for the physician insisted that the President's lady could not be moved, even back to the nearby Capital, without risking complications. On His Excellency's order, the entire incident was kept secret. "It would give needless alarm to the people," he said. But he did not leave Martha's bedside for three days and three nights.

Presumably during those seventy-two hours, while his lady recovered from her indisposition, the President devoted some thought to his hosts, for on the fourth morning he sent black Christopher, his body servant, to summon the Clarkes. They found George Washington by the kitchen fire, shaven and powdered and in immaculate dress, his stern features composed.

"I am told, Farmer Clarke, that you and your good wife refuse reimbursement for the live stock you have slaughtered in the accommodation of our large company."

"You're my President, Sir," said Simeon. "I wouldn't take money."

"We — we wouldn't take money, Your Worship," stammered Sarah.

"Nonetheless, Lady Washington and I would acknowledge your hospitality in some kind. If you give me leave, I shall plant with my own hands a grove of oak saplings behind your house. And beneath one of the saplings I propose to bury two of my personal possessions." Washington's eyes twinkled ever so lightly. "It is my birthday — I feel a venturesome spirit. Come, Farmer Clarke and Mistress Clarke, would you like that?"

"What — what were they?" choked James Ezekiel Patch, the Washington collector. He was pale.

Martha Clarke replied, "The sword at Washington's side, in its white leather scabbard, and a silver coin the President carried in a secret pocket."

"Silver *coin?*" breathed Baroness Tchek, the rare-coin dealer. "What kind of coin, Miss Clarke?"

"The *Diary* calls it 'a half disme,' with an *s*," replied Martha Clarke, frowning. "I guess that's the way they spelled dime in those days. The book's full of queer spellings."

"A United States of America half disme?" asked the Baroness in a very odd way.

"That's what it says, Baroness."

"And this was in February, 1791?"

"Yes."

The Baroness snorted, beginning to rise. "I thought your story was too impossibly romantic, young woman. The United States Mint didn't begin to strike off half dismes until 1792!"

"Half dismes or any other U.S. coinage, I believe," said Ellery. "How come, Miss Clarke?"

"It was an experimental coin," said Miss Clarke coolly. "The *Diary* isn't clear as to whether it was the Mint which struck it off, or some private agency — maybe Washington himself didn't tell Simeon — but the President did say to Simeon that the half disme in his pocket had been coined from silver he himself had furnished and had been presented to him as a keepsake."

"There's a half disme with a story like that behind it in the possession of The American Numismatic Society," muttered the Baroness, "but it's definitely called one of the earliest coins struck off by the Mint. It's possible, I suppose, that in 1791, the preceding year, some specimen coins may have been struck off —"

"Possible my foot," said Miss Clarke. "It's so. The *Diary* says so. I imagine President Washington was pretty interested in the coins to be issued by the new country he was head of."

"Miss Clarke, I — I want that half disme. I mean — I'd like to buy it from you," said the Baroness.

"And I," said Mr. Patch carefully, "would like to ah. . . . purchase Washington's sword."

"The *Diary*," moaned Professor Shaw. "I'll buy *The Diary of Simeon Clarke* from you, Miss Clarke!"

"I'll be happy to sell it to you, Professor — as I said, I found it in the attic and I have it locked up in a highboy in the parlor at home. But as for the other two things. . . ." Martha Clarke paused, and Ellery looked delighted. He thought he knew what was coming. "I'll sell you the sword, Mr. Patch, and you the half disme, Baroness Tchek, providing —" and now Miss Clarke turned her clear eyes on Ellery "— providing you, Mr. Queen, will be kind enough to find them."

* * *

And there was the farmhouse in the frosty Pennsylvania morning, set in the barren winter acres, and looking as bleak as only a little Revolutionary house with a mortgage on its head can look in the month of February.

"There's an apple orchard over there," said Nikki as they got out of Ellery's car. "But where's the grove of oaks? I don't see any!" And then she added, sweetly, "Do you, Ellery?"

Ellery's lips tightened. They tightened further when his solo on the front-door knocker brought no response.

"Let's go around," he said briefly; and Nikki preceded him with cheerful step.

Behind the house there was a barn; and beyond the barn there was comfort, at least for Ellery. For beyond the barn there were twelve ugly holes in the earth, and beside each hole lay either a freshly felled oak tree and its stump, or an ancient stump by itself, freshly uprooted. On one of the stumps sat an old man in earth-stained blue jeans, smoking a corncob pugnaciously.

"Tobias Clarke?" asked Ellery.

"Yump."

"I'm Ellery Queen. This is Miss Porter. Your daughter visited me in New York yesterday —"

"Know all about it."

"May I ask where Martha is?"

"Station. Meetin' them there other folks." Tobias Clark spat and looked away — at the holes. "Don't know what ye're all comin' down here for. Wasn't nothin' under them oaks. Dug 'em all up t'other day. Trees that were standin' and the stumps of the ones that'd fallen years back. Look at them holes. Hired hand and me dug down most to China. Washin'ton's Grove, always been called. Now look at it. Firewood — for someone else, I guess." There was an iron bitterness in his tone. "We're losin' this farm, Mister, unless. . . ." And Tobias Clarke stopped. "Well, maybe we won't," he said. "There's always that there book Martha found."

"Professor Shaw, the rare-book collector, offered your daughter two thousand dollars for it if he's satisfied with it, Mr. Clarke," said Nikki.

"So she told me last night when she got back from New York," said Tobias Clarke. "Two thousand — and we need six." He grinned, and he spat again.

"Well," said Nikki sadly to Ellery, "that's that." She hoped Ellery would immediately get into the car and drive back to New York — immediately.

But Ellery showed no disposition to be sensible. "Perhaps, Mr. Clarke, some trees died in the course of time and just disappeared, stumps, roots, and all. Martha —" Martha! "— said the *Diary* doesn't mention the exact number Washington planted here."

"Look at them holes. Twelve of 'em, ain't there? In a triangle. Man plants trees in a triangle, he plants trees in a triangle. Ye don't see no place between holes big enough for another tree, do ye? Anyways, there was the same distance between all the trees. No, sir, Mister, twelve was all there was ever; and I looked under all twelve."

"What's the extra tree doing in the center of the triangle? You haven't uprooted that one, Mr. Clarke."

Tobias Clarke spat once more. "Don't know much about trees, do he? That's a cherry saplin' I set in myself six years ago. Ain't got nothin' to do with George Washin'ton."

Nikki tittered.

"If you'd sift the earth in those holes —"

"I sifted it. Look, Mister, either somebody dug that stuff up a hundred years ago or the whole yarn's a Saturday night whopper. Which it most likely is. There's Martha now with them other folks." And Tobias Clarke added, spitting for the fourth time, "Don't let me be keepin' ye."

"It reveals Washington rather er. . . . out of character," said James Ezekiel Patch that evening. They were sitting about a fire in the parlor, as heavy with gloom as with Miss Clarke's dinner; and that, at least in Miss Porter's view, was heavy indeed. Baroness Tchek wore the expression of one who is trapped in a cave; there was no further train until morning, and she had not yet resigned herself to a night in a farmhouse bed. The better part of the day had been spent poring over *The Diary of Simeon Clarke,* searching for a clue to the buried Washingtonia. But there was no clue; the pertinent passage referred merely to "a Triangle of Oake Trees behinde the red Barn, distant fifteen yards one from the other, which His Excellency the President did plant with his own Hands, as he had promised me, and then did burie his Sworde and the Half Disme for his Pleasure in a Case of copper beneath one of the Oakes, the which, he said, (the Case) had been fashioned by Mr. Revere of Boston who is experimenting with this Mettle in his Furnasses."

"How out of character, Mr. Patch?" asked Ellery. He had been staring into the fire for a long time, scarcely listening.

"Washington wasn't given to romanticism," said the large man dryly. "No folderol about him. I don't know of anything in his life which prepares us for such a yarn as this. I'm beginning to think —"

"But Professor Shaw himself says the *Diary* is no forgery!" cried Martha Clarke.

"Oh, the book's authentic enough." Professor Shaw seemed unhappy. "But it may simply be a literary hoax, Miss Clarke. The woods are full of them. I'm afraid that unless the story is confirmed by the discovery of that copper case with its contents. . . ."

"Oh, dear," said Nikki impulsively; and for a moment she was sorry for Martha Clarke, she really was.

But Ellery said, "I believe it. Pennsylvania farmers in 1791 weren't given to literary hoaxes, Professor Shaw. As for Washington, Mr. Patch — no man can be so rigidly consistent. And with his wife just recovering from an illness — on his own birthday. . . ." And Ellery fell silent again.

Almost immediately he leaped from his chair. "Mr. Clarke!"

Tobias stirred from his dark corner. "What?"

"Did you ever hear your father, or grandfather — anyone in your family — talk of *another barn behind the house?*"

Martha stared at him. Then she cried, "Papa, that's it! It was a different barn, in a different place, and the original Washington's Grove was cut down, or died —"

"Nope," said Tobias Clarke. "Never was but this one barn. Still got some of its original timbers. Ye can see that date burned into the crosstree. 1761."

Nikki was up early. A steady *hack-hack-hack* borne on frosty air woke her. She peered out of her back window, the coverlet up to her nose, to see Mr. Ellery Queen against the dawn, like a pioneer, wielding an ax powerfully.

Nikki dressed quickly, shivering, flung her mink-dyed muskrat over her shoulders, and ran downstairs, out of the house, and around it past the barn.

"Ellery! What do you think you're doing? It's practically the middle of the night!"

"Chopping," said Ellery, chopping.

"There's *mountains* of firewood stacked against the barn," said Nikki.

"Really, Ellery, I think this is carrying a flirtation too far." Ellery did not reply. "And anyway, there's something — something gruesome and indecent about chopping up trees George Washington planted. It's vandalism."

"Just a thought," panted Ellery, pausing for a moment. "A hundred and fifty-odd years is a long time, Nikki. Lots of queer things could happen, even to a tree, in that time. For instance —"

"The copper case," breathed Nikki, visibly. "The roots grew *around* it. It's *in* one of these stumps!"

"Now you're functioning," said Ellery, and he raised the ax again.

He was still at it two hours later, when Martha Clarke announced breakfast.

At 11:30 A.M. Nikki returned from driving the Professor, the Baroness, and James Ezekiel Patch to the railroad station. She found Mr. Queen seated before the fire in the kitchen in his undershirt, while Martha Clarke caressed his naked right arm.

"Oh!" said Nikki faintly. "I *beg* your pardon."

"Where you going, Nikki?" said Ellery irritably. "Come in. Martha's rubbing liniment into my biceps."

"He's not very accustomed to chopping wood, is he?" asked Martha Clarke in a cheerful voice.

"Reduced those foul 'oakes' to splinters," groaned Ellery. "Martha, ouch!"

"I should think you'd be satisfied *now*," said Nikki coldly. "I suggest we imitate Patch, Shaw, and the Baroness, Ellery — there's a 3:05. We can't impose on Miss Clarke's hospitality forever."

To Nikki's horror, Martha Clarke chose this moment to burst into tears.

"Martha!"

Nikki felt like leaping upon her and shaking the cool look back into her perfidious eyes.

"Here — here, now, Martha." That's right, thought Nikki contemptuously. Embrace her in front of me! "It's those three rats. Running out that way! Don't worry — I'll find that sword and half disme for you yet."

"You'll never find them," sobbed Martha, wetting Ellery's undershirt. "Because they're not here. They *never* were here. When you s-stop to think of it. . . . *burying* that coin, his sword . . . . if the story were true, he'd have *given* them to Simeon and Sarah. . . ."

"Not necessarily, not necessarily," said Ellery with hateful haste. "The old boy had a sense of history, Martha. They all did in those days. They knew they were men of destiny and that the eyes of posterity were upon them. Burying 'em is *just* what Washington would have done!"

"Do you really th-think so?"

Oh. . . . *pfui.*

"But even if he did bury them," Martha sniffled, "it doesn't stand to reason Simeon and Sarah would have let them *stay* buried. They'd have dug that copper box up like rabbits the minute G-George turned his back."

"Two simple country folk?" cried Ellery. "Salt of the earth? The new American earth? Disregard the wishes of His Mightiness, George Washington, First President of the United States? Are you out of your mind? And anyway, what would Simeon do with a dress-sword?"

Beat it into a ploughshare, thought Nikki spitefully — *that's* what he'd do.

"And that half disme. How much could it have been worth in 1791? Martha, they're here under your farm somewhere. You wait and see —"

"I wish I could b-believe it . . . Ellery."

"Shucks, child. Now stop crying —"

From the door Miss Porter said stiffly, "You might put your shirt back on, Superman, before your catch pneumonia."

Mr. Queen prowled about the Clarke acres for the remainder of that day, his nose at a low altitude. He spent some time in the barn. He devoted at least twenty minutes to each of the twelve holes in the earth. He reinspected the oaken wreckage of his axwork, like a paleontologist examining an ancient petrifaction for the impression of a dinosaur foot. He measured off the distance between the holes; and, for a moment, a faint temblor of emotion shook him. George Washington had been a surveyor in his youth; here was evidence that his passion for exactitude had not wearied with the years. As far as Ellery could make out, the oaks had been set into the earth at exactly equal distances, in an equilateral triangle.

It was at this point that Ellery had seated himself upon the seat of a cultivator behind the barn, wondering at his suddenly accelerated circulation. Little memories were knocking at the door. And as he opened to admit them, it was as if he were admitting a personality. It was, of course, at this time that the sense of personal conflict first obtruded. He had merely to shut his eyes in order to materialize a tall, large-featured man carefully pacing off the distances between twelve points — pacing them off in a sort of objective challenge to the unborn future. George Washington. . . .

The man Washington had from the beginning possessed an affinity for numbers. It had remained with him all his life. To count things, not so much for the sake of the things, perhaps, as for the counting, had been of the utmost importance to him. As a boy in Mr. William's school in Westmoreland, he excelled in arithmetic. Long division, subtraction, weights and measures — to calculate cords of wood and pecks of peas, pints and gallons and avoirdupois — young George delighted in these as other boys delighted in horseplay. As a man, he merely directed his passion into the channel of his possessions. Through his possessions he apparently satisfied his curious need for enumeration. He was not content simply to keep accounts of the acreage he owned, its yield, his slaves, his pounds and pence. Ellery recalled the extraordinary case of Washington and the seed. He once calculated the number of seeds in a pound troy weight of red clover. Not appeased by the statistics on red clover, Washington then went to work on a pound of timothy seed. His conclusions were: 71,000 and 298,000. His appetite unsatisfied, he thereupon fell upon the problem of New River grass. Here he tackled a calculation worthy of his prowess: his mathematical labors produced the great, pacifying figure of 844,800.

This man was so obsessed with numbers, Ellery thought, staring at the ruins of Washington's Grove, that he counted the windows in each house of his Mount Vernon estate and the number of "Paynes" in each window of each house, and then triumphantly recorded the exact number of each in his own handwriting.

It was like a hunger, requiring periodic satiation. In 1747, as a boy of fifteen, George Washington drew "A Plan of Major Law: Washingtons Turnip Field as Survey'd by me." In 1786, at the age of fifty-four, General Washington, the most famous man in the world, occupied himself with determining the exact elevation of his piazza above the Potomac's high-water mark. No doubt he experienced a warmer satisfaction thereafter for knowing that when he sat upon his piazza looking down upon the river he was sitting exactly 124 feet 10½ inches above it.

And in 1791, as President of the United States, Ellery mused, he was striding about right here, setting saplings into the ground, "distant fifteen yards one from the other," twelve of them in an equilateral triangle, and beneath one of them he buried a copper case containing his sword and the half disme coined from his own silver. Beneath one of them. . . . But it was not beneath one of them. Or had it been? And had it long ago been dug up by a Clarke? But the story had apparently died with Simeon and Sarah. On the other hand. . . .

Ellery found himself irrationally reluctant to conclude the obvious. George Washington's lifelong absorption with figures kept intruding. Twelve trees, equidistant, in an equilateral triangle.

"What is it?" he kept asking himself, almost angrily. "Why isn't it satisfying me?"

And then, in the gathering dusk, a very odd explanation insinuated itself. *Because it wouldn't have satisfied him!*

That's silly, Ellery said to himself abruptly. It has all the earmarks of a satisfying experience. There is no more satisfying figure in all geometry than an equilateral triangle. It is closed, symmetrical, definite, a whole and balanced and finished thing.

But it wouldn't have satisfied George Washington. . . . for all its symmetry and perfection.

Then perhaps there is a symmetry and perfection beyond the cold beauty of figures?

At this point, Ellery began to question his own postulates . . . . lost in the dark and to his time. . . .

They found him at ten-thirty, crouched on the cultivator seat, numb and staring.

He permitted himself to be led into the house. He suffered Nikki to subject him to the indignity of having his shoes and socks stripped off and his frozen feet rubbed to life, he ate Martha Clarke's dinner — all with a detachment and indifference which alarmed the girls and even made old Tobias look uneasy.

"If it's going to have this effect on him," began Martha, and then she said, "Ellery, give it up. Forget it." But she had to shake him before he heard her.

He shook his head. "They're there."

"*Where?*" cried the girls simultaneously.

"In Washington's Grove."

"Ye found 'em?" croaked Tobias Clarke, half-rising.

"No."

The Clarkes and Nikki exchanged glances. "Then how do you know they're there, Ellery?" asked Nikki gently.

Ellery looked bewildered. "Darned if I know *how* I know," he said, and he even laughed a little. "Maybe George Washington told me." Then he stopped laughing and went into the firelit parlor and — pointedly — slid the doors shut.

At ten minutes past midnight Martha Clarke gave up the contest.

"Isn't he *ever* going to come out of there?" she said, yawning.

"You never can tell what Ellery will do," replied Nikki.

"Well, I can't keep my eyes open another minute."

"Funny," said Nikki. "I'm not the least bit sleepy."

"You city girls."

"You country girls."

They laughed. Then they stopped laughing, and for a moment there was no sound in the kitchen but the patient sentrywalk of the grandfather clock and the snores of Tobias assaulting the ceiling from above.

"Well," said Martha. Then she said, "I just *can't*. Are you staying up, Nikki?"

"For a little while. You go to bed, Martha."

"Yes. Well. Good night."

"Good night, Martha."

At the door Martha turned suddenly: "Did he say *George Washington* told him?"

"Yes."

Martha went rather quickly up the stairs.

Nikki waited fifteen minutes. Then she tiptoed to the foot of the stairs and listened. She heard Tobias snuffling and snorting as he turned over in his bed, and an uneasy moan from the direction of Martha's bedroom, as if she were dreaming an unwholesome dream. Nikki set her jaw grimly and went to the parlor doors and slid them open.

Ellery was on his knees before the fire. His elbows were resting on the floor. His face was propped in his hands. In this attitude his posterior was considerably higher than his head.

"Ellery!"

"Huh?"

"Ellery, what on earth — ?"

"Nikki. I thought you'd gone to bed long ago." In the firelight his face was haggard.

"But what have you been *doing?* You look exhausted!"

"I am. I've been wrestling with a man who could bend a horseshoe with his naked hands. A very strong man. In more ways than one."

"What are you talking about? Who?"

"George Washington. Go to bed, Nikki."

"George. . . . Washington?"

"Go to bed."

". . . .*Wrestling* with him?"

"Trying to break through his defenses. Get into his mind. It's not an easy mind to get into. He's been dead such a long time — that makes the difference. The dead are stubborn, Nikki. Aren't you going to bed?"

Nikki backed out, shivering.

The house *was* icy.

It was even icier when an inhuman bellow accompanied by a thunder that shook the Revolutionary walls of her bedroom brought Nikki out of bed with a yelping leap.

But it was only Ellery.

He was somewhere up the hall, in the first glacial light of the dawn, hammering on Martha Clarke's door.

"Martha. *Martha!* Wake up, damn you, and tell me where I can find a book in this damned house! A biography of Washington — a history of the United States — an almanac. . . . *anything!*"

The parlor fire had long since given up the ghost. Nikki and Martha in wrappers, and Tobias Clarke in an ancient bathrobe over his marbled long underwear, stood around shivering and bewildered as a disheveled, daemonic Ellery leafed eagerly through a 1921 edition of *The Farmer's Fact Book and Complete Compendium.*

"Here it is!" The words shot out of his mouth like bullets, leaving puffs of smoke.

"What is it, Ellery?"

"What on earth are you looking for?"

"He's loony, I tell ye!"

Ellery turned with a look of ineffable peace, closing the book.

"That's it," he said. "That's it."

"What's it?"

"Vermont. The State of Vermont."

"Vermont . . . ?"

"Ver*mont?*"

"Vermont. What in the crawlin' creeper's Vermont got to do with —?"

"Vermont," said Ellery with a tired smile, "did not enter the Union until March fourth, 1791. So that proves it, don't you see?"

"Proves *what?*" shrieked Nikki.

"Where George Washington buried his sword and half disme."

"Because," said Ellery in the rapidly lightening dawn behind the barn, "Vermont was the fourteenth State to do so. The *fourteenth*. Tobias, would you get me an ax, please?"

"An ax," mumbled Tobias. He shuffled away, shaking his head.

"Come on, Ellery, I'm d-dying of c-cold!" chattered Nikki, dancing up and down before the cultivator.

"Ellery," said Martha Clarke piteously, "I don't understand *any* of this."

"It's very simple, Martha — oh, thank you, Tobias — as simple," said Ellery, "as simple arithmetic. Numbers, my dears — numbers tell this remarkable story. Numbers and their influence on our first President who was, above all things, a number-man. That was my key. I merely had to discover the lock to fit it into. Vermont was the lock. And the door's open."

Nikki seated herself on the cultivator. You had to give Ellery his head in a situation like this; you couldn't drive him for beans. Well, she thought grudgingly, seeing how pale and how tired-looking he was after a night's wrestling with George Washington, he's earned it.

"The number was wrong," said Ellery solemnly, leaning on Tobias' ax. "Twelve trees. Washington apparently planted twelve trees — Simeon Clarke's *Diary* never did mention the number twelve, but the evidence seemed unquestionable — there were twelve oaks in an equilateral triangle, each one fifteen yards from its neighbor.

"And yet. . . . I felt that *twelve* oaks couldn't be, perfect as the triangle was. Not if they were planted by George Washington. Not on February the twenty-second, New Style, in the year of our Lord 1791.

"Because on February the twenty-second, 1791 — in fact, until March the fourth, when Vermont entered the Union to swell its original number by one — there was *another* number in the United States so important, so revered, so much a part of the common speech and the common living — and dying — that it was more than a number; it was a solemn and sacred thing; almost not a number at all. It overshadowed other numbers like the still-unborn Paul Bunyan. It was memorialized on the new American flag in the number of its stars and the number of its stripes. It was a number of which George Washington was the standard-bearer! — the head and only recently the strong right arm of the new Republic which had been born out of the blood and muscle of its integers. It was a number which was in the hearts and minds and mouths of all Americans.

"No. If George Washington, who was not merely the living symbol of all this but carried with him that extraordinary compulsion toward numbers which characterized his whole temperament besides, had wished to plant a number of oak trees to commemorate a birthday visit in the year 1791, . . . he would have, he could have, selected only one number out of all the mathematic trillions at his command — *the number thirteen.*"

The sun was looking over the edge of Pennsylvania at Washington's Grove.

"George Washington planted thirteen trees here that day, and under one of them he buried Paul Revere's copper case. Twelve of the trees he arranged in an equilateral triangle, and we know that the historic treasure was not under any of the twelve. Therefore he must have buried the case under the thirteenth — a thirteenth oak sapling which grew to oakhood and, some time during the past century and a half, withered and died and vanished, vanished so utterly that it left no trace, not even its roots.

"Where would Washington have planted that thirteenth oak? Because beneath the spot where it once stood — there lies the copper case containing his sword and the first coin to be struck off in the new United States."

And Ellery glanced tenderly at the cherry sapling which Tobias Clarke had set into the earth in the middle of Washington's Grove six years before.

"Washington the surveyor, the geometer, the man whose mind cried out for integral symmetries? Obviously, in only one place: *In the center of the triangle.* Any other place would be unthinkable."

And Ellery hefted Tobias's ax and strode toward the six-year-old tree. He raised the ax.

But suddenly he lowered it, and turned, and said in a rather startled way: "See here! Isn't today . . . ?"

"Washington's Birthday," said Nikki.

Ellery grinned and began to chop down the cherry tree.

1950

JOHN D. MACDONALD

....

The Homesick Buick

TO GET TO LEEMAN, TEXAS, you go southwest from Beaumont on Route 90 for approximately thirty miles and then turn right on a two-lane concrete farm road. Five minutes from the time you turn, you will reach Leeman. The main part of town is six lanes wide and five blocks long. If the hand of a careless giant should remove the six gas stations, the two theaters, Willows' Hardware Store, the Leeman National Bank, the two big air-conditioned five-and-dimes, the Sears' store, four cafés, Rightsinger's dress shop, and The Leeman House, a twenty-room hotel, there would be very little left except the supermarket and four drugstores.

On October 3, 1949, a Mr. Stanley Woods arrived by bus and carried his suitcase over to The Leeman House. In Leeman there is no social distinction of bus, train, or plane, since Leeman has neither airport facilities nor railroad station.

On all those who were questioned later, Mr. Stanley Woods seemed to have made very little impression. They all spoke of kind of a medium-sized fella in his thirties, or it might be his forties. No, he wasn't fat, but he wasn't thin either. Blue eyes? Could be brown. Wore a gray suit, I think. Can't remember whether his glasses had rims or not. If they did have, they were probably gold.

But all were agreed that Mr. Stanley Woods radiated quiet confidence and the smell of money. According to the cards that were collected here and there, Mr. Woods represented the Groston Precision Tool Company of Atlanta, Georgia. He had deposited in the Leeman National a certified check for twelve hundred dollars, and the bank had made the routine check of looking up the credit standing of Groston. It was Dun & Bradstreet double-A, but, of course, the company explained later that they had never heard of Mr. Stanley Woods. Nor could the fake calling cards be traced. They were of a type of paper and type face which could be duplicated sixty or a hundred times in every big city in the country.

Mr. Woods' story, which all agreed on, was that he was ". . . nosing around to find a good location for a small plant. Decentralization, you know. No, we don't want it right in town."

He rented Tod Bishner's car during the day. Tod works at the Shell station on the corner of Beaumont and Lone Star Streets and doesn't have any use for his Plymouth sedan during the day. Mr. Woods drove around all the roads leading out of town, and, of course, real estate prices were jacked to a considerable degree during his stay.

Mr. Stanley Woods left Leeman rather suddenly on the morning of October 17, under unusual circumstances.

The first person to note a certain oddness was Miss Trilla Price on the switchboard at the phone company. Her local calls were all right, but she couldn't place Charley Anderson's call to Houston, nor, when she tried, could she raise Beaumont. Charley was upset because he wanted to wangle an invitation to go visit his sister over the coming week end.

That was at five minutes of nine. It was probably at the same time that a car with two men in it parked on Beaumont Street, diagonally across from the bank, and one of the two men lifted the hood and began to fiddle with the electrical system.

Nobody agrees from what direction the Buick came into town. There was a man and a girl in it, and they parked near the drugstore. No one seems to know where the third car parked, or even what kind of car it was.

The girl and the man got out of the Buick slowly, just as Stanley Woods came down the street from the hotel.

In Leeman the bank is open on weekdays from nine until two. And so, at nine o'clock, C. F. Hethridge, who is, or was, the chief teller, raised the green shades on the inside of the bank doors and unlocked the doors. He greeted Mr. Woods, who went on over to the high counter at the east wall and began to ponder over his checkbook.

At this point, out on the street, a very peculiar thing happened. One of the two men in the first car strolled casually over and stood beside the Buick. The other man started the motor of the first car, drove down the street, and made a wide U-turn to swing in and park behind the Buick.

The girl and the man had gone over to Bob Kimball's window. Bob is second teller, and the only thing he can remember about the girl is that she was blonde and a little hard-looking around the mouth, and that she wore a great big alligator shoulder bag. The man with her made no impression on Bob at all, except that Bob thinks the man was on the heavy side.

Old Rod Harrigan, the bank guard, was standing beside the front door, yawning, and picking his teeth with a broken match.

At this point, C. F. Hethridge heard the buzzer on the big time vault and went over and swung the door wide and went in to get the money for the cages. He was out almost immediately, carrying Bob's tray over to him. The girl was saying something about cashing a check, and Bob had asked her for identification. She had opened the big shoulder bag as her escort strolled over to the guard. At the same moment the girl pulled out a small, vicious-looking revolver and aimed it between Bob's eyes, her escort sapped old Rod Harrigan with such gusto that it was four that same afternoon before he came out of it enough to talk. And then, or course, he knew nothing.

C. F Hethridge bolted for the vault, and Bob, wondering whether he should step on the alarm, looked over the girl's shoulder just in time to see Stanley Woods aim carefully and bring Hethridge down with a slug through the head, catching him on the fly, so to speak.

Bob says that things were pretty confusing and that the sight of Hethridge dying so suddenly sort of took the heart out of him. Anyway, there was a third car and it contained three men, two of them equipped with empty black-leather suitcases. They went into the vault, acting as though they had been all through the bank fifty times. They stepped over Hethridge on the way in, and on the way out again.

About the only cash they overlooked was the cash right in front of Bob, in his teller's drawer.

As they all broke for the door, Bob dropped and pressed the alarm button. He said later that he held his hands over his eyes, though what good that would do him, he couldn't say.

Henry Willows is the real hero. He was fuddying around in his hardware store when he heard the alarm. With a reaction time remarkable in a man close to seventy, he took a little .22 rifle, slapped a clip into it, trotted to his store door, and quickly analyzed the situation. He saw Mr. Woods, whom he recognized, plus three strangers and a blonde woman coming out of the bank pretty fast. Three cars were lined up, each one with a driver. Two of the men coming out of the bank carried heavy suitcases. Henry leveled on the driver of the lead car, the Buick, and shot him in the left temple, killing him outright. The man slumped over the wheel, his body resting against the horn ring, which, of course, added its blare to the clanging of the bank alarm.

At that point a slug, later identified as having come from a Smith & Wesson Police Positive, smashed a neat hole in Henry's plate-glass store window, radiating cracks in all directions. Henry ducked, and by the time he got ready to take a second shot, the two other cars were gone. The Buick was still there. He saw Bob run out of the bank, and later on he told his wife that he had his finger on the trigger and his sights lined up before it came to him that it was Bob Kimball.

It was agreed that the two cars headed out toward Route 90, and within two minutes Hod Abrams and Lefty Quinn had roared out of town in the same direction in the only police car. They were followed by belligerent amateurs to whom Henry Willows had doled out firearms. But on the edge of town all cars ran into an odd obstacle. The road was liberally sprinkled with metal objects shaped exactly like the jacks that little girls pick up when they bounce a ball, except they were four times normal size and all the points were sharpened. No matter how a tire hit one, it was certain to be punctured.

The police car swerved to a screaming stop, nearly tipping over. The Stein twins, boys of nineteen, managed to avoid the jacks in their souped-up heap until they were hitting eighty. When they finally hit one, the heap rolled over an estimated ten times, killing the twins outright.

So that made four dead. Hethridge, the Stein twins, and one unidentified bank robber.

Nobody wanted to touch the robber, and he stayed right where he was until the battery almost ran down and the horn squawked into silence. Hod Abrams commandeered a car, and he and Lefty rode back into town and took charge. They couldn't get word out by phone, and within a very short time they found that some sharpshooter with a high-powered rifle had gone to work on the towers of local station WLEE and had put the station out of business.

Thus, by the time the Texas Rangers were alerted and ready to set up road blocks, indecision and confusion had permitted an entire hour to pass.

The Houston office of the FBI assigned a detail of men to the case, and from the Washington headquarters, two bank-robbery experts were dispatched by plane to Beaumont. Reporters came from Houston and Beaumont and the two national press services, and Leeman found itself on the front pages all over the country because the planning behind the job seemed to fascinate the average joe.

Mr. Woods left town on that particular Thursday morning. The FBI from Houston was there by noon, and the Washington contingent arrived late Friday. Everyone was very confident. There were a corpse and a car to work on. These would certainly provide the necessary clues to indicate which outfit had pulled the job, even though the method of the robbery did not point to any particular group whose habits were known.

Investigation headquarters were set up in the local police station, and Hod and Lefty, very important in the beginning, had to stand around outside trying to look as though they knew what was going on.

Hethridge, who had been a cold, reserved, unpopular man, had, within twenty-four hours, fifty stories invented about his human kindness and generosity. The Stein twins, heretofore considered to be trash who would be better off in prison, suddenly became proper sons of old Texas.

Special Agent Randolph A. Sternweister, who, fifteen years before, had found a law office to be a dull place, was in charge of the case, being the senior of the two experts who had flown down from Washington. He was forty-one years old, a chain smoker, a chubby man with incongruous hollow cheeks and hair of a shade of gray which his wife, Claire, tells him is distinguished.

The corpse was the first clue. Age, between thirty and thirty-two. Brown hair, thinning on top. Good teeth, with only four small cavities, two of them filled. Height, five feet eight and a quarter; weight, a hundred and forty-eight. No distinguishing scars or tattoos. X-ray plates showed that the right arm had been fractured years before. His clothes were neither new nor old. The suit had been purchased in Chicago. The shirt, underwear, socks, and shoes were all national brands, in the medium-price range. In his pockets they found an almost full pack of cigarettes, a battered Zippo lighter, three fives and a one in a cheap trick billclip, eighty-five cents in change, a book of matches advertising a nationally known laxative, a white bone button, two wooden kitchen matches with blue-and-white heads, and a penciled map, on cheap notebook paper, of the main drag of Leeman — with no indication as to escape route. His fingerprint classification was teletyped to the Central Bureau files, and the answer came back that there was no record of him. It was at this point that fellow workers noted that Mr. Sternweister became a shade irritable.

The next search of the corpse was more minute. No specific occupational calluses were found on his hands. The absence of laundry marks indicated that his linen, if it had been sent out, had been cleaned by a neighborhood laundress. Since Willows had used a .22 hollow-point, the hydraulic pressure on the brain fluids had caused the eyes of Mr. X to bulge in a disconcerting fashion. A local undertaker, experienced in the damage caused by the average Texas automobile accident, replaced the bulging eyeballs and smoothed out the expression for a series of pictures which were sent to many points. The Chicago office reported that the clothing store which had sold the suit was large and that the daily traffic was such that no clerk could identify the customer from the picture; nor was the youngish man known to the Chicago police.

Fingernail scrapings were put in a labeled glassine envelope, as well as the dust vacuumed from pants' cuffs and other portions of the clothing likely to collect dust. The excellent lab in Houston reported back that the dust and scrapings were negative to the extent that the man could not be tied down to any particular locality.

In the meantime the Buick had been the object of equal scrutiny. The outside was a mass of prints from the citizens of Leeman who had peered morbidly in at the man leaning against the horn ring. The plates were Mississippi license plates, and in checking with the Bureau of Motor Vehicle Registration, it was found that the plates had been issued for a 1949 Mercury convertible which had been almost totally destroyed in a head-on collision in June, 1949. The motor number and serial number of the Buick were checked against central records, and it was discovered that the Buick was one which had disappeared from Chapel Hill, North Carolina, on the 5th of July, 1949. The insurance company, having already replaced the vehicle, was anxious to take possession of the stolen car.

Pictures of Mr. X, relayed to Chapel Hill, North Carolina, and to myriad points in Mississippi, drew a large blank. In the meantime a careful dusting of the car had brought out six prints, all different. Two of them turned out to be on record. The first was on record through the cross-classification of Army prints. The man in question was found working in a gas station in Lake Charles, Louisiana. He had a very difficult two hours until a bright police officer had him demonstrate his procedure for brushing out the front of a car. Ex-Sergeant Golden braced his left hand against the dashboard in almost the precise place where the print had been found. He was given a picture of Mr. X to study. By that time has was so thoroughly annoyed at the forces of law and order that it was impossible to ascertain whether or not he had ever seen the man in question. But due to the apparent freshness of the paint, it was established — a reasonable assumption — that the gangsters had driven into Texas from the East.

The second print on record was an old print, visible when dust was carefully blown off the braces under the dismantled front seat. It belonged to a garage mechanic in Chapel Hill, who once had a small misunderstanding with the forces of law and order and who was able to prove, through the garage work orders, that he had repaired the front-seat mechanism when it had jammed in April, 1949.

The samples of road dirt and dust taken from the fender wells and the frame members proved nothing. The dust was proved, spectroscopically, to be from deep in the heart of Texas, and the valid assumption, after checking old weather reports, was that the car had come through some brisk thunderstorms en route.

Butts in the ash tray of the car showed that either two women, or one woman with two brands of lipstick, had ridden recently as a passenger. Both brands of lipstick were of shades which would go with a fair-complexioned blonde, and both brands were available in Woolworth's, Kress', Kresge's, Walgreen's — in fact, in every chain outfit of any importance.

One large crumb of stale whole-wheat bread was found on the floor mat, and even Sternweister could make little of that, despite the fact that the lab was able to report that the bread had been eaten in conjunction with liverwurst.

Attention was given to the oversized jacks which had so neatly punctured the tires. An ex-OSS officer reported that similar items had been scattered on enemy roads in Burma during the late war, and after examining the samples, he stated confidently that the OSS merchandise had been better made. A competent machinist looked them over and stated with assurance that they had been made by cutting eighth-inch rods into short lengths, grinding them on a wheel, putting them in a jig, and spot-welding them. He said that the maker did not do much of a job on either the grinding or the welding, and that the jig itself was a little out of line. An analysis of the steel showed that it was a Jones & Laughlin product that could be bought in quantity at any wholesaler and in a great many hardware stores.

The auditors, after a careful examination of the situation at the bank, reported that the sum of exactly $94,725 had disappeared. They recommended that the balance of $982.80 remaining in Stanley Woods' account be considered as forfeited, thus reducing the loss to $93,742.20. The good citizens of Leeman preferred to think that Stanley had withdrawn his account.

Every person who had a glimpse of the gang was cross-examined. Sternweister was appalled at the difficulty involved in even establishing how many there had been. Woods, the blonde, and the stocky citizen were definite. And then there were two with suitcases — generally agreed upon. Total, so far — five. The big question was whether each car had a driver waiting. Some said no — that the last car in line had been empty. Willows insisted angrily that there had been a driver behind each wheel. Sternweister at last settled for a total of eight, seven of whom escaped.

No one had taken down a single license number. But it was positively established that the other two cars had been either two- or four-door sedans in dark blue, black, green, or maroon, and that they had been either Buicks, Nashes, Oldsmobiles, Chryslers, Pontiacs or Packards — or maybe Hudsons. And one lone woman held out for convertible Cadillacs. For each person that insisted that they had Mississippi registration, there was one equally insistent on Louisiana, Texas, Alabama, New Mexico, and Oklahoma. And one old lady said that she guessed she knew a California plate when she saw one.

On Saturday morning, nine days after the sudden blow to the FDIC, Randolph Sternweister paced back and forth in his suite at the hotel, which he shared with the number-two man from the Washington end, one Buckley Weed. Weed was reading through the transcripts of the testimony of the witnesses, in vain hope of finding something to which insufficient importance had been given. Weed, though lean, a bit stooped, and only thirty-one, had, through osmosis, acquired most of the personal mannerisms of his superior. Sternweister had noticed this and for the past year had been on the verge of mentioning it. As Weed had acquired Sternweister's habit of lighting one cigarette off the last half-inch of the preceding one, any room in which the two of them remained for more than an hour took on the look and smell of any hotel room after a Legion convention.

"Nothing," Sternweister said. "Not one censored, unmentionable, unprintable, unspeakable thing! My God, if I ever want to kill anybody, I'll do it in the Pennsy Station at five-fifteen."

"Yes, at five-fifteen," said Weed.

"The Bureau has cracked cases when the only thing it had to go on was a human hair or a milligram of dust. My God, we've got a whole automobile that weighs nearly two tons, and a whole corpse! They'll think we're down here learning to rope calves. You know what?"

"What, Ran?"

"I think this was done by a bunch of amateurs. There ought to be a law restricting the practice of crime to professionals. A bunch of wise amateurs. And you can bet your loudest argyles, my boy, that they established identity, hide-out, the works, before they knocked off that vault. Right now, blast their souls, they're being seven average citizens in some average community, making no splash with that ninety-four grand. People didn't used to move around so much. Since the war they've been migrating all over the place. See anything in those transcripts?"

"Nothing."

"Then stop rattling paper. I can't think. Since a week ago Thursday, fifty-one stolen cars have been recovered in the South and Southwest. And we don't know which two, if any, belonged to this mob. We don't even know which route they took away from here. Believe it or not — nobody saw 'em!"

As the two specialists stared bleakly at each other, a young man of fourteen named Pink Dee was sidling inconspicuously through the shadows in the rear of Louie's Garage (Tow car service — open 24 hrs.). Pink was considered to have been the least beautiful baby, the most unprepossessing child, in Leeman, and he gave frank promise of growing up to be a rather coarse joke on the entire human race. Born with a milk-blue skin, dead-white hair, little reddish weak eyes, pipe-cleaner bones, narrow forehead, no chin, beaver teeth, a voice like an unoiled hinge, nature had made the usual compensation. His reaction time was exceptional. Plenty of more rugged and more normal children had found out that Pink Dee could hit you by the time you had the word out of your mouth. The blow came from an outsize, knobby fist at the end of a long thin arm, and he swung it with all the abandon of a bag of rocks on the end of a rope. The second important item about Pink Dee came to light when the Leeman School System started giving IQs. Pink's was higher than they were willing to admit the first time, as it did not seem proper that the only genius in Leeman should be old Homer Dee's only son. Pink caught on, and the second time he was rated he got it down into the cretin class. The third rating was ninety-nine, and everybody seemed happy with that.

At fourteen Pink was six feet tall and weighed a hundred and twenty pounds. He peered at the world through heavy lenses and maintained, in the back room of his home on Fountain Street, myriad items of apparatus, some made, some purchased. There he investigated certain electrical and magnetic phenomena, having tired of building radios, and carried on a fairly virulent correspondence on the quantum theory with a Cal Tech professor who was under the impression that he was arguing with someone of more mature years.

Dressed in his khakis, Pink moved through the shadows, inserted the key he had filched into the Buick door, and then into the ignition lock. He turned it to the left to activate the electrical gimmicks, and then turned on the car radio. As soon as it warmed up, he pushed the selective buttons, carefully noting the dial. When he had the readings, he turned it to WLEE to check the accuracy of the dial. When WLEE roared into a farm report, Louie appeared and dragged Pink out by the thin scruff of his neck.

"What the hell?" Louie said.

Being unable to think of any adequate explanation, Pink wriggled away and loped out.

Pink's next stop was WLEE, where he was well known. He found the manual he wanted and spent the next twenty minutes leafing through it.

Having been subjected to a certain amount of sarcasm from both Sternweister and Weed, Hod Abrams and Lefty Quinn were in no mood for the approach Pink Dee used.

"I demand to see the FBI," Pink said firmly, the effect spoiled a bit by the fact that his voice change was so recent that the final syllable was a reversion to his childhood squeaky-hinge voice.

"He demands," Hod said to Lefty.

"Go away, Pink," Lefty growled, "before I stomp on your glasses."

"I am a citizen who wishes to speak to a member of a federal agency," Pink said with dignity.

"A citizen, maybe. A taxpayer, no. You give me trouble, kid, and I'm going to warm your pants right here in this lobby."

Maybe the potential indignity did it. Pink darted for the stairs leading up from the lobby. Hod went roaring up the stairs after him, and Lefty grabbed the elevator. They both snared him outside Sternweister's suite and found that they had a job on their hands. Pink bucked and contorted like a picnic on which a hornet's nest had just fallen.

The door to the suite opened and both Sternweister and Weed glared out, their mouths open.

"Just . . . just a fresh . . . kid," Hod Abrams panted.

"I know where the crooks are!" Pink screamed.

"He's nuts," Lefty yelled.

"Wait a minute," Randolph Sternweister ordered sharply. They stopped dragging Pink but still clung to him. "I admit he doesn't look as though he knew his way home, but you can't tell. You two wait outside. Come in here, young man."

Pink marched erectly into the suite, selected the most comfortable chair, and sank into it, looking very smug.

"Where are they?"

"Well, I don't know exactly —"

"Outside!" Weed said with a thumb motion.

"— but I know how to find out."

"Oh, you know how to find out, eh? Keep talking. I haven't laughed in nine days," Sternweister said.

"Oh, I had to do a little checking first," Pink said in a lofty manner. "I stole the key to the Buick and got into it to test something."

"Kid, experts have been over that car, half-inch by half-inch."

"Please don't interrupt me, sir. And don't take that attitude. Because if it turns out I have something, and I know I have, you're going to look as silly as anything."

Sternweister flushed and then turned pale. He held hard to the edge of a table. "Go ahead," he said thickly.

"I am making an assumption that the people who robbed our bank started out from some hide-out and then went back to the same one. I am further assuming that they were in their hide-out some time — that is, while they were planning the robbery."

Weed and Sternweister exchanged glances. "Go on."

"So my plan has certain possible flaws based on these assumptions, but at least it uncovers one possible pattern of investigation. I know that the car was stolen from Chapel Hill. That was in the paper. And I know the dead man was in Chicago. So I checked Chicago and Chapel Hill a little while ago."

"Checked them?"

"At the radio station, of course. Modern car radios are easy to set to new stations by altering the push buttons. The current settings of the push buttons do not conform either to the Chicago or the Chapel Hill areas. There are six stations that the radio in the Buick is set for, and —"

Sternweister sat down on the couch as though somebody had clubbed him behind the knees. "Agh!" he said.

"So all you have to do," Pink said calmly, "is to check areas against the push-button settings until you find an area *where all six frequencies are represented by radio stations in the immediate geographical vicinity.* It will take a bit of statistical work, of course, and a map of the country, and a supply of push pins should simplify things, I would imagine. Then, after the area is located, I would take the Buick there, and due to variations in individual sets and receiving conditions, you might be able to narrow it down to within a mile or two. Then, by showing the photograph of the dead gangster around at bars and such places —"

And that was why, on the following Wednesday, a repainted Buick with new plates and containing two agents of the Bureau roamed through the small towns near Tampa on the West Florida Coast, and how they found that the car radio in the repainted Buick brought in Tampa, Clearwater, St. Pete, Orlando, Winter Haven, and Dunedin on the push buttons with remarkable clarity the closer they came to a little resort town called Tarpon Springs. On Thursday morning at four, the portable floodlights bathed three beach cottages in a white glare, and the metallic voice of the P.A. system said, "You are surrounded. Come out with your hands high. You are surrounded."

The shots, a few moments later, cracked with a thin bitterness against the heavier sighing of the Gulf of Mexico. Mr. Stanley Woods, or, as the blonde later stated, Mr. Grebbs Fainstock, was shot, with poetic justice, through the head, and that was the end of resistance.

On Pink Dee Day in Leeman, the president of the Leeman National Bank turned over the envelope containing the reward. It came to a bit less than 6 per cent of the recovered funds, and it is ample to guarantee, at some later date, a Cal Tech degree.

In December the Sternweisters bought a new car. When Claire demanded to know why Randolph insisted on delivery *sans* car radio, his only answer was a hollow laugh.

She feels that he has probably been working too hard.

1953

ROSS MACDONALD

....

Gone Girl

IT WAS a Friday night. I was tooling home from the Mexican border in a light blue convertible and a dark blue mood. I had followed a man from Fresno to San Diego and lost him in the maze of streets in Old Town. When I picked up his trail again, it was cold. He had crossed the border, and my instructions went no further than the United States.

Halfway home, just above Emerald Bay, I overtook the worst driver in the world. He was driving a black fishtail Cadillac as if he were tacking a sailboat. The heavy car wove back and forth across the freeway, using two of its four lanes, and sometimes three. It was late, and I was in a hurry to get some sleep. I started to pass it on the right, at a time when it was riding the double line. The Cadillac drifted towards me like an unguided missile, and forced me off the road in a screeching skid.

I speeded up to pass on the left. Simultaneously, the driver of the Cadillac accelerated. My acceleration couldn't match his. We raced neck and neck down the middle of the road. I wondered if he was drunk or crazy or afraid of me. Then the freeway ended. I was doing eighty on the wrong side of a two-lane highway, and a truck came over a rise ahead like a blazing double comet. I floorboarded the gas pedal and cut over sharply to the right, threatening the Cadillac's fenders and its driver's life. In the approaching headlights, his face was as blank and white as a piece of paper, with charred black holes for eyes. His shoulders were naked.

At the last possible second he slowed enough to let me get by. The truck went off onto the shoulder, honking angrily. I braked gradually, hoping to force the Cadillac to stop. It looped past me in an insane arc, tires skittering, and was sucked away into darkness.

When I finally came to a full stop, I had to pry my fingers off the wheel. My knees were remote and watery. After smoking part of a cigarette, I U-turned and drove very cautiously back to Emerald Bay. I was long past the hot-rod age, and I needed rest.

The first motel I came to, the Siesta, was decorated with a vacancy sign and a neon Mexican sleeping luminously under a sombrero. Envying him, I parked on the gravel apron in front of the motel office. There was a light inside. The glass-paned door was standing open, and I went in. The little room was pleasantly furnished with rattan and chintz. I jangled the bell on the desk a few times. No one appeared, so I sat down to wait and lit a cigarette. An electric clock on the wall said a quarter to one.

I must have dozed for a few minutes. A dream rushed by the threshold of my consciousness, making a gentle noise. Death was in the dream. He drove a black Cadillac loaded with flowers. When I woke up, the cigarette was starting to burn my fingers. A thin man in a gray flannel shirt was standing over me with a doubtful look on his face.

He was big-nosed and small-chinned, and he wasn't as young as he gave the impression of being. His teeth were bad, the sandy hair was thinning and receding. He was the typical old youth who scrounged and wheedled his living around motor courts and restaurants and hotels, and hung on desperately to the frayed edge of other people's lives.

"What do you want?" he said. "Who are you? What do you want?" His voice was reedy and changeable like an adolescent's.

"A room."

"Is that all you want?"

From where I sat, it sounded like an accusation. I let it pass. "What else is there? Circassian dancing girls? Free popcorn?"

He tried to smile without showing his bad teeth. The smile was a dismal failure, like my joke. "I'm sorry, sir," he said. "You woke me up. I never make much sense right after I just wake up."

"Have a nightmare?"

His vague eyes expanded like blue bubblegum bubbles. "Why did you ask me that?"

"Because I just had one. But skip it. Do you have a vacancy or don't you?"

"Yessir. Sorry, sir." He swallowed whatever bitter taste he had in his mouth, and assumed an impersonal obsequious manner. "You got any luggage, sir?"

"No luggage."

Moving silently in tennis sneakers like a frail ghost of the boy he once had been, he went behind the counter, and took my name, address, license number, and five dollars. In return, he gave me a key numbered fourteen and told me where to use it. Apparently he despaired of a tip.

Room fourteen was like any other middle-class motel room touched with the California-Spanish mania. Artificially roughened plaster painted adobe color, poinsettia-red curtains, imitation parchment lampshade on a twisted black iron stand. A Rivera reproduction of a sleeping Mexican hung on the wall over the bed. I succumbed to its suggestion right away, and dreamed about Circassian dancing girls.

Along towards morning one of them got frightened, through no fault of mine, and began to scream her little Circassian lungs out. I sat up in bed, making soothing noises, and woke up. It was nearly nine by my wristwatch. The screaming ceased and began again, spoiling the morning like a fire siren outside the window. I pulled on my trousers over the underwear I'd been sleeping in, and went outside.

A young woman was standing on the walk outside the next room. She had a key in one hand and a handful of blood in the other. She wore a wide multi-colored skirt and a low-cut gypsy sort of blouse. The blouse was distended and her mouth was open, and she was yelling her head off. It was a fine dark head, but I hated her for spoiling my morning sleep.

I took her by the shoulders and said, "Stop it."

The screaming stopped. She looked down sleepily at the blood on her hand. It was as thick as axle grease, and almost as dark in color.

"Where did you get that?"

"I slipped and fell in it. I didn't see it."

Dropping the key on the walk, she pulled her skirt to one side with her clean hand. Her legs were bare and brown. Her skirt was stained at the back with the same thick fluid.

"Where? In this room?"

She faltered, "Yes."

Doors were opening up and down the drive. Half a dozen people began to converge on us. A dark-faced man about four and a half feet high came scampering from the direction of the office, his little pointed shoes dancing in the gravel.

"Come inside and show me," I said to the girl.

"I can't. I won't." Her eyes were very heavy, and surrounded by the bluish pallor of shock.

The little man slid to a stop between us, reached up and gripped the upper part of her arm. "What is the matter, Ella? Are you crazy, disturbing the guests?"

She said, "Blood," and leaned against me with her eyes closed.

His sharp glance probed the situation. He turned to the other guests, who had formed a murmuring semicircle around us.

"It is perfectly hokay. Do not be concerned, ladies and gentlemen. My daughter cut herself a little bit. It is perfectly all right."

Circling her waist with one long arm, he hustled her through the open door and slammed it behind him. I caught it on my foot and followed them in.

The room was a duplicate of mine, including the reproduction over the unmade bed, but everything was reversed as in a mirror image. The girl took a few weak steps by herself and sat on the edge of the bed. Then she noticed the blood spots on the sheets. She stood up quickly. Her mouth opened, rimmed with white teeth.

"Don't do it," I said. "We know you have a very fine pair of lungs."

The little man turned on me. "Who do you think you are?"

"The name is Archer. I have the next room."

"Get out of this one, please."

"I don't think I will."

He lowered his greased black head as if he were going to butt me. Under his sharkskin jacket, a hunch protruded from his back like a displaced elbow. He seemed to reconsider the butting gambit, and decided in favor of diplomacy.

"You are jumping to conclusions, mister. It is not so serious as it looks. We had a little accident here last night."

"Sure, your daughter cut herself. She heals remarkably fast."

"Nothing like that." He fluttered one long hand. "I said to the people outside the first thing that came to my mind. Actually, it was a little shuffle. One of the guests suffered a nosebleed."

The girl moved like a sleepwalker to the bathroom door and switched on the light. There was a pool of blood coagulating on the black and white checkerboard linoleum, streaked where she had slipped and fallen in it.

"Some nosebleed," I said to the little man. "Do you run this joint?"

"I am the proprietor of the Siesta motor hotel, yes. My name is Salanda. The gentleman is susceptible to nosebleed. He told me so himself."

"Where is he now?"

"He checked out early this morning."

"In good health?"

"Certainly in good health."

I looked around the room. Apart from the unmade bed with the brown spots on the sheets, it contained no signs of occupancy. Someone had spilled a pint of blood and vanished.

The little man opened to door wide and invited me with a sweep of his arm to leave. "If you will excuse me, sir, I wish to have this cleaned up as quickly as possible. Ella, will you tell Lorraine to get to work on it right away pronto? Then maybe you better like down for a little while, eh?"

"I'm all right now, father. Don't worry about me."

When I checked out a few minutes later, she was sitting behind the desk in the front office, looking pale but composed. I dropped my key on the desk in front of her.

"Feeling better, Ella?"

"Oh. I didn't recognize you with all your clothes on."

"That's a good line. May I use it?"

She lowered her eyes and blushed. "You're making fun of me. I know I acted foolishly this morning."

"I'm not so sure. What do *you* think happened in thirteen last night?"

"My father told you, didn't he?"

"He gave me a version, two of them in fact. I doubt that they're the final shooting script."

Her hand went to the central hollow in her blouse. Her arms and shoulders were slender and brown, the tips of her fingers carmine. "Shooting?"

"A cinema term," I said. "But there might have been a real shooting at that. Don't you think so?"

Her front teeth pinched her lower lip. She looked like somebody's pet rabbit. I restrained an impulse to pat her sleek brown head.

"That's ridiculous. This is a respectable motel. Anyway, father asked me not to discuss it with anybody."

"Why would he do that?"

"He loves this place, that's why. He doesn't want any scandal made out of nothing. If we lost our good reputation here, it would break my father's heart."

"He doesn't strike me as the sentimental type."

She stood up, smoothing her skirt. I saw that she'd changed it. "You leave him alone. He's a dear little man. I don't know what you think you're doing, trying to stir up trouble where there isn't any."

I backed away from her righteous indignation — female indignation is always righteous — and went out to my car. The early spring sun was dazzling. Beyond the freeway and the drifted sugary dunes, the bay was Prussian blue. The road cut inland across the base of the peninsula and returned to the sea a few miles north of the town. Here a wide blacktop parking space shelved off to the left of the highway, overlooking the white beach and whiter breakers. Signs at each end of the turnout stated that this was a County Park, No Beach Fires.

The beach and the blacktop expanse above it were deserted except for a single car, which looked very lonely. It was a long black Cadillac nosed into the cable fence at the edge of the beach. I braked and turned off the highway and got out. The man in the driver's seat of the Cadillac didn't turn his head as I approached him. His chin was propped on the steering wheel, and he was gazing out across the endless blue sea.

I opened the door and looked into his face. It was paper white. The dark brown eyes were sightless. The body was unclothed except for the thick hair matted on the chest, and a clumsy bandage tied around the waist. The bandage was composed of several blood-stained towels, held in place by a knotted piece of nylon fabric whose nature I didn't recognize immediately. Examining it more closely, I saw that it was a woman's slip. The left breast of the garment was embroidered in purple with a heart, containing the name "Fern" in slanting script. I wondered who Fern was.

The man who was wearing her purple heart had dark curly hair, heavy black eyebrows, a heavy chin sprouting black beard. He was rough-looking in spite of his anemia and the lipstick smudged on his mouth.

There was no registration on the steeringpost, and nothing in the glove compartment but a half-empty box of shells for a .38 automatic. The ignition was still turned on. So were the dash and headlights, but they were dim. The gas gauge registered empty. Curlyhead must have pulled off the highway soon after he passed me, and driven all the rest of the night in one place.

I untied the slip, which didn't look as if it would take fingerprints, and went over it for a label. It had one: Gretchen, Palm Springs. It occurred to me that it was Saturday morning and that I'd gone all winter without a week end in the desert. I retied the slip the way I'd found it, and drove back to the Siesta Motel.

Ella's welcome was a few degrees colder than absolute zero. "Well!" She glared down her pretty rabbit nose at me. "I thought we were rid of you."

"So did I. But I just couldn't tear myself away."

She gave me a peculiar look, neither hard nor soft, but mixed. Her hand went to her hair, then reached for a registration card. "I suppose if you want to rent a room, I can't stop you. Only please don't imagine you're making an impression on me. You're not. You leave me cold, mister."

"Archer," I said. "Lew Archer. Don't bother with the card. I came back to use your phone."

"Aren't there any other phones?" She pushed the telephone across the desk. "I guess it's all right, long as it isn't a toll call."

"I'm calling the Highway Patrol. Do you know their local number?"

"I don't remember." She handed me the telephone directory.

"There's been an accident," I said as I dialed.

"A highway accident? Where did it happen?"

"Right here, sister. Right here in room thirteen."

But I didn't tell that to the Highway Patrol. I told them I had found a dead man in a car on the parking lot above the county beach. The girl listened with widening eyes and nostrils. Before I finished she rose in a flurry and left the office by the rear door.

She came back with the proprietor. His eyes were black and bright like nailheads in leather, and the scampering dance of his feet was almost frenzied. "What is this?"

"I came across a dead man up the road a piece."

"So why do you come back here to telephone?" His head was in butting position, his hands outspread and gripping the corners of the desk. "Has it got anything to do with us?"

"He's wearing a couple of your towels."

"What?"

"And he was bleeding heavily before he died. I think somebody shot him in the stomach. Maybe you did."

"You're loco," he said, but not very emphatically. "Crazy accusations like that, they will get you into trouble. What is your business?"

"I'm a private detective."

"You followed him here, is that it? You were going to arrest him, so he shot himself?"

"Wrong on both accounts," I said. "I came here to sleep. And they don't shoot themselves in the stomach. It's too uncertain, and slow. No suicide wants to die of peritonitis."

"So what are you doing now, trying to make scandal for my business?"

"If your business includes trying to cover for murder."

"He shot himself," the little man insisted.

"How do you know?"

"Donny. I spoke to him just now."

"And how does Donny know?"

"The man told him."

"Is Donny your night keyboy?"

"He was. I think I will fire him, for stupidity. He didn't even tell me about this mess. I had to find it out for myself. The hard way."

"Donny means well," the girl said at his shoulder. "I'm sure he didn't realize what happened."

"Who does?" I said. "I want to talk to Donny. But first let's have a look at the register."

He took a pile of cards from a drawer and riffled through them. His large hands, hairy-backed, were calm and expert, like animals that lived a serene life of their own, independent of their emotional owner. They dealt me one of the cards across the desk. It was inscribed in block capitals: Richard Rowe, Detroit, Mich.

I said: "There was a woman with him."

"Impossible."

"Or he was a transvestite."

He surveyed me blankly, thinking of something else. "The HP, did you tell them to come here? They know it happened here?"

"Not yet. But they'll find your towels. He used from for bandage."

"I see. Yes. Of course." He struck himself with a clenched fist on the temple. It made a noise like someone maltreating a pumpkin. "You are a private detective, you say. Now if you informed the police that you were on the trail of a fugitive, a fugitive from justice . . . He shot himself rather than face arrest . . . For five hundred dollars?"

"I'm not that private," I said. "I have some public responsibility. Besides, the cops would do a little checking and catch me out."

"Not necessarily. He *was* a fugitive from justice, you know."

"I hear you telling me."

"Give me a little time, and I can even present you with his record."

The girl was leaning back away from her father, her eyes starred with broken illusions. "Daddy," she said weakly.

He didn't hear her. All of his bright black attention was fixed on me. "Seven hundred dollars?"

"No sale. The higher you raise it, the guiltier you look. Were you here last night?"

"You are being absurd," he said. "I spent the entire evening with my wife. We drove up to Los Angeles to attend the ballet." By way of supporting evidence, he hummed a couple of bars from Tchaikovsky. "We didn't arrive back here in Emerald Bay until nearly two o'clock."

"Alibis can be fixed."

"By criminals, yes," he said. "I am not a criminal."

The girl put a hand on his shoulder. He cringed away, his face creased by monkey fury, but his face was hidden from her.

"Daddy," she said. "Was he murdered, do you think?"

"How do I know?" His voice was wild and high, as if she had touched the spring of his emotion. "I wasn't here. I only know what Donny told me."

The girl was examining me with narrowed eyes, as if I were a new kind of animal she had discovered and was trying to think of a use for.

"This gentleman is a detective," she said, "or claims to be."

I pulled out my photostat and slapped it down on the desk. The little man picked it up and looked from it to my face. "Will you go to work for me?"

"Doing what, telling little white lies?"

The girl answered for him: "See what you can find out about this — this death. On my word of honor, Father had nothing to do with it."

I made a snap decision, the kind you live to regret. "All right. I'll take a fifty-dollar advance. Which is a good deal less than five hundred. My first advice to you is to tell the police everything you know. Provided that you're innocent."

"You insult me," he said.

But he flicked a fifty-dollar bill from the cash drawer and pressed it into my hand fervently, like a love token. I had a queasy feeling that I had been conned into taking his money, not much of it but enough. The feeling deepened when he still refused to talk. I had to use all the arts of persuasion even to get Donny's address out of him.

The keyboy lived in a shack on the edge of a desolate stretch of dunes. I guessed that it had once been somebody's beach house, before sand had drifted like unthawing snow in the angles of the walls and winter storms had broken the tiles and cracked the concrete foundations. Huge chunks of concrete were piled haphazardly on what had been a terrace overlooking the sea.

On one of the tilted slabs, Donny was stretched like a long albino lizard in the sun. The onshore wind carried the sound of my motor to his ears. He sat up blinking, recognized me when I stopped the car, and ran into the house.

I descended flagstone steps and knocked on the warped door. "Open up, Donny."

"Go away," he answered huskily. His eye gleamed like a snail through a crack in the wood.

"I'm working for Mr. Salanda. He wants us to have a talk."

"You can go and take a running jump at yourself, you and Mr. Salanda both."

"Open it or I'll break it down."

I waited for a while. He shot back the bolt. The door creaked reluctantly open. He leaned against the doorpost, searching my face with his eyes, his hairless body shivering from an internal chill. I pushed past him, through a kitchenette that was indescribably filthy, littered with the remnants of old meals, and gaseous with their odors. He followed me silently on bare soles into a larger room whose sprung floorboards undulated under my feet. The picture window had been broken and patched with cardboard. The stone fireplace was choked with garbage. The only furniture was an army cot in one corner where Donny apparently slept.

"Nice homey place you have here. It has that lived-in quality."

He seemed to take it as a compliment, and I wondered if I was dealing with a moron. "It suits me. I never was much of a one for fancy quarters. I like it here, where I can hear the ocean at night."

"What else do you hear at night, Donny?"

He missed the point of the question, or pretended to. "All different things. Big trucks going past on the highway. I like to hear those night sounds. Now I guess I can't go on living here. Mr. Salanda owns it, he lets me live here for nothing. Now he'll be kicking me out of here, I guess."

"On account of what happened last night?"

"Uh-huh." He subsided onto the cot, his doleful head supported by his hands.

I stood over him. "Just what did happen last night, Donny?"

"A bad thing," he said. "This fella checked in about ten o'clock —"

"The man with the dark curly hair?"

"That's the one. He checked in about ten, and I gave him room thirteen. Around about midnight I thought I heard a gun go off from there. It took me a little while to get my nerve up, then I went back to see what was going on. This fella came out of the room, without no clothes on. Just some kind of bandage around his waist. He looked like some kind of a crazy Indian or something. He had a gun in his hand, and he was staggering, and I could see that he was bleeding some. He come right up to me and pushed the gun in my gut and told me to keep my trap shut. He said I wasn't to tell anybody I saw him, now or later. He said if I opened my mouth about it to anybody, that he would come back and kill me. But now he's dead, isn't he?"

"He's dead."

I could smell fear on Donny: there's an unexplained trace of canine in my chromosomes. The hairs were prickling on the back of my neck, and I wondered if Donny's fear was of the past or for the future. The pimples stood out in bas-relief against his pale lugubrious face.

"I think he was murdered, Donny. You're lying, aren't you?"

"Me lying?" But his reaction was slow and feeble.

"The dead man didn't check in alone. He had a woman with him."

"What woman?" he said in elaborate surprise.

"You tell me. Her name was Fern. I think she did the shooting, and you caught her red-handed. The wounded man got out of the room and into his car and away. The woman stayed behind to talk to you. She probably paid you to dispose of his clothes and fake a new registration card for the room. But you both overlooked the blood on the floor of the bathroom. Am I right?"

"You couldn't be wronger, mister. Are you a cop?"

"A private detective. You're in deep trouble, Donny. You'd better talk yourself out of it if you can, before the cops start on you."

"I didn't do anything." His voice broke like a boy's. It went strangely with the glints of gray in his hair.

"Faking the register is a serious rap, even if they don't hang accessory to murder on you."

He began to expostulate in formless sentences that ran together. At the same time his hand was moving across the dirty gray blanket. It burrowed under the pillow and come out holding a crumpled card. He tried to stuff it into his mouth and chew it. I tore it away from between his discolored teeth.

It was a registration card from the motel, signed in a boyish scrawl: Mr. and Mrs. Richard Rowe, Detroit, Mich.

Donny was trembling violently. Below his cheap cotton shorts, his bony knees vibrated like tuning forks. "It wasn't my fault," he cried. "She held a gun on me."

"What did you do with the man's clothes?"

"Nothing. She didn't even let me into the room. She bundled them up and took them away herself."

"Where did she go?"

"Down the highway towards town. She walked away on the shoulder of the road and that was the last I saw of her."

"How much did she pay you, Donny?"

"Nothing, not a cent. I already told you, she held a gun on me."

"And you were so scared you kept quiet until this morning?"

"That's right. I was scared. Who wouldn't be scared?"

"She's gone now," I said. "You can give me a description of her."

"Yeah." He made a visible effort to pull his vague thoughts together. One of his eyes was a little off center, lending his face a stunned, amorphous appearance. "She was a big tall dame with blondey hair."

"Dyed?"

"I guess so, I dunno. She wore it in a braid like, on top of her head. She was kind of fat, built like a lady wrestler, great big watermelons on her. Big legs."

"How was she dressed?"

"I didn't hardly notice, I was so scared. I think she had some kind of a purple coat on, with black fur around the neck. Plenty of rings on her fingers and stuff."

"How old?"

"Pretty old, I'd say. Older than me, and I'm going on thirty-nine."

"And she did the shooting?"

"I guess so. She told me to say if anybody asked me, I was to say that Mr. Rowe shot himself."

"You're very suggestible, aren't you, Donny? It's a dangerous way to be, with people pushing each other around the way they do."

"I didn't get that, mister. Come again." He batted his pale blue eyes at me, smiling expectantly.

"Skip it," I said and left him.

A few hundred yards up the highway I passed an HP car with two uniformed men in the front seat looking grim. Donny was in for it now. I pushed him out of my mind and drove across country to Palm Springs.

Palm Springs is still a one-horse town, but the horse is a Palomino with silver trappings. Most of the girls were Palomino, too. The main street was a cross-section of Hollywood and Vine transported across the desert by some unnatural force and disguised in western costumes which fooled nobody. Not even me.

I found Gretchen's lingerie shop in an expensive-looking arcade built around an imitation flagstone patio. In the patio's center a little fountain gurgled pleasantly, flinging small lariats of spray against the heat. It was late in March, and the season was ending. Most of the shops, including the one I entered, were deserted except for the hired help.

It was a small shop, faintly perfumed by a legion of vanished dolls. Stockings and robes and other garments were coiled on the glass counters or hung like brilliant treesnakes on display stands along the narrow walls. A henna-headed woman emerged from rustling recesses at the rear and came tripping towards me on her toes.

"You are looking for a gift, sir?" she cried with a wilted kind of gaiety. Behind her painted mask, she was tired and aging and it was Saturday afternoon and the lucky ones were dunking themselves in kidney-shaped swimming pools behind walls she couldn't climb.

"Not exactly. In fact, not at all. A peculiar thing happened to me last night. I'd like to tell you about it, but it's kind of a complicated story."

She looked me over quizzically and decided that I worked for a living, too. The phony smile faded away. Another smile took its place, which I liked better. "You look as if you'd had a fairly rough night. And you could do with a shave."

"I met a girl," I said. "Actually she was a mature woman, a statuesque blond to be exact. I picked her up on the beach at Laguna, if you want me to be brutally frank."

"I couldn't bear it if you weren't. What kind of a pitch is this, brother?"

"Wait. You're spoiling my story. Something clicked when we met, in that sunset light, on the edge of the warm summer sea."

"It's always bloody cold when I go in."

"It wasn't last night. We swam in the moonlight and had a gay time and all. Then she went away. I didn't realize until she was gone that I didn't know her telephone number, or even her last name."

"Married woman, eh? What do you think I am, a lonely hearts club?" Still, she was interested, though she probably didn't believe me. "She mentioned me, is that it? What was her first name?"

"Fern."

"Unusual name. You say she was a big blonde?"

"Magnificently proportioned," I said. "If I had a classical education I'd call her Junoesque."

"You're kidding me, aren't you?"

"A little."

"I thought so. Personally I don't mind a little kidding. What did she say about me?"

"Nothing but good. As a matter of fact, I was complimenting her on her — er — garments."

"I see." She was long past blushing. "We had a customer last fall some time, by the name of Fern. Fern Dee. She had some kind of a job at the Joshua Club, I think. But she doesn't fit the description at all. This one was a brunette, a middle-sized brunette, quite young. I remember the name Fern because she wanted it embroidered on all the things she bought. A corny idea if you ask me, but that was her girlish desire and who am I to argue with girlish desires."

"Is she still in town?"

"I haven't seen her lately, not for months. But it couldn't be the woman you're looking for. Or could it?"

"How long ago was she in here?"

She pondered. "Early last fall, around the start of the season. She only came in that once, and made a big purchase, stockings and nightwear and underthings. The works. I remember thinking at the time, here was a girlie who suddenly hit the chips but heavily."

"She might have put on weight since then, and dyed her hair. Strange things can happen to the female form."

"You're telling me," she said. "How old was — your friend?"

"About forty, I'd say, give or take a little."

"It couldn't be the same one then. The girl I'm talking about was twenty-five at the outside, and I don't make mistakes about women's ages. I've seen too many of them in all stages, from Quentin quail to hags, and I certainly do mean hags."

"I bet you have."

She studied me with eyes shadowed by mascara and experience. "You a policeman?"

"I have been."

"You want to tell mother what it's all about?"

"Another time. Where's the Joshua Club?"

"It won't be open yet."

"I'll try it anyway."

She shrugged her thin shoulders and gave me directions. I thanked her.

It occupied a plain-faced one-story building half a block off the main street. The padded leather door swung inward when I pushed it. I passed through a lobby with a retractable roof, which contained a jungle growth of banana trees. The big main room was decorated with tinted desert photomurals. Behind a rattan bar with a fishnet canopy, a white-coated Caribbean type was drying shot-glasses with a dirty towel. His face looked uncommunicative.

On the orchestra dais beyond the piled chairs in the dining area, a young man in shirt sleeves was playing bop piano. His fingers shadowed the tune, ran circles around it, played leapfrog with it, and managed never to hit it on the nose. I stood beside him for a while and listened to him work. He looked up finally, still strumming with his left hand in the bass. He had soft-centered eyes and frozen-looking nostrils and a whistling mouth.

"Nice piano," I said.

"I think so."

"Fifty-second Street?"

"It's the street with the beat and I'm not effete." His left hand struck the same chord three times and dropped away from the keys. "Looking for somebody, friend?"

"Fern Dee. She asked me to drop by some time."

"Too bad. Another wasted trip. She left here end of last year, the dear. She wasn't a bad little nightingale but she was no pro, Joe, you know? She had it but she couldn't project it. When she warbled the evening died, no matter how hard she tried, I don't wanna be snide."

"Where did she lam, Sam, or don't you give a damn?"

He smiled like a corpse in a deft mortician's hands. "I heard the boss retired her to private life. Took her home to live with him. That is what I heard. But I don't mix with the big boy socially, so I couldn't say for sure that she's impure. Is it anything to you?"

"Something, but she's over twenty-one."

"Not more than a couple of years over twenty-one." His eyes darkened, and his thin mouth twisted sideways angrily. "I hate to see it happen to a pretty little twist like Fern. Not that I yearn —"

I broke in on his nonsense rhymes: "Who's the big boss you mentioned, the one Fern went to live with?"

"Angel. Who else?"

"What heaven does he inhabit?"

"You must be new in these parts —" His eyes swiveled and focused on something over my shoulder. His mouth opened and closed.

A grating tenor was behind me: "Got a question you want answered, bud?"

The pianist went back to the piano as if the ugly tenor had wiped me out, annulled my very existence. I turned to its source. He was standing in a narrow doorway behind the drums, a man in his thirties with thick black curly hair and a heavy jaw blue-shadowed by closely shaven beard. He was almost the living image of the dead man in the Cadillac. The likeness gave me a jolt. The heavy black gun in his hand gave me another.

He came around the drums and approached me, bull-shouldered in a fuzzy tweed jacket, holding the gun in front of him like a dangerous gift. The pianist was doing wry things in quickened tempo with the dead march from *Saul*. A wit.

The dead man's almost-double waved his cruel chin and the crueler gun in unison. "Come inside, unless you're a government man. If you are, I'll have a look at your credentials."

"I'm a freelance."

"Inside then."

The muzzle of the automatic came into my solar plexus like a pointing iron finger. Obeying its injunction, I made my way between empty music stands and through the narrow door behind the drums. The iron finger, probing my back, directed me down a lightless corridor to a small square office containing a metal desk, a safe, a filing cabinet. It was windowless, lit by fluorescent tubes in the ceiling. Under their pitiless glare, the face above the gun looked more than ever like the dead man's face. I wondered if I had been mistaken about his deadness, or if the desert heat had addled my brain.

"I'm the manager here," he said, standing so close that I could smell the piney stuff he used on his crisp dark hair. "You got anything to ask about the members of the staff, you ask me."

"Will I get an answer?"

"Try me, bud."

"The name is Archer," I said. "I'm a private detective."

"Working for who?"

"You wouldn't be interested."

"I am, though, very much interested." The gun hopped forward like a toad into my stomach again, with the weight of his shoulder behind it. "Working for who did you say?"

I swallowed anger and nausea, estimating my chances of knocking the gun to one side and taking him bare-handed. The chances seemed pretty slim. He was heavier than I was, and he held the automatic as if it had grown out of the end of his arm. You've seen too many movies, I told myself. I told him: "A motel owner on the coast. A man was shot in one of his rooms last night. I happened to check in there a few minutes later. The old boy hired me to look into the shooting."

"Who was it got himself ventilated?"

"He could be your brother," I said. "Do you have a brother?"

He lost his color. The center of his attention shifted from the gun to my face. The gun nodded. I knocked it up and sideways with a hard left uppercut. Its discharge burned the side of my face and drilled a hole in the wall. My right sank into his neck. The gun thumped the cork floor.

He went down but not out, his spread hand scrabbling for the gun, then closing on it. I kicked his wrist. He grunted but wouldn't let go of it. I threw a punch at the short hairs on the back of his neck. He took it and came up under it with the gun, shaking his head form side to side.

"Up with the hands now," he murmured. He was one of those men whose voices go soft and mild when they are in killing mood. He had the glassy impervious eyes of a killer. "Is Bart dead? My brother?"

"Very dead. He was shot in the belly."

"Who shot him?"

"That's the question."

"Who shot him?" he said in a quite white-faced rage. The single eye of the gun stared emptily at my midriff. "It could happen to you, bud, here and now."

"A woman was with him. She took a quick powder after it happened."

"I heard you say a name to Alfie, the piano-player. Was it Fern?"

"It could have been."

"What do you mean, it could have been?"

"She was there in the room, apparently. If you can give me a description of her?"

His hard brown eyes looked past me. "I can do better than that. There's a picture of her on the wall behind you. Take a look at it. Keep those hands up high."

I shifted my feet and turned uneasily. The wall was blank. I heard him draw a breath and move, and tried to evade his blow. No use. It caught the back of my head. I pitched forward against the blank wall and slid down it into three dimensions of blankness.

The blankness coagulated into colored shapes. The shapes were half human and half beast and they dissolved and reformed. A dead man with a hairy breast climbed out of a hole and doubled and quadrupled. I ran away from them through a twisting tunnel which led to an echo chamber. Under the roaring surge of the nightmare music, a rasping tenor was saying:

"I figure it like this. Vario's tip was good. Bart found her in Acapulco, and he was bringing her back from there. She conned him into stopping off at this motel for the night. Bart always went for her."

"I didn't know that," a dry old voice put in. "This is very interesting news about Bart and Fern. You should have told me before about this. Then I would not have sent him for her and this would not have happened. Would it, Gino?"

My mind was still partly absent, wandering underground in the echoing caves. I couldn't recall the voices, or who they were talking about. I had barely sense enough to keep my eyes closed and go on listening. I was lying on my back on a hard surface. The voices were above me.

The tenor said: "You can't blame Bartolomeo. She's the one, the dirty treacherous lying little bitch."

"Calm yourself, Gino. I blame nobody. But more than ever now, we want her back, isn't that right?"

"I'll kill her," he said softly, almost wistfully.

"Perhaps. It may not be necessary now. I dislike promiscuous killing—"

"Since when, Angel?"

"Don't interrupt, it's not polite. I learned to put first things first. Now what is the most important thing? Why did we want her back in the first place? I will tell you: to shut her mouth. The government heard she left me, they wanted her to testify about my income. We wanted to find her first and shut her mouth, isn't that right?"

"I know how to shut her mouth," the younger man said very quietly.

"First we try a better way, my way. You learn when you're as old as I am there is a use for everything, and not to be wasteful. Not even waste-ful with somebody else's blood. She shot your brother, right? So now we have something on her, strong enough to keep her mouth shut for good. She'd get off with second degree, with what she's got, but even that is five to ten in Tehachapi. I think all I need to do is tell her that. First we have to find her, eh?"

"I'll find her. Bart didn't have any trouble finding her."

"With Vario's tip to help him, no. But I think I'll keep you here with me, Gino. You're too hot-blooded, you and your brother both. I want her alive. Then I can talk to her, and then we'll see."

"You're going soft in your old age, Angel."

"Am I?" There was a light slapping sound, of a blow on flesh. "I have killed many men, for good reasons. So I think you will take that back."

"I take it back."

"And call me Mr. Funk. If I am so old, you will treat my gray hairs with respect. Call me Mr. Funk."

"Mr. Funk."

"All right, your friend here, does he know where Fern is?"

"I don't think so."

"Mr. Funk."

"Mr. Funk." Gino's voice was a whining snarl.

"I think he's coming to. His eyelids fluttered."

The toe of a shoe prodded my side. Somebody slapped my face a number of times. I opened my eyes and sat up. The back of my head was throbbing like an engine fueled by pain. Gino rose from a squatting position and stood over me.

"Stand up."

I rose shakily to my feet. I was in a stone-walled room with a high beamed ceiling, sparsely furnished with stiff old black oak chairs and tables. The room and the furniture seemed to have been built for a race of giants.

The man behind Gino was small and old and weary. He might have been an unsuccessful grocer or a superannuated barkeep who had come to California for his health. Clearly his health was poor. Even in the stifling heat he looked pale and chilly, as if he had caught chronic death from one of his victims. He moved closer to me, his legs shuffling feebly in wrinkled blue trousers that bagged at the knees. His shrunken torso was swathed in a heavy blue turtleneck sweater. He had two days' beard on his chin, like moth-eaten gray plush.

"Gino informs me that you are investigating a shooting." His accent was Middle-European and very faint, as if he had forgotten his origins. "Where did this happen, exactly?"

"I don't think I'll tell you that. You can read it in the papers tomorrow night if you are interested."

"I am not prepared to wait. I am impatient. Do you know where Fern is?"

"I wouldn't be here if I did."

"But you know where she was last night."

"I couldn't be sure."

"Tell me anyway to the best of your knowledge."

"I don't think I will."

"He doesn't think he will," the old man said to Gino.

"I think you better let me out of here. Kidnaping is a tough rap. You don't want to die in the pen."

He smiled at me, with a tolerance more terrible than anger. His eyes were like thin stab-wounds filled with watery blood. Shuffling unhurriedly to the head of the mahogany table behind him, he pressed a spot in the rug with the toe of one felt slipper. Two men in blue serge suits entered the room and stepped towards me briskly. They belonged to the race of giants it had been built for.

Gino moved behind me and reached to pin my arms. I pivoted, landed one short punch, and took a very hard counter below the belt. Something behind me slammed my kidneys with the heft of a trailer truck bumper. I turned on weakening legs and caught a chin with my elbow. Gino's fist, or one of the beams from the ceiling, landed on my neck. My head rang like a gong. Under its clangor, Angel was saying pleasantly:

"Where was Fern last night?"

I didn't say.

The men in blue serge held me upright by the arms while Gino used my head as a punching bag. I rolled with his lefts and rights as well as I could, but his timing improved and mine deteriorated. His face wavered and receded. At intervals Angel inquired politely if I was willing to assist him now. I asked myself confusedly in the hail of fists what I was holding out for or who I was protecting. Probably I was holding out for myself. It seemed important to me not to give in to violence. But my identity was dissolving and receding like the face in front of me.

I concentrated on hating Gino's face. That kept it clear and steady for a while: a stupid square-jawed face barred by a single black brow, two close-set brown eyes staring glassily. His fists continued to rock me like an air-hammer.

Finally Angel placed a clawed hand on his shoulder, and nodded to my handlers. They deposited me in a chair. It swung on an invisible wire from the ceiling in great circles. It swung out wide over the desert, across a bleak horizon, into darkness.

I came to, cursing. Gino was standing over me again. There was an empty water-glass in his hand, and my face was dripping. Angel spoke up beside him, with a trace of irritation in his voice:

"You stand up good under punishment. Why go to all the trouble, though? I want a little information, that is all. My friend, my little girl-friend, ran away. I'm impatient to get her back."

"You're going about it the wrong way."

Gino leaned close, and laughed harshly. He shattered the glass on the arm of my chair, held the jagged base up to my eyes. Fear ran through me, cold and light in my veins. My eyes were my connection with every-thing. Blindness would be the end of me. I closed my eyes, shutting out the cruel edges of the broken thing in his hand.

"Nix, Gino," the old man said. "I have a better idea, as usual. There is heat on, remember."

They retreated to the far side of the table and conferred there in low voices. The young man left the room. The old man came back to me. His storm troopers stood one on each side of me, looking down at him in ignorant awe.

"What is your name, young fellow?"

I told him. My mouth was puffed and lisping, tongue tangled in ropes of blood.

"I like a young fellow who can take it, Mr. Archer. You say that you're a detective. You find people for a living, is that right?"

"I have a client," I said.

"Now you have another. Whoever he is, I can buy and sell him, be-lieve me. Fifty times over." His thin blue hands scoured each other. They made a sound like two dry sticks rubbing together on a dead tree.

"Narcotics?" I said. "Are you the wheel in the heroin racket? I've heard of you."

His watery eyes veiled themselves like a bird's. "Now don't ask foolish questions, or I will lose my respect for you entirely."

"That would break my heart."

"Then comfort yourself with this." He brought an old-fashioned purse out of his hip pocket, abstracted a crumpled bill and smoothed it out on my knee. It was a five-hundred-dollar bill.

"This girl of mine you are going to find for me, she is young and foolish. I am old and foolish, to have trusted her. No matter. Find her for me and bring her back and I will give you another bill like this one. Take it."

"Take it," one of my guards repeated. "Mr. Funk said for you to take it."

I took it. "You're wasting your money. I don't even know what she looks like. I don't know anything about her."

"Gino is bringing a picture. He came across her last fall at a recording studio in Hollywood where Alfie had a date. He gave her an audition and took her on at the club, more for her looks than for the talent she had. As a singer she flopped. But she is a pretty little thing, about five foot four, nice figure, dark brown hair, big hazel eyes. I found a use for her." Lechery flickered briefly in his eyes and went out.

"You find a use for everything."

"That is good economics. I often think if I wasn't what I am, I would make a good economist. Nothing would go to waste." He paused and dragged his dying old mind back to the subject: "She was here for a couple of months, then she ran out on me, silly girl. I heard last week that she was in Acapulco, and the federal Grand Jury was going to subpoena her. I have tax troubles, Mr. Archer, all my life I have tax troubles. Unfortunately I let Fern help with my books a little bit. She could do me great harm. So I sent Bart to Mexico to bring her back. But I meant no harm to her. I still intend her no harm, even now. A little talk, a little realistic discussion with Fern, that is all that will be necessary. So even the shooting of my good friend Bart serves its purpose. Where did it happen, by the way?"

The question flicked out like a hook on the end of a long line.

"In San Diego," I said, "at a place near the airport: the Mission Motel."

He smiled paternally. "Now you are showing good sense."

Gino came back with a silver-framed photograph in his hand. He handed it to Angel, who passed it on to me. It was a studio portrait, of the kind intended for publicity cheesecake. On a black velvet divan, against an artificial night sky, a young woman reclined in a gossamer robe that was split to show one bent leg. Shadows accentuated the lines of her body and the fine bones in her face. Under the heavy makeup which widened the mouth and darkened the half-closed eyes I recognized Ella Salanda. The picture was signed in white, in the lower right-handed corner: "To my Angel, with all my love, Fern."

A sickness assailed me, worse than the sickness induced by Gino's fists. Angel breathed into my face: "Fern Dee is a stage name. Her real name I never learned. She told me one time that if her family knew where she was they would die of shame." He chuckled drily. "She will not want them to know that she killed a man."

I drew away from his charnel-house breath. My guards escorted me out. Gino started to follow, but Angel called him back.

"Don't wait to hear from me," the old man said after me. "I expect to hear from you."

The building stood on a rise in the open desert. It was huge and turreted, like somebody's idea of a castle in Spain. The last rays of the sun washed its wall in purple light and cast long shadows across its barren acreage. It was surrounded by a ten-foot hurricane fence topped with three strands of barbed wire.

Palm Springs was a clutter of white stones in the distance, diamonded by an occasional light. The dull red sun was balanced like a glowing cigar-butt on the rim of the hills above the town. A man with a bulky shoulder harness under his brown suede windbreaker drove me towards it. The sun fell out of sight, and darkness gathered like an impalpable ash on the desert, like a column of blue-gray smoke towering into the sky.

The sky was blue-black and swarming with stars when I got back to Emerald Bay. A black Cadillac followed me out of Palm Springs. I lost it in the winding streets of Pasadena. So far as I could see, I had lost it for good.

The neon Mexican lay peaceful under the stars. A smaller sign at his feet asserted that there was No Vacancy. The lights in the long low stucco buildings behind him shone brightly. The office door was open behind a screen, throwing a barred rectangle of light on the gravel. I stepped into it, and froze.

Behind the registration desk in the office, a woman was avidly reading a magazine. Her shoulders and bosom were massive. Her hair was blond, piled on her head in coroneted braids. There were rings on her fingers, a triple strand of cultured pearls around her thick white throat. She was the woman Donny had described to me.

I pulled the screen door open and said rudely: "Who are you?"

She glanced up, twisting her mouth in a sour grimace. "Well! I'll thank you to keep a civil tongue in your head."

"Sorry. I thought I'd seen you before somewhere."

"Well, you haven't." She looked me over coldly. "What happened to your face, anyway?"

"I had a little plastic surgery done. By an amateur surgeon."

She clucked disapprovingly. "If you're looking for a room, we're full up for the night. I don't believe I'd rent you a room even if we weren't. Look at your clothes."

"Uh-huh. Where's Mr. Salanda?"

"Is it any business of yours?"

"He wants to see me. I'm doing a job for him."

"What kind of a job?"

I mimicked her: "Is it any business of yours?" I was irritated. Under her mounds of flesh she had a personality as thin and hard and abrasive as a rasp.

"Watch who you're getting flip with, sonny boy." She rose, and her shadow loomed immense across the back door of the room. The magazine fell closed on the desk: it was *Teen-age Confessions*. "I am Mrs. Salanda. Are you a handyman?"

"A sort of one," I said. "I'm a garbage collector in the moral field. You look as if you could use me."

The crack went over her head. "Well, you're wrong. And I don't think my husband hired you, either. This is a respectable motel."

"Uh-huh. Are you Ella's mother?"

"I should say not. That little snip is no daughter of mine."

"Her stepmother?"

"Mind your own business. You better get out of here. The police are keeping a close watch on this place tonight, if you're planning any tricks."

"Where's Ella now?"

"I don't know and I don't care. She's probably gallivanting off around the countryside. It's all she's good for. One day at home in the last six months, that's a fine record for a young unmarried girl." Her face was thick and bloated with anger against her stepdaughter. She went on talking blindly, as if she had forgotten me entirely: "I told her father he was an old fool to take her back. How does he know what she's been up to? I say let the ungrateful filly go and fend for herself."

"Is that what you say, Mabel?" Salanda had softly opened the door behind her. He came forward into the room, doubly dwarfed by her blond magnitude. "I say if it wasn't for you, my dear, Ella wouldn't have been driven away from home in the first place."

She turned on him in a blubbering rage. He drew himself up tall and reached to snap his fingers under her nose. "Go back into the house. You are a disgrace to women, a disgrace to motherhood."

"I'm not *her* mother, thank God."

"Thank God," he echoed, shaking his fist at her. She retreated like a schooner under full sail, menaced by a gunboat. The door closed on her. Salanda turned to me:

"I'm sorry, Mr. Archer. I have difficulties with my wife, I am ashamed to say it. I was an imbecile to marry again. I gained a senseless hulk of flesh, and lost my daughter. Old imbecile!" he denounced himself, wagging his great head sadly. "I married in hot blood. Sexual passion has always been my downfall. It runs in my family, this insane hunger for blondeness and stupidity and size." He spread his arms in a wide and futile embrace on emptiness.

"Forget it."

"If I could." He came closer to examine my face. "You are injured, Mr. Archer. Your mouth is damaged. There is blood on your chin."

"I was in a slight brawl."

"On my account?"

"On my own. But I think it's time you leveled with me."

"Leveled with you?"

"Told me the truth. You knew who was shot last night, and who shot him, and why."

He touched my arm, with a quick, tentative grace. "I have only one daughter, Mr. Archer, only the one child. It was my duty to defend her, as best as I could."

"Defend her from what?"

"From shame, from the police, from prison." He flung one arm out, indicating the whole range of human disaster. "I am a man of honor, Mr. Archer. But private honor stands higher with me than public honor. The man was abducting my daughter. She brought him here in the hope of being rescued. Her last hope."

"I think that's true. You should have told me this before."

"I was alarmed, upset. I feared your intentions. Any minute the police were due to arrive."

"But you had a right to shoot him. It wasn't even a crime. The crime was his."

"I didn't know that then. The truth came out to me gradually. I feared that Ella was involved with him." His flat black gaze sought my face and rested on it. "However, I did not shoot him, Mr. Archer. I was not even here at the time. I told you that this morning, and you may take my word for it."

"Was Mrs. Salanda here?"

"No sir, she was not. Why should you ask me that?"

"Donny described the woman who checked in with the dead man. The description fits your wife."

"Donny was lying. I told him to give a false description of the woman. Apparently he was unequal to the task of inventing one."

"Can you prove that she was with you?"

"Certainly I can. We had reserved seats at the theatre. Those who sat around us can testify that the seats were not empty. Mrs. Salanda and I, we are not an inconspicuous couple." He smiled wryly.

"Ella killed him then."

He neither assented, nor denied it. "I was hoping that you were on my side, my side and Ella's. Am I wrong?"

"I'll have to talk to her, before I know myself. Where is she?"

"I do not know, Mr. Archer, sincerely I do not know. She went away this afternoon, after the policemen questioned her. They were suspicious, but we managed to soothe their suspicions. They did not know that she had just come home, from another life, and I did not tell them. Mable wanted to tell them. I silenced her." His white teeth clicked together.

"What about Donny?"

"They took him down to the station for questioning. He told them nothing damaging. Donny can appear very stupid when he wishes. He has the reputation of an idiot, but he is not so dumb. Donny has been with me for many years. He has a deep devotion for my daughter. I got him released tonight."

"You should have taken my advice," I said, "taken the police into your confidence. Nothing would have happened to you. The dead man was a mobster, and what he was doing amounts to kidnaping. Your daughter was a witness against his boss."

"She told me that. I am glad that it is true. Ella has not always told me the truth. She has been a hard girl to bring up, without a good mother to set her an example. Where has she been these last months, Mr. Archer?"

"Singing in a night club in Palm Springs. Her boss was a racketeer."

"A racketeer?" His mouth and nose screwed up, as if he sniffed the odor of corruption.

"Where she was isn't important, compared with where she is now. The boss is still after her. He hired me to look for her."

Salanda regarded me with fear and dislike, as if the odor originated in me. "You let him hire you?"

"It was my best chance of getting out of his place alive. I'm not his boy, if that's what you mean."

"You ask me to believe you?"

"I'm telling you. Ella is in danger. As a matter of fact, we all are." I didn't tell him about the second black Cadillac. Gino would be driving it, wandering the night roads with a ready gun in his armpit and revenge corroding his heart.

"My daughter is aware of the danger," he said. "She warned me of it."

"She must have told you where she was going."

"No. But she may be at the beach house. The house where Donny lives. I will come with you."

"You stay here. Keep your doors locked. If any strangers show and start prowling the place, call the police."

He bolted the door behind me as I went out. Yellow traffic lights cast wan reflections on the asphalt. Streams of cars went by to the north, to the south. To the west, where the sea lay, a great black emptiness opened under the stars. The beach house sat on its white margin, a little over a mile from the motel.

For the second time that day, I knocked on the warped kitchen door. There was light behind it, shining through the cracks. A shadow obscured the light.

"Who is it?" Donny said. Fear or some other emotion had filled his mouth with pebbles.

"You know me, Donny."

The door groaned on his hinges. He gestured dumbly to me to come in, his face a white blur. When he turned his head, and the light from the living room caught his face, I saw that grief was the emotion that marked it. His eyes were swollen as if he had been crying. More than ever he resembled a dilapidated boy whose growing pains had never paid off in manhood.

"Anybody with you?"

Sounds of movement in the living room answered my question. I brushed him aside and went in. Ella Salanda was bent over an open suitcase on the camp cot. She straightened, her mouth thin, eyes wide and dark. The .38 automatic in her hand gleamed dully under the naked bulb suspended form the ceiling.

"I'm getting out of here," she said, "and you're not going to stop me."

"I'm not sure I want to try. Where are you going, Fern?"

Donny spoke behind me, in his grief-thickened voice: "She's going away from me. She promised to stay here if I did what she told me. She promised to be my girl —"

"Shut up, stupid." Her voice cut like a lash, and Donny gasped as if the lash had been laid across his back.

"What did she tell you to do, Donny? Tell me just what you did."

"When she checked in last night with the fella from Detroit, she made a sign I wasn't to let on I knew her. Later on she left me a note. She wrote it with a lipstick on a piece of paper towel. I still got it hidden, in the kitchen."

"What did she write in the note?"

He lingered behind me, fearful of the gun in the girl's hand, more fearful of her anger.

She said: "Don't be crazy, Donny. He doesn't know a thing, not a thing. He can't do anything to either of us."

"I don't care what happens, to me or anybody else," the anguished voice said behind me. "You're running out on me, breaking your promise to me. I always knew it was too good to be true. Now I just don't care any more."

"I care," she said. "I care what happens to me." Her eyes shifted to me, above the unwavering gun. "I won't stay here. I'll shoot you if I have to."

"It shouldn't be necessary. Put it down, Fern. It's Bartolomeo's gun, isn't it? I found the shells to fit it in his glove compartment."

"How do you know so much?"

"I talked to Angel."

"Is he here?" Panic whined in her voice.

"No. I came alone."

"You better leave the same way then, while you can go under your own power."

"I'm staying. You need protection, whether you know it or not. And I need information. Donny, go in the kitchen and bring me that note."

"Don't do it, Donny. I'm warning you."

His sneakered feet made soft indecisive sounds. I advanced on the girl, talking quietly and steadily: "You conspired to kill a man, but you don't have to be afraid. He had it coming. Tell the whole story to the cops, and my guess is they won't even book you. Hell, you can even become famous. The government wants you as a witness in a tax case."

"What kind of a case?"

"A tax case against Angel. It's probably the only kind of rap they can pin on him. You can send him up for the rest of his life like Capone. You'll be a heroine, Fern."

"Don't call me Fern. I hate that name." There were sudden tears in her eyes. "I hate everything connected with that name. I hate myself."

"You'll hate yourself more if you don't put down that gun. Shoot me and it all starts over again. The cops will be on your trail, Angel's troopers will be gunning for you."

Now only the cot was between us, the cot and the unsteady gun facing me above it.

"This is the turning point," I said. "You've made a lot of bum decisions and almost ruined yourself, playing footsie with the evilest men there are. You can go on the way you have been, getting in deeper until you end up in a refrigerated drawer, or you can come back out of it now, into a decent life."

"A decent life? Here? With my father married to Mabel?"

"I don't think Mabel will last much longer. Anyway, I'm not Mabel. I'm on your side."

I waited. She dropped the gun on the blanket. I scooped it up and turned to Donny:

"Let me see that note."

He disappeared through the kitchen door, head and shoulders drooping on the long stalk of his body.

"What could I do?" the girl said. "I was caught. It was Bart or me. All the way up from Acapulco I planned how I could get away. He held a gun in my side when we crossed the border; the same way when we stopped for gas or to eat at the drive-ins. I realized he had to be killed. My father's motel looked like my only chance. So I talked Bart into staying there with me overnight. He had no idea who the place belonged to. I didn't know what I was going to do. I only knew it had to be something drastic. Once I was back with Angel in the desert, that was the end of me. Even if he didn't kill me, it meant I'd have to go on living with him. Anything was better than that. So I wrote a note to Donny in the bathroom, and dropped it out the window. He was always crazy about me."

Her mouth had grown softer. She looked remarkably young and virginal. The faint blue hollows under her eyes were dewy. "Donny shot Bart with Bart's own gun. He had more nerve than I had. I lost my nerve when I went back into the room this morning. I didn't know about the blood in the bathroom. It was the last straw."

She was wrong. Something crashed in the kitchen. A cool draft swept the living room. A gun spoke twice, out of sight. Donny fell backwards through the doorway, a piece of brownish paper clutched in his hand. Blood gleamed on his shoulder like a red badge.

I stepped behind the cot and pulled the girl down to the floor with me. Gino came through the door, his two-colored sports shoe stepping on Donny's laboring chest. I shot the gun out of his hand. He floundered back against the wall, clutching at his wrist.

I sighted carefully for my second shot, until the black bar of his eyebrows was steady in the sights of the .38. The hole it made was invisible. Gino fell loosely forward, prone on the floor beside the man he had killed.

Ella Salanda ran across the room. She knelt, and cradled Donny's head in her lap. Incredible, he spoke, in a loud sighing voice:

"You won't go away again, Ella? I did what you told me. You promised."

"Sure I promised. I won't leave you, Donny. Crazy man. Crazy fool."

"You like me better than you used to? Now?"

"I like you, Donny. You're the most man there is."

She held the poor insignificant head in her hands. He sighed, and his life came out bright-colored at the mouth. It was Donny who went away.

His hand relaxed, and I read the lipstick note she had written him on a piece of porous tissue:

"Donny: This man will kill me unless you kill him first. His gun will be in his clothes on the chair beside the bed. Come in and get it at midnight and shoot to kill. Good luck. I'll stay and be your girl if you do this, just like you always wished. Love. Ella."

I looked at the pair on the floor. She was rocking his lifeless head against her breast. Beside them, Gino looked very small and lonely, a dummy leaking darkness from his brow.

Donny had his wish and I had mine. I wondered what Ella's was.

1955

STANLEY ELLIN

The Moment of Decision

HUGH LOZIER was the exception to the rule that people who are completely sure of themselves cannot be likable. We have all met the sure ones, of course — those controlled but penetrating voices which cut through all others in a discussion, those hard forefingers jabbing home opinions on your chest, those living Final Words on all issues — and I imagine we all share the same amalgam of dislike and envy for them. Dislike, because no one likes to be shouted down or prodded in the chest, and envy, because everyone wishes he himself were so rich in self-assurance that he could do the shouting down and prodding.

For myself, since my work took me regularly to certain places in this atomic world where the only state was confusion and the only steady employment that of splitting political hairs, I found absolute judgments harder and harder to come by. Hugh once observed of this that it was a good thing my superiors in the department were not cut of the same cloth, because God knows what would happen to the country then. I didn't relish that, but — and there was my curse again — I had to grant him his right to say it.

Despite this, and despite the fact that Hugh was my brother-in-law — a curious relationship when you come to think of it — I liked him immensely, just as everyone else did who knew him. He was a big, good-looking man, with clear blue eyes in a ruddy face, and with a quick, outgoing nature eager to appreciate whatever you had to offer. He was overwhelmingly generous, and his generosity was of that rare and excellent kind which makes you feel as if you are doing the donor a favor by accepting it.

I wouldn't say he had any great sense of humor, but plain good humor can sometimes be an adequate substitute for that, and in Hugh's case it was. His stormy side was largely reserved for those times when he thought you might have needed his help in something and failed to call on him for it. Which meant that ten minutes after Hugh had met you and liked you, you were expected to ask him for anything he might be able to offer. A month or so after he married my sister Elizabeth she mentioned to him my avid interest in a fine Copley he had hanging in his gallery at Hilltop, and I can still vividly recall my horror when it suddenly arrived, heavily crated and with his gift card attached, at my barren room-and-a-half. It took considerable effort, but I finally managed to return it to him by forgoing the argument that the picture was undoubtedly worth more than the entire building in which I lived and by complaining that it simply didn't show to advantage on my wall. I think he suspected I was lying, but being Hugh he would never dream of charging me with that in so many words.

Of course, Hilltop and the two hundred years of Lozier tradition that went into it did much to shape Hugh this way. The first Loziers had carved the estate from the heights overlooking the river, had worked hard and flourished exceedingly; its successive generations had invested their income so wisely that money and position eventually erected a towering wall between Hilltop and the world outside. Truth to tell, Hugh was very much a man of the eighteenth century who somehow found himself in the twentieth, and simply made the best of it.

Hilltop itself was almost a replica of the celebrated, but long untenanted, Dane house nearby, and was striking enough to open anybody's eyes at a glance. The house was weathered stone, graceful despite its bulk, and the vast lawns reaching to the river's edge were tended with such fanatic devotion over the years that they had become carpets of purest green which magically changed luster under any breeze. Gardens ranged from the other side of the house down to the groves which half hid the stables and outbuildings, and past the far side of the groves ran the narrow road which led to town. The road was a courtesy road, each estate holder along it maintaining his share, and I think it safe to say that for all the crushed rock he laid in it Hugh made less use of it by far than any of his neighbors.

Hugh's life was bound up in Hilltop; he could be made to leave it only by dire necessity; and if you did meet him away from it you were made acutely aware that he was counting off the minutes until he could return. And if you weren't wary you would more than likely find yourself going along with him when he did return, and totally unable to tear yourself away from the place while the precious weeks rolled by. I know.

I believe I spent more time at Hilltop than at my own apartment after my sister brought Hugh into the family.

At one time I wondered how Elizabeth took to this marriage, considering that before she met Hugh she had been as restless and flighty as she was pretty. When I put the question to her directly, she said, "It's wonderful, darling. Just as wonderful as I knew it would be when I first met him."

It turned out that their first meeting had taken place at an art exhibition, a showing of some ultramodern stuff, and she had been intently studying one of the more bewildering concoctions on display when she became aware of this tall, good-looking man staring at her. And, as she put it, she had been about to set him properly in his place when he said abruptly, "Are you admiring that?"

This was so unlike what she had expected that she was taken completely aback. "I don't know," she said weakly. "Am I supposed to?"

"No," said the stranger, "it's damned nonsense. Come along now, and I'll show you something which isn't a waste of time."

"And," Elizabeth said to me, "I came along like a pup at his heels, while he marched up and down and told me what was good and what was bad, and in a good loud voice, too, so that we collected quite a crowd along the way. Can you picture it, darling?"

"Yes," I said, "I can." By now I had shared similar occasions with Hugh, and learned at firsthand that nothing could dent his cast-iron assurance.

"Well," Elizabeth went on, "I must admit that at first I was a little put off, but then I began to see that he knew exactly what he was talking about, and that he was terribly sincere. Not a bit self-conscious about anything, but just eager for me to understand things the way he did. It's the same way with everything. Everybody else in the world is always fumbling and bumbling over deciding anything — what to order for dinner, or how to manage his job, or whom to vote for — but Hugh always *knows*. It's *not* knowing that makes for all those nerves and complexes and things you hear about, isn't that so? Well, I'll take Hugh, thank you, and leave everyone else to the psychiatrists."

So there it was. An Eden with flawless lawns and no awful nerves and complexes, and not even the glimmer of a serpent in the offing. That is, not a glimmer until the day Raymond made his entrance on the scene.

We were out on the terrace that day, Hugh and Elizabeth and I, slowly being melted into a sort of liquid torpor by the August sunshine, and all of us too far gone to make even a pretence at talk. I lay there with a linen cap over my face, listening to the summer noises around me and being perfectly happy.

There was the low, steady hiss of the breeze through the aspens nearby, the plash and drip of oars on the river below, and now and then the melancholy *tink-tunk* of a sheep bell from one of the flock on the lawn. The flock was a fancy of Hugh's. He swore that nothing was better for a lawn than a few sheep grazing on it, and every summer five or six fat and sleepy ewes were turned out on the grass to serve this purpose and to add a pleasantly pastoral note to the view.

My first warning of something amiss came from the sheep — from the sudden sound of their bells clanging wildly and then baa-ing which suggested an assault by a whole pack of wolves. I heard Hugh say "Damn!" loudly and angrily, and I opened my eyes to see something more incongruous than wolves. It was a large black poodle in the full glory of a clownish haircut, a bright-red collar, and an ecstasy of high spirits as he chased the frightened sheep around the lawn. It was clear the poodle had no intention of hurting them — he probably found them the most wonderful playmates imaginable — but it was just as clear that the panicky ewes didn't understand this, and would very likely end up in the river before the fun was over.

In the bare second it took me to see all this, Hugh had already leaped the low terrace wall and was among the sheep, herding them away from the water's edge, and shouting commands at the dog who had different ideas.

"Down, boy!" he yelled. "Down!" And then as he would to one of his own hounds, he sternly commanded, "Heel!"

He would have done better, I thought, to have picked up a stick or stone and made a threatening gesture, since the poodle paid no attention whatever to Hugh's words. Instead, continuing to bark happily, the poodle made for the sheep again, this time with Hugh in futile pursuit. An instant later the dog was frozen into immobility by a voice from among the aspens near the edge of the lawn.

"Assieds!" the voice called breathlessly. *"Assieds-toi!"*

Then the man appeared, a small, dapper figure trotting across the grass. Hugh stood waiting, his face darkening as we watched.

Elizabeth squeezed my arm. "Let's get down there," she whispered. "Hugh doesn't like being made a fool of."

We got there in time to hear Hugh open his big guns. "Any man," he was saying, "who doesn't know how to train an animal to its place shouldn't own one."

The man's face was all polite attention. It was a good face, thin and intelligent, and webbed with tiny lines at the corners of the eyes. There was also something behind those eyes that couldn't quite be masked. A gentle mockery. A glint of wry perception turned on the world like a camera lens. It was nothing anyone like Hugh would have noticed, but it was there all the same, and I found myself warming to it on the spot. There was also something tantalizingly familiar about the newcomer's face, his high forehead, and his thinning gray hair, but as much as I dug into my memory during Hugh's long and solemn lecture I couldn't come up with an answer. The lecture ended with a few remarks on the best methods of dog training, and by then it was clear that Hugh was working himself into a mood of forgiveness.

"As long as there's no harm done —" he said.

The man nodded soberly. "Still, to get off on the wrong foot with one's new neighbors —"

Hugh looked startled. "Neighbors?" he said almost rudely. "You mean that you live around here?"

The man waved toward the aspens. "On the other side of those woods."

"The *Dane* house?" The Dane house was almost as sacred to Hugh as Hilltop, and he had once explained to me that if he were ever offered a chance to buy the place he would snap it up. His tone now was not so much wounded as incredulous. "I don't believe it!" he exclaimed.

"Oh, yes," the man assured him, "the Dane house. I performed there at a party many years ago, and always hoped that someday I might own it."

It was the word *performed* that gave me my clue — that and the accent barely perceptible under the precise English. He had been born and raised in Marseilles — that would explain the accent — and long before my time he had already become a legend.

"You're Raymond, aren't you?" I said. "Charles Raymond."

"I prefer Raymond alone." He smiled in deprecation of his own small vanity. "And I am flattered that you recognize me."

I don't believe he really was. Raymond the Magician, Raymond the Great would, if anything, expect to be recognized wherever he went. As the master of sleight of hand who had paled Thurston's star, as the escape artist who had almost outshone Houdini, Raymond would not be inclined to underestimate himself.

He had started with the standard box of tricks which makes up the repertoire of most professional magicians; he had gone far beyond that to those feats of escape which, I suppose, are known to us all by now. The lead casket sealed under a foot of lake ice, the welded-steel strait jackets, the vaults of the Bank of England, the exquisite suicide knot which nooses throat and doubles legs together so that the motion of a leg draws the noose tighter around the throat — all these Raymond had known and escaped from. And then at the pinnacle of fame he had dropped from sight and his name had become relegated to the past.

When I asked him why, he shrugged.

"A man works for money or for the love of his work. If he has all the wealth he needs and has no more love for his work, why go on?"

"But to give up a great career —" I protested.

"It was enough to know that the house was waiting here."

"You mean," Elizabeth said, "that you never intended to live any place but here?"

"Never — not once in all these years." He laid a finger along his nose and winked broadly at us. "Of course, I made no secret of this to the Dane estate, and when the time came to sell I was the first and only one approached."

"You don't give up an idea easily," Hugh said in an edged voice.

Raymond laughed. "Idea? It became an obsession really. Over the years I traveled to many parts of the world, but no matter how fine the place, I knew it could not be as fine as that house on the edge of the woods there, with the river at its feet and the hills beyond. Someday, I would tell myself, when my travels are done I will come here, and, like Candide, cultivate my garden."

He ran his hand abstractedly over the poodle's head and looked around with an air of great satisfaction. "And now," he said, "here I am."

Here he was, indeed, and it quickly became clear that his arrival was working a change on Hilltop. Or, since Hilltop was so completely a reflection of Hugh, it was clear that a change was being worked on Hugh. He became irritable and restless, and more aggressively sure of himself than ever. The warmth and good nature were still there — they were as much part of him as his arrogance, but he now had to work a little harder at them. He reminded me of a man who is bothered by a speck in the eye, but can't find it, and must get along with it as best he can.

Raymond, of course, was the speck, and I got the impression at times that he rather enjoyed the role. It would have been easy enough for him to stay close to his own house and cultivate his garden, or paste up his album, or whatever retired performers do, but he evidently found that impossible. He had a way of drifting over to Hilltop at odd times, just as Hugh was led to find his way to the Dane house and spend long and troublesome sessions there.

Both of them must have known that they were so badly suited to each other that the easy and logical solution would have been to stay apart. But they had the affinity of negative and positive forces, and when they were in a room together the crackling of the antagonistic current between them was so strong you could almost see it in the air.

Any subject became a point of contention for them, and they would duel over it bitterly: Hugh armored and weaponed by his massive assurance, Raymond flicking away with a rapier, trying to find a chink in the armor. I think that what annoyed Raymond most was the discovery that there was no chink in the armor. As someone with an obvious passion for searching out all sides to all questions and for going deep into motives and causes, he was continually being outraged by Hugh's single-minded way of laying down the law.

He didn't hesitate to let Hugh know that. "You are positively medieval," he said. "And of all things men should have learned since that time, the biggest is that there are no easy answers, no solutions one can give with a snap of the fingers. I can only hope for you that someday you may be faced with the perfect dilemma, the unanswerable question. You would find that a revelation. You would learn more in that minute than you dreamed possible."

And Hugh did not make matters any better when he coldly answered, "And *I* say, that for any man with a brain and the courage to use it there is no such thing as a perfect dilemma."

It may be that this was the sort of episode that led to the trouble that followed, or it may be that Raymond acted out of the most innocent and aesthetic motives possible. But, whatever the motives, the results were inevitable and dangerous.

They grew from the project Raymond outlined for us in great detail one afternoon. Now that he was living in the Dane house he had discovered that it was too big, too overwhelming. "Like a museum," he explained. "I find myself wandering through it like a lost soul through endless galleries."

The grounds also needed landscaping. The ancient trees were handsome, but, as Raymond put it, there were just too many of them. "Literally," he said, "I cannot see the river for the trees, and I am one devoted to the sight of running water."

Altogether there would be drastic changes. Two wings of the house would come down, the trees would be cleared away to make a broad aisle to the water, the whole place would be enlivened. It would no longer be a museum, but the perfect home he had envisioned over the years.

At the start of this recitative Hugh was slouched comfortably in his chair. Then as Raymond drew the vivid picture of what was to be, Hugh sat up straighter and straighter until he was as rigid as a trooper in the saddle. His lips compressed. His face became blood-red. His hands clenched and unclenched in a slow deadly rhythm. Only a miracle was restraining him from an open outburst, and it was not the kind of miracle to last. I saw from Elizabeth's expression that she understood this, too, but was as helpless as I to do anything about it. And when Raymond, after painting the last glowing strokes of his description, said complacently, "Well, now, what do you think?" there was no holding Hugh.

He leaned forward with deliberation and said, "Do you really want to know what I think?"

"Now, Hugh," Elizabeth said in alarm. "Please, Hugh —"

He brushed that aside.

"Do you really want to know?" he demanded of Raymond.

Raymond frowned. "Of course."

"Then I'll tell you," Hugh said. He took a deep breath. "I think that nobody but a damned iconoclast could even conceive the atrocity you're proposing. I think you're one of those people who take pleasure in smashing apart anything that's stamped with tradition or stability. You'd kick the props from under the whole world if you could!"

"I beg your pardon," Raymond said. He was very pale and angry. "But I think you are confusing change with destruction. Surely, you must comprehend that I do not intend to destroy anything, but only wish to make some necessary changes."

"Necessary?" Hugh gibed. "Rooting up a fine stand of trees that's been there for centuries? Ripping apart a house that's as solid as a rock? *I* call it wanton destruction."

"I'm afraid I do not understand. To refresh a scene, to reshape it —"

"I have no intention of arguing," Hugh cut in. "I'm telling you straight out that you don't have the right to tamper with that property!"

They were on their feet now, facing each other truculently, and the only thing that kept me from being really frightened was the conviction that Hugh would not become violent, and that Raymond was far too level-headed to lose his temper. Then the threatening moment was magically past. Raymond's lips suddenly quirked in amusement, and he studied Hugh with courteous interest.

"I see," he said. "I was quite stupid not to have understood at once. This property, which, I remarked, was a little too much like a museum, is to remain that way, and I am to be its custodian. A caretaker of the past, one might say, a curator of its relics."

He shook his head smilingly. "But I am afraid I am not quite suited to that role. I lift my hat to the past, it is true, but I prefer to court the present. For that reason I will go ahead with my plans, and hope they do not make an obstacle to our friendship."

I remember thinking, when I left next day for the city and a long, hot week at my desk, that Raymond had carried off the affair very nicely, and that, thank God, it had gone no further than it did. So I was completely unprepared for Elizabeth's call at the end of the week.

It was awful, she said. It was the business of Hugh and Raymond and the Dane house, but worse than ever. She was counting on my coming down to Hilltop the next day; there couldn't be any question about that. She had planned a way of clearing up the whole thing, but I simply had to be there to back her up. After all, I was one of the few people Hugh would listen to, and she was depending on me.

"Depending on me for what?" I said. I didn't like the sound of it. "And as for Hugh listening to me, Elizabeth, isn't that stretching it a good deal? I can't see him wanting my advice on his personal affairs."

"If you're going to be touchy about it —"

"I'm *not* touchy about it," I retorted. "I just don't like getting mixed up in this thing. Hugh's quite capable of taking care of himself."

"Maybe too capable."

"And what does that mean?"

"Oh, I can't explain now," she wailed. "I'll tell you everything tomorrow. And, darling, if you have any brotherly feelings you'll be here on the morning train. Believe me, it's serious."

I arrived on the morning train in a bad state. My imagination is one of the overactive kind that can build a cosmic disaster out of very little material, and by the time I arrived at the house I was prepared for almost anything.

But, on the surface, at least, all was serene. Hugh greeted me warmly, Elizabeth was her cheerful self, and we had an amiable lunch and a long talk which never came near the subject of Raymond or the Dane house.

I said nothing about Elizabeth's phone call, but thought of it with a steadily growing sense of outrage until I was alone with her.

"Now," I said, "I'd like an explanation of all this mystery. The Lord knows what I expected to find out here, but it certainly wasn't anything I've seen so far. And I'd like some accounting for the bad time you've given me since that call."

"All right," she said grimly, "and that's what you'll get. Come along."

She led the way on a long walk through the gardens and past the stables and outbuildings. Near the private road which lay beyond the last grove of trees she suddenly said, "When the car drove you up to the house didn't you notice anything strange about this road?"

"No, I didn't."

"I suppose not. The driveway to the house turns off too far away from here. But now you'll have a chance to see for yourself."

I did see for myself. A chair was set squarely in the middle of the road and on the chair sat a stout man placidly reading a magazine. I recognized the man at once: he was one of Hugh's stable hands, and he had the patient look of someone who has been sitting for a long time and expects to sit a good deal longer. It took me only a second to realize what he was there for, but Elizabeth wasn't leaving anything to my deductive powers. When we walked over to him, the man stood up and grinned at us.

"William," Elizabeth said, "would you mind telling my brother what instructions Mr. Lozier gave you?"

"Sure," the man said cheerfully. "Mr. Lozier told us there was always supposed to be one of us sitting right here, and any truck we saw that might be carrying construction stuff or suchlike for the Dane house was to be stopped and turned back. All we had to do was tell them it's private property and they were trespassing. If they laid a finger on us we just call in the police. That's the whole thing."

"Have you turned back any trucks?" Elizabeth asked for my benefit.

The man looked surprised. "Why, you know that, Mrs. Lozier," he said. "There was a couple of them the first day we were out here, and that was all. There wasn't any fuss either," he explained to me. "None of those drivers wants to monkey with trespass."

When we were away from the road again I clapped my hand to my forehead. "It's incredible!" I said. "Hugh must know he can't get away with this. That road is the only one to the Dane place, and it's been in public use so long that it isn't even a private thoroughfare anymore!"

Elizabeth nodded. "And that's exactly what Raymond told Hugh a few days back. He came over here in a fury, and they had quite an argument about it. And when Raymond said something about hauling Hugh off to court, Hugh answered that he'd be glad to spend the rest of his life in litigation over this business. But that wasn't the worst of it. The last thing Raymond said was that Hugh ought to know that force only invites force, and ever since then I've been expecting a war to break out here any minute. Don't you see? That man blocking the road is a constant provocation, and it scares me."

I could understand that. And the more I considered the matter, the more dangerous it looked.

"But I have a plan," Elizabeth said eagerly, "and that's why I wanted you here. I'm having a dinner party tonight, a very small, informal dinner party. It's to be a sort of peace conference. You'll be there, and Dr. Wynant — Hugh likes you both a great deal — and," she hesitated, "Raymond."

"No!" I said. "You mean he's actually coming?"

"I went over to see him yesterday and we had a long talk. I explained everything to him — about neighbors being able to sit down and come to an understanding, and about brotherly love and — oh, it must have sounded dreadfully inspirational and sticky, but it worked. He said he would be there."

I had a foreboding. "Does Hugh know about this?"

"About the dinner? Yes."

"I mean, about Raymond's being here."

"No, he doesn't." And then when she saw me looking hard at her, she burst out defiantly with, "Well, *something* had to be done, and I did it, that's all! Isn't it better than just sitting and waiting for God knows what?"

Until we were all seated around the dining room table that evening I might have conceded the point. Hugh had been visibly shocked by Raymond's arrival, but then, apart from a sidelong glance at Elizabeth which had volumes written in it, he managed to conceal his feelings well enough. He had made the introductions gracefully, kept up his end of the conversation and, all in all, did a creditable job of playing host.

Ironically, it was the presence of Dr. Wynant which made even this much of a triumph possible for Elizabeth, and which then turned it into disaster. The doctor was an eminent surgeon, stocky and gray-haired, with an abrupt, positive way about him. Despite his own position in the world he seemed pleased as a schoolboy to meet Raymond, and in no time at all they were as thick as thieves.

It was when Hugh discovered during dinner that nearly all attention was fixed on Raymond and very little on himself that the mantle of good host started to slip, and the fatal flaws in Elizabeth's plan showed through. There are people who enjoy entertaining lions and who take pleasure in reflected glory, but Hugh was not one of them. Besides, he regarded the doctor as one of his closest friends, and I have noticed that it is the most assured of men who can be the most jealous of their friendships. And when a prized friendship is being impinged on by the man one loathes more than anything else in the world — ! All in all, by simply imagining myself in Hugh's place and looking across the table at Raymond who was gaily and unconcernedly holding forth, I was prepared for the worst.

The opportunity for it came to Hugh when Raymond was deep in a discussion of the devices used in effecting escapes. They were innumerable, he said. Almost anything one could seize on would serve as such a device. A wire, a scrap of metal, even a bit of paper — at one time or another he had used them all.

"But of them all," he said with a sudden solemnity, "there is only one I would stake my life on. Strange, it is one you cannot see, cannot hold in your hand — in fact, for many people it does not even exist. Yet it is the one I have used most often and which has never failed me."

The doctor leaned forward, his eyes bright with interest. "And it is — ?"

"It is a knowledge of people, my friend. Or, as it may be put, a knowledge of human nature. To me it is as vital an instrument as the scalpel is to you."

"Oh?" said Hugh, and his voice was so sharp that all eyes were instantly turned on him. "You make sleight of hand sound like a department of psychology."

"Perhaps," Raymond said, and I saw he was watching Hugh now, gauging him. "You see there is no great mystery in the matter. My profession — my art, as I like to think of it — is no more than the art of misdirection, and I am but one of its many practitioners."

"I wouldn't say there were many escape artists around nowadays," the doctor remarked.

"True," Raymond said, "but you will observe I referred to the art of misdirection. The escape artist, the master of legerdemain, these are a handful who practice the most exotic form of that art. But what of those who engage in the work of politics, of advertising, of salesmanship?" He laid his finger along his nose in the familiar gesture, and winked. "I am afraid they have all made my art their business."

The doctor smiled. "Since you haven't dragged medicine into it I'm willing to go along with you," he said. "But what I want to know is, exactly how does this knowledge of human nature work in your profession?"

"In this way," Raymond said. "One must judge a person carefully. Then, if he finds in that person certain weaknesses he can state a false premise and it will be accepted without question. Once the false premise is swallowed, the rest is easy. The victim will then see only what the magician wants him to see, or will give his vote to that politician, or will buy merchandise because of that advertising." He shrugged. "And that is all there is to it."

"Is it?" Hugh said. "But what happens when you're with people who have some intelligence and won't swallow your false premise? How do you do your tricks then? Or do you keep them on the same level as selling beads to the savages?"

"Now that's uncalled for, Hugh," the doctor said. "The man's expressing his ideas. No reason to make an issue of them."

"Maybe there is," Hugh said, his eyes fixed on Raymond. "I have found he's full of interesting ideas. I was wondering how far he'd want to go in backing them up."

Raymond touched the napkin to his lips with a precise little flick, and then laid it carefully on the table before him. "In short," he said, addressing himself to Hugh, "you want a small demonstration of my art."

"It depends," Hugh said. "I don't want any trick cigarette cases or rabbits out of hats or any damn nonsense like that. I'd like to see something good."

"Something good," echoed Raymond reflectively. He looked around the room, studied it, and then turned to Hugh, pointing toward the huge oak door which was closed between the dining room and the living room, where we had gathered before dinner.

"That door is not locked, is it?"

"No," Hugh said, "it isn't. It hasn't been locked for years."

"But there is a key to it?"

Hugh pulled out his key chain, and with an effort detached a heavy, old-fashioned key. "Yes, it's the same one we use for the butler's pantry." He was becoming interested despite himself.

"Good. No, do not give it to me. Give it to the doctor. You have faith in the doctor's honor, I am sure?"

"Yes," said Hugh dryly, "I have."

"Very well. Now, doctor, will you please go to that door and lock it."

The doctor marched to the door, with his firm, decisive tread, thrust the key into the lock, and turned it. The click of the bolt snapping into place was loud in the silence of the room. The doctor returned to the table holding the key, but Raymond motioned it away. "It must not leave your hand or everything is lost," he warned.

"Now," Raymond said, "for the finale I approach the door, I flick my handkerchief at it" — the handkerchief barely brushed the keyhole — "and presto, the door is unlocked!"

The doctor went to it. He seized the doorknob, twisted it dubiously, and then watched with genuine astonishment as the door swung silently open.

"Well, I'll be damned," he said.

"Somehow," Elizabeth laughed, "a false premise went down easy as an oyster."

Only Hugh reflected a sense of personal outrage. "All right," he demanded, "how was it done? How did you work it?"

"I?" Raymond said reproachfully, and smiled at all of us with obvious enjoyment. "It was you who did it all. I used only my little knowledge of human nature to help you along the way."

I said, "I can guess part of it. That door was set in advance, and when the doctor thought he was locking it, he wasn't. He was really unlocking it. Isn't that the answer?"

Raymond nodded. "Very much the answer. The door *was* locked in advance. I made sure of that, because with a little forethought I suspected there would be such a challenge during the evening, and this was the simplest way of preparing for it. I merely made certain that I was the last one to enter this room, and when I did I used this." He held up his hand so that we could see the sliver of metal in it. "An ordinary skeleton key, of course, but sufficient for an old and primitive lock."

For a moment Raymond looked grave, then he continued brightly, "It was our host himself who stated the false premise when he said the door was unlocked. He was a man so sure of himself that he would not think to test anything so obvious. The doctor is also a man who is sure, and he fell into the same trap. It is, as you now see, a little dangerous always to be so sure."

"I'll go along with that," the doctor said ruefully, "even though it's heresy to admit it in my line of work." He playfully tossed the key he had been holding across the table to Hugh, who let it fall in front of him and made no gesture toward it. "Well, Hugh, like it or not, you must admit the man has proved his point."

"Do I?" said Hugh softly. He sat there smiling a little now, and it was easy to see he was turning some thought over and over in his head.

"Oh, come on, man," the doctor said with some impatience. "You were taken in as much as we were. You know that."

"Of course you were, darling," Elizabeth agreed.

I think that she suddenly saw her opportunity to turn the proceedings into the peace conference she had aimed at, but I could have told her she was choosing her time badly. There was a look in Hugh's eye I didn't like — a veiled look which wasn't natural to him. Ordinarily, when he was really angered, he would blow up a violent storm, and once the thunder and lightning had passed he would be honestly apologetic. But this present mood of his was different. There was a slumbrous quality in it which alarmed me.

He hooked one arm over the back of his chair and rested the other on the table, sitting halfway around to fix his eyes on Raymond. "I seem to be a minority of one," he remarked, "but I'm sorry to say I found your little trick disappointing. Not that it wasn't cleverly done — I'll grant that, all right — but because it wasn't any more than you'd expect from a competent locksmith."

"Now there's a large helping of sour grapes," the doctor jeered.

Hugh shook his head. "No, I'm simply saying that where there's a lock on a door and the key to it in your hand, it's no great trick to open it. Considering our friend's reputation, I thought we'd see more from him than that."

Raymond grimaced. "Since I had hoped to entertain," he said, "I must apologize for disappointing."

"Oh, as far as entertainment goes I have no complaints. But for a real test —"

"A real test?"

"Yes, something a little different. Let's say, a door without any locks or keys to tamper with. A closed door which can be opened with a fingertip, but which is nevertheless impossible to open. How does that sound to you?"

Raymond narrowed his eyes thoughtfully, as if he were considering the picture being presented to him. "It sounds most interesting," he said at last. "Tell me more about it."

"No," Hugh said, and from the sudden eagerness in his voice I felt that this was the exact moment he had been looking for. "I'll do better than that. I'll *show* it to you."

He stood up brusquely and the rest of us followed suit — except Elizabeth, who remained in her seat. When I asked her if she wanted to come along, she only shook her head and sat there watching us hopelessly as we left the room.

We were bound for the cellars, I realized, when Hugh picked up a flashlight along the way, but for a part of the cellars I had never seen before. On a few occasions I had gone downstairs to help select a bottle of wine from the racks there, but now we walked past the wine vault and into a long, dimly lit chamber behind it. Our feet scraped loudly on the rough stone, the walls around us showed the stains of seepage, and warm as the night was outside, I could feel the chill of dampness turning my chest to gooseflesh. When the doctor shuddered and said hollowly, "These are the very tombs of Atlantis," I knew I wasn't alone in my feeling, and felt some relief at that.

We stopped at the very end of the chamber, before what I can best describe as a stone closet built from floor to ceiling in the farthest angle of the walls. It was about four feet wide and not quite twice that in length, and its open doorway showed impenetrable blackness inside. Hugh reached into the blackness and pulled a heavy door into place.

"That's it," he said abruptly. "Plain solid wood, four inches thick, fitted flush into the frame so that it's almost airtight. It's a beautiful piece of carpentry, too, the kind they practiced two hundred years ago. And no locks or bolts. Just a ring set into each side to use as a handle." He pushed the door gently and it swung open noiselessly at his touch. "See that? The whole thing is balanced so perfectly on the hinges that it moves like a feather."

"But what is it for?" I asked. "It must have been made for a reason."

Hugh laughed shortly. "It was. Back in the bad old days, when a servant committed a crime — and I don't suppose it had to be more of a crime than talking back to one of the ancient Loziers — he was put in here to repent. And since the air inside was good for only a few hours at the most, he either repented damn soon or not at all."

"And that door?" the doctor said cautiously. "That impressive door of yours which opens at a touch to provide all the air needed — what prevented the servant from opening it?"

"Look," Hugh said. He flashed his light inside the cell and we crowded behind him to peer in. The circle of light reached across the cell to its far wall and picked out a short, heavy chain hanging a little above head level with a U-shaped collar dangling from its bottom link.

"I see," Raymond said, and they were the first words I had heard him speak since we had left the dining room. "It is truly ingenious. The man stands with his back against the wall, facing the door. The collar is placed around his neck, and then — since it is clearly not made for a lock — it is clamped there, hammered around his neck. The door is closed, and the man spends the next few hours like someone on an invisible rack, reaching out with his feet to catch the ring on the door which is just out of reach. If he is lucky he may not strangle himself in his iron collar, but may live until someone chooses to open the door for him."

"My God," the doctor said. "You make me feel as if I were living through it."

Raymond smiled faintly. "I have lived through many such experiences and, believe me, the reality is always a little worse than the worst imaginings. There is always the ultimate moment of terror, of panic, when the heart pounds so madly you think it will burst through your ribs, and the cold sweat soaks clear through you in the space of one breath. That is when you must take yourself in hand, must dispel all weakness, and remember all the lessons you have ever learned. If not — !" He whisked the edge of his hand across his lean throat. "Unfortunately for the usual victim of such a device," he concluded sadly, "since he lacks the essential courage and knowledge to help himself, he succumbs."

"But you wouldn't," Hugh said.

"I have no reason to think so."

"You mean," and the eagerness was creeping back into Hugh's voice, stronger than ever, "that under the very same conditions as someone chained in there two hundred years ago you could get this door open?"

The challenging note was too strong to be brushed aside lightly. Raymond stood silent for a long minute, face strained with concentration, before he answered.

"Yes," he said. "It would not be easy — the problem is made formidable by its very simplicity — but it could be solved."

"How long do you think it would take you?"

"An hour at the most."

Hugh had come a long way around to get to this point. He asked the question slowly, savoring it. "Would you want to bet on that?"

"Now, wait a minute," the doctor said. "I don't like any part of this."

"And I vote we adjourn for a drink," I put in. "Fun's fun, but we'll all wind up with pneumonia, playing games down here."

Neither Hugh nor Raymond appeared to hear a word of this. They stood staring at each other — Hugh waiting on pins and needles, Raymond deliberating — until Raymond said, "What is this bet you offer?"

"This. If you lose, you get out of the Dane house inside of a month, and sell it to me."

"And if I win?"

It was not easy for Hugh to say it, but he finally got it out. "Then I'll be the one to get out. And if you don't want to buy Hilltop I'll arrange to sell it to the first comer."

For anyone who knew Hugh it was so fantastic, so staggering a statement to hear from him, that none of us could find words at first. It was the doctor who recovered most quickly.

"You're not speaking for yourself, Hugh," he warned. "You're a married man. Elizabeth's feelings have to be considered."

"Is it a bet?" Hugh demanded of Raymond. "Do you want to go through with it?"

"I think before I answer that, there is something to be explained." Raymond paused, then went on slowly, "I am afraid I gave the impression — out of pride, perhaps — that when I retired from my work it was because of a boredom, a lack of interest in it. That was not altogether the truth. In reality, I was required to go to a doctor some years ago, the doctor listened to the heart, and suddenly my heart became the most important thing in the world. I tell you this because, while your challenge strikes me as being a most unusual and interesting way of settling differences between neighbors, I must reject it for reasons of health."

"You were healthy enough a minute ago," Hugh said in a hard voice.

"Perhaps not as much as you would want to think, my friend."

"In other words," Hugh said bitterly, "there's no accomplice handy, no keys in your pocket to help out, and no way of tricking anyone into seeing what isn't there! So you have to admit you're beaten."

Raymond stiffened. "I admit no such thing. All the tools I would need even for such a test as this I have with me. Believe me, they would be enough."

Hugh laughed aloud, and the sound of it broke into small echoes all down the corridors behind us. It was that sound, I am sure — the living contempt in it rebounding from wall to wall around us — which sent Raymond into the cell.

Hugh wielded the hammer, a short-handled but heavy sledge, which tightened the collar into a circlet around Raymond's neck, hitting with hard even strokes at the iron which was braced against the wall. When he had finished I saw the pale glow of the radium-painted numbers on a watch as Raymond studied it in his pitch darkness.

"It is now eleven," he said calmly. "The wager is that by midnight this door must be opened, and it does not matter what means are used. Those are the conditions, and you gentlemen are the witnesses to them."

Then the door was closed, and the walking began.

Back and forth we walked — the three of us — as if we were being compelled to trace every possible geometric figure on that stony floor, the doctor with his quick, impatient step, and I matching Hugh's long, nervous strides. A foolish, meaningless march, back and forth across our own shadows, each of us marking the time by counting off the passing seconds, and each ashamed to be the first to look at his watch.

For a while there was a counterpoint to this scraping of feet from inside the cell. It was a barely perceptible clinking of chain coming at brief, regular intervals. Then there would be a long silence, followed by a renewal of the sound. When it stopped again I could not restrain myself any longer. I held up my watch toward the dim yellowish light of the bulb overhead and saw with dismay that barely twenty minutes had passed.

After that there was no hesitancy in the others about looking at the time and, if anything, this made it harder to bear than just wondering. I caught the doctor winding his watch with small, brisk turns, and then a few minutes later he would try to wind it again, and suddenly drop his hand with disgust as he realized he had already done it. Hugh walked with his watch held up near his eyes, as if by concentration on it he could drag that crawling minute hand faster around the dial.

Thirty minutes had passed.

Forty.

Forty-five.

I remember that when I looked at my watch and saw there were less than fifteen minutes to go I wondered if I could last out even that short time. The chill had sunk so deep into me that I ached with it. I was shocked when I saw that Hugh's face was dripping with sweat, and that beads of it gathered and ran off while I watched.

It was while I was looking at him in fascination that it happened. The sound broke through the walls of the cell like a wail of agony heard from far away, and shivered over us as if it were spelling out the words.

"Doctor!" it cried. *"The air!"*

It was Raymond's voice, but the thickness of the wall blocking it off turned it into a high, thin sound. What was clearest in it was the note of pure terror, the plea growing out of that terror.

"Air!" it screamed, the word bubbling and dissolving into a long-drawn sound which made no sense at all.

And then it was silent.

We leaped for the door together, but Hugh was there first, his back against it, barring the way. In his upraised hand was the hammer which had clinched Raymond's collar.

"Keep back!" he cried. "Don't come any nearer, I warn you!"

The fury in him, brought home by the menace of the weapon, stopped us in our tracks.

"Hugh," the doctor pleaded, "I know what you're thinking, but you can forget that now. The bet's off, and I'm opening the door on my own responsibility. You have my word for that."

"Do I? But do you remember the terms of the bet, doctor? This door must be opened within an hour — *and it doesn't matter what means are used!* Do you understand now? He's fooling both of you. He's faking a death scene, so that you'll push open the door and win his bet for him. But it's my bet, not yours, and I have the last word on it!"

I saw from the way he talked, despite the shaking tension in his voice, that he was in perfect command of himself, and it made everything seem that much worse.

"How do you know he's faking?" I demanded. "The man said he had a heart condition. He said there was always a time in a spot like this when he had to fight panic and could feel the strain of it. What right do you have to gamble with his life?"

"Damn it, don't you see he never mentioned any heart condition until he smelled a bet in the wind? Don't you see he set his trap that way, just as he locked the door behind him when he came into dinner! But this time nobody will spring it for him — nobody!"

"Listen to me," the doctor said, and his voice cracked like a whip. "Do you concede that there's one slim possibility of that man being dead in there, or dying?"

"Yes, it is possible — anything is possible."

"I'm not trying to split hairs with you! I'm telling you that if that man is in trouble every second counts, and you're stealing that time from him. And if that's the case, by God, I'll sit in the witness chair at your trial and swear you murdered him! Is that what you want?"

Hugh's head sank forward on his chest, but his hand still tightly gripped the hammer. I could hear the breath drawing heavily in his throat, and when he raised his head, his face was gray and haggard. The torment of indecision was written in every pale sweating line of it.

And then I suddenly understood what Raymond had meant that day when he told Hugh about the revelation he might find in the face of a perfect dilemma. It was the revelation of what a man may learn about himself when he is forced to look into his own depths, and Hugh had found it at last.

In that shadowy cellar, while the relentless seconds thundered louder and louder in our ears, we waited to see what he would do.

1955

EVAN HUNTER

··

First Offense

HE SAT IN THE police van with the collar of his leather jacket turned up, the bright silver studs sharp against the otherwise unrelieved black. He was seventeen years old, and he wore his hair in a high black crown. He carried his head high and erect because he knew he had a good profile, and he carried his mouth like a switch knife, ready to spring open at the slightest provocation. His hands were thrust deep into his jacket pockets, and his gray eyes reflected the walls of the van. There was excitement in his eyes, too, an almost holiday excitement. He tried to tell himself he was in trouble, but he couldn't quite believe it. His gradual descent to disbelief had been a spiral that had spun dizzily through the range of his emotions. Terror when the cop's flash had picked him out; blind panic when he'd started to run; rebellion when the cop's firm hand had closed around the leather sleeve of his jacket; sullen resignation when the cop had thrown him into the RMP car; and then cocky stubbornness when they'd booked him at the local precinct.

The desk sergeant had looked him over curiously, with a strange aloofness in his Irish eyes.

"What's the matter, Fatty?" he'd asked.

The sergeant stared at him implacably. "Put him away for the night," the sergeant said.

He'd slept overnight in the precinct cell block, and he'd awakened with this strange excitement pulsing through his narrow body, and it was the excitement that had caused his disbelief. Trouble, hell! He'd been in trouble before, but it had never felt like this. This was different. This was a ball, man. This was like being initiated into a secret society some place. His contempt for the police had grown when they refused him the opportunity to shave after breakfast. He was only seventeen, but he had a fairly decent beard, and a man should be allowed to shave in the morning, what the hell! But even the beard had somehow lent to the unreality of the situation, made him appear — in his own eyes — somehow more desperate, more sinister-looking. He knew he was in trouble, but the trouble was glamorous, and he surrounded it with the gossamer lie of make-believe. He was living the storybook legend. He was big time now. They'd caught him and booked him, and he should have been scared but he was excited instead.

There was one other person in the van with him, a guy who'd spent the night in the cell block, too. The guy was an obvious bum, and his breath stank of cheap wine, but he was better than nobody to talk to.

"Hey!" he said.

The bum looked up. "You talking to me?"

"Yeah. Where we going?"

"The line-up, kid," the bum said. "This your first offense?"

"This's the first time I got caught," he answered cockily.

"All felonies go to the line-up," the bum told him. "And also some special types of misdemeanors. You commit a felony?"

"Yeah," he said, hoping he sounded nonchalant. What'd they have this bum in for anyway? Sleeping on a park bench?

"Well, that's why you're going to the line-up. They have guys from every detective squad in the city there, to look you over. So they'll remember you next time. They put you on a stage, and they read off the offense, and the Chief of Detectives starts firing questions at you. What's your name, kid?"

"What's it to you?"

"Don't get smart, punk, or I'll break your arm," the bum said.

He looked at the bum curiously. He was a pretty big guy, with a heavy growth of beard, and powerful shoulders. "My name's Stevie," he said.

"I'm Jim Skinner," the bum said. "When somebody's trying to give you advice, don't go hip on him."

"Yeah, well what's your advice?" he asked, not wanting to back down completely.

"When they get you up there, you don't have to answer anything. They'll throw questions, but you don't have to answer. Did you make a statement at the scene?"

"No," he answered.

"Good. Then don't make no statement now, either. They can't force you to. Just keep your mouth shut, and don't tell them nothing."

"I ain't afraid. They know all about it anyway," Stevie said.

The bum shrugged and gathered around him the sullen pearls of his scattered wisdom. Stevie sat in the van whistling, listening to the accompanying hum of the tires, hearing the secret hum of his blood beneath the other louder sound. He sat at the core of a self-imposed importance, basking in its warm glow, whistling contentedly, secretly happy. Beside him, Skinner leaned back against the wall of the van.

When they arrived at the Centre Street Headquarters, they put them in detention cells, awaiting the line-up which began at nine. At ten minutes to nine, they led him out of his cell, and the cop who'd arrested him originally took him into the special prisoner's elevator.

"How's it feel being an elevator boy?" he asked the cop.

The cop didn't answer him. They went upstairs to the big room where the line-up was being held. A detective in front of them was pinning on his shield so he could get past the cop at the desk. They crossed the large gymnasium-like compartment, walking past the men sitting on folded chairs before the stage.

"Get a nice turnout, don't you?" Stevie said.

"You ever tried vaudeville?" the cop answered.

The blinds in the room had not been drawn yet, and Stevie could see everything clearly. The stage itself with the permanently fixed microphone hanging from a narrow metal tube above; the height markers — four feet, five feet, six feet — behind the mike on the wide white wall. The men in the seats, he knew, were all detectives and his sense of importance suddenly flared again when he realized these bulls had come from all over the city just to look at him. Behind the bulls was a raised platform with a sort of lecturer's stand on it. A microphone rested on the stand, and a chair was behind it, and he assumed this was where the Chief bull would sit. There were uniformed cops stationed here and there around the room, and there was one man in civilian clothing who sat at a desk in front of the stage.

"Who's that?" Stevie asked the cop.

"Police stenographer," the cop answered. "He's going to take down your words for posterity."

They walked behind the stage, and Stevie watched as other felony offenders from all over the city joined them. There was one woman, but all the rest were men, and he studied their faces carefully, hoping to pick up some tricks from them, hoping to learn the subtlety of their expressions. They didn't look like much. He was better-looking than all of them, and the knowledge pleased him. He'd be the star of this little shindig. The cop who'd been with him moved over to talk to a big broad who was obviously a policewoman. Stevie looked around, spotted Skinner and walked over to him.

"What happens now?" he asked.

"They're gonna pull the shades in a few minutes," Skinner said. "Then they'll turn on the spots and start the line-up. The spots won't blind you, but you won't be able to see the faces of any of the bulls out there."

"Who wants to see them mugs?" Stevie asked.

Skinner shrugged. "When your case is called, your arresting officer goes back and stands near the Chief of Detectives, just in case the Chief needs more dope from him. The Chief'll read off your name and the borough where you was pinched. A number'll follow the borough. Like he'll say 'Manhattan one' or 'Manhattan two.' That's just the number of the case from that borough. You're first, you get number one, you follow?"

"Yeah," Stevie said.

"He'll tell the bulls what they got you on, and then he'll say either 'Statement' or 'No statement.' If you made a statement, chances are he won't ask many questions 'cause he won't want you to contradict anything damaging you already said. If there's no statement, he'll fire questions like a machine gun. But you won't have to answer nothing."

"Then what?"

"When he's through, you go downstairs to get mugged and printed. Then they take you over to the Criminal Courts Building for arraignment."

"They're gonna take my picture, huh?" Stevie asked.

"Yeah."

"You think there'll be reporters here?"

"Huh?"

"Reporters."

"Oh. Maybe. All the wire services hang out in a room across the street from where the vans pulled up. They got their own police radio in there, and they get the straight dope as soon as it's happening, in case they want to roll with it. There may be some reporters." Skinner paused. "Why? What'd you do?"

"It ain't so much what I done," Stevie said. "I was just wonderin' if we'd make the papers."

Skinner stared at him curiously. "You're all charged up, ain't you, Stevie?"

"Hell, no. Don't you think I know I'm in trouble?"

"Maybe you don't know just how much trouble," Skinner said.

"What the hell are you talking about?"

"This ain't as exciting as you think, kid. Take my word for it."

"Sure, you know all about it."

"I been around a little," Skinner said drily.

"Sure, on park benches all over the country. I know I'm in trouble, don't worry."

"You kill anybody?"

"No," Stevie said.

"Assault?"

Stevie didn't answer.

"Whatever you done," Skinner advised, "and no matter how long you been doin' it before they caught you, make like it's your first time. Tell them you done it, and then say you don't know why you done it, but you'll never do it again. It might help you, kid. You might get off with a suspended sentence."

"Yeah?"

"Sure. And then keep your nose clean afterwards, and you'll be okay."

"Keep my nose clean! Don't make me laugh, pal."

Skinner clutched Stevie's arm in a tight grip. "Kid, don't be a damn fool. If you can get out, get out now! I coulda got out a hundred times; and I'm still with it, and it's no picnic. Get out before you get started."

Stevie shook off Skinner's hand. "Come on, willya?" he said, annoyed.

"Knock it off there," the cop said. "We're ready to start."

"Take a look at your neighbors, kid," Skinner whispered. "Take a hard look. And then get out of it while you still can."

Stevie grimaced and turned away from Skinner. Skinner whirled him around to face him again, and there was a pleading desperation on the unshaven face, a mute reaching in the red-rimmed eyes before he spoke again. "Kid," he said, "listen to me. Take my advice. I've been . . ."

"Knock it off!" the cop warned again.

He was suddenly aware of the fact that the shades had been drawn and the room was dim. It was very quiet out there, and he hoped they would take him first. The excitement had risen to an almost fever pitch inside him, and he couldn't wait to get on that stage. What the hell was Skinner talking about anyway? "Take a look at your neighbors, kid." The poor jerk probably had a wet brain. What the hell did the police bother with old drunks for, anyway?

A uniformed cop led one of the men from behind the stage, and

Stevie moved a little to his left, so that he could see the stage, hoping none of the cops would shove him back where he wouldn't have a good view. His cop and the policewoman were still talking, paying no attention to him. He smiled, unaware that the smile developed as a smirk, and watched the first man mounting the steps to the stage.

The man's eyes were very small, and he kept blinking them, blinking them. He was bald at the back of his head, and he was wearing a Navy peacoat and dark tweed trousers, and his eyes were red-rimmed and sleepy-looking. He reached to the five-foot-six-inches marker on the wall behind him, and he stared out at the bulls, blinking.

"Assisi," the Chief of Detectives said, "Augustus, Manhattan one. Thirty-three years old. Picked up in a bar on 43rd and Broadway, carrying a .45 Colt automatic. No statement. How about it, Gus?"

"How about what?" Assisi asked.

"Were you carrying a gun?"

"Yes, I was carrying a gun." Assisi seemed to realize his shoulders were slumped. He pulled them back suddenly, standing erect.

"Where, Gus?"

"In my pocket."

"What were you doing with the gun, Gus?"

"I was just carrying it."

"Why?"

"Listen, I'm not going to answer any questions," Assisi said. "You're gonna put me through a third-degree, I ain't answering nothing. I want a lawyer."

"You'll get plenty opportunity to have a lawyer," the Chief of Detectives said. "And nobody's giving you a third-degree. We just want to know what you were doing with a gun. You know that's against the law, don't you?"

"I've got a permit for the gun," Assisi said.

"We checked with Pistol Permits, and they say no. This is a Navy gun, isn't it?"

"Yeah."

"What?"

"I said yeah, it's a Navy gun."

"What were you doing with it? Why were you carrying it around?"

"I like guns."

"Why?"

"Why what? Why do I like guns? Because . . ."

"Why were you carrying it around?"

"I don't know."

"Well, you must have a reason for carrying a loaded .45. The gun *was* loaded, wasn't it?"

"Yeah, it was loaded."

"You have any other guns?"

"No."

"We found a .38 in your room. How about that one?"

"It's no good."

"What?"

"The .38."

"What do you mean, no good?"

"The firin' mechanism is busted."

"You want a gun that works, is that it?"

"I didn't say that."

"You said the .38's no good because it won't fire, didn't you?"

"Well, what good's a gun that won't fire?"

"Why do you need a gun that fires?"

"I was just carrying it. I didn't shoot anybody, did I?"

"No, you didn't. Were you planning on shooting somebody?"

"Sure," Assisi said. "That's just what I was planning."

"Who?"

"I don't know," Assisi said sarcastically. "Anybody. The first guy I saw, all right? Everybody, all right? I was planning on wholesale murder."

"Not murder, maybe, but a little larceny, huh?"

"Murder," Assisi insisted, in his stride now. "I was just going to shoot up the whole town. Okay? You happy now?"

"Where'd you get the gun?"

"In the Navy."

"Where?"

"From my ship."

"It's a stolen gun?"

"No, I found it."

"You stole government property, is that it?"

"I found it."

"When'd you get out of the Navy?"

"Three months ago."

"You worked since?"

"No."

"Where were you discharged?"

"Pensacola."

"Is that where you stole the gun?"

"I didn't steal it."

"Why'd you leave the Navy?"

Assisi hesitated for a long time.

"Why'd you leave the Navy?" the Chief of Detectives asked again.

"They kicked me out!" Assisi snapped.

"Why?"

"I was undesirable!" he shouted.

"Why?"

Assisi did not answer.

"Why?"

There was silence in the darkened room. Stevie watched Assisi's face, the twitching mouth, the blinking eyelids.

"Next case," the Chief of Detectives said.

Stevie watched as Assisi walked across the stage and down the steps on the other side, where the uniformed cop met him. He'd handled himself well, Assisi had. They'd rattled him a little at the end there, but on the whole he'd done a good job. So the guy was lugging a gun around, so what? He was right, wasn't he? He didn't shoot nobody, so what was all the fuss about? Cops! They had nothing else to do, they went around hauling in guys who were carrying guns. Poor bastard was a veteran, too, that was really rubbing it in. But he did a good job up there, even though he was nervous, you could see he was very nervous.

A man and a woman walked past him and onto the stage. The man was very tall, topping the six-foot marker. The woman was shorter, a bleached blonde turning to fat.

"They picked them up together," Skinner whispered. "So they show them together. They figure a pair'll always work as a pair, usually."

"How'd you like that Assisi?" Stevie whispered back. "He really had them bulls on the run, didn't he?"

Skinner didn't answer. The Chief of Detectives cleared his throat.

"MacGregor, Peter, aged forty-five, and Anderson, Marcia, aged forty-two, Bronx one. Got them in a parked car on the Grand Concourse. Back seat of the car was loaded with goods including luggage, a typewriter, a portable sewing machine, and a fur coast. No statements. What about all that stuff, Pete?"

"It's mine."

"The fur coat, too."

"No, that's Marcia's."

"You're not married, are you?"

"No."

"Living together?"

"Well, you know," Pete said.

"What about the stuff?" the Chief of Detectives said again.

"I told you," Pete said. "It's ours."

"What was it doing in the car?"

"Oh. Well, we were . . . uh . . ." The man paused for a long time. "We were going on a trip."

"Where to?"

"Where? Oh. To . . . uh . . ." Again he paused, frowning, and Stevie smiled, thinking what a clown this guy was. This guy was better than a sideshow at Coney. This guy couldn't tell a lie without having to think about it for an hour. And the dumpy broad with him was a hot sketch, too. This act alone was worth the price of admission.

"Uh . . ." Pete said, still fumbling for words. "Uh . . . we were going to . . . uh . . . Denver."

"What for?"

"Oh, just a little pleasure trip, you know," he said, attempting a smile.

"How much money were you carrying when we picked you up?"

"Forty dollars."

"You were going to Denver on forty dollars?"

"Well, it was fifty dollars. Yeah, it was more like fifty dollars."

"Come on, Pete, what were you doing with all that stuff in the car?"

"I told you. We were taking a trip."

"With a sewing machine, huh? You do a lot of sewing, Pete?"

"Marcia does."

"That right, Marcia?"

The blonde spoke in a high reedy voice. "Yeah, I do a lot of sewing."

"That fur coat, Marcia. Is it yours?"

"Sure."

"It has the initials G.D. on the lining. Those aren't your initials, are they, Marcia?"

"No."

"Whose are they?"

"Search me. We bought that coat in a hock shop."

"Where?"

"Myrtle Avenue, Brooklyn. You know where that is?"

"Yes, I know where it is. What about that luggage? It had initials on it, too. And they weren't yours or Pete's. How about it?"

"We got that in a hock shop, too."

"And the typewriter?"

"That's Pete's."

"Are you a typist, Pete?"

"Well, I fool around a little, you know."

"We're going to check all this stuff against our Stolen Goods list, you know that, don't you?"

"We got all that stuff in hock shops," Pete said. "If it's stolen, we don't know nothing about it."

"Were you going to Denver with him, Marcia?"

"Oh, sure."

"When did you both decide to go? A few minutes ago?"

"We decided last week sometime."

"Were you going to Denver by way of the Grand Concourse?"

"Huh?" Pete said.

"Your car was parked on the Grand Concourse. What were you doing there with a carload of stolen goods?"

"It wasn't stolen," Pete said.

"We were on our way to Yonkers," the woman said.

"I thought you were going to Denver."

"Yeah, but we had to get the car fixed first. There was something wrong with the . . ." She paused, turning to Pete. "What was it, Pete? That thing that was wrong?"

Pete waited a long time before answering. "Uh . . . the . . . uh . . . the flywheel, yeah. There's a garage up in Yonkers fixes them good, we heard. Flywheels, I mean."

"If you were going to Yonkers, why were you parked on the Concourse?"

"Well, we were having an argument."

"What kind of an argument."

"Not an argument, really. Just a discussion, sort of."

"About what?"

"About what to eat."

"What!"

"About what to eat. I wanted to eat Chink's, but Marcia wanted a glass of milk and a piece of pie. So we were trying to decide whether we should go to the Chink's or the cafeteria. That's why we were parked on the Concourse."

"We found a wallet in your coat, Pete. It wasn't yours, was it?"

"No."

"Whose was it?"

"I don't know." He paused, then added hastily, "There wasn't no money in it."

"No, but there was identification. A Mr. Simon Granger. Where'd you get it, Pete?"

"I found it in the subway. There wasn't no money in it."

"Did you find all that other stuff in the subway, too?"

"No, sir, I bought that." He paused. "I was going to return the wallet, but I forgot to stick it in the mail."

"Too busy planning for the Denver trip, huh?"

"Yeah, I guess so."

"When's the last time you earned an honest dollar, Pete?"

Pete grinned. "Oh, about two, three years ago, I guess."

"Here's their records," the Chief of Detectives said. "Marcia, 1938, Sullivan Law; 1939, Concealing Birth of Issue; 1940, Possession of Narcotics — you still on the stuff, Marcia?"

"No."

"1942, Dis Cond; 1943, Narcotics again; 1947 — you had enough, Marcia?"

Marcia didn't answer.

"Pete," the Chief of Detectives said, "1940, Attempted Rape; 1941, Selective Service Act; 1942, dis cond; 1943, Attempted Burglary; 1945, Living on Proceeds of Prostitution; 1947, Assault and Battery, did two years at Ossining."

"I never done no time," Pete said.

"According to this, you did."

"I never done no time," he insisted.

"1950," the Chief of Detectives went on, "Carnal Abuse of a Child." He paused. "Want to tell us about that one, Pete?"

"I . . . uh . . ." Pete swallowed. "I got nothing to say."

"You're ashamed of *some* things, that it?"

Pete didn't answer.

"Get them out of here," the Chief of Detectives said.

"See how long he kept them up there?" Skinner whispered. "He knows what they are, wants every bull in the city to recognise them if they . . ."

"Come on," a detective said, taking Skinner's arm.

Stevie watched as Skinner climbed the steps to the stage. Those two had really been something, all right. And just looking at them, you'd never know they were such operators. You'd never know they . . .

"Skinner, James, Manhattan two. Aged fifty-one. Threw a garbage can through the plate glass window of a clothing store on Third Avenue. Arresting officer found him inside the store with a bundle of overcoats. No statement. That right, James?"

"I don't remember," Skinner said.

"Is it, or isn't it?"

"All I remember is waking up in jail this morning."

"You don't remember throwing that ash can through the window?"

"No, sir."

"You don't remember taking those overcoats?"

"No, sir."

"Well, you must have done it, don't you think? The off-duty detective found you inside the store with the coats in your arms."

"I got only his word for that, sir."

"Well, his word is pretty good. Especially since he found you inside the store with your arms full of merchandise."

"I don't remember, sir."

"You've been here before, haven't you?"

"I don't remember, sir."

"What do you do for a living, James?"

"I'm unemployed, sir."

"When's the last time you worked?"

"I don't remember, sir."

"You don't remember much of anything, do you?"

"I have a poor memory, sir."

"Maybe the record has a better memory than you, James," the Chief of Detectives said.

"Maybe so, sir. I couldn't say."

"I hardly know where to start, James. You haven't been exactly an ideal citizen."

"Haven't I, sir?"

"Here's as good a place as any. 1948, Assault and Robbery; 1949, Indecent Exposure; 1951, Burglary; 1952, Assault and Robbery again. You're quite a guy, aren't you, James?"

"If you say so, sir."

"I say so. Now how about that store?"

"I don't remember anything about a store, sir."

"Why'd you break into it?"

"I don't remember breaking into any store, sir."

"Hey, what's this?" the Chief of Detectives said suddenly.

"Sir?"

"Maybe we should've started back a little further, huh, James? Here, on your record. 1938, convicted of first degree murder, sentenced to execution."

The assembled bulls began murmuring among themselves. Stevie leaned forward eagerly, anxious to get a better look at this bum who'd offered him advice.

"What happened there, James?"

"What happened where, sir?"

"You were sentenced to death? How come you're still with us?"

"The case was appealed."

"And never retried?"

"No, sir."

"You're pretty lucky, aren't you?"

"I'm pretty unlucky, sir, if you ask me."

"Is that right? You cheat the chair, and you call that unlucky. Well, the law won't slip up this time."

"I don't know anything about law, sir."

"You don't, huh?"

"No, sir. I only know that if you want to get a police station into action, all you have to do is buy a cheap bottle of wine and drink it quiet, minding your own business."

"And that's what you did, huh, James?"

"That's what I did, sir."

"And you don't remember breaking into that store?"

"I don't remember anything."

"All right, next case."

Skinner turned his head slowly, and his eyes met Stevie's squarely. Again, there was the same mute pleading in his eyes, and then he turned his head away and shuffled off the stage and down the steps into the darkness.

The cop's hand closed around Stevie's biceps. For an instant, he didn't know what was happening, and then he realized his case was the next one. He shook off the cop's hand, squared his shoulders, lifted his head, and began climbing the steps.

He felt taller all at once. He felt like an actor coming on after his cue. There was an aura of unreality about the stage and the darkened room beyond it, the bulls sitting in that room.

The Chief of Detectives was reading off the information about him, but he didn't hear it. He kept looking at the lights, which weren't really so bright, they didn't blind him at all. Didn't they have brighter lights?

Couldn't they put more lights on him, so they could see him when he told his story?

He tried to make out the faces of the detectives, but he couldn't see them clearly, and he was aware of the Chief of Detectives' voice droning on and on, but he didn't hear what the man was saying, he heard only the hum of his voice. He glanced over his shoulder, trying to see how tall he was against the markers, and then he stood erect, his shoulders back, moving closer to the hanging microphone, wanting to be sure his voice was heard when he began speaking.

". . . no statement," the Chief of Detectives concluded. There was a long pause, and Stevie waited, holding his breath. "This your first offense, Steve?" the Chief of Detectives asked.

"Don't you know?" Stevie answered.

"I'm asking you."

"Yeah, it's my first offense."

"You want to tell us all about it?"

"There's nothing to tell. You know the whole story, anyway."

"Sure, but do you."

"What are you talking about?"

"Tell us the story, Steve."

"Whatya makin' a big federal case out of a lousy stick-up for? Ain't you got nothing better to do with your time?"

"We've got plenty of time, Steve."

"Well, I'm in a hurry."

"You're not going any place, kid. Tell us about it."

"What's there to tell? There was a candy store stuck up, that's all."

"Did you stick it up?"

"That's for me to know and you to find out."

"We know you did."

"Then don't ask me stupid questions."

"Why'd you do it?"

"I ran out of butts."

"Come on, kid."

"I done it 'cause I wanted to."

"Why?"

"Look, you caught me cold, so let's get this over with, huh? Whatya wastin' time with me for?"

"We want to hear what you've got to say. Why'd you pick this particular candy store?"

"I just picked it. I put slips in a hat and picked this one out."

"You didn't really, did you, Steve?"

"No, I didn't really. I picked it 'cause there's an old crumb who runs it, and I figured it was a pushover."

"What time did you enter the store, Steve?"

"The old guy told you all this already, didn't he? Look, I know I'm up here so you can get a good look at me. All right, take your good look, and let's get it over with."

"What time, Steve?"

"I don't have to tell you nothing."

"Except that we know it already."

"Then why do you want to hear it again? Ten o'clock, all right? How does that fit?"

"A little early, isn't it?"

"How's eleven? Try that one for size."

"Let's make it twelve, and we'll be closer."

"Make it whatever you want to," Stevie said, pleased with the way he was handling this. They knew all about it, anyway, so he might as well have himself a ball, show them they couldn't shove him around.

"You went into the store at twelve, is that right?"

"If you say so, Chief."

"Did you have a gun?"

"No."

"What then?"

"Nothing."

"Nothing at all?"

"Just me, I scared him with a dirty look, that's all."

"You had a switch knife, didn't you?"

"You found one on me, so why ask?"

"Did you use the knife?"

"No."

"You didn't tell the old man to open the cash register or you'd cut him up? Isn't that what you said?"

"I didn't make a tape recording of what I said."

"But you did threaten him with the knife. You did force him to open the cash register, holding the knife on him."

"I suppose so."

"How much money did you get?"

"You've got the dough. Why don't you count it?"

"We already have. Twelve dollars, is that right?"

"I didn't get a chance to count it. The Law showed."

"When did the Law show?"

"When I was leaving. Ask the cop who pinched me. He knows when."

"Something happened before you left, though."

"Nothing happened. I cleaned out the register and then blew. Period."

"Your knife had blood on it."

"Yeah? I was cleaning chickens last night."

"You stabbed the owner of that store, didn't you?"

"Me? I never stabbed nobody in my whole life."

"Why'd you stab him?"

"I didn't."

"Where'd you stab him?"

"I didn't stab him."

"Did he start yelling?"

"I don't know what you're talking about."

"You stabbed him, Steve. We know you did."

"You're full of crap."

"Don't get smart, Steve."

"Ain't you had your look yet? What the hell more do you want?"

"We want you to tell us why you stabbed the owner of that store."

"And I told you I didn't stab him."

"He was taken to the hospital last night with six knife wounds in his chest and abdomen. Now how about that, Steve?"

"Save your questioning for the detective squadroom. I ain't saying another word."

"You had your money. Why'd you stab him?"

Stevie did not answer.

"Were you afraid?"

"Afraid of what?" Stevie answered defiantly.

"I don't know. Afraid he'd tell who held him up? Afraid he'd start yelling? What were you afraid of, kid?"

"I wasn't afraid of nothing. I told the old crumb to keep his mouth shut. He shoulda listened to me."

"He didn't keep his mouth shut?"

"Ask him."

"I'm asking you!"

"No, he didn't keep his mouth shut. He started yelling. Right after I'd cleaned out the drawer. The damn jerk, for a lousy twelve bucks he starts yelling."

"What'd you do?"

"I told him to shut up."

"And he didn't."

"No, he didn't. So I hit him, and he still kept yelling. So — so I gave him the knife."

"Six times?"

"I don't know how many times. I just — gave it to him. He shouldn't have yelled. You ask him if I did any harm to him before that. Go ahead, ask him. He'll tell you. I didn't even touch the crumb before he started yelling. Go to the hospital and ask him if I touched him. Go ahead, ask him."

"We can't, Steve."

"Wh . . ."

"He died this morning."

"He . . ." For a moment, Stevie could not think clearly. Died? Is that what he'd said? The room was curiously still now. It had been silent attentive before, but this was something else, something different, and the stillness suddenly chilled him, and he looked down at his shoes.

"I . . . I didn't mean him to pass away," he mumbled.

The police stenographer looked up. "To what?"

"To pass away," a uniformed cop repeated, whispering.

"What?" the stenographer asked again.

"He didn't mean him to pass away!" the cop shouted.

The cop's voice echoed in the silent room. The stenographer bent his head and began scribbling in his pad.

"Next case," the Chief of Detectives said.

Stevie walked off the stage, his mind curiously blank, his feet strangely leaden. He followed the cop to the door, and then walked with him to the elevator. They were both silent as the doors closed.

"You picked an important one for your first one," the cop said.

"He shouldn't have died on me," Stevie answered.

"You shouldn't have stabbed him," the cop said.

He tried to remember what Skinner had said to him before the lineup, but the noise of the elevator was loud in his ears, and he couldn't think clearly. He could only remember the word "neighbors" as the elevator dropped to the basement to join them.

1957

MARGARET MILLAR

....

The Couple Next Door

IT WAS BY ACCIDENT that they lived next door to each other, but by design that they became neighbors — Mr. Sands, who had retired to California after a life of crime investigation, and the Rackhams, Charles and Alma. Rackham was a big, innocent-looking man in his fifties. Except for the accumulation of a great deal of money, nothing much had ever happened to Rackham, and he liked to listen to Sands talk, while Alma sat with her knitting, plump and contented, unimpressed by any tale that had no direct bearing on her own life. She was half Rackham's age, but the fullness of her figure, and her air of having withdrawn from life quietly and without fuss, gave her the stamp of middle-age.

Two or three times a week Sands crossed the concrete driveway, skirted the eugenia hedge, and pressed the Rackhams' door chime. He stayed for tea or for dinner, to play gin or Scrabble, or just to talk. "That reminds me of a case I had in Toronto," Sands would say, and Rackham would produce martinis and an expression of intense interest, and Alma would smile tolerantly, as if she didn't really believe a single thing Sands, or anyone else, ever said.

They made good neighbors: the Rackhams, Charles younger than his years, and Alma older than hers, and Sands who could be any age at all . . .

It was the last evening of August and through the open window of Sands' study came the scent of jasmine and the sound of a woman's harsh, wild weeping.

He thought at first that the Rackhams had a guest, a woman on a crying jag, perhaps, after a quarrel with her husband.

He went out into the front yard to listen, and Rackham came around the corner of the eugenia hedge, dressed in a bathrobe.

He said, sounding very surprised, "Alma's crying."

"I heard."

"I asked her to stop. I begged her. She won't tell me what's the matter."

"Women have cried before."

"Not Alma." Rackham stood on the damp grass, shivering, his forehead streaked with sweat. "What do you think we should do about it?"

The *I* had become *we*, because they were good neighbors, and along with the games and the dinners and the scent of jasmine, they shared the sound of a woman's grief.

"Perhaps you could talk to her," Rackham said.

"I'll try."

"I don't think there is anything physically the matter with her. We both had a check-up at the Tracy clinic last week. George Tracy is a good friend of mine — he'd have told me if there was anything wrong."

"I'm sure he would."

"If anything ever happened to Alma I'd kill myself."

Alma was crouched in a corner of the davenport in the living room, weeping rhythmically, methodically, as if she had accumulated a hoard of tears and must now spend them all in one night. Her fair skin was blotched with patches of red, like strawberry birthmarks, and her eyelids were blistered from the heat of her tears. She looked like a stranger to Sands, who had never seen her display any emotion stronger than ladylike distress over a broken teacup or an overdone roast.

Rackham went over and stroked her hair. "Alma, dear. What is the matter?"

"Nothing . . . nothing . . ."

"Mr. Sands is here, Alma. I thought he might be able — we might be able —"

But no one was able. With a long shuddering sob, Alma got up and lurched across the room, hiding her blotched face with her hands. They heard her stumble up the stairs.

Sands said, "I'd better be going."

"No, please don't. I — the fact is, I'm scared. I'm scared stiff. Alma's always been so quiet."

"I know that."

"You don't suppose — there's no chance she's losing her mind?"

If they had not been good neighbors Sands might have remarked that Alma had little mind to lose. As it was, he said cautiously, "She might have had bad news, family trouble of some kind."

"She has no family except me."

"If you're worried, perhaps you'd better call your doctor."

"I think I will."

George Tracy arrived within half an hour, a slight, fair-haired man in his early thirties, with a smooth unhurried manner that imparted confidence. He talked slowly, moved slowly, as if there was all the time in the world to minister to desperate women.

Rackham chafed with impatience while Tracy removed his coat, placed it carefully across the back of the chair, and discussed the weather with Sands.

"It's a beautiful evening," Tracy said, and Alma's moans sliding down the stairs distorted his words, altered their meaning: *a terrible evening, an awful evening.* "There's a touch of fall in the air. You live in these parts, Mr. Sands?"

"Next door."

"For heaven's sake, George," Rackham said, "will you hurry up? For all you know, Alma might be dying."

"That I doubt. People don't die as easily as you might imagine. She's in her room?"

"Yes. Now will you *please —*"

"Take it easy, old man."

Tracy picked up his medical bag and went towards the stairs, leisurely, benign.

"He's always like that." Rackham turned to Sands scowling. "Exasperating son-of-a-gun. You can bet that if he had a wife in Alma's condition he'd be taking those steps three at a time."

"Who knows? — perhaps he has."

"*I* know," Rackham said crisply. "He's not even married. Never had time for it, he told me. He doesn't look it but he's very ambitious."

"Most doctors are."

"Tracy is, anyway."

Rackham mixed a pitcher of martinis, and the two men sat in front of the unlit fire, waiting and listening. The noises from upstairs gradually ceased, and pretty soon the doctor came down again.

Rackham rushed across the room to meet him. "How is she?"

"Sleeping. I gave her a hypo."

"Did you talk to her? Did you ask her what was the matter?"

"She was in no condition to answer questions."

"Did you find anything wrong with her?"

"Not physically. She's a healthy young woman."

"Not *physically*. Does that mean — ?"

"Take it easy, old man."

Rackham was too concerned with Alma to notice Tracy's choice of words, but Sands noticed, and wondered if it had been conscious or unconscious: Alma's a healthy young woman . . . Take it easy, old man.

"If she's still depressed in the morning," Tracy said, "bring her down to the clinic with you when you come in for your X-rays. We have a good neurologist on our staff." He reached for his coat and hat. "By the way, I hope you followed the instructions."

Rackham looked at him stupidly. "What instructions?"

"Before we can take specific X-rays, certain medication is necessary."

"I don't know what you're talking about."

"I made it very clear to Alma," Tracy said, sounding annoyed. "You were to take one ounce of sodium phosphate after dinner tonight, and report to the X-ray department at 8 o'clock tomorrow morning without breakfast."

"She didn't tell me."

"Oh."

"It must have slipped her mind."

"Yes. Obviously. Well, it's too late now." He put on his coat, moving quickly for the first time, as if he were in a rush to get away. The change made Sands curious. He wondered why Tracy was suddenly so anxious to leave, and whether there was any connection between Alma's hysteria and her lapse of memory about Rackham's X-rays. He looked at Rackham and guessed, from his pallor and his worried eyes, that Rackham had already made a connection in his mind.

"I understood," Rackham said carefully, "that I was all through at the clinic. My heart, lungs, metabolism — everything fit as a fiddle."

"People," Tracy said, "are not fiddles. Their tone doesn't improve with age. I will make another appointment for you and send you specific instructions by mail. Is that all right with you?"

"I guess it will have to be."

"Well, good night, Mr. Sands, pleasant meeting you." And to Rackham, "Good night, old man."

When he had gone, Rackham leaned against the wall, breathing hard. Sweat crawled down the sides of his face like worms and hid in the collar of his bathrobe. "You'll have to forgive me, Sands. I feel — I'm not feeling very well."

"Is there anything I can do?"

"Yes," Rackham said. "Turn back the clock."

"Beyond my powers, I'm afraid."

"Yes . . . Yes, I'm afraid."

"Good night, Rackham." *Good night, old man.*

"Good night, Sands." *Good night old man to you, too.*

Sands shuffled across the concrete driveway, his head bent. It was a dark night, with no moon at all.

From his study Sands could see the lighted windows of Rackham's bedroom. Rackham's shadow moved back and forth behind the blinds as if seeking escape from the very light that gave it existence. Back and forth, in search of nirvana.

Sands read until far into the night. It was one of the solaces of growing old — if the hours were numbered, at least fewer of them need be wasted in sleep. When he went to bed, Rackham's bedroom light was still on.

They had become good neighbors by design; now, also by design, they became strangers. Whose design it was, Alma's or Rackham's, Sands didn't know.

There was no definite break, no unpleasantness. But the eugenia hedge seemed to have grown taller and thicker, and the concrete driveway a mile wide. He saw the Rackhams occasionally; they waved or smiled or said, "Lovely weather," over the backyard fence. But Rackham's smile was thin and painful, Alma waved with a leaden arm, and neither of them cared about the weather. They stayed indoors most of the time, and when they did come out they were always together, arm in arm, walking slowly and in step. It was impossible to tell whose step led, and whose followed.

At the end of the first week in September, Sands met Alma by accident in a drug store downtown. It was the first time since the night of the doctor's visit that he'd seen either of the Rackhams alone.

She was waiting at the prescription counter wearing a flowery print dress that emphasized the fullness of her figure and the bovine expression of her face. A drug-store length away, she looked like a rather dull, badly dressed young woman with a passion for starchy foods, and it was hard to understand what Rackham had seen in her. But then Rackham had never stood a drug-store length away from Alma; he saw her only in close-up, the surprising, intense blue of her eyes, and the color and texture of her skin, like whipped cream. Sands wondered whether it was her skin and eyes, or her quality of serenity which had appealed most to Rackham, who was quick and nervous and excitable.

She said, placidly, "Why, hello there."

"Hello, Alma."

"Lovely weather, isn't it?"

"Yes . . . How is Charles?"

"You must come over for dinner one of these nights."

"I'd like to."

"Next week, perhaps. I'll give you a call — I must run now, Charles is waiting for me. See you next week."

But she did not run, she walked; and Charles was not waiting for her, he was waiting for Sands. He had let himself into Sands' house and was pacing the floor of the study, smoking a cigarette. His color was bad, and he had lost weight, but he seemed to have acquired an inner calm. Sands could not tell whether it was the calm of a man who had come to an important decision, or that of a man who had reached the end of his rope and had stopped struggling.

They shook hands, firmly, pressing the past week back into shape.

Rackham said, "Nice to see you again, old man."

"I've been here all along."

"Yes. Yes, I know . . . I had things to do, a lot of thinking to do."

"Sit down. I'll make you a drink."

"No, thanks. Alma will be home shortly, I must be there."

Like a Siamese twin, Sands thought, *separated by a miracle, but returning voluntarily to the fusion — because the fusion was in a vital organ.*

"I understand," Sands said.

Rackham shook his head. "No one can understand, really, but you come very close sometimes, Sands. Very close." His cheeks flushed, like a boy's. "I'm not good at words or expressing my emotions, but I wanted to thank you before we leave, and tell you how much Alma and I have enjoyed your companionship."

"You're taking a trip?"

"Yes. Quite a long one."

"When are you leaving?"

"Today."

"You must let me see you off at the station."

"No, no," Rackham said quickly. "I couldn't think of it. I hate last-minute depot farewells. That's why I came over this afternoon to say goodbye."

"Tell me something of your plans."

"I would if I had any. Everything is rather indefinite. I'm not sure where we'll end up."

"I'd like to hear from you now and then."

"Oh, you'll hear from me, of course." Rackham turned away with an impatient twitch of his shoulders as if he was anxious to leave, anxious to start the trip right now before anything happened to prevent it.

"I'll miss you both," Sands said. "We've had a lot of laughs together."

Rackham scowled out of the window. "Please, no farewell speeches. They might shake my decision. My mind is already made up, I want no second thoughts."

"Very well."

"I must go now. Alma will be wondering —"

"I saw Alma earlier this afternoon," Sands said.

"Oh?"

"She invited me for dinner next week."

Outside the open window two hummingbirds fought and fussed, darting with crazy accuracy in and out of the bougainvillaea vine.

"Alma," Rackham said carefully, "can be very forgetful sometimes."

"Not that forgetful. She doesn't know about this trip you've planned, does she? . . . Does she, Rackham?"

"I wanted it to be a surprise. She's always had a desire to see the world. She's still young enough to believe that one place is different from any other place. . . . You and I know better."

"Do we?"

"Goodbye, Sands."

At the front door they shook hands again and Rackham again promised to write, and Sands promised to answer his letters. Then Rackham crossed the lawn and the concrete driveway, head bent, shoulders hunched. He didn't look back as he turned the corner of the eugenia hedge.

Sands went over to his desk, looked up a number in the telephone directory, and dialed.

A girl's voice answered, "Tracy clinic, X-ray department."

"This is Charles Rackham," Sands said.

"Yes, Mr. Rackham."

"I'm leaving town unexpectedly. If you'll tell me the amount of my bill I'll send you a check before I go."

"The bill hasn't gone through, but the standard price for a lower gastrointestinal is twenty-five dollars."

"Let's see, I had that done on the —"

"The fifth. Yesterday."

"But my original appointment was for the first, wasn't it?"

The girl gave a does-it-really-matter sigh. "Just a moment, sir, and I'll check." Half a minute later she was back on the line.

"We have no record of an appointment for you on the first, sir."

"You're sure of that?"

"Even without the record book, I'd be sure. The first was a Monday. We do only gall bladders on Monday."

"Oh. Thank you."

Sands went out and got into his car. Before he pulled away from the curb he looked over at Rackham's house and saw Rackham pacing up and down the veranda, waiting for Alma.

The Tracy clinic was less impressive than Sands had expected, a converted two-story stucco house with a red tile roof. Some of the tiles were broken and the whole building needed paint, but the furnishings inside were smart and expensive.

At the reception desk a nurse wearing a crew cut and a professional smile told Sands that Dr. Tracy was booked solid for the entire afternoon. The only chance of seeing him was to sit in the second-floor waiting room and catch him between patients.

Sands went upstairs and took a chair in a little alcove at the end of the hall, near Tracy's door. He sat with his face half hidden behind an open magazine. After a while the door of Tracy's office opened and over the top of his magazine Sands saw a woman silhouetted in the door frame — a plump, fair-haired young woman in a flowery print dress.

Tracy followed her into the hall and the two of them stood looking at each other in silence. Then Alma turned and walked away, passing Sands without seeing him because her eyes were blind with tears.

Sands stood up. "Dr. Tracy?"

Tracy turned sharply, surprise and annoyance pinching the corners of his mouth. "Well? Oh, it's Mr. Sands."

"May I see you a moment?"

"I have quite a full schedule this afternoon."

"This is an emergency."

"Very well. Come in."

They sat facing each other across Tracy's desk.

"You look pretty fit," Tracy said with a wry smile, "for an emergency case."

"The emergency is not mine. It may be yours."

"If it's mine, I'll handle it alone, without the help of a poli — I'll handle it myself."

Sands leaned forward. "Alma has told you, then, that I used to be a policeman."

"She mentioned it in passing."

"I saw Alma leave a few minutes ago. . . . She'd be quite a nice-looking woman if she learned to dress properly."

"Clothes are not important in a woman," Tracy said, with a slight flush. "Besides, I don't care to discuss my patients."

"Alma is a patient of yours?"

"Yes."

"Since the night Rackham called you when she was having hysterics?"

"Before then."

Sands got up, went to the window, and looked down at the street.

People were passing, children were playing on the sidewalk, the sun shone, the palm trees rustled with wind — everything outside seemed normal and human and real. By contrast, the shape of the idea that was forming in the back of his mind was so grotesque and ugly that he wanted to run out of the office, to join the normal people passing on the street below. But he knew he could not escape by running. The idea would follow him, pursue him until he turned around and faced it.

It moved inside his brain like a vast wheel, and in the middle of the wheel, impassive, immobile, was Alma.

Tracy's harsh voice interrupted the turning of the wheel. "Did you come here to inspect my view, Mr. Sands?"

"Let's say, instead, your viewpoint."

"I'm a busy man. You're wasting my time."

"No. I'm giving you time."

"To do what?"

"Think things over."

"If you don't leave my office immediately, I'll have you thrown out." Tracy glanced at the telephone but he didn't reach for it, and there was no conviction in his voice.

"Perhaps you shouldn't have let me in. Why did you?"

"I thought you might make a fuss if I didn't."

"Fusses aren't in my line." Sands turned from the window. "Liars are, though."

"What are you implying?"

"I've thought a great deal about that night you came to the Rackhams' house. In retrospect, the whole thing appeared too pat, too contrived: Alma had hysterics and you were called in to treat her. Natural enough, so far."

Tracy stirred but didn't speak.

"The interesting part came later. You mentioned casually to Rackham that he had an appointment for some X-rays to be taken the following day, September the first. It was assumed that Alma had forgotten to tell him. Only Alma *hadn't* forgotten. There was nothing to forget. I checked with your X-ray department half an hour ago. They have no record of any appointment for Rackham on September the first."

"Records get lost."

"This record wasn't lost. It never existed. You lied to Rackham. The lie itself wasn't important, it was the *kind* of lie. I could have understood a lie of vanity, or one to avoid punishment or to gain profit. But this seemed such a silly, senseless, little lie. It worried me. I began to wonder about Alma's part in the scene that night. Her crying was most unusual for a woman of Alma's inert nature. What if her crying was also a lie? And what was to be gained by it?"

"Nothing," Tracy said wearily. "Nothing was gained."

"But something was *intended* — and I think I know what it was. The scene was played to worry Rackham, to set him up for an even bigger scene. If that next scene has already been played, I am wasting my time here. Has it?"

"You have a vivid imagination."

"No. The plan was yours — I only figured it out."

"Very poor figuring, Mr. Sands." But Tracy's face was gray, as if mold had grown over his skin.

"I wish it were. I had become quite fond of the Rackhams."

He looked down at the street again, seeing nothing but the wheel turning inside his head. Alma was no longer in the middle of the wheel, passive and immobile; she was revolving with the others — Alma and Tracy and Rackham, turning as the wheel turned, clinging to its perimeter.

Alma, devoted wife, a little on the dull side. . . . What sudden passion of hate or love had made her capable of such consummate deceit? Sands imagined the scene the morning after Tracy's visit to the house. Rackham, worried and exhausted after a sleepless night: *"Are you feeling better now, Alma?"*

"Yes."

"What made you cry like that?"

"I was worried."

"About me?"

"Yes."

"Why didn't you tell me about my X-ray appointment?"

"I couldn't. I was frightened. I was afraid they would discover some-thing serious the matter with you."

"Did Tracy give you any reason to think that?"

"He mentioned something about a blockage. Oh, Charles I'm scared! If anything ever happened to you, I'd die. I couldn't live without you!"

For an emotional and sensitive man like Rackham, it was a perfect set-up: his devoted wife was frightened to the point of hysterics, his good friend and physician had given her reason to be frightened. Rack-ham was ready for the next step. . . .

"According to the records in your X-ray department," Sands said, "Rackham had a lower gastrointestinal X-ray yesterday morning. What was the result?"

"Medical ethics forbid me to —"

"You can't hide behind a wall of medical ethics that's already full of holes. What was the result?"

There was a long silence before Tracy spoke. "Nothing."

"You found nothing the matter with him?"

"That's right."

"Have you told Rackham that?"

"He came in earlier this afternoon, alone."

"Why alone?"

"I didn't want Alma to hear what I had to say."

"Very considerate of you."

"No, it was not considerate," Tracy said dully. "I had decided to back out of our — our agreement — and I didn't want her to know just yet."

"The agreement was to lie to Rackham, convince him that he had a fatal disease?"

"Yes."

"Did you?"

"No. I showed him the X-rays, I made it clear that there was nothing wrong with him. . . . I tried. I tried my best. It was no use."

"What do you mean?"

"He wouldn't believe me! He thought I was trying to keep the real truth from him." Tracy drew in his breath, sharply. "It's funny, isn't it? — after days of indecision and torment I made up my mind to do the right thing. But it was too late. Alma had played her role too well. She's the only one Rackham will believe."

The telephone on Tracy's desk began to ring but he made no move to answer it, and pretty soon the ringing stopped and the room was quiet again.

Sands said, "Have you asked Alma to tell him the truth?"

"Yes, just before you came in."

"She refused?"

Tracy didn't answer.

"She wants him to think he is fatally ill?"

"I — yes."

"In the hope that he'll kill himself, perhaps?"

Once again Tracy was silent. But no reply was necessary.

"I think Alma miscalculated," Sands said quietly. "Instead of planning suicide, Rackham is planning a trip. But before he leaves, he's going to hear the truth — from you and from Alma." Sands went towards the door. "Come on, Tracy. You have a house call to make."

"No. I can't." Tracy grasped the desk with both hands, like a child resisting the physical force of removal by a parent. "I won't go."

"You have to."

"No! Rackham will ruin me if he finds out. That's how this whole thing started. We were afraid, Alma and I, afraid of what Rackham would do if she asked him for a divorce. He's crazy in love with her, he's obsessed!"

"And so are you?"

"Not the way he is. Alma and I both want the same things — a little peace, a little quiet together. We are alike in many ways."

"That I can believe," Sands said grimly. "You wanted the same things, a little peace, a little quiet — and a little of Rackham's money?"

"The money was secondary."

"A very close second. How did you plan on getting it?"

Tracy shook his head from side to side, like an animal in pain. "You keep referring to plans, ideas, schemes. We didn't start out with plans or schemes. We just fell in love. We've been in love for nearly a year, not daring to do anything about it because I knew how Rackham would react if we told him. I have worked hard to build up his clinic; Rackham could destroy it, and me, within a month."

"That's a chance you'll have to take. Come on, Tracy."

Sands opened the door and the two men walked down the hall, slowly and in step, as if they were handcuffed together.

A nurse in uniform met them at the top of the stairs. "Dr. Tracy, are you ready for your next — ?"

"Cancel all my appointments, Miss Leroy."

"But that's imposs —"

"I have a very important house call to make."

"Will it take long?"

"I don't know."

The two men went down the stairs, past the reception desk, and out into the summer afternoon. Before he got into Sands' car, Tracy looked back at the clinic, as if he never expected to see it again.

Sands turned on the ignition and the car sprang forward like an eager pup.

After a time Tracy said, "Of all the people in the world who could have been at the Rackhams' that night, it had to be an ex-policeman."

"It's lucky for you that I was there."

"Lucky." Tracy let out a harsh little laugh. "What's lucky about financial ruin?"

"It's better than some other kinds of ruin. If your plan had gone through, you could never have felt like a decent man again."

"You think I will anyway?"

"Perhaps, as the years go by."

"The years." Tracy turned, with a sigh. "What are you going to tell Rackham?"

"Nothing. You will tell him yourself."

"I can't. You don't understand, I'm quite fond of Rackham, and so is Alma. We — it's hard to explain."

"Even harder to understand." Sands thought back to all the times he had seen the Rackhams together and envied their companionship, their mutual devotion. Never, by the slightest glance or gesture of impatience or slip of the tongue, had Alma indicated that she was passionately in love with another man. He recalled the games of Scrabble, the dinners, the endless conversations with Rackham, while Alma sat with her knitting, her face reposeful, content. Rackham would ask, "Don't you want to play too, Alma?" And she would reply, "No, thank you, dear, I'm quite happy with my thoughts."

Alma, happy with her thoughts of violent delights and violent ends.

Sands said, "Alma is equally in love with you?"

"Yes." He sounded absolutely convinced. "No matter what Rackham says or does, we intend to have each other."

"I see."

"I wish you did."

The blinds of the Rackham house were closed against the sun. Sands led the way up the veranda steps and pressed the door chime, while Tracy stood, stony-faced and erect, like a bill collector or a process server.

Sands could hear the chimes pealing inside the house and feel their vibrations beating under his feet.

He said, "They may have gone already."

"Gone where?"

"Rackham wouldn't tell me. He just said he was planning the trip as a surprise for Alma."

"He can't take her away! He can't force her to leave if she doesn't want to go!"

Sands pressed the door chime again, and called out, "Rackham? Alma?" But there was no response.

He wiped the sudden moisture off his forehead with his coat sleeve. "I'm going in."

"I'm coming with you."

"No."

The door was unlocked. He stepped into the empty hall and shouted up the staircase, "Alma? Rackham? Are you there?"

The echo of his own voice teased him from the dim corners.

Tracy had come into the hall. "They've left, then?"

"Perhaps not. They might have just gone out for a drive. It's a nice day for a drive."

"Is it?"

"Go around to the back and see if their car's in the garage."

When Tracy had gone, Sands closed the door behind him and shot the bolt. He stood for a moment listening to Tracy's nervous footsteps on the concrete driveway. Then he turned and walked slowly into the living room, knowing the car would be in the garage, no matter how nice a day it was for a drive.

The drapes were pulled tight across the windows and the room was cool and dark, but alive with images and noisy with the past:

"I wanted to thank you before we leave, Sands."

"You're taking a trip?"

"Yes, quite a long one."

"When are you leaving?"

"Today."

"You must let me see you off at the station. . . ."

But no station had been necessary for Rackham's trip. He lay in front of the fireplace in a pool of blood, and beside him was his companion on the journey, her left arm curving around his waist.

Rackham had kept his promise to write. The note was on the mantel, addressed not to Sands, but to Tracy.

> *Dear George:*
>
> *You did your best to foil me but I got the truth from Alma. She could never hide anything from me; we are too close to each other. This is the easiest way out. I am sorry that I must take Alma along, but she told me so often that she could not live without me. I cannot leave her behind to grieve.*
>
> *Think of us now and then, and try not to judge me too harshly.*
>
> *Charles Rackham*

Sands put the note back on the mantel. He stood quietly, his heart pierced by the final splinter of irony: before Rackham had used the gun on himself, he had lain down on the floor beside Alma and placed her dead arm lovingly around his waist.

From outside came the sound of Tracy's footsteps returning along the driveway, and then the pounding of his fists on the front door.

"Sands, I'm locked out. Open the door. Let me in! Sands, do you hear me? Open this door!"

Sands went and opened the door.

1957

HENRY SLESAR

The Day of the Execution

WHEN THE JURY FOREMAN stood up and read the verdict, Warren Selvey, the prosecuting attorney, listened to the pronouncement of guilt as if the words were a personal citation of merit. He heard in the foreman's somber tones, not a condemnation of the accused man who shriveled like a burnt match on the courtroom chair, but a tribute to Selvey's own brilliance. "*Guilty as charged . . .*" No, Warren Selvey thought triumphantly, guilty as I've proved . . .

For a moment, the judge's melancholy eye caught Selvey's and the old man on the bench showed shock at the light of rejoicing that he saw there. But Selvey couldn't conceal his flush of happiness, his satisfaction with his own efforts, with his first major conviction.

He gathered up his documents briskly, fighting to keep his mouth appropriately grim, though it ached to smile all over his thin, brown face. He put his briefcase beneath his arm, and when he turned, faced the buzzing spectators. "Excuse me," he said soberly, and pushed his way through to the exit doors, thinking now only of Doreen.

He tried to visualize her face, tried to see the red mouth that could be hard or meltingly soft, depending on which one of her many moods happened to be dominant. He tried to imagine how she would look when she heard his good news, how her warm body would feel against his, how her arms would encompass him.

But this imagined foretaste of Doreen's delights was interrupted. There were men's eyes seeking his now, and men's hands reaching towards him to grip his hand in congratulation. Garson, the district attorney, smiling heavily and nodding his lion's head in approval of his cub's behavior. Vance, the assistant D.A., grinning with half a mouth, not altogether pleased to see his junior in the spotlight. Reporters, too, and photographers, asking for statements, requesting poses.

Once, all this would have been enough for Warren Selvey. This moment, and these admiring men. But now there was Doreen, too, and thought of her made him eager to leave the arena of his victory for a quieter, more satisfying reward.

But he didn't make good his escape. Garson caught his arm and steered him into the gray car that waited at the curb.

"How's it feel?" Garson grinned, thumping Selvey's knee as they drove off.

"Feels pretty good," Selvey said mildly, trying for the appearance of modesty. "But, hell, I can't take all the glory, Gar. Your boys made the conviction."

"You don't really mean that." Garson's eyes twinkled. "I watched you through the trial, Warren. You were tasting blood. You were an avenging sword. You put him on the waiting list for the chair, not me."

"Don't say that!" Selvey said sharply. "He was guilty as sin, and you know it. Why, the evidence was clear-cut. The jury did the only thing it could."

"That's right. The way you handled things, they did the only thing they could. But let's face it, Warren. With another prosecutor, maybe they would have done something else. Credit where credit's due, Warren."

Selvey couldn't hold back the smile any longer. It illumined his long, sharp-chinned face, and he felt the relief of having it relax his features. He leaned back against the thick cushion of the car.

"Maybe so," he said. "But I thought he was guilty, and I tried to convince everybody else. It's not just A-B-C evidence that counts, Gar. That's law school sophistry, you know that. Sometimes you just *feel . . .*"

"Sure." The D.A. looked out of the window "How's the bride, Warren?"

"Oh, Doreen's fine."

"Glad to hear it. Lovely woman, Doreen."

She was lying on the couch when he entered the apartment. He hadn't imagined this detail of his triumphant homecoming.

He came over to her and shifted slightly on the couch to let his arms surround her.

He said: "Did you hear, Doreen? Did you hear what happened?"

"I heard it on the radio."

"Well? Don't you know what it means? I've got my conviction. My first conviction, and a big one. I'm no junior anymore, Doreen."

"What will they do to that man?"

He blinked at her, tried to determine what her mood might be. "I asked for the death penalty," he said. "He killed his wife in cold blood. Why should he get anything else?"

"I just asked, Warren." She put her cheek against his shoulder.

"Death is part of the job," he said. "You know that as well as I do, Doreen. You're not holding that against me?"

She pushed him away for a moment, appeared to be deciding whether to be angry or not. Then she drew him quickly to her, her breath hot and rapid in his ear.

They embarked on a week of celebration. Quiet, intimate celebration, in dim supper clubs and with close acquaintances. It wouldn't do for Selvey to appear publicly gay under the circumstances.

On the evening of the day the convicted Murray Rodman was sentenced to death, they stayed at home and drank hand-warmed brandy from big glasses. Doreen got drunk and playfully passionate, and Selvey thought he could never be happier. He had parlayed a mediocre law school record and an appointment as a third-class member of the state legal department into a position of importance and respect. He had married a beautiful, pampered woman and could make her whimper in his arms. He was proud of himself. He was grateful for the opportunity Murray Rodman had given him.

It was on the day of Rodman's scheduled execution that Selvey was approached by the stooped, gray-haired man with the grease-spotted hat.

He stepped out of the doorway of a drug store, his hands shoved into the pockets of his dirty tweed overcoat, his hat low over his eyes. He had white stubble on his face.

"Please," he said, "can I talk to you a minute?"

Selvey looked him over, and put a hand in his pocket for change.

"No," the man said quickly. "I don't want a handout. I just want to talk to you, Mr. Selvey."

"You know who I am?"

"Yeah, sure, Mr. Selvey. I read all about you."

Selvey's hard glance softened. "Well, I'm kind of rushed right now. Got an appointment."

"This is important, Mr. Selvey. Honest to God. Can't we go some-place? Have coffee maybe? Five minutes is all."

"Why don't you drop me a letter, or come down to the office? We're on Chambers Street —"

"It's about that man, Mr. Selvey. The one they're executing tonight."

The attorney examined the man's eyes. He saw how intent and pene-trating they were.

"All right," he said. "There's a coffee shop down the street. But only five minutes, mind you."

It was almost two-thirty; the lunchtime rush at the coffee shop was over. They found a booth in the rear, and sat silently while a waiter cleared the remnants of a hasty meal from the table.

Finally, the old man leaned forward and said: "My name's Arlington, Phil Arlington. I've been out of town, in Florida, else I wouldn't have let things go this far. I didn't see a paper, hear a radio, nothing like that."

"I don't get you, Mr. Arlington. Are you talking about the Rodman trial?"

"Yeah, the Rodman business. When I came back and heard what hap-pened, I didn't know what to do. You can see that, can't you? It hurt me, hurt me bad to read what was happening to that poor man. But I was afraid. You can understand that. I was afraid."

"Afraid of what?"

The man talked to his coffee. "I had an awful time with myself, trying to decide what to do. But then I figured — hell, this Rodman is a young man. What is he, thirty-eight? I'm sixty-four, Mr. Selvey. Which is better?"

"Better for what?" Selvey was getting annoyed; he shot a look at his watch. "Talk sense, Mr. Arlington. I'm a busy man."

"I thought I'd ask your advice." The gray-haired man licked his lips. "I was afraid to go to the police right off, I thought I should ask you. Should I tell them what I did, Mr. Selvey? Should I tell them I killed that woman? Tell me. Should I?"

The world suddenly shifted on its axis. Warren Selvey's hands grew cold around the coffee cup. He stared at the man across from him.

"What are you talking about?" he said. "Rodman killed his wife. We proved that."

"No, no, that's the point. I was hitchhiking east. I got a lift into Wilford. I was walking around town, trying to figure out where to get food, a job, anything. I knocked on this door. This nice lady answered. She didn't have no job, but she gave me a sandwich. It was a ham sandwich."

"What house? How do you know it was Mrs. Rodman's house?"

"I know it was. I seen her picture, in the newspapers. She was a nice lady. If she hadn't walked into that kitchen after, it would have been okay."

"What, what?" Selvey snapped.

"I shouldn't have done it. I mean, she was real nice to me, but I was so broke. I was looking around the jars in the cupboard. You know how women are; they're always hiding dough in the jars, house money they call it. She caught me at it and got mad. She didn't yell or anything, but I could see she meant trouble. That's when I did it, Mr. Selvey. I went off my head."

"I don't believe you," Selvey said. "Nobody saw any — anybody in the neighborhood. Rodman and his wife quarreled all the time —"

The gray-haired man shrugged. "I wouldn't know anything about that, Mr. Selvey. I don't know anything about those people. But that's what happened, and that's why I want your advice." He rubbed his forehead. "I mean, if I confess now, what would they do to me?"

"Burn you," Selvey said coldly. "But you instead of Rodman. Is that what you want?"

Arlington paled. "No. Prison, okay. But not that."

"Then just forget about it. Understand me, Mr. Arlington? I think you dreamed the whole thing, don't you? Just think of it that way. A bad dream. Now get back on the road and forget it."

"But that man. They're killing him tonight —"

"Because he's guilty." Selvey's palm hit the table. "I *proved* him guilty. Understand?"

The man's lip trembled.

"Yes sir," he said.

Selvey got up and tossed a five on the table.

"Pay the bill," he said curtly. "Keep the change."

That night, Doreen asked him the hour for the fourth time.

"Eleven," he said sullenly.

"Just another hour." She sank deep into the sofa cushions. "I wonder how he feels right now . . ."

"Cut it out!"

"My, we're jumpy tonight."

"My part's done with, Doreen. I told you that again and again. Now the State's doing its job."

She held the tip of her pink tongue between her teeth, thoughtfully. "But you put him where he is, Warren. You can't deny that."

"The jury put him there!"

"You don't have to shout at *me*, attorney."

"Oh, Doreen . . ." He leaned across to make some apologetic gesture, but the telephone rang.

He picked it up angrily.

"Mr. Selvey? This is Arlington."

All over Selvey's body, a pulse throbbed.

"What do you want?"

"Mr. Selvey, I been thinking it over. What you told me today. Only I don't think it would be right, just forgetting about it. I mean —"

"Arlington, listen to me. I'd like to see you at my apartment. I'd like to see you right now."

From the sofa, Doreen said: "Hey!"

"Did you hear me, Arlington? Before you do anything rash, I want to talk to you, tell you where you stand legally. I think you owe that to yourself."

There was a pause at the other end.

"Guess maybe you're right, Mr. Selvey. Only I'm way downtown, and by the time I get there —"

"You can make it. Take the IRT subway, it's quickest. Get off at 86th Street."

When he hung up, Doreen was standing.

"Doreen, wait. I'm sorry about this. This man is — an important witness in a case I'm handling. The only time I can see him is now."

"Have fun," she said airily, and went to the bedroom.

"Doreen —"

The door closed behind her. For a moment, there was silence. Then she clicked the lock.

Selvey cursed his wife's moods beneath his breath, and stalked over to the bar.

By the time Arlington sounded the door chimes, Selvey had downed six inches of bourbon.

Arlington's grease-spotted hat and dirty coat looked worse than ever in the plush apartment. He took them off and looked around timidly.

"We've only got three-quarters of a hour," he said. "I've just go to do something, Mr. Selvey."

"I know what you can do," the attorney smiled. "You can have a drink and talk things over."

"I don't think I should —" But the man's eyes were already fixed on the bottle in Selvey's hands. The lawyer's smile widened.

By eleven-thirty, Arlington's voice was thick and blurred, his eyes no longer so intense, his concern over Rodman no longer so compelling.

Selvey kept his visitor's glass filled.

The old man began to mutter. He muttered about his childhood, about some past respectability, and inveighed a string of strangers who had done him dirt. After a while, his shaggy head began to roll on his shoulders, and his heavy lidded eyes began to close.

He was jarred out of his doze by the mantel clock's chiming.

"Whazzat?"

"Only the clock," Selvey grinned.

"Clock? What time? What time?"

"Twelve, Mr. Arlington. Your worries are over. Mr. Rodman's already paid for his crime."

"No!" The old man stood up, circling wildly. "No, that's not true. I killed that woman. Not him! They can't kill him for something he —"

"Relax, Mr. Arlington. Nothing you can do about it now."

"Yes, yes! Must tell them — the police —"

"But why? Rodman's been executed. As soon as that clock struck, he was dead. What good can you do him now?"

"Have to!" the old man sobbed. "Don't you see? Couldn't live with myself, Mr. Selvey. Please —"

He tottered over to the telephone. Swiftly, the attorney put his hand on the receiver.

"Don't," he said.

Their hands fought for the instrument, and the younger man's won easily.

"You won't stop me, Mr. Selvey. I'll go down there myself. I'll tell them all about it. And I'll tell them about you —"

He staggered towards the door. Selvey's arm went out and spun him around.

"You crazy old tramp! You're just asking for trouble. Rodman's dead —"

"I don't care!"

Selvey's arm lashed out and his hand cracked across the sagging, white-whiskered face. The old man sobbed at the blow, but persisted in his attempt to reach the door. Selvey's anger increased and he struck out again, and after the blow, his hands dropped to the old man's scrawny neck. The next idea came naturally. There wasn't much life throbbing in the old throat. A little pressure, and Selvey could stop the frantic breathing, the hoarse, scratchy voice, the damning words . . .

Selvey squeezed, harder and harder.

And then his hands let him go. The old man swayed and slid against Selvey's body to the floor.

In the doorway, rigid, icy-eyed: Doreen.

"Doreen, listen —"

"You choked him," she said.

"Self-defense!" Selvey shouted. "He broke in here, tried to rob the apartment."

She slammed the door shut, twisted the inside lock. Selvey raced across the carpet and pounded desperately on the door. He rattled the knob and called her name, but there was no answer. Then he heard the sound of a spinning telephone dial.

It was bad enough, without having Vance in the crowd that jammed the apartment. Vance, the assistant D.A., who hated his guts anyway. Vance, who was smart enough to break down his burglar story without any trouble, who had learned that Selvey's visitor had been expected. Vance, who would delight in his predicament.

But Vance didn't seem delighted. He looked puzzled. He stared down at the dead body on the floor of Selvey's apartment and said: "I don't get it, Warren. I just don't get it. What did you want to kill a harmless old guy like that for?"

"Harmless? *Harmless?*"

"Sure. Harmless. That's old Arlington, I'd know him any place."

"You know him?" Selvey was stunned.

"Sure, I met up with him when I was working out of Bellaire County. Crazy old guy goes around confessing to murders. But why kill him, Warren? What for?"

1962

PATRICIA HIGHSMITH

....

The Terrapin

VICTOR heard the elevator door open, his mother's quick footsteps in the hall, and he flipped his book shut. He shoved it under the sofa pillow out of sight, and winced as he heard it slip between sofa and wall to the floor with a thud. Her key was in the lock.

"Hello, Vee-ector-r!" she cried, raising one arm in the air. Her other arm circled a brown paper bag, her hand held a cluster of little bags. "I have been to my publisher and to the market and also to the fish market," she told him. "Why aren't you out playing? It's a lovely, lovely day!"

"I was out," he said. "For a little while. I got cold."

"Ugh!" She was unloading the grocery bag in the tiny kitchen off the foyer. "You are seeck, you know that? In the month of October, you are cold? I see all kinds of children playing on the sidewalk. Even, I think, that boy you like. What's his name?"

"I don't know," Victor said. His mother wasn't really listening anyway. He pushed his hands into the pockets of his short, too small shorts, making them tighter than ever, and walked aimlessly around the living-room, looking down at his heavy, scuffed shoes. At least his mother had to buy him shoes that fit him, and he rather liked these shoes, because they had the thickest soles of any he had ever owned, and they had heavy toes that rose up a little, like mountain climbers' shoes. Victor paused at the window and looked straight out at a toast-coloured apartment building across Third Avenue. He and his mother lived on the eighteenth floor, next to the top floor where the penthouses were. The building across the street was even taller than this one. Victor had liked their Riverside Drive apartment better. He had liked the school he had gone to there better. Here they laughed at his clothes. In the other school, they had finally got tired of laughing at them.

"You don't want to go out?" asked his mother, coming into the living-room, wiping her hands briskly on a paper bag. She sniffed her palms. "Ugh! That stee-enk!"

"No, Mama," Victor said patiently.

"Today is Saturday."

"I know."

"Can you say the days of the week?"

"Of course."

"Say them."

"I don't want to say them. I know them." His eyes began to sting around the edges with tears. "I've known them for years. Years and years. Kids five years old can say the days of the week."

But his mother was not listening. She was bending over the drawing-table in the corner of the room. She had worked late on something last night. On his sofa bed in the opposite corner of the room, Victor had not been able to sleep until two in the morning, when his mother had gone to bed on the studio couch.

"Come here, Veector. Did you see this?"

Victor came on dragging feet, hands still in his pockets. No, he hadn't even glanced at her drawing-board this morning, hadn't wanted to.

"This is Pedro, the little donkey. I invented him last night. What do you think? And this is Miguel, the little Mexican boy who rides him. They ride and ride all over Mexico, and Miguel thinks they are lost, but Pedro knows the way home all the time, and . . ."

Victor did not listen. He deliberately shut his ears in a way he had learned to do from many years of practice, but boredom, frustration — he knew the word frustration, had read all about it — clamped his shoulders, weighted like a stone in his body, pressed hatred and tears up to his eyes, as if a volcano were churning in him. He had hoped his mother might take a hint from his saying that he was cold in his silly short shorts. He had hoped his mother might remember what he had told her, that the fellow he had wanted to get acquainted with down-stairs, a fellow who looked about his own age, eleven, had laughed at his short pants on Monday afternoon. *They make you wear your kid brother's pants or something?* Victor had drifted away, mortified. What if the fellow knew he didn't even own any longer pants, not even a pair of knickers, much less *long* pants, even blue jeans! His mother, for some cock-eyed reason, wanted him to look "French," and made him wear short shorts and stockings that came to just below his knees, and dopey shirts with round collars. His mother wanted him to stay about six years old, for ever, all his life. She liked to test out her drawings on him. *Veector is my sounding board,* she sometimes said to her friends. *I show my drawings to Veector and I* know *if children will like them.* Often Victor said he liked stories that he did not like, or drawings that he was indifferent to, because he felt sorry for his mother and because it put her in a better mood if he said he liked them. He was quite tired now of children's book illustrations, if he had ever in his life liked them — he really couldn't remember — and now he had two favourites: Howard Pyle's illustrations in some of Robert Louis Stevenson's books and Cruikshank's in Dickens'. It was too bad, Victor thought, that he was absolutely the last person of whom his mother should have asked an opinion, because he simply *hated* children's illustrations. And it was a wonder his mother didn't see this, because she hadn't sold any illustrations for books for years and years, not since *Wimple-Dimple,* a book whose jacket was all torn and turning yellow now from age, which sat in the centre of the bookshelf in a little cleared spot, propped up against the back of the bookcase so everyone could see it. Victor had been seven years old when that book was printed. His mother liked to tell people and remind him, too, that he had told her what he had wanted to see her draw, had watched her make every drawing, had shown his opinion by laughing or not, and that she had been absolutely guided by him. Victor doubted this very much, because first of all the story was somebody else's and had been written before his mother did the drawings, and her drawings had had to follow the story, naturally. Since then, his mother had done only a few illustrations now and then for magazines for children, how to make paper pumpkins and black paper cats for Hallowe'en and things like that, though she took her portfolio around to publishers all the time. Their income came from his father, who was a wealthy businessman in France, an exporter of perfumes. His mother said he was very wealthy and very handsome. But he married again, he never wrote, and Victor had no interest in him, didn't even care if he never saw a picture of him, and he never had. His father was French with some Polish, and his mother was Hungarian with some French. The word Hungarian made Victor think of gypsies, but when he had asked his mother once, she had said emphatically that she hadn't any gypsy blood, and she had been annoyed that Victor brought the question up.

And now she was sounding him out again, poking him in the ribs to make him wake up, as she repeated:

"Listen to me! Which do you like better, Veector? 'In all Mexico there was no bur-r-ro as wise as Miguel's Pedro,' or 'Miguel's Pedro was the wisest bur-r-ro in all Mexico'?"

"I think — I like it the first way better."

"Which way is that?" demanded his mother, thumping her palm down on the illustration.

Victor tried to remember the wording, but realized he was only staring at the pencil smudges, the thumbprints on the edge of his mother's illustration board. The coloured drawing in the centre did not interest him at all. He was not-thinking. This was a frequent, familiar sensation to him now, there was something exciting and important about not-thinking, Victor felt, and he thought one day he would find something about it — perhaps under another name — in the Public Library or in the psychology books around the house that he browsed in when his mother was out.

"Veec-tor! What are you doing?"

"Nothing, Mama!"

"That's exactly it! Nothing! Can you not even *think?*"

A warm shame spread through him. It was as if his mother read his thoughts about not-thinking. "I am thinking," he protested. "I'm thinking about *not*-thinking." His tone was defiant. What could she do about it, after all?

"About what?" Her black, curly head tilted, her mascaraed eyes narrowed at him.

"Not-thinking."

His mother put her jewelled hands on her hips. "Do you know, Veector, you are a little bit strange in the head?" She nodded. "You are seeck. Psychologically seeck. And retarded, do you know that? You have the behaviour of a leetle boy five years old," she said slowly and weightily. "It is just as well you spend your Saturdays indoors. Who knows if you would not walk in front of a car, eh? But that is why I love you, little Veector." She put her arm around his shoulders, pulled him against her and for an instant Victor's nose pressed into her large, soft bosom. She was wearing her flesh-coloured dress, the one you could see through a little where her breast stretched it out.

Victor jerked his head away in a confusion of emotions. He did not know if he wanted to laugh or cry.

His mother was laughing gaily, her head back. "Seeck you are! Look at you! My lee-tle boy still, lee-tle short pants — Ha! Ha!"

Now the tears showed in his eyes, he supposed, and his mother acted

as if she were enjoying it! Victor turned his head away so she would not
see his eyes. Then suddenly he faced her. "Do you think I like these
pants? *You* like them, not me, so why do you have to make fun of
them?"

"A lee-tle boy who's crying!" she went on, laughing.

Victor made a dash for the bathroom, then swerved away and dived
on to the sofa, his face toward the pillows. He shut his eyes tight and
opened his mouth, crying but not-crying in a way he had learned
through practice also. With his mouth open, his throat tight, not
breathing for nearly a minute, he could somehow get the satisfaction of
crying, screaming even, without anybody knowing it. He pushed his
nose, his open mouth, his teeth, against the tomato-red sofa pillow, and
though his mother's voice went on in a lazily mocking tone, and her
laughter went on, he imagined that it was getting fainter and more distant from him. He imagined, rigid in every muscle, that he was suffering the absolute worst that any human being could suffer. He imagined
that he was dying. But he did not think of death as an escape, only as a
concentrated and a painful incident. This was the climax of his not-crying. Then he breathed again, and his mother's voice intruded:

"Did you hear me? — *Did you hear me?* Mrs. Badzerkian is coming
for tea. I want you to wash your face and put on a clean shirt. I want you
to recite something for her. Now what are you going to recite?"

"In winter when I go to bed," said Victor. She was making him mem-
orize every poem in *A Child's Garden of Verses.* He had said the first one
that came into his head, and now there was an argument, because he
had recited that one the last time. "I said it, because I couldn't think of
any other one right off the bat!" Victor shouted.

"Don't yell at me!" his mother cried, storming across the room at
him.

She slapped his face before he knew what was happening.

He was up on one elbow on the sofa, on his back, his long, knobby-
kneed legs splayed out in front of him. All right, he thought, if that's the
way it is, that's the way it is. He looked at her with loathing. He would
not show the slap had hurt, that it still stung. No more tears for today, he swore, no more even not-crying. He would finish the day, go
through the tea, like a stone, like a soldier, not wincing. His mother
paced around the room, turning one of her rings round and round,
glancing at him from time to time, looking quickly away from him. But
his eyes were steady on her. He was not afraid. She could even slap him
again and he wouldn't care.

At last, she announced that she was going to wash her hair, and she went into the bathroom.

Victor got up from the sofa and wandered across the room. He wished he had a room of his own to go to. In the apartment on Riverside Drive, there had been three rooms, a living-room, and his and his mother's rooms. When she was in the living-room, he had been able to go into his bedroom and vice versa, but here . . . They were going to tear down the old building they had lived in on Riverside Drive. It was not a pleasant thing for Victor to think about. Suddenly remembering the book that had fallen, he pulled out the sofa and reached for it. It was Menninger's *The Human Mind,* full of fascinating case histories of people. Victor put it back on the bookshelf between an astrology book and *How to Draw.* His mother did not like him to read psychology books, but Victor loved them, especially ones with case histories in them. The people in the case histories did what they wanted to do. They were natural. Nobody bossed them. At the local branch library, he spent hours browsing through the psychology shelves. They were in the adults' section, but the librarian did not mind his sitting at the tables there, because he was quiet.

Victor went into the kitchen and got a glass of water. As he was standing there drinking it, he heard a scratching noise coming from one of the paper bags on the counter. A mouse, he thought, but when he moved a couple of the bags, he didn't see any mouse. The scratching was coming from inside one of the bags. Gingerly, he opened the bag with his fingers, and waited for something to jump out. Looking in, he saw a white paper carton. He pulled it out slowly. Its bottom was damp. It opened like a pastry box. Victor jumped in surprise. It was a turtle on its back, a live turtle. It was wriggling its legs in the air, trying to turn over. Victor moistened his lips, and frowning with concentration, took the turtle by its sides with both hands, turned him over and let him down gently into the box again. The turtle drew in its feet then, and its head stretched up a little and it looked straight at him. Victor smiled. Why hadn't his mother told him she'd brought him a present? A live turtle. Victor's eyes glazed with anticipation as he thought of taking the turtle down, maybe with a leash around its neck, to show the fellow who'd laughed at his short pants. He might change his mind about being friends with him, if he found he owned a turtle.

"Hey, Mama! Mama!" Victor yelled at the bathroom door. "You brought me a tur-rtle?"

"A what?" The water shut off.

"A turtle! In the kitchen!" Victor had been jumping up and down in the hall. He stopped.

His mother had hesitated, too. The water came on again, and she said in a shrill tone, "C'est une terrapène! Pour un ragoût!"

Victor understood, and a small chill went over him because his mother had spoken in French. His mother addressed him in French when she was giving an order that had to be obeyed, or when she anticipated resistance from him. So the terrapin was for a stew. Victor nodded to himself with a stunned resignation, and went back to the kitchen. For a stew. Well, the terrapin was not long for this world, as they say. What did the terrapin like to eat? Lettuce? Raw bacon? Boiled potato? Victor peered into the refrigerator.

He held a piece of lettuce near the terrapin's horny mouth. The terrapin did not open its mouth, but it looked at him. Victor held the lettuce near the two little dots of its nostrils, but if the terrapin smelled it, it showed no interest. Victor looked under the sink and pulled out a large wash pan. He put two inches of water into it. Then he gently dumped the terrapin into the pan. The terrapin paddled for a few seconds, as if it had to swim, then finding that its stomach sat on the bottom of the pan, it stopped, and drew its feet in. Victor got down on his knees and studied the terrapin's face. Its upper lip overhung the lower, giving it a rather stubborn and unfriendly expression, but its eyes — they were bright and shining. Victor smiled when he looked hard at them.

"Okay, monsieur terrapène," he said, "just tell me what you'd like to eat and we'll get it for you! — Maybe some tuna?"

They had had tuna fish salad yesterday for dinner, and there was a small bowl of it left over. Victor got a little chunk of it in his fingers and presented it to the terrapin. The terrapin was not interested. Victor looked around the kitchen, wondering, then seeing the sunlight on the floor of the living-room, he picked up the pan and carried it to the living-room and set it down so the sunlight would fall on the terrapin's back. All turtles liked sunlight, Victor thought. He lay down on the floor on his side, propped up on an elbow. The terrapin stared at him for a moment, then very slowly and with an air of forethought and caution, put out its legs and advanced, found the circular boundary of the pan, and moved to the right, half its body out of the shallow water. It wanted out, and Victor took it on one hand, by the sides, and said:

"You can come out and have a little walk."

He smiled as the terrapin started to disappear under the sofa. He caught it easily, because it moved so slowly. When he put it down on the carpet, it was quite still, as if it had withdrawn a little to think what it should do next, where it should go. It was a brownish green. Looking at it, Victor thought of river bottoms, of river water flowing. Or maybe oceans. Where did terrapins come from? He jumped up and went to the dictionary on the bookshelf. The dictionary had a picture of a terrapin, but it was a dull, black and white drawing, not so pretty as the live one. He learned nothing except that the name was of Algonquian origin, that the terrapin lived in fresh or brackish water, and that it was edible. Edible. Well, that was bad luck, Victor thought. But he was not going to eat any terrapène tonight. It would be all for his mother, that ragoût, and even if she slapped him and made him learn an extra two or three poems, he would not eat any terrapin tonight.

His mother came out of the bathroom. "What are you doing there? — Veector?"

Victor put the dictionary back on the shelf. His mother had seen the pan. "I'm looking at the terrapin," he said, then realized the terrapin had disappeared. He got down on hands and knees and looked under the sofa.

"Don't put him on the furniture. He makes spots," said his mother. She was standing in the foyer, rubbing her hair vigorously with a towel.

Victor found the terrapin between the wastebasket and the wall. He put him back in the pan.

"Have you changed your shirt?" asked his mother.

Victor changed his shirt, and then at his mother's order sat down on the sofa with *A Child's Garden of Verses* and tackled another poem, a brand new one for Mrs. Badzerkian. He learned two lines at a time, reading it aloud in a soft voice to himself, then repeating it, then putting two, four and six lines together, until he had the whole thing. He recited it to the terrapin. Then Victor asked his mother if he could play with the terrapin in the bathtub.

"No! And get your shirt all splashed?"

"I can put on my other shirt."

"No! It's nearly four o'clock now. Get that pan out of the living-room!"

Victor carried the pan back to the kitchen. His mother took the terrapin quite fearlessly out of the pan, put it back into the white paper box, closed its lid, and stuck the box in the refrigerator. Victor jumped a little as the refrigerator door slammed. It would be awfully cold in there for the terrapin. But then, he supposed, fresh or brackish water was cold now and then, too.

"Veector, cut the lemon," said his mother. She was preparing the big round tray with cups and saucers. The water was boiling in the kettle.

Mrs. Badzerkian was prompt as usual, and his mother poured the tea as soon as she had deposited her coat and pocketbook on the foyer chair and sat down. Mrs. Badzerkian smelled of cloves. She had a small, straight mouth and a thin moustache on her upper lip which fascinated Victor, as he had never seen one on a woman before, not one at such short range, anyway. He never had mentioned Mrs. Badzerkian's moustache to his mother, knowing it was considered ugly, but in a strange way, her moustache was the thing he liked best about her. The rest of her was dull, uninteresting, and vaguely unfriendly. She always pretended to listen carefully to his poetry recitals, but he felt that she fidgeted, thought of other things while he spoke, and was glad when it was over. Today, Victor recited very well and without any hesitation, standing in the middle of the living-room floor and facing the two women, who were then having their second cups of tea.

"Très bien," said his mother. "Now you may have a cookie."

Victor chose from the plate a small round cookie with a drop of orange goo in its centre. He kept his knees close together when he sat down. He always felt Mrs. Badzerkian looked at his knees and with distaste. He often wished she would make some remark to his mother about his being old enough for long pants, but she never had, at least not within his hearing. Victor learned from his mother's conversation with Mrs. Badzerkian that the Lorentzes were coming for dinner tomorrow evening. It was probably for them that the terrapin stew was going to be made. Victor was glad that he would have the terrapin one more day to play with. Tomorrow morning, he thought, he would ask his mother if he could take the terrapin down on the sidewalk for a while, either on a leash or in the paper box, if his mother insisted.

"— like a chi-ild!" his mother was saying, laughing, with a glance at him, and Mrs. Badzerkian smiled shrewdly at him with her small, tight mouth.

Victor had been excused, and was sitting across the room with a book on the studio couch. His mother was telling Mrs. Badzerkian how he had played with the terrapin. Victor frowned down at his book, pretending not to hear. His mother did not like him to open his mouth to her or her guests once he had been excused. But now she was calling him her "lee-tle ba-aby Veec-tor . . ."

He stood up with his finger in the place in his book. "I don't see why it's childish to look at a terrapin!" he said, flushing with sudden anger. "They are very interesting animals, they —"

His mother interrupted him with a laugh, but at once the laugh disappeared and she said sternly, "Veector, I thought I had excused you. Isn't that correct?"

He hesitated, seeing in a flash the scene that was going to take place when Mrs. Badzerkian had left. "Yes, Mama. I'm sorry," he said. Then he sat down and bent over his book again. Twenty minutes later, Mrs. Badzerkian left. His mother scolded him for being rude, but it was not a five- or ten-minute scolding of the kind he had expected. It lasted hardly two minutes. She had forgotten to buy heavy cream, and she wanted Victor to go downstairs and get some. Victor put on his grey woollen jacket and went out. He always felt embarrassed and conspicuous in the jacket, because it came just a little bit below his short pants, and he looked as if he had nothing on underneath the coat.

Victor looked around for Frank on the sidewalk, but he didn't see him. He crossed Third Avenue and went to a delicatessen in the big building that he could see from the living-room window. On his way back, he saw Frank walking along the sidewalk, bouncing a ball. Now Victor went right up to him.

"Hey," Victor said. "I've got a terrapin upstairs."

"A what?" Frank caught the ball and stopped.

"A terrapin. You know, like a turtle. I'll bring him down tomorrow morning and show you, if you're around. He's pretty big."

"Yeah? — why don't you bring him down now?"

"Because we're gonna eat now," said Victor. "See you." He went into his building. He felt he had achieved something. Frank had looked really interested. Victor wished he could bring the terrapin down now, but his mother never liked him to go out after dark, and it was practically dark now.

When Victor got upstairs, his mother was still in the kitchen. Eggs were boiling and she had put a big pot of water on a back burner. "You took him out again!" Victor said, seeing the terrapin's box on the counter.

"Yes, I prepare the stew tonight," said his mother. "That is why I needed the cream."

Victor looked at her. "You're going to — You have to kill it tonight?"

"Yes, my little one. Tonight." She jiggled the pot of eggs.

"Mama, can I take him downstairs to show Frank?" Victor asked quickly. "Just for five minutes, Mama. Frank's down there now."

"Who is Frank?"

"He's that fellow you asked me about today. The blond fellow we always see. Please, Mama."

His mother's black eyebrows frowned. "Take the terrapène downstairs? Certainly not. Don't be absurd, my baby! The terrapène is not a toy!"

Victor tried to think of some other lever of persuasion. He had not removed his coat. "You wanted me to get acquainted with Frank —"

"Yes. What has that got to do with a terrapin?"

The water on the back burner began to boil.

"You see, I promised him I'd —" Victor watched his mother lift the terrapin from the box, and as she dropped it into the boiling water, his mouth fell open. *Mama!*

"What is this? What is this noise?"

Victor, open-mouthed, stared at the terrapin whose legs were now racing against the steep sides of the pot. The terrapin's mouth opened, its eyes looked directly at Victor for an instant, its head arched back in torture, the open mouth sank beneath the seething water — and that was the end. Victor blinked. It was dead. He came closer, saw the four legs and the tail stretched out in the water, its head. He looked at his mother.

She was drying her hands on a towel. She glanced at him, then said, "Ugh!" She smelled her hands, then hung the towel back.

"Did you have to kill him like that?"

"How else? The same way you kill a lobster. Don't you know that? It doesn't hurt them."

He stared at her. When she started to touch him, he stepped back. He thought of the terrapin's wide open mouth, and his eyes suddenly flooded with tears. Maybe the terrapin had been screaming and it hadn't been heard over the bubbling of the water. The terrapin had looked at him, wanting him to pull him out, and he hadn't moved to help him. His mother had tricked him, done it so fast, he couldn't save him. He stepped back again. "No, don't touch me!"

His mother slapped his face, hard and quickly.

Victor set his jaw. Then he about-faced and went to the closet and threw his jacket on to a hanger and hung it up. He went into the living-room and fell down on the sofa. He was not crying now, but his mouth opened against the sofa pillow. Then he remembered the terrapin's mouth and he closed his lips. The terrapin had suffered, otherwise it would not have moved its legs fast to get out. Then he wept, soundlessly as the terrapin, his mouth open. He put both hands over his face, so as not to wet the sofa. After a long while, he got up. In the kitchen, his mother was humming, and every few minutes he heard her quick, firm steps as she went about her work. Victor had set his teeth again. He walked slowly to the kitchen doorway.

The terrapin was out on the wooden chopping board, and his mother, after a glance at him, still humming, took a knife and bore down on its blade, cutting off the terrapin's little nails. Victor half closed his eyes, but he watched steadily. The nails, with bits of skin attached to them, his mother scooped off the board into her palm and dumped into the garbage bag. Then she turned the terrapin on to its back and with the same sharp, pointed knife, she began to cut away the pale bottom shell. The terrapin's neck was bent sideways. Victor wanted to look away, but still he stared. Now the terrapin's insides were all exposed, red and white and greenish. Victor did not listen to what his mother was saying, about cooking terrapins in Europe, before he was born. Her voice was gentle and soothing, not at all like what she was doing.

"All right, don't look at me like that!" she suddenly threw at him, stomping her foot. "What's the matter with you? Are you crazy? Yes, I think so! You are seeck, you know that?"

Victor could not touch any of his supper, and his mother could not force him to, even though she shook him by the shoulders and threatened to slap him. They had creamed chipped beef on toast. Victor did not say a word. He felt very remote from his mother, even when she screamed right into his face. He felt very odd, the way he did sometimes when he was sick at his stomach, but he was not sick at his stomach. When they went to bed, he felt afraid of the dark. He saw the terrapin's face very large, its mouth open, its eyes wide and full of pain. Victor wished he could walk out the window and float, go anywhere he wanted to, disappear, yet be everywhere. He imagined his mother's hands on his shoulders, jerking him back, if he tried to step out the window. He hated his mother.

He got up and went quietly into the kitchen. The kitchen was absolutely dark, as there was no window, but he put his hand accurately on the knife rack and felt gently for the knife he wanted. He thought of the terrapin, in little pieces now, all mixed up in the sauce of cream and egg yolks and sherry in the pot in the refrigerator.

His mother's cry was not silent; it seemed to tear his ears off. His second blow was in her body, and then he stabbed her throat again. Only tiredness made him stop, and by then people were trying to bump the door in. Victor at last walked to the door, pulled the chain bolt back, and opened it for them.

He was taken to a large, old building full of nurses and doctors. Victor was very quiet and did everything he was asked to do, and answered the questions they put to him, but only those questions, and since they didn't ask him anything about a terrapin, he did not bring it up.

1965

SHIRLEY JACKSON

....

The Possibility of Evil

MISS ADELA STRANGEWORTH came daintily along Main Street on her way to the grocery. The sun was shining, the air was fresh and clear after the night's heavy rain, and everything in Miss Strangeworth's little town looked washed and bright. Miss Strangeworth took keep breaths and thought that there was nothing in the world like a fragrant summer day.

She knew everyone in town, of course; she was fond of telling strangers — tourists who sometimes passed through the town and stopped to admire Miss Strangeworth's roses — that she had never spent more than a day outside this town in all her long life. She was seventy-one, Miss Strangeworth told the tourists, with a pretty little dimple showing by her lip, and she sometimes found herself thinking that the town belonged to her. "My grandfather built the first house on Pleasant Street," she would say, opening her blue eyes wide with the wonder of it. "This house, right here. My family has lived here for better than a hundred years. My grandmother planted these roses, and my mother tended them, just as I do. I've watched my town grow; I can remember when Mr. Lewis, Senior, opened the grocery store, and the year the river flooded out the shanties on the low road, and the excitement when some young folks wanted to move the park over to the space in front of where the new post office is today. They wanted to put up a statue of Ethan Allen" — Miss Strangeworth would frown a little and sound stern — "but it should have been a statue of my grandfather. There wouldn't have been a town here at all if it hadn't been for my grandfather and the lumber mill."

Miss Strangeworth never gave away any of her roses, although the tourists often asked her. The roses belonged on Pleasant Street, and it bothered Miss Strangeworth to think of people wanting to carry them away, to take them into strange towns and down strange streets. When the new minister came, and the ladies were gathering flowers to decorate the church, Miss Strangeworth sent over a great basket of gladioli; when she picked the roses at all, she set them in bowls and vases around the inside of the house her grandfather had built.

Walking down Main Street on a summer morning, Miss Strangeworth had to stop every minute or so to say good morning to someone or to ask after someone's health. When she came into the grocery, half a dozen people turned away from the shelves and the counters to wave at her or call out good morning.

"And good morning to you, too, Mr. Lewis," Miss Strangeworth said at last. The Lewis family had been in the town almost as long as the Strangeworths; but the day young Lewis left high school and went to work in the grocery, Miss Strangeworth had stopped calling him Tommy and started calling him Mr. Lewis, and he had stopped calling her Addie and started calling her Miss Strangeworth. They had been in high school together, and had gone to picnics together, and to high-school dances and basketball games; but now Mr. Lewis was behind the counter in the grocery, and Miss Strangeworth was living alone in the Strangeworth house on Pleasant Street.

"Good morning," Mr. Lewis said, and added politely, "Lovely day."

"It is a very nice day," Miss Strangeworth said, as though she had only just decided that it would do after all. "I would like a chop, please, Mr. Lewis, a small, lean veal chop. Are those strawberries from Arthur Parker's garden? They're early this year."

"He brought them in this morning," Mr. Lewis said.

"I shall have a box," Miss Strangeworth said. Mr. Lewis looked worried, she thought, and for a minute she hesitated, but then she decided that he surely could not be worried over the strawberries. He looked very tired indeed. He was usually so chipper, Miss Strangeworth thought, and almost commented, but it was far too personal a subject to be introduced to Mr. Lewis, the grocer, so she only said, "And a can of cat food and, I think, a tomato."

Silently, Mr. Lewis assembled her order on the counter, and waited. Miss Strangeworth looked at him curiously and then said, "It's Tuesday, Mr. Lewis. You forgot to remind me."

"Did I? Sorry."

"Imagine your forgetting that I always buy my tea on Tuesday," Miss Strangeworth said gently. "A quarter pound of tea, please, Mr. Lewis."

"Is that all, Miss Strangeworth?"

"Yes, thank you, Mr. Lewis. Such a lovely day, isn't it?"

"Lovely," Mr. Lewis said.

Miss Strangeworth moved slightly to make room for Mrs. Harper at the counter. "Morning, Adela," Mrs. Harper said, and Miss Strangeworth said, "Good morning, Martha."

"Lovely day," Mrs. Harper said, and Miss Strangeworth said, "Yes, lovely," and Mr. Lewis, under Mrs. Harper's glance, nodded.

"Ran out of sugar for my cake frosting," Mrs. Harper explained. Her hand shook slightly as she opened her pocketbook. Miss Strangeworth wondered, glancing at her quickly, if she had been taking proper care of herself. Martha Harper was not as young as she used to be, Miss Strangeworth thought. She probably could use a good strong tonic.

"Martha," she said, "you don't look well."

"I'm perfectly all right," Mrs. Harper said shortly. She handed her money to Mr. Lewis, took her change and her sugar, and went out without speaking again. Looking after her, Miss Strangeworth shook her head slightly. Martha definitely did *not* look well.

Carrying her little bag of groceries, Miss Strangeworth came out of the store into the bright sunlight and stopped to smile down on the Crane baby. Don and Helen Crane were really the two most infatuated young parents she had ever known, she thought indulgently, looking at the delicately embroidered baby cap and the lace-edged carriage cover.

"That little girl is going to grow up expecting luxury all her life," she said to Helen Crane.

Helen laughed. "That's the way we want her to feel," she said. "Like a princess."

"A princess can see a lot of trouble sometimes," Miss Strangeworth said dryly. "How old is Her Highness now?"

"Six months next Tuesday," Helen Crane said, looking down with rapt wonder at her child. "I've been worrying though, about her. Don't you think she ought to move around more? Try to sit up, for instance?"

"For plain and fancy worrying," Miss Strangeworth said, amused, "give me a new mother every time."

"She just seems — slow," Helen Crane said.

"Nonsense. All babies are different. Some of them develop much more quickly than others."

"That's what my mother says." Helen Crane laughed, looking a little bit ashamed.

"I suppose you've got young Don all upset about the fact that his daughter is already six months old and hasn't yet begun to learn to dance?"

"I haven't mentioned it to him. I suppose she's just so precious that I worry about her all the time."

"Well, apologize to her right now," Miss Strangeworth said. "*She* is probably worrying about why you keep jumping around all the time." Smiling to herself and shaking her old head, she went on down the sunny street, stopping once to ask little Billy Moore why he wasn't out riding in his daddy's shiny new car, and talking for a few minutes outside the library with Miss Chandler, the librarian, about the new novels to be ordered and paid for by the annual library appropriation. Miss Chandler seemed absent-minded and very much as though she were thinking about something else. Miss Strangeworth noticed that Miss Chandler had not taken much trouble with her hair that morning, and sighed. Miss Strangeworth hated sloppiness.

Many people seemed disturbed recently, Miss Strangeworth thought. Only yesterday the Stewarts' fifteen-year-old Linda had run crying down her own front walk and all the way to school, not caring who saw her. People around town thought she might have had a fight with the Harris boy, but they showed up together at the soda shop after school as usual, both of them looking grim and bleak. Trouble at home, people concluded, and sighed over the problems of trying to raise kids right these days.

From halfway down the block Miss Strangeworth could catch the heavy scent of her roses, and she moved a little more quickly. The perfume of roses meant home, and home meant the Strangeworth House on Pleasant Street. Miss Strangeworth stopped at her own front gate, as she always did, and looked with deep pleasure at her house, with the red and pink and white roses massed along the narrow lawn, and the rambler going up along the porch; and the neat, the unbelievably trim lines of the house itself, with its slimness and its washed white look. Every window sparkled, every curtain hung stiff and straight, and even the stones of the front walk were swept and clear. People around town wondered how old Miss Strangeworth managed to keep the house looking the way it did, and there was a legend about a tourist once mistaking it for the local museum and going all through the place without finding out about his mistake. But the town was proud of Miss Strangeworth and her roses and her house. They had all grown together.

Miss Strangeworth went up her front steps, unlocked her front door with her key, and went into the kitchen to put away her groceries. She debated about having a cup of tea and then decided that it was too close to midday dinnertime; she would not have the appetite for her little chop if she had tea now. Instead she went into the light, lovely sitting room, which still glowed from the hands of her mother and her grandmother, who had covered the chairs with bright chintz and hung the curtains. All the furniture was spare and shining, and the round hooked rugs on the floor had been the work of Miss Strangeworth's grandmother and her mother. Miss Strangeworth had put a bowl of her red roses on the low table before the window, and the room was full of their scent.

Miss Strangeworth went to the narrow desk in the corner and unlocked it with her key. She never knew when she might feel like writing letters, so she kept her notepaper inside and the desk locked. Miss Strangeworth's usual stationery was heavy and cream-colored with STRANGEWORTH HOUSE engraved across the top, but, when she felt like writing her other letters, Miss Strangeworth used a pad of various-colored paper bought from the local newspaper shop. It was almost a town joke, that colored paper, layered in pink and green and blue and yellow; everyone in town bought it and used it for odd, informal notes and shopping lists. It was usual to remark, upon receiving a note written on a blue page, that so-and-so would be needing a new pad soon — here she was, down to the blue already. Everyone used the matching envelopes for tucking away recipes, or keeping odd little things in, or even to hold cookies in the school lunchboxes. Mr. Lewis sometimes gave them to the children for carrying home penny candy.

Although Miss Strangeworth's desk held a trimmed quill pen which had belonged to her grandfather, and a gold-frosted fountain pen which had belonged to her father, Miss Strangeworth always used a dull stub of pencil when she wrote her letters, and she printed them in a childish block print. After thinking for a minute, although she had been phrasing the letter in the back of her mind all the way home, she wrote on a pink sheet: DIDN'T YOU EVER SEE AN IDIOT CHILD BEFORE? SOME PEOPLE JUST SHOULDN'T HAVE CHILDREN SHOULD THEY?

She was pleased with the letter. She was fond of doing things exactly right. When she made a mistake, as she sometimes did, or when the letters were not spaced nicely on the page, she had to take the discarded page to the kitchen stove and burn it at once. Miss Strangeworth never delayed when things had to be done.

After thinking for a minute, she decided that she would like to write another letter, perhaps to go to Mrs. Harper, to follow up the ones she had already mailed. She selected a green sheet this time and wrote quickly: Have YOU FOUND OUT YET WHAT THEY WERE ALL LAUGH-ING ABOUT AFTER YOU LEFT THE BRIDGE CLUB ON THURSDAY? OR IS THE WIFE REALLY ALWAYS THE LAST ONE TO KNOW?

Miss Strangeworth never concerned herself with facts; her letters all dealt with the more negotiable stuff of suspicion. Mr. Lewis would never have imagined for a minute that his grandson might be lifting petty cash from the store register if he had not had one of Miss Strangeworth's letters. Miss Chandler, the librarian, and Linda Stewart's parents would have gone unsuspectingly ahead with their lives, never aware of possible evil lurking nearby, if Miss Strangeworth had not sent letters opening their eyes. Miss Strangeworth would have been genu-inely shocked if there *had* been anything between Linda Stewart and the Harris boy, but, as long as evil existed unchecked in the world, it was Miss Strangeworth's duty to keep her town alert to it. It was far more sensible for Miss Chandler to wonder what Mr. Shelley's first wife had really died of than to take a chance on not knowing. There were so many wicked people in the world and only one Strangeworth left in the town. Besides, Miss Strangeworth liked writing her letters.

She addressed an envelope to Don Crane after a moment's thought, wondering curiously if he would show the letter to his wife, and using a pink envelope to match the pink paper. Then she addressed a second envelope, green, to Mrs. Harper. Then an idea came to her and she se-lected a blue sheet and wrote: You NEVER KNOW ABOUT DOCTORS. RE-MEMBER THEY'RE ONLY HUMAN AND NEED MONEY LIKE THE REST OF US. SUPPOSE THE KNIFE SLIPPED ACCIDENTALLY. WOULD DR. BURNS GET HIS FEE AND A LITTLE EXTRA FROM THAT NEPHEW OF YOURS?

She addressed the blue envelope to old Mrs. Foster, who was having an operation next month. She had thought of writing one more letter, to the head of the school board, asking how a chemistry teacher like Billy Moore's father could afford a new convertible, but, all at once, she was tired of writing letters. The three she had done would do for one day. She could write more tomorrow; it was not as though they all had to be done at once.

She had been writing her letters — sometimes two or three every day for a week, sometimes no more than one in a month — for the past year. She never got any answers, of course, because she never signed her name. If she had been asked, she would have said that her name, Adela Strangeworth, a name honored in the town for so many years, did not belong on such trash. The town where she lived had to be kept clean and sweet, but people everywhere were lustful and evil and degraded, and needed to be watched; the world was so large, and there was only one Strangeworth left in it. Miss Strangeworth sighed, locked her desk, and put the letters into her big black leather pocketbook, to be mailed when she took her evening walk.

She broiled her little chop nicely, and had a sliced tomato and a good cup of tea ready when she sat down to her midday dinner at the table in her dining room, which could be opened to seat twenty-two, with a second table, if necessary, in the hall. Sitting in the warm sunlight that came through the tall windows of the dining room, seeing her roses massed outside, handling the heavy, old silverware and the fine, translucent china, Miss Strangeworth was pleased; she would not have cared to be doing anything else. People must live graciously, after all, she thought, and sipped her tea. Afterward, when her plate and cup and saucer were washed and dried and put back onto the shelves where they belonged, and her silverware was back in the mahogany silver chest, Miss Strangeworth went up the graceful staircase and into her bedroom, which was the front room overlooking the roses, and had been her mother's and her grandmother's. Their Crown Derby dresser set and furs had been kept here, their fans and silver-backed brushes and their own bowls of roses; Miss Strangeworth kept a bowl of white roses on the bed table.

She drew the shades, took the rose satin spread from the bed, slipped out of her dress and her shoes, and lay down tiredly. She knew that no doorbell or phone would ring; no one in town would dare to disturb Miss Strangeworth during her afternoon nap. She slept, deep in the rich smell of roses.

After her nap she worked in her garden for a little while, sparing herself because of the heat; then she came in to her supper. She ate asparagus from her own garden, with sweet-butter sauce and a soft-boiled egg, and, while she had her supper, she listened to a late-evening news broadcast and then to a program of classical music on her small radio. After her dishes were done and her kitchen set in order, she took up her hat — Miss Strangeworth's hats were proverbial in the town; people believed that she had inherited them from her mother and her grandmother — and, locking the front door of her house behind her, set off on her evening walk, pocketbook under her arm. She nodded to Linda Stewart's father, who was washing his car in the pleasantly cool evening. She thought that he looked troubled.

There was only one place in town where she could mail her letters, and that was the new post office, shiny with red brick and silver letters. Although Miss Strangeworth had never given the matter any particular thought, she had always made a point of mailing her letters very secretly; it would, of course, not have been wise to let anyone see her mail them. Consequently, she timed her walk so she could reach the post office just as darkness was starting to dim the outlines of the trees and the shapes of people's faces, although no one could ever mistake Miss Strangeworth, with her dainty walk and her rustling skirts.

There was always a group of young people around the post office, the very youngest roller-skating upon its driveway, which went all the way around the building and was the only smooth road in town; and the slightly older ones already knowing how to gather in small groups and chatter and laugh and make great, excited plans for going across the street to the soda shop in a minute or two. Miss Strangeworth had never had any self-consciousness before the children. She did not feel that any of them were staring at her unduly or longing to laugh at her; it would have been most reprehensible for their parents to permit their children to mock Miss Strangeworth of Pleasant Street. Most of the children stood back respectfully as Miss Strangeworth passed, silenced briefly in her presence, and some of the older children greeted her, saying soberly, "Hello, Miss Strangeworth."

Miss Strangeworth smiled at them and quickly went on. It had been a long time since she had known the name of every child in town. The mail slot was in the door of the post office. The children stood away as Miss Strangeworth approached it, seemingly surprised that anyone should want to use the post office after it had been officially closed up for the night and turned over to the children. Miss Strangeworth stood by the door, opening her black pocketbook to take out the letters, and heard a voice which she knew at once to be Linda Stewart's. Poor little Linda was crying again, and Miss Strangeworth listened carefully. This was, after all, her town, and these were her people; if one of them was in trouble she ought to know about it.

"I can't tell you, Dave," Linda was saying — so she *was* talking to the Harris boy, as Miss Strangeworth had supposed — "I just *can't*. It's just *nasty*."

"But why won't your father let me come around any more? What on earth did I do?"

"I can't tell you. I just wouldn't tell you for *any*thing. You've got to have a dirty, dirty mind for things like that."

"But something's happened. You've been crying and crying, and your father is all upset. Why can't *I* know about it, too? Aren't I like one of the family?"

"Not any more, Dave, not any more. You're not to come near our house again; my father said so. He said he'd horsewhip you. That's all I can tell you: You're not to come near our house any more."

"But I didn't *do* anything."

"Just the same, my father said . . ."

Miss Strangeworth sighed and turned away. There was so much evil in people. Even in a charming little town like this one, there was still so much evil in people.

She slipped her letters into the slot, and two of them fell inside. The third caught on the edge and fell outside, onto the ground at Miss Strangeworth's feet. She did not notice it because she was wondering whether a letter to the Harris boy's father might not be of some service in wiping out this potential badness. Wearily Miss Strangeworth turned to go home to her quiet bed in her lovely house, and never heard the Harris boy calling to her to say that she had dropped something.

"Old lady Strangeworth's getting deaf," he said, looking after her and holding in his hand the letter he had picked up.

"Well, who cares?" Linda said. "Who cares any more, anyway?"

"It's for Don Crane," the Harris boy said, "this letter. She dropped a letter addressed to Don Crane. Might as well take it on over. We pass his house anyway." He laughed. "Maybe it's got a check or something in it and he'd be just as glad to get it tonight instead of tomorrow."

"Catch old Lady Strangeworth sending anybody a check," Linda said. "Throw it in the post office. Why do anyone a favor?" She sniffled. "Doesn't seem to me anybody around here cares about us," she said. "Why should we care about them?"

"I'll take it over anyway," the Harris boy said. "Maybe it's good news for them. Maybe they need something happy tonight, too. Like us."

Sadly, holding hands, they wandered off down the dark street, the Harris boy carrying Miss Strangeworth's pink envelope in his hand.

Miss Strangeworth awakened the next morning with a feeling of intense happiness and, for a minute, wondered why, and then remembered that this morning three people would open her letters. Harsh, perhaps, at first, but wickedness was never easily banished, and a clean heart was a scoured heart. She washed her soft old face and brushed her teeth, still sound in spite of her seventy-one years, and dressed herself carefully in her sweet, soft clothes and buttoned shoes. Then, coming downstairs and reflecting that perhaps a little waffle would be agreeable for breakfast in the sunny dining room, she found the mail on the hall floor and bent to pick it up. A bill, the morning paper, a letter in a green envelope that looked oddly familiar. Miss Strangeworth stood perfectly still for a minute, looking down at the green envelope with the penciled printing, and thought: It looks like one of my letters. Was one of my letters sent back? No, because no one would know where to send it. How did this get here?

Miss Strangeworth was a Strangeworth of Pleasant Street. Her hand did not shake as she opened the envelope and unfolded the sheet of green paper inside. She began to cry silently for the wickedness of the world when she read the words: Look out at what used to be your roses.

1965

FLANNERY O'CONNOR

The Comforts of Home

THOMAS WITHDREW to the side of the window and with his head between the wall and the curtain he looked down on the driveway where the car had stopped. His mother and the little slut were getting out of it. His mother emerged slowly, stolid and awkward, and then the little slut's long slightly bowed legs slid out, the dress pulled above the knees. With a shriek of laughter she ran to meet the dog, who bounded, overjoyed, shaking with pleasure, to welcome her. Rage gathered throughout Thomas's large frame with a silent ominous intensity, like a mob assembling.

It was now up to him to pack a suitcase, go to the hotel, and stay there until the house should be cleared.

He did not know where a suitcase was, he disliked to pack, he needed his books, his typewriter was not portable, he was used to an electric blanket, he could not bear to eat in restaurants. His mother, with her daredevil charity, was about to wreck the peace of the house.

The back door slammed and the girl's laugh shot up from the kitchen, through the back hall, up the stairwell and into his room, making for him like a bolt of electricity. He jumped to the side and stood glaring about him. His words of the morning had been unequivocal: "If you bring that girl back into this house, I leave. You can choose — her or me."

She had made her choice. An intense pain gripped his throat. It was the first time in his thirty-five years . . . He felt a sudden burning moisture behind his eyes. Then he steadied himself, overcome by rage. On the contrary: she had not made any choice. She was counting on his attachment to his electric blanket. She would have to be shown.

The girl's laughter rang upward a second time and Thomas winced.

He saw again her look of the night before. She had invaded his room. He had waked to find his door open and her in it. There was enough light from the hall to make her visible as she turned toward him. The face was like a comedienne's in a musical comedy — a pointed chin, wide apple cheeks and feline empty eyes. He had sprung out of his bed and snatched a straight chair and then he had backed her out the door, holding the chair in front of him like an animal trainer driving out a dangerous cat. He had driven her silently down the hall, pausing when he reached it to beat on his mother's door. The girl, with a gasp, turned and fled into the guest room.

In a moment his mother had opened her door and peered out apprehensively. Her face, greasy with whatever she put on it at night, was framed in pink rubber curlers. She looked down the hall where the girl had disappeared. Thomas stood before her, the chair still lifted in front of him as if he were about to quell another beast. "She tried to get in my room," he hissed, pushing in. "I woke up and she was trying to get in my room." He closed the door behind him and his voice rose in outrage. "I won't put up with this! I won't put up with it another day!"

His mother, backed by him to her bed, sat down on the edge of it. She had a heavy body on which sat a thin, mysteriously gaunt and incongruous head.

"I'm telling you for the last time," Thomas said, "I won't put up with this another day." There was an observable tendency in all of her actions. This was, with the best intentions in the world, to make a mockery of virtue, to pursue it with such a mindless intensity that everyone involved was made a fool of and virtue itself became ridiculous. "Not another day," he repeated.

His mother shook her head emphatically, her eyes still on the door.

Thomas put the chair on the floor in front of her and sat down on it. He leaned forward as if he were about to explain something to a defective child.

"That's just another way she's unfortunate," his mother said. "So awful, so awful. She told me the name of it but I forget what it is but it's something she can't help. Something she was born with. Thomas," she said and put her hand to her jaw, "suppose it were you?"

Exasperation blocked his windpipe. "Can't I make you see," he croaked, "that if she can't help herself you can't help her?"

His mother's eyes, intimate but untouchable, were the blue of great distances after sunset. "Nimpermaniac," she murmured.

"Nymphomaniac," he said fiercely. "She doesn't need to supply you with any fancy names. She's a moral moron. That's all you need to know. Born without the moral faculty — like somebody else would be born without a kidney or a leg. Do you understand?"

"I keep thinking it might be you," she said, her hand still on her jaw. "If it were you, how do you think I'd feel if nobody took you in? What if you were a nimpermaniac and not a brilliant smart person and you did what you couldn't help and . . ."

Thomas felt a deep unbearable loathing for himself as if he were turning slowly into the girl.

"What did she have on?" she asked abruptly, her eyes narrowing.

"Nothing!" he roared. "Now will you get her out of here!"

"How can I turn her out in the cold?" she said. "This morning she was threatening to kill herself again."

"Send her back to jail," Thomas said.

"I would not send *you* back to jail, Thomas," she said.

He got up and snatched the chair and fled the room while he was still able to control himself.

Thomas loved his mother. He loved her because it was his nature to do so, but there were times when he could not endure her love for him. There were times when it became nothing but pure idiot mystery and he sensed about him forces, invisible currents entirely out of his control. She proceeded always from the tritest of considerations — it was the *nice thing to do* — into the most foolhardy engagements with the devil, whom, of course, she never recognized.

The devil for Thomas was only a manner of speaking, but it was a manner appropriate to the situations his mother got into. Had she been in any degree intellectual, he could have proved to her from early Christian history that no excess of virtue is justified, that a moderation of good produces likewise a moderation in evil, that if Antony of Egypt had stayed at home and attended to his sister, no devils would have plagued him.

Thomas was not cynical and so far from being opposed to virtue, he saw it as the principle of order and the only thing that makes life bearable. His own life was made bearable by the fruits of his mother's saner virtues — by the well-regulated house she kept and the excellent meals she served. But when virtue got out of hand with her, as now, a sense of devils grew upon him, and these were not mental quirks in himself or the old lady, they were denizens with personalities, present though not visible, who might any moment be expected to shriek or rattle a pot.

The girl had landed in the county jail a month ago on a bad check charge and his mother had seen her picture in the paper. At the break-fast table she had gazed at it for a long time and then had passed it over the coffee pot to him. "Imagine," she said, "only nineteen years old and in that filthy jail. And she doesn't look like a bad girl."

Thomas glanced at the picture. It showed the face of a shrewd raga-muffin. He observed that the average age for criminality was steadily lowering.

"She looks like a wholesome girl," his mother said.

"Wholesome people don't pass bad checks," Thomas said.

"You don't know what you'd do in a pinch."

"I wouldn't pass a bad check," Thomas said.

"I think," his mother said, "I'll take her a little box of candy."

If then and there he had put his foot down, nothing else would have happened. His father, had he been living, would have put his foot down at that point. Taking a box of candy was her favorite nice thing to do. When anyone within her social station moved to town, she called and took a box of candy; when any of her friends' children had babies or won a scholarship, she called and took a box of candy; when an old per-son broke his hip, she was at his bedside with a box of candy. He had been amused at the idea of her taking a box of candy to the jail.

He stood now in his room with the girl's laugh rocketing away in his head and cursed his amusement.

When his mother returned from the visit to the jail, she had burst into his study without knocking and had collapsed full-length on his couch, lifting her small swollen feet up on the arm of it. After a mo-ment, she recovered herself enough to sit up and put a newspaper un-der them. Then she fell back again. "We don't know how the other half lives," she said.

Thomas knew that though her conversation moved from cliché to cliché there were real experiences behind them. He was less sorry for the girl's being in jail than for his mother having to see her there. He would have spared her all unpleasant sights. "Well," he said and put away his journal, "you had better forget it now. The girl has ample rea-son to be in jail."

"You can't imagine what all she's been through," she said, sitting up again, "listen." The poor girl, Star, had been brought up by a stepmother with three children of her own, one an almost grown boy who had taken advantage of her in such dreadful ways that she had been forced to run away and find her real mother. Once found, her real mother had sent her to various boarding schools to get rid of her. At each of these she had been forced to run away by the presence of perverts and sadists so monstrous that their acts defied description. Thomas could tell that his mother had not been spared the details that she was sparing him. Now and again when she spoke vaguely, her voice shook and he could tell that she was remembering some horror that had been put to her graphically. He had hoped that in a few days the memory of all this would wear off, but it did not. The next day she returned to the jail with Kleenex and cold-cream and a few days later, she announced that she had consulted a lawyer.

It was at these times that Thomas truly mourned the death of his father though he had not been able to endure him in life. The old man would have had none of this foolishness. Untouched by useless compassion, he would (behind her back) have pulled the necessary strings with his crony, the sheriff, and the girl would have been packed off to the state penitentiary to serve her time. He had always been engaged in some enraged action until one morning when (with an angry glance at his wife as if she alone were responsible) he had dropped dead at the breakfast table. Thomas had inherited his father's reason without his ruthlessness and his mother's love of good without her tendency to pursue it. His plan for all practical action was to wait and see what developed.

The lawyer found that the story of the repeated atrocities was for the most part untrue, but when he explained to her that the girl was a psychopathic personality, not insane enough for the asylum, not criminal enough for the jail, not stable enough for society, Thomas's mother was more deeply affected than ever. The girl readily admitted that her story was untrue on account of her being a congenital liar; she lied, she said, because she was insecure. She had passed through the hands of several psychiatrists who had put the finishing touches to her education. She knew there was no hope for her. In the presence of such an affliction as this, his mother seemed bowed down by some painful mystery that nothing would make endurable but a redoubling of effort. To his annoyance, she appeared to look on *him* with compassion, as if her hazy charity no longer made distinctions.

A few days later she burst in and said that the lawyer had got the girl paroled — to her.

Thomas rose from his Morris chair, dropping the review he had been reading. His large bland face contracted in anticipated pain. "You are not," he said, "going to bring that girl here!"

"No, no," she said, "calm yourself, Thomas." She had managed with difficulty to get the girl a job in a pet shop in town and a place to board with a crotchety old lady of her acquaintance. People were not kind. They did not put themselves in the place of someone like Star who had everything against her.

Thomas sat down again and retrieved his review. He seemed just to have escaped some danger which he did not care to make clear to himself. "Nobody can tell you anything," he said, "but in a few days that girl will have left town, having got what she could out of you. You'll never hear from her again."

Two nights later he came home and opened the parlor door and was speared by a shrill depthless laugh. His mother and the girl sat close to the fireplace where the gas logs were lit. The girl gave the immediate impression of being physically crooked. Her hair was cut like a dog's or an elf's and she was dressed in the latest fashion. She was training on him a long familiar sparkling stare that turned after a second into an intimate grin.

"Thomas!" his mother said, her voice firm with the injunction not to bolt. "This is Star you've heard so much about. Star is going to have supper with us."

The girl called herself Star Drake. The lawyer had found that her real name was Sarah Ham.

Thomas neither moved nor spoke but hung in the door in what seemed a savage perplexity. Finally he said, "How do you do, Sarah," in a tone of such loathing that he was shocked at the sound of it. He reddened, feeling it beneath him to show contempt for any creature so pathetic. He advanced into the room, determined at least on a decent politeness and sat down heavily in a straight chair.

"Thomas writes history," his mother said with a threatening look at him. "He's president of the local Historical Society this year."

The girl leaned forward and gave Thomas an even more pointed attention. "Fabulous!" she said in a throaty voice.

"Right now Thomas is writing about the first settlers in this country," his mother said.

"Fabulous!" the girl repeated.

Thomas by an effort of will managed to look as if he were alone in the room.

"Say, you know who he looks like?" Star asked, her head on one side, taking him in at an angle.

"Oh some one very distinguished!" his mother said archly.

"This cop I saw in the movie I went to last night," Star said.

"Star," his mother said, "I think you ought to be careful about the kind of movies you go to. I think you ought to see only the best ones. I don't think crime stories would be good for you."

"Oh this was a crime-does-not-pay," Star said, "and I swear this cop looked exactly like him. They were always putting something over on the guy. He would look like he couldn't stand it a minute longer or he would blow up. He was a riot. And not bad looking," she added with an appreciative leer at Thomas.

"Star," his mother said, "I think it would be grand if you developed a taste for music."

Thomas sighed. His mother rattled on and the girl, paying no attention to her, let her eyes play over him. The quality of her look was such that it might have been her hands, resting now on his knees, now on his neck. Her eyes had a mocking glitter and he knew that she was well aware he could not stand the sight of her. He needed nothing to tell him he was in the presence of the very stuff of corruption, but blameless corruption because there was no responsible faculty behind it. He was looking at the most unendurable form of innocence. Absently he asked himself what the attitude of God was to this, meaning if possible to adopt it.

His mother's behavior throughout the meal was so idiotic that he could barely stand to look at her and since he could less stand to look at Sarah Ham, he fixed on the sideboard across the room a continuous gaze of disapproval and disgust. Every remark of the girl's his mother met as if it deserved serious attention. She advanced several plans for the wholesome use of Star's spare time. Sarah Ham paid no more attention to this advice than if it came from a parrot. Once when Thomas inadvertently looked in her direction, she winked. As soon as he had swallowed the last spoonful of dessert, he rose and muttered, "I have to go, I have a meeting."

"Thomas," his mother said, "I want you to take Star home on your way. I don't want her riding in taxis by herself at night."

For a moment Thomas remained furiously silent. Then he turned and left the room. Presently he came back with a look of obscure determination on his face. The girl was ready, meekly waiting at the parlor door. She cast up at him a great look of admiration and confidence. Thomas did not offer his arm but she took it anyway and moved out of the house and down the steps, attached to what might have been a miraculously moving monument.

"Be good!" his mother called.

Sarah Ham snickered and poked him in the ribs.

While getting his coat he had decided that this would be his opportunity to tell the girl that unless she ceased to be a parasite on his mother, he would see to it, personally, that she was returned to jail. He would let her know that he understood what she was up to, that he was not an innocent and that there were certain things he would not put up with. At his desk, pen in hand, none was more articulate than Thomas. As soon as he found himself shut into the car with Sarah Ham, terror seized his tongue.

She curled her feet up under her and said, "Alone at last," and giggled.

Thomas swerved the car away from the house and drove fast toward the gate. Once on the highway, he shot forward as if he were being pursued.

"Jesus!" Sarah Ham said, swinging her feet off the seat. "Where's the fire?"

Thomas did not answer. In a few seconds he could feel her edging closer. She stretched, eased nearer, and finally hung her hand limply over his shoulder. "Tomsee doesn't like me," she said, "but I think he's fabulously cute."

Thomas covered the three and a half miles into town in a little over four minutes. The light at the first intersection was red but he ignored it. The old woman lived three blocks beyond. When the car screeched to a halt at the place, he jumped out and ran around to the girl's door and opened it. She did not move from the car and Thomas was obliged to wait. After a moment one leg emerged, then her small white crooked face appeared and stared up at him. There was something about the look of it that suggested blindness but it was the blindness of those who don't know that they cannot see. Thomas was curiously sickened. The empty eyes moved over him. "Nobody likes me," she said in a sullen tone. "What if you were me and I couldn't stand to ride you three miles?"

"My mother likes you," he muttered.

"Her!" the girl said. "She's just about seventy-five years behind the times!"

Breathlessly Thomas said, "If I find you bothering her again, I'll have you put back in jail." There was a dull force behind his voice though it came out barely above a whisper.

"You and who else?" she said and drew back in the car as if now she did not intend to get out at all. Thomas reached into it, blindly grasped the front of her coat, pulled her out by it and released her. Then he lunged back to the car and sped off. The other door was still hanging open and her laugh, bodiless but real, bounded up the street as if it were about to jump in the open side of the car and ride away with him. He reached over and slammed the door and then drove toward home, too angry to attend his meeting. He intended to make his mother well-aware of his displeasure. He intended to leave no doubt in her mind. The voice of his father rasped in his head.

Numbskull, the old man said, put your foot down now. Show her who's boss before she shows you.

But when Thomas reached home, his mother, wisely, had gone to bed.

The next morning he appeared at the breakfast table, his brow lowered and the thrust of his jaw indicating that he was in a dangerous humor. When he intended to be determined, Thomas began like a bull that, before charging, backs with his head lowered and paws the ground. "All right now listen," he began, yanking out his chair and sitting down, "I have something to say to you about that girl and I don't intend to say it but once." He drew breath. "She's nothing but a little slut. She makes fun of you behind your back. She means to get everything she can out of you and you are nothing to her."

His mother looked as if she too had spent a restless night. She did not dress in the morning but wore her bathrobe and a grey turban around her head, which gave her face a disconcerting omniscient look. He might have been breakfasting with a sibyl.

"You'll have to use canned cream this morning," she said, pouring his coffee. "I forgot the other."

"All right, did you hear me?" Thomas growled.

"I'm not deaf," his mother said and put the pot back on the trivet. "I know I'm nothing but an old bag of wind to her."

"Then why do you persist in this foolhardy . . ."

"Thomas," she said, and put her hand to the side of her face, "it might be . . ."

"It is not me!" Thomas said, grasping the table leg at his knee.

She continued to hold her face, shaking her head slightly. "Think of all you have," she began. "All the comforts of home. And morals, Thomas. No bad inclinations, nothing bad you were born with."

Thomas began to breathe like someone who feels the onset of asthma. "You are not logical," he said in a limp voice. "*He* would have put his foot down."

The old lady stiffened. "You," she said, "are not like him."

Thomas opened his mouth silently.

"However," his mother said, in a tone of such subtle accusation that she might have been taking back the compliment, "I won't invite her back again since you're so dead set against her."

"I am not set against her," Thomas said. "I am set against your making a fool of yourself."

As soon as he left the table and closed the door of his study on himself, his father took up a squatting position in his mind. The old man had had the countryman's ability to converse squatting, though he was no countryman but had been born and brought up in the city and only moved to a smaller place later to exploit his talents. With steady skill he had made them think him one of them. In the midst of a conversation on the courthouse lawn, he would squat and his two or three companions would squat with him with no break in the surface of the talk. By gesture he had lived his lie; he had never deigned to tell one.

Let her run over you, he said. You ain't like me. Not enough to be a man.

Thomas began vigorously to read and presently the image faded. The girl had caused a disturbance in the depths of his being, somewhere out of the reach of his power of analysis. He felt as if he had seen a tornado pass a hundred yards away and had an intimation that it would turn again and head directly for him. He did not get his mind firmly on his work until mid-morning.

Two nights later, his mother and he were sitting in the den after their supper, each reading a section of the evening paper, when the telephone began to ring with the brassy intensity of a fire alarm. Thomas reached for it. As soon as the receiver was in his hand, a shrill female voice screamed into the room, "Come get this girl! Come get her! Drunk! Drunk in my parlor and I won't have it! Lost her job and come back here drunk! I won't have it!"

His mother leapt up and snatched the receiver.

The ghost of Thomas's father rose before him. Call the sheriff, the old man prompted. "Call the sheriff," Thomas said in a loud voice. "Call the sheriff to go there and pick her up."

"We'll be right there," his mother was saying. "We'll come and get her right away. Tell her to get her things together."

"She ain't in no condition to get nothing together," the voice screamed. "You shouldn't have put something like her off on me! My house is respectable!"

"Tell her to call the sheriff," Thomas shouted.

His mother put the receiver down and looked at him. "I wouldn't turn a dog over to that man," she said.

Thomas sat in the chair with his arms folded and looked fixedly at the wall.

"Think of the poor girl, Thomas," his mother said, "with nothing. Nothing. And we have everything."

When they arrived, Sarah Ham was slumped spraddle-legged against the banister on the boarding house front-steps. Her tam was down on her forehead where the old woman had slammed it and her clothes were bulging out of her suitcase where the old woman had thrown them in. She was carrying on a drunken conversation with herself in a low personal tone. A streak of lipstick ran up one side of her face. She allowed herself to be guided by his mother to the car and put in the back seat without seeming to know who the rescuer was. "Nothing to talk to all day but a pack of goddamned parakeets," she said in a furious whisper.

Thomas, who had not got out of the car at all, or looked at her after the first revolted glance, said, "I'm telling you, once and for all, the place to take her is the jail."

His mother, sitting on the back seat, holding the girl's hand, did not answer.

"All right, take her to the hotel," he said.

"I cannot take a drunk girl to a hotel, Thomas," she said. "You know that."

"Then take her to a hospital."

"She doesn't need a jail or a hotel or a hospital," his mother said, "she needs a home."

"She does not need mine," Thomas said.

"Only for tonight, Thomas," the old lady sighed. "Only for tonight."

Since then eight days had passed. The little slut was established in the guest room. Every day his mother set out to find her a job and a place to board, and failed, for the old woman had broadcast a warning. Thomas kept to his room or the den. His home was to him home, workshop, church, as personal as the shell of a turtle and as necessary. He could not believe that it could be violated in this way. His flushed face had a constant look of stunned outrage.

As soon as the girl was up in the morning, her voice throbbed out in a blues song that would rise and waver, then plunge low with insinuations of passion about to be satisfied and Thomas, at his desk, would

lunge up and begin frantically stuffing his ears with Kleenex. Each time
he started from one room to another, one floor to another, she would
be certain to appear. Each time he was half way up or down the stairs,
she would either meet him and pass, cringing coyly, or go up or down
behind him, breathing small tragic spearmint-flavored sighs. She appeared to adore Thomas's repugnance to her and to draw it out of him
every chance she got as if it added delectably to her martyrdom.

The old man — small, wasp-like, in his yellowed Panama hat, his
seer-sucker suit, his pink carefully-soiled shirt, his small string tie —
appeared to have taken up his station in Thomas's mind and from
there, usually squatting, he shot out the same rasping suggestion every
time the boy paused from his forced studies. Put your foot down. Go to
see the sheriff.

The sheriff was another edition of Thomas's father except that he
wore a checkered shirt and a Texas type hat and was ten years younger.
He was as easily dishonest, and he had genuinely admired the old man.
Thomas, like his mother, would have gone far out of his way to avoid
his glassy pale blue gaze. He kept hoping for another solution, for a
miracle.

With Sarah Ham in the house, meals were unbearable.

"Tomsee doesn't like me," she said the third or fourth night at the
supper table and cast her pouting gaze across at the large rigid figure of
Thomas, whose face was set with the look of a man trapped by insufferable odors. "He doesn't want me here. Nobody wants me anywhere."

"Thomas's name is Thomas," his mother interrupted. "Not Tomsee."

"I made Tomsee up," she said. "I think it's cute. He hates me."

"Thomas does not hate you," his mother said. "We are not the kind of
people who hate," she added, as if this were an imperfection that had
been bred out of them generations ago.

"Oh, I know when I'm not wanted," Sarah Ham continued. "They
didn't even want me in jail. If I killed myself I wonder would God
want me?"

"Try it and see," Thomas muttered.

The girl screamed with laughter. Then she stopped abruptly, her face
puckered and she began to shake. "The best thing to do," she said, her
teeth clattering, "is to kill myself. Then I'll be out of everybody's way. I'll
go to hell and be out of God's way. And even the devil won't want me.
He'll kick me out of hell, not even in hell . . ." she wailed.

Thomas rose, picked up his plate and knife and fork and carried
them to the den to finish his supper. After that, he had not eaten an-

other meal at the table but had had his mother serve him at his desk. At these meals, the old man was intensely present to him. He appeared to be tipping backwards in his chair, his thumbs beneath his galluses, while he said such things as, She never ran me away from my own table.

A few nights later, Sarah Ham slashed her wrists with a paring knife and had hysterics. From the den where he was closeted after supper, Thomas heard a shriek, then a series of screams, then his mother's scurrying footsteps through the house. He did not move. His first instant of hope that the girl had cut her throat faded as he realized she could not have done it and continue to scream the way she was doing. He returned to his journal and presently the screams subsided. In a moment his mother burst in with his coat and hat. "We have to take her to the hospital," she said. "She tried to do away with herself. I have a tourniquet on her arm. Oh Lord, Thomas," she said, "imagine being so low you'd do a thing like that!"

Thomas rose woodenly and put on his hat and coat. "We will take her to the hospital," he said, "and we will leave her there."

"And drive her to despair again?" the old lady cried. "Thomas!"

Standing in the center of his room now, realizing that he had reached the point where action was inevitable, that he must pack, that he must leave, that he must go, Thomas remained immovable.

His fury was directed not at the little slut but at his mother. Even though the doctor had found that she had barely damaged herself and had raised the girl's wrath by laughing at the tourniquet and putting only a streak of iodine on the cut, his mother could not get over the incident. Some new weight of sorrow seemed to have been thrown across her shoulders, and not only Thomas, but Sarah Ham was infuriated by this, for it appeared to be a general sorrow that would have found another object no matter what good fortune came to either of them. The experience of Sarah Ham had plunged the old lady into mourning for the world.

The morning after the attempted suicide, she had gone through the house and collected all the knives and scissors and locked them in a drawer. She emptied a bottle of rat poison down the toilet and took up the roach tablets from the kitchen floor. Then she came to Thomas's study and said in a whisper, "Where is that gun of his? I want you to lock it up."

"The gun is in my drawer," Thomas roared, "and I will not lock it up. If she shoots herself, so much the better!"

"Thomas," his mother said, "she'll hear you!"

"Let her hear me!" Thomas yelled. "Don't you know she has no intention of killing herself? Don't you know her kind never kill themselves? Don't you . . ."

His mother slipped out the door and closed it to silence him and Sarah Ham's laugh, quite close in the hall, came rattling into his room. "Tomsee'll find out. I'll kill myself and then he'll be sorry he wasn't nice to me. I'll use his own lil gun, his own lil ol' pearl-handled revollervuh!" she shouted and let out a loud tormented-sounding laugh in imitation of a movie monster.

Thomas ground his teeth. He pulled out his desk drawer and felt for the pistol. It was an inheritance from the old man, whose opinion it had been that every house should contain a loaded gun. He had discharged two bullets one night into the side of a prowler, but Thomas had never shot anything. He had no fear that the girl would use the gun on herself and he closed the drawer. Her kind clung tenaciously to life and were able to wrest some histrionic advantage from every moment.

Several ideas for getting rid of her had entered his head but each of these had been suggestions whose moral tone indicated that they had come from a mind akin to his father's, and Thomas had rejected them. He could not get the girl locked up again until she did something illegal. The old man would have been able with no qualms at all to get her drunk and send her out on the highway in his car, meanwhile notifying the highway patrol of her presence on the road, but Thomas considered this below his moral stature. Suggestions continued to come to him, each more outrageous than the last.

He had not the vaguest hope that the girl would get the gun and shoot herself, but that afternoon when he looked in the drawer, the gun was gone. His study locked from the inside, not the out. He cared nothing about the gun, but the thought of Sarah Ham's hands sliding among his papers infuriated him. Now even his study was contaminated. The only place left untouched by her was his bedroom.

That night she entered it.

In the morning at breakfast, he did not eat and did not sit down. He stood beside his chair and delivered his ultimatum while his mother sipped her coffee as if she were both alone in the room and in great pain. "I have stood this," he said, "for as long as I am able. Since I see plainly that you care nothing about me, about my peace or comfort or working conditions, I am about to take the only step open to me. I will give you one more day. If you bring the girl back into this house this afternoon, I leave. You can choose — her or me." He had more to say but at that point his voice cracked and he left.

At ten o'clock his mother and Sarah Ham left the house.

At four he heard the car wheels on the gravel and rushed to the window. As the car stopped, the dog stood up, alert, shaking.

He seemed unable to take the first step that would set him walking to the closet in the hall to look for the suitcase. He was like a man handed a knife and told to operate on himself if he wished to live. His huge hands clenched helplessly. His expression was a turmoil of indecision and outrage. His pale blue eyes seemed to sweat in his broiling face. He closed them for a moment and on the back of his lids, his father's image leered at him. Idiot! the old man hissed, idiot! The criminal slut stole your gun! See the sheriff! See the sheriff!

It was a moment before Thomas opened his eyes. He seemed newly stunned. He stood where he was for at least three minutes, then he turned slowly like a large vessel reversing its direction and faced the door. He stood there a moment longer, then he left, his face set to see the ordeal through.

He did not know where he would find the sheriff. The man made his own rules and kept his own hours. Thomas stopped first at the jail, where his office was, but he was not in it. He went to the courthouse and was told by a clerk that the sheriff had gone to the barber-shop across the street. "Yonder's the deppity," the clerk said and pointed out the window to the large figure of a man in a checkered shirt, who was leaning against the side of a police car, looking into space.

"It has to be the sheriff," Thomas said and left for the barber-shop. As little as he wanted anything to do with the sheriff, he realized that the man was at least intelligent and not simply a mound of sweating flesh.

The barber said the sheriff had just left. Thomas started back to the courthouse and as he stepped on to the sidewalk from the street, he saw a lean, slightly stooped figure gesticulating angrily at the deputy.

Thomas approached with an aggressiveness brought on by nervous agitation. He stopped abruptly three feet away and said in an over-loud voice, "Can I have a word with you?" without adding the sheriff's name, which was Farebrother.

Farebrother turned his sharp creased face just enough to take Thomas in, and the deputy did likewise, but neither spoke. The sheriff removed a very small piece of cigaret from his lip and dropped it at his feet. "I told you what to do," he said to the deputy. Then he moved off with a slight nod that indicated Thomas could follow him if he wanted to see him. The deputy slunk around the front of the police car and got inside.

Farebrother, with Thomas following, headed across the courthouse square and stopped beneath a tree that shaded a quarter of the front lawn. He waited, leaning slightly forward, and lit another cigaret.

Thomas began to blurt out his business. As he had not had time to prepare his words, he was barely coherent. By repeating the same thing over several times, he managed at length to get out what he wanted to say. When he finished, the sheriff was still leaning slightly forward, at an angle to him, his eyes on nothing in particular. He remained that way without speaking.

Thomas began again, slower and in a lamer voice, and Farebrother let him continue for some time before he said, "We had her oncet." He then allowed himself a slow, creased, all-knowing, quarter smile.

"I had nothing to do with that," Thomas said. "That was my mother."

Farebrother squatted.

"She was trying to help the girl," Thomas said. "She didn't know she couldn't be helped."

"Bit off more than she could chew, I reckon," the voice below him mused.

"She has nothing to do with this," Thomas said. "She doesn't know I'm here. The girl is dangerous with that gun."

"*He,*" the sheriff said, "never let anything grow under his feet. Particularly nothing a woman planted."

"She might kill somebody with that gun," Thomas said weakly, looking down at the round top of the Texas type hat.

There was a long time of silence.

"Where's she got it?" Farebrother asked.

"I don't know. She sleeps in the guest room. It must be in there, in her suitcase probably," Thomas said.

Farebrother lapsed into silence again.

"You could come search the guest room," Thomas said in a strained voice. "I can go home and leave the latch off the front door and you can come in quietly and go upstairs and search her room."

Farebrother turned his head so that his eyes looked boldly at Thomas's knees. "You seem to know how it ought to be done," he said. "Want to swap jobs?"

Thomas said nothing because he could not think of anything to say, but he waited doggedly. Farebrother removed the cigaret butt from his lips and dropped it on the grass. Beyond him on the courthouse porch a group of loiterers who had been leaning at the left of the door moved over to the right where a patch of sunlight had settled. From one of the upper windows a crumpled piece of paper blew out and drifted down.

"I'll come along about six," Farebrother said. "Leave the latch off the door and keep out of my way — yourself and them two women too."

Thomas let out a rasping sound of relief meant to be "Thanks," and struck off across the grass like someone released. The phrase, "them two women," stuck like a burr in his brain — the subtlety of the insult to his mother hurting him more than any of Farebrother's references to his own incompetence. As he got into his car, his face suddenly flushed. Had he delivered his mother over to the sheriff — to be a butt for the man's tongue? Was he betraying her to get rid of the little slut? He saw at once that this was not the case. He was doing what he was doing for her own good, to rid her of a parasite that would ruin their peace. He started his car and drove quickly home but once he had turned in the driveway, he decided it would be better to park some distance from the house and go quietly in by the back door. He parked on the grass and on the grass walked in a circle toward the rear of the house. The sky was lined with mustard-colored streaks. The dog was asleep on the back doormat. At the approach of his master's step, he opened one yellow eye, took him in, and closed it again.

Thomas let himself into the kitchen. It was empty and the house was quiet enough for him to be aware of the loud ticking of the kitchen clock. It was a quarter to six. He tiptoed hurriedly through the hall to the front door and took the latch off it. Then he stood for a moment listening. From behind the closed parlor door, he heard his mother snoring softly and presumed that she had gone to sleep while reading. On the other side of the hall, not three feet from his study, the little slut's black coat and red pocketbook were slung on a chair. He heard water running upstairs and decided she was taking a bath.

He went into his study and sat down at his desk to wait, noting with distaste that every few moments a tremor ran through him. He sat for a minute or two doing nothing. Then he picked up a pen and began to draw squares on the back of an envelope that lay before him. He looked at his watch. It was eleven minutes to six. After a moment he idly drew the center drawer of the desk out over his lap. For a moment he stared at the gun without recognition. Then he gave a yelp and leaped up. She had put it back!

Idiot! his father hissed, idiot! Go plant it in her pocketbook. Don't just stand there. Go plant it in her pocketbook!

Thomas stood staring at the drawer.

Moron! the old man fumed. Quick while there's time! Go plant it in her pocketbook.

Thomas did not move.

Imbecile! his father cried.

Thomas picked up the gun.

Make haste, the old man ordered.

Thomas started forward, holding the gun away from him. He opened the door and looked at the chair. The black coat and red pocketbook were lying on it almost within reach.

Hurry up, you fool, his father said.

From behind the parlor door the almost inaudible snores of his mother rose and fell. They seemed to mark an order of time that had nothing to do with the instants left to Thomas. There was no other sound.

Quick, you imbecile, before she wakes up, the old man said.

The snores stopped and Thomas heard the sofa springs groan. He grabbed the red pocketbook. It had a skin-like feel to his touch and as it opened, he caught an unmistakable odor of the girl. Wincing, he thrust in the gun and then drew back. His face burned an ugly dull red.

"What is Tomsee putting in my purse?" she called and her pleased laugh bounced down the staircase. Thomas whirled.

She was at the top of the stair, coming down in the manner of a fashion model, one bare leg and then the other thrusting out the front of her kimona in a definite rhythm. "Tomsee is being naughty," she said in a throaty voice. She reached the bottom and cast a possessive leer at Thomas whose face was now more grey than red. She reached out, pulled the bag open with her finger and peered at the gun.

His mother opened the parlor door and looked out.

"Tomsee put his pistol in my bag!" the girl shrieked.

"Ridiculous," his mother said, yawning. "What would Thomas want to put his pistol in your bag for?"

Thomas stood slightly hunched, his hands hanging helplessly at the wrists as if he had just pulled them up out of a pool of blood.

"I don't know what for," the girl said, "but he sure did it," and she proceeded to walk around Thomas, her hands on her hips, her neck thrust forward and her intimate grin fixed on him fiercely. All at once her expression seemed to open as the purse had opened when Thomas touched it. She stood with her head cocked on one side in an attitude of disbelief. "Oh boy," she said slowly, "is he a case."

At that instant Thomas damned not only the girl but the entire order of the universe that made her possible.

"Thomas wouldn't put a gun in your bag," his mother said. "Thomas is a gentleman."

The girl made a chortling noise. "You can see it in there," she said and pointed to the open purse.

You *found* it in her bag, you dimwit! the old man hissed.

"I found it in her bag!" Thomas shouted. "The dirty criminal slut stole my gun!"

His mother gasped at the sound of the other presence in his voice. The old lady's sybil-like face turned pale.

"Found it my eye!" Sarah Ham shrieked and started for the pocketbook, but Thomas, as if his arm were guided by his father, caught it first and snatched the gun. The girl in a frenzy lunged at Thomas's throat and would actually have caught him around the neck had not his mother thrown herself forward to protect her.

Fire! the old man yelled.

Thomas fired. The blast was like a sound meant to bring an end to evil in the world. Thomas heard it as a sound that would shatter the laughter of sluts until all shrieks were stilled and nothing was left to disturb the peace of perfect order.

The echo died away in waves. Before the last one had faded, Farebrother opened the door and put his head inside the hall. His nose wrinkled. His expression for some few seconds was that of a man unwilling to admit surprise. His eyes were clear as glass, reflecting the scene. The old lady lay on the floor between the girl and Thomas.

The sheriff's brain worked instantly like a calculating machine. He saw the facts as if they were already in print: the fellow had intended all along to kill his mother and pin it on the girl. But Farebrother had been too quick for him. They were not yet aware of his head in the door. As he scrutinized the scene, further insights were flashed to him. Over her body, the killer and the slut were about to collapse into each other's arms. The sheriff knew a nasty bit when he saw it. He was accustomed to enter upon scenes that were not as bad as he had hoped to find them, but this one met his expectations.

1967

JEROME WEIDMAN

....

Good Man, Bad Man

ONE THING about the obituary page. It starts people talking. Men and women who for years have been afraid to open their mouths, they read a four-line item on the obituary page, and suddenly they become garrulous. I'm no exception.

Yesterday, if you had mentioned the name Jazz L. McCabe to me, I would have given you an innocent look and said, "Who?" Today, try and shut me up. This morning's *Times* reports that McCabe died last night at Mt. Sinai Hospital. A coronary at the age of seventy-three. High time.

His name was James, but down on East Fourth Street we called him Jazz because that's the way he signed his name: *Jas. L. McCabe.* The first time I saw *Jas. L. McCabe,* it was written at the bottom of a letter. The letter was typed. That threw my mother into a panic. She thought it was a *moof tzettle,* which is Yiddish for eviction notice. These were just about the only typewritten communications that arrived on East Fourth Street in those days.

"It's not from the court," I said, after studying the letter. "It has nothing to do with our rent."

"What is it, then?" my mother said.

"It's for Natie Goodman," I said.

"Then why did the letter carrier put it in our box?"

"Well, it's for Natie and me," I said. "The both of us."

This was not strictly true, but my mother was a peasant woman from a remote corner of Hungary, and she had come to America only a couple of years before I was born. Things went on in this country that she did not understand, and at the age of almost fourteen I had not yet developed any great desire to waste my time enlightening her.

Let me go back to before that letter came, to when I was only twelve.

I had a friend named Nathan Goodman. His father owned a grocery store at the corner of Lewis and Fourth streets, and the Goodmans lived two floors above us in a huge, dirty-gray tenement that faced the store. Natie was a great reader. Most kids on East Fourth Street were. A borrower's card for the Hamilton Fish Park branch of the New York Public Library was standard equipment for every kid on the block. The reason was simple. Art Acord in *The Oregon Trail* at the movie theater on Second Street cost a dime. *David Copperfield* cost nothing, not if you got to the front door of the library at nine o'clock on Saturday morning. Dickens was big stuff on East Fourth Street.

What got me involved with Jazz L. McCabe was Natie Goodman's laziness. Natie was a tough kid to get out of bed in the morning. He was late for *Nicholas Nickleby*. Some other kid got it. What Natie got was a book called *The Boy Scouts of Bob's Hill*.

My wife doesn't believe me. But I swear. There once was a book called *The Boy Scouts of Bob's Hill*, and it changed my life.

"I want you to read this," Natie said to me the day after he missed out on *Nicholas Nickelby*, and he handed me the book.

"Why?" I said. I was working my way through *Great Expectations*, and hated to be deflected.

"You wait and see," Natie said.

I didn't have to wait long. *The Boy Scouts of Bob's Hill* was a short book. It told the story of a group of boys, about the same age as Natie and me, who formed a Boy Scout troop with headquarters in a cave at a placed called Bob's Hill. Don't ask me where Bob's Hill was. Probably somewhere in New England or out West, maybe even in California. Wherever it was, it was about as different from East Fourth Street as Addis Ababa is from Radio City. Furthermore, until I read this book I had never even heard of Boy Scouts. But I had never heard of London either, until I read *Martin Chuzzlewit*. The effect was the same. It was immediate, and it has lasted. I still feel about London the way Troilus felt about Cressida. The moment I finished reading *The Boy Scouts of Bob's Hill*, I ran down to the grocery store to find Natie Goodman. He was stacking empty cartons out in back, a chore for which his father paid him twenty-five cents a week.

"I know what you're going to say," he said, "and I'm way ahead of you. Let's start a Scout troop."

I had been going to say only that I liked *The Boy Scouts of Bob's Hill* and intended to hotfoot it right over to the library and see if maybe it was one of a series of books, because if it was, I wanted to read them all.

But, as Natie had said, he was way ahead of me — and not for the first time, either.

"How can we do that?" I said.

"We write to the national headquarters," Natie said. "I looked it up in the telephone book. It's right here in New York."

Natie wrote the letter, but I helped with the phrasing, and we chipped in for the stamp. It cost two cents, and no nonsense about zones or zip codes. Two cents, no matter where you were writing to, Seattle or the Bronx. Actually, Natie and I were writing to Two Park Avenue, but the answer came from a man in New Rochelle.

It was a short, handwritten letter, and it was signed *Lester Osterweil*. Mr. Osterweil said that the National Council of the Boy Scouts of America had advised him that Master Nathan Goodman and a friend, both of East Fourth Street in New York City, had inquired about organizing a Boy Scout troop in their neighborhood, and that he, Mr. Osterweil, had been asked to pursue the matter because he worked not too far from East Fourth Street. Mr. Osterweil asked if we knew the location of the Hamilton Fish Park branch of the New York Public Library (which was like asking Gertrude Ederle if she knew the location of the English Channel), because that was where he would like to meet us the following Tuesday at 6:00 P.M., a time he hoped was convenient for us, but if it wasn't he would be pleased to make a more convenient arrangement. In the meantime he begged to remain yours for more and better Scouting, sincerely Lester Osterweil.

In those days, when life was still uncomplicated, anything that I didn't have to explain to my mother was convenient for me, and to make things convenient for himself all Natie had to do was steer clear of the grocery store in which his father and mother were trapped until almost midnight, every day except Friday, when they closed at sundown.

The following Tuesday evening, Natie and I were on the front steps of the library by five thirty, and at six o'clock a tall, thin, hatless man with a sad face, wearing a dirty raincoat, came down the block and introduced himself to us.

Looking back on it now, I would guess that Mr. Osterweil was then around thirty, give or take a couple of years, but to me and Natie, who had just turned twelve, he looked as old as Calvin Coolidge. He talked like Coolidge, too. Not that I ever heard Coolidge talk, but there were a lot of jokes in those days about how rarely he opened his mouth and, when he did, how little came out.

The first thing Mr. Osterweil said was an explanation of what he'd meant when he wrote that he worked not too far from East Fourth Street. He was the manager of the F. W. Woolworth store on Avenue B between Fifth and Sixth streets, about a five-minute walk from the Hamilton Fish Park branch library. Mr. Osterweil's next words put me and Natie Goodman in his pocket forever. He asked how we'd like a couple of ice cream sodas.

Between that night, when he came into my life, and the night, about two years later, when he left it, I learned a lot about Mr. Osterweil, but I don't remember how I learned it. For example, I don't know how I learned he was a bachelor and lived with his mother in New Rochelle in the house where both of them had been born. Not that at twelve I was what you would call shy, exactly, but I can't believe I ever asked Mr. Osterweil for this piece of information.

I have a theory — which I can't prove, but which I will never stop defending — that if you feel strongly about anybody, if you really love or really hate, you pick up information about them without trying, the way a blue serge suit picks up lint, because all your pores are always open, so to speak. Maybe I don't mean pores but antennae.

Whatever I mean, this much I know: What I remember about Lester Osterweil I remember because I was crazy about him, and what I remember about Jazz L. McCabe I remember because for almost forty years, until this morning when I read his obituary in the *Times*, I have hated the bastard. He was something, Jazz L. McCabe was. Something rotten.

Lester Osterweil was just the opposite. Goodness came out of him the way hot air comes out of politicians. He didn't even have to try. Maybe that's what drew him to the Boy Scout movement. There is something simple about it. Like the Golden Rule. If you want boys to be decent, if you care about helping them grow up to be good men — why, just get them out into the open, take them on hikes, teach them to tie knots, to make fire with flint and steel, to believe that the Kingdom of Heaven is not a bull stock market but a khaki uniform that a boy wins by proving he has accepted the ludicrous belief that it is admirable to be trustworthy, loyal, helpful, friendly, courteous, kind, obedient, cheerful, thrifty, brave, clean, and reverent. Silly, of course. I shudder to think what an ass I must have been at the age of twelve to believe such stuff. I have, however, a good excuse. I was corrupted by Lester Osterweil.

Not only did Mr. Osterweil believe all this, he built his life around his belief. He had very little money. This is no reflection on the F. W. Woolworth Company. I'm sure they paid their store managers a fair wage, that Lester Osterweil was paid as much as he deserved. If the money didn't go as far as he wanted it to go, that was his fault, not Woolworth's. Lester Osterweil wanted his money to go to the boys of East Fourth Street, but he didn't have enough to go around because his mother lived in a wheelchair and earned very little by sewing for her New Rochelle neighbors. Mr. Osterweil did pretty well, though.

He helped me and Natie Goodman and a dozen other kids to buy our first Scout uniforms. Troop 224, which met every Saturday night in the downstairs reading room of the Hamilton Fish Park library, always met as a troop should meet — every member properly dressed, every member wearing the insignia to which he is entitled. I still get a kick out of remembering the day I gave Mr. Osterweil four quarters, a dime, and a nickel, the last payment I owed on the $3.50 he had advanced so I could buy a new shirt and a merit-badge sash to wear at the troop ceremony when I was made Senior Patrol Leader. I earned the money by taking over Natie Goodman's job, which Natie hated, of stacking empties for his father. I wore that merit-badge sash the way King Arthur wore Excalibur. For the man who made it possible for me to wear it, I would have killed.

Before what happened happened, there were good times with Mr. Osterweil. Pretty damn near a year and a half of them.

The weekly meetings. The new skills. The merit badges. The useless knowledge picked up for the fun of it. I don't know why, but I still enjoy knowing that the poplar *tremuloides* can also be identified as the trembling aspen. Or that the square knot is used for typing ropes of equal thickness. If they are of unequal thickness, you'd better use a sheet bend, and I still do. Morse code? I can wigwag ten words a minute with a single flag, assuming there is still anyone around who can read wig-wagged Morse. If there isn't, I san send it electronically, almost as fast as AP bulletins come in on a news ticker. I haven't stopped much arterial bleeding lately by calling on my knowledge of the proper pressure points, but not too long ago a neighbor's son, chasing a long fly across our lawn, crashed through our kitchen window, and when the ambulance came an intern complimented me on the spiral reverse bandage I'd put around the kid's forearm. Just a few of the things I learned from Mr. Osterweil.

But the best things were the Sunday hikes. That's what I remember clearest. The Sunday hikes.

Getting out of the bed I shared with my kid brother, and out of the house without waking him or my mother, who thought Mr. Osterweil was an American militarist working to turn me and Natie and the other boys of Troop 224 into *pogromniks,* her word for all people who wore uniforms, whether they worked for the New York Sanitation Department or Czar Nicholas II. Meeting Natie in the grocery store, which would not open officially for another hour (we'd sneak in with a key Natie was not supposed to have). Stuffing our knapsacks with stale rolls, a little jar of butter scooped out of the big wooden tub in the icebox, a block of silver-wrapped cream cheese, a can of baked beans. *No, let's take two. Baked beans are the best. . . . But what about your old man? . . . Aah, I'll push the other cans to the front of the shelf. He won't notice we took two.* I think Mr. Goodman did notice. But I also think he didn't mind. He was proud of the way Natie's merit badges kept piling up. Mr. Goodman had come to America when he was still a young man. He was not as scared as my mother.

Knapsacks loaded, there was the long walk across town to the Astor Place subway station. Except that it never seemed long, not at seven o'clock on those Sunday mornings. The streets empty and quiet, except for the sparrows screaming their heads off, their screaming somehow making it all seem even quieter. On First Avenue, the sun coming across the El, putting golden covers on the garbage cans. On Seventh Street, beyond Second Avenue, the young priest getting ready for early mass, sweeping the steps of the church, his skirts hiked up to avoid the dust. On Third Avenue, in the slatted shade from the El, the sleeping drunks looking friendly and curiously clean. And the sky, like a long wedding canopy over the tenements, smooth and blue as Waterman's ink.

Then the troop gathering slowly outside the subway kiosk. The comparison of knapsack contents. The arrival of Mr. Osterweil. The long ride in the almost empty subway car, up to Dyckman Street. The ferry crossing the Hudson, standing at the gate up front, catching the spray in your face when she hit a big one. On the New Jersey side, the briefing by Mr. Osterweil. Tall, skinny, his Adam's apple bobbing in and out of his khaki collar, his yellow hair blowing in the wind, his sad face looking sadder with the seriousness of his instructions. We needed flint for our fire sets; he'd heard there was quite a lot of it lying around as a result of the blasting they were doing for this new bridge, so would we keep our eyes open?

We kept our eyes open. By the time we arrived at our campsite, we were loaded down with flint. I've often wondered how they managed to get the George Washington Bridge finished without it.

Then the fires. And the cooking. And the smell of roasting hot dogs.

And lying around on the grass, digesting the baked beans, while Mr. Osterweil read aloud from the Scout *Handbook*. Watching the traffic on the river. Skipping stones out toward the sailboats. And finally, the sinking sun.

I never realized I was doing anything more than having the time of my life, and then we won the annual All-Manhattan rally. All of a sudden, I was famous. Well, Troop 224 was famous. The day after I won eight of our winning forty-nine points for speed knot tying, and Natie Goodman rolled up sixteen for flint-and-steel and two-flag semaphore, a picture of Troop 224 appeared in the New York *Graphic*. All thirty-three of us, grouped around Mr. Osterweil, who looked as though he thought the cameraman was pointing a gun at him. The *Jewish Daily Forward* ran a somewhat smaller picture, but my face and Natie's were clearly visible, and the paper called Mr. Osterweil — in Yiddish, of course — "a fine influence on the young people of the neighborhood."

All this was very surprising and very pleasant. None of it was a preparation for the appearance in our lives of Jazz L. McCabe. His typewritten letter, the one that scared my mother because she thought it was a *moof tzettle,* was in our mailbox a few days after the pictures appeared in the *Graphic* and the *Forward.* The letter was addressed to me, as the troop's Senior Patrol Leader. I stared at it for a while, then took it over to the Goodmans' store, where Natie stared at it for a while.

"There's something fishy about this," he said finally.

It was the *mot juste,* all right. The letter advised me that Mr. Lester Osterweil had resigned as Scoutmaster of Troop 224, and that our new Scoutmaster would be the man whose name appeared at the bottom of the letter and who looked forward eagerly to seeing me and the other Scouts at our next weekly meeting: *Jas. L. McCabe.*

"Why should Mr. Osterweil resign?" I said.

"I don't know," Natie said. "Who is this Jazz L. McCabe?"

"I don't know," I said.

"Let's go find out," Natie said.

Mr. Osterweil had asked us long ago never to visit him during working hours. He did not think it was fair to his employers to devote to Scouting any of the time for which he was paid by the F. W. Woolworth Company. We had always obeyed Mr. Osterweil's rule, but Natie and I agreed that Jazz L. McCabe's letter was important enough to justify breaking it. We did not, however, get the chance. Mr. Osterweil, we learned when we got to the store, had not showed up for work that day.

But he did show up at the troop meeting the following night. When

Natie and I came into the room. Mr. Osterweil was standing at the table up front, talking to a man we had never seen before. He called us over.

"This is Mr. McCabe," he said. "He says he wrote you a letter."

"Yes, sir," I said.

I pulled the letter from my pocket and handed it over. While Mr. Osterweil read it, Natie and I studied Mr. Jazz L. McCabe.

I have always had a tendency, which I'm sure is fairly common, to form mental pictures of people I have not yet met from the sound and appearance of their names. Seeing the *Jas. L. McCabe* at the bottom of his letter, my mind had at once constructed an image of a large, bluff, hearty Irishman. I was wrong.

Jas. L. McCabe, when I saw him for the first time that Saturday night, reminded me of the man pictured on the bottle of Ed. Pinaud's Eau De Cologne that stood on the marble shelf in Mr. Raffeto's barbershop on Lewis Street.

Jas. L. McCabe was small, neat, and dapper. He wore a tight double-breasted sharkskin suit and highly polished black shoes with pointed toes. A diamond stickpin in the form of a tiny horseshoe held his tightly knotted black tie in an elegant little fop's bulge under his stiff white collar. His face was round; it seemed plump because his collar was so tight that the flesh of his neck bulged. His black hair was parted in the middle and slicked back with some sort of ointment that gleamed in the glaring electric light. The sharp points of a waxed moustache gave Mr. McCabe something to do with his nervously darting hands, and he kept them busy doing it, so that he seemed to be swatting flies.

He didn't look as though he had ever heard of a sheet bend, much less knew how to tie one. Jas. L. McCabe looked as though he was ready at any moment to whip an apron over you and give you a haircut. What he gave me and Natie Goodman that night was the willies.

Mr. Osterweil's face was pale when he looked up from the letter. "This letter is a lie," he said to us. "I have not resigned as Scoutmaster of this troop."

What happened next was startling. Jas. L. McCabe stopped looking like a foolish barber. He looked suddenly like one of those Sicilian bodyguards who were always following Edward G. Robinson around in the movies.

"OK, you bastard," he said in a cold voice to Lester Osterweil. "You asked for it."

He stalked — no, he sort of hopped — furiously out of the meeting room, and slammed the door.

"Do you want this back?" Mr. Osterweil said.

A moment went by before I realized he was talking about the letter. "No, sir," I said.

Slowly, deliberately, as though he wanted me and Natie to realize his movements held a message for us, Mr. Osterweil tore Jazz L. McCabe's letter into small pieces, and dropped them into the wastebasket.

"All right, Senior Patrol Leader," he said. "You may call the meeting to order."

I did, but it was not a success. Neither was the next day's hike. Everything was the same, and yet everything was different. Even the sky, on the long walk across town to the Astor Place subway station, did not look smooth and blue as Waterman's ink. The unexpected, troubling appearance of Jazz L. McCabe had spoiled everything, even the feel and smell of those mornings.

I did not realize how upset we were until the next day. I was in the back of the Goodman grocery store, helping Natie stack the empties, when his father asked what we were talking so noisily about. We told him about the letter from Jazz L. McCabe, and the scene that had taken place at the troop meeting.

"What kind of a name this is, a man should call himself Jazz, this I don't know," Mr. Goodman said. "But what it means, what he wants, this anybody with a head on his shoulders can see."

"What does it mean?" Natie said.

"You boys won the rally, so you got Mr. Osterweil's picture in the papers," Mr. Goodman said. "This Jazz L. McCabe, he's one of the new Democratic district leaders, and what a district leader wants is votes. You don't get votes if nobody knows who you are. But if you get your picture in the papers, that's how people learn who you are. So this Jazz L. McCabe, he figures if he gets rid of Mr. Osterweil and becomes the Scoutmaster himself, the next time you and the troop you win something, the *Jewish Daily Forward* will be saying about this Jazz L. McCabe, not about Mr. Osterweil. They'll be saying it's Jazz L. McCabe who is a fine influence on the young people of the neighborhood."

Nobody ever got around to saying that. Not in my presence, anyway. Or Natie's.

Two days later I got another typewritten letter. This one was from the Manhattan Council of the Boy Scouts of America. Over a dramatically illegible signature, Natie Goodman and I were asked if we would be good enough to appear at the Manhattan Council offices uptown on

Lexington Avenue on the following day at 4:00 P.M. It was a matter of the utmost urgency.

I was impressed. Not just because this was a typewritten letter. I was impressed because this was the first time I had ever seen the word "utmost" on anything but a page written by Charles Dickens.

When Natie and I got to the offices of the Manhattan Council the next day, we found Mr. Osterweil waiting on a bench in the anteroom. He looked sad. Under ordinary circumstances this would not have made an impression on me. Mr. Osterweil always looked sad. But sad in a nice way. As though the cause of his sadness was not something bad that had happened to him, but his troubled concern that something bad might happen to you. These were not, however, ordinary circumstances.

This was a man who had changed my life. He had brought something into it that I had never known existed. And I don't mean only the knowledge that the poplar *tremuloides* can also be properly called the trembling aspen. He had broken down the walls that until his arrival had always surrounded East Fourth Street. He had let in the sunlit world outside the ghetto. I did not, at the time, understand all that. But I felt it.

"Mr. Osterweil," I said, "what are we all doing here?"

"Well," he said slowly, "I'm not sure, but I think it's because Mr. McCabe wants to take over Troop 224."

"But why did they ask *us* to come here?" Natie said. "Not you, Mr. Osterweil. *Us.*"

The Scoutmaster's Adam's apple bobbed a couple of times, and then he said, "If the boys in the troop want me to stay on as Scoutmaster, the Council will have to let me stay on."

"You mean," Natie said, "if we say the word, it's nuts to this Jazz L. McCabe?"

"Pretty much, yes," Mr. Osterweil said.

"OK," Natie said grimly. "You got nothing to worry about, sir."

For forty years, every time that I have found myself hating Jazz L. McCabe, I have also found myself hearing again the sound of Natie's voice as he uttered those words: *You got nothing to worry about, sir.* If you want to feel confidence in the power of decency and justice to direct the forces that rule the world, the best time to take a shot at it is when you're thirteen going on fourteen. After that, it's an uphill fight.

I didn't realize that, of course, when a door opened at the far side of the anteroom and a secretary said, "Mr. Osterweil, please?"

He stood up and followed her out of the room, and the door closed behind him.

"When he comes out," Natie said, "I think it would be a good idea if we talked to him for a couple of minutes before we go in."

It was an excellent idea, but when the door opened again, about a half hour later, the secretary was alone.

Natie and I both stood up, but she only wanted me. "This way, please," she said.

Wondering what had happened to Mr. Osterweil, I followed the girl into a corridor. At the far end she opened a door on the right and smiled encouragingly at me. I stepped through, and she pulled the door shut behind me.

I was in a room that reminded me of the "Closed Shelf Section" in the Hamilton Fish Park library, except that the walls were lined not with books but with pictures of men like Dan Beard and Lord Baden-Powell. But there was that same feeling of a room in which nobody lived, but which people visited for a special purpose.

At a long table between the windows sat three men. I had never seen men like these in real life, but I had seen hundreds of pictures of them in the newspapers. These were the faces, photographed by Underwood & Underwood, that appeared in the financial section of the *Times* when the corporations for which they worked appointed them to vice-presidencies and board chairmanships. They looked prosperous and well scrubbed. They were all smiling kindly at me. They all had good teeth.

"Please don't be afraid," said the man in the middle. "We just want to ask you a few questions."

"Yes, sir," I said.

"Why don't you sit down," said the man on the left, pointing to a chair facing the table.

"Thank you, sir," I said.

"It was you and Scout Goodman who were responsible for the founding of Troop 224, were you not?" said the man on the left.

"Yes, sir," I said.

"May we congratulate you on your fine showing at the recent All-Manhattan rally," said the man on the right.

"Thank you, sir."

I don't think, looking back on it, that I was usually all that polite at the age of thirteen going on fourteen. But there was that fifth point of the Scout Law, which came out squarely in favor of courtesy, and I was at that moment seated close to the heartland of the American Scout movement.

"Now, then," said the man in the middle, and even if he had not hiked himself forward in his chair and leaned across the table, I would have known the preliminaries were over. There was a main-bout sound to that "Now, then."

"We have asked you to come here today because we are faced with a very painful problem," said the man in the middle. "It has to do with Mr. Osterweil."

"Yes, sir," I said.

"Do you think he is a good Scoutmaster?"

"Yes, sir."

"Good," said the man in the middle. "We would be very sorry to hear that your troop had not been assigned a good Scoutmaster. What's that?"

I jumped slightly in my chair before I realized that the last two words had not been addressed to me. The man on the left had leaned forward and was whispering to the man in the middle.

"Right," the man in the middle said finally to the man on the left. Then he said to me, "You understand, of course, that to be a good Scoutmaster requires more than a knowledge of the various skills in which Scouts are trained. He must also be a good man in the moral sense. Do you understand what I mean?"

"Yes, sir," I said, and it is possible that I did, but I think my main concern was not to cause trouble by appearing stupid. Feeling my way without advice, so to speak, I felt the best thing I could do for Mr. Osterweil, as well as for myself and Natie, was to look calm and act as though nothing unusual had happened during all the time Mr. Osterweil had been our Scoutmaster, because, with a man like that in charge, how could anything unusual happen?

"Mr. Osterweil was assigned to your troop," the man in the middle said, "because we had every reason to believe he was a morally upright person. Otherwise, of course, he would not have been admitted to the Scout movement. However, we have received a communication from a man named McCabe. Do you know him?"

"Yes, sir," I said. "Jazz."

"What?"

I sensed I had made a mistake, so I said quickly, "It's the way he spells his name, sir."

The man on the left leaned forward again, holding out a sheet of paper and pointing to something at the bottom. The man in the middle adjusted his glasses, leaned over the sheet, peered at it for a moment, then leaned back and nodded at me.

"I see," he said. "Well, Mr. McCabe wrote to us that he had recently assumed certain political duties in your neighborhood, and that in his efforts to learn as much as he could about the people he would be serving, he had made a thorough investigation of the area. He wrote that he had discovered a number of parents were worried about the relationship between the Scoutmaster of Troop 224 and the boys in the troop. Are you aware of this?"

Of course I was aware of it. But I wasn't going to tell a man with an Underwood & Underwood face that because we wore uniforms my mother believed Mr. Osterweil was training us all to be *pogromniks*.

I said, "No, sir."

The man on the right leaned over and whispered to the man in the middle, who said, "Good point," and turned back to me. "What about your relationship with Mr. Osterweil? Is it a friendly one?"

"Yes, sir."

"How friendly, may I ask?"

I thought about what it was like — lying around the campfire on Sundays, watching the boats on the river and digesting roasted hot dogs and baked beans and listening to the sound of Mr. Osterweil's voice as he read aloud from the Scout *Handbook*. But I didn't know how to put all that into words. Not for those faces out of *The New York Times* financial section. I tried with something I felt they would understand.

"Well," I said, "Mr. Osterweil lent me three and a half dollars to buy a new shirt and a merit-badge sash."

"You say he lent you the money?"

"Yes, sir."

"You're sure he didn't give it to you as a present?"

"No, sir," I said. "I paid him back by stacking empties."

"By doing what?"

I explained about Natie's father's grocery store, and the job I'd taken over from Natie.

"Oh, I see," said the man in the middle. He seemed disappointed in my answer. "Just a moment, please."

Now both the man on the right and the man on the left leaned forward. There was a whispered conference.

"Good point," the man in the middle said finally, and the other two leaned back. "I'm now going to ask you something very important," he said to me. "Please think carefully before you answer, and please answer with complete honesty, on your honor as a Scout. Will you do that?"

"Yes, sir," I said.

"On your honor as a Scout, remember."

"Yes, sir."

"Has Mr. Osterweil ever made any attempt to molest you?"

I thought that over. Not because I didn't understand the question. I knew what the word "molest" meant. Miss Marine, my English teacher, had said more than once that I had the best vocabulary in her class. But I was here for a purpose, and that was to keep Mr. Osterweil as our Scoutmaster. Just saying no, he had never molested me, was not enough. I had to do better than that.

"No, sir, he never did," I said. "Just the opposite."

"How do you mean, just the opposite."

"Mr. Osterweil is very friendly."

"In what way?"

I knew it sounded a little silly, but I wanted to counteract that crack about molesting, which I knew had come out of that bastard McCabe's letter, so I said, "Mr. Osterweil puts his arms around us."

"He does, does he?"

"Yes, sir."

Again the heads on the left and right joined the one in the middle for a hurried conference, but this time I wasn't worried. I could tell from the excitement in the unintelligible whispers that I had given the right answer. The heads separated.

"Could you . . ." the man in the middle said, then paused and cleared his throat. "On your word of honor now, as a Scout, tell us how often — and yes, with whom, any particular boys? — does Mr. Osterweil put his arms around you?"

I thought about how proud and happy Mr. Osterweil was when any one of us did something good. Like when we won the rally. Or like when I was made Senior Patrol Leader.

"Oh, he does it a lot," I said. "All the time. He likes all of us."

They didn't bother to call Natie in; that was the end of the interview. It was also the end of Mr. Osterweil, but I didn't know that at the mo-

ment. Even when I found out, three days later, I didn't put it all together. I merely thought, through the pain that was to turn into all
those years of hatred for Jazz L. McCabe, I merely thought stupidly:
What a funny way to become a part of history. The Empire State Building, completed only a few months before, had just been opened to the
public. Mr. Osterweil had gone up to the hundred-and-second floor
and jumped from the observation deck.

1969

JOE GORES

....

Goodbye, Pops

I GOT OFF THE GREYHOUND and stopped to draw icy Minnesota air
into my lungs. A bus had brought me from Springfield, Illinois to Chicago the day before; a second bus had brought me here. I caught my
passing reflection in the window of the old-fashioned depot — a tall,
hard man with a white and savage face, wearing an ill-fitting overcoat.
I caught another reflection, too, one that froze my guts: a cop in uniform. Could they already know it was someone else in that burned-out
car?

Then the cop turned away, chafing his arms with gloved hands
through his blue stormcoat, and I started breathing again. I went
quickly over to the cab line. Only two hackies were waiting there; the
front one rolled down his window as I came up.

"You know the Miller place north of town?" I asked.

He looked me over. "I know it. Five bucks — now."

I paid him from the money I'd rolled a drunk for in Chicago and
eased back against the rear seat. As he nursed the cab out into ice-rimed
Second Street, my fingers gradually relaxed from their rigid chopping
position. I deserved to go back inside if I let a clown like this get to me.

"Old man Miller's pretty sick, I hear." He half-turned to catch me
with a corner of an eye. "You got business with him?"

"Yeah. My own."

That ended that conversation. It bothered me that Pops was sick
enough for this clown to know about it; but maybe my brother Rod being vice-president at the bank would explain that. There was a lot of
new construction and a freeway west of town with a tricky overpass to
the old county road. A mile beyond a new sub-division were the 200
wooded hilly acres I knew so well.

After my break from the Federal pen at Terre Haute, Indiana two days before, I'd gotten outside their cordon through woods like these. I'd gone out in a prison truck, in a pail of swill meant for the prison farm pigs, had headed straight west, across the Illinois line. I'm good in open country, even when I'm in prison condition, so by dawn I was in a hayloft near Paris, Illinois, some 20 miles from the pen. You can do what you have to do.

The cabby stopped at the foot of the private road, looking dubious. "Listen, buddy, I know that's been plowed, but it looks damned icy. If I try it and go into the ditch —"

"I'll walk from here."

I waited beside the road until he'd driven away, then let the north wind chase me up the hill and into the leafless hardwoods. The cedars that Pops and I had put in as a windbreak were taller and fuller; rabbit paths were pounded hard into the snow under the barbed-wire tangles of wild raspberry bushes. Under the oaks at the top of the hill was the old-fashioned, two-story house, but I detoured to the kennels first. The snow was deep and undisturbed inside them. No more foxhounds. No cracked corn in the bird feeder outside the kitchen window, either. I rang the front doorbell.

My sister-in-law Edwina, Rod's wife, answered it. She was three years younger than my 35, and she'd started wearing a girdle.

"Good Lord! Chris!" Her mouth tightened. "We didn't —"

"Ma wrote that the old man was sick." She'd written, all right. *Your father is very ill. Not that you have ever cared if any of us lives or dies. . . .* And then Edwina decided that my tone of voice had given her something to get righteous about.

"I'm amazed you'd have the nerve to come here, even if they did let you out on parole or something." So nobody had been around asking yet. "If you plan to drag the family name through the mud again —"

I pushed by her into the hallway. "What's wrong with the old man?" I called him Pops only inside myself, where no one could hear.

"He's dying, that's what's wrong with him."

She said it with a sort of baleful pleasure. It hit me, but I just grunted and went by into the living room. Then the old girl called down from the head of the stairs.

"Eddy? What — who is it?"

"Just — a salesman, Ma. He can wait until Doctor's gone."

Doctor. As if some damned croaker was generic physician all by himself. When he came downstairs Edwina tried to hustle him out before I could see him, but I caught his arm as he poked it into his overcoat sleeve.

"Like to see you a minute, Doc. About old man Miller."

He was nearly six feet, a couple of inches shorter than me, but outweighing me by 40 pounds. He pulled his arm free.

"Now see here, fellow —"

I grabbed his lapels and shook him, just enough to pop a button off his coat and put his glasses awry on his nose. His face got red.

"Old family friend, Doc." I jerked a thumb at the stairs. "What's the story?"

It was dumb, dumb as hell, of course, asking him; at any second the cops would figure out that the farmer in the burned-out car wasn't me after all. I'd dumped enough gasoline before I struck the match so they couldn't lift prints off anything except the shoe I'd planted: but they'd make him through dental charts as soon as they found out he was missing. When they did they'd come here asking questions, and then the croaker would realize who I was. But I wanted to know whether Pops was as bad off as Edwina said he was, and I've never been a patient man.

The croaker straightened his suitcoat, striving to regain lost dignity. "He — Judge Miller is very weak, too weak to move. He probably won't last out the week." His eyes searched my face for pain, but there's nothing like a Federal pen to give you control. Disappointed, he said, "His lungs. I got to it much too late, of course. He's resting easily."

I jerked the thumb again. "You know your way out."

Edwina was at the head of the stairs, her face righteous again. It seems to run in the family, even with those who married in. Only Pops and I were short of it.

"Your father is very ill. I forbid you —"

"Save it for Rod; it might work on him."

In the room I could see the old man's arm hanging limply over the edge of the bed, with smoke from the cigarette between his fingers running up to the ceiling in a thin unwavering blue line. The upper arm, which once had measured an honest 18 and had swung his small tight fist against the side of my head a score of times, could not even hold a cigarette up in the air. It gave me the same wrench as finding a good foxhound that's gotten mixed up with a bobcat.

The old girl came out of her chair by the foot of the bed, her face blanched. I put my arms around her. "Hi, Ma," I said. She was rigid inside my embrace, but I knew she wouldn't pull away. Not there in Pops' room.

He had turned his head at my voice. The light glinted from his silky white hair. His eyes, translucent with imminent death, were the pure, pale blue of birch shadows on fresh snow.

"Chris," he said in a weak voice. "Son of a biscuit, boy . . . I'm glad to see you."

"You ought to be, you lazy devil," I said heartily. I pulled off my suit jacket and hung it over the back of the chair, and tugged off my tie. "Getting so lazy that you let the foxhounds go!"

"That's enough, Chris." She tried to put steel into it.

"I'll just sit here a little, Ma," I said easily. Pops wouldn't have long, I knew, and any time I got with him would have to do me. She stood in the doorway, a dark indecisive shape; then she turned and went silently out, probably to phone Rod at the bank.

For the next couple of hours I did most of the talking; Pops just lay there with his eyes shut, like he was asleep. But then he started in, going way back, to the trapline he and I had run when I'd been a kid; to the big white-tail buck that followed him through the woods one rutting season until Pops whacked it on the nose with a tree branch. It was only after his law practice had ripened into a judgeship that we began to draw apart; I guess that in my twenties I was too wild, too much what he'd been himself 30 years before. Only I kept going in that direction.

About seven o'clock my brother Rod called from the doorway. I went out, shutting the door behind me. Rod was taller than me, broad and big-boned, with an athlete's frame — but with mush where his guts should have been. He had close-set pale eyes and not quite enough chin, and hadn't gone out for football in high school.

"My wife reported the vicious things you said to her." It was his best give-the-teller-hell voice. "We've talked this over with mother and we want you out of here tonight. We want —"

"*You* want? Until he kicks off it's still the old man's house, isn't it?"

He swung at me then — being Rod, it was a right-hand lead — and I blocked it with an open palm. Then I back-handed him, hard, twice across the face each way, jerking his head from side to side with the slaps and crowding him up against the wall. I could have fouled his groin to bend him over, then driven locked hands down on the back of his neck as I jerked a knee into his face; and I wanted to. The need to get away before they came after me was gnawing at my gut like a weasel in a trap gnawing off his own paw to get loose. But I merely stepped away from him.

"You — you murderous animal!" He had both hands up to his

cheeks like a woman might have done. Then his eyes widened theatrically, as the realization struck him. I wondered why it had taken so long. "You've *broken out*!" he gasped. "*Escaped*! A fugitive from — from justice!"

"Yeah. And I'm staying that way. I know you, kid, all of you. The last thing any of you want is for the cops to take me here." I tried to put his tones into my voice. "*Oh*! The *scandal*!"

"But they'll be after you —"

"They think I'm dead," I said flatly. "I went off an icy road in a stolen car in down-state Illinois, and it rolled and burned with me inside."

His voice was hushed, almost horror-stricken. "You mean — that there *is* a body in the car?"

"Right."

I knew what he was thinking, but I didn't bother to tell him the truth — that the old farmer who was driving me to Springfield, because he thought my doubled-up fist in the overcoat pocket was a gun, hit a patch of ice and took the car right off the lonely country road. He was impaled on the steering post, so I took his shoes and put one of mine on his foot. The other I left, with my fingerprints on it, lying near enough so they'd find it but not so near that it'd burn along with the car. Rod wouldn't have believed the truth anyway. If they caught me, who would?

I said, "Bring me up a bottle of bourbon and a carton of cigarettes. And make sure Eddy and Ma keep their mouths shut if anyone asks about me." I opened the door so Pops could hear. "Well, thanks, Rod. It *is* nice to be home again."

Solitary in the pen makes you able to stay awake easily or snatch sleep easily, whichever is necessary. I stayed awake for the last 37 hours that Pops had, leaving the chair by his bed only to go to the bathroom and to listen at the head of the stairs whenever I heard the phone or the doorbell ring. Each time I thought: *this is it*. But my luck held. If they'd just take long enough so I could stay until Pops went; the second that happened, I told myself, I'd be on my way.

Rod and Edwina and Ma were there at the end, with Doctor hovering in the background to make sure he got paid. Pops finally moved a pallid arm and Ma sat down quickly on the edge of the bed — a small, erect, rather indomitable woman with a face made for wearing a lorgnette. She wasn't crying yet; instead, she looked purely luminous in a way.

"Hold my hand, Eileen." Pops paused for the terrible strength to speak again. "Hold my hand. Then I won't be frightened."

She took his hand and he almost smiled, and shut his eyes. We waited, listening to his breathing get slower and slower and then just stop, like a grandfather clock running down. Nobody moved, nobody spoke. I looked around at them, so soft, so unused to death, and I felt like a marten in a brooding house. Then Ma began to sob.

It was a blustery day with snow flurries. I parked the jeep in front of the funeral chapel and went up the slippery walk with wind plucking at my coat, telling myself for the hundredth time just how nuts I was to stay for the service. By now they *had* to know that the dead farmer wasn't me; by now some smart prison censor *had* to remember Ma's letter about Pops being sick. He was two days dead, and I should have been in Mexico by this time. But it didn't seem complete yet, somehow. Or maybe I was kidding myself, maybe it was just the old need to put down authority that always ruins guys like me.

From a distance it looked like Pops but up close you could see the cosmetics and that his collar was three sizes too big. I felt his hand: it was a statue's hand, unfamiliar except for the thick, slightly down-curved fingernails.

Rod came up behind me and said, in a voice meant only for me, "After today I want you to leave us alone. I want you out of my house."

"Shame on you, brother," I grinned. "Before the will is even read, too."

We followed the hearse through snowy streets at the proper funeral pace, lights burning. Pallbearers wheeled the heavy casket out smoothly on oiled tracks, then set it on belts over the open grave. Snow whipped and swirled from a gray sky, melting on the metal and forming rivulets down the sides.

I left when the preacher started his scam, impelled by the need to get moving, get away, yet impelled by another urgency, too. I wanted something out of the house before all the mourners arrived to eat and guzzle. The guns and ammo already had been banished to the garage, since Rod never had fired a round in his life; but it was easy to dig out the beautiful little .22 target pistol with the long barrel. Pops and I had spent hundreds of hours with that gun, so the grip was worn smooth and the blueing was gone from the metal that had been out in every sort of weather.

Putting the jeep on four-wheel I ran down through the trees to a cut between the hills, then went along on foot through the darkening hardwoods. I moved slowly, evoking memories of Korea to neutralize the icy bite of the snow through my worn shoes. There was a flash of brown as a cotton-tail streaked from under a deadfall toward a rotting woodpile I'd stacked years before. My slug took him in the spine, paralyzing the back legs. He jerked and thrashed until I broke his neck with the edge of my hand.

I left him there and moved out again, down into the small marshy triangle between the hills. It was darkening fast as I kicked at the frozen tussocks. Finally a ringneck in full plumage burst out, long tail fluttering and stubby pheasant wings beating to raise his heavy body. He was quartering up and just a bit to my right, and I had all the time in the world. I squeezed off in mid-swing, knowing it was perfect even before he took that heart-stopping pinwheel tumble.

I carried them back to the jeep; there was a tiny ruby of blood on the pheasant's beak, and the rabbit was still hot under the front legs. I was using headlights when I parked on the curving cemetery drive. They hadn't put the casket down yet, so the snow had laid a soft blanket over it. I put the rabbit and pheasant on top and stood without moving for a minute or two. The wind must have been strong, because I found that tears were burning on my cheeks.

Goodbye, Pops. Goodbye to deer-shining out of season in the hardwood belt across the creek. Goodbye to jump-shooting mallards down in the river bottoms. Goodbye to woodsmoke and mellow bourbon by firelight and all the things that made a part of you mine. The part they could never get at.

I turned away, toward the jeep — and stopped dead. I hadn't even heard them come up. Four of them, waiting patiently as if to pay their respects to the dead. In one sense they were: to them that dead farmer in the burned-out car was Murder One. I tensed, my mind going to the .22 pistol that they didn't know about in my overcoat pocket. Yeah. Except that it had all the stopping power of a fox's bark. If only Pops had run to handguns of a little heavier caliber. But he hadn't.

Very slowly, as if my arms suddenly had grown very heavy, I raised my hands above my head.

1973

HARLAN ELLISON

···

The Whimper of Whipped Dogs

ON THE NIGHT after the day she had stained the louvered window shutters of her new apartment on East 52nd Street, Beth saw a woman slowly and hideously knifed to death in the courtyard of her building. She was one of twenty-six witnesses to the ghoulish scene, and, like them, she did nothing to stop it.

She saw it all, every moment of it, without break and with no impediment to her view. Quite madly, the thought crossed her mind as she watched in horrified fascination, that she had the sort of marvelous line of observation Napoleon had sought when he caused to have constructed at the *Comédie-Française* theaters, a curtained box at the rear, so he could watch the audience as well as the stage. The night was clear, the moon was full, she had just turned off the 11:30 movie on Channel 2 after the second commercial break, realizing she had already seen Robert Taylor in *Westward the Women,* and had disliked it the first time; and the apartment was quite dark.

She went to the window, to raise it six inches for the night's sleep, and she saw the woman stumble into the courtyard. She was sliding along the wall, clutching her left arm with her right hand. Con Ed had installed mercury-vapor lamps on the poles; there had been sixteen assaults in seven months; the courtyard was illuminated with a chill purple glow that made the blood streaming down the woman's left arm look black and shiny. Beth saw every detail with utter clarity, as though magnified a thousand power under a microscope, solarized as if it had been a television commercial.

The woman threw back her head, as if she were trying to scream, but there was no sound. Only the traffic on First Avenue, late cabs foraging for singles paired for the night at Maxwell's Plum and Friday's and

Adam's Apple. But that was over there, beyond. Where *she* was, down there seven floors below, in the courtyard, everything seemed silently suspended in an invisible force-field.

Beth stood in the darkness of her apartment, and realized she had raised the window completely. A tiny balcony lay just over the low sill; now not even glass separated her from the sight; just the wrought-iron balcony railing and seven floors to the courtyard below.

The woman staggered away from the wall, her head still thrown back, and Beth could see she was in her mid-thirties, with dark hair cut in a shag; it was impossible to tell if she was pretty: terror had contorted her features and her mouth was a twisted black slash, opened but emitting no sound. Cords stood out in her neck. She had lost one shoe, and her steps were uneven, threatening to dump her to the pavement.

The man came around the corner of the building, into the courtyard. The knife he held was enormous — or perhaps it only seemed so: Beth remembered a bonehandled fish knife her father had used one summer at the lake in Maine: it folded back on itself and locked, revealing eight inches of serrated blade. The knife in the hand of the dark man in the courtyard seemed to be similar.

The woman saw him and tried to run, but he leaped across the distance between them and grabbed her by the hair and pulled her head back as though he would slash her throat in the next reaper-motion.

Then the woman screamed.

The sound skirled up into the courtyard like bats trapped in an echo chamber, unable to find a way out, driven mad. It went on and on . . .

The man struggled with her and she drove her elbows into his sides and he tried to protect himself, spinning her around by her hair, the terrible scream going up and up and never stopping. She came loose and he was left with a fistful of hair torn out by the roots. As she spun out, he slashed straight across and opened her up just below the breasts. Blood sprayed through her clothing and the man was soaked; it seemed to drive him even more berserk. He went at her again, as she tried to hold herself together, the blood pouring down over her arms.

She tried to run, teetered against the wall, slid sidewise, and the man struck the brick surface. She was away, stumbling over a flower bed, falling, getting to her knees as he threw himself on her again. The knife came up in a flashing arc that illuminated the blade strangely with purple light. And still she screamed.

Lights came on in dozens of apartments and people appeared at windows.

He drove the knife to the hilt into her back, high on the right shoulder. He used both hands.

Beth caught it all in jagged flashes — the man, the woman, the knife, the blood, the expressions on the faces of those watching from the windows. Then lights clicked off in the windows, but they still stood there, watching.

She wanted to yell, to scream, "What are you doing to that woman?" But her throat was frozen, two iron hands that had been immersed in dry ice for ten thousand years clamped around her neck. She could feel the blade sliding into her own body.

Somehow — it seemed impossible but there it was down there, happening somehow — the woman struggled erect and *pulled* herself off the knife. Three steps, she took three steps and fell into the flower bed again. The man was howling now, like a great beast, the sounds inarticulate, bubbling up from his stomach. He fell on her and the knife went up and came down, then again, and again, and finally it was all a blur of motion, and her scream of lunatic bats went on till it faded off and was gone.

Beth stood in the darkness, trembling and crying, the sight filling her eyes with horror. And when she could no longer bear to look at what he was doing down there to the unmoving piece of meat over which he worked, she looked up and around at the windows of darkness where the others still stood — even as she stood — and somehow she could see their faces, bruise-purple with the dim light from the mercury lamps, and there was a universal sameness to their expressions. The women stood with their nails biting into the upper arms of their men, their tongues edging from the corners of their mouths; the men were wild-eyed and smiling. They all looked as though they were at cock fights. Breathing deeply. Drawing some sustenance from the grisly scene below. An exhalation of sound, deep, deep, as though from caverns beneath the earth. Flesh pale and moist.

And it was then that she realized the courtyard had grown foggy, as though mist off the East River had rolled up 52nd Street in a veil that would obscure the details of what the knife and the man were still doing . . . endlessly doing it . . . long after there was any joy in it . . . still doing it . . . again and again . . .

But the fog was unnatural, thick and gray and filled with tiny scintillas of light. She stared at it, rising up in the empty space of the courtyard. Bach in the cathedral, stardust in a vacuum chamber.

Beth saw eyes.

There, up there, at the ninth floor and higher, two great eyes, as surely as night and the moon, there were *eyes*. And — a face? Was that a face, could she be sure, was she imagining it . . . a face? In the roiling vapors of chill fog something lived, something brooding and patient and utterly malevolent had been summoned up to witness what was happening down there in the flower bed. Beth tried to look away, but could not. The eyes, those primal burning eyes, filled with an abysmal antiquity yet frighteningly bright and anxious like the eyes of a child; eyes filled with tomb depths, ancient and new, chasm-filled, burning, gigantic and deep as an abyss, holding her, compelling her. The shadow play was being staged not only for the tenants in their windows, watching and drinking of the scene, but for some *other*. Not on frigid tundra or waste moors, not in subterranean caverns or on some faraway world circling a dying sun, but here, in the city, here the eyes of that *other* watched.

Shaking with the effort, Beth wrenched her eyes from those burning depths up there beyond the ninth floor, only to see again the horror that had brought that *other*. And she was struck for the first time by the awfulness of what she was witnessing, she was released from the immobility that had held her like a coelacanth in shale, she was filled with the blood thunder pounding against the membranes of her mind: she had *stood* there! She had done nothing, nothing! A woman had been butchered and she had said nothing, done nothing. Tears had been useless, tremblings had been pointless, she *had done nothing*!

Then she heard hysterical sounds midway between laughter and giggling, and as she stared up into that great face rising in the fog and chimneysmoke of the night, she heard *herself* making those deranged gibbon noises and from the man below a pathetic, trapped sound, like the whimper of whipped dogs.

She was staring up into that face again. She hadn't wanted to see it again — ever. But she was locked with those smoldering eyes, overcome with the feeling that they were childlike, though she *knew* they were incalculably ancient.

Then the butcher below did an unspeakable thing and Beth reeled with dizziness and caught the edge of the window before she could tumble out onto the balcony; she steadied herself and fought for breath.

She felt herself being looked at, and for a long moment of frozen terror she feared she might have caught the attention of that face up there in the fog. She clung to the window, feeling everything growing faraway and dim, and stared straight across the court. She *was* being watched. Intently. By the young man in the seventh-floor window across from her own apartment. Steadily, he was looking at her. Through the strange fog with its burning eyes feasting on the sight below, he was staring at her.

As she felt herself blacking out, in the moment before unconsciousness, the thought flickered and fled that there was something terribly familiar about his face.

It rained the next day. East 52nd Street was slick and shining with the oil rainbows. The rain washed the dog turds into the gutters and nudged them down and down to the catch-basin openings. People bent against the slanting rain, hidden beneath umbrellas, looking like enormous, scurrying black mushrooms. Beth went out to get the newspapers after the police had come and gone.

The news reports dwelled with loving emphasis on the twenty-six tenants of the building who had watched in cold interest as Leona Ciarelli, 37, of 455 Fort Washington Avenue, Manhattan, had been systematically stabbed to death by Burton H. Wells, 41, an unemployed electrician, who had been subsequently shot to death by two off-duty police officers when he burst into Michael's Pub on 55th Street, covered with blood and brandishing a knife that authorities later identified as the murder weapon.

She had thrown up twice that day. Her stomach seemed incapable of retaining anything solid, and the taste of bile lay along the back of her tongue. She could not blot the scenes of the night before from her mind; she re-ran them again and again, every movement of that reaper arm playing over and over as though on a short loop of memory. The woman's head thrown back for silent screams. The blood. Those eyes in the fog.

She was drawn again and again to the window, to stare down into the courtyard and the street. She tried to superimpose over the bleak Manhattan concrete the view from her window in Swann House at Bennington: the little yard and another white, frame dormitory; the fantastic apple trees; and from the other window the rolling hills and gorgeous Vermont countryside; her memory skittered through the change of seasons. But there was always concrete and the rain-slick streets; the rain on the pavement was black and shiny as blood.

She tried to work, rolling up the tambour closure of the old rolltop desk she had bought on Lexington Avenue and hunching over the graph sheets of choreographer's charts. But Labanotation was merely a Jackson Pollock jumble of arcane hieroglyphics to her today, instead of the careful representation of eurhythmics she had studied four years to perfect. And before that, Farmington.

The phone rang. It was the secretary from the Taylor Dance Company, asking when she would be free. She had to beg off. She looked at her hand, lying on the graph sheets of figures Laban had devised, and she saw her fingers trembling. She had to beg off. Then she called Guzman at the Downtown Ballet Company, to tell him she would be late with the charts.

"My God, lady, I have ten dancers sitting around in a rehearsal hall getting their leotards sweaty! What do you expect me to do?"

She explained what had happened the night before. And as she told him, she realized the newspapers had been justified in holding that tone against the twenty-six witnesses to the death of Leona Ciarelli. Paschal Guzman listened, and when he spoke again, his voice was several octaves lower, and he spoke more slowly. He said he understood and she could take a little longer to prepare the charts. But there was a distance in his voice, and he hung up while she was thanking him.

She dressed in an argyle sweater vest in shades of dark purple, and a pair of fitted khaki gabardine trousers. She had to go out, to walk around. To do what? To think about other things. As she pulled on the Fred Braun chunky heels, she idly wondered if that heavy silver bracelet was still in the window of Georg Jensen's. In the elevator, the young man from the window across the courtyard stared at her. Beth felt her body begin to tremble again. She went deep into the corner of the box when he entered behind her.

Between the fifth and fourth floors, he hit the *off* switch and the elevator jerked to a halt.

Beth stared at him and he smiled innocently.

"Hi. My name's Gleeson, Ray Gleeson, I'm in 714."

She wanted to demand he turn the elevator back on, by what right did he *presume* to do such a thing, what did he mean by this, turn it on at once or suffer the consequences. That was what she *wanted* to do. Instead, from the same place she had heard the gibbering laughter the night before, she heard her voice, much smaller and much less possessed than she had trained it to be, saying, "Beth O'Neill, I live in 701."

The thing about it, was that *the elevator was stopped*. And she was frightened. But he leaned against the paneled wall, very well dressed, shoes polished, hair combed and probably blown dry with a hand drier, and he *talked* to her as if they were across a table at L'Argenteuil. "You just moved in, huh?"

"About two months ago."

"Where did you go to school? Bennington or Sarah Lawrence?"

"Bennington. How did you know?"

He laughed, and it was a nice laugh. "I'm an editor at a religious book publisher; every year we get half a dozen Bennington, Sarah Lawrence, Smith girls. They come hopping in like grasshoppers, ready to revolutionize the publishing industry."

"What's wrong with that? You sound like you don't care for them."

"Oh, I *love* them, they're marvelous. They think they know how to write better than the authors we publish. Had one darlin' little item who was given galleys of three books to proof, and she rewrote all three. I think she's working as a table-swabber in a Horn & Hardart's now."

She didn't reply to that. She would have pegged him as an anti-feminist, ordinarily, if it had been anyone else speaking. But the eyes. There was something terribly familiar about his face. She was enjoying the conversation; she rather liked him.

"What's the nearest big city to Bennington?"

"Albany, New York. About sixty miles."

"How long does it take to drive there?"

"From Bennington? About an hour and a half."

"Must be a nice drive, that Vermont country, really pretty. They went coed, I understand. How's that working out?"

"I don't know, really."

"You don't know?"

"It happened around the time I was graduating."

"What did you major in?"

"I was a dance major, specializing in Labanotation. That's the way you write choreography."

"It's all electives, I gather. You don't have to take anything required, like sciences, for example." He didn't change tone as he said, "That was a terrible thing last night. I saw you watching. I guess a lot of us were watching. It was a really terrible thing."

She nodded dumbly. Fear came back.

"I understand the cops got him. Some nut, they don't even know why he killed her, or why he went charging into that bar. It was really an awful thing. I'd very much like to have dinner with you one night soon, if you're not attached."

"That would be all right."

"Maybe Wednesday. There's an Argentinian place I know. You might like it."

"That would be all right."

"Why don't you turn on the elevator, and we can go," he said, and smiled again. She did it, wondering why she had stopped the elevator in the first place.

On her third date with him, they had their first fight. It was at a party thrown by a director of television commercials. He lived on the ninth floor of their building. He had just done a series of spots for *Sesame Street* (the letters "U" for Underpass, "T" for Tunnel, lowercase "b" for boats, "c" for cars; the numbers 1 to 6 and the numbers 1 to 20; the words *light* and *dark*) and was celebrating his move from the arena of commercial tawdriness (and its attendant $75,000 a year) to the sweet fields of educational programming (and its accompanying descent into low-pay respectability). There was a logic in his joy Beth could not quite understand, and when she talked with him about it, in a far corner of the kitchen, his arguments didn't seem to parse. But he seemed happy, and his girlfriend, a long-legged ex-model from Philadelphia, continued to drift to him and away from him, like some exquisite undersea plant, touching his hair and kissing his neck, murmuring words of pride and barely submerged sexuality. Beth found it bewildering, though the celebrants were all bright and lively.

In the living room, Ray was sitting on the arm of the sofa, hustling a stewardess named Luanne. Beth could tell he was hustling; he was trying to look casual. When he *wasn't* hustling, he was always intense, about everything. She decided to ignore it, and wandered around the apartment, sipping at a Tanqueray and tonic.

There were framed prints of abstract shapes clipped from a calendar printed in Germany. They were in metal Bonniers frames.

In the dining room a huge door from a demolished building somewhere in the city had been handsomely stripped, teaked and refinished. It was now the dinner table.

A Lightolier fixture attached to the wall over the bed swung out, levered up and down, tipped, and its burnished globe-head revolved a full three hundred and sixty degrees.

She was standing in the bedroom, looking out the window, when she realized *this* had been one of the rooms in which light had gone on, gone off; one of the rooms that had contained a silent watcher at the death of Leona Ciarelli.

When she returned to the living room, she looked around more carefully. With only three or four exceptions — the stewardess, a young married couple from the second floor, a stockbroker from Hemphill, Noyes — *everyone* at the party had been a witness to the slaying.

"I'd like to go," she told him.

"Why, aren't you having a good time?" asked the stewardess, a mocking smile crossing her perfect little face.

"Like all Bennington ladies," Ray said, answering for Beth, "she is enjoying herself most by not enjoying herself at all. It's a trait of the anal retentive. Being here in someone else's apartment, she can't empty ashtrays or rewind the toilet paper roll so it doesn't hang a tongue, and being tightassed, her nature demands we go.

"All right, Beth, let's say our goodbyes and take off. The Phantom Rectum strikes again."

She slapped him and the stewardess's eyes widened. But the smile remained frozen where it had appeared.

He grabbed her wrist before she could do it again. "Garbanzo beans, baby," he said, holding her wrist tighter than necessary.

They went back to her apartment, and after sparring silently with kitchen cabinet doors slammed and the television being tuned too loud, they got to her bed, and he tried to perpetuate the metaphor by fucking her in the ass. He had her on elbows and knees before she realized what he was doing; she struggled to turn over and he rode her bucking and tossing without a sound. And when it was clear to him that she would never permit it, he grabbed her breast from underneath and squeezed so hard she howled in pain. He dumped her on her back, rubbed himself between her legs a dozen times, and came on her stomach.

Beth lay with her eyes closed and an arm thrown across her face. She wanted to cry, but found she could not. Ray lay on her and said nothing. She wanted to rush to the bathroom and shower, but he did not move, till long after his semen had dried on their bodies.

"Who did you date at college?" he asked.

"I didn't date anyone very much." Sullen.

"No heavy makeouts with wealthy lads from Williams and Dartmouth . . . no Amherst intellectuals begging you to save them from creeping faggotry by permitting them to stick their carrots in your sticky little slit?"

"Stop it!"

"Come on, baby, it couldn't all have been knee socks and little round circle-pins. You don't expect me to believe you didn't get a little mouthful of cock from time to time. It's only, what? about fifteen miles to Williamstown? I'm sure the Williams werewolves were down burning the highway to your cunt on weekends; you can level with old Uncle Ray. . . ."

"*Why are you like this?!*" She started to move, to get away from him, and he grabbed her by the shoulder, forced her to lie down again. Then he rose up over her and said, "I'm like this because I'm a New Yorker, baby. Because I live in this fucking city every day. Because I have to play patty-cake with the ministers and other sanctified holy-joe assholes who want their goodness and lightness tracts published by the Blessed Sacrament Publishing and Storm Window Company of 277 Park Avenue, when what I *really* want to do is toss the stupid psalm-suckers out the thirty-seventh-floor window and listen to them quote chapter-and-worse all the way down. Because I've lived in this great big snapping dog of a city all my life and I'm mad as a mudfly, for chrissakes!"

She lay unable to move, breathing shallowly, filled with a sudden pity and affection for him. His face was white and strained, and she knew he was saying things to her that only a bit too much Almadén and exact timing would have let him say.

"What do you expect from me," he said, his voice softer now, but no less intense, "do you expect kindness and gentility and understanding and a hand on *your* hand when the smog burns your eyes? I can't do it, I haven't got it. No one has it in this cesspool of a city. Look around you; what do you think is happening here? They take rats and they put them in boxes and when there are too many of them, some of the little fuckers go out of their minds and start gnawing the rest to death. *It ain't no different here, baby!* It's rat time for everybody in this madhouse. You can't expect to jam as many people into this stone thing as we do, with buses and taxis and dogs shitting themselves scrawny and noise night and day and no money and not enough places to live and no place to go to have a decent think . . . you can't do it without making the time right for some godforsaken other kind of thing to be born! You can't hate everyone around you, and kick every beggar and nigger and *mestizo* shithead, you can't have cabbies stealing from you and taking tips they don't deserve, and then cursing you, you can't walk in the soot till your collar turns black, and your body stinks with the smell of flaking brick and decaying brains, you can't do it without calling up some kind of awful —"

He stopped.

His face bore the expression of a man who has just received brutal word of the death of a loved one. He suddenly lay down, rolled over, and turned off.

She lay beside him, trembling, trying desperately to remember where she had seen his face before.

He didn't call her again, after the night of the party. And when they met in the hall, he pointedly turned away, as though he had given her some obscure chance and she had refused to take it. Beth thought she understood: though Ray Gleeson had not been her first affair, he had been the first to reject her so completely. The first to put her not only out of his bed and his life, but even out of his world. It was as though she were invisible, not even beneath contempt, simply not there.

She busied herself with other things.

She took on three new charting jobs for Guzman and a new group that had formed on Staten Island, of all places. She worked furiously and they gave her new assignments; they even paid her.

She tried to decorate the apartment with a less precise touch. Huge poster blowups of Merce Cunningham and Martha Graham replaced the Brueghel prints that had reminded her of the view looking down the hill toward Williams. The tiny balcony outside her window, the balcony she had steadfastly refused to stand upon since the night of the slaughter, the night of the fog with eyes, that balcony she swept and set about with little flower boxes in which she planted geraniums, petunias, dwarf zinnias, and other hardy perennials. Then, closing the window, she went to give herself, to involve herself in this city to which she had brought her ordered life.

And the city responded to her overtures:

Seeing off an old friend from Bennington, at Kennedy International, she stopped at the terminal coffee shop to have a sandwich. The counter — like a moat — surrounded a center service island that had huge advertising cubes rising above it on burnished poles. The cubes proclaimed the delights of Fun City. *New York Is a Summer Festival,* they said, and *Joseph Papp Presents Shakespeare in Central Park* and *Visit the Bronx Zoo* and *You'll Adore Our Contentious but Lovable Cabbies.* The food emerged from a window far down the service area and moved slowly on a conveyor belt through the hordes of screaming waitresses who slathered the counter with redolent washcloths. The lunchroom had all the charm and dignity of a steel-rolling mill, and approximately the same noise level. Beth ordered a cheeseburger that cost a dollar and a quarter, and a glass of milk.

When it came, it was cold, the cheese unmelted, and the patty of meat resembling nothing so much as a dirty scouring pad. The bun was cold and untoasted. There was no lettuce under the patty.

Beth managed to catch the waitress's eye. The girl approached with an annoyed look. "Please toast the bun and may I have a piece of lettuce?" Beth said.

"We dun' do that," the waitress said, turning half away as though she would walk in a moment.

"You don't do what?"

"We dun' toass the bun here."

"Yes, but I *want* the bun toasted," Beth said firmly.

"An' you got to pay for extra lettuce."

"If I was asking for *extra* lettuce," Beth said, getting annoyed, "I would pay for it, but since there's *no* lettuce here, I don't think I should be charged extra for the first piece."

"We dun' do that."

The waitress started to walk away. "Hold it," Beth said, raising her voice just enough so the assembly-line eaters on either side stared at her. "You mean to tell me I have to pay a dollar and a quarter and I can't get a piece of lettuce or even get the bun toasted?"

"Ef you dun' like it . . ."

"Take it back."

"You gotta pay for it, you order it."

"I said take it back, I don't want the fucking thing!"

The waitress scratched it off the check. The milk cost 27¢ and tasted going-sour. It was the first time in her life that Beth had said *that* word aloud.

At the cashier's stand, Beth said to the sweating man with the felt-tip pens in his shirt pocket, "Just out of curiosity, are you interested in complaints?"

"No!" he said, snarling, quite literally snarling. He did not look up as he punched out 73¢ and it came rolling down the chute.

The city responded to her overtures:

It was raining again. She was trying to cross Second Avenue, with the light. She stepped off the curb and a car came sliding through the red and splashed her. "Hey!" she yelled.

"Eat shit, sister!" the driver yelled back, turning the corner.

Her boots, her legs and her overcoat were splattered with mud. She stood trembling on the curb.

The city responded to her overtures:

She emerged from the building at One Astor Place with her big brief-case full of Laban charts; she was adjusting her rain scarf about her head. A well-dressed man with an attaché case thrust the handle of his umbrella up between her legs from the rear. She gasped and dropped her case.

The city responded and responded and responded.

Her overtures altered quickly.

The old drunk with the stippled cheeks extended his hand and mumbled words. She cursed him and walked on up Broadway past the beaver film houses.

She crossed against the lights on Park Avenue, making hackies slam their brakes to avoid hitting her; she used *that* word frequently now.

When she found herself having a drink with a man who had elbowed up beside her in the singles' bar, she felt faint and knew she should go home.

But Vermont was so far away.

Nights later. She had come home from the Lincoln Center ballet, and gone straight to bed. Lying half-asleep in her bedroom, she heard an alien sound. One room away, in the living room, in the dark, there was a sound. She slipped out of bed and went to the door between the rooms. She fumbled silently for the switch on the lamp just inside the living room, and found it, and clicked it on. A black man in a leather car coat was trying to get *out* of the apartment. In that first flash of light filling the room she noticed the television set beside him on the floor as he struggled with the door, she noticed the police lock and bar had been broken in a new and clever manner *New York* magazine had not yet reported in a feature article on apartment ripoffs, she noticed that he had gotten his foot tangled in the telephone cord that she had requested be extra-long so she could carry the instrument into the bathroom, I don't want to miss any business calls when the shower is running; she noticed all things in perspective and one thing with sharpest clarity: the expression on the burglar's face.

There was something familiar in that expression.

He almost had the door open, but now he closed it, and slipped the police lock. He took a step toward her.

Beth went back, into the darkened bedroom.

The city responded to her overtures.

She backed against the wall at the head of the bed. Her hand fumbled in the shadows for the telephone. His shape filled the doorway, light, all light behind him.

In silhouette it should not have been possible to tell, but somehow she knew he was wearing gloves and the only marks he would leave would be deep bruises, very blue, almost black, with the tinge under them of blood that had been stopped in its course.

He came for her, arms hanging casually at his sides. She tried to climb over the bed, and he grabbed her from behind, ripping her nightgown. Then he had a hand around her neck and he pulled her backward. She fell off the bed, landed at his feet and his hold was broken. She scuttled across the floor and for a moment she had the respite to feel terror. She was going to die, and she was frightened.

He trapped her in the corner between the closet and the bureau and kicked her. His foot caught her in the thigh as she folded tighter, smaller, drawing her legs up. She was cold.

Then he reached down with both hands and pulled her erect by her hair. He slammed her head against the wall. Everything slid up in her sight as though running off the edge of the world. He slammed her head against the wall again, and she felt something go soft over her right ear.

When he tried to slam her a third time she reached out blindly for his face and ripped down with her nails. He howled in pain and she hurled herself forward, arms wrapping themselves around his waist. He stumbled backward and in a tangle of thrashing arms and legs they fell out onto the little balcony.

Beth landed on the bottom, feeling the window boxes jammed up against her spine and legs. She fought to get to her feet, and her nails hooked into his shirt under the open jacket, ripping. Then she was on her feet again and they struggled silently.

He whirled her around, bent her backward across the wrought-iron railing. Her face was turned outward.

They were standing in their windows, watching.

Through the fog she could see them watching. Through the fog she recognized their expressions. Through the fog she heard them breathing in unison, bellows breathing of expectation and wonder. Through the fog.

And the black man punched her in the throat. She gagged and started to black out and could not draw air into her lungs. Back, back, he bent her further back and she was looking up, straight up, toward the ninth floor and higher . . .

Up there: eyes.

The words Ray Gleeson had said in a moment filled with what he had become, with the utter hopelessness and finality of the choice the city had forced on him, the words came back. *You can't live in this city and survive unless you have protection . . . you can't live this way, like rats driven mad, without making the time right for some godforsaken other kind of thing to be born . . . you can't do it without calling up some kind of awful . . .*

God! A new God, an ancient God come again with the eyes and hunger of a child, a deranged blood God of fog and street violence. A God who needed worshippers and offered the choices of death as a victim or life as an eternal witness to the deaths of *other* chosen victims. A God to fit the times, a God of streets and people.

She tried to shriek, to appeal to Ray, to the director in the bedroom window of his ninth-floor apartment with his long-legged Philadelphia model beside him and his fingers inside her as they worshipped in their holiest of ways, to the others who had been at the party that had been Ray's offer of a chance to join their congregation. She wanted to be saved from having to make that choice.

But the black man had punched her in the throat, and now his hands were on her, one on her chest, the other in her face, the smell of leather filling her where the nausea could not. And she understood Ray had *cared*, had wanted her to take the chance offered; but she had come from a world of little white dormitories and Vermont countryside; it was not a real world. *This* was the real world and up there was the God who ruled this world, and she had rejected him, had said no to one of his priests and servitors. *Save me! Don't make me do it!*

She knew she had to call out, to make appeal, to try and win the approbation of that God. *I can't . . . save me!*

She struggled and made terrible little mewling sounds trying to summon the words to cry out, and suddenly she crossed a line, and screamed up into the echoing courtyard with a voice Leona Ciarelli had never known enough to use.

"Him! Take him! Not me! I'm yours, I love you, I'm yours! Take him, not me, please not me, take him, take him, I'm yours!"

And the black man was suddenly lifted away, wrenched off her, and off the balcony, whirled straight up into the fog-thick air in the courtyard, as Beth sank to her knees on the ruined flower boxes.

She was half-conscious, and could not be sure she saw it just that way, but up he went, end over end, whirling and spinning like a charred leaf.

And the form took firmer shape. Enormous paws with claws and shapes that no animal she had ever seen had ever possessed, and the burglar, black, poor, terrified, whimpering like a whipped dog, was stripped of his flesh. His body was opened with a thin incision, and there was a rush as all the blood poured from him like a sudden cloudburst, and yet he was still alive, twitching with the involuntary horror of a frog's leg shocked with an electric current. Twitched, and twitched again as he was torn piece by piece to shreds. Pieces of flesh and bone and half a face with an eye blinking furiously, cascaded down past Beth, and hit the cement below with sodden thuds. And still he was alive, as his organs were squeezed and musculature and bile and shit and skin were rubbed, sandpapered together and let fall. It went on and on, as the death of Leona Ciarelli had gone on and on, and she understood with the blood-knowledge of survivors *at any cost* that the reason the witnesses to the death of Leona Ciarelli had done nothing was not that they had been frozen with horror, that they didn't want to get involved, or that they were inured to death by years of television slaughter.

They were worshippers at a black mass the city had demanded be staged; not once, but a thousand times a day in this insane asylum of steel and stone.

Now she was on her feet, standing half-naked in her ripped nightgown, her hands tightening on the wrought-iron railing, begging to see more, to drink deeper.

Now she was one of them, as the pieces of the night's sacrifice fell past her, bleeding and screaming.

Tomorrow the police would come again, and they would question her, and she would say how terrible it had been, that burglar, and how she had fought, afraid he would rape her and kill her, and how he had fallen, and she had no idea how he had been so hideously mangled and ripped apart, but a seven-storey fall, after all . . .

Tomorrow she would not have to worry about walking in the streets, because no harm could come to her. Tomorrow she could even remove the police lock. Nothing in the city could do her any further evil, because she had made the only choice. She was now a dweller in the city, now wholly and richly a part of it. Now she was taken to the bosom of her God.

She felt Ray beside her, standing beside her, holding her, protecting her, his hand on her naked backside, and she watched the fog swirl up and fill the courtyard, fill the city, fill her eyes and her soul and her heart with its power. As Ray's naked body pressed tightly inside her, she drank deeply of the night, knowing whatever voices she heard from this moment forward would be the voices not of whipped dogs, but those of strong, meat-eating beasts.

At last she was unafraid, and it was so good, so very good *not* to be afraid.

When inward life dries up, when feeling decreases and apathy increases, when one cannot affect or even genuinely touch another person, violence flares up as a daimonic necessity for contact, a mad drive forcing touch in the most direct way possible.

Rollo May, *Love and Will*

1973

ROBERT L. FISH

....

The Wager

I SUPPOSE if I were watching television coverage of the return of a lunar mission and Kek Huuygens climbed out of the command module after splashdown, I shouldn't be greatly surprised. I'd be even less surprised to see Kek hustled aboard the aircraft carrier and given a thorough search by a suspicious Customs official. Kek, you see, is one of those men who turn up at very odd times in unexpected places. Also, he is rated by the customs services of nearly every nation in the world as the most talented smuggler alive. Polish by birth, Dutch by adopted name, the holder of a valid U.S. passport, multilingual, a born sleight-of-hand artist, Kek is an elusive target for the stolid bureaucrat who thinks in terms of hollow shoe heels and suitcases with false bottoms. Now and then over the years, Kek has allowed me to publish a little of his lore in my column. When I came across him last, however, he was doing something very ordinary in a commonplace setting. Under the critical eye of a waiter, he was nursing a beer at a table in that little sunken-garden affair in Rockefeller Center.

Before I got to his table, I tried to read the clues. Kek had a good tan and he looked healthy. But his suit had a shine that came from wear rather than from silk thread. A neat scissors trim didn't quite conceal the fact that his cuffs were frayed. He was not wearing his usual boutonniere.

"I owe you three cognacs from last time — Vaduz, wasn't it — and I'm buying," I said as I sat down.

"You are a man of honor," he said and called to the waiter, naming a most expensive cognac. Then he gave me his wide, friendly smile. "Yes, you have read the signs and they are true — but not for any reasons you might imagine. Sitting before you, you can observe the impoverishment that comes from total success. Failure can be managed, but success can be a most difficult thing to control . . ."

Hidden inside every Kek Huuygens aphorism there is a story somewhere. But if you want it produced, you must pretend complete indifference. "Ah, yes," I said, "failure is something you know in your heart. Success is something that lies in the eye of the beholder. I think —"

"Do you want to hear the story or don't you?" Kek said. "You can't use it in your column, though, I warn you."

"Perhaps in time?"

"Perhaps in time, all barbarous customs regulations will be repealed," he said. "Perhaps the angels will come down to rule the earth. Until then, you and I alone will share this story." That was Kek's way of saying "Wait until things have cooled off."

It all began in Las Vegas (Huuygens said) and was primarily caused by two unfortunate factors: one, that I spoke the word banco aloud and, two, that it was heard. I am still not convinced that the player against me wasn't the world's best card manipulator, but at any rate, I found myself looking at a jack and a nine, while the best I could manage for myself was a six. So I watched my money disappear, got up politely to allow the next standee to take my place and started for the exit. I had enough money in the hotel safe to pay my bill and buy me a ticket back to New York — a simple precaution I recommend to all who never learn to keep quiet in a baccarat game — and a few dollars in my pocket, but my financial position was not one any sensible banker would have lent money against. I was sure something would turn up, as it usually did, and in this case it turned up even faster than usual, because I hadn't even reached the door before I was stopped.

The man who put his hand on my arm did so in a completely friendly manner, and I recalled him as being one of the group standing around the table during the play. There was something faintly familiar about him, but even quite famous faces are disregarded at a baccarat table; one is not there to collect autographs. The man holding my arm was short, heavy, swarthy and of a type to cause instant distaste on the part of any discerning observer. What caught and held my attention was that he addressed me by name — and in French. "M'sieu Huuygens?" he said. To my absolute amazement, he pronounced it correctly. I acknowledged that I was, indeed, M'sieu Kek Huuygens. "I should like to talk with you a moment and to buy you a drink," he said.

"I could use one," I admitted, and I allowed him to lead me into the bar. As we went, I noticed two men who had been standing to one side studying their fingernails; they now moved with us and took up new positions to each side, still studying their nails. One would think that fingernails were a subject that could quickly bore, but apparently not to those two. As I sat down beside my chubby host, I looked at him once more, and suddenly recognition came.

He saw the light come on in the little circle over my head and smiled, showing a dazzling collection of white teeth, a tribute to the art of the dental laboratory.

"Yes," he said, "I am Antoine Duvivier," and waved over a waiter. We ordered and I returned my attention to him. Duvivier, as you must know — even newspapermen listen to the radio, I assume — was the president of the island of St. Michel in the Caribbean, or had been until his loyal subjects decided that presidents should be elected, after which he departed in the middle of the night, taking with him most of his country's treasury. He could see the wheels turning in my head as I tried to see how I could use this information to my advantage, and I must say he waited politely enough while I was forced to give up on the problem. Then he said, "I have watched you play at baccarat."

We received our drinks and I sipped, waiting for him to go on.

"You are quite a gambler, M'sieu Huuygens," he said, "but, of course, you would have to be, in your line of work." He saw my eyebrows go up and added quite coolly, "Yes, M'sieu Huuygens, I have had you investigated, and thoroughly. But please permit me to explain that it was not done from idle curiosity. I am interested in making you a proposition."

I find, in situations like this, the less said the better, so I said nothing.

"Yes," he went on, "I should like to offer you —" He paused, as if reconsidering his words, actually looking embarrassed, as if he were guilty of a *gaffe*. "Let me rephrase that," he said and searched for a better approach. At last he found it. "What I meant was, I should like to make a *wager* with you, a wager I am sure should be most interesting to a gambler such as yourself."

This time, of course, I had to answer, so I said, "Oh?"

"Yes," he said, pleased at my instant understanding. "I should like to wager twenty thousand dollars of my money, against two dollars of yours, that you will *not* bring a certain object from the Caribbean through United States Customs and deliver it to me in New York City."

I must admit I admire bluntness, even though the approach was not particularly unique. "The odds are reasonable," I admitted. "One might even say generous. What type of object are we speaking of?"

He lowered his voice. "It is a carving," he said. "A Tien Tse Huwai, dating back to eight centuries before Christ. It is of ivory and is not particularly large; I imagine it could fit into your coat pocket, although, admittedly, it would be bulky. It depicts a village scene — but you, I understand, are an art connoisseur; you may have heard of it. In translation, its name is *The Village Dance.*" Normally, I can control my features, but my surprise must have shown, for Duvivier went on in the same soft voice. "Yes, I have it. The carving behind that glass case in the St. Michel National Gallery is a copy — a plastic casting, excellently done, but a copy. The original is at the home of a friend in Barbados. I could get it that far, but I was afraid to attempt bringing it the rest of the way; to have lost it would have been tragic. Since then, I have been looking for a man clever enough to get it into the States without being stopped by Customs." He suddenly grinned, those white blocks of teeth almost blinding me. "I am offering ten-thousand-to-one odds that that clever man is *not* you."

It was a cute ploy, but that was not what interested me at the moment.

"M'sieu," I said simply, "permit me a question: I am familiar with the Tien *Village Dance.* I have never seen it, but it received quite a bit of publicity when your National Gallery purchased it, since it was felt — if you will pardon me — that the money could have been used better elsewhere. However, my surprise a moment ago was not that you have the carving; it was at your offer. The Tien, many years in the future, may, indeed, command a large price, but the figure your museum paid when you bought it was, as I recall, not much more than the twenty thousand dollars you are willing to — ah — wager to get it into this country. And that value could only be realized at a legitimate sale, which would be difficult, it seems to me, under the circumstances."

Duvivier's smile had been slowly disappearing as I spoke. Now he was looking at me in disappointment.

"You do not understand, M'sieu," he said, and there was a genuine touch of sadness in his voice at my incogitancy. "To you, especially after your losses tonight, I am sure the sum of twenty thousand dollars seems a fortune, but, in all honesty, to me it is not. I am not interested in the monetary value of the carving; I have no intention of selling it. I simply wish to own it." He looked at me with an expression I have seen many times before — the look of a fanatic, a zealot. A Collector, with a capital C. "You cannot possibly comprehend," he repeated, shaking his head. "It is such an incredibly lovely thing . . ."

Well, of course, he was quite wrong about my understanding, or lack of it; I understood perfectly. For a moment, I almost found myself liking the man; but only for a moment. And a wager is a wager, and I had to admit I had never been offered such attractive odds before in my life. As for the means of getting the carving into the United States, especially from Barbados, I had a thought on that, too. I was examining my idea in greater detail when his voice broke in on me.

"Well?" he asked, a bit impatiently.

"You have just made yourself a bet," I said. "But it will require a little time."

"How much time?" Now that I was committed, the false friendliness was gone from both voice and visage; for all practical purposes, I was now merely an employee.

I thought a moment. "It's hard to say. It depends," I said at last. "Less than two months but probably more than one."

He frowned. "Why so long?" I merely shrugged and reached for my glass. "All right," he said grudgingly. "And how do you plan on getting it through Customs?" My response to this was to smile at him gently, so he gave up. "I shall give you a card to my friend in Barbados, which will release the carving into your care. After that" — he smiled again, but this time it was a bit wolfish for my liking — "our wager will be in effect. We will meet at my apartment in New York."

He gave me his address, together with his telephone number, and then handed me a second card with a scrawl on it to a name in Barbados, and that was that. We drank up, shook hands and I left the bar, pleased to be working again and equally pleased to be quitted of Duvivier, if only for a while.

Huuygens paused and looked at me with his satanic eyebrows tilted sharply. I recognized the expression and made a circular gesture over our glasses, which was instantly interpreted by our waiter. Kek waited until we were served, thanked me gravely and drank. I settled back to listen, sipping. When next Huuygens spoke, however, I thought at first he was changing the subject, but I soon learned this was not the case.

Anyone who says the day of travel by ship has passed (Huuygens went on) has never made an examination of the brochures for Caribbean cruises that fill and overflow the racks of travel agencies. It appears that between sailings from New York and sailings from Port Everglades — not to mention Miami, Baltimore, Norfolk and others — almost everything afloat must be pressed into service to transport those Americans with credit cards and a little free time to the balmy breezes and shimmering sands of the islands. They have trips for all seasons, as well as for every taste and pocketbook. There are bridge cruises to St. Lucia, canasta cruises to Trinidad, golf cruises to St. Croix. There are seven-day cruises to the Bahamas, eight-day cruises to Jamaica, thirteen-day cruises to Martinique; there are even — I was not surprised to see — three-day cruises to nowhere. And it struck me that even though it was approaching summer, a cruise would be an ideal way to travel; it had been one of my principal reasons for requiring so much time to consummate the deal.

So I went to the travel agency in the hotel lobby and was instantly inundated with schedules and pamphlets. I managed to get the reams of propaganda to my room without a bellboy, sat down on the bed and carefully made my selection. When I had my trip laid out to my satisfaction, I descended once again to the hotel lobby and presented my program to the travel agent there. He must have thought I was insane, but I explained I suffered from Widget Syndrome and required a lot of salt air, after which he shrugged and picked up the phone to confirm my reservations through New York. They readily accepted my credit card for the bill — which I sincerely hoped to be able to honor by the time it was presented — and two days later, I found myself in Miami, boarding the *M. V. Andropolis* for a joyous sixteen-day cruise. It was longer than I might have chosen, but it was the only one that fit my schedule and I felt that I had — or would, shortly — earn the rest.

I might as well tell you right now that it was a delightful trip. I should have preferred to have taken along my own feminine companionship, but my finances would not permit it; there are, after all, such hard-cash outlays as bar bills and tips. However, there was no lack of unattached women aboard, some even presentable, and the days — as they say — fairly flew. We had the required rum punch in Ocho Rios, fought off the beggars in Port-au-Prince, visited Bluebeard's Castle in Charlotte Amalie and eventually made it to Barbados.

Barbados is a lovely island, with narrow winding roads that skirt the ocean and cross between the Caribbean and Atlantic shores through high stands of sugar cane that quite efficiently hide any view of approaching traffic; but my rented car and I managed to get to the address I had been given without brushing death more than three or four times. The man to whom I presented the ex-president's card was not in the least perturbed to be giving up the carving; if anything, he seemed relieved to be rid of its responsibility. It was neatly packaged in straw, wrapped in brown paper and tied with twine, and I left it exactly that way as I drove back to the dock through the friendly islanders, all of whom demonstrated their happy, carefree insouciance by walking in the middle of the road.

There was no problem about carrying the package aboard. Other passengers from the M. V. Andropolis were forming a constant line, like ants, to and from the ship, leaving empty-handed to return burdened with Wedgwood, Hummel figures, camera lenses and weirdly woven straw hats that did not fit. I gave up my boarding pass at the gangplank, climbed to my proper deck and locked myself in my stateroom, interested in seeing this carving upon which M'sieu Antoine Duvivier was willing to wager the princely sum of twenty thousand United States dollars.

The paper came away easily enough. I eased the delicate carving from its bed of straw and took it to the light of my desk lamp. At first I was so interested in studying the piece for its authenticity that the true beauty of the carving didn't strike me; but when I finally came to concede that I was, indeed, holding a genuine Tien Tse Huwai in my hands and got down to looking at the piece itself, I had to admit that M'sieu Duvivier, whatever his other failings, was a man of excellent taste. I relished the delicate nuances with which Tien had managed his intricate subject, the warmth he had been able to impart to his cold medium, the humor he had been genius enough to instill in the ivory scene. Each figure in the relaxed yet ritualistic village dance had his own posture, and although there were easily forty or fifty men and women involved, carved with infinite detail on a plaque no larger than six by eight inches and possibly three inches in thickness, there was no sense of crowding. One could allow himself to be drawn into the carving, to almost imagine movement or hear the flutes. I enjoyed the study of the masterpiece for another few minutes and then carefully rewrapped it and tucked it into the air-conditioning duct of my stateroom, pleased that the first portion of my assignment had been completed with such ease. I replaced the grillwork and went upstairs to the bar, prepared to enjoy the remaining three or four days of balmy breezes — if not shimmering sands, since Barbados had been our final port.

The trip back to Miami was enjoyable but uneventful. I lost in the shuffleboard tournament, largely due to a nearsighted partner, but in compensation I picked up a record number of spoons from the bottom of the swimming pool and received in reward, at the captain's party, a crystal ashtray engraved with a design of Triton either coming up or going down for the third time. What I am trying to say is that, all in all, I enjoyed myself completely and the trip was almost compensation for the thorough — and humiliating — search I had to suffer when I finally went through Customs in Miami. As usual, they did everything but disintegrate my luggage, and they handled my person in a manner I normally accept only from young ladies. But at last I was free of Customs — to their obvious chagrin — and I found myself in the street in one piece. So I took myself and my luggage to a hotel for the night.

And the next morning I reboarded the *M. V. Andropolis* for its next trip — in the same cabin — a restful three-day cruise to nowhere . . .

Huuygens smiled at me gently. My expression must have caused the waiter concern — he probably thought I had left my wallet at home — for he hurried over. To save myself embarrassment, I ordered another round and then went back to staring Huuygens.

I see (Kek went on, his eyes twinkling) that intelligence has finally forced its presence upon you. I should have thought it was rather obvious. These Caribbean cruise ships vary their schedules, mixing trips to the islands with these short cruises to nowhere, where they merely wander aimlessly upon the sea and eventually find their way back — some say with considerable luck — to their home port. Since they touch no foreign shore, and since even the ships' shops are closed during these cruises, one is not faced with the delay or embarrassment of facing a Customs agent upon one's return. Therefore, if one were to take a cruise *preceding* a cruise to nowhere and were to be so careless as to inadvertently leave a small object — in the air-conditioning duct of his stateroom, for example — during the turnaround, he could easily retrieve it on the second cruise and walk off the ship with it in his pocket, with no fear of discovery.

Which, of course, is what I did . . .

The flight to New York was slightly anticlimatic, and I called M'sieu Duvivier as soon as I landed at Kennedy. He was most pleasantly surprised, since less than a month had actually elapsed, and said he would expect me as fast as I could get there by cab.

The ex-president of St. Michel lived in a lovely apartment on Central Park South, and as I rode up in the elevator, I thought of how pleasant it must be to have endless amounts of money at one's disposal; but before I had a chance to dwell on that thought too much, we had arrived and I found myself pushing what I still think was a lapis-lazuli doorbell set in a solid-gold frame. It made one want to weep. At any rate, Duvivier himself answered the door, as anxious as any man I have ever seen. He didn't even wait to ask me in or inquire as to my taste in apéritifs.

"You have it?" he asked, staring at my coat pocket.

"Before we go any further," I said, "I should like you to repeat the exact terms of our wager. The *exact* terms, if you please."

He looked at me in irritation, as if I were being needlessly obstructive.

"All right," he said shortly. "I wagered you twenty thousand dollars of my money against two dollars of your that you would *not* bring me a small carving from Barbados through United States Customs and deliver it to me in New York. Is that correct?"

I sighed. "Perfectly correct," I said and reached into my pocket. "You are a lucky man. You won." And I handed him his two dollars . . .

I stared across the table at Huuygens. I'm afraid my jaw had gone slack. He shook his head at me, a bit sad at my lack of comprehension.

"You can't possibly understand," he said, almost petulantly. "It is so incredibly lovely . . ."

1973

JOYCE CAROL OATES

....

Do with Me What You Will

"THEN WHAT?"

"I got very . . . I got very excited and. . . ."

"Did she look at you?"

"Yeah. And it made me want to. . . . It made me want to go after her,
you know, like grab hold of her. . . . Because she was thinking the same
thing. She was afraid of me and she was thinking. . . ."

"She kept looking back at you?"

"Oh, yes, she did. Yes. Back over her shoulder. I got so excited that I
just followed her, I mean I must of followed her, I don't even remember
my legs going. . . . It was just her, looking back over her shoulder at me,
like checking on me, and me following her, just her and me and nobody
else on the street. I never saw nobody else. I just saw her ahead of me,
but I didn't even see her face, I was too excited."

"When did she start to run?"

"Oh, my, I don't know, I. . . . I guess it was by . . . uh . . . that drugstore
there, what is it, some drugstore that. . . . Well, it was closed, of course,
because of the late hour. Uh . . . some name you see all the time. . . ."

"Cunningham's."

"Oh, yes, yes. Cunningham's. But I don't know if I really saw that, Mr.
Morrissey, so clear as that . . . any place at all . . . like I know the neighborhood upward and downward, but I wasn't watching too close at the
time. Because I had my eye on her, you know, to see she couldn't get
away. She was like a fox would be, going fast all of a sudden, and damn
scared. That makes them clever, when they're scared."

"Then she started to run? Where was this?"

"The other side of the drugstore . . . across a street. . . . I don't know the names, but they got them written down, the police. They could tell you."

"I don't want any information from them, I want it from you. The intersection there is St. Ann and Ryan Boulevard. Is that where she started running?"

"If that's what they said. . . ."

"That's what she said. She told them. When she started to run, did you run?"

"Yeah."

"Right away?"

"Yeah, right away."

"Did you start running before she did?"

"No. I don't know."

"But only after she started running . . . ?"

"I think so."

"Did you? After she started running, but not before?"

"Yeah."

"Were there any cars waiting for the light to change at that intersection?"

"I don't know . . . I was in a frenzy. . . . You know how you get, when things happen fast, and you can't pay attention. . . . I. . . . I saw her running and I thought to myself, *You ain't going to get away!* I was almost ready to laugh or to scream out, it was so. . . . It was so high-strung a few minutes for me. . . ."

"Did she run across the street, or out into the street?"

"She . . . uh . . . she started screaming. . . . That was when she started screaming. But it didn't scare me off. She ran out into the middle of the street . . . yeah, I can remember that now . . . out into the middle, where it was very wide. . . . I remember some cars waiting for the light to change, now. But I didn't pay much attention to them then."

"Then what happened?"

"Well, uh, she got out there and something like, like her shoe was broke, the heel was snapped . . . and she was yelling at this guy in a car, that waited for the light to change but then couldn't get away because she was in front of the car. And . . . uh . . . that was a . . . a Pontiac Tempest, a nice green car. . . . And it was a man and a woman, both white. She was yelling for them to let her in. But when she ran around to the side of the car, and grabbed the door handle, well, it was locked, of course, and she couldn't get it open and I was just waiting by the curb to see how it would go . . . and the guy, he just pressed down that accelerator and got the hell out of there. Man, he shot off like a rocket, I had to laugh. And she looked over her shoulder at me where I was waiting, you know, and. . . ."

"Yes, then what?"

"Well, then. Then I, uh, I got her. There wasn't anything to it, she was pretty tired by then, and. . . . I just grabbed her and dragged her back somewhere, you know, the way they said . . . she told them all the things that happened. . . . I can't remember it too clear myself, because I was crazylike, like laughing because I was so high, you know. I wasn't scared, either. I felt like a general or somebody in a movie, where things go right, like I came to the edge of a country or a whole continent, you know, and naturally I wouldn't want the movie to end just yet. . . ."

"But you don't remember everything that happened?"

"I don't know. Maybe. But no. I guess not, I mean. . . . You know how you get in a frenzy. . . ."

"You signed a confession."

"Yeah, I s'pose so. I mean, I wanted to cooperate a little. I figured they had me anyway, and anyway I was still so high, I couldn't come in for a landing. I wasn't scared or anything and felt very good. So I signed it."

"Did they tell you you had the right to call an attorney?"

"Yeah, maybe."

"You had the right to counsel . . . ? Did the police tell you that?"

"*Right to counsel.* . . . Yeah, I heard something like that. I don't know. Maybe I was a little scared. My mouth was bleeding down my neck."

"From being struck?"

"Before they got the handcuffs on me, I was trying to get away. So somebody got me in the face."

"Did it hurt?"

"No, naw. I didn't feel it. I started getting wet, then one of the policemen, in the car, he wiped me off with a rag, because it was getting on him. I don't know if it hurt or not. Later on it hurt. The tooth was loose and I fooled around with it, wiggling it, in jail, and took it out myself; so I wouldn't swallow it or something at night. My whole face swoll up afterward. . . ."

"So you waived your right to counsel?"

"I don't know. I guess so. If they said that, then I did."

"Why did you waive your right to counsel?"

"I don't know."

"Were you pressured into it?"

"What? I don't know. I . . . uh . . . I was mixed up and a little high. . . ."

"Did you say, maybe, that you didn't have any money for a lawyer?"

"Uh . . . yeah. In fact, I did say that, yeah. I did."

"You did?"

"I think so."

"You did say that."

"I think I said it. . . ."

"You told them you couldn't afford a lawyer."

"Yeah."

"And did they say you had the right to counsel anyway? Did they say that if you were indigent, counsel would be provided for you?"

"Indigent . . . ?"

"Yes, indigent. If you didn't have money for a lawyer, you'd be given one anyway. Didn't they explain that to you?"

"What was that . . . ? *In* . . . ?"

"Indigent. They didn't explain that to you, did they?"

"About what?"

"If you were indigent, counsel would be provided for you."

"Indigent. . . ."

"Indigent. Did they use that word? Do you remember it?"

"Well, uh. . . . Lots of words got used. . . . I. . . ."

"Did they use the word *indigent?* Did they explain your situation to you?"

"What situation? . . . I was kind of mixed up and excited and. . . ."

"And they had been banging you around, right? Your tooth was knocked out . . . your face was cut . . . your face swelled up. . . . So you signed a confession, right? After Mrs. Donner made her accusation, you agreed with her, you signed a confession for the police, in order to co-operate with them and not be beaten any more. I think that was a very natural thing to do under the circumstances. Do you know which one of the police hit you?"

"Oh, they all did, they was all scrambling around after me. . . . Damn lucky I didn't get shot. I was fearless, I didn't know shit how close I came to getting killed. Jesus. Never come in for a landing till the next day, I was so high. Pulled the tooth out by the roots and never felt it. But later on it hurt like hell. . . . I couldn't remember much."

"Were you examined by a doctor?"

"No."

"A dentist?"

"Hell, no."

"Let's see your mouth. . . . What about those missing teeth on the side there? What happened to them?"

"Them, they been gone a long time."

"It looks raw there."

"Yeah, well, I don't know. . . . It looks what?"

"It looks sore."

"Well, it might be sore. I don't know. My gums is sore sometimes. They bleed sometimes by themselves."

"What happened to your mouth?"

"I got kicked there. Two, three years back."

"Your mother told me you'd had some trouble back in your neighborhood, off and on, and I see you were arrested for some incidents, but what about some trouble with a girl . . . ? Did you ever get into trouble with a girl?"

"What girl?"

"Your mother says it was a girl in the neighborhood."

"Yeah."

"Yeah what?"

"Yeah, it was a girl, a girl. She never made no trouble for me. Her father was out after me, but he got in trouble himself. So I don't know, I mean, it passed on by. She was. . . . She didn't want no trouble, it was her old man tried to make a fuss. What's my mother been telling you, that old news? That's damn old news; that's last year's news."

"You weren't arrested for rape, were you?"

"No. I tole you, it was only her father; then he had to leave town."

"Before this you've been arrested twice, right? And put on probation twice? And no jail sentence."

"That's a way of looking at it."

"How do you look at it?"

"I hung around a long time waiting to get out . . . waiting for the trial. . . . You know, the trial or the hearing or whatever it was. Then the judge let me go anyway."

"You waited in jail, you mean."

"Sure I waited in jail."

"Why couldn't you get bond?"

"My momma said the hell with me."

"According to the record, you were arrested for theft twice. You pleaded guilty. What about the assault charges?"

"From roughing somebody up? Well, uh, that stuff got put aside. There was a deal made."

"So you got off on probation twice."

"Yeah, that worked out OK."

"You were arrested for the first time when you were nineteen years old, right?"

"If that's what it says."

"That isn't bad. Nineteen years old . . . that's a pretty advanced age for a first offense. . . . And no jail sentence, just probation. Now, tell me, is all this accurate: Your father served a five-year sentence for armed robbery, right? — then he left Detroit? Your mother has been on ADC from 1959 until the present, right? You have four brothers and two sisters, two children are still living at home with your mother, and your sister has a baby herself? — and you don't live at home, but nearby somewhere? And you give her money when you can?"

"Yeah."

"It says here you're unemployed. Were you ever employed?"

"Sure I been employed."

"It isn't down here. What kind of job did you have?"

"How come it ain't down there?"

"I don't know. What kind of job did you have?"

"Look, you write it in yourself, Mr. Morrissey, because I sure was employed. . . . I call that an insult. I was kind of a delivery boy off and on, I could get references to back me up."

"This is just a photostat copy of your files from Welfare; I can't write anything in . . . Where did you work?"

"Some store that's closed up now."

"Whose was it?"

"I disremember the exact name."

"You're unemployed at the present time, at the age of twenty-three?"

"Well, I can't help that. I. . . . Mr. Morrissey, you going to make a deal for me?"

"I won't have to make a deal."

"Huh? Well, that woman is awful mad at me. She's out to get me."

"Don't worry about her."

"In the police station she was half-crazy, she was screaming so. . . . Her clothes was all ripped. I don't remember none of that. The front of her was all blood. Jesus, I don't know, I must of gone crazy or something. . . . When they brought me in, she was already there, waiting, and she took one look at me and started screaming. That was the end."

"She might reconsider, she might think all this over carefully. Don't worry about her. Let me worry about her. In fact, you have no necessary reason to believe that the woman who identified you was the woman you followed and attacked. . . . It might have been another woman. You didn't really see her face. All you know is that she was white, and probably all she knows about her attacker is that he was black. I won't have to make a deal for you. Don't worry about that."

"She's awful mad at me, she ain't going to back down. . . ."

"Let me worry about her. Tell me: How did the police happen to pick you up? Did they have a warrant for your arrest?"

"Hell, no. It was a goddamn asshole accident like a joke. . . . I, uh, I was running away from her, where I left her . . . and . . . and. . . . I just run into the side of the squad car. Like that. Was running like hell and run into the side of the car, where it was parked, without no lights on. So they picked me up like that."

"Because you were running, they picked you up, right?"

"I run into the side of their goddamn fucking car."

"So they got out and arrested you?"

"One of them chased me."

"Did he fire a shot?"

"Sure he fired a shot."

"So you surrendered?"

"I hid somewhere, by a cellar window. But they found me. It was just a goddamn stupid accident. . . . Jesus, I don't know. I must of been flying so high, couldn't see the car where it was parked. They had it parked back from the big street, with the lights out. I saw one of them with a paper cup, some coffee that got spilled down his front, when I banged into the door. He was surprised."

"So they brought you into the station and the woman was brought in also, this Mrs. Donner, and she identified you. Is that it? She took one look at you and seemed to recognize you?"

"Started screaming like hell."

"She identified you absolutely, in spite of her hysterical state?"

"I guess so."

"And you admitted attacking her?"

"I guess so."

"Was that really the correct woman, though? This 'Mrs. Donner' who is accusing you of rape?"

"Huh?"

"Could you have identified her?"

"Me? I don't know. No. I don't know."

"Let's go back to the bar. You said there were three women there, all white women. Did they look alike to you, or what?"

"I don't know."

"Did one of them catch your attention?"

"Maybe. I don't know. One of them . . . she kind of was watching me, I thought. They was all horsing around."

"It was very crowded in the bar? And this woman, this particular woman, looked at you. Did she smile at you?"

"They was all laughing, you know, and if they looked around the place, why, it would seem they was smiling. . . . I don't know which one it was. I'm all mixed up on that."

"Would you say that this woman, let's call her 'Mrs. Donner' temporarily, this woman was behaving in a way that was provocative? She was looking at you or toward you, and at other men?"

"There was a lot of guys in there, black guys, and some white guys, too. I liked the tone of that place. There was a good feeling there. I wasn't drunk, but. . . ."

"Yes, you were drunk."

"Naw, I was high on my own power, I only had a few drinks."

"You were drunk; that happens to be a fact. That's an important fact. Don't forget it."

"I was drunk . . . ?"

"Yes. You were drunk. And a white woman did smile at you, in a bar on Gratiot; let's say it was this 'Mrs. Donner' who is charging you with rape. Do you know anything about her? No. I'll tell you: She's married, separated from her husband, the husband's whereabouts are unknown, she's been on and off welfare since 1964, she worked for a while at Leonard's Downtown, the department store, and was discharged because she evidently took some merchandise home with her . . . and she's been unemployed since September of last year, but without any visible means of support; no welfare. So she won't be able to account for her means of support since September, if that should come up in court."

"Uh. . . . You going to make a deal with them, then?"

"I don't have to make a deal. I told you to let me worry about her. She has to testify against you, and she has to convince a jury that she didn't deserve to be followed by you, that she didn't entice you, she didn't smile at you. She has to convince a jury that she didn't deserve whatever happened to her. . . . She did smile at you?"

"Well, uh, you know how it was . . . a lot of guys crowding around, shifting around. . . . I don't know which one of the women for sure looked at me, there was three of them, maybe they all did . . . or maybe just one . . . or. . . . It was confused. Some guys was buying them drinks and I couldn't get too close, I didn't know anybody there. I liked the tone of the place, but I was on the outside, you know? I was having my own party in my head. Then I saw this one woman get mad and put on her coat —"

"A light-colored coat? An imitation-fur coat?"

"Jesus, how do I know? Saw her put her arm in a sleeve. . . ."

"And she walked out? Alone?"

"Yeah. So I . . . I got very jumpy. . . . I thought I would follow her, you know, just see what happens. . . ."

"But you didn't follow her with the intention of committing rape."

"I. . . ."

"You wanted to talk to her, maybe? She'd smiled at you and you wanted to talk to her?"

"I don't know if. . . ."

"This white woman, whose name you didn't know, had smiled at you. She then left the bar — that is, Carson's Tavern — at about midnight, completely alone, unescorted, and she walked out along the street. Is this true?"

"Yes."

"When did she notice that you were following her?"

"Right away."

"Then what happened?"

"She started walking faster."

"Did she pause or give any sign to you? You mentioned that she kept looking over her shoulder at you —"

"Yeah."

"Then she started to run?"

"Yeah."

"She tried to get someone to stop, to let her in his car, but he wouldn't. He drove away. She was drunk, wasn't she, and screaming at him?"

"She was screaming. . . ."

"She was drunk, too. That happens to be a fact. You were both drunk, those are facts. This 'Mrs. Donner' who is accusing you of rape was drunk at the time. So. . . . The driver in the Pontiac drove away and you approached her. Was it the same woman who had smiled at you in the tavern?"

"I think . . . uh. . . . I don't know. . . ."

"She was the woman from the tavern?"

"That got mad and put her coat on? Sure. She walked out. . . ."

"Did all three women more or less behave in the same manner? They were very loud, they'd been drinking, you really couldn't distinguish between them . . . ?"

"I don't know."

"When you caught up to the woman, what did she say to you?"

"Say? Nothing. No words."

"She was screaming?"

"Oh, yeah."

"What did you say to her?"

"Nothing."

"Could you identify her?"

"I . . . uh. . . . That's where I get mixed up."

"Why?"

"I don't remember no face to her."

"Why not?"

"Must not of looked at it."

"Back in the bar, you didn't look either?"

"Well, yes . . . but I. . . . It's all a smear, like. Like a blur."

"This 'Mrs. Donner' says you threatened to kill her. Is that true?"

"If she says so. . . ."

"No, hell. Don't worry about what she says. What do *you* say?"

"I don't remember."

"*Lay still or I'll kill you.* Did you say that?"

"Is that what they have down?"

"Did you say it? *Lay still or I'll kill you?*"

"That don't sound like me."

"You didn't say anything to her, did you?"

"When? When we was fighting?"

"At any time."

"I don't remember."

"In the confusion of struggling, it isn't likely you said anything to her, is it? — anything so distinct as that? Or maybe it was another man, another black man, who attacked this 'Mrs. Donner' and she's confusing him with you . . . ?"

"Uh. . . ."

"Did you intend to kill her?"

"No."

"What did you have in mind, when you followed her out of the tavern?"

"Oh, you know . . . I was kind of high-strung. . . ."

"She had smiled at you, so you thought she might be friendly? A pretty white woman like that, only twenty-nine years old, with her hair fixed up and a fancy imitation-fur coat, who had smiled at you, a stranger, in a bar . . . ? You thought she might be friendly, wasn't that it?"

"Friendly? Jesus! I never expected no friendship, that's for sure."

"Well, put yourself back in that situation. Don't be so sure. If a white woman smiled at you, and you followed her out onto the street, it would be logical you might expect her to be friendly toward you. Keep your mind clear. You don't have to believe what other people tell you about yourself; you don't have to believe that you assaulted that woman just because she says you did. Things aren't so simple. Did you expect her to fight you off?"

"Don't know."

"If she hadn't fought you, there wouldn't be any crime committed, would there? She resisted you, she provoked you into a frenzy. . . . But don't think about that. I'll think about that angle. I'm the one who's going to question Mrs. Donner, and then we'll see who's guilty of what. . . . But one important thing: Why didn't you tell the police that you really didn't recognize the woman, yourself?"

"Huh? Jesus, they'd of been mad as hell —"

"Yes, they would have been mad, they might have beaten you some more. You were terrified of a further beating. So, of course, you didn't protest, you didn't say anything. Because she's a white woman and you're black. Isn't that the real reason?"

"I don't know."

"There weren't any black men in the station. You were the only black man there. So you thought it would be the safest, most prudent thing to confess to everything, because this white woman and the white police had you, they had you, and you considered yourself fair game. And already you'd been beaten, your mouth was bleeding, and you didn't know you had the right to an attorney, to any help at all. You were completely isolated. They could do anything to you they wanted. . . . Your instincts told you to go along with them, to cooperate. Nobody can blame you for that; that's how you survived. Does any of this sound familiar to you?"

"Some kind of way, yes. . . . Yes, I think so."

"And the police demonstrated their antagonism toward you, their

automatic assumption of your guilt, even though the woman who accused you of rape was a probable prostitute, a woman of very doubtful
reputation who led you on, who enticed you out into the street . . . and
then evidently changed her mind, or became frightened when she saw
how excited you were. Is that it? Why do you think she identified you so
quickly, why was she so certain?"

"Must of seen my face."

"How did she see your face, if you didn't see hers?"

"I saw hers but didn't take it in, you know, I kind of blacked out . . .
she was fighting me off and that drove me wild . . . it was good luck she
stopped, or . . . or something else might of happened. . . . You know how
frenzied you get. There was a streetlight there, and I thought to myself,
She ain't going to forget me."

"Why not?"

"Gave her a good look at my face. My face is important to me."

1978

STEPHEN KING

··

Quitters, Inc.

MORRISON WAS WAITING for someone who was hung up in the air traffic jam over Kennedy International when he saw a familiar face at the end of the bar and walked down.

"Jimmy? Jimmy McCann?"

It was. A little heavier than when Morrison had seen him at the Atlanta Exhibition the year before, but otherwise he looked awesomely fit. In college he had been a little thin, pallid chain smoker buried behind huge horn-rimmed glasses. He had apparently switched to contact lenses.

"Dick Morrison?"

"Yeah. You look great." He extended his hand and they shook.

"So do you," McCann said, but Morrison knew it was a lie. He had been overworking, overeating, and smoking too much. "What are you drinking?"

"Bourbon and bitters," Morrison said. He hooked his feet around a bar stool and lighted a cigarette. "Meeting someone, Jimmy?"

"No. Going to Miami for a conference. A heavy client. Bills six million. I'm supposed to hold his hand because we lost out on a big special next spring."

"Are you still with Crager and Barton?"

"Executive veep now."

"Fantastic! Congratulations! When did all this happen?" He tried to tell himself that the little worm of jealousy in his stomach was just acid indigestion. He pulled out a roll of antacid pills and crunched one in his mouth.

"Last August. Something happened that changed my life." He looked speculatively at Morrison and sipped his drink. "You might be interested."

My God, Morrison thought with an inner wince. Jimmy McCann's got religion.

"Sure," he said, and gulped at his drink when it came.

"I wasn't in very good shape," McCann said. "Personal problems with Sharon, my dad died — heart attack — and I'd developed this hacking cough. Bobby Crager dropped by my office one day and gave me a fatherly little pep talk. Do you remember what those are like?"

"Yeah." He had worked at Crager and Barton for eighteen months before joining the Morton Agency. "Get your butt in gear or get your butt out."

McCann laughed. "You know it. Well, to put the capper on it, the doc told me I had an incipient ulcer. He told me to quit smoking." McCann grimaced. "Might as well tell me to quit breathing."

Morrison nodded in perfect understanding. Nonsmokers could afford to be smug. He looked at his own cigarette with distaste and stubbed it out, knowing he would be lighting another in five minutes.

"Did you quit?" he asked.

"Yes, I did. At first I didn't think I'd be able to — I was cheating like hell. Then I met a guy who told me about an outfit over on Forty-sixth Street. Specialists. I said what do I have to lose and went over. I haven't smoked since."

Morrison's eyes widened. "What did they do? Fill you full of some drug?"

"No." He had taken out his wallet and was rummaging through it. "Here it is. I knew I had one kicking around." He laid a plain white business card on the bar between them.

QUITTERS, INC.

Stop Going Up in Smoke!

237 East 46th Street

Treatments by Appointment

"Keep it, if you want," McCann said. "They'll cure you. Guaranteed."

"How?"

"I can't tell you," McCann said.

"Huh? Why not?"

"It's part of the contract they make you sign. Anyway, they tell you how it works when they interview you."

"You signed a *contract?*"

McCann nodded.

"And on the basis of that —"

"Yep." He smiled at Morrison, who thought: Well, it's happened. Jim McCann has joined the smug bastards.

"Why the great secrecy if this outfit is so fantastic? How come I've never seen any spots on TV, billboards, magazine ads —"

"They get all the clients they can handle by word of mouth."

"You're an advertising man, Jimmy. You can't believe that."

"I do," McCann said. "They have a ninety-eight percent cure rate."

"Wait a second," Morrison said. He motioned for another drink and lit a cigarette. "Do these guys strap you down and make you smoke until you throw up?"

"No."

"Give you something so that you get sick every time you light —"

"No, it's nothing like that. Go and see for yourself." He gestured at Morrison's cigarette. "You don't really like that, do you?"

"Nooo, but —"

"Stopping really changed things for me," McCann said. "I don't suppose it's the same for everyone, but with me it was just like dominoes falling over. I felt better and my relationship with Sharon improved. I had more energy, and my job performance picked up."

"Look, you've got my curiosity aroused. Can't you just —"

"I'm sorry, Dick. I really can't talk about it." His voice was firm.

"Did you put on any weight?"

For a moment he thought Jimmy McCann looked almost grim. "Yes. A little too much, in fact. But I took it off again. I'm about right now. I was skinny before."

"Flight 206 now boarding at Gate 9," the loudspeaker announced.

"That's me," McCann said, getting up. He tossed a five on the bar. "Have another, if you like. And think about what I said, Dick. Really." And then he was gone, making his way through the crowd to the escalators. Morrison picked up the card, looked at it thoughtfully, then tucked it away in his wallet and forgot it.

The card fell out of his wallet and onto another bar a month later. He had left the office early and had come here to drink the afternoon away. Things had not been going well at the Morton Agency. In fact, things were bloody horrible.

He gave Henry a ten to pay for his drink, then picked up the small card and reread it — 237 East Forty-sixth Street was only two blocks over; it was a cool, sunny October day outside, and maybe, just for chuckles —

When Henry brought his change, he finished his drink and then went for a walk.

Quitters, Inc., was in a new building where the monthly rent on the office space was probably close to Morrison's yearly salary. From the directory in the lobby, it looked to him like their offices took up one whole floor, and that spelled money. Lots of it.

He took the elevator up and stepped off into a lushly carpeted foyer and from there into a gracefully appointed reception room with a wide window that looked out on the scurrying bugs below. Three men and one woman sat in the chairs along the walls, reading magazines. Business types, all of them. Morrison went to the desk.

"A friend gave me this," he said, passing the card to the receptionist. "I guess you'd say he's an alumnus."

She smiled and rolled a form into her typewriter. "What is your name, sir?"

"Richard Morrison."

Clack-clackety-clack. But very muted clacks; the typewriter was an IBM.

"Your address?"

"Twenty-nine Maple Lane, Clinton, New York."

"Married?"

"Yes."

"Children?"

"One." He thought of Alvin and frowned slightly. "One" was the wrong word. "A half" might be better. His son was mentally retarded and lived at a special school in New Jersey.

"Who recommended us to you, Mr. Morrison?"

"An old school friend. James McCann."

"Very good. Will you have a seat? It's been a very busy day."

"All right."

He sat between the woman, who was wearing a severe blue suit, and a young executive type wearing a herringbone jacket and modish sideburns. He took out his pack of cigarettes, looked around, and saw there were no ashtrays.

He put the pack away again. That was all right. He would see this little game through and then light up while he was leaving. He might even tap some ashes on their maroon shag rug if they made him wait long enough. He picked up a copy of *Time* and began to leaf through it.

He was called a quarter of an hour later, after the woman in the blue suit. His nicotine center was speaking quite loudly now. A man who had come in after him took out a cigarette case, snapped it open, saw there were no ashtrays, and put it away — looking a little guilty, Morrison thought. It made him feel better.

At last the receptionist gave him a sunny smile and said, "Go right in, Mr. Morrison."

Morrison walked through the door beyond her desk and found himself in an indirectly lit hallway. A heavyset man with white hair that looked phony shook his hand, smiled affably, and said, "Follow me, Mr. Morrison."

He led Morrison past a number of closed, unmarked doors and then opened one of them about halfway down the hall with a key. Beyond the door was an austere little room walled with drilled white cork panels. The only furnishings were a desk with a chair on either side. There was what appeared to be a small oblong window in the wall behind the desk, but it was covered with a short green curtain. There was a picture on the wall to Morrison's left — a tall man with iron-gray hair. He was holding a sheet of paper in one hand. He looked vaguely familiar.

"I'm Vic Donatti," the heavyset man said. "If you decide to go ahead with our program, I'll be in charge of your case."

"Pleased to know you," Morrison said. He wanted a cigarette very badly.

"Have a seat."

Donatti put the receptionist's form on the desk, and then drew another form from the desk drawer. He looked directly into Morrison's eyes. "Do you want to quit smoking?"

Morrison cleared his throat, crossed his legs, and tried to think of a way to equivocate. He couldn't. "Yes," he said.

"Will you sign this?" He gave Morrison the form. He scanned it quickly. The undersigned agrees not to divulge the methods or techniques or et cetera, et cetera.

"Sure," he said, and Donatti put a pen in his hand. He scratched his name, and Donatti signed below it. A moment later the paper disappeared back into the desk drawer. Well, he thought ironically, I've taken the pledge. He had taken it before. Once it had lasted for two whole days.

"Good," Donatti said. "We don't bother with propaganda here, Mr. Morrison. Questions of health or expense or social grace. We have no interest in why you want to stop smoking. We are pragmatists."

"Good," Morrison said blankly.

"We employ no drugs. We employ no Dale Carnegie people to sermonize you. We recommend no special diet. And we accept no payment until you have stopped smoking for one year."

"My God," Morrison said.

"Mr. McCann didn't tell you that?"

"No."

"How is Mr. McCann, by the way? Is he well?"

"He's fine."

"Wonderful. Excellent. Now . . . just a few questions, Mr. Morrison. These are somewhat personal, but I assure you that your answers will be held in strictest confidence."

"Yes?" Morrison asked noncommittally.

"What is your wife's name?"

"Lucinda Morrison. Her maiden name was Ramsey."

"Do you love her?"

Morrison looked up sharply, but Donatti was looking at him blandly. "Yes, of course," he said.

"Have you ever had marital problems? A separation, perhaps?"

"What has that got to do with kicking the habit?" Morrison asked. He sounded a little angrier than he had intended, but he wanted — hell, he *needed* — a cigarette.

"A great deal," Donatti said. "Just bear with me."

"No. Nothing like that." Although things *had* been a little tense just lately.

"You just have the one child?"

"Yes. Alvin. He's in a private school."

"And which school is it?"

"That," Morrison said grimly, "I'm not going to tell you."

"All right," Donatti said agreeably. He smiled disarmingly at Morrison. "All your questions will be answered tomorrow at your first treatment."

"How nice," Morrison said, and stood.

"One final question," Donatti said. "You haven't had a cigarette for over an hour. How do you feel?"

"Fine," Morrison lied. "Just fine."

"Good for you!" Donatti exclaimed. He stepped around the desk and opened the door. "Enjoy them tonight. After tomorrow, you'll never smoke again."

"Is that right?"

"Mr. Morrison," Donatti said solemnly, "we guarantee it."

He was sitting in the outer office of Quitters, Inc., the next day promptly at three. He had spent most of the day swinging between skipping the appointment the receptionist had made for him on the way out and going in a spirit of mulish cooperation — *Throw your best pitch at me, buster.*

In the end, something Jimmy McCann had said convinced him to keep the appointment — *It changed my whole life.* God knew his own life could do with some changing. And then there was his own curiosity. Before going up in the elevator, he smoked a cigarette down to the filter. Too damn bad if it's the last one, he thought. It tasted horrible.

The wait in the outer office was shorter this time. When the receptionist told him to go in, Donatti was waiting. He offered his hand and smiled, and to Morrison the smile looked almost predatory. He began to feel a little tense, and that made him want a cigarette.

"Come with me," Donatti said, and led the way down to the small room. He sat behind the desk again, and Morrison took the other chair.

"I'm very glad you came," Donatti said. "A great many prospective clients never show up again after the initial interview. They discover they don't want to quit as badly as they thought. It's going to be a pleasure to work with you on this."

"When does the treatment start?" Hypnosis, he was thinking. It must be hypnosis.

"Oh, it already has. It started when we shook hands in the hall. Do you have cigarettes with you, Mr. Morrison?"

"Yes."

"May I have them, please?"

Shrugging, Morrison handed Donatti his pack. There were only two or three left in it, anyway.

Donatti put the pack on the desk. Then, smiling into Morrison's eyes, he curled his right hand into a fist and began to hammer it down on the pack of cigarettes, which twisted and flattened. A broken cigarette end flew out. Tobacco crumbs spilled. The sound of Donatti's fist was very loud in the closed room. The smile remained on his face in spite of the

force of the blows, and Morrison was chilled by it. Probably just the effect they want to inspire, he thought.

At last Donatti ceased pounding. He picked up the pack, a twisted
and battered ruin. "You wouldn't believe the pleasure that gives me," he
said, and dropped the pack into the wastebasket. "Even after three years
in the business, it still pleases me."

"As a treatment, it leaves something to be desired," Morrison said
mildly. "There's a newsstand in the lobby of this very building. And
they sell all brands."

"As you say," Donatti said. He folded his hands. "Your son, Alvin
Dawes Morrison, is in the Paterson School for Handicapped Children.
Born with cranial brain damage. Tested IQ of 46. Not quite in the edu-
cable retarded category. Your wife —"

"How did you find that out?" Morrison barked. He was startled and
angry. "You've got no goddamn right to go poking around my —"

"We know a lot about you," Donatti said smoothly. "But, as I said, it
will all be held in strictest confidence."

"I'm getting out of here," Morrison said thinly. He stood up.

"Stay a bit longer."

Morrison looked at him closely. Donatti wasn't upset. In fact, he
looked a little amused. The face of a man who has seen this reaction
scores of times — maybe hundreds.

"All right. But it better be good."

"Oh, it is." Donatti leaned back. "I told you we were pragmatists here.
As pragmatists, we have to start by realizing how difficult it is to cure an
addiction to tobacco. The relapse rate is almost eighty-five percent. The
relapse rate for heroin addicts is lower than that. It is an extraordinary
problem. *Extraordinary.*"

Morrison glanced into the wastebasket. One of the cigarettes, although twisted, still looked smokeable. Donatti laughed good-
naturedly, reached into the wastebasket, and broke it between his
fingers.

"State legislatures sometimes hear a request that the prison systems
do away with the weekly cigarette ration. Such proposals are invariably
defeated. In a few cases where they have passed, there have been fierce
prison riots. *Riots,* Mr. Morrison. Imagine it."

"I," Morrison said, "am not surprised."

"But consider the implications. When you put a man in prison you
take away any normal sex life, you take away his liquor, his politics, his

freedom of movement. No riots — or few in comparison to the number of prisons. But when you take away his *cigarettes* — wham! bam!" He slammed his fist on the desk for emphasis.

"During World War I, when no one on the German home front could get cigarettes, the sight of German aristocrats picking butts out of the gutter was a common one. During World War II, many American women turned to pipes when they were unable to obtain cigarettes. A fascinating problem for the true pragmatist, Mr. Morrison."

"Could we get to the treatment?"

"Momentarily. Step over here, please." Donatti had risen and was standing by the green curtains Morrison had noticed yesterday. Donatti drew the curtains, discovering a rectangular window that looked into a bare room. No, not quite bare. There was a rabbit on the floor, eating pellets out of a dish.

"Pretty bunny," Morrison commented.

"Indeed. Watch him." Donatti pressed a button by the windowsill. The rabbit stopped eating and began to hop about crazily. It seemed to leap higher each time its feet struck the floor. Its fur stood out spikily in all directions. Its eyes were wild.

"Stop that! You're electrocuting him!"

Donatti released the button. "Far from it. There's a very low-yield charge in the floor. Watch the rabbit, Mr. Morrison!"

The rabbit was crouched about ten feet away from the dish of pellets. His nose wriggled. All at once he hopped away into a corner.

"If the rabbit gets a jolt often enough while he's eating," Donatti said, "he makes the association very quickly. Eating causes pain. Therefore, he won't eat. A few more shocks, and the rabbit will starve to death in front of his food. It's called aversion training."

Light dawned in Morrison's head.

"No, thanks." He started for the door.

"Wait, please, Mr. Morrison."

Morrison didn't pause. He grasped the doorknob . . . and felt it slip solidly through his hand. "Unlock this."

"Mr. Morrison, if you'll just sit down —"

"Unlock this door or I'll have the cops on you before you can say Marlboro Man."

"*Sit down.*" The voice was cold as shaved ice.

Morrison looked at Donatti. His brown eyes were muddy and frightening. My God, he thought, I'm locked in here with a psycho. He licked his lips. He wanted a cigarette more than he ever had in his life.

"Let me explain the treatment in more detail," Donatti said.

"You don't understand," Morrison said with counterfeit patience. "I don't want the treatment. I've decided against it."

"No, Mr. Morrison. *You're* the one who doesn't understand. You don't have any choice. When I told you the treatment had already begun, I was speaking the literal truth. I would have thought you'd tipped to that by now."

"You're crazy," Morrison said wonderingly.

"No. Only a pragmatist. Let me tell you all about the treatment."

"Sure," Morrison said. "As long as you understand that as soon as I get out of here I'm going to buy five packs of cigarettes and smoke them all the way to the police station." He suddenly realized he was biting his thumbnail, sucking on it, and made himself stop.

"As you wish. But I think you'll change your mind when you see the whole picture."

Morrison said nothing. He sat down again and folded his hands.

"For the first month of the treatment, our operatives will have you under constant supervision," Donatti said. "You'll be able to spot some of them. Not all. But they'll always be with you. *Always.* If they see you smoke a cigarette, I get a call."

"And I suppose you bring me here and do the old rabbit trick," Morrison said. He tried to sound cold and sarcastic, but he suddenly felt horribly frightened. This was a nightmare.

"Oh, no," Donatti said. "Your wife gets the rabbit trick, not you."

Morrison looked at him dumbly.

Donatti smiled. "You," he said, "get to watch."

After Donatti let him out, Morrison walked for over two hours in a complete daze. It was another fine day, but he didn't notice. The monstrousness of Donatti's smiling face blotted out all else.

"You see," he had said, "a pragmatic problem demands pragmatic solutions. You must realize we have your best interests at heart."

Quitters, Inc., according to Donatti, was a sort of foundation — a nonprofit organization begun by the man in the wall portrait. The gentleman had been extremely successful in several family businesses — including slot machines, massage parlors, numbers, and a brisk (although clandestine) trade between New York and Turkey. Mort "Three-Fingers" Minelli had been a heavy smoker — up in the three-pack-a-day range. The paper he was holding in the picture was a doctor's diagnosis: lung cancer. Mort had died in 1970, after endowing Quitters, Inc., with family funds.

"We try to keep as close to breaking even as possible," Donatti had said. "But we're more interested in helping our fellow man. And of course, it's a great tax angle."

The treatment was chillingly simple. A first offense and Cindy would be brought to what Donatti called "the rabbit room." A second offense, and Morrison would get the dose. On a third offense, both of them would be brought in together. A fourth offense would show grave cooperation problems and would require sterner measures. An operative would be sent to Alvin's school to work the boy over.

"Imagine," Donatti said, smiling, "how horrible it will be for the boy. He wouldn't understand it even if someone explained. He'll only know someone is hurting him because Daddy was bad. He'll be very frightened."

"You bastard," Morrison said helplessly. He felt close to tears. "You dirty, filthy bastard."

"Don't misunderstand," Donatti said. He was smiling sympathetically. "I'm sure it won't happen. Forty percent of our clients never have more than three falls from grace. Those are reassuring figures, aren't they?"

Morrison didn't find them reassuring. He found them terrifying.

"Of course, if you transgress a *fifth* time —"

"What do you mean?"

Donatti beamed. "The room for you and your wife, a second beating for your son, and a beating for your wife."

Morrison, driven beyond the point of rational consideration, lunged over the desk at Donatti. Donatti moved with amazing speed for a man who had apparently been completely relaxed. He shoved the chair backward and drove both of his feet over the desk and into Morrison's belly. Gagging and coughing, Morrison staggered backward.

"Sit down, Mr. Morrison," Donatti said benignly. "Let's talk this over like rational men."

When he could catch his breath, Morrison did as he was told. Nightmares had to end sometime, didn't they?

Quitters, Inc., Donatti had explained further, operated on a ten-step punishment scale. Steps six, seven, and eight consisted of further trips to the rabbit room (and increased voltage) and more serious beating. The ninth step would be the breaking of his son's arms.

"And the tenth?" Morrison asked, his mouth dry.

Donatti shook his head sadly. "Then we give up, Mr. Morrison. You become part of the unregenerate two percent."

"You really give up?"

"In a manner of speaking." He opened one of the desk drawers and laid a silenced .45 on the desk. He smiled into Morrison's eyes. "But even the unregenerate two percent never smoke again. We guarantee it."

The Friday Night Movie was *Bullitt*, one of Cindy's favorites, but after an hour of Morrison's mutterings and fidgetings, her concentration was broken.

"What's the matter with you?" she asked during station identification.

"Nothing . . . everything," he growled. "I'm giving up smoking."

She laughed. "Since when? Five minutes ago?"

"Since three o'clock this afternoon."

"You really haven't had a cigarette since then?"

"No," he said, and began to gnaw his thumbnail. It was ragged, down to the quick.

"That's wonderful! What ever made you decide to quit?"

"You," he said. "And . . . and Alvin."

Her eyes widened, and when the movie came back on, she didn't notice. Dick rarely mentioned their retarded son. She came over, looked at the empty ashtray by his right hand, and then into his eyes. "Are you really trying to quit, Dick?"

"Really." *And if I go to the cops,* he added mentally, *the local goon squad will be around to rearrange your face, Cindy.*

"I'm glad. Even if you don't make it, we both thank you for the thought, Dick."

"Oh, I think I'll make it," he said, thinking of the muddy, homicidal look that had come into Donatti's eyes when he kicked him in the stomach.

He slept badly that night, dozing in and out of sleep. Around three o'clock he woke up completely. His craving for a cigarette was like a low-grade fever. He went downstairs and to his study. The room was in the middle of the house. No windows. He slid open the top drawer of his desk and looked in, fascinated by the cigarette box. He looked around and licked his lips.

Constant supervision during the first month, Donatti had said.

Eighteen hours a day during the next two — but he would never know *which* eighteen. During the fourth month, the month when most clients backslid, the "service" would return to twenty-four hours a day. Then twelve hours of broken surveillance each day for the rest of the year. After that? Random surveillance for the rest of the client's life.

For the rest of his life.

"We may audit you every other month," Donatti said. "Or every other day. Or constantly for one week two years from now. The point is, *you won't know.* If you smoke, you'll be gambling with loaded dice. Are they watching? Are they picking up my wife or sending a man after my son right now? Beautiful, isn't it? And if you do sneak a smoke, it'll taste awful. It will taste like your son's blood."

But they couldn't be watching now, in the dead of night, in his own study. The house was grave-quiet.

He looked at the cigarettes in the box for almost two minutes, unable to tear his gaze away. Then he went to the study door, peered out into the empty hall, and went back to look at the cigarettes some more. A horrible picture came: his life stretching before him and not a cigarette to be found. How in the name of God was he ever going to be able to make another tough presentation to a wary client, without that cigarette burning nonchalantly between his fingers as he approached the charts and layouts? How would he be able to endure Cindy's endless garden shows without a cigarette? How could he even get up in the morning and face the day without a cigarette to smoke as he drank his coffee and read the paper?

He cursed himself for getting into this. He cursed Donatti. And most of all, he cursed Jimmy McCann. How could he have done it? The son of a bitch had *known.* His hands trembled in their desire to get hold of Jimmy Judas McCann.

Stealthily, he glanced around the study again. He reached into the drawer and brought out a cigarette. He caressed it, fondled it. What was the old slogan? *So round, so firm, so fully packed.* Truer words had never been spoken. He put the cigarette in his mouth and then paused, cocking his head.

Had there been the slightest noise from the closet? A faint shifting? Surely not. But —

Another mental image — that rabbit hopping crazily in the grip of electricity. The thought of Cindy in that room —

He listened desperately and heard nothing. He told himself that all he had to do was to go to the closet door and yank it open. But he was too afraid of what he might find. He went back to bed but didn't sleep for a long time.

In spite of how lousy he felt in the morning, breakfast tasted good. After a moment's hesitation, he followed his customary bowl of cornflakes with scrambled eggs. He was grumpily washing out the pan when Cindy came downstairs in her robe.

"Richard Morrison! You haven't eaten an egg for breakfast since Hector was a pup."

Morrison grunted. He considered *since Hector was a pup* to be one of Cindy's stupider sayings, on a par with *I should smile and kiss a pig.*

"Have you smoked yet?" she asked, pouring orange juice.

"No."

"You'll be back on them by noon," she proclaimed airily.

"Lot of goddamn help you are!" he rasped, rounding on her. "You and anyone else who doesn't smoke, you all think . . . ah, never mind."

He expected her to be angry, but she was looking at him with something like wonder. "You're really serious," she said. "You really are."

"You bet I am." *You'll never know* how *serious. I hope.*

"Poor baby," she said, going to him. "You look like death warmed over. But I'm very proud."

Morrison held her tightly.

Scenes from the life of Richard Morrison, October–November:

Morrison and a crony from Larkin Studios at Jack Dempsey's bar. Crony offers a cigarette. Morrison grips his glass a little more tightly and says: *I'm quitting.* Crony laughs and says: *I give you a week.*

Morrison waiting for the morning train, looking over the top of the *Times* at a young man in a blue suit. He sees the young man almost every morning now, and sometimes at other places. At Onde's, where he is meeting a client. Looking at 45s in Sam Goody's, where Morrison is looking for a Sam Cooke album. Once in a foursome behind Morrison's group at the local golf course.

Morrison getting drunk at a party, wanting a cigarette — but not quite drunk enough to take one.

Morrison visiting his son, bringing him a large ball that squeaked when you squeezed it. His son's slobbering, delighted kiss. Somehow not as repulsive as before. Hugging his son tightly, realizing what Donatti and his colleagues had so cynically realized before him: love is the most pernicious drug of all. Let the romantics debate its existence. Pragmatists accept it and use it.

Morrison losing the physical compulsion to smoke little by little, but never quite losing the psychological craving, or the need to have something in his mouth — cough drops, Life Savers, a toothpick. Poor substitutes, all of them.

And finally, Morrison hung up in a colossal traffic jam in the Midtown Tunnel. Darkness. Horns blaring. Air stinking. Traffic hopelessly snarled. And suddenly, thumbing open the glove compartment and seeing the half-open pack of cigarettes in there. He looked at them for a moment, then snatched one and lit it with the dashboard lighter. If anything happens, it's Cindy's fault, he told himself defiantly. I told her to get rid of all the damn cigarettes.

The first drag made him cough smoke out furiously. The second made his eyes water. The third made him feel lightheaded and swoony. It tastes awful, he thought.

And on the heels of that: My God, what am I doing?

Horns blatted impatiently behind him. Ahead, the traffic had begun to move again. He stubbed the cigarette out in the ashtray, opened both front windows, opened the vents, and then fanned the air helplessly like a kid who had just flushed his first butt down the john.

He joined the traffic flow jerkily and drove home.

"Cindy?" he called. "I'm home."

No answer.

"Cindy? Where are you, hon?"

The phone rang, and he pounced on it. "Hello? Cindy?"

"Hello, Mr. Morrison," Donatti said. He sounded pleasantly brisk and businesslike. "It seems we have a small business matter to attend to. Would five o'clock be convenient?"

"Have you got my wife?"

"Yes, indeed." Donatti chuckled indulgently.

"Look, let her go," Morrison babbled. "It won't happen again. It was a slip, just a slip, that's all. I only had three drags and for God's sake *it didn't even taste good!*"

"That's a shame. I'll count on you for five then, shall I?"

"Please," Morrison said, close to tears. "Please —"

He was speaking to a dead line.

At 5 P.M. the reception room was empty except for the secretary, who gave him a twinkly smile that ignored Morrison's pallor and disheveled appearance. "Mr. Donatti?" she said into the intercom. "Mr. Morrison to see you." She nodded to Morrison. "Go right in."

Donatti was waiting outside the unmarked room with a man who was wearing a SMILE sweatshirt and carrying a .38. He was built like an ape.

"Listen," Morrison said to Donatti. "We can work something out, can't we? I'll pay you. I'll —"

"Shaddap," the man in the SMILE sweatshirt said.

"It's good to see you," Donatti said. "Sorry it has to be under such adverse circumstances. Will you come with me? We'll make this as brief as possible. I can assure you your wife won't be hurt . . . this time."

Morrison tensed himself to leap at Donatti.

"Come, come," Donatti said, looking annoyed. "If you do that, Junk here is going to pistol-whip you and your wife is still going to get it. Now where's the percentage in that?"

"I hope you rot in hell," he told Donatti.

Donatti sighed. "If I had a nickel for every time someone expressed a similar sentiment, I could retire. Let it be a lesson to you, Mr. Morrison. When a romantic tries to do a good thing and fails they give him a medal. When a pragmatist succeeds, they wish him in hell. Shall we go?"

Junk motioned with the pistol.

Morrison preceded them into the room. He felt numb. The small green curtain had been pulled. Junk prodded him with the gun. This is what being a witness at the gas chamber must have been like, he thought.

He looked in. Cindy was there, looking around bewilderedly.

"Cindy!" Morrison called miserably. "Cindy, they —"

"She can't hear or see you," Donatti said. "One-way glass. Well, let's get it over with. It really was a very small slip. I believe thirty seconds should be enough. Junk?"

Junk pressed the button with one hand and kept the pistol jammed firmly into Morrison's back with the other.

It was the longest thirty seconds of his life.

When it was over, Donatti put a hand on Morrison's shoulder and said, "Are you going to throw up?"

"No," Morrison said weakly. His forehead was against the glass. His legs were jelly. "I don't think so." He turned around and saw that Junk was gone.

"Come with me," Donatti said.

"Where?" Morrison asked apathetically.

"I think you have a few things to explain, don't you?"

"How can I face her? How can I tell her that I . . . I . . ."

"I think you're going to be surprised," Donatti said.

The room was empty except for a sofa. Cindy was on it, sobbing helplessly.

"Cindy?" he said gently.

She looked up, her eyes magnified by tears. "Dick?" she whispered. "Dick? Oh . . . Oh God . . ." He held her tightly. "Two men," she said against his chest. "In the house and at first I thought they were burglars and then I thought they were going to rape me and then they took me someplace with a blindfold over my eyes and . . . and . . . oh it was *h-horrible* —"

"Shhh," he said. "Shhh."

"But why?" she asked, looking up at him. "Why would they —"

"Because of me," he said. "I have to tell you a story, Cindy —"

When he had finished he was silent a moment and then said, "I suppose you hate me. I wouldn't blame you."

He was looking at the floor, and she took his face in both hands and turned it to hers. "No," she said. "I don't hate you."

He looked at her in mute surprise.

"It was worth it," she said. "God bless these people. They've let you out of prison."

"Do you mean that?"

"Yes," she said, and kissed him. "Can we go home now? I feel much better. Ever so much."

The phone rang one evening a week later, and when Morrison recognized Donatti's voice, he said, "Your boys have got it wrong. I haven't even been near a cigarette."

"We know that. We have a final matter to talk over. Can you stop by tomorrow afternoon?"

"Is it —"

"No, nothing serious. Bookkeeping really. By the way, congratulations on your promotion."

"How did you know about that?"

"We're keeping tabs," Donatti said noncommittally, and hung up.

When they entered the small room, Donatti said, "Don't look so nervous. No one's going to bite you. Step over here, please."

Morrison saw an ordinary bathroom scale. "Listen, I've gained a little weight, but —"

"Yes, seventy-three percent of our clients do. Step up, please."

Morrison did, and tipped the scales at one-seventy-four.

"Okay, fine. You can step off. How tall are you, Mr. Morrison?"

"Five-eleven."

"Okay, let's see." He pulled a small card laminated in plastic from his breast pocket. "Well, that's not too bad. I'm going to write you a prescrip for some highly illegal diet pills. Use them sparingly and according to directions. And I'm going to set your maximum weight at . . . let's see . . ." He consulted the card again. "One eighty-two, how does that sound? And since this is December first, I'll expect you the first of every month for a weigh-in. No problem if you can't make it, as long as you call in advance."

"And what happens if I go over one-eighty-two?"

Donatti smiled. "We'll send someone out to your house to cut off your wife's little finger," he said. "You can leave through this door, Mr. Morrison. Have a nice day."

Eight months later:

Morrison runs into the crony from the Larkin Studios at Dempsey's bar. Morrison is down to what Cindy proudly calls his fighting weight: one-sixty-seven. He works out three times a week and looks as fit as whipcord. The crony from Larkin, by comparison, looks like something the cat dragged in.

Crony: Lord, how'd you ever stop? I'm locked into this damn habit tighter than Tillie. The crony stubs his cigarette out with real revulsion and drains his scotch.

Morrison looks at him speculatively and then takes a small white business card out of his wallet. He puts it on the bar between them. You know, he says, these guys changed my life.

*   *   *

Twelve months later:

Morrison receives a bill in the mail. The bill says:

QUITTERS, INC.
237 East 46th Street
New York, N.Y. 10017

1 Treatment	$2500.00
Counselor (Victor Donatti)	$2500.00
Electricity	$ .50
total (Please pay this amount)	$5000.50

Those sons of bitches! he explodes. They charged me for the electricity they used to . . . to . . .

Just pay it, she says, and kisses him.

Twenty months later:

Quite by accident, Morrison and his wife meet the Jimmy McCanns at the Helen Hayes Theatre. Introductions are made all around. Jimmy looks as good, if not better, than he did on that day in the airport terminal so long ago. Morrison has never met his wife. She is pretty in the radiant way plain girls sometimes have when they are very, very happy.

She offers her hand and Morrison shakes it. There is something odd about her grip, and halfway through the second act, he realizes what it was. The little finger on her right hand is missing.

1981

JACK RITCHIE

··

The Absence of Emily

THE PHONE RANG and I picked up the receiver. "Yes?"

"Hello, darling, this is Emily."

I hesitated. "Emily who?"

She laughed lightly. "Oh, come now, darling. Emily, your wife."

"I'm sorry, you must have a wrong number." I hung up, fumbling a bit as I cradled the phone.

Millicent, Emily's cousin, had been watching me. "You look white as a sheet."

I glanced covertly at a mirror.

"I don't mean in actual *color*, Albert. I mean figuratively. In attitude. You seem frightened. Shocked."

"Nonsense."

"Who phoned?"

"It was a wrong number."

Millicent sipped her coffee. "By the way, Albert, I thought I saw Emily in town yesterday, but, of course, that was impossible."

"Of course it was impossible. Emily is in San Francisco."

"Yes, but *where* in San Francisco?"

"She didn't say. Just visiting friends."

"I've known Emily all her life. She has very few secrets from me. She doesn't *know* anybody in San Francisco. When will she be back?"

"She might be gone a rather long time."

"How long?"

"She didn't know."

Millicent smiled. "You have been married before, haven't you, Albert?"

"Yes."

"As a matter of fact, you were a widower when you met Emily?"

"I didn't try to keep that fact a secret."

"Your first wife met her death in a boating accident five years ago? She fell overboard and drowned?"

"I'm afraid so. She couldn't swim a stroke."

"Wasn't she wearing a life preserver?"

"No. She claimed they hindered her movements."

"It appears that you were the only witness to the accident."

"I believe so. At least no one else ever came forward."

"Did she leave you any money, Albert?"

"That's none of your business, Millicent."

Cynthia's estate had consisted of a fifty-thousand-dollar life-insurance policy, of which I was the sole beneficiary, some forty-thousand dollars in sundry stocks and bonds, and one small sailboat.

I stirred my coffee. "Millicent, I thought I'd give you first crack at the house."

"First crack?"

"Yes. We've decided to sell this place. It's really too big for just the two of us. We'll get something smaller. Perhaps even an apartment. I thought you might like to pick up a bargain. I'm certain we can come to satisfactory terms."

She blinked. "Emily would never sell this place. It's her home. I'd have to hear the words from her in person."

"There's no need for that. I have her power of attorney. She has no head for business, you know, but she trusts me implicitly. It's all quite legal and aboveboard."

"I'll think it over." She put down her cup. "Albert, what did you do for a living before you met Emily? Or Cynthia, for that matter?"

"I managed."

When Millicent was gone, I went for my walk on the back grounds of the estate. I went once again to the dell and sat down on the fallen log. How peaceful it was here. Quiet. A place to rest. I had been coming here often in the last few days.

Millicent and Emily. Cousins. They occupied almost identical large homes on spacious grounds next to each other. And, considering that fact, one might reasonably have supposed that they were equally wealthy. Such, however, was not the case, as I discovered after my marriage to Emily.

Millicent's holdings must certainly reach far into seven figures, since they require the full-time administrative services of Amos Eberly, her attorney and financial advisor.

Emily, on the other hand, owned very little more than the house and the grounds themselves and she had borrowed heavily to keep them going. She had been reduced to two servants, the Brewsters. Mrs. Brewster, a surly creature, did the cooking and desultory dusting, while her husband, formerly the butler, had been reduced to a man-of-all-work, who pottered inadequately about the grounds. The place really required the services of two gardeners.

Millicent and Emily. Cousins. Yet it was difficult to imagine two people more dissimilar in either appearance or nature.

Millicent is rather tall, spare, and determined. She fancies herself an intellect and she has the tendency to rule and dominate all those about her, and that had certainly included Emily. It is obvious to me that Millicent deeply resents the fact that I removed Emily from under her thumb.

Emily. Shorter than average. Perhaps twenty-five pounds overweight. An amiable disposition. No claim to blazing intelligence. Easily dominated, yes, though she had a surprising stubborn streak when she set her mind to something.

When I returned to the house, I found Amos Eberly waiting. He is a man in his fifties and partial to gray suits.

"Where is Emily?" he asked.

"In Oakland." He gave that thought.

"I meant San Francisco. Oakland is just across the bay, isn't it? I usually think of them as one, which, I suppose, is unfair to both."

He frowned. "San Francisco? But I saw her in town just this morning. She was looking quite well."

"Impossible."

"Impossible for her to be looking well?"

"Impossible for you to have seen her. She is still in San Francisco."

He sipped his drink. "I know Emily when I see her. She wore a lilac dress with a belt. And a sort of gauzy light-blue scarf."

"You were mistaken. Besides, women don't wear gauzy light-blue scarves these days."

"Emily did. Couldn't she have come back without letting you know?"

"No."

Eberly studied me. "Are you ill or something, Albert? Your hands seem to be shaking."

"Touch of the flu," I said quickly. "Brings out the jitters in me. What brings you here anyway, Amos?"

"Nothing in particular, Albert. I just happened to be in the neighborhood and thought I'd drop in and see Emily."

"Damn it, I told you she isn't here."

"All right, Albert," he said soothingly. "Why should I doubt you? If you say she isn't here, she isn't here."

It has become my habit on Tuesday and Thursday afternoons to do the household food shopping, a task which I pre-empted from Mrs. Brewster when I began to suspect her arithmetic.

As usual, I parked in the supermarket lot and locked the car. When I looked up, I saw a small, slightly stout woman across the street walking toward the farther end of the block. She wore a lilac dress and a light-blue scarf. It was the fourth time I'd seen her in the last ten days.

I hurried across the street. I was still some seventy-five yards behind her when she turned the corner.

Resisting the temptation to shout at her to stop, I broke into a trot.

When I reached the corner, she was nowhere in sight. She could have disappeared into any one of a dozen shop fronts.

I stood there, trying to regain my breath, when a car pulled to the curb.

It was Millicent. "Is that you, Albert?"

I regarded her without enthusiasm. "Yes."

"What in the world are you doing? I saw you running and I've never seen you run before."

"I was *not* running. I was merely trotting to get my blood circulating. A bit of jogging is supposed to be healthy, you know."

I volunteered my adieu and strode back to the supermarket.

The next morning when I returned from my walk to the dell, I found Millicent in the drawing room, pouring herself coffee and otherwise making herself at home — a habit from the days when only Emily occupied the house.

"I've been upstairs looking over Emily's wardrobe," Millicent said. "I didn't see anything missing."

"Why should anything be missing? Has there been a thief in the house? I suppose you know every bit and parcel of her wardrobe?"

"Not every bit and parcel, but almost. Almost. And very little, if anything, seems to be missing. Don't tell me that Emily went off to San Francisco without any luggage."

"She had luggage. Though not very much."

"What was she wearing when she left?"

Millicent had asked that question before. This time I said, "I don't remember."

Millicent raised an eyebrow. "You don't remember?" She put down her cup. "Albert, I'm holding a seance at my place tonight. I thought perhaps you'd like to come."

"I will not go to any damn seance."

"Don't you want to communicate with any of your beloved dead?"

"I believe in letting the dead rest. Why bother them with every trifling matter back here."

"Wouldn't you want to speak to your first wife?"

"Why the devil would I want to communicate with Cynthia? I have absolutely nothing to say to her anyway."

"But perhaps she has something to say to you."

I wiped my forehead. "I'm not going to your stupid seance and that's final."

That evening, as I prepared for bed, I surveyed the contents of Emily's closet. How would I dispose of her clothes? Probably donate them to some worthy charity, I thought.

I was awakened at two A.M. by the sound of music.

I listened. Yes, it was plainly Emily's favorite sonata being played on the piano downstairs.

I stepped into my slippers and donned my dressing robe. In the hall, I snapped on the lights.

I was halfway down the stairs when the piano-playing ceased. I completed my descent and stopped at the music room doors. I put my ear to one of them. Nothing. I slowly opened the door and peered inside.

There was no one at the piano. However, two candles in holders flickered on its top. The room seemed chilly. Quite chilly.

I found the source of the draft behind some drapes and closed the French doors to the terrace. I snuffed out the candles and left the room.

I met Brewster at the head of the stairs.

"I thought I heard a piano being played, sir," he said. "Was that you?"

I wiped the palms of my hands on my robe. "Of course."

"I didn't know you played the piano, sir."

"Brewster, there are a lot of things you don't know about me and never will."

I went back to my room, waited half an hour, and then dressed. In the bright moonlight outside, I made my way to the garden shed. I unbolted its door, switched on the lights, and surveyed the gardening equipment. My eyes went to the tools in the wall racks.

I pulled down a long-handled irrigating shovel and knocked a bit of dried mud from its tip. I slung the implement over my shoulder and began walking toward the dell.

I was nearly there when I stopped and sighed heavily. I shook my head and returned to the shed. I put the shovel back into its place on the rack, switched off the lights, and returned to bed.

The next morning, Millicent dropped in as I was having breakfast.

"How are you this morning, Albert?"

"I have felt better."

Millicent sat down at the table and waited for Mrs. Brewster to bring her a cup.

Mrs. Brewster also brought the morning mail. It included a number of advertising fliers, a few bills, and one small blue envelope addressed to me.

I examined it. The handwriting seemed familiar and so did the scent. The postmark was town.

I slit open the envelope and pulled out a single sheet of notepaper.

> *Dear Albert:*
> *You have no idea how much I miss you. I shall return*
> *home soon, Albert. Soon.*
>
> > *Emily*

I put the note back into the envelope and slipped both into my pocket.

"Well?" Millicent asked.

"Well, what?"

"I thought I recognized Emily's handwriting on the envelope. Did she say when she'd be back?"

"That is *not* Emily's handwriting. It is a note from my aunt in Chicago."

"I didn't know you had an aunt in Chicago."

"Millicent, rest assured. I *do* have an aunt in Chicago."

That night I was in bed, but awake, when the phone on my night table rang. I picked up the receiver.

"Hello, darling. This is Emily."

I let five seconds pass. "You are *not* Emily. You are an impostor."

"Now, Albert, why are you being so stubborn? Of course this is me. Emily."

"You couldn't be."

"Why couldn't I be?"

"*Because.*"

"Because why?"

"Where are you calling from?"

She laughed. "I think you'd be surprised."

"You couldn't be Emily. I *know* where she is and she couldn't — *wouldn't* — make a phone call at this hour of the night just to say hello. It's well past midnight."

"You think you know where I am, Albert? No, I'm not there any more. It was so uncomfortable, so dreadfully uncomfortable. And so I left, Albert. I left."

I raised my voice. "Damn you, I can *prove* you're still there."

She laughed. "Prove? How can you prove anything like that, Albert? Good night." She hung up.

I got out of bed and dressed. I made my way downstairs and detoured into the study. I made myself a drink, consumed it slowly, and then made another.

When I consulted my watch for the last time it was nearly one A.M. I put on a light jacket against the chill of the night and made my way to the garden shed. I opened the doors, turned on the lights, and pulled the long-handled shovel from the rack.

This time I went all the way to the dell. I paused beside a huge oak and stared at the moonlit clearing.

I counted as I began pacing. "One, two, three, four —" I stopped at sixteen, turned ninety degrees, and then paced off eighteen more steps.

I began digging.

I had been at it for nearly five minutes when suddenly I heard the piercing blast of a whistle and immediately I became the focus of perhaps a dozen flashlight beams and approaching voices.

I shielded my eyes against the glare and recognized Millicent. "What the devil is this?"

She showed cruel teeth. "You had to make sure she was really dead, didn't you, Albert? And the only way you could do that was to return to her grave."

I drew myself up. "I am looking for Indian arrowheads. There's an ancient superstition that if one is found under the light of the moon it will bring luck for the finder for several weeks."

Millicent introduced the people gathered about me. "Ever since I began suspecting what really has happened to Emily you've been under twenty-four-hour surveillance by private detectives."

She indicated the others. "Miss Peters. She is quite a clever mimic and was the voice of Emily you heard over the phone. She also plays piano. And Mrs. McMillan. She reproduced Emily's handwriting and was the woman in the lilac dress and the blue scarf."

Millicent's entire household staff seemed to be present. I also recognized Amos Eberly and the Brewsters. I would fire them tomorrow.

The detectives had brought along their own shovels and spades, and two of them superseded me in my shallow depression. They began digging.

"See here," I said, exhibiting indignation. "You have no right to do that. This is *my* property. At the very least you need a search warrant."

Millicent found that amusing. "This is *not* your property, Albert. It is *mine*. You stepped over the dividing line six paces back."

I wiped my forehead. "I'm going back to the house."

"You are under arrest, Albert."

"Nonsense, Millicent. I do not see a *proper* uniformed policeman among these people. And in this state private detectives do not have the right to arrest anyone at all."

For a moment she seemed stymied, but then saw light. "You are under *citizen's* arrest, Albert. Any citizen has the power to make a citizen's arrest and I am a citizen."

Millicent twirled the whistle on its chain. "We knew we were getting to you, Albert. You almost dug her up last night, didn't you? But then you changed your mind. But that was just as well. Last night I couldn't have produced as many witnesses. Tonight we were ready and waiting."

The detectives dug for some fifteen minutes and then paused for a rest. One of them frowned. "You'd think the digging would be easier. This ground looks like it's never been dug up before."

They resumed their work and eventually reached a depth of six feet before they gave up. The spade man climbed out of the excavation. "Hell, nothing's been buried here. The only thing we found was an Indian arrowhead."

Millicent had been glaring at me for the last half hour.

I smiled. "Millicent, what makes you think that I *buried* Emily?"

With that I left them and returned to the house.

When had I first become aware of Millicent's magnificent maneuverings and the twenty-four-hour surveillance? Almost from the very beginning, I suspect. I'm rather quick on the uptake.

What had been Millicent's objective? I suppose she envisioned reducing me to such a state of fear that eventually I'd break down and confess to the murder of Emily.

Frankly, I would have regarded the success of such a scheme as farfetched, to say the least. However, once I was aware of what Millicent was attempting, I got into the spirit of the venture.

Millicent may have initiated the enterprise, the play, but it is I who led her to the dell.

There were times when I thought I overdid it just a bit — wiping at nonexistent perspiration, trotting after the elusive woman in the lilac dress, that sort of thing — but on the other hand I suppose these reactions were rather expected of me and I didn't want to disappoint any eager watchers.

Those brooding trips to the dell had been quite a good touch, I thought. And the previous night's halfway journey there, with the shovel over my shoulder, had been intended to assure a large audience at the finale twenty-four hours later.

I had counted eighteen witnesses, excluding Millicent.

I pondered. Defamation of character? Slander? Conspiracy? False arrest? Probably a good deal more.

I would threaten to sue for a large and unrealistic amount. That was the fashion nowadays, wasn't it? Twenty million? It didn't really matter, of course, because I doubted very much if the matter would ever reach court.

No, Millicent wouldn't be able to endure the publicity. She couldn't let the world know what a total fool she'd made of herself. She couldn't bear to be the laughingstock of her circle, her peers.

She would, of course, attempt to hush it up as best she could. A few dollars here and a few there to buy the silence of the witnesses. But could one seriously hope to buy the total silence of eighteen individual people? Probably not. However, when the whispers began to circulate, it would be a considerable help to Millicent if the principal player involved would join her in vehemently denying that any such ridiculous event had ever taken place at all.

And I would do that for Millicent. For a consideration. A *large* consideration.

At the end of the week, my phone rang.

"This is Emily. I'm coming home now, dear."

"Wonderful."

"Did anyone miss me?"

"You have no idea."

"You haven't told anyone where I've been these last four weeks, have you, Albert? Especially not Millicent?"

"Especially not Millicent."

"What *did* you tell her?"

"I said you were visiting friends in San Francisco."

"Oh, dear. I don't *know* anybody in San Francisco. Do you suppose she got suspicious?"

"Well, maybe just a little bit."

"She thinks I have absolutely no will power, but I really have. But just the same, I didn't want her laughing at me if I didn't stick it out. Oh, I suppose going to a health farm is cheating, in a way. I mean you can't be tempted because they control all of the food. But I really stuck it out. I could have come home any time I wanted to."

"You have marvelous will power, Emily."

"I've lost *thirty* pounds, Albert! And it's going to *stay* off. I'll bet I'm every bit as slim now as Cynthia ever was."

I sighed. There was absolutely no reason for Emily to keep comparing herself to my first wife. The two of them are separate entities and each has her secure compartment in my affections.

Poor Cynthia. She had insisted on going off by herself in that small craft. I had been at the yacht-club window sipping a martini and watching the cold gray harbor.

Cynthia's boat seemed to have been the only one on the water on that inhospitable day and there had apparently been an unexpected gust of wind. I had seen the boat heel over sharply and Cynthia thrown overboard. I'd raised the alarm immediately, but by the time we got out there it had been too late.

Emily sighed too. "I suppose I'll have to get an entire new wardrobe. Do you think we can really afford one, Albert?"

We could now. And then some.

1984

LAWRENCE BLOCK

···

By the Dawn's Early Light

ALL THIS HAPPENED a long time ago.

Abe Beame was living in Gracie Mansion, although even he seemed to have trouble believing he was really the Mayor of the City of New York. Ali was in his prime, and the Knicks still had a year or so left in Bradley and DeBusschere. I was still drinking in those days, of course, and at the time it seemed to be doing more for me than it was doing to me.

I had already left my wife and kids, my home in Syosset, and the NYPD. I was living in the hotel on West Fifty-seventh Street where I still live, and I was doing most of my drinking around the corner in Jimmy Armstrong's saloon. Billie was the nighttime bartender, his own best customer for the twelve-year-old Jameson. A Filipino youth named Dennis was behind the stick most days.

And Tommy Tillary was one of the regulars.

He was big, probably six-two, full in the chest, big in the belly, too. He rarely showed up in a suit but always wore a jacket and a tie, usually a navy and burgundy blazer with gray flannel slacks, or white duck pants in warmer weather. He had a loud voice that boomed from his barrel chest, and a big cleanshaven face that was innocent around the pouting mouth and knowing around the eyes. He was somewhere in his late forties, and he drank a lot of top-shelf Scotch. Chivas, as I remember it, but it could have been Johnny Black. Whatever it was, his face was beginning to show it, with patches of permanent flush at the cheekbones and a tracery of broken capillaries across the bridge of the nose.

We were saloon friends. We didn't speak every time we ran into each other, but at least we always acknowledged one another with a nod or a wave. He told a lot of dialect jokes and told them reasonably well, and I laughed at my share of them. Sometimes I was in a mood to reminisce about my days on the force, and when my stories were funny his laugh was as loud as anyone's.

Sometimes he showed up alone, sometimes with male friends. About a third of the time he was in the company of a short and curvy blonde named Carolyn. "Caro-lyn from the Caro-line," was the way he occasionally introduced her, and she did have a faint southern accent that became more pronounced as the drink got to her. Generally they came in together, but sometimes he got there first and she joined him later.

Then one morning I picked up the *Daily News* and read that burglars had broken into a house on Colonial Road, in the Bay Ridge section of Brooklyn. They had stabbed to death the only occupant present, one Margaret Tillary. Her husband, Thomas J. Tillary, a salesman, was not at home at the time.

It's an uncommon name. There's a Tillary Street in Brooklyn, not far from the entrance to the Brooklyn Bridge, but I've no idea what war hero or ward heeler they named it after, or if he's a relative of Tommy's. I hadn't known Tommy was a salesman, or that he'd had a wife. He did wear a wide yellow gold band on the appropriate finger, and it was clear that he wasn't married to Carolyn from the Caroline, and it now looked as though he was a widower. I felt vaguely sorry for him, vaguely sorry for the wife I'd never even known of, but that was the extent of it. I drank enough back then to avoid feeling any emotion very strongly.

And then, two or three nights later, I walked into Armstrong's and there was Carolyn. She didn't look to be waiting for him or anyone else, nor did she look as though she'd just breezed in a few minutes ago. She had a stool by herself at the bar and she was drinking something dark from a lowball glass.

I took a seat a few stools down from her. I ordered two double shots of bourbon, drank one, and poured the other into the cup of black coffee Billie brought me. I was sipping the coffee when a voice with a Piedmont softness to it said, "I forget your name."

I looked up.

"I believe we were introduced," she said, "but I don't recall your name."

"It's Matt," I said, "and you're right, Tommy introduced us. You're Carolyn."

"Carolyn Cheatham. Have you seen him?"

"Tommy? Not since it happened."

"Neither have I. Were you-all at the funeral?"

"No. When was it?"

"This afternoon. Neither was I. There. Matt. Whyn't you buy me a drink? Or I'll buy you one, but come sit next to me so's I don't have to shout. Please?"

She was drinking Amaretto, sweet almond liqueur that she took on the rocks. It tastes like dessert but it's as strong as whiskey.

"He told me not to come," she said. "To the funeral. It was someplace in Brooklyn, that's a whole foreign nation to me, Brooklyn, but a lot of people went from the office. I could have had a ride, I could have been part of the office crowd, come to pay our respects. But he said not to, he said it wouldn't look right."

"Because —"

"He said it was a matter of respect for the dead." She picked up her glass and stared into it. I've never known what people hope to see there, although it's a gesture I've performed often enough myself.

"Respect," she said. "What's he care about respect? I would have just been part of the office crowd, we both work at Tannahill, far as anyone there knows we're just friends. And all we ever were is friends, you know."

"Whatever you say."

"Oh, *shit*," she said. "Ah don't mean Ah wasn't fucking him, for the Lord's sake. Ah mean it was just laughs and good times. He was married and he went home to Mama every night and that was jes fine, because who in her right mind'd want Tommy Tillary around by the dawn's early light? Christ in the foothills, did Ah spill this or drink it?"

We agreed that she was drinking them a little too fast. Sweet drinks, we told each other, had a way of sneaking up on a person. It was this fancy New York Amaretto shit, she maintained, not like the bourbon she'd grown up on. You knew where you stood with bourbon.

I told her I was a bourbon drinker myself, and it pleased her to learn this. Alliances have been forged on thinner bonds than that, and ours served to propel us out of Armstrong's, with a stop down the block for a fifth of Maker's Mark — her choice — and a four-block walk to her apartment. There were exposed brick walls, I remember, and candles stuck in straw-wrapped bottles, and several travel posters from Sabena, the Belgian airline.

We did what grownups do when they find themselves alone together. We drank our fair share of the Maker's Mark and went to bed. She made a lot of enthusiastic noises and more than a few skillful moves, and afterward she cried some.

A little later she dropped off to sleep. I was tired myself, but I put on my clothes and sent myself home. Because who in her right mind'd want Matt Scudder around by the dawn's early light?

Over the next couple of days, I wondered every time I entered Armstrong's if I'd run into her, and each time I was more relieved than disappointed when I didn't. I didn't encounter Tommy either, and that too was a relief, and in no sense disappointing.

Then one morning I picked up the *News* and read that they'd arrested a pair of young Hispanics from Sunset Park for the Tillary burglary and homicide. The paper ran the usual photo — two skinny kids, their hair unruly, one of them trying to hide his face from the camera, the other smirking defiantly, and each of them handcuffed to a broad-shouldered grimfaced Irishman in a suit. You didn't need the careful caption to tell the good guys from the bad guys.

Sometime in the middle of the afternoon I went over to Armstrong's for a hamburger and drank a beer with it, then got the day going with a round or two of laced coffee. The phone behind the bar rang and Dennis put down the glass he was wiping and answered it. "He was here a minute ago," he said. "I'll see if he stepped out." He covered the mouthpiece with his hand and looked quizzically at me. "Are you still here?" he asked. "Or did you slip away while my attention was somehow diverted?"

"Who wants to know?"

"Tommy Tillary."

You never know what a woman will decide to tell a man, or how a man will react to it. I didn't want to find out, but I was better off learning over the phone than face to face. I nodded and took the phone from Dennis.

I said, "Matt Scudder, Tommy. I was sorry to hear about your wife."

"Thanks, Matt. Jesus, it feels like it happened a year ago. It was what, a week?"

"At least they got the bastards."

There was a pause. Then he said, "Jesus. You haven't seen a paper, huh?"

"That's where I read about it. Two. Spanish kids."

"You read the *News* this morning."

"I generally do. Why?"

"You didn't happen to see this afternoon's *Post*."

"No. Why, what happened? They turn out to be clean?"

Another pause. Then he said, "I figured you'd know. The cops were over early this morning, even before I saw the story in the *News*. It'd be easier if you already knew."

"I'm not following you, Tommy."

"The two Spics. Clean? Shit, they're about as clean as the men's room in the Times Square subway station. The cops hit their place and found stuff from my house everywhere they looked. Jewelry they had descriptions of, a stereo that I gave them the serial number, everything. Monogrammed shit. I mean that's how clean they were, for Christ's sake."

"So?"

"They admitted the burglary but not the murder."

"That's common, Tommy."

"Lemme finish, huh? They admitted the burglary, but according to them it was a put-up job. According to them I hired them to hit my place. They could keep whatever they got and I'd have everything out and arranged for them, and in return I got to clean up on the insurance by over-reporting the loss."

"What did the loss amount to?"

"Shit, *I* don't know. There were twice as many things turned up in their apartment as I ever listed when I made out a report. There's things I missed a few days after I filed the report and others I didn't know were gone until the cops found them. You don't notice everything right away, at least I don't, and on top of it how could I think straight with Peg dead? You know?"

"It hardly sounds like an insurance set-up."

"No, of course it wasn't. How the hell could it be? All I had was a standard homeowner's policy. It covered maybe a third of what I lost. According to them, the place was empty when they hit it. Peg was out."

"And?"

"And I set them up. They hit the place, they carted everything away, and I came home with Peg and stabbed her six, eight times, whatever it was, and left her there so it'd look like it happened in a burglary."

"How could the burglars testify that you stabbed your wife?"

"They couldn't. All they said was they didn't and she wasn't home when they were there, and that I hired them to do the burglary. The cops pieced the rest of it together."

"What did they do, arrest you?"

"No. They came over to the house, it was early, I don't know what time. It was the first I knew that the Spics were arrested, let alone that they were trying to do a job on me. They just wanted to talk, the cops, and at first I talked to them, and then I started to get the drift of what they were trying to put onto me. So I wasn't saying anything more without my lawyer present, and I called him, and he left half his breakfast on the table and came over in a hurry, and he wouldn't let me say a word."

"And the cops didn't take you in or book you?"

"No."

"Did they buy your story?"

"No way. I didn't really tell 'em a story because Kaplan wouldn't let me say anything. They didn't drag me in because they don't have a case yet, but Kaplan says they're gonna be building one if they can. They told me not to leave town. You believe it? My wife's dead, the *Post* headline says *Quiz Husband in Burglary Murder*, and what the hell do they think I'm gonna do? Am I going fishing for fucking trout in Montana? 'Don't leave town.' You see this shit on television, you think nobody in real life talks this way. Maybe television's where they get it from."

I waited for him to tell me what he wanted from me. I didn't have long to wait.

"Why I called," he said, "is Kaplan wants to hire a detective. He figured maybe these guys talked around the neighborhood, maybe they bragged to their friends, maybe there's a way to prove they did the killing. He says the cops won't concentrate on that end if they're too busy nailing the lid shut on me."

I explained that I didn't have any official standing, that I had no license and filed no reports.

"That's okay," he insisted. "I told Kaplan what I want is somebody I can trust, and somebody who'll do the job for me. I don't think they're gonna have any kind of a case at all, Matt, but the longer this drags on the worse it is for me. I want it cleared up, I want it in the papers that these Spanish assholes did it all and I had nothing to do with anything. You name a fair fee and I'll pay it, me to you, and it can be cash in your hand if you don't like checks. What do you say?"

He wanted somebody he could trust. Had Carolyn from the Caroline told him how trustworthy I was?

What did I say? I said yes.

*   *   *

I met Tommy Tillary and his lawyer in Drew Kaplan's office on Court Street a few blocks from Brooklyn's Borough Hall. There was a Syrian restaurant next door, and at the corner a grocery store specializing in Middle Eastern imports stood next to an antique shop overflowing with stripped oak furniture and brass lamps and bedsteads. Kaplan's office ran to wood paneling and leather chairs and oak file cabinets. His name and the names of two partners were painted on the frosted glass door in old-fashioned gold and black lettering. Kaplan himself looked conservatively up-to-date, with a three-piece striped suit that was better cut than mine. Tommy wore his burgundy blazer and gray flannel trousers and loafers. Strain showed at the corners of his blue eyes and around his mouth. His complexion was off, too, as if anxiety had drawn the blood inward, leaving the skin sallow.

"All we want you to do," Drew Kaplan said, "is find a key in one of their pants pockets, Herrera's or Cruz's, and trace it to a locker in Penn Station, and in the locker there's a footlong knife with their prints and her blood on it."

"Is that what it's going to take?"

He smiled. "It wouldn't hurt. No, actually we're not in such bad shape. They got some shaky testimony from a pair of Latins who've been in and out of trouble since they got weaned to Tropicana. They got what looks to them like a good motive on Tommy's part."

"Which is?"

I was looking at Tommy when I talked. His eyes slipped away from mine. Kaplan said, "A marital triangle, a case of the shorts, and a strong money motive. Margaret Tillary inherited a little over a quarter of a million dollars six or eight months ago. An aunt left a million two and it got cut four ways. What they don't bother to notice is he loved his wife, and how many husbands cheat? What is it they say? Ninety percent cheat and ten percent lie?"

"That's good odds."

"One of the killers, Angel Herrera, did some odd jobs at the Tillary house last March or April. Spring cleaning, he hauled stuff out of the basement and attic, a little donkey work for hourly wages. According to common sense, that's how Herrera and his buddy Cruz knew the house and what was in it and how to gain access."

"The case against Tommy sounds pretty thin."

"It is," Kaplan said. "The thing is, you go to court with something like this and you lose even if you win. For the rest of your life everybody remembers you stood trial for murdering your wife, never mind that you won an acquittal. All that means, some Jew lawyer bought a judge or tricked a jury."

"So I'll get a guinea lawyer," Tommy said. "And they'll think he threatened the judge and beat up the jury."

"Besides," the lawyer said, "you never know which way a jury's going to jump. Tommy's alibi is he was with another lady at the time of the burglary. The woman's a colleague, they could see it as completely above-board, but who says they're going to? What they sometimes do, they decide they don't believe the alibi because it's his girlfriend lying for him, and at the same time they label him a scumbag for screwing around while his wife's getting killed."

"You keep it up," Tommy said, "I'll find myself guilty, the way you make it sound."

"Plus he's hard to get a sympathetic jury for. He's a big handsome guy, a sharp dresser, and you'd love him in a gin joint but how much do you love him in a courtroom? He's a telephone securities salesman, he's beautiful on the phone, and that means every clown whoever lost a hundred dollars on a stock tip or bought magazine subscriptions over the phone is going to walk into the courtroom with a hard-on for him. I'm telling you, I want to stay the hell *out* of court. I'll *win* in court, I know that, or the worst that'll happen is I'll win on appeal, but who needs it? This is a case that shouldn't be in the first place, and I'd love to clear it up before they even go so far as presenting a bill to the Grand Jury."

"So from me you want —"

"Whatever you can find, Matt. Whatever discredits Cruz and Herrera. I don't know what's there to be found, but you were a cop and now you're a private, and you can get down in the streets and nose around."

I nodded. I could do that. "One thing," I said. "Wouldn't you be better off with a Spanish-speaking detective? I know enough to buy a beer in a bodega, but I'm a long ways from fluent."

Kaplan shook his head. "Tommy says he wants somebody he can trust," he said. "I think he's right. A personal relationship's worth more than a dime's worth of '*Me llamo Matteo y como está usted?*'"

"That's the truth," Tommy Tillary said. "Matt, I know I can count on you."

I wanted to tell him all he could count on was his fingers. I didn't really see what I could expect to uncover that wouldn't turn up in a regular police investigation. But I'd spent enough time carrying a shield to know not to push away money when somebody wants to give it to you. I felt comfortable taking a fee. The man was inheriting a quarter of a million dollars, plus whatever insurance she carried. If he was willing to spread some of it around, I was willing to take it.

So I went to Sunset Park and spent some time in the streets and some more time in the bars. Sunset Park is in Brooklyn, of course, on the borough's western edge above Bay Ridge and south and west of Greenwood Cemetery. These days there's a lot of brownstoning going on there, with young urban professionals renovating the old houses and gentrifying the neighborhood. Back then the upwardly mobile young had not yet discovered Sunset Park, and the area was a mix of Latins and Scandinavians, most of the former Puerto Ricans, most of the latter Norwegians. The balance was gradually shifting from Europe to the islands, from light to dark, but this was a process that had been going on for ages and there was nothing hurried about it.

I talked to Herrera's landlord and Cruz's former employer and one of his recent girlfriends. I drank beer in bars and the back rooms of bodegas. I went to the local stationhouse — they hadn't caught the Margaret Tillary murder case, that had been a matter for the local precinct in Bay Ridge and some detectives from Brooklyn Homicide. I read the sheets on both of the burglars and drank coffee with the cops and picked up some of the stuff that doesn't get on the yellow sheets.

I found out that Miguelito Cruz once killed a man in a tavern brawl over a woman. There were no charges pressed; a dozen witnesses reported the dead man had gone after Cruz first with a broken bottle. Cruz had most likely been carrying the knife, but several witnesses insisted it had been tossed to him by an anonymous benefactor, and there hadn't been enough evidence to make a case of weapons possession, let alone homicide.

I learned that Herrera had three children living with their mother in Puerto Rico. He was divorced, but wouldn't marry his current girlfriend because he regarded himself as still married to his ex-wife in the eyes of God. He sent money to his children, when he had any to send.

I learned other things. They didn't seem terribly consequential then and they've faded from memory altogether by now, but I wrote them down in my pocket notebook as I learned them, and every day or so I duly reported my findings to Drew Kaplan. He always seemed pleased with what I told him.

*   *   *

Some nights I stayed fairly late in Sunset Park. There was a dark beery tavern called The Fjord that served as a comfortable enough harbor after I tired of playing Sam Spade. But I almost invariably managed a stop at Armstrong's before I called it a night. Billie would lock the door around two, but he'd keep serving until four and he'd let you in if he knew you.

One night she was there, Carolyn Cheatham, drinking bourbon this time instead of Amaretto, her face frozen with stubborn old pain. It took her a blink or two to recognize me. Then tears started to form in the corners of her eyes, and she used the back of one hand to wipe them away.

I didn't approach her until she beckoned. She patted the stool beside hers and I eased myself onto it. I had coffee with bourbon in it, and bought a refill for her. She was pretty drunk already, but that's never been enough reason to turn down a drink.

She talked about Tommy. He was being nice to her, she said. Calling up, sending flowers. Because he might need to testify that he'd been with her when his wife was killed, and he'd need her to back him up.

But he wouldn't see her because it wouldn't look right, not for a new widower, not for a man who'd been publicly accused of murder.

"He sends flowers with no card enclosed," she said. "He calls me from pay phones. The son of a bitch."

Billie called me aside. "I didn't want to put her out," he said, "a nice woman like that, shitfaced as she is. But I thought I was gonna have to. You'll see she gets home?"

I said I would.

First I had to let her buy us another round. She insisted. Then I got her out of there and a cab came along and saved us the walk. At her place, I took the keys from her and unlocked the door. She half sat, half sprawled on the couch. I had to use the bathroom, and when I came back her eyes were closed and she was snoring lightly.

I got her coat and shoes off, put her to bed, loosened her clothing and covered her with a blanket. I was tired from all that and sat down on the couch for a minute, and I almost dozed off myself. Then I snapped awake and let myself out. Her door had a spring lock. All I had to do was close it and it was locked.

Much of the walk back to my hotel disappeared in blackout. I was crossing Fifty-seventh Street, and then it was morning and I was stretched out in my own bed, my clothes a tangle on the straight-backed chair. That happened a lot in those days, that kind of before-bed blackout, and I used to insist it didn't bother me. What ever happened on the way home? Why waste brain cells remembering the final fifteen minutes of the day?

I went back to Sunset Park the next day. I learned that Cruz had been in trouble as a youth. With a gang of neighborhood kids, he used to go into the city and cruise Greenwich Village, looking for homosexuals to beat up. He'd had a dread of homosexuality, probably flowing as it generally does out of a fear of a part of himself, and he stifled that dread by fag-bashing.

"He still doan like them," a woman told me. She had glossy black hair and opaque eyes, and she was letting me pay for her rum and orange juice. "He's pretty, you know, and they come on to him, an' he doan like it."

I called that item in, along with a few others equally earth-shaking. I bought myself a steak dinner at the Slate over on Tenth Avenue that night, then finished up at Armstrong's, not drinking very hard, just coasting along on bourbon and coffee.

Twice, the phone rang for me. Once it was Tommy Tillary, telling me how much he appreciated what I was doing for him. It seemed to me that all I was doing was taking his money, but he had me believing that my loyalty and invaluable assistance were all he had to cling to.

The second call was from Carolyn. More praise. I was a gentleman, she assured me, and a hell of a fellow all around. And I should forget that she'd been bad-mouthing Tommy. Everything was going to be fine with them.

I told her I'd never doubted it for a minute, and that I couldn't really remember what she'd said anyway.

I took the next day off. I think I went to a movie, and it may have been *The Sting*, with Newman and Redford achieving vengeance through swindling.

The day after that I did another tour of duty over in Brooklyn. And the day after that I picked up the *News* first thing in the morning. The headline was nonspecific, something like *Kill Suspect Hangs Self in Cell*, but I knew it was my case before I turned to the story on Page Three.

Miguelito Cruz had torn his clothing into strips, knotted the strips together, stood his iron bedstead on its side, climbed onto it, looped his homemade rope around an overhead pipe, and jumped off the upended bedstead and into the next world.

That evening's six o'clock TV news had the rest of the story. Informed of his friend's death, Angel Herrera had recanted his original story and admitted that he and Cruz had conceived and executed the Tillary burglary on their own. It had been Miguelito who had stabbed the Tillary woman when she walked in on them. He'd picked up a kitchen knife while Herrera watched in horror. Miguelito always had a short temper, Herrera said, but they were friends, even cousins, and they had hatched their story to protect Miguelito. But now that he was dead, Herrera could admit what had really happened.

I was in Armstrong's that night, which was not remarkable. I had it in mind to get drunk, though I could not have told you why, and that was remarkable, if not unheard of. I got drunk a lot those days, but I rarely set out with that intention. I just wanted to feel a little better, a little more mellow, and somewhere along the way I'd wind up waxed.

I wasn't drinking particularly hard or fast, but I was working at it, and then somewhere around ten or eleven the door opened and I knew who it was before I turned around. Tommy Tillary, well dressed and freshly barbered, making his first appearance in Jimmy's place since his wife was killed.

"Hey, look who's here!" he called out, and grinned that big grin. People rushed over to shake his hand. Billie was behind the stick, and he'd no sooner set one up on the house for our hero than Tommy insisted on buying a round for the bar. It was an expensive gesture, there must have been thirty or forty people in there, but I don't think he cared if there were three or four hundred.

I stayed where I was, letting the others mob him, but he worked his way over to me and got an arm around my shoulders. "This is the man," he announced. "Best fucking detective ever wore out a pair of shoes. This man's money —" he told Billie "— is no good at all tonight. He can't buy a drink, he can't buy a cup of coffee, if you went and put in pay toilets since I was last here, he can't use his own dime."

"The john's still free," Billie said, "but don't give the boss any ideas."

"Oh, don't tell me he didn't already think of it," Tommy said. "Matt, my boy, I love you. I was in a tight spot, I didn't want to walk out of my house, and you came through for me."

What the hell had I done? I hadn't hanged Miguelito Cruz or coaxed a confession out of Angel Herrera. I hadn't even set eyes on either man. But he was buying the drinks, and I had a thirst, so who was I to argue?

I don't know how long we stayed there. Curiously, my drinking slowed down even as Tommy's picked up speed. Carolyn, I noticed, was not present, nor did her name find its way into the conversation. I wondered if she would walk in — it was, after all, her neighborhood bar, and she was apt to drop in on her own. I wondered what would happen if she did.

I guess there were a lot of things I wondered about, and perhaps that's what put the brakes on my own drinking. I didn't want any gaps in my memory, any gray patches in my awareness.

After a while Tommy was hustling me out of Armstrong's. "This is celebration time," he told me. "We don't want to sit in one place till we grow roots. We want to bop a little."

He had a car, and I just went along with him without paying too much attention to exactly where we were. We went to a noisy Greek club on the East Side, I think, where the waiters looked like mob hitmen. We went to a couple of trendy singles joints. We wound up somewhere in the Village, in a dark beery cave that reminded me, I realized after a while, of the Norwegian joint in Sunset Park. The Fjord? Right.

It was quiet there, and conversation was possible, and I found myself asking him what I'd done that was so praiseworthy. One man had killed himself and another had confessed, and where was my role in either incident?

"The stuff you came up with," he said.

"What stuff? I should have brought back fingernail parings, you could have had someone work voodoo on them."

"About Cruz and the fairies."

"He was up for murder. He didn't kill himself because he was afraid they'd get him for fag-bashing when he was a juvenile offender."

Tommy took a sip of Scotch. He said, "Couple days ago, black guy comes up to Cruz in the chow line. Huge spade, built like the Seagram's Building. 'Wait'll you get up to Green Haven,' he tells him. 'Every blood there's gonna have you for a girlfriend. Doctor gonna have to cut you a brand-new asshole, time you get outta there.'"

I didn't say anything.

"Kaplan," he said. "Drew talked to somebody who talked to somebody, and that did it. Cruz took a good look at the idea of playin' Drop the Soap for half the jigs in captivity, and the next thing you know the murderous little bastard was dancing on air. And good riddance to him."

I couldn't seem to catch my breath. I worked on it while Tommy went to the bar for another round. I hadn't touched the drink in front of me but I let him buy for both of us.

When he got back I said, "Herrera."

"Changed his story. Made a full confession."

"And pinned the killing on Cruz."

"Why not? Cruz wasn't around to complain. Who knows which one of 'em did it, and for that matter who cares? The thing is, you gave us the lever."

"For Cruz," I said. "To get him to kill himself."

"And for Herrera. Those kids of his in Santurce. Drew spoke to Herrera's lawyer and Herrera's lawyer spoke to Herrera, and the message was, look, you're going up for burglary whatever you do, and probably for murder, but if you tell the right story you'll draw shorter time and on top of that, that nice Mr. Tillary's gonna let bygones be bygones and every month there's a nice check for your wife and kiddies back home in Puerto Rico."

At the bar, a couple of old men were reliving the Louis-Schmeling fight, the second one, where Louis punished the German champion. One of the old fellows was throwing roundhouse punches in the air, demonstrating.

I said, "Who killed your wife?"

"One or the other of them. If I had to bet I'd say Cruz. He had those little beady eyes, you looked at him up close and you got that he was a killer."

"When did you look at him up close?"

"When they came and cleaned the house, the basement and the attic. Not when they came and cleaned me out, that was the second time."

He smiled, but I kept looking at him until the smile lost its certainty. "That was Herrera who helped around the house," I said. "You never met Cruz."

"Cruz came along, gave him a hand."

"You never mentioned that before."

"Oh, sure I did, Matt. What difference does it make, anyway?"

"Who killed her, Tommy?"

"Hey, let it alone, huh?"

"Answer the question."

"I already answered it."

"You killed her, didn't you?"

"What are you, crazy? Cruz killed her and Herrera swore to it, isn't that enough for you?"

"Tell me you didn't kill her."

"I didn't kill her."

"Tell me again."

"I didn't fucking kill her. What's the matter with you?"

"I don't believe you."

"Oh, Jesus," he said. He closed his eyes, put his head in his hands. He sighed and looked up and said, "You know, it's a funny thing with me. Over the telephone, I'm the best salesman you could ever imagine. I swear I could sell sand to the Arabs, I could sell ice in the winter, but face to face I'm no good at all. Why do you figure that is?"

"You tell me."

"I don't know. I used to think it was my face, the eyes and the mouth, I don't know. It's easy over the phone. I'm talking to a stranger, I don't know who he is or what he looks like, and he's not lookin' at me, and it's a cinch. Face to face, especially with someone I know, it's a different story." He looked at me. "If we were doin' this over the phone, you'd buy the whole thing."

"It's possible."

"It's fucking certain. Word for word, you'd buy the package. Suppose I was to tell you I did kill her, Matt. You couldn't prove anything. Look, the both of us walked in there, the place was a mess from the burglary, we got in an argument, tempers flared, something happened."

"You set up the burglary. You planned the whole thing, just the way Cruz and Herrera accused you of doing. And now you wriggled out of it."

"And you helped me, don't forget that part of it."

"I won't."

"And I wouldn't have gone away for it anyway, Matt. Not a chance. I'da beat it in court, only this way I don't have to go to court. Look, this is just the booze talkin', and we can both forget it in the morning, right? I didn't kill her, you didn't accuse me, we're still buddies, everything's fine. Right?"

Blackouts are never there when you want them. I woke up the next day and remembered all of it, and I found myself wishing I didn't. He'd killed his wife and he was getting away with it. And I'd helped him. I'd taken his money, and in return I'd shown him how to set one man up for suicide and pressure another into making a false confession.

And what was I going to do about it?

I couldn't think of a thing. Any story I carried to the police would speedily be denied by Tommy and his lawyer, and all I had was the thinnest of hearsay evidence, my own client's own words when he and I both had a skinful of booze. I went over it for a few days, looking for ways to shake something loose, and there was nothing. I could maybe interest a newspaper reporter, maybe get Tommy some press coverage that wouldn't make him happy, but why? And to what purpose?

It rankled. But I would just have a couple of drinks, and then it wouldn't rankle so much.

Angel Herrera pleaded to burglary, and in return the Brooklyn D.A.'s office dropped all homicide charges. He went upstate to serve five-to-ten.

And then I got a call in the middle of the night. I'd been sleeping a couple of hours but the phone woke me and I groped for it. It took me a minute to recognize the voice on the other end.

It was Carolyn Cheatham.

"I had to call you," she said, "on account of you're a bourbon man and a gentleman. I owed it to you to call you."

"What's the matter?"

"He ditched me," she said, "and he got fired out of Tannahill & Co. so he won't have to look at me around the office. Once he didn't need me he let go of me, and do you know he did it over the phone?"

"Carolyn —"

"It's all in the note," she said. "I'm leaving a note."

"Look, don't do anything yet," I said. I was out of bed, fumbling for my clothes. "I'll be right over. We'll talk about it."

"You can't stop me, Matt."

"I won't try to stop you. We'll talk first, and then you can do anything you want."

The phone clicked in my ear.

I threw my clothes on, rushed over there, hoping it would be pills, something that took its time. I broke a small pane of glass in the downstairs door and let myself in, then used an old credit card to slip the bolt of her spring lock. If she had engaged the dead bolt lock I would have had to kick the door in.

The room smelled of cordite. She was on the couch she'd passed out on the last time I saw her. The gun was still in her hand, limp at her side, and there was a black-rimmed hole in her temple.

There was a note, too. An empty bottle of Maker's Mark stood on the coffee table, an empty glass beside it. The booze showed in her hand-writing, and in the sullen phrasing of the suicide note.

I read the note. I stood there for a few minutes, not for very long, and then I got a dish towel from the pullman kitchen and wiped the bottle and the glass. I took another matching glass, rinsed it out and wiped it, and put it in the drainboard of the sink.

I stuffed the note in my pocket. I took the gun from her fingers, checked routinely for a pulse, then wrapped a sofa pillow around the gun to muffle its report. I fired one round into her chest, another into her open mouth.

I dropped the gun into a pocket and left.

They found the gun in Tommy Tillary's house, stuffed between the cushions of the living room sofa, clean of prints inside and out. Ballistics got a perfect match. I'd aimed for soft tissue with the round shot into her chest because bullets can fragment on impact with bone. That was one reason I'd fired the extra shots. The other was to rule out the possibility of suicide.

After the story made the papers, I picked up the phone and called Drew Kaplan. "I don't understand it," I said. "He was free and clear, why the hell did he kill the girl?"

"Ask him yourself," Kaplan said. He did not sound happy. "You want my opinion, he's a lunatic. I honestly didn't think he was. I figured maybe he killed his wife, maybe he didn't. Not my job to try him. But I didn't figure he was a homicidal maniac."

"It's certain he killed the girl?"

"Not much question. The gun's pretty strong evidence. Talk about finding somebody with the smoking pistol in his hand, here it was in Tommy's couch. The idiot."

"Funny he kept it."

"Maybe he had other people he wanted to shoot. Go figure a crazy man. No, the gun's evidence, and there was a phone tip, a man called in the shooting, reported a man running out of there and gave a description that fitted Tommy pretty well. Even had him wearing that red blazer he wears, tacky thing makes him look like an usher at the Paramount."

"It sounds tough to square."

"Well, somebody else'll have to try to do it," Kaplan said. "I told him I can't defend him this time. What it amounts to, I wash my hands of him."

I thought of this when I read that Angel Herrera got out just the other day. He served all ten years because he was as good at getting into trouble inside the walls as he'd been on the outside.

Somebody killed Tommy Tillary with a homemade knife after he'd served two years and three months of a manslaughter stretch. I wondered at the time if that was Herrera getting even, and I don't suppose I'll ever know. Maybe the checks stopped going to Santurce and Herrera took it the wrong way. Or maybe Tommy said the wrong thing to somebody else, and said it face to face instead of over the phone.

I don't think I'd do it that way now. I don't drink any more, and the impulse to play God seems to have evaporated with the booze.

But then a lot of things have changed. Billie left Armstrong's not long after that, left New York too; the last I heard he was off drink himself, living in Sausalito and making candles.

I ran into Dennis the other day in a bookstore on lower Fifth Avenue, full of odd volumes on yoga and spiritualism and holistic healing. And Armstrong's is scheduled to close the end of next month. The lease is up for renewal, and I suppose the next you know the old joint'll be another Korean fruit market.

I still light a candle now and then for Carolyn Cheatham and Miguelito Cruz. Not very often. Just every once in a while.

1984

STEPHEN GREENLEAF

....

Iris

THE BUICK TRUDGED toward the summit, each step slower than the last, the automatic gearing slipping ever-lower as the air thinned and the grade steepened and the trucks were rendered snails. At the top the road leveled, and the Buick spent a brief sigh of relief before coasting thankfully down the other side, atop the stiff gray strap that was Interstate 5. As it passed from Oregon to California the car seemed cheered. Its driver shared the mood, though only momentarily.

He blinked his eyes and shrugged his shoulders and twisted his head. He straightened his leg and shook it. He turned up the volume of the radio, causing a song to be sung more loudly than it merited. But the acid fog lay still behind his eyes, eating at them. As he approached a roadside rest area he decided to give both the Buick and himself a break.

During the previous week he had chased a wild goose in the shape of a rumor all the way to Seattle, with tantalizing stops in Eugene and Portland along the way. Eight hours earlier, when he had finally recognized the goose for what it was, he had headed home, hoping to make it in one day but realizing as he slowed for the rest area that he couldn't reach San Francisco that evening without risking more than was sensible in the way of vehicular manslaughter.

He took the exit, dropped swiftly to the bank of the Klamath River and pulled into a parking slot in the Randolph Collier safety rest area. After making use of the facilities, he pulled out his map and considered where to spend the night. Redding looked like the logical place, out of the mountains, at the head of the soporific valley that separated him from home. He was reviewing what he knew about Redding when a voice, aggressively gay and musical, greeted him from somewhere near the car. He glanced to his side, sat up straight and rolled down the window. "Hi," the thin voice said again.

"Hi."

She was blond, her long straight tresses misbehaving in the wind that tumbled through the river canyon. Her narrow face was white and seamless, as though it lacked flesh, was only skull. Her eyes were blue and tardy. She wore a loose green blouse gathered at the neck and wrists and a long skirt of faded calico, fringed in white ruffles. Her boots were leather and well-worn, their tops disappearing under her skirt the way the tops of the mountains at her back disappeared into a disc of cloud.

He pegged her for a hitchhiker, one who perpetually roams the roads and provokes either pity or disapproval in those who pass her by. He glanced around to see if she was fronting for a partner, but the only thing he saw besides the picnic and toilet facilities and travelers like himself was a large bundle resting atop a picnic table at the far end of the parking lot. Her worldly possessions, he guessed; her only aids to life. He looked at her again and considered whether he wanted to share some driving time and possibly a motel room with a girl who looked a little spacy and a little sexy and a lot heedless of the world that delivered him his living.

"My name's Iris," she said, wrapping her arms across her chest, shifting her weight from foot to foot, shivering in the autumn chill.

"Mine's Marsh."

"You look tired." Her concern seemed genuine, his common symptoms for some reason alarming to her.

"I am," he admitted.

"Been on the road long?"

"From Seattle."

"How far is that about?" The question came immediately, as though she habitually erased her ignorance.

"Four hundred miles. Maybe a little more."

She nodded as though the numbers made him wise. "I've been to Seattle."

"Good."

"I've been lots of places."

"Good."

She unwrapped her arms and placed them on the door and leaned toward him. Her musk was unadulterated. Her blouse dropped open to reveal breasts sharpened to twin points by the mountain air. "Where you headed, Marsh?"

"South."

"L.A.?"

He shook his head. "San Francisco."

"Good. Perfect."

He expected it right then, the flirting pitch for a lift, but her request was slightly different. "Could you take something down there for me?"

He frowned and thought of the package on the picnic table. Drugs? "What?" he asked.

"I'll show you in a sec. Do you think you could, though?"

He shook his head. "I don't think so. I mean, I'm kind of on a tight schedule, and . . ."

She wasn't listening. "It goes to . . ." She pulled a scrap of paper from the pocket of her skirt and uncrumpled it. "It goes to 95 Albosa Drive, in Hurley City. That's near Frisco, isn't it? Marvin said it was."

He nodded. "But I don't . . ."

She put up a hand. "Hold still. I'll be right back."

She skipped twice, her long skirt hopping high above her boots to show a shaft of gypsum thigh, then trotted to the picnic table and picked up the bundle. Halfway back to the car she proffered it like a prize soufflé.

"Is this what you want me to take?" he asked as she approached.

She nodded, then looked down at the package and frowned. "I don't like this one," she said, her voice dropping to a dismissive rasp.

"Why not?"

"Because it isn't happy. It's from the B Box, so it can't help it, I guess, but all the same it should go back, I don't care *what* Marvin says."

"What is it? A puppy?"

She thrust the package through the window. He grasped it reflexively, to keep it from dropping to his lap. As he secured his grip the girl ran off. "Hey! Wait a minute," he called after her. "I can't take this thing. You'll have to . . ."

He thought the package moved. He slid one hand beneath it and with the other peeled back the cotton strips that swaddled it. A baby — not canine but human — glared at him and screamed. He looked frantically for the girl and saw her climbing into a gray Volkswagen bug that was soon scooting out of the rest area and climbing toward the freeway.

He swore, then rocked the baby awkwardly for an instant, trying to quiet the screams it formed with every muscle. When that didn't work, he placed the child on the seat beside him, started the car and backed out. As he started forward he had to stop to avoid another car, and then to reach out wildly to keep the child from rolling off the seat.

He moved the gear to park and gathered the seat belt on the passenger side and tried to wrap it around the baby in a way that would be more safe than throttling. The result was not reassuring. He unhooked the belt and put the baby on the floor beneath his legs, put the car in gear and set out after the little gray VW that had disappeared with the child's presumptive mother. He caught it only after several frantic miles, when he reached the final slope that descended to the grassy plain that separated the Siskiyou range from the lordly aspect of Mt. Shasta.

The VW buzzed toward the mammoth mountain like a mad mouse assaulting an elephant. He considered overtaking the car, forcing Iris to stop, returning the baby, then getting the hell away from her as fast as the Buick would take him. But something in his memory of her look and words made him keep his distance, made him keep Iris in sight while he waited for her to make a turn toward home.

The highway flattened, then crossed the high meadow that nurtured sheep and cattle and horses below the lumps of the southern Cascades and the Trinity Alps. Traffic was light, the sun low above the western peaks, the air a steady splash of autumn. He checked his gas gauge. If Iris didn't turn off in the next fifty miles he would either have to force her to stop or let her go. The piercing baby sounds that rose from beneath his knees made the latter choice impossible.

They reached Yreka, and he closed to within a hundred yards of the bug, but Iris ignored his plea that the little city be her goal. Thirty minutes later, after he had decided she was nowhere near her destination, Iris abruptly left the interstate, at the first exit to a village that was handmaiden to the mountain, a town reputed to house an odd collection of spiritual seekers and religious zealots.

The mountain itself, volcanic, abrupt, spectacular, had been held by the Indians to be holy, and the area surrounding it was replete with hot springs and mud baths and other prehistoric marvels. Modern mystics had accepted the mantle of the mountain, and the crazy girl and her silly bug fit with what he knew about the place and those who gathered there. What didn't fit was the baby she had foisted on him.

He slowed and glanced at his charge once again and failed to receive anything resembling contentment in return. Fat little arms escaped the blanket and pulled the air like taffy. Spittle dribbled down its chin. A translucent bubble appeared at a tiny nostril, then broke silently and vanished.

The bug darted through the north end of town, left, then right, then left again, quickly, as though it sensed pursuit. He lagged behind, hoping Iris was confident she had ditched him. He looked at the baby again, marveling that it could cry so loud, could for so long expend the major portion of its strength in unrequited pleas. When he looked at the road again the bug had disappeared.

He swore and slowed and looked at driveways, then began to plan what to do if he had lost her. Houses dwindled, the street became dirt, then flanked the log decks and lumber stacks and wigwam burners of a sawmill. A road sign declared it unlawful to sleigh, toboggan or ski on a county road. He had gasped the first breaths of panic when he saw the VW nestled next to a ramshackle cabin on the back edge of town, empty, as though it had been there always.

A pair of firs sheltered the cabin and the car, made the dwindling day seem night. The driveway was mud, the yard bordered by a falling wormwood fence. He drove to the next block and stopped his car, the cabin now invisible.

He knew he couldn't keep the baby much longer. He had no idea what to do, for it or with it, had no idea what it wanted, no idea what awaited it in Hurley City, had only a sense that the girl, Iris, was goofy, perhaps pathologically so, and that he should not abet her plan.

Impossibly, the child cried louder. He had some snacks in the car — crackers, cookies, some cheese — but he was afraid the baby was too young for solids. He considered buying milk, and a bottle, and playing parent. The baby cried again, gasped and sputtered, then repeated its protest.

He reached down and picked it up. The little red face inflated, contorted, mimicked a steam machine that continuously whistled. The puffy cheeks, the tiny blue eyes, the round pug nose, all were engorged in scarlet fury. He cradled the baby in his arms as best he could and rocked it. The crying dimmed momentarily, then began again.

His mind ran the gauntlet of childhood scares — diphtheria, smallpox, measles, mumps, croup, even a pressing need to burp. God knew what ailed it. He patted its forehead and felt the sticky heat of fever.

Shifting position, he felt something hard within the blanket, felt for it, finally drew it out. A nippled baby bottle, half-filled, body-warm. He shook it and presented the nipple to the baby, who sucked it as its due. Giddy at his feat, he unwrapped his package further, enough to tell him he was holding a little girl and that she seemed whole and healthy except for her rage and fever. When she was feeding steadily he put her back on the floor and got out of the car.

The stream of smoke it emitted into the evening dusk made the cabin seem dangled from a string. Beneath the firs the ground was moist, a spongy mat of rotting twigs and needles. The air was cold and damp and smelled of burning wood. He walked slowly up the drive, courting silence, alert for the menace implied by the hand-lettered sign, nailed to the nearest tree, that ordered him to KEEP OUT.

The cabin was dark but for the variable light at a single window. The porch was piled high with firewood, both logs and kindling. A maul and wedge leaned against a stack of fruitwood piled next to the door. He walked to the far side of the cabin and looked beyond it for signs of Marvin.

A tool shed and a broken-down school bus filled the rear yard. Between the two a tethered nanny goat grazed beneath a line of drying clothes, silent but for her neck bell, the swollen udder oscillating easily beneath her, the teats extended like accusing fingers. Beyond the yard a thicket of berry bushes served as fence, and beyond the bushes a stand of pines blocked further vision. He felt alien, isolated, exposed, threatened, as Marvin doubtlessly hoped all strangers would.

He thought about the baby, wondered if it was all right, wondered if babies could drink so much they got sick or even choked. A twinge of fear sent him trotting back to the car. The baby was fine, the bottle empty on the floor beside it, its noises not wails but only muffled whimpers. He returned to the cabin and went onto the porch and knocked at the door and waited.

Iris wore the same blouse and skirt and boots, the same eyes too shallow to hold her soul. She didn't recognize him; her face pinched only with uncertainty.

He stepped toward her and she backed away and asked him what he wanted. The room behind her was a warren of vague shapes, the only source of light far in the back by a curtain that spanned the room.

"I want to give you your baby back," he said.

She looked at him more closely, then opened her mouth in silent exclamation, then slowly smiled. "How'd you know where I lived?"

"I followed you."

"Why? Did something happen to it already?"

"No, but I don't want to take it with me."

She seemed truly puzzled. "Why not? It's on your way, isn't it? Almost?"

He ignored the question. "I want to know some more about the baby."

"Like what?"

"Like whose is it? Yours?"

Iris frowned and nibbled her lower lip. "Sort of."

"What do you mean, 'sort of?' Did you give birth to it?"

"Not exactly." Iris combed her hair with her fingers, then shook it off her face with an irritated twitch. "What are you asking all these questions for?"

"Because you asked me to do you a favor and I think I have the right to know what I'm getting into. That's only fair, isn't it?"

She paused. Her pout was dubious. "I guess."

"So where did you get the baby?" he asked again.

"Marvin got it."

"From whom?"

"Those people in Hurley City. So I don't know why you won't take it back, seeing as how it's theirs and all."

"But why . . ."

His question was obliterated by a high glissando, brief and piercing. He looked at Iris, then at the shadowy interior of the cabin.

There was no sign of life, no sign of anything but the leavings of neglect and a spartan bent. A fat gray cat hopped off a shelf and sauntered toward the back of the cabin and disappeared behind the blanket that was draped on the rope that spanned the rear of the room. The cry echoed once again. "What's that?" he asked her.

Iris giggled. "What does it sound like?"

"Another baby?"

Iris nodded.

"Can I see it?"

"Why?"

"Because I like babies."

"If you like them, why won't you take the one I gave you down to Hurley City?"

"Maybe I'm changing my mind. Can I see this one?"

"I'm not supposed to let anyone in here."

"It'll be okay. Really. Marvin isn't here, is he?"

She shook her head. "But he'll be back any time. He just went to town."

He summoned reasonableness and geniality. "Just let me see your baby for a second, Iris. Please? Then I'll go. And take the other baby with me. I promise."

She pursed her lips, then nodded and stepped back. "I got more than one," she suddenly bragged. "Let me show you." She turned and walked quickly toward the rear of the cabin and disappeared behind the blanket.

When he followed he found himself in a space that was half-kitchen and half-nursery. Opposite the electric stove and Frigidaire, along the wall between the wood stove and the rear door, was a row of wooden boxes, seven of them, old orange crates, dividers removed, painted different colors and labeled A to G. Faint names of orchards and renderings of fruits rose through the paint on the stub ends of the crates. Inside boxes C through G were babies, buried deep in nests of rags and scraps of blanket. One of them was crying. The others slept soundly, warm and toasty, healthy and happy from all the evidence he had.

"My God," he said.

"Aren't they beautiful? They're just the best little things in the whole world. Yes they are. Just the best little babies in the whole wide world. And Iris loves them all a bunch. Yes, she does. Doesn't she?"

Beaming, Iris cooed to the babies for another moment, then her face darkened. "The one I gave you, she wasn't happy here. That's because she was a B Box baby. My B babies are always sad, I don't know why. I treat them all the same, but the B babies are just contrary. That's why the one I gave you should go back. Where is it, anyway?"

"In the car."

"By itself?"

He nodded.

"You shouldn't leave her there like that," Iris chided. "She's pouty enough already."

"What about these others?" he asked, looking at the boxes. "Do they stay here forever?"

Her whole aspect solidified. "They stay till Marvin needs them. Till he does, I give them everything they want. Everything they need. No one could be nicer to my babies than me. *No* one."

The fire in the stove lit her eyes like ice in sunlight. She gazed raptly at the boxes, one by one, and received something he sensed was sexual in return. Her breaths were rapid and shallow, her fists clenched at her sides. "Where'd you get these babies?" he asked softly.

"Marvin gets them." She was only half-listening.

"Where?"

"All over. We had one from Nevada one time, and two from Idaho I think. Most are from California, though. And Oregon. I think that C Box baby's from Spokane. That's Oregon, isn't it?"

He didn't correct her. "Have there been more besides these?"

"Some."

"How many?"

"Oh, maybe ten. No, more than that. I've had three of all the babies except G babies."

"And Marvin got them all for you?"

She nodded and went to the stove and turned on a burner. "You want some tea? It's herbal. Peppermint."

He shook his head. "What happened to the other babies? The ones that aren't here any more?"

"Marvin took them." Iris sipped her tea.

"Where?"

"To someone that wanted to love them." The declaration was as close as she would come to gospel.

The air in the cabin seemed suddenly befouled, not breathable. "Is that what this is all about, Iris? Giving babies to people that want them?"

"That want them and will *love* them. See, Marvin gets these babies from people that *don't* want them, and gives them to people that *do*. It's his business."

"Does he get paid for it?"

She shrugged absently. "A little, I think."

"Do you go with Marvin when he picks them up?"

"Sometimes. When it's far."

"And where does he take them? To Idaho and Nevada, or just around here?"

She shrugged again. "He doesn't tell me where they go. He says he doesn't want me to try and get them back." She smiled peacefully. "He knows how I am about my babies."

"How long have you and Marvin been doing this?"

"I been with Marvin about three years."

"And you've been trading in babies all that time?"

"Just about."

She poured some more tea into a ceramic cup and sipped it. She gave no sign of guile or guilt, no sign that what he suspected could possibly be true.

"Do you have any children of your own, Iris?"

Her hand shook enough to spill her tea. "I *almost* had one once."

"What do you mean?"

She made a face. "I got pregnant, but nobody wanted me to keep it so I didn't."

"Did you put it up for adoption?"

She shook her head.

"Abortion?"

Iris nodded, apparently in pain, and mumbled something. He asked her what she'd said. "I did it myself," she repeated. "That's what I can't live with. I scraped it out of there myself. I passed out. I . . ."

She fell silent. He looked back at the row of boxes that held her penance. When she saw him look she began to sing a song. "Aren't they just perfect?" she said when she was through. "Aren't they all just perfect?"

"How do you know where the baby you gave me belongs?" he asked quietly.

"Marvin's got a book that keeps track. I sneaked a look at it one time when he was stoned."

"Where's he keep it?"

"In the van. At least that's where I found it." Iris put her hands on his chest and pushed. "You better go before Marvin gets back. You'll take the baby, won't you? It just don't belong here with the others. It fusses all the time and I can't love it like I should."

He looked at Iris's face, at the firelight washing across it, making it alive. "Where are you from, Iris?"

"Me? Minnesota."

Did you come to California with Marvin?"

She shook her head. "I come with another guy. I was tricking for him when I got knocked up. After the abortion I told him I wouldn't trick no more so he ditched me. Then I did a lot of drugs for a while, till I met Marvin at a commune down by Mendocino."

"What's Marvin's last name?"

"Hessel. Now you got to go. Really. Marvin's liable to do something crazy if he finds you here." She walked toward him and he retreated.

"Okay, Iris. Just one thing. Could you give me something for the baby to eat? She's real hungry."

Iris frowned. "She only likes goat's milk, is the problem, and I haven't milked today." She walked to the Frigidaire and returned with a bottle. "This is all I got. Now, git."

He nodded, took the bottle from her, then retreated to his car.

He opened the door on the stinging smell of ammonia. The baby greeted him with screams. He picked it up, rocked it, talked to it, hummed a tune, finally gave it the second bottle, which was the only thing it wanted.

As it sucked its sustenance he started the car and let the engine warm, and a minute later flipped the heater switch. When it seemed prudent, he unwrapped the child and unpinned her soggy diaper and patted her dumplinged bottom dry with a tissue from the glove compartment. After covering her with her blanket he got out of the car, pulled his suitcase from the trunk and took out his last clean T-shirt, then returned to the car and fashioned a bulky diaper out of the cotton shirt and affixed it to the child, pricking his finger in the process, spotting both the garment and the baby with his blood. Then he sat for a time, considering his obligations to the children that had suddenly littered his life.

He should go to the police, but Marvin might return before they responded and might learn of Iris' deed and harm the children or flee with them. He could call the police and wait in place for them to come, but he doubted his ability to convey his precise suspicions over the phone. As he searched for other options, headlights ricocheted off his mirror and into his eyes, then veered off. When his vision was re-established he reached into the glove compartment for his revolver. Shoving it into his pocket, he got out of the car and walked back to the driveway and disobeyed the sign again.

A new shape had joined the scene, rectangular and dark. Marvin's van, creaking as it cooled. He waited, listened, and when he sensed no other presence he approached it. A converted bread truck, painted Navy blue, with sliding doors into the driver's cabin and hinged doors at the back. The right fender was dented, the rear bumper wired in place. A knobby-tired motorcycle was strapped to a rack on the top. The door on the driver's side was open, so he climbed in.

The high seat was rotted through, its stuffing erupting like white weeds through the dirty vinyl. The floorboards were littered with food wrappers and beer cans and cigarette butts. He activated his pencil flash and pawed through the refuse, pausing at the only pristine object in the van — a business card, white with black engraving, taped to a corner of the dash: 'J. Arnold Rasker, Attorney at Law. Practice in all Courts. Initial Consultation Free. Phone day or night.'

He looked through the cab for another minute, found nothing resembling Marvin's notebook and nothing else of interest. After listening for Marvin's return and hearing nothing he went through the narrow doorway behind the driver's seat into the cargo area in the rear, the yellow ball that dangled from his flash bouncing playfully before him.

The entire area had been carpeted, ceiling included, in a matted pink plush that was stained in unlikely places and coming unglued in others. A roundish window had been cut into one wall by hand, then covered with plasticine kept in place with tape. Two upholstered chairs were bolted to the floor on one side of the van, and an Army cot stretched out along the other. Two orange crates similar to those in the cabin, though empty, lay between the chairs. Above the cot a picture of John Lennon was tacked to the carpeted wall with a rusty nail. A small propane bottle was strapped into one corner, an Igloo cooler in another. Next to the Lennon poster a lever-action rifle rested in two leather slings. The smells were of gasoline and marijuana and unwashed flesh. Again he found no notebook.

He switched off his light and backed out of the van and walked to the cabin, pausing on the porch. Music pulsed from the interior, heavy metal, obliterating all noises including his own. He walked to the window and peered inside.

Iris, carrying and feeding a baby, paced the room, eyes closed, mumbling, seemingly deranged. Alone momentarily, she was soon joined by a wide and woolly man, wearing cowboy boots and Levi's, a plaid shirt, full beard, hair to his shoulders. A light film of grease coated flesh and clothes alike, as though he had just been dipped. Marvin strode through the room without speaking, his black eyes angry, his shoulders tipping to the frenetic music as he sucked the final puffs of a joint held in an oddly dainty clip.

Both Marvin and Iris were lost in their tasks. When their paths crossed they backed away as though they feared each other. He watched them for five long minutes. When they disappeared behind the curtain in the back he hurried to the door and went inside the cabin.

The music paused, then began again, the new piece indistinguishable from the old. The heavy fog of dope washed into his lungs and lightened his head and braked his brain. Murmurs from behind the curtain erupted into a swift male curse. A pan clattered on the stove; wood scraped against wood. He drew his gun and moved to the edge of the room and sidled toward the curtain and peered around its edge.

Marvin sat in a chair at a small table, gripping a bottle of beer. Iris was at the stove, her back to Marvin, opening a can of soup. Marvin guzzled half the bottle, banged it on the table, and swore again. "How could you be so fucking stupid?"

"Don't, Marvin. Please?"

"Just tell me who you gave it to. That's all I want to know. It was your buddy Gretel, wasn't it? Had to be, she's the only one around here as loony as you."

"It wasn't anyone you know. Really. It was just a guy."

"What guy?"

"Just *a guy.* I went out to a rest area way up by Oregon, and I talked to him and he said he was going to Frisco so I gave it to him and told him where to take it. You *know* it didn't belong here, Marvin. You know how puny it was."

Marvin stood up, knocking his chair to the floor. "You stupid bitch." His hand raised high, Marvin advanced on Iris with beer dribbling from his chin. "I'll break your jaw, woman. I swear I will."

"Don't hit me, Marvin. Please don't hit me again."

"Who was it? I want a name."

"I don't *know,* I told you. Just some guy going to Frisco. His name was Mark, I think."

"And he took the kid?"

Iris nodded. "He was real nice."

"You bring him here? Huh? Did you bring the son-of-a-bitch to the cabin? Did you tell him about the others?"

"No. Marvin. No. I swear. You know I'd never do that."

"Lying bitch."

Marvin grabbed Iris by the hair and dragged her away from the stove and slapped her across the face. She screamed and cowered. Marvin raised his hand to strike again.

Sucking a breath, he raised his gun and stepped from behind the curtain. "Hold it," he told Marvin. "Don't move."

Marvin froze, twisted his head, took in the gun and released his grip on Iris and backed away from her, his black eyes glistening. A slow smile exposed dark and crooked teeth. "Well, now," Marvin drawled. "Just who might you be besides a fucking trespasser? Don't tell me; let me guess. You're the nice man Iris gave a baby to. The one she swore she didn't bring out here. Right?"

"She didn't bring me. I followed her."

Both men glanced at Iris. Her hand was at her mouth and she was nibbling a knuckle. "I thought you went to Frisco," was all she said.

"Not yet."

"What do you want?" Her question assumed a fearsome answer.

Marvin laughed. "You stupid bitch. He wants the *rest* of them. Then he wants to throw us in jail. He wants to be a hero, Iris. And to be a hero he has to put you and me behind bars for the rest of our fucking lives." Marvin took a step forward.

"Don't be dumb." He raised the gun to Marvin's eyes.

Marvin stopped, frowned, then grinned again. "You look like you used that piece before."

"Once or twice."

"What's your gig?"

"Detective. Private."

Marvin's lips parted around his crusted teeth. "You must be kidding. Iris flags down some bastard on the freeway and he turns out to be a private cop?"

"That's about it."

Marvin shook his head. "Judas H. Priest. And here you are. A professional hero, just like I said."

He captured Marvin's eyes. "I want the book."

"What book?" Marvin burlesqued ignorance.

"The book with the list of babies and where you got them and where you took them."

Marvin looked at Iris, stuck her with his stare. "You're dead meat, you know that? You bring the bastard here and tell him all about it and expect him to just take off and not try to *stop* us? You're too fucking dumb to breathe, Iris. I got to put you out of your misery."

"I'm sorry, Marvin."

"He's going to take them *back,* Iris. Get it? He's going to take those sweet babies away from you and give them back to the assholes that don't want them. And then he's going to the cops and they're going to say you *kidnapped* those babies, Iris, and that you were bad to them and should go to jail because of what you did. Don't you see that, you brain-fried bitch? *Don't you see what he's going to do?*"

"I . . ." Iris stopped, overwhelmed by Marvin's incantation. "Are you?" she asked, finally looking away from Marvin.

"I'm going to do what's best for the babies, Iris. That's all."

"What's best for them is with me and Marvin."

"Not any more," he told her. "Marvin's been shucking you, Iris. He steals those babies. Takes them from their parents, parents who love them. He roams up and down the coast stealing children and then he sells them, Iris. Either back to the people he took them from or to people desperate to adopt. I think he's hooked up with a lawyer named Rasker, who arranges private adoptions for big money and splits the take with Marvin. He's not interested in who loves those kids, Iris. He's only interested in how much he can sell them for."

Something had finally activated Iris' eyes. "Marvin? Is that true?"

"No, baby. The guy's blowing smoke. He's trying to take the babies away from you and then get people to believe you did something bad, just like that time with the abortion. He's trying to say you did bad things to babies again, Iris. We can't let him do that."

He spoke quickly, to erase Marvin's words. "People don't give away babies, Iris. Not to guys like Marvin. There are agencies that arrange that kind of thing, that check to make sure the new home is in the best interests of the child. Marvin just swipes them and sells them to the highest bidder, Iris. That's all he's in it for."

"I don't believe you."

"It doesn't matter. Just give me Marvin's notebook and we can check it out, contact the parents and see what they say about their kids. Ask if they wanted to be rid of them. That's fair, isn't it?"

"I don't know. I guess."

"Iris?"

"What, Marvin?"

"I want you to pick up that pan and knock this guy on the head. Hard. Go on, Iris. He won't shoot you, you know that. Hit him on the head so he can't put us in jail."

He glanced at Iris, then as quickly to Marvin and to Iris once again. "Don't do it, Iris. Marvin's trouble. I think you know that now." He looked away from Iris and gestured at her partner. "Where's the book?"

"Iris?"

Iris began to cry. "I can't, Marvin. I can't do that."

"The book," he said to Marvin again. "Where is it?"

Marvin laughed. "You'll never know, detective."

"Okay. We'll do it your way. On the floor. Hands behind your head. Legs spread. Now."

Marvin didn't move. When he spoke the words were languid. "You don't look much like a killer, detective, and I've known a few, believe me. So I figure if you're not gonna shoot me I don't got to do what you say. I figure I'll just take that piece away from you and feed it to you inch by inch. Huh? Why don't I do just that?"

He took two quick steps to Marvin's side and sliced open Marvin's cheek with a quick swipe of the gun barrel. "Want some more?"

Marvin pawed at his cheek with a grimy hand, then examined his bloody fingers. "You bastard. Okay. I'll get the book. It's under here."

Marvin bent toward the floor, twisting away from him, sliding his hands toward the darkness below the stove. He couldn't tell what Marvin was doing, so he squinted, then moved closer. When Marvin began to stand he jumped back, but Marvin wasn't attacking, Marvin was holding a baby, not a book, holding a baby by the throat.

"Okay, pal," Marvin said through his grin. "Now, you want to see this kid die before your eyes, you just keep hold of that gun. You want to see it breathe some more, you drop it."

He froze, his eyes on Marvin's fingers, which inched further around the baby's neck and began to squeeze.

"The baby gurgled, gasped, twitched, was silent. Its face reddened; its eyes bulged. The tendons in Marvin's hand stretched taut. Between grimy gritted teeth, Marvin wheezed in rapid streams of glee.

He dropped his gun. Marvin told Iris to pick it up. She did, and exchanged the gun for the child. Her eyes lapped Marvin's face, as though to renew its acquaintance. Abruptly, she turned and ran around the curtain and disappeared.

"Well, now." Marvin's words slid easily. "Looks like the worm has turned, detective. What's your name, anyhow?"

"Tanner."

"Well, Tanner, your ass is mine. No more John Wayne stunts for you. You can kiss this world good-bye."

Marvin fished in the pocket of his jeans, then drew out a small spiral notebook and flashed it. "It's all in here, Tanner. Where they came from; where they went. Now watch."

Gun in one hand, notebook in the other, Marvin went to the wood stove and flipped open the heavy door. The fire made shadows dance.

"Don't."

"Watch, bastard."

Marvin tossed the notebook into the glowing coals, fished in the box beside the stove for a stick of kindling, then tossed it in after the notebook and closed the iron door. "Bye-bye babies." Marvin's laugh was quick and cruel. "Now turn around. We're going out back."

He did as he was told, walking toward the door, hearing only a silent shuffle at his back. As he passed her he glanced at Iris. She hugged the baby Marvin had threatened, crying, not looking at him. "Remember the one in my car," he said to her. She nodded silently, then turned away.

Marvin prodded him in the back and he moved to the door. Hand on the knob, he paused, hoping for a magical deliverance, but none came. Marvin prodded him again and he moved outside, onto the porch then into the yard. "Around back," Marvin ordered. "Get in the bus."

He staggered, tripping over weeds, stumbling over rocks, until he reached the rusting bus. The moon and stars had disappeared; the night was black and still but for the whistling wind, clearly Marvin's ally. The nanny goat laughed at them, then trotted out of reach. He glanced back at Marvin. In one hand was a pistol, in the other a blanket. "Go on in. Just pry the door open."

He fit his finger between the rubber edges of the bus door and opened it. The first step was higher than he thought, and he tripped and almost fell. "Watch it. I almost blasted you right then."

He couldn't suppress a giggle. For reasons of his own, Marvin matched his laugh. "Head on back, Tanner. Pretend you're on a field trip to the zoo."

He walked down the aisle between the broken seats, smelling rot and rust and the lingering scent of skunk. "Why here?" he asked as he reached the rear.

"Because you'll keep in here just fine till I get time to dig a hole out back and open that emergency door and dump you in. Plus it's quiet. I figure with the bus and the blanket no one will hear a thing. Sit."

He sat, Marvin draped the blanket across the arm that held the gun, then extended the shrouded weapon toward his chest. He had no doubt that Marvin would shoot without a thought or fear. "Any last words, Tanner? Any parting thoughts?"

"Just that you forgot something."

"What?"

"You left the door open."

Marvin glanced quickly toward the door in the front of the bus. He dove for Marvin's legs, sweeping at the gun with his left hand as he did so, hoping to dislodge it into the folds of the blanket where it would lie useless and unattainable.

"Cocksucker."

Marvin wrested the gun from his grasp and raised it high, tossing off the blanket in the process. He twisted frantically to protect against the blow he knew was coming, but Marvin was too heavy and strong, retained the upper hand by kneeling on his chest. The revolver glinted in the darkness, a missile poised to descend.

Sound split the air, a piercing scream of agony from the cabin or somewhere near it. "What the hell?" Marvin swore, started to retreat, then almost thoughtlessly clubbed him with the gun, once, then again. After a flash of pain a broad black creature held him down for a length of time he couldn't calculate.

When he was aware again he was alone in the bus, lying in the aisle. His head felt crushed to pulp. He put a hand to his temple and felt blood. Midst throbbing pain he struggled to his feet and made his way outside and stood leaning against the bus while the night air struggled to clear his head.

He took a step, staggered, took another and gained an equilibrium, then lost it and sat down. Back on his feet, he trudged toward the porch and opened the door. Behind him, the nanny laughed again.

The cabin was dark, the only light the faint flicker from the stove behind the curtain. He walked carefully, trying to avoid the litter on the floor, the shapes in the room. Halfway to the back his foot struck something soft. As he bent to shove it out of his way it made a human sound. He knelt, saw that it was Iris, then found a lamp and turned it on.

She was crumpled, face down, in the center of the room, arms and legs folded under her, her body curled to avoid assault. He knelt again, heard her groan once more, and saw that what he'd thought was a piece of skirt was in fact a pool of blood and what he'd thought was shadow was a broad wet trail of the selfsame substance leading toward the rear of the cabin.

He ran his hands down her body, feeling for wounds. Finding none, he rolled Iris to her side, then to her back. Blood bubbled from a point beneath her sternum. Her eyelids fluttered, open, closed, then open again. "He shot me," she said. "It hurt so bad I couldn't stop crying so he shot me."

"I know. Don't try to talk."

"Did he shoot the babies, too? I thought I heard. . . ."

"I don't know."

"Would you look? Please?"

He nodded, stood up, fought a siege of vertigo, then went behind the curtain, then returned to Iris. "They're all right."

She tried to smile her thanks. "Something scared him off. I think some people were walking by outside and heard the shot and went for help. I heard them yelling."

"Where would he go, Iris?"

"Up in the woods. On his dirt bike. He knows lots of people up there. They grow dope, live off the land. The cops'll never find him." Iris moaned again. "I'm dying, aren't I?"

"I don't know. Is there a phone here?"

She shook her head. "Down at the end of the street. By the market."

"I'm going down and call an ambulance. And the cops. How long ago did Marvin leave?"

She closed her eyes. "I blacked out. Oh, God. It's real bad now, Mr. Tanner. Real bad."

"I know, Iris. You hang on. I'll be back in a second. Try to hold this in place." He took out his handkerchief and folded it into a square and placed it on her wound. "Press as hard as you can." He took her left hand and placed it on the compress, then stood up.

"Wait. I have to . . ."

He spoke above her words. "You have to get to a hospital. I'll be back in a minute and we can talk some more."

"But . . ."

"Hang on."

He ran from the cabin and down the drive, spotted the lights of the convenience market down the street and ran to the phone booth and placed his calls. The police said they'd already been notified and a car was on the way. The ambulance said it would be six minutes. As fast as he could he ran back to the cabin, hoping it would be fast enough.

Iris had moved. Her body was straightened, her right arm outstretched toward the door, the gesture of a supplicant. The sleeve of her blouse was tattered, burned to a ragged edge above her elbow. Below the sleeve her arm was red in spots, blistered in others, dappled like burned food. The hand at its end was charred and curled into a crusty fist that was dusted with gray ash. Within the fingers was an object, blackened, burned, and treasured.

He pried it from her grasp. The cover was burned away, and the edges of the pages were curled and singed, but they remained decipherable, the written scrawl preserved. The list of names and places was organized to match the gaily painted boxes in the back. Carson City. Boise. Grant's Pass. San Bernardino. Modesto. On and on, a gazetteer of crime.

"I saved it," Iris mumbled. "I saved it for my babies."

He raised her head to his lap and held it till she died. Then he went to his car and retrieved his B Box baby and placed her in her appointed crib. For the first time since he'd known her the baby made only happy sounds, an irony that was lost on the five dead children at her flank and on the just dead woman who had feared it all.

1984

SARA PARETSKY

Three-Dot Po

CINDA GOODRICH AND I were jogging acquaintances. A professional photographer, she kept the same erratic hours as a private investigator; we often met along Belmont Harbor in the late mornings. By then we had the lakefront to ourselves; the hip young professionals run early so they can make their important eight o'clock meetings.

Cinda occasionally ran with her boyfriend, Jonathan Michaels, and always with her golden retriever, Three-Dot Po, or Po. The dog's name meant something private to her and Jonathan; they only laughed and shook their heads when I asked about it.

Jonathan played the piano, often at late-night private parties. He was seldom up before noon and usually left exercise to Cinda and Po. Cinda was a diligent runner, even on the hottest days of summer and the coldest of winter. I do twenty-five miles a week in a grudging fight against age and calories, but Cinda made a ten-mile circuit every morning with religious enthusiasm.

One December I didn't see her out for a week and wondered vaguely if she might be sick. The following Saturday, however, we met on the small promontory abutting Belmont Harbor — she returning from her jaunt three miles farther north, and I just getting ready to turn around for home. As we jogged together, she explained that Eli Burton, the fancy North Michigan Avenue department store, had hired her to photograph children talking to Santa. She made a face. "Not the way Eric Lieberman got his start, but it'll finance January in the Bahamas for Jonathan and me." She called to Po, who was inspecting a dead bird on the rocks by the water, and moved on ahead of me.

The week before Christmas the temperature dropped suddenly and left us with the bitterest December on record. My living room was so cold I couldn't bear to use it; I handled all my business bundled in bed, even moving the television into the bedroom. I didn't go out at all on Christmas Eve.

Christmas Day I was supposed to visit friends in one of the northern suburbs. I wrapped myself in a blanket and went to the living room to scrape a patch of ice on a window. I wanted to see how badly snowed over Halsted Street was, assuming my poor little Omega would even start.

I hadn't run for five days, since the temperature first fell. I was feeling flabby, knew I should force myself outside, but felt too lazy to face the weather. I was about to go back to the bedroom and wrap some presents when I caught sight of a golden retriever moving smartly down the street. It was Po; behind her came Cinda, warm in an orange down vest, face covered with a ski mask.

"Ah, nuts," I muttered. If she could do it, I could do it. Layering on thermal underwear, two pairs of wool socks, sweatshirts, and a down vest, I told myself encouragingly, "Quitters never win and winners never quit," and "It's not the size of the dog in the fight that counts but the size of the fight in the dog."

The slogans got me out the door, but they didn't prepare me for the shock of cold. The wind sucked the air out of my lungs and left me gasping. I staggered back into the entryway and tied a scarf around my face, adjusted earmuffs and a wool cap, and put on sunglasses to protect my eyes.

Even so, it was bitter going. After the first mile the blood was flowing well and my arms and legs were warm, but my feet were cold, and even heavy muffling couldn't keep the wind from scraping the skin on my cheeks. Few cars were on the streets, and no other people. It was like running through a wasteland. This is what it would be like after a nuclear war: no people, freezing cold, snow blowing across in fine pelting particles like a desert sandstorm.

The lake made an even eerier landscape. Steam rose from it as from a giant cauldron. The water was invisible beneath the heavy veils of mist. I paused for a moment in awe, but the wind quickly cut through the layers of clothes.

The lake path curved around as it led to the promontory so that you could only see a few yards ahead of you. I kept expecting to meet Cinda and Po on their way back, but the only person who passed me was a solitary male jogger, anonymous in a blue ski mask and khaki down jacket.

At the far point of the promontory the wind blew unblocked across the lake. It swept snow and frozen mist pellets with it, blowing in a high persistent whine. I was about to turn and go home when I heard a dog barking above the keening wind. I hesitated to go down to the water, but what if it was Po, separated from her mistress?

The rocks leading down to the lake were covered with ice. I slipped and slid down, trying desperately for hand- and toe-holds — even if someone were around to rescue me I wouldn't survive a bath in subzero water.

I found Po on a flat slab of rock. She was standing where its edge hung over the mist-covered water, barking furiously. I called to her. She turned her head briefly but wouldn't come.

By now I had a premonition of what would meet me when I'd picked my way across the slab. I lay flat on the icy rock, gripping my feet around one end, and leaned over it through the mist to peer in the water. As soon as I showed up, Po stopped barking and began an uneasy pacing and whining.

Cinda's body was just visible beneath the surface. It was a four-foot drop to the water from where I lay. I couldn't reach her and I didn't dare get down in the water. I thought furiously and finally unwound a long muffler from around my neck. Tying it to a jagged spur near me I wrapped the other end around my waist and prayed. Leaning over from the waist gave me the length I needed to reach into the water. I took a deep breath and plunged my arms in. The shock of the water was almost more than I could bear; I concentrated on Cinda, on the dog, thought of Christmas in the northern suburbs, of everything possible but the cold which made my arms almost useless. "You only have one chance, Vic. Don't blow it."

The weight of her body nearly dragged me in on top of Cinda. I slithered across the icy rock, scissoring my feet wildly until they caught on the spur where my muffler was tied. Po was no help, either. She planted herself next to me, whimpering with anxiety as I pulled her mistress from the water. With water soaked in every garment, Cinda must have weighed two hundred pounds. I almost lost her several times, almost lost myself, but I got her up. I tried desperately to revive her, Po anxiously licking her face, but there was no hope. I finally realized I was going to die of exposure myself if I didn't get away from there. I tried calling Po to come with me, but she wouldn't leave Cinda. I ran as hard as I could back to the harbor, where I flagged down a car. My teeth were

chattering so hard I almost couldn't speak, but I got the strangers to realize there was a dead woman back on the promontory point. They
drove me to the Town Hall police station.

I spent most of Christmas Day in bed, layered in blankets, drinking
hot soup prepared by my friend Dr. Lotty Herschel. I had some frostbite
in two of my fingers, but she thought they would recover. Lotty left at
seven to eat dinner with her nurse, Carol Alvarado, and her family.

The police had taken Cinda away, and Jonathan had persuaded Po to
go home with him. I guess it had been a fairly tragic scene — Jonathan
crying, the dog unwilling to let Cinda's body out of her sight. I hadn't
been there myself, but one of my newspaper friends told me about it.

It was only eight o'clock when the phone next to my bed began ringing, but I was deep in sleep, buried in blankets. It must have rung nine
or ten times before I even woke up, and another several before I could
bring myself to stick one of my sore arms out to answer it.

"Hello?" I said groggily.

"Vic. Vic, I hate to bother you, but I need help."

"Who is this?" I started coming to.

"Jonathan Michaels. They've arrested me for killing Cinda. I only get
the one phone call." He was trying to speak jauntily, but his voice
cracked.

"Killing Cinda?" I echoed. "I thought she slipped and fell."

"Apparently someone strangled her and pushed her in after she was
dead. Don't ask me how they know. Don't ask me why they thought I
did it. The problem is — the problem is — Po. I don't have anyone to
leave her with."

"Where are you now?" I swung my legs over the bed and began pulling on longjohns. He was at their apartment, four buildings up the
street from me, on his way downtown for booking and then to Cook
County jail. The arresting officer, not inhuman on Christmas Day,
would let him wait for me if I could get there fast.

I was half dressed by the time I hung up and quickly finished pulling
on jeans, boots, and a heavy sweater. Jonathan and two policemen were
standing in the entryway of his building when I ran up. He handed me
his apartment keys. In the distance I would hear Po's muffled barking.

"Do you have a lawyer?" I demanded.

Ordinarily a cheerful, bearded young man with long golden hair,
Jonathan now looked rather bedraggled. He shook his head dismally.

"You need one. I can find someone for you, or I can represent you
myself until we come up with someone better. I don't practice anymore,

so you need someone who's active, but I can get you through the formalities."

He accepted gratefully, and I followed him into the waiting police car. The arresting officers wouldn't answer any of my questions. When we got down to the Eleventh Street police headquarters, I insisted on seeing the officer in charge, and was taken in to Sergeant John McGonnigal.

McGonnigal and I had met frequently. He was a stocky young man, very able, and I had a lot of respect for him. I'm not sure he reciprocated it. "Merry Christmas, Sergeant. It's a terrible day to be working, isn't it?"

"Merry Christmas, Miss Warshawski. What are you doing here?"

I represent Jonathan Michaels. Seems someone got a little confused and thinks he pushed Ms. Goodrich into Lake Michigan this morning."

"We're not confused. She was strangled and pushed into the lake. She was dead before she went into the water. He has no alibi for the relevant time."

"No alibi! Who in this city does have an alibi?"

There was more to it than that, he explained stiffly. Michaels and Cinda had been heard quarreling late at night by their neighbors across the hall and underneath. They had resumed their fight in the morning. Cinda had finally slammed out of the house with the dog around nine-thirty.

"He didn't follow her, Sergeant."

"How do you know?"

I explained that I had watched Cinda from my living room. "And I didn't run into Mr. Michaels out on the point. I only met one person."

He pounced on that. How could I be sure it wasn't Jonathan? Finally agreeing to get a description of his clothes to see if he owned a navy ski mask or a khaki jacket, McGonnigal also pointed out that there were two ways to leave the lakefront — Jonathan could have gone north instead of south.

"Maybe. But you're spinning a very thin thread, Sergeant. It's not going to hold up. Now I need some time alone with my client."

He was most unhappy to let me represent Michael, but there wasn't much he could do about it. He left us alone in a small interrogation room.

"I'm taking it on faith that you didn't kill Cinda," I said briskly. "But for the record, did you?"

He shook his head. "No way. Even if I had stopped loving her, which I hadn't, I don't solve my problems that way." He ran a hand through his long hair. "I can't believe this. I can't even really believe Cinda is dead. It's all happened too fast. And now they're arresting me." His hands were beautiful, with long strong fingers. Strong enough to strange someone, certainly.

"What were you fighting about this morning?"

"Fighting?"

"Don't play dumb with me, Jonathan: I'm the only help you've got. Your neighbors heard you — that's why the police arrested you."

He smiled a little foolishly. "It all seems so stupid now. I keep thinking, if I hadn't gotten her mad, she wouldn't have gone out there. She'd be alive now."

"Maybe. Maybe not. What were you fighting about?"

He hesitated. "Those damned Santa Claus pictures she took. I never wanted her to do it, anyway. She's too good — she was too good a photographer to be wasting her time on that kind of stuff. Then she got mad and started accusing me of being Lawrence Welk, and who was I to talk. It all started because someone phoned her at one this morning. I'd just gotten back from a gig —" he grinned suddenly, painfully "— a Lawrence Welk gig, and this call came in. Someone who had been in one of her Santa shots. Said he was very shy, and wanted to make sure he wasn't in the picture with his kid, so would she bring him the negatives?"

"She had the negatives? Not Burton's?"

"Yeah. Stupid idiot. She was developing the film herself. Apparently this guy called Burton's first. Anyway, to make a long story short, she agreed to meet him today and give him the negatives, and I was furious. First of all, why should she go out on Christmas to satisfy some moron's whim? And why was she taking those dumb-assed pictures anyway?"

Suddenly his face cracked and he started sobbing. "She was so beautiful and I loved her so much. Why did I have to fight with her?"

I patted his shoulder and held his hand until the tears stopped. "You know, if that was her caller she was going to meet, that's probably the person who killed her."

"I thought of that. And that's what I told the police. But they say it's the kind of thing I'd be bound to make up under the circumstances."

I pushed him through another half hour of questions. What had she said about her caller? Had he given his name? She didn't know his name. Then how had she known which negatives were his? She didn't — just the day and the time he'd been there, so she was taking over the negative for that morning. That's all he knew; she'd been too angry to tell him what she was taking with her. Yes, she had taken negatives with her.

He gave me detailed instructions on how to look after Po. Just dry dog food. No table scraps. As many walks as I felt like giving her — she was an outdoor dog and loved snow and water. She was very well trained; they never walked her with a leash. Before I left, I talked to McGonnigal. He told me he was going to follow up on the story about the man in the photograph at Burton's the next day but he wasn't taking it too seriously. He told me they hadn't found any film on Cinda's body, but that was because she hadn't taken any with her — Jonathan was making up that, too. He did agree, though, to hold Jonathan at Eleventh Street overnight. He could get a bail hearing in the morning and maybe not have to put his life at risk among the gang members who run Cook County jail disguised as prisoners.

I took a taxi back to the north side. The streets were clear and we moved quickly. Every mile or so we passed a car abandoned on the roadside, making the Arctic landscape appear more desolate than ever.

Once at Jonathan's apartment it took a major effort of will to get back outside with the dog. Po went with me eagerly enough, but kept turning around, looking at me searchingly as though hoping I might be transformed into Cinda.

Back in the apartment, I had no strength left to go home. I found the bedroom, let my clothes drop where they would on the floor and tumbled into bed.

Holy Innocents' Day, lavishly celebrated by my Polish Catholic relatives, was well advanced before I woke up again. I found Po staring at me with reproachful brown eyes, panting slightly. "All right, all right," I grumbled, pulling the covers back and staggering to my feet.

I'd been too tired the night before even to locate the bathroom. Now I found it, part of a large darkroom. Cinda apparently had knocked down a wall connecting it to the dining room; she had a sink and built-in shelves all in one handy location. Prints were strung around the room, and chemicals and lingerie jostled one another incongruously. I borrowed a toothbrush, cautiously smelling the toothpaste to make sure it really held Crest, not developing chemicals.

I put my clothes back on and took Po around the block. The weather had moderated considerably; a bank thermometer on the corner stood at 9 degrees. Po wanted to run to the lake, but I didn't feel up to going that far this morning, and called her back with difficulty. After lunch, if I could get my car started, we might see whether any clues lay hidden in the snow.

I called Lotty from Cinda's apartment, explaining where I was and why. She told me I was an idiot to have gotten out of bed the night before, but if I wasn't dead of exposure by now I would probably survive until someone shot me. Somehow that didn't cheer me up.

While I helped myself to coffee and toast in Cinda's kitchen I started calling various attorneys to see if I could find someone to represent Jonathan. Tim Oldham, who'd gone to law school with me, handled a good-sized criminal practice. He wasn't too enthusiastic about taking a client without much money, but I put on some not very subtle pressure about a lady I'd seen him with on the Gold Coast a few weeks ago who bore little resemblance to his wife. He promised me Jonathan would be home by supper time, called me some unflattering names and hung up.

Besides the kitchen, bedroom, and darkroom, the apartment had one other room, mostly filled by a grand piano. Stacks of music stood on the floor — Jonathan either couldn't afford shelves or didn't think he needed them. The walls were hung with poster-sized photographs of Jonathan playing, taken by Cinda. They were very good.

I went back into the darkroom and poked around at the pictures. Cinda had put all her Santa Claus photographs in neatly marked envelopes. She'd carefully written the name of each child next to the number of the exposure on that roll of film. I switched on a light table and started looking at them. She'd taken pictures every day for three weeks, which amounted to thousands of shots. It looked like a needle-in-the-haystack type task. But most of the pictures were of children. The only others were ones Cinda had taken for her own amusement, panning the crowd, or artsy shots through glass at reflecting lights. Presumably her caller was one of the adults in the crowd.

After lunch I took Po down to my car. She had no hesitation about going with me and leaped eagerly into the backseat. "You have too trusting a nature," I told her. She grinned at me and panted heavily. The Omega started, after a few grumbling moments, and I drove north to Bryn Mawr and back to get the battery well charged before turning into the lot at Belmont Harbor. Po was almost beside herself with excitement, banging her tail against the rear window until I got the door open and let her out. She raced ahead of me on the lake path. I didn't try to call her back; I figured I'd find her at Cinda's rock.

I moved slowly, carefully scanning the ground for traces of — what?

Film? A business card? The wind was so much calmer today and the air enough warmer that visibility was good, but I didn't see anything.

At the lake the mist had cleared away, leaving the water steely gray, moving uneasily under its iron bands of cold. Po stood as I expected, on the rock where I'd found her yesterday. She was the picture of dejection. She clearly had expected to find her mistress there.

I combed the area carefully and at last found one of those gray plastic tubes that film comes in. It was empty. I pocketed it, deciding I could at least show it to McGonnigal and hope he would think it important. Po left the rocks with utmost reluctance. Back on the lake path, she kept turning around to look for Cinda. I had to lift her into the car. During the drive to police headquarters, she kept turning restlessly in the back of the car, a trying maneuver since she was bigger than the seat.

McGonnigal didn't seem too impressed with the tube I'd found, but he took it and sent it to the forensics department. I asked him what he'd learned from Burton's; they didn't have copies of the photographs. Cinda had all those. If someone ordered one, they sent the name to Cinda and she supplied the picture. They gave McGonnigal a copy of the list of the seven hundred people requesting pictures and he had someone going through to see if any of them were known criminals, but he obviously believed it was a waste of time. If it weren't for the fact that his boss, Lieutenant Robert Mallory, had been a friend of my father's, he probably wouldn't even have made this much of an effort.

I stopped to see Jonathan, who seemed to be in fairly good spirits. He told me Tim Oldham had been by. "He thinks I'm a hippy and not very interesting compared to some of the mob figures he represents, but I can tell he's doing his best." He was working out the fingering to a Schubert score, using the side of the bed as a keyboard. I told him Po was well, but waiting for me in the car outside, so I'd best be on my way.

I spent the rest of the afternoon going through Cinda's Santa photographs. I'd finished about a third of them at five when Tim Oldham phoned to say that Jonathan would have to spend another night in jail: because of the Christmas holidays he hadn't been able to arrange for bail.

"You owe me, Vic; this has been one of the more thankless ways I've spent a holiday."

"You're serving justice, Tim," I said brightly. "What more could you ask for? Think of the oath you swore when you became a member of the bar."

"I'm thinking of the oaths I'd like to swear at you," he grumbled.

I laughed and hung up. I took Po for one last walk, gave her her evening food and drink and prepared to leave for my own place. As soon as the dog saw me putting my coat back on, she abandoned her dinner and started dancing around my feet, wagging her tail, to show that she was always ready to play. I kept yelling "No" to her with no effect. She grinned happily at me as if to say this was a game she often played — she knew humans liked to pretend they didn't want her along, but they always took her in the end.

She was very upset when I shoved her back into the apartment behind me. As I locked the door, she began barking. Retrievers are quiet dogs; they seldom bark and never whine. But their voices are deep and full-bodied, coming straight from their huge chests. Good diaphragm support, the kind singers seldom achieve.

Cinda's apartment was on the second floor. When I got to the ground floor, I could still hear Po from the entryway. She was clearly audible outside the front door. "Ah, nuts!" I muttered. How long could she keep this up? Were dogs like babies? Did you just ignore them for a while and discipline them into going to sleep? Did that really work with babies? After standing five minutes in the icy wind I could still hear Po. I swore under my breath and let myself back into the building.

She was totally ecstatic at seeing me, jumping up on my chest and licking my face to show there were no hard feelings. "You're shameless and a fraud," I told her severely. She wagged her tail with delight. "Still, you're an orphan; I can't treat you too harshly."

She agreed and followed me down the stairs and back to my apartment with unabated eagerness. I took a bath and changed my clothes, made dinner and took care of my mail, then walked Po around the block to a little park, and back up the street to her own quarters. I brought my own toothbrush with me this time; there didn't seem much point in trying to leave the dog until Jonathan got out of jail.

Cinda and Jonathan had few furnishings, but they owned a magnificent stereo system and a large record collection. I put some Britten quartets on, found a novel buried in the stack of technical books next to Cinda's side of the bed, and purloined a bottle of burgundy. I curled up on a beanbag chair with the book and the wine. Po lay at my feet, panting happily. Altogether a delightful domestic scene. Maybe I should get a dog.

I finished the book and the bottle of wine a little after midnight and went to bed. Po padded into the bedroom after me and curled up on a rug next to the bed. I went to sleep quickly.

A single sharp bark from the dog woke me about two hours later. "What is it, girl? Nightmares?" I started to turn over to go back to sleep when she barked again. "Quiet, now!" I commanded.

I heard her get to her feet and start toward the door. And then I heard the sound that her sharper ears had caught first. Someone was trying to get into the apartment. It couldn't be Jonathan; I had his keys, and this was someone fumbling, trying different keys, trying to pick the lock. In about thirty seconds I pulled on jeans, boots, and a sweatshirt, ignoring underwear. My intruder had managed the lower lock and was starting on the upper.

Po was standing in front of the door, hackles raised on her back. Obedient to my whispered command she wasn't barking. She followed me reluctantly into the darkroom-bathroom. I took her into the shower stall and pulled the curtain across as quietly as I could.

We waited there in the dark while our intruder finished with locks. It was an unnerving business listening to the rattling, knowing someone would be on us momentarily. I wondered if I'd made the right choice; maybe I should have dashed down the back stairs with the dog and gotten the police. It was too late now, however; we could hear a pair of boots moving heavily across the living room. Po gave a deep, mean growl in the back of her throat.

"Doggy? Doggy? Are you in here, Doggy?" The man knew about Po, but not whether she was here. He must not have heard her two short barks earlier. He had a high tenor voice with a trace of a Spanish accent.

Po continued to growl, very softly. At last the far door to the darkroom opened and the intruder came in. He had a flashlight which he shone around the room; through the curtain I could see its point of light bobbing.

Satisfied that no one was there, he turned on the overhead switch. This was connected to a ventilating fan, whose noise was loud enough to mask Po's continued soft growling.

I couldn't see him, but apparently he was looking through Cinda's photograph collection. He flipped on the switch at the light table and then spent a long time going through the negatives. I was pleased with Po; I wouldn't have expected such patience from a dog. The intruder must have sat for an hour while my muscles cramped and water dripped on my head, and she stayed next to me quietly the whole time.

At last he apparently found what he needed. He got up and I heard more paper rustling, then the light went out.

"Now!" I shouted at Po. She raced out of the room and found the intruder as he was on his way out the far door. Blue light flashed; a gun barked. Po yelped and stopped momentarily. By that time I was across the room, too. The intruder was on his way out the apartment door.

I pulled my parka from the chair where I'd left it and took off after him. Po was bleeding slightly from her left shoulder, but the bullet must only have grazed her because she ran strongly. We tumbled down the stairs together and out the front door into the icy December night. As we went outside, I grabbed the dog and rolled over with her. I heard the gun go off a few times but we were moving quickly, too quickly to make a good target.

Street lamps showed our man running away from us down Halsted to Belmont. He wore the navy ski mask and khaki parka of the solitary runner I'd seen at the harbor yesterday morning.

Hearing Po and me behind him he put on a burst of speed and made it to a car waiting at the corner. We were near the Omega now; I bundled the dog into the backseat, sent up a prayer to the patron saint of Delco batteries, and turned on the engine.

The streets were deserted. I caught up with the car, a dark Lincoln, where Sheridan Road crossed Lake Shore Drive at Belmont. Instead of turning onto the drive, the Lincoln cut straight across to the harbor.

"This is it, girl," I told Po. "You catch this boy, then we take you in and get that shoulder stitched up. And then you get your favorite dinner — even if it's a whole cow."

The dog was leaning over the front seat, panting, her eyes gleaming. She was a retriever, after all. The Lincoln stopped at the end of the harbor parking lot. I halted the Omega some fifty yards away and got out with the dog. Using a row of parked cars as cover, we ran across the lot, stopping near the Lincoln in the shelter of a van. At that point, Po began her deep, insistent barking.

This was a sound which would attract attention, possibly even the police, so I made no effort to stop her. The man in the Lincoln reached the same conclusion; a window opened and he began firing at us. This was just a waste of ammunition, since we were sheltered behind the van.

The shooting only increased Po's vocal efforts. It also attracted attention from Lake Shore Drive; out of the corner of my eye I saw the flashing blue lights which herald the arrival of Chicago's finest.

Our attacker saw them, too. A door opened and the man in the ski mask slid out. He took off along the lake path, away from the harbor entrance, out toward the promontory. I clapped my hands at Po and started running after him. She was much faster than me; I lost sight of her in the dark as I picked my way more cautiously along the icy path, shivering in the bitter wind, shivering at the thought of the dark freezing water to my right. I could hear it slapping ominously against the ice-covered rocks, could hear the man pounding ahead of me. No noise from Po. Her tough pads picked their way sure and silent across the frozen gravel.

As I rounded the curve toward the promontory I could hear the man yelling in Spanish at Po, heard a gun go off, heard a loud splash in the water. Rage at him for shooting the dog gave me a last burst of speed. I rounded the end of the point. Saw his dark shape outlined against the rocks and jumped on top of him.

He was completely unprepared for me. We fell heavily, rolling down the rocks. The gun slipped from his hand, banged loudly as it bounced against the ice and fell into the water. We were a foot away from the water, fighting recklessly — the first person to lose a grip would be shoved in to die.

Our parkas weighted our arms and hampered our swings. He lunged clumsily at my throat. I pulled away, grabbed hold of his ski mask and hit his head against the rocks. He grunted and drew back, trying to kick me. As I moved away from his foot I lost my hold on him and slid backwards across the ice. He followed through quickly, giving a mighty shove which pushed me over the edge of the rock. My feet landed in the water. I swung them up with an effort, two icy lumps, and tried to back away.

As I scrabbled for a purchase, a dark shape came out of the water and climbed onto the rock next to me. Po. Not killed after all. She shook herself, spraying water over me and over my assailant. The sudden bath took him by surprise. He stopped long enough for me to get well away and gain my breath and a better position.

The dog, shivering violently, stayed close to me. I ran a hand through her wet fur. "Soon, kid. We'll get you home and dry soon."

Just as the attacker launched himself at us, a searchlight went on overhead. "This is the police," a loudspeaker boomed. "Drop your guns and come up."

The dark shape hit me, knocked me over. Po let out a yelp and sunk her teeth into his leg. His yelling brought the police to our sides.

They carried strong flashlights. I could see a sodden mass of paper, a small manila envelope with teethmarks in it. Po wagged her tail and picked it up again.

"Give me that!" our attacker yelled in his high voice. He fought with the police to try to reach the envelope. "I threw that in the water. How can this be? How did she get it?"

"She's a retriever," I said.

Later, at the police station, we looked at the negatives in the envelope Po had retrieved from the water. They showed a picture of the man in the ski mask looking on with intense, brooding eyes while Santa Claus talked to his little boy. No wonder Cinda found him worth photographing.

"He's a cocaine dealer," Sergeant McGonnigal explained to me. "He jumped a ten-million-dollar bail. No wonder he didn't want any photographs of him circulating around. We're holding him for murder this time."

A uniformed man brought Jonathan into McGonnigal's office. The sergeant cleared his throat uncomfortably. "Looks like your dog saved your hide, Mr. Michaels."

Po. who had been lying at my feet, wrapped in a police horse blanket, gave a bark of pleasure. She staggered to her feet, trailing the blanket, and walked stiffly over to Jonathan, tail wagging.

I explained our adventure to him, and what a heroine the dog had been. "What about that empty film container I gave you this afternoon, Sergeant?"

Apparently Cinda had brought that with her to her rendezvous, not knowing how dangerous her customer was. When he realized it was empty, he'd flung it aside and attacked Cinda. "We got a complete confession," McGonnigal said. "He was so rattled by the sight of the dog with the envelope full of negatives in her mouth that he completely lost his nerve. I know he's got good lawyers — one of them's your friend Oldham — but I hope we have enough to convince a judge not to set bail."

Jonathan was on his knees fondling the dog and talking to her. He looked over his shoulder at McGonnigal. "I'm sure Oldham's relieved that you caught the right man — a murderer who can afford to jump a ten-million-dollar bail is a much better client than one who can hardly keep a retriever in dog food." He turned back to the dog. "But we'll blow our savings on a steak; you get the steak and I'll eat Butcher's Blend tonight, Miss Three-Dot Po of Blackstone, People's Heroine, and winner of the Croix de Chien for valor." Po panted happily and licked his face.

1986

SUE GRAFTON

....

The Parker Shotgun

THE CHRISTMAS HOLIDAYS had come and gone, and the new year was underway. January, in California, is as good as it gets — cool, clear, and green, with a sky the color of wisteria and a surf that thunders like a volley of gunfire in a distant field. My name is Kinsey Millhone. I'm a private investigator, licensed, bonded, insured; white, female, age thirty-two, unmarried, and physically fit. That Monday morning, I was sitting in my office with my feet up, wondering what life would bring, when a woman walked in and tossed a photograph on my desk. My introduction to the Parker shotgun began with a graphic view of its apparent effect when fired at a formerly nice-looking man at close range. His face was still largely intact, but he had no use now for a pocket comb. With effort, I kept my expression neutral as I glanced up at her.

"Somebody killed my husband."

"I can see that," I said.

She snatched the picture back and stared at it as though she might have missed some telling detail. Her face suffused with pink, and she blinked back tears. "Jesus. Rudd was killed five months ago, and the cops have done shit. I'm so sick of getting the runaround I could scream."

She sat down abruptly and pressed a hand to her mouth, trying to compose herself. She was in her late twenties, with a gaudy prettiness. Her hair was an odd shade of brown, like cherry Coke, worn shoulder length and straight. Her eyes were large, a lush mink brown; her mouth was full. Her complexion was all warm tones, tanned, and clear. She didn't seem to be wearing makeup, but she was still as vivid as a magazine illustration, a good four-color run on slick paper. She was seven months pregnant by the look of her; not voluminous yet, but rotund. When she was calmer, she identified herself as Lisa Osterling.

"That's a crime lab photo. How'd you come by it?" I said when the preliminaries were disposed of.

She fumbled in her handbag for a tissue and blew her nose. "I have my little ways," she said morosely. "Actually I know the photographer and I stole a print. I'm going to have it blown up and hung on the wall just so I won't forget. The police are hoping I'll drop the whole thing, but I got news for *them*." her mouth was starting to tremble again, and a tear splashed onto her skirt as though my ceiling had a leak.

"What's the story?" I said. "The cops in this town are usually pretty good." I got up and filled a paper cup with water from my Sparklett's dispenser, passing it over to her. She murmured a thank you and drank it down, staring into the bottom of the cup as she spoke. "Rudd was a cocaine dealer until a month or so before he died. They haven't said as much, but I know they've written him off as some kind of small-time punk. What do they care? They'd like to think he was killed in a drug deal — a double cross or something like that. He wasn't, though. He'd given it all up because of this."

She glanced down at the swell of her belly. She was wearing a kelly green T-shirt with an arrow down the front. The word "Oops!" was written across her breasts in machine embroidery.

"What's your theory?" I asked. Already I was leaning toward the official police version of events. Drug dealing isn't synonymous with longevity. There's too much money involved and too many amateurs getting into the act. This was Santa Teresa — ninety-five miles north of the big time in L.A., but there are still standards to maintain. A shotgun blast is the underworld equivalent of a bad annual review.

"I don't have a theory. I just don't like theirs. I want you to look into it so I can clear Rudd's name before the baby comes."

I shrugged. "I'll do what I can, but I can't guarantee the results. How are you going to feel if the cops are right?"

She stood up, giving me a flat look. "I don't know why Rudd died, but it had nothing to do with drugs," she said. She opened her handbag and extracted a roll of bills the size of a wad of socks. "What do you charge?"

"Thirty bucks an hour plus expenses."

She peeled off several hundred-dollar bills and laid them on the desk. I got out a contract.

*   *   *

My second encounter with the Parker shotgun came in the form of a dealer's appraisal slip that I discovered when I was nosing through Rudd Osterling's private possessions an hour later at the house. The address she'd given me was on the Bluffs, a residential area on the west side of town, overlooking the Pacific. It should have been an elegant neighborhood, but the ocean generated too much fog and too much corrosive salt air. The houses were small and had a temporary feel to them, as though the occupants intended to move on when the month was up. No one seemed to get around to painting the trim, and the yards looked like they were kept by people who spent all day at the beach. I followed her in my car, reviewing the information she'd given me as I urged my ancient VW up Capilla Hill and took a right on Presipio.

The late Rudd Osterling had been in Santa Teresa since the sixties, when he migrated to the West Coast in search of sunshine, good surf, good dope, and casual sex. Lisa told me he'd lived in vans and communes, working variously as a roofer, tree trimmer, bean picker, fry cook, and forklift operator — never with any noticeable ambition or success. He'd started dealing cocaine two years earlier, apparently netting more money than he was accustomed to. Then he'd met and married Lisa, and she'd been determined to see him clean up his act. According to her, he'd retired from the drug trade and was just in the process of setting himself up in a landscape maintenance business when someone blew the top of his head off.

I pulled into the driveway behind her, glancing at the frame and stucco bungalow with its patchy grass and dilapidated fence. It looked like one of those households where there's always something under construction, probably without permits and not up to code. In this case, a foundation had been laid for an addition to the garage, but the weeds were already growing up through cracks in the concrete. A wooden outbuilding had been dismantled, the old lumber tossed in an unsightly pile. Closer to the house, there were stacks of cheap pecan wood paneling, sun-bleached in places and warped along one edge. It was all hapless and depressing, but she scarcely looked at it.

I followed her into the house.

"We were just getting the house fixed up when he died," she remarked.

"When did you buy the place?" I was manufacturing small talk, trying to cover my distaste at the sight of the old linoleum counter, where a line of ants stretched from a crust of toast and jelly all the way out the back door.

"We didn't really. This was my mother's. She and my stepdad moved back to the Midwest last year."

"What about Rudd? Did he have any family out here?"

"They're all in Connecticut, I think, real la-di-dah. His parents are dead, and his sisters wouldn't even come out to the funeral."

"Did he have a lot of friends?"

"All cocaine dealers have friends."

"Enemies?"

"Not that I ever heard about."

"Who was his supplier?"

"I don't know that."

"No disputes? Suits pending? Quarrels with the neighbors? Family arguments about the inheritance?"

She gave me a "no" on all four counts.

I had told her I wanted to go through his personal belongings, so she showed me into the tiny back bedroom, where he'd set up a card table and some cardboard file boxes. A real entrepreneur. I began to search while she leaned against the doorframe, watching.

I said, "Tell me about what was going on the week he died." I was sorting through canceled checks in a Nike shoe box. Most were written to the neighborhood supermarket, utilities, telephone company.

She moved to the desk chair and sat down. "I can't tell you much because I was at work. I do alterations and repairs at a dry cleaner's up at Presipio Mall. Rudd would stop in now and then when he was out running around. He'd picked up a few jobs already, but he really wasn't doing the gardening full time. He was trying to get all his old business squared away. Some kid owed him money. I remember that."

"He sold cocaine on *credit?*"

She shrugged. "Maybe it was grass or pills. Somehow the kid owed him a bundle. That's all I know."

"I don't suppose he kept any records."

"Nuh-uh. It was all in his head. He was too paranoid to put anything down in black and white."

The file boxes were jammed with old letters, tax returns, receipts. It all looked like junk to me.

"What about the day he was killed? Were you at work then?"

She shook her head. "It was a Saturday. I was off work, but I'd gone to the market. I was out maybe an hour and a half, and when I got home, police cars were parked in front, and the paramedics were here. Neighbors were standing out on the street." She stopped talking, and I was left to imagine the rest.

"Had he been expecting anyone?"

"If he was, he never said anything to me. He was in the garage, doing I don't know what. Chauncy, next door, heard the shotgun go off, but by the time he got here to investigate, whoever did it was gone."

I got up and moved toward the hallway. "Is this the bedroom down here?"

"Right. I haven't gotten rid of his stuff yet. I guess I'll have to eventually. I'm going to use his office for the nursery."

I moved into the master bedroom and went through his hanging clothes. "Did the police find anything?"

"They didn't look. Well, one guy came through and poked around some. About five minutes' worth."

I began to check through the drawers she indicated were his. Nothing remarkable came to light. On top of the chest was one of those brass and walnut caddies, where Rudd apparently kept his watch, keys, loose change. Almost idly, I picked it up. Under it there was a folded slip of paper. It was a partially completed appraisal form from a gun shop out in Colgate, a township to the north of us. "What's a Parker?" I said when I'd glanced at it. She peered over the slip.

"Oh. That's probably the appraisal on the shotgun he got."

"The one he was killed with?"

"Well, I don't know. They never found the weapon, but the homicide detective said they couldn't run it through ballistics, anyway — or whatever it is they do."

"Why'd he have it appraised in the first place?"

"He was taking it in trade for a big drug debt, and he needed to know if it was worth it."

"Was this the kid you mentioned before or someone else?"

"The same one, I think. At first, Rudd intended to turn around and sell the gun, but then he found out it was a collector's item so he decided to keep it. The gun dealer called a couple of times after Rudd died, but it was gone by then."

"And you told the cops all this stuff?"

"Sure. They couldn't have cared less."

I doubted that, but I tucked the slip in my pocket anyway. I'd check it out and then talk to Dolan in homicide.

*   *   *

The gun shop was located on a narrow side street in Colgate, just off the main thoroughfare. Colgate looks like it's made up of hardware stores, U-haul rentals, and plant nurseries; places that seem to have half their merchandise outside, surrounded by chain link fence. The gun shop had been set up in someone's front parlor in a dinky white frame house. There were some glass counters filled with gun paraphernalia, but no guns in sight.

The man who came out of the back room was in his fifties, with a narrow face and graying hair, gray eyes made luminous by rimless glasses. He wore a dress shirt with the sleeves rolled up and a long gray apron tied around his waist. He had perfect teeth, but when he talked I could see the rim of pink where his upper plate was fit, and it spoiled the effect. Still, I had to give him credit for a certain level of good looks, maybe a seven on a scale of ten. Not bad for a man his age. "Yes ma'am," he said. He had a trace of an accent, Virginia, I thought.

"Are you Avery Lamb?"

"That's right. What can I help you with?"

"I'm not sure. I'm wondering what you can tell me about this appraisal you did." I handed him the slip.

He glanced down and then looked up at me. "Where did you get this?"

"Rudd Osterling's widow," I said.

"She told me she didn't have the gun."

"That's right."

His manner was a combination of confusion and wariness. "What's your connection to the matter?"

I took out a business card and gave it to him. "She hired me to look into Rudd's death. I thought the shotgun might be relevant since he was killed with one."

He shook his head. "I don't know what's going on. This is the second time it's disappeared."

"Meaning what?"

"Some woman brought it in to have it appraised back in June. I made an offer on it then, but before we could work out a deal, she claimed the gun was stolen."

"I take it you had some doubts about that."

"Sure I did. I don't think she ever filed a police report, and I suspect she knew damn well who took it but didn't intend to pursue it. Next thing I knew, this Osterling fellow brought the same gun in. It had a beavertail fore-end and an English grip. There was no mistaking it."

"Wasn't that a bit of a coincidence? His bringing the gun in to you?"

"Not really. I'm one of the few master gunsmiths in this area. All he had to do was ask around the same way she did."

"Did you tell her the gun had showed up?"

He shrugged with his mouth and a lift of his brows. "Before I could talk to her, he was dead and the Parker was gone again."

I checked the date on the slip. "That was in August?"

"That's right, and I haven't seen the gun since."

"Did he tell you how he acquired it?"

"Said he took it in trade. I told him this other woman showed up with it first, but he didn't seem to care about that."

"How much was the Parker worth?"

He hesitated, weighing his words. "I offered him six thousand."

"But what's its value out in the marketplace?"

"Depends on what people are willing to pay."

I tried to control the little surge of impatience he had sparked. I could tell he'd jumped into his crafty negotiator's mode, unwilling to tip his hand in case the gun showed up and he could nick it off cheap. "Look," I said, "I'm asking you in confidence. This won't go any further unless it becomes a police matter, and then neither one of us will have a choice. Right now, the gun's missing anyway, so what difference does it make?"

He didn't seem entirely convinced, but he got my point. He cleared his throat with obvious embarrassment. "Ninety-six."

I stared at him. "Thousand dollars?"

He nodded.

"Jesus. That's a lot for a gun, isn't it?"

His voice dropped. "Ms. Millhone, that gun is priceless. It's an A-1 Special 28-gauge with a two-barrel set. There were only two of them made."

"But why so much?"

"For one thing, the Parker's a beautifully crafted shotgun. There are different grades, of course, but this one was exceptional. Fine wood. Some of the most incredible scrollwork you'll ever see. Parker had an Italian working for him back then who'd spend sometimes five thousand hours on the engraving alone. The company went out of business around 1942, so there aren't any more to be had."

"You said there were two. Where's the other one, or would you know?"

"Only what I've heard. A dealer in Ohio bought the one at auction a couple years back for ninety-six. I understand some fella down in Texas has it now, part of a collection of Parkers. The gun Rudd Osterling brought in has been missing for years. I don't think he knew what he had on his hands."

"And you didn't tell him."

Lamb shifted his gaze. "I told him enough," he said carefully. "I can't help it if the man didn't do his homework."

"How'd you know it was the missing Parker?"

"The serial number matched, and so did everything else. It wasn't a fake, either. I examined the gun under heavy magnification, checking for fill-in welds and traces of markings that might have been over-stamped. After I checked it out, I showed it to a buddy of mine, a big gun buff, and he recognized it, too."

"Who else knew about it besides you and this friend?"

"Whoever Rudd Osterling got it from, I guess."

"I'll want the woman's name and address if you've still got it. Maybe she knows how the gun fell into Rudd's hands."

Again he hesitated for a moment, and then he shrugged. "I don't see why not." He made a note on a piece of scratch paper and pushed it across the counter to me. "I'd like to know if the gun shows up," he said.

"Sure, as long as Mrs. Osterling doesn't object."

I didn't have any other questions for the moment. I moved toward the door, then glanced back at him. "How could Rudd have sold the gun if it was stolen property? Wouldn't he have needed a bill of sale for it? Some proof of ownership?"

Avery Lamb's face was devoid of expression. "Not necessarily. If an avid collector got hold of that gun, it would sink out of sight, and that's the last you'd ever see of it. He'd keep it in his basement and never show it to a soul. It'd be enough if he knew he had it. You don't need a bill of sale for that."

I sat out in my car and made some notes while the information was fresh. Then I checked the address Lamb had given me, and I could feel the adrenaline stir. It was right back in Rudd's neighborhood.

The woman's name was Jackie Barnett. The address was two streets over from the Osterling house and just about parallel; a big corner lot planted with avocado trees and bracketed with palms. The house itself was yellow stucco with flaking brown shutters and a yard that needed mowing. The mailbox read "Squires," but the house number seemed to match. There was a basketball hoop nailed up above the two-car garbage and a dismantled motorcycle in the driveway.

I parked my car and got out. As I approached the house, I saw an old man in a wheelchair planted in the side yard like a lawn ornament. He was parchment pale, with baby-fine white hair and rheumy eyes. The left half of his face had been disconnected by a stroke, and his left arm and hand rested uselessly in his lap. I caught sight of a woman peering through the window, apparently drawn by the sound of my car door slamming shut. I crossed the yard, moving toward the front porch. She opened the door before I had a chance to knock.

"You must be Kinsey Millhone. I just got off the phone with Avery. He said you'd be stopping by."

"That was quick. I didn't realize he'd be calling ahead. Saves me an explanation. I take it you're Jackie Barnett."

"That's right. Come in if you like. I just have to check on him," she said, indicating the man in the yard.

"Your father?"

She shot me a look. "Husband," she said. I watched her cross the grass toward the old man, grateful for a chance to recover from my gaffe. I could see now that she was older than she'd first appeared. She must have been in her fifties — at that stage where women wear too much makeup and dye their hair too bold a shade of blonde. She was buxom, clearly overweight, but lush. In a seventeenth-century painting, she'd have been depicted supine, her plump naked body draped in sheer white. Standing over her, something with a goat's rear end would be poised for assault. Both would look coy but excited at the prospects. The old man was beyond the pleasures of the flesh, yet the noises he made — garbled and indistinguishable because of the stroke — had the same intimate quality as sounds uttered in the throes of passion, a disquieting effect.

I looked away from him, thinking of Avery Lamb instead. He hadn't actually told me the woman was a stranger to him, but he'd certainly implied as much. I wondered now what their relationship consisted of.

Jackie spoke to the old man briefly, adjusting his lap robe. Then she came back and we went inside.

"Is your name Barnett or Squires?" I asked.

"Technically it's Squires, but I still use Barnett for the most part," she said. She seemed angry, and I thought at first the rage was directed at me. She caught my look. "I'm sorry," she said, "but I've about had it with him. Have you ever dealt with a stroke victim?"

"I understand it's difficult."

"It's impossible! I know I sound hard-hearted, but he was always short-tempered and now he's frustrated on top of that. Self-centered, demanding. Nothing suits him. Nothing. I put him out in the yard sometimes just so I won't have to fool with him. Have a seat, hon."

I sat. "How long has he been sick?"

"He had the first stroke in June. He's been in and out of the hospital ever since."

"What's the story on the gun you took out to Avery's shop?"

"Oh, that's right. He said you were looking into some fellow's death. He lived right here on the Bluffs, too, didn't he?"

"Over on Whitmore . . ."

"That was terrible. I read about it in the papers, but I never did hear the end of it. What went on?"

"I wasn't given the details," I said briefly. "Actually, I'm trying to track down a shotgun that belonged to him. Avery Lamb says it was the same gun you brought in."

She had automatically proceeded to get out two cups and saucers, so her answer was delayed until she'd poured coffee for us both. She passed a cup over to me, and then she sat down, stirring milk into hers. She glanced at me self-consciously. "I just took that gun to spite *him*," she said with a nod toward the yard. "I've been married to Bill for six years and miserable for every one of them. It was my own damn fault. I'd been divorced for ages and I was doing fine, but somehow when I hit fifty, I got in a panic. Afraid of growing old alone, I guess. I ran into Bill, and he looked like a catch. He was retired, but he had loads of money, or so he said. He promised me the moon. Said we'd travel. Said he'd buy me clothes and a car and I don't know what all. Turns out he's a penny-pinching miser with a mean mouth and a quick fist. At least he can't do that anymore." She paused to shake her head, staring down at her coffee cup.

"The gun was his?"

"Well, yes, it was. He has a collection of shotguns. I swear he took better care of them than he did of me. I just despise guns. I was always after him to get rid of them. Makes me nervous to have them in the house. Anyway, when he got sick, it turned out he had insurance, but it only paid eighty percent. I was afraid his whole life savings would go up in smoke. I figured he'd go on for years, using up all the money, and then I'd be stuck with his debts when he died. So I just picked up one of the guns and took it out to that gun place to sell. I was going to buy me some clothes."

"What made you change your mind?"

"Well, I didn't think it'd be worth but eight or nine hundred dollars. Then Avery said he'd give me six thousand for it, so I had to guess it was worth at least twice that. I got nervous and thought I better put it back."

"How soon after that did the gun disappear?"

"Oh, gee, I don't know. I didn't pay much attention until Bill got out of the hospital the second time. He's the one who noticed it was gone," she said. "Of course, he raised pluperfect hell. You should have seen him. He had a conniption fit for two days, and then he had another stroke and had to be hospitalized all over again. Served him right if you ask me. At least I had Labor Day weekend to myself. I needed it."

"Do you have any idea who might have taken the gun?"

She gave me a long, candid look. Her eyes were very blue and couldn't have appeared more guileless. "Not the faintest."

I let her practice her wide-eyed stare for a moment, and then I laid out a little bait just to see what she'd do. "God, that's too bad," I said. "I'm assuming you reported it to the police."

I could see her debate briefly before she replied. Yes or no. Check one. "Well, of course," she said.

She was one of those liars who blush from lack of practice.

I kept my tone of voice mild. "What about the insurance? Did you put in a claim?"

She looked at me blankly, and I had the feeling I'd taken her by surprise on that one. She said, "You know, it never even occurred to me. But of course he probably would have it insured, wouldn't he?"

"Sure, if the gun's worth that much. What company is he with?"

"I don't remember offhand. I'd have to look it up."

"I'd do that if I were you," I said. "You can file a claim, and then all you have to do is give the agent the case number."

"Case number?"

"The police will give you that from their report."

She stirred restlessly, glancing at her watch. "Oh, lordy, I'm going to have to give him his medicine. Was there anything else you wanted to ask while you were here?" Now that she'd told me a fib or two, she was anxious to get rid of me so she could assess the situation. Avery Lamb had told me she'd never reported it to the cops. I wondered if she'd call him up now to compare notes.

"Could I take a quick look at his collection?" I said, getting up.

"I suppose that'd be all right. It's in here," she said. She moved toward a small paneled den, and I followed, stepping around a suitcase near the door.

A rack of six guns was enclosed in a glass-fronted cabinet. All of them were beautifully engraved, with fine wood stocks, and I wondered how a priceless Parker could really be distinguished. Both the cabinet and the rack were locked, and there were no empty slots. "Did he keep the Parker in here?"

She shook her head. "The Parker had its own case." She hauled out a handsome wood case from behind the couch and opened it for me, demonstrating its emptiness as though she might be setting up a magic trick. Actually, there was a set of barrels in the box, but nothing else.

I glanced around. There was a shotgun propped in one corner, and I picked it up, checking the manufacturer's imprint on the frame. L. C. Smith. Too bad. For a moment I'd thought it might be the missing Parker. I'm always hoping for the obvious. I set the Smith back in the corner with regret.

"Well, I guess that'll do," I said. "Thanks for the coffee."

"No trouble. I wish I could be more help." She started easing me toward the door.

I held out my hand. "Nice meeting you," I said. "Thanks again for your time."

She gave my hand a perfunctory shake. "That's all right. Sorry I'm in such a rush, but you know how it is when you have someone sick."

Next thing I knew, the door was closing at my back and I was heading toward my car, wondering what she was up to.

I'd just reached the driveway when a white Corvette came roaring down the street and rumbled into the drive. The kid at the wheel flipped the ignition key and cantilevered himself up onto the seat top. "Hi. You know if my mom's here?"

"Who, Jackie? Sure," I said, taking a flyer. "You must be Doug."

He looked puzzled. "No, Eric. Do I know you?"

I shook my head. "I'm just a friend passing through."

He hopped out of the Corvette. I moved on toward my car, keeping an eye on him as he headed toward the house. He looked about seventeen, blond, blue-eyed, with good cheekbones, a moody, sensual mouth, lean surfer's body. I pictured him in a few years, hanging out in resort hotels, picking up women three times his age. He'd do well. So would they.

Jackie had apparently heard him pull in, and she came out onto the porch, intercepting him with a quick look at me. She put her arm through his, and the two moved into the house. I looked over at the old man. He was making noises again, plucking aimlessly at his bad hand with his good one. I felt a mental jolt, like an interior tremor shifting the ground under me. I was beginning to get it.

I drove the two blocks to Lisa Osterling's. She was in the backyard, stretched out on a chaise in a sunsuit that made her belly look like a watermelon in a laundry bag. Her face and arms were rosy, and her tanned legs glistened with tanning oil. As I crossed the grass, she raised a hand to her eyes, shading her face from the winter sunlight so she could look at me. "I didn't expect to see you back so soon."

"I have a question," I said, "and then I need to use your phone. Did Rudd know a kid named Eric Barnett?"

"I'm not sure. What's he look like?"

I gave her a quick rundown, including a description of the white Corvette. I could see the recognition in her face as she sat up.

"Oh, him. Sure. He was over here two or three times a week. I just never knew his name. Rudd said he lived around here somewhere and stopped by to borrow tools so he could work on his motorcycle. Is he the one who owed Rudd the money?"

"Well, I don't know how we're going to prove it, but I suspect he was."

"You think he killed him?"

"I can't answer that yet, but I'm working on it. Is the phone in here?" I was moving toward the kitchen. She struggled to her feet and followed me into the house. There was a wall phone near the back door. I tucked the receiver against my shoulder, pulling the appraisal slip out of my pocket. I dialed Avery Lamb's gun shop. The phone rang twice.

Somebody picked up on the other end. "Gun shop."

"Mr. Lamb?"

"This is Orville Lamb. Did you want me or my brother, Avery?"

"Avery, actually, I have a quick question for him."

"Well, he left a short while ago, and I'm not sure when he'll be back. Is it something I can help you with?"

"Maybe so," I said. "If you had a priceless shotgun — say, an Ithaca or a Parker, one of the classics — would you shoot a gun like that?"

"You could," he said dubiously, "but it wouldn't be a good idea, especially if it was in mint condition to begin with. You wouldn't want to take a chance on lowering the value. Now if it'd been in use previously, I don't guess it would matter much, but still I wouldn't advise it — just speaking for myself. Is this a gun of yours?"

But I'd hung up. Lisa was right behind me, her expression anxious. "I've got to go in a minute," I said, "but here's what I think went on. Eric Barnett's stepfather has a collection of fine shotguns, one of which turns out to be very, very valuable. The old man was hospitalized, and Eric's mother decided to hock one of the guns in order to do a little something for herself before he'd blown every asset he had on his medical bills. She had no idea the gun she chose was worth so much, but the gun dealer recognized it as the find of a lifetime. I don't know whether he told her that or not, but when she realized it was more valuable than she thought, she lost her nerve and put it back."

"Was that the same gun Rudd took in trade?"

"Exactly. My guess is that she mentioned it to her son, who saw a chance to square his drug debt. He offered Rudd the shotgun in trade, and Rudd decided he'd better get the gun appraised, so he took it out to the same place. The gun dealer recognized it when he brought it in."

She stared at me. "Rudd was killed over the gun itself, wasn't he?" she said.

"I think so, yes. It might have been an accident. Maybe there was a struggle and the gun went off."

She closed her eyes and nodded. "Okay. Oh, wow. That feels better. I can live with that." Her eyes came open, and she smiled painfully. "Now what?"

"I have one more hunch to check out, and then I think we'll know what's what."

She reached over and squeezed my arm. "Thanks."

"Yeah, well, it's not over yet, but we're getting there."

When I got back to Jackie Barnett's, the white Corvette was still in the driveway, but the old man in the wheelchair had apparently been moved into the house. I knocked, and after an interval, Eric opened the door, his expression altering only slightly when he saw me.

I said, "Hello again. Can I talk to your mom?"

"Well, not really. She's gone right now."

"Did she and Avery go off together?"

"Who?"

I smiled briefly. "You can drop the bullshit, Eric. I saw the suitcase in the hall when I was here the first time. Are they gone for good or just for a quick jaunt?"

"They said they'd be back by the end of the week," he mumbled. It was clear he looked a lot slicker than he really was. I almost felt bad that he was so far outclassed.

"Do you mind if I talk to your stepfather?"

He flushed. "She doesn't want him upset."

"I won't upset him."

He shifted uneasily, trying to decide what to do with me.

I thought I'd help him out. "Could I just make a suggestion here? According to the California penal code, grand theft is committed when the real or personal property taken is of a value exceeding two hundred dollars. Now that includes domestic fowl, avocados, olives, citrus, nuts, and artichokes. Also shotguns, and it's punishable by imprisonment in the county jail or state prison for not more than one year. I don't think you'd care for it."

He stepped away from the door and let me in.

The old man was huddled in his wheelchair in the den. The rheumy eyes came up to meet mine, but there was no recognition in them. Or maybe there was recognition but no interest. I hunkered beside his wheelchair. "Is your hearing okay?"

He began to pluck aimlessly at his pant leg with his good hand, looking away from me. I've seen dogs with the same expression when they've done pottie on the rug and know you've got a roll of newspaper tucked behind your back.

"Want me to tell you what I think happened?" I didn't really need to wait. He couldn't answer in any mode that I could interpret. "I think when you came home from the hospital the first time and found out the gun was gone, the shit hit the fan. You must have figured out that Eric took it. He'd probably taken other things if he'd been doing cocaine for long. You probably hounded him until you found out what he'd done with it, and then you went over to Rudd's to get it. Maybe you took the L. C. Smith with you the first time, or maybe you came back for it when he refused to return the Parker. In either case, you blew his head off and then came back across the yards. And then you had another stroke."

I became aware of Eric in the doorway behind me. I glanced back at him. "You want to talk about this stuff?" I asked.

"Did he kill Rudd?"

"I think so," I said. I stared at the old man.

His face had taken on a canny stubbornness, and what was I going to do? I'd have to talk to Lieutenant Dolan about the situation, but the cops would probably never find any real proof, and even if they did, what could they do to him? He'd be lucky if he lived out the year.

"Rudd was a nice guy," Eric said.

"God, Eric. You *all* must have guessed what happened," I said snappishly.

He had the good grace to color up at that, and then he left the room. I stood up. To save myself, I couldn't work up any righteous anger at the pitiful remainder of a human being hunched in front of me. I crossed to the gun cabinet.

The Parker shotgun was in the rack, three slots down, looking like the other classic shotguns in the case. The old man would die, and Jackie would inherit it from his estate. Then she'd marry Avery and they'd all have what they wanted. I stood there for a moment, and then I started looking through the desk drawers until I found the keys. I unlocked the cabinet and then unlocked the rack. I substituted the L. C. Smith for the Parker and then locked the whole business up again. The old man was whimpering, but he never looked at me, and Eric was nowhere in sight when I left.

The last I saw of the Parker shotgun, Lisa Osterling was holding it somewhat awkwardly across her bulky midriff. I'd talk to Lieutenant Dolan all right, but I wasn't going to tell him everything. Sometimes justice is served in other ways.

1989

DONALD E. WESTLAKE

....

Too Many Crooks

"DID YOU HEAR SOMETHING?" Dortmunder whispered.

"The wind," Kelp said.

Dortmunder twisted around in his seated position and deliberately shone the flashlight in the kneeling Kelp's eyes. "What wind? We're in a tunnel."

"There's underground rivers," Kelp said, squinting, "so maybe there's underground winds. Are you through the wall there?"

"Two more whacks," Dortmunder told him. Relenting, he aimed the flashlight past Kelp back down the empty tunnel, a meandering, messy gullet, most of it less than three feet in diameter, wriggling its way through rocks and rubble and ancient middens, traversing 40 tough feet from the rear of the basement of the out-of-business shoe store to the wall of the bank on the corner. According to the maps Dortmunder had gotten from the water department by claiming to be with the sewer department, and the maps he'd gotten from the sewer department by claiming to be with the water department, just the other side of this wall was the bank's main vault. Two more whacks and this large, irregular square of concrete that Dortmunder and Kelp had been scoring and scratching at for some time now would at last fall away onto the floor inside, and there would be the vault.

Dortmunder gave it a whack.

Dortmunder gave it another whack.

The block of concrete fell onto the floor of the vault. "Oh, thank God," somebody said.

What? Reluctant but unable to stop himself, Dortmunder dropped sledge and flashlight and leaned his head through the hole in the wall and looked around.

It was the vault, all right. And it was full of people.

A man in a suit stuck his hand out and grabbed Dortmunder's and shook it while pulling him through the hole and on into the vault. "Great work, Officer," he said. "The robbers are outside."

Dortmunder had thought he and Kelp were the robbers. "They are?"

A round-faced woman in pants and a Buster Brown collar said, "Five of them. With machine guns."

"Machine guns," Dortmunder said.

A delivery kid wearing a mustache and an apron and carrying a flat cardboard carton containing four coffees, two decafs and a tea said, "We all hostages, mon. I gonna get fired."

"How many of you are there?" the man in the suit asked, looking past Dortmunder at Kelp's nervously smiling face.

"Just the two," Dortmunder said, and watched helplessly as willing hands dragged Kelp through the hole and set him on his feet in the vault. It was really very full of hostages.

"I'm Kearney," the man in the suit said. "I'm the bank manager, and I can't tell you how glad I am to see you."

Which was the first time any bank manager had said *that* to Dortmunder, who said, "Uh-huh, uh-huh," and nodded, and then said, "I'm, uh, Officer Diddums, and this is Officer, uh, Kelley."

Kearney, the bank manager, frowned. "Diddums, did you say?"

Dortmunder was furious with himself. Why did I call myself Diddums? Well, I didn't know I was going to need an alias inside a bank vault, did I? Aloud, he said, "Uh-huh. Diddums. It's Welsh."

"Ah," said Kearney. Then he frowned again and said, "You people aren't even armed."

"Well, no," Dortmunder said. "We're the, uh, the hostage-rescue team; we don't want any shots fired, increase the risk for you, uh, civilians."

"Very shrewd," Kearney agreed.

Kelp, his eyes kind of glassy and his smile kind of fixed, said, "Well, folks, maybe we should leave here now, single file, just make your way in an orderly fashion through —"

"They're coming!" hissed a stylish woman over by the vault door.

Everybody moved. It was amazing; everybody shifted at once. Some people moved to hide the new hole in the wall, some people moved to get farther away from the vault door and some people moved to get behind Dortmunder, who suddenly found himself the nearest person in the vault to that big, round, heavy metal door, which was easing massively and silently open.

It stopped halfway, and three men came in. They wore black ski masks and black leather jackets and black work pants and black shoes. They carried Uzi submachine guns at high port. Their eyes looked cold and hard, and their hands fidgeted on the metal of the guns, and their feet danced nervously, even when they were standing still. They looked as though anything at all might make them overreact.

"Shut up!" one of them yelled, though nobody'd been talking. He glared around at his guests and said, "Gotta have somebody to stand out front, see can the cops be trusted." His eye, as Dortmunder had known it would, lit on Dortmunder. "You," he said.

"Uh-huh," Dortmunder said.

"What's your name?"

Everybody in the vault had already heard him say it, so what choice did he have? "Diddums," Dortmunder said.

The robber glared at Dortmunder through his ski mask. "Diddums?"

"It's Welsh," Dortmunder explained.

"Ah," the robber said, and nodded. He gestured with the Uzi. "Outside, Diddums."

Dortmunder stepped forward, glancing back over his shoulder at all the people looking at him, knowing every goddamn one of them was glad he wasn't him — even Kelp, back there pretending to be four feet tall — and then Dortmunder stepped through the vault door, surrounded by all those nervous maniacs with machine guns, and went with them down a corridor flanked by desks and through a doorway to the main part of the bank, which was a mess.

The time at the moment, as the clock high on the wide wall confirmed, was 5:15 in the afternoon. Everybody who worked at the bank should have gone home by now; that was the theory Dortmunder had been operating from. What must have happened was, just before closing time at three o'clock (Dortmunder and Kelp being already then in the tunnel, working hard, knowing nothing of events on the surface of the planet), these gaudy showboats had come into the bank waving their machine guns around.

And not just waving them, either. Lines of ragged punctures had been drawn across the walls and the Lucite upper panel of the tellers' counter, like connect-the-dot puzzles. Wastebaskets and a potted Ficus had been overturned, but fortunately, there were no bodies lying around; none Dortmunder could see, anyway. The big plate-glass front windows had been shot out, and two more of the black-clad robbers were crouched down, one behind the OUR LOW LOAN RATES poster and the other behind the OUR HIGH IRA RATES poster, staring out at the street, from which came the sound of somebody talking loudly but indistinctly through a bullhorn.

So what must have happened, they'd come in just before three, waving their guns, figuring a quick in and out, and some brown-nose employee looking for advancement triggered the alarm, and now they had a stalemate hostage situation on their hands; and, of course, everybody in the world by now has seen *Dog Day Afternoon* and therefore knows that if the police get the drop on a robber in circumstances such as these circumstances right here, they'll immediately shoot him dead, so now hostage negotiation is trickier than ever. This isn't what I had in mind when I came to the bank, Dortmunder thought.

The boss robber prodded him along with the barrel of his Uzi, saying, "What's your first name, Diddums?"

Please don't say Dan, Dortmunder begged himself. Please, please, somehow, anyhow, manage not to say Dan. His mouth opened. "John," he heard himself say, his brain having turned desperately in this emergency to that last resort, the truth, and he got weak-kneed with relief.

"OK, John, don't faint on me," the robber said. "This is very simple what you got to do here. The cops say they want to talk, just talk, nobody gets hurt. Fine. So you're gonna step out in front of the bank and see do the cops shoot you."

"Ah," Dortmunder said.

"No time like the present, huh, John?" the robber said, and poked him with the Uzi again.

"That kind of hurts," Dortmunder said.

"I apologize," the robber said, hard-eyed. "Out."

One of the other robbers, eyes red with strain inside the black ski mask, leaned close to Dortmunder and yelled, "You wanna shot in the foot first? You wanna *crawl* out there?"

"I'm going," Dortmunder told him. "See? Here I go."

The first robber, the comparatively calm one, said, "You go as far as the sidewalk, that's all. You take one step off the curb, we blow your head off."

"Got it," Dortmunder assured him, and crunched across broken glass to the sagging-open door and looked out. Across the street was parked a line of buses, police cars, police trucks, all in blue and white with red gumdrops on top, and behind them moved a seething mass of armed cops. "Uh," Dortmunder said. Turning back to the comparatively calm robber, he said, "You wouldn't happen to have a white flag or anything like that, would you?"

The robber pressed the point of the Uzi to Dortmunder's side. "Out," he said.

"Right," Dortmunder said. He faced front, put his hands way up in the air and stepped outside.

What a *lot* of attention he got. From behind all those blue-and-whites on the other side of the street, tense faces stared. On the roof-tops of the red-brick tenements, in this neighborhood deep in the residential heart of Queens, sharp-shooters began to familiarize themselves through their telescopic sights with the contours of Dortmunder's furrowed brow. To left and right, the ends of the block were sealed off with buses parked nose to tail pipe, past which ambulances and jumpy white-coated medics could be seen. Everywhere, rifles and pistols jittered in nervous fingers. Adrenaline ran in the gutters.

"I'm not with *them!*" Dortmunder shouted, edging across the sidewalk, arms upraised, hoping this announcement wouldn't upset the other bunch of armed hysterics behind him. For all he knew, they had a problem with rejection.

However, nothing happened behind him, and what happened out front was that a bullhorn appeared, resting on a police-car roof, and roared at him, *"You a hostage?"*

"I sure am!" yelled Dortmunder.

"What's your name?"

Oh, not again, thought Dortmunder, but there was nothing for it. "Diddums," he said.

"What?"

"Diddums!"

A brief pause: *"Diddums?"*

"It's Welsh!"

"Ah."

There was a little pause while whoever was operating the bullhorn conferred with his compatriots, and then the bullhorn said, *"What's the situation in there?"*

What kind of question was that? "Well, uh," Dortmunder said, and remembered to speak more loudly, and called, "kind of tense, actually."

"Any of the hostages been harmed?"

"Uh-uh. No. Definitely not. This is a . . . this is a . . . nonviolent confrontation." Dortmunder fervently hoped to establish that idea in everybody's mind, particularly if he were going to be out here in the middle much longer.

"Any change in the situation?"

Change? "Well," Dortmunder answered, "I haven't been in there that long, but it seems like —"

"Not that long? What's the matter with you, Diddums? You've been in that bank over two hours now!"

"Oh, yeah!" Forgetting, Dortmunder lowered his arms and stepped forward to the curb. "That's right!" he called. "Two hours! *More* than two hours! Been in there a long time!"

"Step out here away from the bank!"

Dortmunder looked down and saw his toes hanging ten over the edge of the curb. Stepping back at a brisk pace, he called, "I'm not supposed to do that!"

"Listen, Diddums, I've got a lot of tense men and women over here. I'm telling you, step away from the bank!"

"The fellas inside," Dortmunder explained, "they don't want me to step off the curb. They said they'd, uh, well, they just don't want me to do it."

"Psst! Hey, Diddums!"

Dortmunder paid no attention to the voice calling from behind him. He was concentrating too hard on what was happening right now out front. Also, he wasn't that used to the new name yet.

"Diddums!"

"Maybe you better put your hands up again."

"Oh, yeah!" Dortmunder's arms shot up like pistons blowing through an engine block. "There they are!"

"Diddums, goddamn it, do I have to shoot *you to get you to pay attention?"*

Arms dropping, Dortmunder spun around. "Sorry! I wasn't — I was — here I am!"

"Get those goddamn hands up!"

Dortmunder turned sideways, arms up so high his sides hurt. Peering sidelong to his right, he called to the crowd across the street, "Sirs, they're talking to me inside now." Then he peered sidelong to his left, saw the comparatively calm robber crouched beside the broken doorframe and looking less calm than before, and he said, "Here I am."

"We're gonna give them our demands now," the robber said. "Through you."

"That's fine," Dortmunder said. "That's great. Only, you know, how come you don't do it on the phone? I mean, the way it's normally —"

The red-eyed robber, heedless of exposure to the sharpshooters across the street, shouldered furiously past the comparatively calm robber, who tried to restrain him as he yelled at Dortmunder, "You're rubbing it in, are ya? OK, I made a mistake! I got excited and I shot up the switchboard! You want me to get excited again?"

"No, no!" Dortmunder cried, trying to hold his hands straight up in the air and defensively in front of his body at the same time. "I forgot! I just forgot!"

The other robbers all clustered around to grab the red-eyed robber, who seemed to be trying to point his Uzi in Dortmunder's direction as he yelled, "I did it in front of everybody! I humiliated myself in front of everybody! And now you're making fun of me!"

"I *forgot!* I'm sorry!"

"You can't forget that! Nobody's ever gonna forget that!"

The three remaining robbers dragged the red-eyed robber back away from the doorway, talking to him, trying to soothe him, leaving Dortmunder and the comparatively calm robber to continue their conversation. "I'm sorry," Dortmunder said. "I just forgot. I've been kind of distracted lately. Recently."

"You're playing with fire here, Diddums," the robber said. "Now tell them they're gonna get our demands."

Dortmunder nodded, and turned his head the other way, and yelled, "They're gonna tell you their demands now. I mean, I'm gonna tell you their demands. *Their* demands. Not *my* demands. *Their* de —"

"*We're willing to listen, Diddums, only so long as none of the hostages get hurt.*"

"That's good!" Dortmunder agreed, and turned his head the other way to tell the robber, "That's reasonable, you know, that's sensible, that's a very good thing they're saying."

"Shut up," the robber said.

"Right," Dortmunder said.

The robber said, "First, we want the riflemen off the roofs."

"Oh, so do I," Dortmunder told him, and turned to shout, "They want the riflemen off the roofs!"

"*What else?*"

"What else?"

"And we want them to unblock that end of the street, the — what is it? — the north end."

Dortmunder frowned straight ahead at the buses blocking the intersection. "Isn't that east?" he asked.

"Whatever it is," the robber said, getting impatient. "That end down
there to the left."

"OK." Dortmunder turned his head and yelled, "They want you to
unblock the east end of the street!" Since his hands were way up in the
sky somewhere, he pointed with his chin.

"Isn't that north?"

"I knew it was," the robber said.

"Yeah, I guess so," Dortmunder called. "That end down there to the
left."

"The right, you mean."

"Yeah, that's right. Your right, my left. *Their* left."

"What else?"

Dortmunder sighed, and turned his head. "What else?"

The robber glared at him. "I can *hear* the bullhorn, Diddums. I can
hear him say 'What else?' You don't have to repeat everything he says.
No more translations."

"Right," Dortmunder said. "Gotcha. No more translations."

"We'll want a car," the robber told him. "A station wagon. We're
gonna take three hostages with us, so we want a big station wagon. And
nobody follows us."

"Gee," Dortmunder said dubiously, "are you sure?"

The robber stared. "Am I *sure?*"

"Well, you know what they'll do," Dortmunder told him, lowering
his voice so the other team across the street couldn't hear him. "What
they do in these situations, they fix a little radio transmitter under the
car, so then they don't have to *follow* you, exactly, but they know where
you are."

Impatient again, the robber said, "So you'll tell them not to do that.
No radio transmitters, or we kill the hostages."

"Well, I suppose," Dortmunder said doubtfully.

"What's wrong *now?*" the robber demanded. "You're too goddamn
picky, Diddums; you're just the messenger here. You think you know my
job better than I do?"

I know I do, Dortmunder thought, but it didn't seem a judicious
thing to say aloud, so instead, he explained, "I just want things to go
smooth, that's all. I just don't want bloodshed. And I was thinking, The
New York City police, you know, well, they've got helicopters."

"Damn," the robber said. He crouched low to the littered floor, behind the broken doorframe, and brooded about his situation. Then he looked up at Dortmunder and said, "OK, Diddums, you're so smart. What *should* we do?"

Dortmunder blinked. "You want *me* to figure out your getaway?"

"Put yourself in our position," the robber suggested. "Think about it."

Dortmunder nodded. Hands in the air, he gazed at the blocked intersection and put himself in the robbers' position. "Hoo, boy," he said. "You're in a real mess."

"We *know* that, Diddums."

"Well," Dortmunder said, "I tell you what maybe you could do. You make them give you one of those buses they've got down there blocking the street. They give you one of those buses right now, then you know they haven't had time to put anything cute in it, like time-release tear-gas grenades or anyth —"

"Oh, my God," the robber said. His black ski mask seemed to have paled slightly.

"Then you take *all* the hostages," Dortmunder told him. "Everybody goes in the bus, and one of you people drives, and you go somewhere real crowded, like Times Square, say, and then you stop and make all the hostages get out and run."

"Yeah?" the robber said. "What good does that do us?"

"Well," Dortmunder said, "you drop the ski masks and the leather jackets and the guns, and *you* run, too. Twenty, thirty people all running away from the bus in different directions, in the middle of Times Square in rush hour, everybody losing themselves in the crowd. It might work."

"Jeez, it might," the robber said. "OK, go ahead and — what?"

"What?" Dortmunder echoed. He strained to look leftward, past the vertical column of his left arm. The boss robber was in excited conversation with one of his pals; not the red-eyed maniac, a different one. The boss robber shook his head and said, "Damn!" Then he looked up at Dortmunder. "Come back in here, Diddums," he said.

Dortmunder said, "But don't you want me to —"

"Come back in here!"

"Oh," Dortmunder said. "Uh, I better tell them over there that I'm gonna move."

"Make it fast," the robber told him. "Don't mess with me, Diddums. I'm in a bad mood right now."

"OK." Turning his head the other way, hating it that his back was to-

ward this bad-mooded robber for even a second, Dortmunder called,
"They want me to go back into the bank now. Just for a minute." Hands
still up, he edged sideways across the sidewalk and through the gaping
doorway, where the robbers laid hands on him and flung him back
deeper into the bank.

He nearly lost his balance but saved himself against the sideways-
lying pot of the tipped-over Ficus. When he turned around, all five of
the robbers were lined up looking at him, their expressions intent, focused, almost hungry, like a row of cats looking in a fish-store window.
"Uh," Dortmunder said.

"He's it now," one of the robbers said.

Another robber said, "But *they* don't know it."

A third robber said, "They will soon."

"They'll know it when nobody gets on the bus," the boss robber said,
and shook his head at Dortmunder. "Sorry, Diddums. Your idea doesn't
work anymore."

Dortmunder had to keep reminding himself that he wasn't actually
part of this string. "How come?" he asked.

Disgusted, one of the other robbers said, "The rest of the hostages
got away, that's how come."

Wide-eyed, Dortmunder spoke without thinking: "The tunnel!"

All of a sudden, it got very quiet in the bank. The robbers were now
looking at him like cats looking at a fish with no window in the way.
"The tunnel?" repeated the boss robber slowly. "You *know* about the
tunnel?"

"Well, kind of," Dortmunder admitted. "I mean, the guys digging it,
they got there just before you came and took me away."

"And you never mentioned it."

"Well," Dortmunder said, very uncomfortable, "I didn't feel like I
should."

The red-eyed maniac lunged forward, waving that submachine gun
again, yelling, "*You're* the guy with the tunnel! It's your tunnel!" And he
pointed the shaking barrel of the Uzi at Dortmunder's nose.

"Easy, easy!" the boss robber yelled. "This is our only hostage; don't
use him up!"

The red-eyed maniac reluctantly lowered the Uzi, but he turned to
the others and announced, "*Nobody's* gonna forget when I shot up the
switchboard. Nobody's *ever* gonna forget that. He wasn't *here!*"

All of the robbers thought that over. Meantime, Dortmunder was
thinking about his own position. He might be a hostage, but he wasn't

your normal hostage, because he was also a guy who had just dug a tunnel to a bank vault, and there were maybe 30 eyeball witnesses who could identify him. So it wasn't enough to get away from these bank robbers; he was also going to have to get away from the police. Several thousand police.

So did that mean he was locked to these second-rate smash-and-grabbers? Was his own future really dependent on *their* getting out of this hole? Bad news, if true. Left to their own devices, these people couldn't escape from a merry-go-round.

Dortmunder sighed. "OK," he said. "The first thing we have to do is —"

"We?" the boss robber said. "Since when are you in this?"

"Since you dragged me in," Dortmunder told him. "And the first thing we have to do is —"

The red-eyed maniac lunged at him again with the Uzi, shouting, "Don't you tell us what to do! *We* know what to do!"

"I'm your only hostage," Dortmunder reminded him. "Don't use me up. Also, now that I've seen you people in action, I'm your only hope of getting out of here. So this time, listen to me. The first thing we have to do is close and lock the vault door."

One of the robbers gave a scornful laugh. "The hostages are *gone*," he said. "Didn't you hear that part? Lock the vault door after the hostages are gone. Isn't that some kind of old saying?" And he laughed and laughed.

Dortmunder looked at him. "It's a two-way tunnel," he said quietly.

The robbers stared at him. Then they all turned and ran toward the back of the bank. They *all* did.

They're too excitable for this line of work, Dortmunder thought as he walked briskly toward the front of the bank. *Clang* went the vault door, far behind him, and Dortmunder stepped through the broken doorway and out again to the sidewalk, remembering to stick his arms straight up in the air as he did.

"Hi!" he yelled, sticking his face well out, displaying it for all the sharpshooters to get a really *good* look at. "Hi, it's me again! Diddums! Welsh!"

"Diddums!" screamed an enraged voice from deep within the bank. "Come back here!"

Oh, no. Ignoring that, moving steadily but without panic, arms up, face forward, eyes wide, Dortmunder angled leftward across the sidewalk, shouting, "I'm coming out again! And I'm *escaping!*" And he dropped his arms, tucked his elbows in and ran hell for leather toward those blocking buses.

Gunfire encouraged him: sudden burst behind him of *ddrrritt, ddrrritt,* and then *kopp-kopp-kopp,* and then a whole symphony of *fooms* and *thug-thugs* and *padapows.* Dortmunder's toes, turning into high-tension steel springs, kept him bounding through the air like the Wright brothers' first airplane, swooping and plunging down the middle of the street, that wall of buses getting closer and closer.

"Here! In here!" Uniformed cops appeared on both sidewalks, waving to him, offering sanctuary in the forms of open doorways and police vehicles to crouch behind, but Dortmunder was *escaping.* From everything.

The buses. He launched himself through the air, hit the blacktop hard and rolled under the nearest bus. Roll, roll, roll, hitting his head and elbows and knees and ears and nose and various other parts of his body against any number of hard, dirty objects, and then he was past the bus and on his feet, staggering, staring at a lot of goggle-eyed medics hanging around beside their ambulances, who just stood there and gawked back.

Dortmunder turned left. *Medics* weren't going to chase him; their franchise didn't include healthy bodies running down the street. The cops couldn't chase him until they'd moved their buses out of the way. Dortmunder took off like the last of the dodoes, flapping his arms, wishing he knew how to fly.

The out-of-business shoe store, the other terminus of the tunnel, passed on his left. The getaway car they'd parked in front of it was long gone, of course. Dortmunder kept thudding on, on, on.

Three blocks later, a gypsy cab committed a crime by picking him up even though he hadn't phoned the dispatcher first; in the city of New York, only licensed medallion taxis are permitted to pick up customers who hail them on the street. Dortmunder, panting like a Saint Bernard on the lumpy back seat, decided not to turn the guy in.

His faithful companion May came out of the living room when Dortmunder opened the front door of his apartment and stepped into his hall. "*There* you are!" she said. "Thank goodness. It's all over the radio *and* the television."

"I may never leave the house again," Dortmunder told her. "If Andy Kelp ever calls, says he's got this great job, easy, piece of cake, I'll just tell him I've retired."

"Andy's here," May said. "In the living room. You want a beer?"

"Yes," Dortmunder said simply.

May went away to the kitchen and Dortmunder limped into the living room, where Kelp was seated on the sofa holding a can of beer and looking happy. On the coffee table in front of him was a mountain of money.

Dortmunder stared. "What's *that?*"

Kelp grinned and shook his head. "It's been too long since we scored, John," he said. "You don't even recognize the stuff anymore. This is money."

"But — from the vault? How?"

"After you were taken away by those other guys — they were caught, by the way," Kelp interrupted himself, "without loss of life — anyway, I told everybody in the vault there, the way to keep the money safe from the robbers was we'd all carry it out with us. So we did. And then I decided what we should do is put it all in the trunk of my unmarked police car in front of the shoe store, so I could drive it to the precinct for safekeeping while they all went home to rest from their ordeal."

Dortmunder looked at his friend. He said, "You got the hostages to carry the money from the vault."

"And put it in our car," Kelp said. "Yeah, that's what I did."

May came in and handed Dortmunder a beer. He drank deep, and Kelp said, "They're looking for you, of course. Under that other name."

May said, "That's the one thing I don't understand. Diddums?"

"It's Welsh," Dortmunder told her. Then he smiled upon the mountain of money on the coffee table. "It's not a bad name," he decided. "I may keep it."

1996

JAMES CRUMLEY

....

Hot Springs

AT NIGHT, even in the chill mountain air, Mona Sue insisted on crank-
ing the air conditioner all the way up. Her usual temperature always
ran a couple of degrees higher than normal, and she claimed that
the baby she carried made her constant fever even worse. She kept the
cabin cold enough to hang meat. During the long, sleepless nights
Benbow spooned to her naked, burning skin, trying to stay warm.

In the mornings, too, Mona Sue forced him into the cold. The modern cabin sat on a bench in the cool shadow of Mount Nihart, and they
broke their fast with a room-service breakfast on the deck, a robe
wrapped loosely about her naked body while Benbow bundled into
both sweats and a robe. She ate furiously, stoking a furnace, and re-
counted her dreams as if they were gospel, effortlessly consuming most
of the spread of exotic cheeses and expensively unseasonable fruits, a
loaf of sourdough toast and four kinds of meat, all the while aimlessly
babbling through the events of her internal night, the dreams of a teenage girl, languidly symbolic and vaguely frightening. She dreamt of her
mother, young and lovely, devouring her litter of barefoot boys in the
dark Ozark hollows. And her father, home from a Tennessee prison, his
crooked member dangling against her smooth cheek.

Benbow suspected she left the best parts out and did his best to listen
to the soft southern cadences without watching her face. He knew what
happened when he watched her talk, watched the soft moving curve of
her dark lips, the wise slant of her gray eyes. So he picked at his breakfast and tried to focus his stare downslope at the steam drifting off the
large hot-water pool behind the old shagbark lodge.

But then she switched to her daydreams about their dubious future,
which were as deadly specific as a .45 slug in the brainpan: after the

baby, they could flee to Canada; nobody would follow them up there. He listened and watched with the false patience of a teenage boy involved in his first confrontation with pure lust and hopeless desire.

Mona Sue ate with the precise and delicate greed of a heart surgeon, the pad of her spatulate thumb white on the handle of her spoon as she carved a perfect curled ball from the soft orange meat of her melon. Each bite of meat had to be balanced with an equal weight of toast before being crushed between her tiny white teeth. Then she examined each strawberry poised before her darkly red lips as if it might be a jewel of great omen and she some ancient oracle, then sank her shining teeth into the fleshy fruit as if it were the mortal truth. Benbow's heart rolled in his chest as he tried to fill his lungs with the cold air to fight off the heat of her body.

Fall had come to the mountains, now. The cottonwoods and alders welcomed the change with garish mourning dress, and in the mornings a rime of ice covered the windshield of the gray Taurus he had stolen at the Denver airport. New snow fell each night, moving slowly down the ridges from the high distant peaks of the Hard Rock Range and slipped closer each morning down the steep ridge behind them. Below the bench the old lodge seemed to settle more deeply into the narrow canyon, as if hunkering down for eons of snow, and the steam from the hot springs mixed with wood smoke and lay flat and sinuous among the yellow creek willows.

Benbow suspected, too, that the scenery was wasted on Mona Sue. Her dark eyes seemed turned inward to a dreamscape of her life, her husband, R. L. Dark, the pig farmer, his bullnecked son, Little R. L., and the lumpy Ozark offal of her large worthless family.

"Coach," she'd say — she thought it funny to call him Coach — interrupting the shattered and drifting narrative of her dreams. Then she would sweep back the thick black Indian hair from her face, tilt her narrow head on the slender column of her neck, and laugh. "Coach, that ol' R. L., he's a-comin'. You stole somethin' belonged to him, and you can bet he's on his way. Lit'l R. L., too, prob'ly, 'cause he tol' me once he'd like to string your guts on a bob-wire fence," she recited like a sprightly but not very bright child.

"Sweetheart, R. L. Dark can just barely cipher the numbers on a dollar bill or the spots on a card," Benbow answered, as he had each morning for the six months they'd been on the run, "he can't read a map that he hasn't drawn himself, and by noon he's too drunk to fit his ass in a tractor seat and find his hog pens. . . ."

"You know, Puddin', an ol' boy's got enough a them dollar bills, or stacks a them Franklins like we do," she added, laughing, "he can hire-out that readin' part, and the map part too. So he's a-comin'. You can put that in your momma's piggy bank."

This was a new wrinkle in their morning ritual, and Benbow caught himself glancing down at the parking lot behind the lodge and at the single narrow road up Hidden Springs Canyon, but he shook it off quickly. When he made the fateful decision to take Mona Sue and the money, he vowed to go for it, never glancing over his shoulder, living in the moment.

And this was it. Once more. Leaving his breakfast untouched, again, he slipped his hand through the bulky folds of Mona Sue's terry cloth robe to cradle the warm ripening fullness of her breasts and the long, thick nipples, already rock hard before his touch, and he kissed her mouth, sweet with strawberry and melon. Once again, he marveled at the deep passionate growl from the base of her throat as he pressed his lips into the hollow, then Benbow lifted her small frame — she nestled the baby high under the smooth vault of her rib cage and even at seven months the baby barely showed — and carried her to the bedroom.

Benbow knew, from recent experience, that the horse wrangler who doubled as room-service waiter would be waiting to clear the picnic table when they came out of the house to finish the coffee. The wrangler might have patience with horses but not with guests who spent their mornings in bed. But he would wait for long minutes, silent as an Sioux scout, as Mona Sue searched her robe for his tip, occasionally exposing the rising contour of a breast or the clean scissoring of her long legs. Benbow had given him several hard looks, which the wrangler ignored as if the blunt stares were spoken in a foreign tongue. But nothing helped. Except to take the woman inside and avoid the wrangler altogether.

This morning Benbow laid Mona Sue on the feather bed like a gift, opened her robe, kissed the soft curve of her swollen belly, then blew softly on her feathery pubic hair. Mona Sue sobbed quickly, coughed as if she had a catfish bone caught in her throat, her long body arching. Benbow sobbed, too, his hunger for her more intense than the hunger growling in his empty stomach.

While Mona Sue had swelled through her pregnancy, Benbow had shed twenty-seven pounds from his blocky frame. Sometimes, just after they made love, it seemed as if her burning body had stolen the baby from his own muscled flesh, something stolen during the tangle of love, something growing hard and tight in her smooth, slim body.

As usual, they made love, then finished the coffee, ordered a fresh pot, tipped the wrangler, then made love again before her morning nap.

While Mona Sue slept, usually Benbow would drink the rest of the coffee as he read the day-old Meriwether newspaper, then slip into his sweats and running shoes, and jog down the switchbacks to the lodge to laze in the hot waters of the pools. He loved it there, floating in the water that seemed heavier than normal, thicker but cleaner, clearer. He almost felt whole there, cleansed and healthy and warm, taking the waters like some rich foreign prince, fleeing his failed life.

Occasionally, Benbow wished Mona Sue would interrupt her naps to join him, but she always said it might hurt the baby and she was already plenty hot with her natural fevers. As the weeks passed, Benbow learned to treasure his time alone in the hot pool and stopped asking her.

So their days wound away routinely, spooling like silk ribbons through their fingers, as placid as the deeply still waters of the pool.

But this noon, exhausted from the run and the worry, the lack of sleep and food, Benbow slipped effortlessly into the heated gravity of Mona Sue's sleeping body and slept, only to wake suddenly, sweating in spite of the chill, when the air conditioner was switched off.

R. L. Dark stood at the foot of their bed. Grinning. The old man stretched his crinkled neck, sniffing the air like an ancient snapping turtle, testing the air for food or fun, since he had no natural enemies except for teenage boys with .22's R. L. had dressed for the occasion. He wore a new Carhart tin coat and clean bib overalls with the old Webley .455 revolver hanging on a string from his neck and bagging the bib pocket.

Two good ol' boys flanked him, one bald and the other wildly hirsute, both huge and dressed in Kmart flannel plaid. The bald one held up a small ballpeen hammer like a trophy. They weren't grinning. A skinny man in a baggy white suit shifted from foot to foot behind them, smiling weakly like a gun-shy pointer pup.

"Well, piss on the fire, boys, and call the dogs," R. L. Dark said, hustling the extra .455 rounds in his pocket as if they were his withered privates, "this hunt's done." The old man's cackle sounded like the sunrise cry of a cannibalistic rooster. "Son, they say you coulda been some kinda football coach, and I know you're one hell of a poker player, but I'd a never thought you'd come to this sorry end — a simpleminded

thief and a chicken-fuckin' wife stealer." Then R. L. brayed like one of
the old plow mules he kept in the muddy bottoms of the White. "But
you can run right smart, son. Gotta say that. Sly as an old boar coon. We
might still be a-lookin' if'n Baby Doll there ain't a called her momma.
Collect. To brag 'bout the baby."

Jesus, Benbow thought. Her mother. A toothless woman, now,
shaped like a potato dumpling, topped with greasy hair, seasoned with
moles.

Mona Sue woke, rubbing her eyes like a child, murmuring, "How you
been, Daddy Honey?"

And Benbow knew he faced a death even harder than his unlucky life,
knew even before the monster on the right popped him behind the ear
with the ballpeen hammer and jerked his stunned body out of bed as if
he were a child and handed him to his partner, who wrapped him in a
full nelson. The bald one flipped the hammer and rapped his nuts
smartly with it, then flipped it again and began breaking the small
bones of Benbow's right foot with the round knob of the hammerhead.

Before Benbow fainted, harsh laughter raked his throat. Maybe this
was the break he had been waiting for all his life.

Actually, it had all been Little R. L.'s fault. Sort of. Benbow had spotted
the hulking bowlegged kid with the tiny ears and the thick neck three
years earlier when the downward spiral of his football coaching career
had led him to Alabamphilia, a small town on the edge of the Ozarks, a
town without hope or dignity or even any convincing religious fervor, a
town that smelled of chicken guts, hog manure, and rampant incest,
which seemed to be the three main industries.

Benbow first saw Little R. L. in a pickup touch football game played
on the hardscrabble playground and knew from the first moment that
the boy had the quick grace of a deer, combined with the strength of a
wild boar. This kid was one of the best natural running backs he'd ever
seen. Benbow also found out just as quickly that Little R. L. was one of
the redheaded Dark boys, and the Dark boys didn't play football.

Daddy R. L. thought football was a silly game, a notion with which
Benbow agreed, and too much like work not to draw wages, with which
once again Benbow agreed, and if'n his boys were going to work for
free, they were damn well going to work for him and his hog operation,
not some dirt-poor pissant washed-up football bum. Benbow had to
agree with that, too, right to R. L.'s face, had to eat the old man's shit to
get to the kid. Because this kid could be Benbow's ticket out of this

Ozark hell, and he intended to have him. This was the one break Benbow needed to save his life. Once again.

It had always been that way for Benbow, needing that one break that never seemed to come. During his senior year at the small high school in western Nebraska, after three and a half years of mostly journeyman work as a blocking back in a pass-crazy offense, Benbow's mother had worked double shifts at the truck-stop café — his dad had been dead so long nobody really remembered him — so they could afford to put together a video-tape of his best efforts as a running back and pass receiver to send down to the university coaches in Lincoln. Once they had agreed to send a scout up for one game, Benbow had badgered his high school coach into a promise to let him carry the ball at least twenty times that night.

But the weather screwed him. On what should have been a lovely early October Friday night, a storm raced in from Canada, days early, and its icy wind blew Benbow's break right out of the water. Before the game, it rained two hard inches, then the field froze. During the first half it rained again, then hailed, and at the end of the second quarter it became a blinding snow squall.

Benbow had gained sixty yards, sure, but none of it pretty. And at halftime the Nebraska scout came by to apologize but if he was to get home in this weather, he had to start now. The lumpy old man invited Benbow to try a walk-on. Right, Benbow thought. Without a scholarship, he didn't have the money to register for fall semester. *Damn,* Benbow thought as he kicked the water cooler, and *damn it to hell,* he thought as his big toe shattered and his senior season ended.

So he played football for some pissant Christian college in the Dakotas where he didn't bother to take a degree. With his fused toe, he had lost a step in the open-field and his cuts lost their precision, so he haunted the weight room, forced thick muscle over his running back's body, and made himself into a solid if small fullback, but good enough to wrangle an invitation to one of the postseason senior bowl games. Then the first-string fullback, who was sure to be drafted by the pros, strained his knee in practice and refused to play. Oh, God, Benbow thought, another break.

But God foxed this one. The backfield coach was a born-again fundamentalist named Culpepper, and once he caught Benbow neither bowing his head nor even bothering to close his eyes during a lengthy team prayer, the coach became determined to convert the boy. Benbow played along, choking on his anger at the self-righteous bastard until his stomach cramped, swallowing the anger until he was throwing up three times a day, twice during practice and once before lights-out. By game day he'd lost twelve pounds and feared he wouldn't have the strength to play.

But he did. He had a first half to praise the football gods, if not the Christian one: two rushing touchdowns, one three yards dragging a linebacker and a corner, the other thirty-nine yards of fluid grace and power; and one receiving, twenty-two yards. But the quarterback had missed the handoff at the end of the first half, jammed the ball against Benbow's hip, and a blitzing linebacker picked it out of the air, then scored.

In the locker room at halftime, Culpepper was all over him like stink on shit. *Pride goeth before a fall!* he shouted. *We're never as tall as we are on our knees before Jesus!* And all the other soft-brain clichés. Benbow's stomach knotted like a rawhide rope, then rebelled. Benbow caught that bit of vomit and swallowed it. But the second wave was too much. He turned and puked into a nearby sink. Culpepper went mad. Accused him of being out of shape, of drinking, smoking, and fornicating. When Benbow denied the charges, Culpepper added another, screamed *Prevaricator!* his foamy spittle flying into Benbow's face. And that was that.

Culpepper lost an eye from the single punch and nearly died during the operation to rebuild his cheekbone. Everybody said Benbow was lucky not to do time, like his father, who had killed a corrupt weighmaster down in Texas with his tire thumper, and was then killed himself by a bad Houston drug dealer down in the Ellis Unit at Huntsville when Benbow was six. Benbow was lucky, he guessed, but marked "Uncoachable" by the pro scouts and denied tryouts all over the league. Benbow played three years in Canada, then destroyed his knee in a bar fight with a Chinese guy in Vancouver. Then he was out of the game. Forever.

Benbow drifted west, fighting fires in the summers and dealing poker in the winter, taking the occasional college classes until he finally finished a PE teaching degree at Northern Montana and garnered an assistant coach's job at a small town in the Sweetgrass Hills, where he discovered he had an unsuspected gift for coaching, as he did for poker: a quick mind and no fear. A gift, once discovered, that became an addiction to the hard work, long hours, loving the game, and paying the price to win.

Head coach in three years, then two state championships, and a move to a larger school in Washington State. Where his mother came to live with him. Or die with him, as it were. The doctors said it was her heart, but Benbow knew that she died of truck-stop food, cheap whiskey, and long-haul drivers whose souls were as full of stale air as their tires.

But he coached a state championship team the next year and was considering offers from a football power down in northern California when he was struck down by a scandalous lawsuit. His second-string quarterback had become convinced that Benbow was sleeping with his mother, which of course he was. When the kid attacked Benbow at practice with his helmet, Benbow had to hit the kid to keep him off. He knew this part of his life was over when he saw the kid's eye dangling out of its socket on the grayish pink string of the optic nerve.

Downhill, as they say, from there. Drinking and fighting as often as coaching, low-rent poker games and married women, usually married to school-board members or dumb-shit administrators. Downhill all the way to Alabamphilia.

Benbow came back to this new world propped in a heap on the couch in the cottage's living room with a dull ache behind his ear and a thousand sharp pains in his foot, which was propped in a white cast on the coffee table, the fresh cast the size of a watermelon. Benbow didn't have to ask what purpose it served. The skinny man sat beside him, a syringe in hand. Across the room, R. L.'s bulk stood black against a fiery sunset, Mona Sue sitting curled in a chair in his shadow, slowly filing her nails. Through the window, Benbow could see the Kmart twins walking slow guard tours back and forth across the deck.

"He's comin' out of it, Mr. Dark," the old man said, his voice as sharp as his pale nose.

"Well, give him another dose, Doc," R. L. said without turning. "We don't want that boy a-hurtin' none. Not yet."

Benbow didn't understand what R. L. meant as the doctor stirred beside him, releasing a thin, dry stench like a limestone cavern or an open grave. Benbow had heard that death supposedly hurt no more than having a tooth pulled and he wondered who had brought back that bit of information as the doctor hit him in the shoulder with a blunt needle, then he slipped uneasily into an enforced sleep like a small death.

When he woke again, Benbow found little changed but the light. Mona Sue still curled in her chair, sleeping now, below her husband's hulk against the full dark sky. The doctor slept, too, leaning the fragile bones of his skull against Benbow's sore arm. And Benbow's leg was also asleep, locked in position by the giant cast resting on the coffee table. He sat very still for as long as he could, waiting for his mind to clear, willing his dead leg to awaken, and wondering why he wasn't dead too.

"Don't be gettin' no ideas, son," R. L. said without turning.

Of all the things Benbow had hated during the long Sundays shoveling pig shit or dealing cards for R. L. Dark — that was the trade he and the old man had made for Little R. L.'s football services — he hated the bastard calling him "son."

"I'm not your 'son,' you fucking old bastard."

R. L. ignored him, didn't even bother to turn. "How hot's that there water?" he asked calmly as the doctor stirred.

Benbow answered without thinking. "Somewhere between ninety-eight and one-oh-two. Why?"

"How 'bout half a dose, Doc?" R. L. said, turning now. "And see 'bout makin' that boy's cast waterproof. I'm thinkin' that hot water might take the edge off my rheumatism and I for sure want the coach there to keep me company. . . ."

Once again Benbow found the warm, lazy path back to the darkness at the center of his life, half listening to the old man and Mona Sue squabble over the air conditioner.

After word of his bargain with R. L. Dark for the gridiron services of his baby son spread throughout every tuck and hollow of the county, Benbow could no longer stop after practice for even a single quiet beer at any one of the rank honky-tonks that surrounded the dry town without hearing snickers as he left. It seemed that whatever he might have gained in sympathy, he surely lost in respect. And the old man treated worse than a farting joke.

On the Saturdays that first fall, when Benbow began his days exchanging his manual labor for Little R. L.'s rushing talents, the old man dogged him all around the hog farm on a small John Deere tractor, endlessly pointing out Benbow's total ignorance of the details of trading bacon for bread and his general inability to perform hard work, complaining at great length, then cackling wildly and jacking the throttle on the tractor as if this was the funniest thing he'd ever seen. Even knowing that Little R. L. was lying on the couch in front of the television and soothing his sore muscles with a pint jar of 'shine, couldn't make Benbow even begin to resent his bargain, and he never even bothered to look at the old man, knowing that this was his only escape.

Sundays, though, the old man left him alone. Sunday was Poker Day.

Land-rich farmers, sly country lawyers with sharp eyes and soft hands, and small-town bankers with the souls of slave traders came from as far away as West Memphis, St. Louis, and Fort Smith to gather in R. L.'s double-wide for a table stakes hold 'em game, a game famous in at least four states, and occasionally in northern Mexico.

On the sabbath he was on his own, except for the surly, lurking presence of Little R. L., who seemed to blame his coach for every ache and pain, and the jittery passage of a slim, petulant teenage girl who slopped past him across the muddy farmyard in a shapeless feed-sack dress and oversized rubber boots, trailing odd, throaty laughter, the same laughter she had when one of the sows decided to dine on her litter. Benbow should have listened.

But these seemed minor difficulties when balanced against the fact that Little R. L. gained nearly a hundred yards a game his freshman year.

The next fall, the shit-shoveling and the old man's attitude seemed easier to bear. Then when Benbow casually let slip that he had once dealt and played poker professionally, R. L.'s watery blue eyes suddenly glistened with greed, and the Sunday portion of Benbow's bargain became both easier and more complicated. Not that the old man needed him to cheat. R. L. Dark always won. The only times the old man signaled him to deal seconds was to give hands to his competitors to keep them in the game so the old man could skin them even deeper.

The brutal and dangerous monotony of Benbow's life continued, controlled and hopeful until the fall of Little R. L.'s junior year when everything came apart. Then back together with a terrible rush. A break, a dislocation, and a connection.

On the Saturday afternoon after Little R. L. broke the state rushing record the night before, the teenage girl stopped chuckling long enough to ask a question. "How long you have to go to college, Coach, to figure out how to scoot pig shit off concrete with a fire hose?"

When she laughed, Benbow finally asked, "Who the fuck are you, honey?"

"Mrs. R. L. Dark, Senior," she replied, the perfect arch of her nose in the air, "that's who." And Benbow looked at her for the first time, watched the thrust of her hard, marvelous body naked beneath the thin fabric of her cheap dress.

Then Benbow tried to make conversation with Mona Sue, made the mistake of asking Mona Sue why she wore rubber boots. "Hookworms," she said, pointing at his sockless feet in old Nikes. *Jesus,* he thought.

Then *Jesus wept* that night as he watched the white worms slither through his dark, bloody stool. Now he knew what the old man had been laughing about.

On Sunday a rich Mexican rancher tried to cover one of R. L.'s raises with a Rolex, then the old man insisted on buying the fifteen-thousand-dollar watch with five K cash, and when he opened the small safe set in the floor of the trailer's kitchen, Benbow glimpsed the huge pile of banded stacks of one-hundred-dollar bills that filled the safe.

The next Friday night Little R. L. broke his own rushing record with more than a quarter left in the game, which was good because in the fourth quarter the turf gave way under his right foot, which then slid under a pursuing tackle. Benbow heard the *pop* all the way from the sidelines as the kid's knee dislocated.

Explaining to R. L. that a bargain was a bargain, no matter what happened with the kid's knee, the next day Benbow went about his chores just long enough to lure Mona Sue into a feed shed and out of her dress. But not her rubber boots. Benbow didn't care. He just fucked her. The revenge he planned on R. L. Dark a frozen hell in his heart. But the soft hunger of her mouth and the touch of her astonishing body — diamond-hard nipples, fast-twitch cat muscle slithering under human skin, her cunt like a silken bag of rich, luminous seed pearls suspended in heavenly fucking fire — destroyed his hope of vengeance. Now he simply wanted her. No matter the cost.

Two months later, just as her pregnancy began to show, Benbow cracked the safe with a tablespoon of nitro, took all the money, and they ran.

Although he was sure Mona Sue still dreamed, she'd lost her audience. Except for the wrangler, who still watched her as if she were some heathen idol. But every time she tried to talk to the dark cowboy, the old man pinched her thigh with horny fingers so hard it left blood blisters.

Their mornings were much different now. They all went to the hot water. The doctor slept on a poolside bench behind Mona Sue who sat on the side of the pool, her feet dangling in the water, her blotched thighs exposed, and her eyes as vacant as her half-smile. R. L. Dark, Curly, and Bald Bill, wearing cutoffs and cheap T-shirts, stood neck-deep in the steamy water, loosely surrounding Benbow, anchored by his plastic-shrouded cast, which loomed like a giant boulder under the heavy water.

A vague sense of threat, like an occasional sharp sniff of sulphur, came off the odd group and kept the other guests at a safe distance, and the number of guests declined every day as the old man rented each cabin and room at the lodge as it came empty. The rich German twins who owned the place didn't seem to care who paid for their cocaine.

During the first few days, nobody had much bothered to speak to Benbow, not even to ask where he had hidden the money. The pain in his foot had retreated to a dull ache, but the itch under the cast had become unbearable. One morning, the doctor had taken pity on him and searched the kitchen drawers for something for Benbow to use to scratch beneath the cast, finally coming up with a cheap shish kebab skewer. Curly and Bald Bill had examined the thin metal stick as if it might be an Arkansas toothpick or a bowie knife, then laughed and let Benbow have it. He kept it holstered in his cast, waiting, scratching the itch. And a deep furrow in the rear of the cast.

Then one morning as they stood silent and safe in the pool, a storm cell drifted slowly down the mountain to fill the canyon with swirling squalls of thick, wet snow, the old man raised his beak into the flakes and finally spoke: "I always meant to come back to this country," he said.

"What?"

Except for the wrangler slowly gathering damp towels and a dark figure in a hooded sweatshirt and sunglasses standing inside the bar, the pool and the deck had emptied when the snow began. Benbow had been watching the snow gather in the dark waves of Mona Sue's hair as she tried to catch a spinning flake on her pink tongue. Even as he faced death, she still stirred the banked embers glowing in Benbow's crotch.

"During WW Two," the old man said softly, "I got in some trouble over at Fort Chaffee — stuck a noncom with a broomstick — so the Army sent me up here to train with the Tenth Mountain. Stupid assholes thought it was some kinda punishment. Always meant to come back someday. . . ."

But Benbow watched the cold wind ripple the stolid surface of the hot water as the snowflakes melted into it. The rising steam became a thick fog.

"I always liked it," Benbow said, glancing up at the mountains as it appeared and disappeared behind the roiling clouds of snow. "Great hunting weather," he added. "There's a little herd of elk bedded just behind that first ridge." As his keepers' eyes followed his upslope, he drifted slowly through the fog toward Mona Sue's feet aimlessly stirring the water. "If you like it so much, you old bastard, maybe you should buy it."

"Watch your tongue, boy," Curly said as he cuffed Benbow on the head. Benbow stumbled closer to Mona Sue.

"I just might do that, son," the old man said, cackling, "just to piss you off. Not that you'll be around to be pissed off."

"So what the fuck are we hanging around here for?" Benbow asked, turning on the old man, which brought him even closer to Mona Sue.

The old man paused as if thinking. "Well, son, we're waitin' for that baby. If'n that baby has red hair and you tell us where you hid the money, we'll just take you home, kill you easy, then feed you to the hogs."

"And if it doesn't have red hair, since I'm not about to tell you where to find the money?"

"We'll just find a hungry sow, son, and feed you to her," the old man said, "startin' with your good toes."

Everybody laughed then: R. L. Dark threw back his head and howled; the hulks exchanged high fives and higher giggles; and Benbow collapsed underwater. Even Mona Sue chuckled deep in her throat. Until Benbow jerked her off the side of the pool. Then she choked. The poor girl had never learned to swim.

Before either the old man or his bodyguards could move, though, the dark figure in the hooded sweatshirt burst through the bar door in a quick, limping dash and dove into the pool, then lifted the struggling girl onto the deck and knelt beside her while enormous amounts of steaming water poured from her nose and mouth before she began breathing. Then the figure swept the hood from the flaming red hair and held Mona Sue close to his chest.

"Holy shit, boy," the old man asked unnecessarily as Bald Bill helped him out of the pool. "What the fuck you doin' here?"

"Goddammit, baby, lemme go," Mona Sue screamed, "it's a-coming!"

Which roused the doctor from his sleepy rest. And the wrangler from his work. Both of them covered the wide wooden bench with dry towels, upon which Little R. L. gently placed Mona Sue's racked body. Curly scrambled out of the pool, warning Benbow to stay put, and joined the crowd of men around her sudden and violent contractions. Bald Bill helped the old man into his overalls and the pistol's thong as Little R. L helped the doctor hold Mona Sue's body, arched with sudden pain, on the bench.

"Oh, Lordy me!" she screamed, "it's tearin' me up!"

"Do somethin', you pissant," the old man said to the wiry doctor, then slapped him soundly.

Benbow slipped to the side of the pool, holding on to the edge with one hand as he dug frantically at the cast with the other. Bits of plaster of paris and swirls of blood rose through the hot water. Then it was off, and the skewer in his hand. He planned to roll out of the pool, drive the sliver of metal through the old man's kidney, then grab the Webley. After that, he'd call the shots.

But life should have taught him not to plan.

As Bald Bill helped his boss into the coat, he noticed Benbow at the edge of the pool and stepped over to him. Bald Bill saw the bloody cast floating at Benbow's chest. "What the fuck?" he said, kneeling down to reach for him.

Benbow drove the thin shaft of metal with the strength of a lifetime of disappointment and rage into the bottom of Bald Bill's jaw, up through the root of his tongue, then up through his soft palate, horny brainpan, mushy gray matter, and the thick bones of his skull. Three inches of the skewer poked like a steel finger bone out of the center of his bald head.

Bald Bill didn't make a sound. Just blinked once dreamily, smiled, then stood up. After a moment, swaying, he began to walk in small airless circles at the edge of the deck until Curly noticed his odd behavior.

"Bubba?" he said as he stepped over to his brother.

Benbow leapt out of the water; one hand grabbed an ankle and the other dove up the leg of Curly's trunks to grab his nut sack and jerk the giant toward the pool. Curly's grunt and the soft clunk of his head against the concrete pool edge was lost as Mona Sue delivered the child with a deep sigh, and the old man shouted boldly, "Goddamn, it's a girl! A black-headed girl!"

Benbow had slithered out of the pool and limped halfway to the old man's back as he watched the doctor lay the baby on Mona Sue's heaving chest. "Shit fire and save the matches," the old man said, panting deeply as if the labor had been his.

Little R. L. turned and jerked his father toward him by the front of his coat, hissing, "Shut the fuck up, old man." Then he shoved him violently away, smashing the old man's frail body into Benbow's shoulder. Something cracked inside the old man's body, and he sank to his knees, snapping at the cold air with his bloody beak like a gut-shot turtle. Benbow grabbed the pistol's thong off his neck before the old man tumbled dead into the water.

Benbow cocked the huge pistol with a soft metallic click, then his sharp bark of laughter cut through the snowy air like a gunshot. Everything slowed to a stop. The doctor finished cutting the cord. The wrangler's hands held a folded towel under Mona Sue's head. Little R. L. held his gristled body halfway into a mad charge. Bald Bill stopped his aimless circling long enough to fall into the pool. Even Mona Sue's cooing sighs died. Only the cold wind moved, whipping the steamy fog across the pool as the snowfall thickened.

Then Mona Sue screamed, "No!" and broke the frozen moment.

The bad knee gave Benbow time to get off a round. The heavy slug took Little R. L. in the top of his shoulder, tumbled through his chest, and exited just above his kidney in a shower of blood, bone splinters, and lung tissue, and dropped him like a side of beef on the deck. But the round had already gone on its merry way through the sternum of the doctor as if he weren't there. Which, in moments, he wasn't.

Benbow threw the pistol joyfully behind him, heard it splash in the pool, and hurried to Mona Sue's side. As he kissed her blood-spattered face, she moaned softly. He leaned closer, but only mistook her moans for passion until he understood what she was saying. Over and over. The way she once called his name. And Little R. L.'s. Maybe even the old man's. "Cowboy, Cowboy, Cowboy," she whispered.

Benbow wasn't even mildly surprised when he felt the arm at his throat or the blade tickle his short ribs. "I took you for a backstabber," he said, "the first time I laid eyes on your sorry ass."

"Just tell me where the money is, *old man*," the wrangler whispered, "and you can die easy."

"You can have the money," Benbow sobbed, trying for one final break, "just leave me the woman." But the flash of scorn in Mona Sue's eyes was the only answer he needed. "Fuck it," Benbow said, almost laughing, "let's do it the hard way."

Then he fell backward onto the hunting knife, driving the blade to the hilt above his short ribs before the wrangler could release the handle. He stepped back in horror as Benbow stumbled toward the hot waters of the pool.

At first, the blade felt cold in Benbow's flesh, but the flowing blood quickly warmed it. Then he eased himself into the hot water and lay back against its compassionate weight like the old man the wrangler had called him. The wrangler stood over Benbow, his eyes like coals glowing through the fog and thick snow. Mona Sue stepped up beside the wrangler, Benbow's baby whimpering at her chest, snow melting on her shoulders.

"Fuck it," Benbow whispered, drifting now, "it's in the air conditioner."

"Thanks, old man," Mona Sue said, smiling.

"Take care," Benbow whispered, thinking, *This is the easy part,* then leaned farther back into the water, sailing on the pool's wind-riffled, snow-shot surface, eyes closed, happy in the hot, heavy water, moving his hands slightly to stay afloat, his fingers tangled in dark, bloody streams, the wind pushing him toward the cool water at the far end of the pool, blinking against the soft cold snow, until his tired body slipped, unwatched, beneath the hot water to rest.

1996

BRENDAN DUBOIS

The Dark Snow

WHEN I GET TO THE STEPS of my lakeside home, the door is open. I slowly walk in, my hand reaching for the phantom weapon at my side, everything about me extended and tingling as I enter the strange place that used to be mine. I step through the small kitchen, my boots crunching the broken glassware and dishes on the tile floor. Inside the living room with its cathedral ceiling the furniture has been upended, as if an earthquake had struck.

I pause for a second, looking out the large windows and past the enclosed porch, down to the frozen waters of Lake Marie. Off in the distance are the snow-covered peaks of the White Mountains. I wait, trembling, my hand still curving for that elusive weapon. They are gone, but their handiwork remains. The living room is a jumble of furniture, torn books and magazines, shattered pictures and frames. On one clear white plaster wall, next to the fireplace, two words have been written in what looks to be ketchup: GO HOME.

This is my home. I turn over a chair and drag it to the windows. I sit and look out at the crisp winter landscape, my legs stretched out, holding both hands still in my lap, which is quite a feat.

For my hands at that moment want to be wrapped around someone's throat.

After a long time wandering, I came to Nansen, New Hampshire, in the late summer and purchased a house along the shoreline of Lake Marie. I didn't waste much time, and I didn't bargain. I made an offer that was about a thousand dollars below the asking price, and in less than a month it belonged to me.

At first I didn't know what to do with it. I had never had a residence that was actually mine. Everything before this had been apartments, hotel rooms, or temporary officer's quarters. The first few nights I couldn't sleep inside. I would go outside to the long dock that extends into the deep blue waters of the lake, bundle myself up in a sleeping bag over a thin foam mattress, and stare up at the stars, listening to the loons getting ready for their long winter trip. The loons don't necessarily fly south; the ones here go out to the cold Atlantic and float with the waves and currents, not once touching land the entire winter.

As I snuggled in my bag I thought it was a good analogy for what I'd been doing. I had drifted too long. It was time to come back to dry land.

After getting the power and other utilities up and running and moving in the few boxes of stuff that belonged to me, I checked the bulky folder that had accompanied my retirement and pulled out an envelope with a doctor's name on it. Inside were official papers that directed me to talk to him, and I shrugged and decided it was better than sitting in an empty house getting drunk. I phoned and got an appointment for the next day.

His name was Ron Longley and he worked in Manchester, the state's largest city and about an hour's drive south of Lake Marie. His office was in a refurbished brick building along the banks of the Merrimack River. I imagined I could still smell the sweat and toil of the French Canadians who had worked here for so many years in the shoe, textile, and leather mills until their distant cousins in Georgia and Alabama took their jobs away.

I wasn't too sure what to make of Ron during our first session. He showed me some documents that made him a Department of Defense contractor and gave his current classification level, and then, after signing the usual insurance nonsense, we got down to it. He was about ten years younger than I, with a mustache and not much hair on top. He wore jeans, a light blue shirt, and a tie that looked as if about six tubes of paint had been squirted onto it, and he said, "Well, here we are."

"That we are," I said. "And would you believe I've already forgotten if you're a psychologist or a psychiatrist?"

That made for a good laugh. With a casual wave of his hand, he said, "Makes no difference. What would you like to talk about?"

"What should I talk about?"

A shrug, one of many I would eventually see. "Whatever's on your mind."

"Really?" I said, not bothering to hide the challenge in my voice. "Try this one on then, doc. I'm wondering what I'm doing here. And another thing I'm wondering about is paperwork. Are you going to be making a report down south on how I do? You working under some deadline, some pressure?"

His hands were on his belly and he smiled. "Nope."

"Not at all?"

"Not at all," he said. "If you want to come in here and talk baseball for fifty minutes, that's fine with me."

I looked at him and those eyes. Maybe it's my change of view since retirement, but there was something trustworthy about him. I said, "You know what's really on my mind?"

"No, but I'd like to know."

"My new house," I said. "It's great. It's on a big lake and there aren't any close neighbors, and I can sit on the dock at night and see stars I haven't seen in a long time. But I've been having problems sleeping."

"Why's that?" he asked, and I was glad he wasn't one of those stereotypical head docs, the ones who take a lot of notes.

"Weapons."

"Weapons?"

I nodded. "Yeah, I miss my weapons." A deep breath. "Look, you've seen my files, you know the places Uncle Sam has sent me and the jobs I've done. All those years, I had pistols or rifles or heavy weapons, always at my side, under my bed or in a closet. But when I moved into that house, well, I don't have them anymore."

"How does that make you feel?" Even though the question was friendly, I knew it was a real doc question and not a from-the-next-bar-stool type of question.

I rubbed my hands. "I really feel like I'm changing my ways. But damn it. . . . "

"Yes?"

I smiled. "I sure could use a good night's sleep."

As I drove back home, I thought, Hell, it's only a little white lie.

The fact is, I did have my weapons.

They were locked up in the basement, in strongboxes with heavy combination locks. I couldn't get to them quickly, but I certainly hadn't tossed them away.

I hadn't been lying when I told Ron I couldn't sleep. That part was entirely true.

I thought, as I drove up the dirt road to my house, scaring a possum that scuttled along the side of the gravel, that the real problem with living in my new home was so slight that I was embarrassed to bring it up to Ron.

It was the noise.

I was living in a rural paradise, with clean air, clean water, and views of the woods and lake and mountains that almost broke my heart each time I climbed out of bed, stiff with old dreams and old scars. The long days were filled with work and activities I'd never had time for. Cutting old brush and trimming dead branches. Planting annuals. Clearing my tiny beach of leaves and other debris. Filling bird feeders. And during the long evenings on the front porch or on the dock, I tackled thick history books.

But one night after dinner — I surprised myself at how much I enjoyed cooking — I was out on the dock, sitting in a fifties-era web lawn chair, a glass of red wine in my hand and a history of the Apollo space program in my lap. Along the shoreline of Lake Marie, I could see the lights of the cottages and other homes. Every night there were fewer and fewer lights, as more of the summer people boarded up their places and headed back to suburbia.

I was enjoying my wine and the book and the slight breeze, but there was also a distraction: three high-powered speedboats, racing around on the lake and tossing up great spray and noise. They were dragging people along in inner tubes, and it was hard to concentrate on my book. After a while the engines slowed and I was hoping the boats would head back to their docks, but they drifted together and ropes were exchanged, and soon they became a large raft. A couple of grills were set up and there were more hoots and yells, and then a sound system kicked in, with rock music and a heavy bass that echoed among the hills.

It was then too dark to read and I'd lost interest in the wine. I was sitting there, arms folded tight against my chest, trying hard to breathe. The noise got louder and I gave up and retreated into the house, where the heavy *thump-thump* of the bass followed me in. If I'd had a boat I could have gone out and asked them politely to turn it down, but that would have meant talking with people and putting myself in the way, and I didn't want to do that.

Instead, I went upstairs to my bedroom and shut the door and windows. Still, that *thump-thump* shook the beams of the house. I lay down with a pillow wrapped about my head and tried not to think of what was in the basement.

Later that night I got up for a drink of water, and there was still noise and music. I walked out onto the porch and could see movement on the lake and hear laughter. On a tree near the dock was a spotlight that the previous owners had installed and which I had rarely used. I flipped on the switch. Some shouts and shrieks. Two powerboats, tied together, had drifted close to my shore. The light caught a young muscular man with a fierce black mustache standing on the stern of his powerboat and urinating into the lake. His half a dozen companions, male and female, yelled and cursed in my direction. The boats started up and two men and a young woman stumbled to the side of one and dropped their bathing suits, exposing their buttocks. A couple others gave me a one-fingered salute, and there was a shower of bottles and cans tossed over the side as they sped away.

I spent the next hour on the porch, staring into the darkness.

The next day I made two phone calls, to the town hall and the police department of Nansen. I made gentle and polite inquiries and got the same answers from each office. There was no local or state law about boats coming to within a certain distance of shore. There was no law forbidding boats from mooring together. Nansen being such a small town, there was also no noise ordinance.

Home sweet home.

On my next visit Ron was wearing a bow tie, and we discussed necktie fashions before we got into the business at hand. He said, "Still having sleeping problems?"

I smiled. "No, not at all."

"Really?"

"It's fall," I said. "The tourists have gone home, most of the cottages along the lake have been boarded up and nobody takes out boats anymore. It's so quiet at night I can hear the house creak and settle."

"That's good, that's really good," Ron said, and I changed the subject. A half-hour later, I was heading back to Nansen, thinking about my latest white lie. Well, it wasn't really a lie. More of an oversight.

I hadn't told Ron about the hang-up phone calls. Or how trash had twice been dumped in my driveway. Or how a week ago, when I was shopping, I had come back to find a bullet hole through one of my windows. Maybe it had been a hunting accident. Hunting season hadn't started, but I knew that for some of the workingmen in this town, it didn't matter when the state allowed them to do their shooting.

I had cleaned up the driveway, shrugged off the phone calls, and cut away brush and saplings around the house, to eliminate any hiding spots for . . . hunters.

Still, I could sit out on the dock, a blanket around my legs and a mug of tea in my hand, watching the sun set in the distance, the reddish pink highlighting the strong yellows, oranges, and reds of the fall foliage. The water was a slate gray, and though I missed the loons, the smell of the leaves and the tang of woodsmoke from my chimney seemed to settle in just fine.

As it grew colder, I began to go into town for breakfast every few days. The center of Nansen could be featured in a documentary on New Hampshire small towns. Around the green common with its Civil War statue are a bank, a real estate office, a hardware store, two gas stations, a general store, and a small strip of service places with everything from a plumber to video rentals and Gretchen's Kitchen. At Gretchen's I read the paper while letting the mornings drift by. I listened to the old-timers at the counter pontificate on the ills of the state, nation, and world, and watched harried workers fly in to grab a quick meal. Eventually, a waitress named Sandy took some interest in me.

She was about twenty years younger than I, with raven hair, a wide smile, and a pleasing body that filled out her regulation pink uniform. After a couple weeks of flirting and generous tips on my part, I asked her out, and when she said yes, I went to my pickup truck and burst out laughing. A real date. I couldn't remember the last time I had had a real date.

The first date was dinner a couple of towns over, in Montcalm, the second was dinner and a movie outside Manchester, and the third was dinner at my house, which was supposed to end with a rented movie in the living room but instead ended up in the bedroom. Along the way I learned that Sandy had always lived in Nansen, was divorced with two young boys, and was saving her money so she could go back to school and become a legal aide. "If you think I'm going to keep slinging hash and waiting for Billy to send his support check, then you're a damn fool," she said on our first date.

After a bedroom interlude that surprised me with its intensity, we sat on the enclosed porch. I opened a window for Sandy, who needed a smoke. The house was warm and I had on a pair of shorts; she had wrapped a towel around her torso. I sprawled in an easy chair while she sat on the couch, feet in my lap. Both of us had glasses of wine and I felt comfortable and tingling. Sandy glanced at me as she worked on her cigarette. I'd left the lights off and lit a couple of candles, and in the hazy yellow light, I could see the small tattoo of a unicorn on her right shoulder.

Sandy looked at me and asked, "What were you doing when you was in the government?"

"Traveled a lot and ate bad food."

"No, really," she said. "I want a straight answer."

Well, I thought, as straight as I can be. I said, "I was a consultant, to foreign armies. Sometimes they needed help with certain weapons or training techniques. That was my job."

"Were you good?"

Too good, I thought. "I did all right."

"You've got a few scars there."

"That I do."

She shrugged, took a lazy puff off her cigarette. "I've seen worse."

I wasn't sure where this was headed. Then she said, "When are you going to be leaving?"

Confused, I asked her, "You mean, tonight?"

"No," she said. "I mean, when are you leaving Nansen and going back home?"

I looked around the porch and said, "This is my home."

She gave me a slight smile, like a teacher correcting a fumbling but eager student. "No, it's not. This place was built by the Gerrish family. It's the Gerrish place. You're from away, and this ain't your home."

I tried to smile, though my mood was slipping. "Well, I beg to disagree."

She said nothing for a moment, just studied the trail of smoke from her cigarette. Then she said, "Some people in town don't like you. They think you're uppity, a guy that don't belong here."

I began to find it quite cool on the porch. "What kind of people?"

"The Garr brothers. Jerry Tompkins. Kit Broderick. A few others. Guys in town. They don't particularly like you."

"I don't particularly care," I shot back.

A small shrug as she stubbed out her cigarette. "You will."

The night crumbled some more after that, and the next morning, while sitting in the corner at Gretchen's, I was ignored by Sandy. One of the older waitresses served me, and my coffee arrived in a cup stained with lipstick, the bacon was charred black, and the eggs were cold. I got the message. I started making breakfast at home, sitting alone on the porch, watching the leaves fall and days grow shorter.

I wondered if Sandy was on her own or if she had been scouting out enemy territory on someone's behalf.

At my December visit, I surprised myself by telling Ron about something that had been bothering me.

"It's the snow," I said, leaning forward, hands clasped between my legs. "It's going to start snowing soon. And I've always hated the snow, especially since . . . "

"Since when?"

"Since something I did once," I said. "In Serbia."

"Go on," he said, fingers making a tent in front of his face.

"I'm not sure I can."

Ron tilted his head quizzically. "You know I have the clearances."

I cleared my throat, my eyes burning a bit. "I know. It's just that it's . . . Ever see blood on snow, at night?"

I had his attention. "No," he said, "no, I haven't."

"It steams at first, since it's so warm," I said. "And then it gets real dark, almost black. Dark snow, if you can believe it. It's something that stays with you, always."

He looked steadily at me for a moment, then said, "Do you want to talk about it some more?"

"No."

I spent all of one gray afternoon in my office cubbyhole, trying to get a new computer up and running. When at last I went downstairs for a quick drink, I looked outside and there they were, big snowflakes lazily drifting to the ground. Forgetting about the drink, I went out to the porch and looked at the pure whiteness of everything, of the snow covering the bare limbs, the shrubbery, and the frozen lake. I stood there and hugged myself, admiring the softly accumulating blanket of white and feeling lucky.

Two days after the snowstorm I was out on the frozen waters of Lake Marie, breathing hard and sweating and enjoying every second of it. The day before I had driven into Manchester to a sporting goods store and had come out with a pair of cross-country skis. The air was crisp and still, and the sky was a blue so deep I half-expected to see brush-strokes. From the lake, I looked back at my home and liked what I saw. The white paint and plain construction made me smile for no particular reason. I heard not a single sound, except for the faint drone of a distant airplane. Before me someone had placed signs and orange ropes in the snow, covering an oval area at the center of the lake. Each sign said the same thing: DANGER! THIN ICE! I remembered the old-timers at Gretchen's Kitchen telling a story about a hidden spring coming up through the lake bottom, or some damn thing, that made ice at the center of the lake thin, even in the coldest weather. I got cold and it was time to go home.

About halfway back to the house is where it happened.

At first it was a quiet sound, and I thought that it was another airplane. Then the noise got louder and louder, and separated, becoming distinct. Snowmobiles, several of them. I turned and they came speeding out of the woods, tossing up great rooster tails of snow and ice. They were headed straight for me. I turned away and kept up a steady pace, trying to ignore the growing loudness of the approaching engines. An itchy feeling crawled up my spine to the base of my head, and the noise exploded in pitch as they raced by me.

Even over the loudness of the engines I could make out the yells as the snowmobiles roared by, hurling snow in my direction. There were two people to each machine and they didn't look human. Each was dressed in a bulky jump suit, heavy boots, and a padded helmet. They raced by and, sure enough, circled around and came back at me. This time I flinched. This time, too, a couple of empty beer cans were thrown my way.

By the third pass, I was getting closer to my house. I thought it was almost over when one of the snowmobiles broke free from the pack and raced across about fifty feet in front of me. The driver turned so that the machine was blocking me and sat there, racing the throttle. Then he pulled off his helmet, showing an angry face and thick mustache, and I recognized him as the man on the powerboat a few months earlier. He handed his helmet to his passenger, stepped off the snowmobile, and unzipped his jump suit. It took only a moment as he marked the snow in a long, steaming stream, and there was laughter from the others as he got back on the machine and sped away. I skied over the soiled snow and took my time climbing up the snow-covered shore. I entered my home, carrying my skis and poles like weapons over my shoulder.

That night, and every night afterward, they came back, breaking the winter stillness with the throbbing sounds of engines, laughter, drunken shouts, and music from portable stereos. Each morning I cleared away their debris and scuffed fresh snow over the stains. In the quiet of my house, I found myself constantly on edge, listening, waiting for the noise to suddenly return and break up the day. Phone calls to the police department and town hall confirmed what I already knew: Except for maybe littering, no ordinances or laws were being broken.

On one particularly loud night, I broke a promise to myself and went to the tiny, damp cellar to unlock the green metal case holding a pistol-shaped device. I went back upstairs to the enclosed porch, and with the lights off, I switched on the night-vision scope and looked at the scene below me. Six snowmobiles were parked in a circle on the snow-covered ice, and in the center, a fire had been made. Figures stumbled around in the snow, talking and laughing. Stereos had been set up on the seats of two of the snowmobiles, and the loud music with its bass *thump-thump-thump* echoed across the flat ice. Lake Marie is one of the largest bodies of water in this part of the country, but the camp was set up right below my windows.

I watched for a while as they partied. Two of the black-suited figures started wrestling in the snow. More shouts and laughter, and then the fight broke up and someone turned the stereos even louder. *Thump-thump-thump.*

I switched off the nightscope, returned it to its case in the cellar, and went to bed. Even with foam rubber plugs in my ears, the bass noise reverberated inside my skull. I put the pillow across my face and tried to ignore the sure knowledge that this would continue all winter, the noise and the littering and the aggravation, and when the spring came, they would turn in their snowmobiles for boats, and they'd be back, all summer long.

Thump-thump-thump.

At the next session with Ron, we talked about the weather until he pierced me with his gaze and said, "Tell me what's wrong."

I went through half a dozen rehearsals of what to tell him, and then skated to the edge of the truth and said, "I'm having a hard time adjusting, that's all."

"Adjusting to what?"

"To my home," I said, my hands clasped before me. "I never thought I would say this, but I'm really beginning to get settled, for the first time in my life. You ever been in the military, Ron?"

"No, but I know —"

I held up my hand. "Yes, I know what you're going to say. You've worked as a consultant, but you've never been one of us, Ron. Never. You can't know what it's like, constantly being ordered to uproot yourself and go halfway across the world to a new place with a different language, customs, and weather, all within a week. You never settle in, never really get into a place you call home."

He swiveled a bit in his black leather chair. "But that's different now?"

"It sure is," I said.

There was a pause as we looked at each other, and Ron said, "But something is going on."

"Something is."

"Tell me."

And then I knew I wouldn't. A fire wall had already been set up between Ron and the details of what was going on back at my home. If I let him know what was really happening, I knew that he would make a report, and within the week I'd be ordered to go somewhere else. If I'd been younger and not so dependent on a monthly check, I would have put up a fight.

But now, no more fighting. I looked past Ron and said, "An adjustment problem, I guess."

"Adjusting to civilian life?"

"More than that," I said. "Adjusting to Nansen. It's a great little town, but . . . I feel like an outsider."

"That's to be expected."

"Sure, but I still don't like it. I know it will take some time, but . . . well, I get the odd looks, the quiet little comments, the cold shoulders."

Ron seemed to choose his words carefully. "Is that proving to be a serious problem?"

Not even a moment of hesitation as I lied: "No, not at all."

"And what do you plan on doing?"

An innocent shrug. "Not much. Just try to fit in, try to be a good neighbor."

"That's all?"

I nodded firmly. "That's all."

It took a bit of research, but eventually I managed to put a name to the face of the mustached man who had pissed on my territory. Jerry Tompkins. Floor supervisor for a computer firm outside Manchester, married with three kids, an avid boater, snowmobiler, hunter, and all-around guy. His family had been in Nansen for generations, and his dad was one of the three selectmen who ran the town. Using a couple of old skills, I tracked him down one dark afternoon and pulled my truck next to his in the snowy parking lot of a tavern on the outskirts of Nansen. The tavern was called Peter's Pub and its windows were barred and blacked out.

I stepped out of my truck and called to him as he walked to the entrance of the pub. He turned and glared at me. "What?"

"You're Jerry Tompkins, aren't you."

"Sure am," he said, hands in the pockets of his dark-green parka. "And you're the fella that's living up in the old Gerrish place."

"Yes, and I'd like to talk with you for a second."

His face was rough, like he had spent a lot of time outdoors in the wind and rain and an equal amount indoors, with cigarette smoke and loud country music. He rocked back on his heels with a little smile and said, "Go ahead. You got your second."

"Thanks," I said. "Tell you what, Jerry, I'm looking for something."

"And what's that?"

"I'm looking for a treaty."

He nodded, squinting his eyes. "What kind of treaty?"

"A peace treaty. Let's cut out the snowmobile parties on the lake by my place and the trash dumped in the driveway and the hang-up calls. Let's start fresh and just stay out of each other's way. What do you say? Then, this summer, you can all come over to my place for a cookout. I'll even supply the beer."

He rubbed at the bristles along his chin. "Seems like a one-sided deal. Not too sure what I get out of it."

"What's the point in what you're doing now?"

A furtive smile. "It suits me."

I felt like I was beginning to lose it. "You agree with the treaty, we all win."

"Still don't see what I get out of it," he said.

"That's the purpose of a peace treaty," I said. "You get peace."

"Feel pretty peaceful right now."

"That might change," I said, instantly regretting the words.

His eyes darkened. "Are you threatening me?"

A retreat, recalling my promise to myself when I'd come here. "No, not a threat, Jerry. What do you say?"

He turned and walked away, moving his head to keep me in view. "Your second got used up a long time ago, pal. And you better be out of this lot in another minute, or I'm going inside and coming out with a bunch of my friends. You won't like that."

No, I wouldn't, and it wouldn't be for the reason Jerry believed. If they did come out I'd be forced into old habits and old actions, and I'd promised myself I wouldn't do that. I couldn't.

"You got it," I said, backing away. "But remember, Jerry. Always."

"What's that?"

"The peace treaty," I said, going to the door of my pickup truck. "I offered."

Another visit to Ron, on a snowy day. The conversation meandered along, and I don't know what got into me, but I looked out the old mill windows and said, "What do people expect, anyway?"

"What do you mean?" he asked.

"You take a tough teenager from a small Ohio town, and you train him and train him and train him. You turn him into a very efficient hunter, a meat eater. Then, after twenty or thirty years, you say thank you very much and send him back to the world of quiet vegetarians, and you expect him to start eating cabbages and carrots with no fuss or muss. A hell of a thing, thinking you can expect him to put away his tools and skills."

"Maybe that's why we're here," he suggested.

"Oh, please," I said. "Do you think this makes a difference?"

"Does it make a difference to you?"

I kept looking out the window. "Too soon to tell, I'd say. Truth is, I wonder if this is meant to work, or is just meant to make some people feel less guilty. The people who did the hiring, training, and discharging."

"What do you think?"

I turned to him. "I think for the amount of money you charge Uncle Sam, you ask too many damn questions."

* * *

Another night at two A.M. I was back outside, beside the porch, again with the nightscope in my hands. They were back, and if anything, the music and the engines blared even louder. A fire burned merrily among the snowmobiles, and as the revelers pranced and hollered, I wondered if some base part of their brains was remembering thousand-year-old rituals. As I looked at their dancing and drinking figures, I kept thinking of the long case at the other end of the cellar. Nice heavy-duty assault rifle with another night-vision scope, this one with crosshairs. Scan and track. Put a crosshair across each one's chest. Feel the weight of a fully loaded clip in your hand. Know that with a silencer on the end of the rifle, you could quietly take out that crew in a fistful of seconds. Get your mind back into the realm of possibilities, of cartridges and windage and grains and velocities. How long could it take between the time you said go and the time you could say mission accomplished? Not long at all.

"No," I whispered, switching off the scope.

I stayed on the porch for another hour, and as my eyes adjusted, I saw more movements. I picked up the scope. A couple of snow machines moved in, each with shapes on the seats behind the drivers. They pulled up to the snowy bank and the people moved quickly, intent on their work. Trash bags were tossed on my land, about eight or nine, and to add a bit more fun, each bag had been slit several times with a knife so it could burst open and spew its contents when it hit the ground. A few more hoots and hollers and the snowmobiles growled away, leaving trash and the flickering fire behind. I watched the lights as the snowmobiles roared across the lake and finally disappeared, though their sound did not.

The nightscope went back onto my lap. The rifle, I thought, could have stopped the fun right there with a couple of rounds through the engines. Highly illegal, but it would get their attention, right?

Right.

In my next session with Ron, I got to the point. "What kind of reports are you sending south?"

I think I might have surprised him. "Reports?"

"How I'm adjusting, that sort of thing."

He paused for a moment, and I knew there must be a lot of figuring going on behind those smiling eyes. "Just the usual things, that's all. That you're doing fine."

"Am I?"

"Seems so to me."

"Good." I waited for a moment, letting the words twist about on my tongue. "Then you can send them this message. I haven't been a hundred percent with you during these sessions, Ron. Guess it's not in my nature to be so open. But you can count on this. I won't lose it. I won't go into a gun shop and then take down a bunch of civilians. I'm not going to start hanging around 1600 Pennsylvania Avenue. I'm going to be all right."

He smiled. "I have never had any doubt."

"Sure you've had doubts," I said, smiling back. "But it's awfully polite of you to say otherwise."

On a bright Saturday, I tracked down the police chief of Nansen at one of the two service stations in town, Glen's Gas & Repair. His cruiser, ordinarily a dark blue, was now a ghostly shade of white from the salt used to keep the roads clear. I parked at the side of the garage, and walking by the service bays, I could sense that I was being watched. I saw three cars with their hoods up, and I also saw a familiar uniform: black snowmobile jump suits.

The chief was overweight and wearing a heavy blue jacket with a black Navy watch cap. His face was open and friendly, and he nodded in all the right places as I told him my story.

"Not much I can do, I'm afraid," he said, leaning against the door of his cruiser, one of two in the entire town. "I'd have to catch 'em in the act of trashing your place, and that means surveillance, and that means overtime hours, which I don't have."

"Surveillance would be a waste of time anyway," I replied. "These guys, they aren't thugs, right? For lack of a better phrase, they're good old boys, and they know everything that's going on in Nansen, and they'd know if you were setting up surveillance. And then they wouldn't show."

"You might think you're insulting me, but you're not," he said gently. "That's just the way things are done here. It's a good town and most of us get along, and I'm not kept that busy, not at all."

"I appreciate that, but you should also appreciate my problem," I said. "I live here and pay taxes, and people are harassing me. I'm looking for some assistance, that's all, and a suggestion of what I can do."

"You could move," the chief said, raising his coffee cup.

"Hell of a suggestion."

"Best one I can come up with. Look, friend, you're new here, you've got no family, no ties. You're asking me to take on some prominent families just because you don't get along with them. So why don't you move on? Find someplace smaller, hell, even someplace bigger, where you don't stand out so much. But face it, it's not going to get any easier."

"Real nice folks," I said, letting an edge of bitterness into my voice.

That didn't seem to bother the chief. "That they are. They work hard and play hard, and they pay taxes, too, and they look out for one another. I know they look like hell-raisers to you, but they're more than that. They're part of the community. Why, just next week, a bunch of them are going on a midnight snow run across the lake and into the mountains, raising money for the children's camp up at Lake Montcalm. People who don't care wouldn't do that."

"I just wish they didn't care so much about me."

He shrugged and said, "Look, I'll see what I can do. . . . " but the tone of his voice made it clear he wasn't going to do a damn thing.

The chief clambered into his cruiser and drove off, and as I walked past the bays of the service station, I heard snickers. I went around to my pickup truck and saw the source of the merriment.

My truck was resting heavily on four flat tires.

At night I woke up from cold and bloody dreams and let my thoughts drift into fantasies. By now I knew who all of them were, where all of them lived. I could go to their houses, every one of them, and bring them back and bind them in the basement of my home. I could tell them who I was and what I've done and what I can do, and I would ask them to leave me alone. That's it. Just give me peace and solitude and everything will be all right.

And they would hear me out and nod and agree, but I would know that I had to convince them. So I would go to Jerry Tompkins, the mustached one who enjoyed marking my territory, and to make my point, break a couple of his fingers, the popping noise echoing in the dark confines of the tiny basement.

Nice fantasies.

I asked Ron, "What's the point?"

He was comfortable in his chair, hands clasped over his little potbelly. "I'm sorry?"

"The point of our sessions?"

His eyes were unflinching. "To help you adjust."

"Adjust to what?"

"To civilian life."

I shifted on the couch. "Let me get this. I work my entire life for this country, doing service for its civilians. I expose myself to death and injury every week, earning about a third of what I could be making in the private sector. And when I'm through, I have to adjust, I have to make allowances for civilians. But civilians, they don't have to do a damn thing. Is that right?"

"I'm afraid so."

"Hell of a deal."

He continued a steady gaze. "Only one you've got."

So here I am, in the smelly rubble that used to be my home. I make a few half-hearted attempts to turn the furniture back over and do some cleanup work, but I'm not in the mood. Old feelings and emotions are coursing through me, taking control. I take a few deep breaths and then I'm in the cellar, switching on the single lightbulb that hangs down from the rafters by a frayed black cord. As I maneuver among the packing cases, undoing combination locks, my shoulder strikes the lightbulb, causing it to swing back and forth, casting crazy shadows on the stone walls.

The night air is cool and crisp, and I shuffle through the snow around the house as I load the pickup truck, making three trips in all. I drive under the speed limit and halt completely at all stop signs as I go through the center of town. I drive around, wasting minutes and hours, listening to the radio. This late at night and being so far north, a lot of the stations that I can pick up are from Quebec, and there's a joyous lilt to the French-Canadian music and words that makes something inside me ache with longing.

When it's almost a new day, I drive down a street called Mast Road. Most towns around here have a Mast Road, where colonial surveyors marked tall pines that would eventually become masts for the Royal Navy. Tonight there are no surveyors, just the night air and darkness and a skinny rabbit racing across the cracked asphalt. When I'm near the target, I switch off the lights and engine and let the truck glide the last few hundred feet or so. I pull up across from a darkened house. A pickup truck and a Subaru station wagon are in the driveway. Gray smoke is wafting up from the chimney.

I roll down the window, the cold air washing over me like a wave of water. I pause, remembering what has gone on these past weeks, and then I get to work.

The nightscope comes up and clicks into action, and the name on the mailbox is clear enough in the sharp green light. TOMPKINS, in silver and black stick-on letters. I scan the two-story Cape Cod, checking out the surroundings. There's an attached garage to the right and a sunroom to the left. There is a front door and two other doors in a breezeway that runs from the garage to the house. There are no rear doors.

I let the nightscope rest on my lap as I reach toward my weapons. The first is a grenade launcher, with a handful of white phosphorus rounds clustered on the seat next to it like a gathering of metal eggs. Next to the grenade launcher is a 9mm Uzi, with an extended wooden stock for easier use. Another night-vision scope with crosshairs is attached to the Uzi.

Another series of deep breaths. Easy enough plan. Pop a white phosphorus round into the breezeway and another into the sunroom. In a minute or two both ends of the house are on fire. Our snowmobiler friend and his family wake up and, groggy from sleep and the fire and the noise, stumble out the front door onto the snow-covered lawn.

With the Uzi in my hand and the crosshairs on a certain face, a face with a mustache, I take care of business and drive to the next house.

I pick up the grenade launcher and rest the barrel on the open window. It's cold. I rub my legs together and look outside at the stars. The wind comes up and snow blows across the road. I hear the low *hoo-hoo-hoo* of an owl.

I bring the grenade launcher up, resting the stock against my cheek. I aim. I wait.

It's very cold.

The weapon begins trembling in my hands and I let it drop to the front seat.

I sit on my hands, trying to warm them while the cold breeze blows. Idiot. Do this and how long before you're in jail, and then on trial before a jury of friends or relatives of those fine citizens you gun down tonight?

I start up the truck and let the heater sigh itself on, and then I roll up the window and slowly drive away, lights still off.

"Fool," I say to myself, "remember who you are." And with the truck's lights now on, I drive home. To what's left of it.

Days later, there's a fresh smell to the air in my house, for I've done a lot of cleaning and painting, trying not only to bring everything back to where it was but also to spruce up the place. The only real problem has been in the main room, where the words GO HOME were marked in bright red on the white plaster wall. It took me three coats to cover that up, and of course I ended up doing the entire room.

The house is dark and it's late. I'm waiting on the porch with a glass of wine in my hand, watching a light snow fall on Lake Marie. Every light in the house is off and the only illumination comes from the fireplace, which needs more wood.

But I'm content to dawdle. I'm finally at peace after these difficult weeks in Nansen. Finally, I'm beginning to remember who I really am.

I sip my wine, waiting, and then comes the sound of the snowmobiles. I see their wavering dots of light racing across the lake, doing their bit for charity. How wonderful. I raise my glass in salute, the noise of the snowmobiles getting louder as they head across the lake in a straight line.

I put the wineglass down, walk into the living room, and toss the last few pieces of wood onto the fire. The sudden heat warms my face in a pleasant glow. The wood isn't firewood, though. It's been shaped and painted by man, and as the flames leap up and devour the lumber, I see the letters begin to fade: DANGER! THIN ICE!

I stroll back to the porch, pick up the wineglass, and wait.

Below me, on the peaceful ice of Lake Marie, my new home for my new life, the headlights go by.

And then, one by one, they blink out, and the silence is wonderful.

1996

MICHAEL MALONE

....

Red Clay

UP ON ITS SHORT SLOPE the columned front of our courthouse was wavy in the August sun, like a courthouse in lake water. The leaves hung from maples, and the flag of North Carolina wilted flat against its metal pole. Heat sat sodden over Devereux County week by relentless week; they called the weather "dog days," after the star, Sirius, but none of us knew that. We thought they meant no dog would leave shade for street on such days — no dog except a mad one. I was ten that late August in 1959; I remembered the summer because of the long heat wave, and because of Stella Doyle.

When they pushed open the doors, the policemen and lawyers flung their arms up to their faces to block the sun and stopped there in the doorway as if the hot light were shoving them back inside. Stella Doyle came out last, a deputy on either side to walk her down to where the patrol car, orange as Halloween candles, waited to take her away until the jury could make up its mind about what had happened two months earlier out at Red Hills. It was the only house in the county big enough to have a name. It was where Stella Doyle had, maybe, shot her husband, Hugh Doyle, to death.

Excitement over Doyle's murder had swarmed through the town and stung us alive. No thrill would replace it until the assassination of John F. Kennedy. Outside the courthouse, sidewalk heat steaming up through our shoes, we stood patiently waiting to hear Mrs. Doyle found guilty. The news stood waiting, too, for she was, after all, not merely the murderer of the wealthiest man we knew; she was Stella Doyle. She was the movie star.

Papa's hand squeezed down on my shoulder and there was a tight line to his mouth as he pulled me into the crowd and said, "Listen now,

Buddy, if anybody ever asks you, when you're grown, 'Did you ever see the most beautiful woman God made in your lifetime,' son, you say 'Yes, I had that luck, and her name was Stella Dora Doyle.'" His voice got louder, right there in the crowd for everybody to hear. "You tell them how her beauty was so bright, it burned back the shame they tried to heap on her head, burned it right on back to scorch their faces."

Papa spoke these strange words looking up the steps at the almost plump woman in black the deputies were holding. His arms were folded over his seersucker vest, his fingers tight on the sleeves of his shirt. People around us had turned to stare and somebody snickered.

Embarrassed for him, I whispered, "Oh, Papa, she's nothing but an old murderer. Everybody knows how she got drunk and killed Mr. Doyle. She shot him right through the head with a gun."

Papa frowned. "You don't know that."

I kept on. "Everybody says she was so bad and drunk all the time, she wouldn't let his folks even live in the same house with her. She made him throw out his own mama and papa."

Papa shook his head at me. "I don't like to hear ugly gossip coming out of your mouth, all right, Buddy?"

"Yes, sir."

"She didn't kill Hugh Doyle."

"Yes, sir."

His frown scared me; it was so rare. I stepped closer and took his hand, took his stand against the rest. I had no loyalty to this woman Papa thought so beautiful. I just could never bear to be cut loose from the safety of his good opinion. I suppose that from that moment on, I felt toward Stella Doyle something of what my father felt, though in the end perhaps she meant less to me, and stood for more. Papa never had my habit of symbolizing.

The courthouse steps were wide, uneven stone slabs. As Mrs. Doyle came down, the buzzing of the crowd hushed. All together, like trained dancers, people stepped back to clear a half-circle around the orange patrol car. Newsmen shoved their cameras to the front. She was rushed down so fast that her shoe caught in the crumbling stone and she fell against one of the deputies.

"She's drunk!" hooted a woman near me, a country woman in a flowered dress belted with a strip of painted rope. She and the child she jiggled against her shoulder were puffy with the fat of poverty. "Look'it her" — the woman pointed — "look at that dress. She thinks she's still out there in Hollywood." The woman beside her nodded, squinting out from under the visor of the kind of hat pier fishermen wear. "I went and killed my husband, wouldn't no rich lawyers come running to weasel me out of the law." She slapped at a fly's buzz.

Then they were quiet and everybody else was quiet and our circle of sun-stunned eyes fixed on the woman in black, stared at the wonder of one as high as Mrs. Doyle about to be brought so low.

Holding to the stiff, tan arm of the young deputy, Mrs. Doyle reached down to check the heel of her shoe. Black shoes, black suit and purse, wide black hat — they all sinned against us by their fashionableness, blazing wealth as well as death. She stood there, arrested a moment in the hot immobility of the air, then she hurried down, rushing the two big deputies down with her, to the open door of the orange patrol car. Papa stepped forward so quickly that the gap filled with people before I could follow him. I squeezed through, fighting with my elbows, and I saw that he was holding his straw hat in one hand, and offering the other hand out to the murderer. "Stella, how are you? Clayton Hayes."

As she turned, I saw the strawberry gold hair beneath the hat; then her hand, bright with a big diamond, took away the dark glasses. I saw what Papa meant. She was beautiful. Her eyes were the color of lilacs, but darker than lilacs. And her skin held the light like the inside of a shell. She was not like other pretty women, because the difference was not one of degree. I have never seen anyone else of her kind.

"Why, Clayton! God Almighty, it's been years."

"Well, yes, a long time now, I guess," he said, and shook her hand.

She shook the hand in both of hers. "You look the same as ever. Is this your boy?" she said. The violet eyes turned to me.

"Yes, this is Buddy. Ada and I have six so far, three of each."

"Six? Are we that old, Clayton?" She smiled. "They said you'd married Ada Hackney."

A deputy cleared his throat. "Sorry, Clayton, we're going to have to get going."

"Just a minute, Lonnie. Listen, Stella, I just wanted you to know I'm sorry as I can be about your losing Hugh."

Tears welled in her eyes. "He did it himself, Clayton," she said.

"I know that. I know you didn't do this." Papa nodded slowly again and again, the way he did when he was listening. "I know that. Good luck to you."

She swatted tears away. "Thank you."

"I'm telling everybody I'm sure of that."

"Clayton, thank you."

Papa nodded again, then tilted his head back to give her his slow, peaceful smile. "You call Ada and me if there's ever something we can do to help you, you hear?" She kissed his cheek and he stepped back with me into the crowd of hostile, avid faces as she entered the police car. It moved slow as the sun through the sightseers. Cameras pushed against its windows.

A sallow man biting a pipe skipped down the steps to join some other reporters next to us. "Jury sent out for food," he told them. "No telling with these yokels. Could go either way." He pulled off his jacket and balled it under his arm. "Jesus, it's hot."

A younger reporter with thin, wet hair disagreed. "They all think Hollywood's Babylon and she's the whore. Hugh Doyle was the local prince, his daddy kept the mills open in the bad times, quote unquote half the rednecks in the county. They'll fry her. For that hat if nothing else."

"Could go either way," grinned the man with the pipe. "She was born in a shack six miles from here. Hat or no hat, that makes her one of them. So what if she did shoot the guy, he was dying of cancer anyhow, for Christ's sake. Well, she never could act worth the price of a bag of popcorn, but Jesus damn she was something to look at!"

Now that Stella Doyle was gone, people felt the heat again and went back to where they could sit still in the shade until the evening breeze and wait for the jury's decision. Papa and I walked back down Main Street to our furniture store. Papa owned a butcher shop, too, but he didn't like the meat business and wasn't very good at it, so my oldest brother ran it while Papa sat among the mahogany bedroom suites and red maple dining-room sets in a big rocking chair and read, or talked to friends who dropped by. The rocker was actually for sale but he had sat in it for so long now that it was just Papa's chair. Three ceiling fans stirred against the quiet, shady air while he answered my questions about Stella Doyle.

He said that she grew up Stella Dora Hibble on Route 19, in a three-room, tin-roofed little house propped off the red clay by concrete blocks — the kind of saggy-porched, pinewood house whose owners leave on display in their dirt yard, like sculptures, the broken artifacts of their aspirations and the debris of their unmendable lives: the doorless refrigerator and the rusting car, the pyre of metal and plastic that tells drivers along the highway "Dreams don't last."

Stella's mother, Dora Hibble, had believed in dreams anyhow. Dora had been a pretty girl who'd married a farmer and worked harder than she had the health for, because hard work was necessary just to keep from going under. But in the evenings Mrs. Hibble had looked at movie magazines. She had believed the romance was out there and she wanted it, if not for her, for her children. At twenty-seven, Dora Hibble died during her fifth labor. Stella was eight when she watched from the door of the bedroom as they covered her mother's face with a thin blanket. When Stella was fourteen, her father died when a machine jammed at Doyle Mills. When Stella was sixteen, Hugh Doyle, Jr., who was her age, my father's age, fell in love with her.

"Did you love her, too, Papa?"

"Oh, yes. All us boys in town were crazy about Stella Dora, one time or another. I had my attack of it, same as the rest. We were sweethearts in seventh grade. I bought a big-size Whitman's Sampler on Valentine's. I remember it cost every cent I had."

"Why were y'all crazy about her?"

"I guess you'd have to worry you'd missed out on being alive if you didn't feel that way about Stella, one time or another."

I was feeling a terrible emotion I later defined as jealousy. "But didn't you love Mama?"

"Well, now, this was before it was my luck to meet your mama."

"And you met her coming to town along the railroad track and you told your friends 'That's the girl for me and I'm going to marry her,' didn't you?"

"Yes, sir, and I was right on both counts." Papa rocked back in the big chair, his hands peaceful on the armrests.

"Was Stella Dora still crazy about you after you met Mama?"

His face crinkled into the lines of his ready laughter. "No, sir, she wasn't. She loved Hugh Doyle, minute she laid eyes on him, and he felt the same. But Stella had this notion about going off to get to be somebody in the movies. And Hugh couldn't hold her back, and I guess she couldn't get him to see what it was made her want to go off so bad either."

"What was it made her want to go?"

Papa smiled at me. "Well, I don't know, son. What makes you want to go off so bad? You're always saying you're going here, and there, 'cross the world, up to the moon. I reckon you're more like Stella than I am."

"Do you think she was wrong to want to go be in the movies?"

"No."

"You don't think she killed him?"

"No, sir, I don't."

"Somebody killed him."

"Well, Buddy, sometimes people lose hope and heart, and feel like they can't go on living."

"Yeah, I know. Suicide."

Papa's shoes tapped the floor as the rocker creaked back and forth. "That's right. Now you tell me, why're you sitting in here? Why don't you ride your bike on over to the ballpark and see who's there?"

"I want to hear about Stella Doyle."

"You want to hear. Well. Let's go get us a Coca-Cola, then. I don't guess somebody's planning to show up in this heat to buy a chest of drawers they got to haul home."

"You ought to sell air conditioners, Papa. People would buy air conditioners."

"I guess so."

So Papa told me the story. Or at least his version of it. He said Hugh and Stella were meant for each other. From the beginning it seemed to the whole town a fact as natural as harvest that so much money and so much beauty belonged together, and only Hugh Doyle with his long, free, easy stride was rich enough to match the looks of Stella Dora. But even Hugh Doyle couldn't hold her. He was only halfway through the state university, where his father had told him he'd have to go before he married Stella, if he wanted a home to bring her to, when she quit her job at Coldsteam's beauty parlor and took the bus to California. She was out there for six years before Hugh broke down and went after her.

By then every girl in the county was cutting Stella's pictures out of the movie magazines and reading how she got her lucky break, how she married a big director, and divorced him, and married a big star, and how that marriage broke up even quicker. Photographers traveled all the way to Thermopylae to take pictures of where she was born. People tried to tell them her house was gone, had fallen down and been used for firewood, but they just took photographs of Reverend Ballister's house instead and said Stella had grown up in it. Before long, even local girls would go stand in front of the Ballister house like a shrine, sometimes they'd steal flowers out of the yard. The year that *Fever,* her best movie, came to the Grand Theater on Main Street, Hugh Doyle flew out to Los Angeles and won her back. He took her down to Mexico to divorce the baseball player she'd married after the big star. Then Hugh married her himself and put her on an ocean liner and took her all over the world. For a whole two years, they didn't come home to Thermopylae. Everybody in the county talked about this two-year honeymoon, and Hugh's father confessed to some friends that he was disgusted by his son's way of life.

But when the couple did come home, Hugh walked right into the mills and turned a profit. His father confessed to the same friends that he was flabbergasted Hugh had it in him. But after the father died Hugh started drinking and Stella joined him. The parties got a little wild. The fights got loud. People talked. They said he had other women. They said Stella'd been locked up in a sanitorium. They said the Doyles were breaking up.

And then one June day a maid at Red Hills, walking to work before the morning heat, fell over something that lay across a path to the stables. And it was Hugh Doyle in riding clothes with a hole torn in the side of his head. Not far from his gloved hand, the police found Stella's pistol, already too hot from the sun to touch. The cook testified that the Doyles had been fighting like cats and dogs all night long the night before, and Hugh's mother testified that he wanted to divorce Stella but she wouldn't let him, and so Stella was arrested. She said she was innocent, but it was her gun, she was his heir, and she had no alibi. Her trial lasted almost as long as that August heat wave.

A neighbor strolled past the porch, where we sat out the evening heat, waiting for the air to lift. "Jury's still out," he said. Mama waved her hand at him. She pushed herself and me in the big green wood swing that hung from two chains to the porch roof, and answered my questions about Stella Doyle. She said, "Oh, yes, they all said Stella was specially pretty. I never knew her to talk to myself."

"But if Papa liked her so much, why didn't y'all get invited out to their house and everything?"

"Her and your papa just went to school together, that's all. That was a long time back. The Doyles wouldn't ask folks like us over to Red Hills."

"Why not? Papa's family used to have a *whole* lot of money. That's what you said. And Papa went right up to Mrs. Doyle at the courthouse today, right in front of everybody. He told her, You let us know if there's anything we can do."

Mama chuckled the way she always did about Papa, a low ripple like a pigeon nesting, a little exasperated at having to sit still so long. "You know your papa'd offer to help out anybody he figured might be in trouble, white or black. That's just him; that's not any Stella Dora Doyle. Your papa's just a good man. You remember that, Buddy."

Goodness was Papa's stock-in-trade; it was what he had instead of
money or ambition, and Mama often reminded us of it. In him she kept
safe all the kindness she had never felt she could afford for herself. She,
who could neither read nor write, who had stood all day in a cigarette
factory from the age of nine until the morning Papa married her, was a
fighter. She wanted her children to go farther than Papa had. Still, for
years after he died, she would carry down from the attic the yellow mil-
dewed ledgers where his value was recorded in more than $75,000 of
out-of-date bills he had been unwilling to force people in trouble to
pay. Running her sun-spotted finger down the brown wisps of names
and the money they'd owed, she would sigh that proud, exasperated
ripple, and shake her head over foolish, generous Papa.

Through the front parlor window I could hear my sisters practicing
the theme from *The Apartment* on the piano. Someone across the street
turned on a light. Then we heard the sound of Papa's shoes coming a
little faster than usual down the sidewalk. He turned at the hedge carrying the package of shiny butcher's paper in which he brought meat
home every evening. "Verdict just came in!" he called out happily. "Not
guilty! Jury came back about forty minutes ago. They already took her
home."

Mama took the package and sat Papa down in the swing next to her.
"Well, well," she said. "They let her off."

"Never ought to have come up for trial in the first place, Ada, like I
told everybody all along. It's like her lawyers showed. Hugh went down
to Atlanta, saw that doctor, found out he had cancer, and he took his
own life. Stella never even knew he was sick."

Mama patted his knee. "Not guilty; well, well."

Papa made a noise of disgust. "Can you believe some folks out on
Main Street tonight are all fired up *because* Stella got off! Adele Simpson
acted downright indignant!"

Mama said, "And you're surprised?" And she shook her head with me
at Papa's innocence.

Talking of the trial, my parents made one shadow along the wood
floor of the porch, while inside my sisters played endless variations of
"Chopsticks," the notes handed down by ghostly creators long passed
away.

A few weeks later, Papa was invited to Red Hills, and he let me come
along; we brought a basket of sausage biscuits Mama had made for Mrs.
Doyle.

As soon as Papa drove past the wide white gate, I learned how money could change even weather. It was cooler at Red Hills, and the grass was the greenest grass in the county. A black man in a black suit let us into the house, then led us down a wide hallway of pale yellow wood into a big room shuttered against the heat. She was there in an armchair almost the color of her eyes. She wore loose-legged pants and was pouring whiskey from a bottle into a glass.

"Clayton, thanks for coming. Hello there, little Buddy. Look, I hope I didn't drag you from business."

Papa laughed. "Stella, I could stay gone a week and never miss a customer." It embarrassed me to hear him admit such failure to her.

She said she could tell I liked books, so maybe I wouldn't mind if they left me there to read while she borrowed my daddy for a little bit. There were white shelves in the room, full of books. I said I didn't mind but I did; I wanted to keep on seeing her. Even with the loose shirt soiled and rumpled over a waist she tried to hide, even with her face swollen from heat and drink and grief, she was something you wanted to look at as long as possible.

They left me alone. On the white piano were dozens of photographs of Stella Doyle in silver frames. From a big painting over the mantelpiece her remarkable eyes followed me around the room. I looked at that painting as sun deepened across it, until finally she and Papa came back. She had a tissue to her nose, a new drink in her hand. "I'm sorry, honey," she said to me. "Your daddy's been sweet letting me run on. I just needed somebody to talk to for a while about what happened to me." She kissed the top of my head and I could feel her warm lips at the part in my hair.

We followed her down the wide hall out onto the porch. "Clayton, you'll forgive a fat old souse talking your ear off and bawling like a jackass."

"No such thing, Stella."

"And you *never* thought I killed him, even when you first heard. My God, thank you."

Papa took her hand again. "You take care now," he said.

Then suddenly she was hugging herself, rocking from side to side. Words burst from her like a door flung open by wind. "I could kick him in the ass, that bastard! Why didn't he tell me? To quit, to *quit*, and use *my* gun, and just about get me strapped in the gas chamber, that goddamn bastard, and never say a word!" Her profanity must have shocked Papa as much as it did me. He never used it, much less ever heard it from a woman.

But he nodded and said, "Well, good-bye, I guess, Stella. Probably won't be seeing you again."

"Oh, Lord, Clayton, I'll be back. The world's so goddamn little."

She stood at the top of the porch, tears wet in those violet eyes that the movie magazines had loved to talk about. On her cheek a mosquito bite flamed like a slap. Holding to the big white column, she waved as we drove off into the dusty heat. Ice flew from the glass in her hand like diamonds.

Papa was right; they never met again. Papa lost his legs from diabetes, but he'd never gone much of anywhere even before that. And afterward, he was one of two places — home or the store. He'd sit in his big wood wheelchair in the furniture store, with his hands peaceful on the arm-rests, talking with whoever came by.

I did see Stella Doyle again; the first time in Belgium, twelve years later. I went farther than Papa.

In Bruges there are small restaurants that lean like elegant elbows on the canals and glance down at passing pleasure boats. Stella Doyle was sitting, one evening, at a table in the crook of the elbow of one of them, against an iron railing that curved its reflection in the water. She was alone there when I saw her. She stood, leaned over the rail, and slipped the ice cubes from her glass into the canal. I was in a motor launch full of tourists passing below. She waved with a smile at us and we waved back. It had been a lot of years since her last picture, but probably she waved out of habit. For the tourists motoring past, Stella in white against the dark restaurant was another snapshot of Bruges. For me, she was home and memory. I craned to look back as long as I could, and leapt from the boat at the next possible stop.

When I found the restaurant, she was yelling at a well-dressed young man who was leaning across the table, trying to soothe her in French. They appeared to be quarreling over his late arrival. All at once she hit him, her diamond flashing into his face. He filled the air with angry ges-tures, then turned and left, a white napkin to his cheek. I was made very shy by what I'd seen — the young man was scarcely older than I was. I stood unable to speak until her staring at me jarred me forward. I said, "Mrs. Doyle? I'm Buddy Hayes. I came out to see you at Red Hills with my father Clayton Hayes one time. You let me look at your books."

She sat back down and poured herself a glass of wine. "You're *that* lit-tle boy? God Almighty, how old am I? Am I a hundred yet?" Her laugh had been loosened by the wine. "Well, a Red Clay rambler, like me. How 'bout that. Sit down. What are *you* doing over here?"

I told her, as nonchalantly as I could manage, that I was traveling on college prize money, a journalism award. I wrote a prize essay about a murder trial.

"Mine?" she asked, and laughed.

A waiter, plump and flushed in his neat black suit, trotted to her side. He shook his head at the untouched plates of food. "Madame, your friend has left, then?"

Stella said, "Mister, I helped him along. And turns out, he was no friend."

The waiter then turned his eyes, sad and reproachful, to the trout on the plate.

"How about another bottle of that wine and a great big bucket of ice?" Stella asked.

The waiter kept flapping his fat quick hands around his head, entreating us to come inside. "*Les moustiques, madame!*"

"I just let them bite," she said. He went away grieved.

She was slender now, and elegantly dressed. And while her hands and throat were older, the eyes hadn't changed, nor the red-gold hair. She was still the most beautiful woman God had made in my lifetime, the woman of whom my father had said that any man who had not desired her had missed out on being alive, the one for whose honor my father had turned his back on the whole town of Thermopylae. Because of Papa, I had entered my adolescence daydreaming about fighting for Stella Doyle's honor; we had starred together in a dozen of her movies: I dazzled her jury; I cured Hugh Doyle while hiding my own noble love for his wife. And now here I sat drinking wine with her on a veranda in Bruges; me, the first Hayes ever to win a college prize, ever to get to college. Here I sat with a movie star.

She finished her cigarette, dropped it spinning down into the black canal. "You look like him," she said. "Your papa. I'm sorry to hear that about the diabetes."

"I look like him, but I don't think like him," I told her.

She tipped the wine bottle upside down in the bucket. "You want the world," she said. "Go get it, honey."

"That's what my father doesn't understand."

"He's a good man," she answered. She stood up slowly. "And I think Clayton would want me to get you to your hotel."

All the fenders of her Mercedes were crushed. She said, "When I've had a few drinks, I need a strong car between me and the rest of the cockeyed world."

The big car bounced over the moon-white street. "You know what, Buddy? Hugh Doyle gave me my first Mercedes, one morning in Paris. At breakfast. He held the keys out in his hand like a damn daffodil he'd picked in the yard. He gave me *this* goddamn thing." She waved her finger with its huge diamond. "This damn thing was tied to my big toe one Christmas morning!" And she smiled up at the stars as if Hugh Doyle were up there tying diamonds on them. "He had a beautiful grin, Buddy, but he was a son of a bitch."

The car bumped to a stop on the curb outside my little hotel. "Don't miss your train tomorrow," she said. "And you listen to me, don't go back home; go on to Rome."

"I'm not sure I have time."

She looked at me. "*Take* time. Just take it. Don't get scared, honey."

Then she put her hand in my jacket pocket and the moon came around her hair, and my heart panicked crazily, thudding against my shirt, thinking she might kiss me. But her hand went away, and all she said was, "Say hi to Clayton when you get home, all right? Even losing his legs and all, your daddy's lucky, you know that?"

I said, "I don't see how."

"Oh, I didn't either till I was a lot older than you. And had my damn in-laws trying to throw me into the gas chamber. Go to bed. So long, Red Clay."

Her silver car floated away. In my pocket, I found a large wad of French money, enough to take me to Rome, and a little ribboned box, clearly a gift she had decided not to give the angry young man in the beautiful suit who'd arrived too late. On black velvet lay a man's wristwatch, reddish gold.

It's an extremely handsome watch, and it still tells me the time.

I only went home to Thermopylae for the funerals. It was the worst of the August dog days when Papa died in the hospital bed they'd set up next to his and Mama's big four poster in their bedroom. At his grave, the clots of red clay had already dried to a dusty dull color by the time we shoveled them down upon him, friend after friend taking a turn at the shovel. The petals that fell from roses fell limp to the red earth, wilted like the crowd who stood by the grave while Reverend Ballister told us that Clayton Hayes was "a good man." Behind a cluster of

Mama's family, I saw a woman in black turn away and walk down the grassy incline to a car, a Mercedes.

After the services I went driving, but I couldn't outtravel Papa in Devereux County. The man at the gas pump listed Papa's virtues as he cleaned my windshield. The woman who sold me the bottle of bourbon said she'd owed Papa $215.00 since 1944, and when she'd paid him back in 1966 he'd forgotten all about it. I drove along the highway where the foundations of tin-roofed shacks were covered now by the parking lots of minimalls; beneath the asphalt, somewhere, was Stella Doyle's birthplace. Stella Dora Hibble, Papa's first love.

Past the white gates, the Red Hills lawn was as parched as the rest of the county. Paint blistered and peeled on the big white columns. I waited a long time before the elderly black man I'd met twenty years before opened the door irritably.

I heard her voice from the shadowy hall yelling, "Jonas! Let him in."

On the white shelves the books were the same. The photos on the piano as young as ever. She frowned so strangely when I came into the room, I thought she must have been expecting someone else and didn't recognize me.

"I'm Buddy Hayes, Clayton's —"

"I know who you are."

"I saw you leaving the cemetery. . . ."

"I know you did."

I held out the bottle.

Together we finished the bourbon in memory of Papa, while shutters beat back the sun, hid some of the dirty glasses scattered on the floor, hid Stella Doyle in her lilac armchair. Cigarette burns scarred the armrests, left their marks on the oak floor. Behind her the big portrait showed Time up for the heartless bastard he is. Her hair was cropped short, and gray. Only the color of her eyes had stayed the same; they looked as remarkable as ever in the swollen face.

"I came out here to bring you something."

"What?"

I gave her the thin, cheap, yellowed envelope I'd found in Papa's desk with his special letters and papers. It was addressed in neat, cursive pencil to "Clayton." Inside was a silly Valentine card. Betty Boop popping bonbons in her pouty lips, exclaiming "Ooooh, I'm sweet on you." It was childish and lascivious at the same time, and it was signed with a lipstick blot, now brown with age, and with the name "Stella," surrounded by a heart.

I said, "He must have kept this since the seventh grade."

She nodded. "Clayton was a good man." Her cigarette fell from her ashtray onto the floor. When I came over to pick it up, she said, "Goodness is luck; like money, like looks. Clayton was lucky that way." She went to the piano and took more ice from the bucket there; one piece she rubbed around the back of her neck, then dropped into her glass. She turned, the eyes wet, like lilac stars. "You know, in Hollywood, they said, '*Hibble?!* What kind of hick name is that, we can't use that!' So I said, 'Use Doyle, then.' I mean, I took Hugh's name six years before he ever came out to get me. Because I knew he'd come. The day I left Thermopylae he kept yelling at me, 'You can't have both!' He kept yelling it while the bus was pulling out. 'You can't have me and it both!' He wanted to rip my heart out for leaving, for *wanting* to go." Stella moved along the curve of the white piano to a photograph of Hugh Doyle in a white open shirt, grinning straight out at the sun. She said, "But I could have both. There were only two things I *had* to have in this little world, and one was the lead in a movie called *Fever,* and the other one was Hugh Doyle." She put the photograph down carefully. "I didn't know about the cancer till my lawyers found out he'd been to see that doctor in Atlanta. Then it was easy to get the jury to go for suicide." She smiled at me. "Well, not easy. But we turned them around. I think your papa was the only man in town who *never* thought I was guilty."

It took me a while to take it in. "Well, he sure convinced me," I said.

"I expect he convinced a lot of people. Everybody thought so much of Clayton."

"You killed your husband."

We looked at each other. I shook my head. "Why?"

She shrugged. "We had a fight. We were drunk. He was sleeping with my fucking maid. I was crazy. Lots of reasons, no reason. I sure didn't plan it."

"You sure didn't confess it either."

"What good would that have done? Hugh was dead. I wasn't about to let his snooty-assed mother shove me in the gas chamber and pocket the money."

I shook my head. "Jesus. And you've never felt a day's guilt, have you?"

Her head tilted back, smoothing her throat. The shuttered sun had fallen down the room onto the floor, and evening light did a movie fade and turned Stella Doyle into the star in the painting behind her. "Ah, baby, don't believe it," she said. The room stayed quiet.

I stood up and dropped the empty bottle in the wastebasket. I said, "Papa told me how he was in love with you."

Her laugh came warmly through the shuttered dusk. "Yes, and I guess I was sweet on him, too, boop boop dedoo."

"Yeah, Papa said no man could say he'd been alive if he'd seen you and not felt that way. I just wanted to tell you I know what he meant." I raised my hand to wave good-bye.

"Come over here," she said, and I went to her chair and she reached up and brought my head down to her and kissed me full and long on the mouth. "So long, Buddy." Slowly her hand moved down my face, the huge diamond radiant.

News came over the wire. The tabloids played with it for a few days on back pages. They had some pictures. They dug up the Hugh Doyle trial photos to put beside the old studio glossies. The dramatic death of an old movie star was worth sending a news camera down to Thermopylae, North Carolina, to get a shot of the charred ruin that had once been Red Hills. A shot of the funeral parlor and the flowers on the casket.

My sister phoned me that there was even a crowd at the coroner's inquest at the courthouse. They said Stella Doyle had died in her sleep after a cigarette set fire to her mattress. But rumors started that her body had been found at the foot of the stairs, as if she'd been trying to escape the fire, but had fallen. They said she was drunk. They buried her beside Hugh Doyle in the family plot, the fanciest tomb in the Methodist cemetery, not far from where my parents were buried. Not long after she died, one of the cable networks did a night of her movies. I stayed up to watch *Fever* again.

My wife said, "Buddy, I'm sorry, but this is the biggest bunch of sentimental slop I ever saw. The whore'll sell her jewels and get the medicine and they'll beat the epidemic but she'll die to pay for her past and then the town'll see she was really a saint. Am I right?"

"You're right."

She sat down to watch awhile. "You know, I can't decide if she's a really lousy actress or a really good one. It's weird."

I said, "Actually, I think she was a much better actress than anyone gave her credit for."

My wife went to bed, but I watched through the night. I sat in Papa's old rocking chair that I'd brought north with me after his death. Finally at dawn I turned off the set, and Stella's face disappeared into a star, and went out. The reception was awful and the screen too small. Besides, the last movie was in black and white; I couldn't see her eyes as well as I could remember the shock of their color, when she first turned toward me at the foot of the courthouse steps, that hot August day when I was ten, when my father stepped forward out of the crowd to take her hand, when her eyes were lilacs turned up to his face, and his straw hat in the summer sun was shining like a knight's helmet.

1998

TOM FRANKLIN

Poachers

AT DAWN, on the first day of April, the three Gates brothers banked their ten-foot aluminum boat in a narrow slough of dark water. They tied their hounds, strapped on their rifles and stepped out, ducking black magnolia branches heavy with rain and Spanish moss. The two thin younger brothers, denim overalls tucked into their boots, lugged between them a Styrofoam cooler of iced fish, coons and possums. The oldest brother — twenty, bearded, heavyset — carried a Sunbeam Bread sack of eels in his coat pocket. Hooked over his left shoulder was the pink body of a fawn they'd shot and skinned and, over the right, a stray dog to which they'd done the same. With the skins and heads gone and the dog's tail chopped off, they were difficult to tell apart.

The Gateses climbed the hill, clinging to vines and saplings, slipping in the red clay, their boots coated and enormous by the time they stepped out of the woods. For a moment they stood in the road, looking at the gray sky, the clouds piling up. The two younger ones, Scott and Wayne, set the cooler down. Kent, the oldest, removed his limp cap and squeezed the water from it. He nodded, and his brothers picked up the cooler.

They rounded a curve and crossed a one-lane bridge, stopping to piss over the rail into creek water high from all the rain, then went on, passing houses on either side: dark warped boards with knotholes big enough to look through and cement blocks for steps. Black men appeared in doors and windows to watch them go by — to most of these people they were something not seen often, something nocturnal and dangerous. Along this stretch of the Alabama River, everyone knew that the brothers' father, Boo Gates, had married a girl named Anna when he was thirty and she was seventeen, and that the boys had been born in quick succession, with less than a year between them.

But few outside the family knew that a fourth child — a daughter, unnamed — had been stillborn, and that Boo had buried her in an unmarked grave in a clearing in the woods behind their house. Anna died the next day, and the three boys, dirty and naked, watched their father's stoop-shouldered descent into the earth as he dug her grave. By the time he'd finished it was dark and the moon had come up out of the trees and the boys lay asleep upon one another in the dirt like wolf pups.

The name of this community, if it could be called that, was Lower Peach Tree, though as far as anybody knew there'd never been an Upper Peach Tree. Scattered along the leafy banks of the river were ragged houses, leaning and drafty, many empty, caving in, so close to the water they'd been built on stilts. Each April floods came and the crumbling land along the riverbank would disappear and each May, when the floodwaters receded, a house or two would be gone.

Upriver, near the lock and dam, stood an old store, a slanting building with a steep, rusty tin roof and a stovepipe in the back. Behind the store the mimosa trees sagged, waterlogged. In front, beside the gas pump, long green steps led up to the door, where a red sign said OPEN. Inside to the right, like a bar, a polished maple counter covered the entire wall. Behind the counter hung a rack with wire pegs for tools, hardware, fishing tackle. The condoms, bullets, tobacco products and rat poison were beneath the counter.

The store owner, old Kirxy, had bad knees, and this weather settled around his joints like rot. For most of his life he'd been married and lived in a nice two-story house on the highway, fireplaces in every bedroom, a china cabinet. But when his wife died two years ago — cancer — he found it easier to avoid the house, to keep the bills paid and the grass mowed but the door locked, to spend nights in the store, to sleep in the back room on the army cot and to warm his meals of corned beef and beef stew on a hot plate. He didn't mind that people had all but stopped coming to the store. As long as he served a few long-standing customers, he thought he'd stick around. He had his radio and one good station and money enough. He liked the area, knew his regulars weren't the kind to drive an hour to the nearest town. For those few people, Kirxy would go once a week to Grove Hill to shop for goods he'd resell, marking up the price just enough for a reasonable profit. He didn't need the money, it was just good business.

Liquor-wise, the county was dry, but that didn't stop Kirxy. For his regulars, he would serve plastic cups of the cheap whiskey he bought in the next county or bottles of beer he kept locked in the old refrigerator in back. For these regulars, he would break packages of cigarettes and keep them in a cigar box and sell them for a dime apiece, a nickel stale. Aspirins were seven cents each, Tylenol tablets nine. He would open boxes of shotgun shells or cartridges and sell them for amounts that varied according to caliber, and he'd been known to find specialty items — paperback novels, explosive and, once, a rotary telephone.

At Euphrates Morrisette's place, the Gates brothers pounded on the back door. In his yard a cord of wood was stacked between two fence posts and covered by a green tarp, brick halves holding the tarp down. A tire swing, turning slowly and full of rainwater, hung from a white oak. When Morrisette appeared — he was a large, bald black man — Kent held out the fawn and dog. Morrisette put on glasses and squinted at both. "Hang back," he said, and closed the door. Kent sat on the porch edge and his brothers on the steps.

The door opened and Morrisette came out with three pint jars of homemade whiskey. Each brother took a jar and unscrewed its lid, sniffed the clear liquid. Morrisette set his steaming coffee cup on the windowsill. He fastened his suspenders, looking at the carcasses hanging over the rail. The brothers were already drinking.

"Where's that girl?" Kent asked, his face twisted from the sour whiskey.

"My stepdaughter, you mean?" Morrisette's Adam's apple pumped in his throat. "She inside."

Far away a rooster crowed.

"Get her out here," Kent said. He drank again, shuddered.

"She ain't but fifteen."

Kent scratched his beard. "Just gonna look at her."

When they left, the stepdaughter was standing on the porch in her white nightgown, barefoot and rubbing the sleep from her eyes. The brothers backed away, clanking with hardware and grinning at her, Morrisette's jaw clenched.

Sipping from their jars, they took the bag of eels down the road to the

half blind conjure woman, who waited on her porch. Her house, with
its dark drapes and empty parrot cages dangling from the eaves, seemed
to be slipping off into the gully. She snatched the eels from Kent, squinting into the bag with her good eye. Grunting, she paid them from a
dusty cloth sack on her apron and muttered to herself as they went up
the dirt road. Wayne, the youngest, looked back.

They peddled the rest of the things from their cooler, then left
through the dump, stumbling down the ravine in the rain, following
the water's edge to their boat. In the back, Kent wedged his jar between
his thighs and ran the silent trolling motor with his foot. His brothers
leaned against the walls of the boat, facing opposite banks, no sound
but rain and the low hum of the motor. They drank silently, holding the
burning whiskey in their mouths before gathering the will to swallow.
Along the banks, fallen trees held thick strands of cottonmouth, black
sparkling creatures dazed and slow from winter, barely able to move. If
not for all the rain, they might still be hibernating, comatose in the
banks of the river or beneath the soft yellow underbellies of rotten logs.

Rounding a bend, the brothers saw a small boat downriver, its engine
clear, loud and unfamiliar. Heading this way. The man in the boat lifted
a hand in greeting. He wore a green poncho and a dark hat covered
with plastic. Kent shifted his foot, turning the trolling motor, and
steered them toward the bank, giving the stranger a wide berth. He felt
for their outboard's crank rope while Scott and Wayne faced forward
and sat on the boat seats. The man drawing closer didn't look much
older than Kent. He cut his engine and coasted up beside them, smiling.

"Morning, fellows," he said, showing a badge. "New district game
warden."

The brothers looked straight ahead, as if he weren't there. The warden's engine was steaming, a flock of geese passed overhead. Wayne
slipped his hands inside the soft leather collars of two dogs, who'd begun to growl.

"You fellows oughta know," the warden said, pointing his long chin
to the rifle in Scott's hands, "that it's illegal to have those guns loaded
on the river. I'm gonna have to check 'em. I'll need to see some licenses,
too."

When he stood, the dogs jumped forward, toenails scraping aluminum. Wayne pulled them back, glancing at his brothers.

Kent spat into the brown water. He met the warden's eyes and in an
instant knew the man had seen the telephone in the floor of their boat.

"Pull to the bank!" the warden yelled, drawing a pistol. "Y'all are under arrest for poaching!"

The Gateses didn't move. One of the dogs began to claw the hull and the others joined him. A howl rose.

"Shut those dogs up!" The warden's face had grown blotchy and red.

The spotted hound broke free and sprang over the gunnel, slobber strung from its teeth, and the man most surprised by the game warden's shot was the game warden himself. His face drained of color as the noise echoed off the water and died in the bent black limbs and the cattails. The bullet had passed through the front dog's neck and smacked into the bank behind them, missing Wayne by inches. The dog collapsed, and there was an instant of silence before the others, now loose, clattered overboard into the water, red-eyed, tangled in their leashes, trying to swim.

"Pull to the goddamn bank!" the warden yelled. "Right now!"

Scowling, Kent leaned and spat. He laid his 30-30 aside. Using the shoulders of his brothers for balance, he made his way to the prow. Scott, flecked with dog blood, moved to the back to keep the boat level. At the front, Kent reached into the water and took the first dog by its collar, lifted the kicking form and set it streaming and shivering behind him. His brothers turned their faces away as it shook off the water, rocking the boat. Kent grabbed the rope that led to the big three-legged hound and pulled it in hand over hand until he could work his fingers under its collar. He gave Wayne a sidelong look and together they hauled it in. Then Kent grabbed for the smaller bitch while Wayne got the black and tan.

The warden watched them, his hips swaying with the rise and fall of the current. Rain fell harder now, spattering against the boats. Kneeling among the dogs, Kent unsnapped the leash and tossed the spotted hound overboard. It sank, then resurfaced and floated on its side, trailing blood. Kent's lower lip twitched. Wayne whispered to the dogs and placed his hands on two of their heads to calm them — they were retching and trembling and rolling their eyes fearfully at the trees.

Scott stood up with his hands raised, as if to surrender. When the man looked at him, Kent jumped from his crouch into the other boat, his big fingers closing around the game warden's neck.

Later that morning, Kirxy had just unlocked the door and hung out the OPEN sign when he heard the familiar rattle of the Gates truck. He sipped his coffee and limped behind the counter, sat on his stool. The boys came several times a week, usually in the afternoon, before they started their evenings of hunting and fishing. Kirxy would give them the supplies they needed — bullets, fishing line, socks, a new cap to replace one lost in the river. They would fill their truck and cans with gas. Eighteen-year-old Wayne would get the car battery from the charger near the wood-burning stove and replace it with the drained one from their boat's trolling motor. Kirxy would serve them coffee or Cokes — never liquor, not to minors — and they'd eat whatever they chose from the shelves, usually candy bars or potato chips, ignoring Kirxy's advice that they ought to eat healthier, Vienna sausages, Dinty Moore or Chef Boyardee.

Today they came in looking a little spooked, Kirxy thought. Scott stayed near the door, peering out, the glass fogging by his face. Wayne went to the candy aisle and selected several Hershey's bars. He left a trail of muddy boot prints behind him. Kirxy would mop later.

"Morning, boys," he said. "Coffee?"

Wayne nodded. Kirxy filled a Styrofoam cup then grinned as the boy loaded it with sugar.

"You take coffee with your sweetener?" he asked.

Kent leaned on the counter, inspecting the hardware items on their pegs, a hacksaw, a set of Allen wrenches. A gizmo with several uses, knife, measuring tape, awl. Kirxy could smell the booze on the boys.

"Ya'll need something?" he asked.

"That spotted one you give us?" Kent said, not meeting his eyes. "Won't bark no more."

"She won't?"

"Naw. Tree 'em fine, but won't bark nary a time. Gonna have to shoot her."

His mouth full of chocolate, Wayne looked at Kirxy. By the door, Scott unfolded his arms.

"No," Kirxy said. "Ain't no need for that, Kent. Do what that conjure woman recommends. Go out in the woods, find you a locust shell stuck to a tree. This is the time of year for 'em, if I'm not mistaken."

"Locust shell?" Kent asked.

"Yeah. Bring it back home and crunch it up in the dog's scraps, and that'll make her bark like she ought to."

Kent nodded to Kirxy and walked to the door. He went out, his brothers following.

"See you," Kirxy called. "You're welcome."

Wayne waved with a Hershey's bar and closed the door.

Kirxy stared after them for a time. It had been more than a year since they'd paid him anything, but he couldn't bring himself to ask for money; he'd even stopped writing down what they owed.

He got his coffee and limped from behind the counter to the easy chair by the stove. He shook his head at the muddy footprints in the candy aisle. He sat slowly, tucked a blanket around his legs, took out his bottle and added a splash to his coffee. Sipping, he picked up a novel — Louis L'Amour, *Sackett's Land* — and reached in his apron pocket for his glasses.

Though she had been once, the woman named Esther wasn't much of a regular in Kirxy's store these days. She lived two miles upriver in a shambling white house with magnolia trees in the yard. The house had a wraparound porch, and when it flooded you could fish from the back, sitting in the tall white rocking chairs, though you weren't likely to catch anything, a baby alligator maybe, or sometimes bullfrogs. Owls nested in the trees along her part of the river, but in this weather they seemed quiet. She missed their hollow calling.

Esther was fifty. She'd had two husbands and six children who were gone and had ill feelings toward her. She'd had her female parts removed in an operation. Now she lived alone and, most of the time, drank alone. If the Gates boys hadn't passed out in their truck somewhere in the woods, they might stop by after a night's work. Esther would make them strong coffee and feed them salty fried eggs and greasy link sausages, and some mornings, like today, she would get a faraway look in her eyes and take Kent's shirt collar in her fingers and lead him upstairs and watch him close the bathroom door and listen to the sounds of his bathing.

She smiled, knowing these were the only baths he ever took.

When he emerged, his long hair stringy, his chest flat and hard, she led him down the hall past the telephone nook to her bedroom. He crawled into bed and watched her take off her gown and step out of her underwear. Bending, she looked in the mirror to fluff her hair, then climbed in beside him. He was gentle at first, curious, then rougher, the way she liked him to be. She closed her eyes, the bed frame rattling and bumping, her father's old pocket watch slipping off the nightstand. Water gurgled in the pipework in the walls as the younger brothers took baths, too, hoping for a turn of their own, which had never happened. At least not yet.

"Slow, baby," Esther whispered in Kent's ear. "It's plenty of time. . . ."

On April third it was still raining. Kirxy put aside his crossword to answer the telephone.

"Can you come on down to the lock and dam?" Goodloe asked. "We got us a situation here."

Kirxy disliked smart-assed Goodloe, but something in the sheriff's voice told him it was serious. He'd heard on the news that the new game warden had been missing for two days. The authorities had dragged the river all night and had three helicopters in the air. Kirxy sat forward in his chair, waiting for his back to loosen a bit. He added a shot of whiskey to his coffee and gulped it down as he shrugged into his denim jacket, zipping it up to his neck because he stayed cold when it rained. He put cotton balls in his ears, set his cap on his bald head, and took his walking cane from beside the door.

In his truck, the four-wheel-drive engaged and the defroster on high, he sank and rose in the deep ruts, gobs of mud flying past his windows, the wipers swishing across his view. The radio announcer said it was sixty degrees, more rain on the way. Conway Twitty began to sing. A mile from the lock and dam Kirxy passed the Grove Hill ambulance, axle-deep in mud. A burly black paramedic wedged a piece of two-by-four beneath one of the rear tires while the bored-looking driver sat behind the wheel, smoking and racing the engine.

Kirxy slowed and rolled down his window. "Y'all going after a live one or a dead one?"

"Dead, Mr. Kirxy," the black man answered.

Kirxy nodded and accelerated. At the lock and dam, he could see a crowd of people and umbrellas and beyond them he saw the dead man, lying on the ground under a black raincoat. Some onlooker had begun to direct traffic. Goodloe and three deputies in yellow slickers stood near the body with their hands in their pockets.

Kirxy climbed out and people nodded somberly and parted to let him through. Goodloe, who'd been talking to his deputies, ceased as Kirxy approached and they stood looking at the raincoat.

"Morning, Sugarbaby," Kirxy said, using the childhood nickname Goodloe hated. "Is this who I think it is?"

"Yep," Goodloe muttered. "Rookie game warden of the year."

With his cane, Kirxy pulled back the raincoat to reveal the white face. "Young fellow," he said.

There was a puddle beneath the dead man, twigs in his hair and a clove of moss in his breast pocket. With the rubber tip of his cane, Kirxy brushed a leech from the man's forehead. He bent and looked into the warden's left eye, which was partly open. He noticed his throat, the dark bruises there.

Goodloe unfolded a handkerchief and blew his nose then wiped it. "Don't go abusing the evidence, Kirxy." He stuffed the handkerchief into his back pocket.

"Evidence? Now, Sugarbaby."

Goodloe exhaled and looked at the sky. "Don't shit me, Kirxy. You know good and well who done this. I expect they figure the law don't apply up here on this part of the river, the way things is been all these years. Them other wardens scared of 'em. But I reckon that's fixing to change." He paused. "I had to place me a call to the capital this morning. To let 'em know we was all outta game wardens. And you won't believe who they patched me through to."

Kirxy adjusted the cotton in his right ear.

"Old Frank David himself," the sheriff said. "Ain't nothing ticks him off more than this kind of thing."

A dread stirred in Kirxy's belly. "Frank David. Was he a relation of this fellow?"

"Teacher," Goodloe said. "Said he's been giving lessons to young game wardens over at the forestry service. He asked me a whole bunch of questions. Regular interrogation. Said this here young fellow was the cream of the crop. Best new game warden there was."

"Wouldn't know it from this angle," Kirxy said.

Goodloe grunted.

A photographer from the paper was studying the corpse. He glanced at the sky as if gauging the light. When he snapped the first picture, Kirxy was in it like a sportsman.

"What'd you want from me?" he asked Goodloe.

"You tell them boys I need to ask 'em some questions, and I ain't fixing to traipse all over the county. I'll drop by the store this evening."

"If they're there, they're there," Kirxy said. "I ain't their damn father."

Goodloe followed him to the truck. "You might think of getting 'em a lawyer," he said through the window.

Kirxy started the engine. "Shit, Sugarbaby. Them boys don't need a lawyer. They just need to stay in the woods, where they belong. Folks oughta know to let 'em alone by now."

Goodloe stepped back from the truck. He smacked his lips. "I don't reckon anybody got around to telling that to the deceased."

Driving, Kirxy turned off the radio. He remembered the Gates brothers when they were younger, before their father shot himself. He pictured the three blond heads in the front of Boo's boat as he motored upriver past the store, lifting a solemn hand to Kirxy where he stood with a broom on his little back porch. After Boo's wife and newborn daughter had died, he'd taught those boys all he knew about the woods, about fishing, tracking, hunting, killing. He kept them in his boat all night as he telephoned catfish and checked his trotlines and jugs and shot things on the bank. He'd given each of his sons a specific job to do, one dialing the phone, another netting the stunned catfish, the third adjusting the chains that generated electricity from a car battery into the water. Boo would tie a piece of rope around each of his sons' waists and loop the other end to his own ankle in case one of the boys fell overboard. Downriver, Kent would pull in the trotlines while Wayne handed him a cricket or catalpa worm for the hook. Scott took the bass, perch or catfish Kent gave him and slit its soft cold belly with a fillet knife and ran two fingers up into the fish and drew out its palmful of guts and dumped them overboard. Sometimes on warm nights cottonmouths or young alligators would follow them, drawn by blood. A danger was catching a snake or snapping turtle on the trotline, and each night Boo whispered for Kent to be careful, to lift the line with a stick and see what he had there instead of using his bare hand.

During the morning they would leave the boat tied and the boys would follow their father through the trees from trap to trap, stepping when he stepped, not talking. Boo emptied the traps and rebaited them while behind him Kent put the carcass in his squirrel pouch. In the afternoons, they gutted and skinned what they'd brought home. What time was left before dark they spent sleeping in the featherbed in the cabin where their mother and sister had died.

After Boo's suicide, Kirxy had tried to look after the boys, their ages twelve, thirteen and fourteen — just old enough, Boo must've thought, to raise themselves. For a while Kirxy let them stay with him and his wife, who'd never had a child. He tried to send them to school, but they were past learning to read and write and got expelled the first day for fighting, ganging up on a black kid. They were past the kind of life

Kirxy's wife was used to living. They scared her, the way they watched her with eyes narrowed into black lines, the way they ate with their hands, the way they wouldn't talk. What she didn't know was that from those years of wordless nights on the river and silent days in the woods they had developed a kind of language of their own, a language of the eyes, of the fingers, of the way a shoulder moved, a nod of the head.

Because his wife's health wasn't good in those days, Kirxy had returned the boys to their cabin in the woods. He spent most Saturday's with them, trying to take up where Boo had left off, bringing them food and milk, clothes and new shoes, reading them books, teaching them things and tellings stories. He'd worked out a deal with Esther, who took hot food to them in the evenings and washed their clothes for them.

Slowing to let two buzzards hop away from a dead deer, Kirxy lit a cigarette and wiped his foggy windshield with the back of his hand. He thought of Frank David, Alabama's legendary game warden. There were dozens of stories about the man — Kirxy had heard and told them for years, had repeated them to the Gates boys, even made some up to scare them. Now the true ones and the fictions were confused in his mind. He remembered one: A dark, moonless night, and two poachers use a spotlight to freeze a buck in the darkness and shoot it. They take hold of its wide rack of horns and struggle to drag the big deer when suddenly they realize that now three men are pulling. The first poacher jumps and says, "Hey, it ain't supposed to be but two of us dragging this deer!"

And Frank David says, "Ain't supposed to be none of y'all dragging it."

The Gates boys came in the store just before closing, smelling like the river. Nodding to Kirxy, they went to the shelves and began selecting cans of things to eat. Kirxy poured himself a generous shot of whiskey. He'd stopped by their cabin earlier and, not finding them there, left a quarter on the steps. An old signal he hadn't used in years.

"Goodloe's coming by tonight," he said to Kent. "Wants to ask if y'all know anything about that dead game warden."

Kent shot the other boys a look.

"Now I don't know if y'all've ever even seen that fellow," Kirxy said, "and I'm not asking you to tell me." He paused, in case they wanted to. "But that's what old Sugarbaby's gonna want to know. If I was y'all, I just wouldn't tell him anything. Just say I was at home, that I don't know nothing about any dead game warden. Nothing at all."

Kent shrugged and walked down the aisle he was on and stared out the back window, though there wasn't anything to see except the trees, ghostly and bent, when the lightning came. His brothers took seats by the stove and began to eat. Kirxy watched them, remembering when he used to read to them, *Tarzan of the Apes* and *The Return of Tarzan.* The boys had wanted to hear the books over and over — they loved the jungle, the elephants, rhinos, gorillas, the anacondas thirty feet long. They would listen intently, their eyes bright in the light of the stove, Wayne holding in his small dirty hand the Slinky Kirxy had given him as a Christmas present, his lips moving along with Kirxy's voice, mouthing some of the words: *the great apes; Numa the lion; La, Queen of Opar, the Lost City.*

They had listened to his Frank David stories the same way: the game warden appearing beside a tree on a night when there wasn't a moon, a tracker so keen he could see in the dark, could follow a man through the deepest swamp by smelling the fear in his sweat, by the way the water swirled: a bent-over shadow slipping between the beaver lairs, the cypress trees, the tangle of limb and vine, parting the long wet bangs of Spanish moss with his rifle barrel, creeping toward the glowing windows of the poacher's cabin, the deer hides nailed to the wall, the gator pelts, the fish with their grim smiles hooked to a clothesline, turtle shells like army helmets drying on the windowsills. Any pit bull or mutt meant to guard the place lying behind him with its throat slit, Frank David slips out of the fog with fog still clinging to the brim of his hat. He circles the cabin, peers in each window, mounts the porch. Puts his shoulder through the front door. Stands with wood splinters landing on the floor at his feet. A hatted man of average height, clean-shaven: no threat until the big hands come up, curl into fists, the knuckles scarred, blue, sharp.

Kirxy finished his drink and poured another. It burned pleasantly in his belly. He looked at the boys, occupied by their bags of corn curls. A Merle Haggard song ended on the radio and Kirxy clicked it off, sparing the boys the evening news.

In the quiet, Kirxy heard Goodloe's truck. He glanced at Kent, who'd probably been hearing it for a while. Outside, Goodloe slammed his door. He hurried up the steps and tapped on the window. Kirxy exaggerated his limp and took his time letting him in.

"Good evening," Goodloe said, shaking the water from his hands. He took off his hat and hung it on the nail by the door, then hung up his yellow slicker.

"Evening, Sugarbaby," Kirxy said.

"If I can use a little understatement here," Goodloe said, "it's a tad wet tonight."

"Yep." Kirxy went behind the counter and refilled his glass. "You just caught the tail end of happy hour. That is, if you're off the wagon again. Can I sell you a tonic? Warm you up?"

"You know we're a dry county, Kirxy."

"Would that be a no?"

"It's a watch your ass." Goodloe looked at the brothers. "Just wanted to ask these boys some questions."

"Have at it, Sugarbaby."

Goodloe walked to the Lance rack and detached a package of Nip-Chee crackers. He opened it, offered the pack to each of the boys. Only Wayne took one. Smiling, Goodloe bit a cracker in half and turned a chair around and sat with his elbows across its back. He looked over toward Kent, half hidden by shadow. He chewed slowly. "Come on out here so I can see you, boy. I ain't gonna bite nothing but these stale-ass cheese crackers."

Kent moved a step closer.

Goodloe took out a notepad. "Where was y'all between the hours of four and eight A.M. two days ago?"

Kent looked at Scott. "Asleep."

"Asleep," Scott said.

Goodloe snorted. "Now come on, boys. The whole dern county knows y'all ain't slept a night in your life. Y'all was out on the river, weren't you? Making a few telephone calls?"

"You saying he's a liar?" Kirxy asked.

"I'm posing the questions here." Goodloe chewed another cracker. "Hell, everybody knows the other game wardens has been letting y'all get away with all kinds of shit. I reckon this new fellow had something to prove."

"Sounds like he oughta used a life jacket," Kirxy said, wiping the counter.

"It appears —" Goodloe studied Kent — "that he might've been strangled. You got a alibi, boy?"

Kent looked down.

Goodloe sighed. "I mean — Christ — is there anybody can back up what you're saying?"

The windows flickered.

"Yeah," Kirxy said. "I can."

Goodloe turned and faced the storekeeper. "You."

"That's right. They were here with me. Here in the store."

Goodloe looked amused. "They was, was they. Okay, Mr. Kirxy. How come you didn't mention that to me this morning? Saved us all a little time?"

Kirxy sought Kent's eyes but saw nothing there, no understanding, no appreciation. No fear. He went back to wiping the counter. "Well, I guess because they was passed out drunk, and I didn't want to say anything, being as I was, you know, giving alcohol to young'uns."

"But now that it's come down to murder, you figured you'd better just own up."

"Something like that."

Goodloe stared at Kirxy for a long time; neither would look away. Then the sheriff turned to the boys. "Y'all ever heard of Frank David?"

Wayne nodded.

"Well," Goodloe said. "Looks like he's aiming to be this district's game warden. I figure he pulled some strings, what he did."

Kirxy came from behind the counter. "That all your questions? It's past closing and these young'uns need to go home and get some sleep." He went to the door and opened it, stood waiting.

"All righty then," the sheriff said, standing. "I expect I oughta be getting back to the office anyhow." He winked at Kirxy. "See you or these boys don't leave the county for a few days. This ain't over yet." He put the crackers in his coat. "I expect y'all might be hearing from Frank David, too," he said, watching the boys' faces. But there was nothing to see.

Alone later, Kirxy put out the light and bolted the door. He went to adjust the stove and found himself staring out the window, looking into the dark where he knew the river was rising and swirling, tires and plastic garbage can lids and deadwood from upriver floating past. He struck a match and lit a cigarette, the glow of his ash reflected in the window, and he saw himself years ago, telling the boys those stories.

How Frank David would sit so still in the woods waiting for poachers that dragonflies would perch on his nose, gnats would walk over his eyeballs. Nobody knew where he came from, but Kirxy had heard he'd been orphaned as a baby in a fire and found half-starved in the swamp by a Cajun woman. She'd raised him on the slick red clay banks of the Tombigbee River, among lean black poachers and white trash moonshiners. He didn't even know how old he was, people said. And they said he was the best poacher ever, the craftiest, the meanest. That he cut

a drunk logger's throat in a juke joint knifefight one night. That he fled
south and, underage, joined the marines in Mobile and wound up in
Korea, the infantry, where because of his shooting ability and his stealth
they made him a sniper. Before he left that country, he'd registered over
a hundred kills, Communists half a world away who never saw him
coming.

Back home in Alabama, he disappeared for a few years then showed
up at the state game warden's office, demanding a job. Some people had
heard that in the intervening time he'd gotten religion.

"What makes you think I ought to hire you?" the head warden asked.

"Because I spent ten years of my life poaching right under your
nose," Frank David said.

The Gates boys' pickup was the same old Ford their father had shot
himself in several years before, heartbroken over their mother's death.
The bullet hole in the roof had rusted out but was now covered with a
strip of duct tape from Kirxy's store. Spots of the truck's floor were
rusted away, too, so things in the road often flew up into their laps:
rocks, Budweiser cans, a king snake they were trying to run over. The
truck was older than any of them, only one thin prong left of the steering wheel and the holes of missing knobs in the dash. It was a three-
speed, a column shifter, the gearshift covered with a buck's dried ball
sack. The windows and windshield, busted or shot out years before,
hadn't been replaced because most of their driving took them along
back roads after dark or in fields, and the things they came upon were
easier shots without glass.

Though he'd never had a license, Kent drove, had since he was eight.
Scott rode shotgun. Tonight both were drinking, and in the back Wayne
stood holding his rifle and trying to keep his balance. Below the soles of
his boots the floor was soft, a tarry black from the blood of all the animals they'd killed. You could see spike antlers, forelegs and hooves of
deer. Teeth, feathers and fur. The brittle beaks and beards of turkeys and
the delicate, hinged leg bone of something molded in the sludge like a
fossil.

Just beyond a No Trespassing sign, Kent swerved off the road and
they bounced and slid through a field in the rain, shooting at rabbits.
Then they split up, the younger boys checking traps, one on each side of
the river, and Kent in the boat rebaiting their trotlines the way his father
had shown him.

They met at the truck just before midnight, untied the dogs and

tromped down a steep logging path, Wayne on one end of four leashes
and the lunging hounds on the other. When they got to the bottom-
land, he unclipped the leashes and loosed the dogs and the brothers followed the baying ahead in the dark, aiming their flashlights into the
black mesh of trees where the eyes of coons and possums gleamed like
rubies. The hounds bayed and frothed, clawed the trunks of trees and
leaped into the air and landed and leaped again, their sides pumping,
ribs showing — hounds that, given the chance, would eat until their
stomachs burst.

When the Gateses came to the river two hours later, the dogs were
lapping water and panting. Wayne bent and rubbed their ears and let
them lick his cheeks. His brothers rested and drank, belching at the sky.
After a time, they leashed the hounds and staggered downstream to the
live oak where their boat was tied. They loaded the dogs in and shoved
off into the fog and trolled over the still water.

In the middle, Scott lowered the twin chains beside the boat and began dialing the old telephone. Wayne netted the stunned catfish — you
couldn't touch them with your hand or they'd come to — and threw
them into the cooler, where in a few seconds the waking fish would begin to thrash. In the rear, Kent fingered his rifle and watched the bank
in case a coyote wandered down, hunting bullfrogs.

They climbed out of the woods into a dirt road in the misty dawn,
plying through the muddy yards and pissing by someone's front porch
in plain sight of the black face inside. A few houses down, Morrisette
didn't come to his door, and when Kent tried the handle it was locked.
He looked at Scott, then put his elbow through the glass and reached
in and unlocked it.

While his brothers searched for the liquor, Wayne ate the biscuits he
found wrapped in tinfoil on the stove. He found a box of corn flakes in
a cabinet and ate most of them, too. He ate a plate of cold fried liver.
Scott was in a bedroom looking under the bed. In the closet. He was going through drawers, his dirty fingers among the white cloth. In the
back of the house Kent found a door locked from the inside. He jimmied it open with his knife, and when he came into the kitchen, he had
a gallon jar of whiskey under his arm and Euphrates' stepdaughter by
the wrist.

Wayne stopped chewing, crumbs falling from his mouth. He approached the girl and put his hand out to touch her, but Kent pushed
him hard, into the wall. Wayne stayed there, a clock ticking beside
his head, a string of spit linking his two opened lips, watching as his

brother ran his rough hands up and down the girl's trembling body, over the nipples that showed through the thin cloth. Her eyes were closed, lips moving in prayer. Looking down, Kent saw the puddle spreading around her bare feet.

"Shit," he said, a hand cupping her breast. "Pissed herself."

He let her go and she shrank back against the wall, behind the door. She was still there, along with a bag of catfish on the table, when her stepfather came back half an hour later, ten gallons of whiskey under the tarp in his truck.

On that same Saturday Kirxy drove to the chicken fights, held in Heflin Bradford's bulging barn, deep in woods cloudy with mosquitoes. He passed the handpainted sign that'd been there forever, as long as he could remember, nailed to a tree. It said JESUS IS NOT COMING.

Kirxy climbed out of his truck and buttoned his collar, his ears full of cotton. Heflin's wife worked beneath a rented awning, grilling chicken and sausages, selling Cokes and beer. Gospel music played from a portable eight-track tape player by her head. Heflin's grandson Nolan took the price of admission at the barn door and stamped the backs of white hands and the cracked pink palms of black ones. Men in overalls and baseball caps that said CAT DIESEL POWER or STP stood at the tailgates of their pickups, smoking cigarettes, stooping to peer into the dark cages where roosters paced. The air was filled with windy rain spits and the crowing of roosters, the ground littered with limp, dead birds.

A group of men discussed Frank David, and Kirxy paused to listen.

"He's the one caught that bunch over in Warshington County," one man said. "Them alligator poachers."

"Sugarbaby said two of 'em wound up in the intensive care," another claimed. "Said they pulled a gun and old Frank David went crazy with a axe handle."

Kirxy moved on and paid the five-dollar admission. In the barn, there were bleachers along the walls and a big circular wooden fence in the center, a dome of chicken wire over the top. Kirxy found a seat at the bottom next to the back door, near a group of mean old farts he'd known for forty years. People around them called out bets and bets were accepted. Cans of beer lifted. Kirxy produced a thermos of coffee and a dented tin cup. He poured the coffee then added whiskey from a bottle that went back into his coat pocket. The tin cup warmed his fingers as he squinted through his bifocals to see which bird to bet on.

In separate corners of the barn, two bird handlers doused their roost-

ers' heads and asses with rubbing alcohol to make them fight harder.
They tightened the long, steel curved spurs. When the referee in the
center of the ring indicated it was time, the handlers entered the pen,
each cradling his bird in his arms. They flashed the roosters at each
other until their feathers had ruffled with blood lust and rage, the
roosters pedaling the air, stretching their necks toward each other. The
handlers kept them a breath apart for a second, then withdrew them to
their corners, whispering in their ears. When the referee tapped the
ground three times with his stick, the birds were unleashed on each
other. They charged and rose in the center of the ring, gouging with
spur and beak, the handlers circling the fight like crabs, blood on their
forearms and faces, ready to seize their roosters at the referee's cry of
"Handle!"

A clan of Louisiana Cajuns watched. They'd emerged red-eyed from
a van in a marijuana cloud: skinny, shirtless men with oily ponytails
and goatees and tattoos of symbols of black magic. Under their arms,
they carried thick, white, hooded roosters to pit against the reds and
blacks of the locals. Their women had stumbled out of the van behind
them, high yellow like gypsies, big-lipped, big-chested girls in halter
tops tied at their bellies and miniskirts and red heels.

In the ring the Cajuns kissed their birds on the beaks, and one tall,
completely bald Cajun wearing gold earrings in both ears put his bird's
whole head in his mouth. His girl, too, came barefoot into the ring, tattoo of a snake on her shoulder, and took the bird's head into her mouth.

"Bet on them white ones," a friend whispered to Kirxy. "These ones
around here ain't ever seen a white rooster. They don't know what
they're fighting."

That evening, checking traps in the woods north of the river, Wayne
kept hearing things. Little noises. Leaves. Twigs.

Afraid, he forced himself to go on so his brothers wouldn't laugh at
him. Near dark, in a wooden trap next to an old fence-row, he was surprised to find the tiny white fox they'd once seen cross the road in front
of their truck. He squatted before the trap and poked a stick through
the wire at the thin snout, his hand steady despite the way the fox
snapped at the stick and bit off the end. Would the witch woman want
this alive? At the thought of her he looked around. It felt like she was
watching him, as if she were hiding in a tree in the form of some animal, a possum, a swamp rat. He stood and dragged the trap through the
mud and over the land while the fox jumped in circles, growling.

A mile upstream, Scott had lost a boot to the mud and was hopping back one-footed to retrieve it. It stood alone, buried to the ankle. He wrenched it free, then sat with his back against a sweet gum to scrape off the mud. He'd begun to lace the boot when he saw a hollow tree stump, something moving inside. With his rifle barrel, he rolled the thing out — it was most of the body of a dead catfish, the movement from the maggots devouring it. When he kicked it, they spilled from the fish like rice pellets and lay throbbing in the mud.

Downstream, as night came and the rain fell harder, Kent trolled their boat across the river, flashlight in his mouth, using a stick to pull up a trotline length by length and removing the fish or turtles and re-baiting the hooks and dropping them back into the water. Near the bank, approaching the last hook, he heard something. He looked up with the flashlight in his teeth to see the thing untwirling in the air. It wrapped around his neck like a rope, and for an instant he thought he was being hanged. He grabbed the thing. It flexed and tightened, then his neck burned and went numb and he felt dizzy, his fingertips buzzing, legs weak, a tree on the bank distorting, doubling, tripling into a whole line of fuzzy shapes, turning sideways, floating.

Kent blinked. Felt his eyes bulging, his tongue swelling. His head about to explode. Then a bright light.

His brothers found the boat at dawn, four miles downstream, lodged on the far side in a fallen tree. They exchanged a glance then looked back across the river. A heavy gray fog hooded the water and the boat appeared and dissolved in the ghostly limbs around it. Scott sat on a log and took off his boots and left them standing by the log. He removed his coat and laid it over the boots. He handed his brother his rifle without looking at him, left him watching as he climbed down the bank and, hands and elbows in the air like a believer, waded into the water.

Wayne propped the second rifle against a tree and stood on the bank holding his own gun, casting his frightened eyes up and down the river. From far away a woodpecker drummed. Crows began to collect in a pecan tree downstream. After a while Wayne squatted, thinking of their dogs, tied to the bumper of their truck. They'd be under the tailgate, probably, trying to keep dry.

Soon Scott had trolled the boat back across. Together they pulled it out of the water and stood looking at their brother, who lay across the floor among the fish and turtles he'd caught. One greenish terrapin, still alive, a hook in its lip, stared back. They both knew what they were supposed to think — the blood and the sets of twin fang marks, the black bruises and shriveled skin, the neck swollen like mumps, the purple bulb of tongue between his lips. They were supposed to think *cotton-mouth*. Kent's hands were squeezed into fists and they'd hardened that way, the skin wrinkled, eyes half open. His rifle lay unfired in the boat, as if indeed a snake had done this.

But it wasn't the tracks of a snake they found when they went to get the white fox. The fox was gone, the trap empty, its catch sprung. Scott knelt and ran his knuckles along the rim of a boot print in the mud — not a very wide track, not very far from the next one. He put his finger in the black water that'd already begun to fill the track: not too deep. He looked up at Wayne. The print of an average-size man. In no hurry. Scott rose and they began.

Above them, the sky cracked and flickered.

Silently, quickly — no time to get the dogs — they followed the trail back through the woods, losing it once, twice, backtracking, working against the rain that fell and fell harder, that puddled blackly and crept up their legs, until they stood in water to their calves, rain beading on the brims of their caps. They gazed at the ground, the sky, at the rain streaming down each other's muddy face.

At the truck, Wayne jumped in the driver's seat and reached for the keys. Scott appeared in the window, shaking his head. When Wayne didn't scoot over, the older boy hit him in the jaw then slung open the door and pulled Wayne out, sent him rolling over the ground. Scott climbed in and had trouble getting the truck choked. By the time he had the hang of it, Wayne had gotten into the back and sat among the wet dogs, staring at his dead brother.

At their cabin, they carried Kent into the woods. They laid him on the ground and began digging near where their sister, mother and father were buried in their unmarked graves. For three hours they worked, the dogs coming from under the porch and sniffing around Kent and watching the digging, finally slinking off and crawling back under the porch, out of the rain. An hour later the dogs came boiling out again and stood in a group at the edge of the yard, baying. The boys paused but saw or heard nothing. When the dogs kept making noise, Scott got his rifle and fired into the woods several times. He nodded to his brother and they went back to digging. By the time they'd finished, it was late afternoon and the hole was full of slimy water and they were black with mud. They each took off one of Kent's boots and Scott got the things from his pockets. They stripped off his shirt and pants and lowered him into the hole. When he bobbed to the top of the water, they got stones and weighted him down. Then shoveled mud into the grave.

They showed up at Esther's, black as tar.

"Where's Kent?" she asked, holding her robe closed at her throat.

"We buried him," Scott said, moving past her into the kitchen. She put a hand over her mouth, and as Scott told her what they'd found she slumped against the door, looking outside. An owl flew past in the floodlights. She thought of calling Kirxy but decided to wait until morning — the old bastard thought she was a slut and a corruption. For tonight she'd just keep them safe in her house.

Scott went to the den. He turned on the TV, the reception bad because of the weather. Wayne, a bruise on his left cheek, climbed the stairs. He went into one of the bedrooms and closed the door behind him. It was chilly in the room and he noticed pictures of people on the wall, children and a tall man and a younger woman he took to be Esther. She'd been pretty then. He stood dripping on the floor, looking into her black-and-white face, searching for signs of the woman he knew now. Soon the door opened behind him and she came in. And though he still wore his filthy wet clothes, she steered him to the bed and guided him down onto it. She unbuckled his belt, removed his hunting knife and stripped the belt off. She unbuttoned his shirt and rubbed her fingers across his chest, the hair just beginning to thicken there. She undid his pants and ran the zipper down its track. She worked them over his thighs, knees and ankles and draped them across the back of a chair. She pulled off his boots and socks. Pried a finger beneath the elastic of his underwear, felt that he'd already come.

He looked at her face. His mouth opened. Esther touched his chin, the scratch of whiskers, his breath on her hand.

"Hush now," she said, and watched him fall asleep.

Downstairs, the TV went off.

When Goodloe knocked, Esther answered, a cold sliver of her face in the cracked door. "The hell you want?"

"Good evening to you, too. The Gateses here?"

"No."

Goodloe glanced behind him. "I believe that's their truck. It's kinda hard to mistake, especially for us trained lawmen."

She tried to close the door but Goodloe had his foot in it. He glanced at the three deputies who stood importantly by the Blazer. They dropped their cigarettes and crushed them out. They unsnapped their holsters and strode across the yard, standing behind Goodloe with their hands on their revolvers and their legs apart like TV deputies.

"Why don't y'all just let 'em alone?" Esther said. "Ain't they been through enough?"

"Tell 'em I'd like to see 'em," Goodloe said. "Tell 'em get their boots."

"You just walk straight to hell, mister."

Wayne appeared behind her, lines from the bed linen on his face.

"Whoa, Nellie," Goodloe said. "Boy, you look plumb terrible. Why don't you let us carry you on down to the office for a little coffee. Little cake." He glanced back at one of the deputies. "We got any of that cinnamon roll left, Dave?"

"You got a warrant for their arrest?" Esther asked.

"No, I ain't got a warrant for their arrest. They ain't under arrest. They fixing to get questioned, is all. Strictly informal." Goodloe winked. "You reckon you could do without 'em for a couple of hours?"

"Fuck you, Sugarbaby."

The door slammed. Goodloe nodded down the side of the house and two deputies went to make sure nobody escaped from the back. But in a minute Wayne came out dressed, his hands in his pockets, and followed Goodloe down the stairs, the deputies watching him closely, and watching the house.

"Where's your brothers?" Goodloe asked.

He looked down.

Goodloe nodded to the house and two deputies went in, guns drawn. They came out a few minutes later, frowning.

"Must've heard us coming," Goodloe said. "Well, we got this one. We'll find them other two tomorrow." They got into the Blazer and Goodloe looked at Wayne, sitting in the back.

"Put them cuffs on him," Goodloe said.

Holding his rifle, Scott came out of the woods when the Blazer was gone. He returned to the house.

"They got Wayne," Esther said. "Why didn't you come tell him they was out there?"

"He got to learn," Scott said. He went to the cabinet where she kept the whiskey and took the bottle. She watched him go to the sofa and sit down in front of the blank TV. Soon she joined him, bringing glasses. He filled both, and when they emptied them he filled them again.

They spent the night like that, and at dawn they were drunk. Wearing her robe, Esther began clipping her fingernails, a cigarette smoking in the ashtray beside her. She'd forgotten about calling Kirxy.

Scott was telling her about the biggest catfish they'd ever called up: a hundred pounds, he swore, a hundred fifty. "You could of put your whole head in that old cat's mouth," he said, sipping his whiskey. "Back fin long as your damn arm."

He stood. Walked to the front window. There were toads in the yard — with the river swelling they were everywhere. In the evenings there were rainfrogs. The yard had turned into a pond and each night the rainfrogs sang. It was like no other sound. Esther said it kept her up at night.

"That, and some other things," she said.

Scott heard a fingernail ring the ashtray. He rubbed his hand across his chin, felt the whiskers there. He watched the toads as they huddled in the yard, still as rocks, bloated and miserable-looking.

"That catfish was green," Scott said, sipping. "I swear to God. Green as grass."

"Them goddamn rainfrogs," she said. "I just lay there at night with my hands over my ears."

A clipping rang the ashtray.

He turned and went to her on the sofa. "They was moss growing on his nose," he said, putting his hand on her knee.

"Go find your brother," she said. She got up and walked unsteadily across the floor and went into the bathroom, closed the door. When she came out, he and the bottle were gone.

Without Kent, Scott felt free to do what he wanted, which was to drive very fast. He got the truck started and spun off, aiming for every mud hole he could. He shot past a house with a washing machine on the front porch, two thin black men butchering a hog hanging from a tree. One of the men waved with a knife. Drinking, Scott drove through the mountains of trash at the dump and turned the truck in circles, kicking up muddy rooster tails. He swerved past the Negro church and the graveyard where a group of blacks huddled, four warbling poles over an open grave, the wind tearing the preacher's hat out of his hands and a woman's umbrella reversing.

When he tired of driving, he left the truck in their hiding place and, using trees for balance, stumbled down the hill to their boat. He carried Kent's rifle, which he'd always admired. On the river, he fired up the outboard and accelerated, the boat prow lifting and leveling out, the buzz of the motor rising in the trees. The water was nearly orange from mud, the cypress knees nothing but knobs and tips because of the floods. Nearing the old train trestle, he cut the motor and coasted to a stop. He sat listening to the rain, to the distant barking of a dog, half a mile away. Chasing something, maybe a deer. As the dog charged through the woods, Scott closed his eyes and imagined the terrain, marking where he thought the dog was now and where he thought it was now. Then the barking stopped, suddenly, as if the dog had run smack into a tree.

Scott clicked on the trolling motor and moved the boat close to the edge of the river, the rifle across his knees. He scanned the banks, and when the rain started to fall harder he accelerated toward the trestle. From beneath the cross ties, he smelled creosote and watched the rain as it stirred the river. He looked into the gray trees and thought he would drive into town later, see about getting Wayne. Kent had never wanted to go to Grove Hill — their father had warned them of the po-lice, of jail.

Scott picked up one of the catfish from the night before. It was stiff, as if carved out of wood. He stared at it, watching the green blowflies hover above his fist, then threw it over into the cattails along the bank.

The telephone rig was under the seat. He lifted the chains quietly, considering what giant catfish might be passing beneath the boat this very second, a thing as large as a man's thigh, with eyes the size of ripe plums and skin the color of mud. Catfish, their father had taught them, have long whiskers that make them the only fish you can "call." Kirxy had told Scott and his brothers that if a game warden caught you tele-phoning, all you needed to do was dump your rig overboard. But, Kirxy warned, Frank David would handcuff you and jump overboard and swim around the bottom of the river until he found your rig.

Scott spat a stream of tobacco into the brown water. Minnows ap-peared and began to investigate, nibbling at the dark yolk of spit as it elongatted and dissolved. With his rifle's safety off, he lowered the chains into the water, a good distance apart. He checked the connec-tions — the battery, the telephone. He lifted the phone and began to dial. "Hello?" he whispered, the thing his father had always said, grin-ning in the dark. The wind picked up a bit, he heard it rattling in the trees, and he dialed faster, had just seen the first silver body bob to the surface when something landed with a clatter in his boat. He glanced over.

A bundle of dynamite, sparks shooting off the end, fuse already gone. He looked above him, the trestle, but nobody was there. He moved to grab the dynamite, but his cheeks ballooned with hot red wind and his hands caught fire.

When the smoke cleared and the water stopped boiling, silver bodies began to bob to the surface — largemouth bass, bream, gar, suckers, white perch, polliwogs, catfish — some only stunned but others dead, in pieces, pink fruitlike things, the water blooming darkly with mud.

Kirxy's telephone rang for the second time in one day, a rarity that proved what his wife had always said: Bad news came over the phone. The first call had been Esther, telling him of Kent's death, Wayne's arrest, Scott's disappearance. This time Kirxy heard Goodloe's voice telling him that somebody — or maybe a couple of somebodies — had been blown up out on the trestle.

"Scott," Kirxy said, sitting.

He arrived at the trestle, and with his cane hobbled over the uneven tracks. Goodloe's deputies and three ambulance drivers in rubber gloves and waders were scraping pieces off the cross ties with spoons, dropping the parts in Ziploc bags. The boat, two flattened shreds of aluminum, lay on the bank. In the water, minnows darted about, nibbling.

"Christ," Kirxy said. He brought a handkerchief to his lips. Then he went to where Goodloe stood on the bank, writing in his notebook.

"What do you aim to do about this?" Kirxy demanded.

"Try to figure out who it was, first."

"You know goddamn well who it was."

"I expect it's either Kent or Scott Gates."

"It's Scott," Kirxy said.

"How do you know that?"

Kirxy told him that Kent was dead.

Goodloe studied the storekeeper. "I ain't seen the body."

Kirxy's blood pressure was going up. "Fuck, Sugarbaby. Are you one bit aware what's going on here?"

"Fishing accident," Goodloe said. "His bait exploded."

From the bank, a deputy called that he'd found most of a boot. "Foot's still in it," he said, holding it up by the lace.

"Tag it," Goodloe said, writing something down. "Keep looking."

Kirxy poked Goodloe in the shoulder with his cane. "You really think Scott'd blow himself up?"

Goodloe looked at his shoulder, the muddy cane print, then at the storekeeper. "Not on purpose, I don't." He paused. "Course, suicide does run in their family."

"What about Kent?"

"What about him?"

"Christ, Sugarbaby —"

Goodloe held up his hand. "Just show me, Kirxy."

They left the ambulance drivers and the deputies and walked the other way without talking. When they came to Goodloe's Blazer, they got in and drove without talking. Soon they stopped in front of the Gates cabin. Instantly hounds surrounded the truck, barking viciously and jumping with muddy paws against the glass. Goodloe blew the horn until the hounds slunk away, heads low, fangs bared. The sheriff opened his window and fired several times in the air, backing the dogs up. When he and Kirxy got out, Goodloe had reloaded.

The hounds kept to the edge of the woods, watching.

His eye on them, Kirxy led Goodloe behind the decrepit cabin. Rusty screens covered some windows, rags of drape others. Beneath the house, the dogs paced them. "Back here," Kirxy said, heading into the trees. Esther had said they'd buried Kent, and this was the logical place. He went slowly, careful not to bump a limb and cause a small down-pour. Sure enough, there lay the grave. You could see where the dogs had been scratching around it.

Goodloe went over and toed the dirt. "You know the cause of death?"

"Yeah, I know the cause of death. His name's Frank fucking David."

"I meant how he was killed."

"The boys said snakebite. Three times in the neck. But I'd do an autopsy."

"You would." Goodloe exhaled. "Okay. I'll send Roy and Avery over here to dig him up. Maybe shoot these goddern dogs."

"I'll tell you what you better do first. You better keep Wayne locked up safe."

"I can't hold him much longer," Goodloe said. "Unless he confesses."

Kirxy pushed him from behind, and at the edge of the woods the dogs tensed. Goodloe backed away, raising his pistol, the grave between them.

"You crazy, Kirxy? You been locked in that store too long?"

"Goodloe," Kirxy gasped. The cotton in his left ear had come out and suddenly air was roaring through his head. "Even you can't be this stupid. You let that boy out and he's that cold-blooded fucker's next target —"

"Target, Kirxy? Shit. Ain't nothing to prove anybody killed them dern boys. This one snake-bit, you said so yourself. That other one blowing himself up. Them dern Gateses has fished with dynamite their whole life. You oughta know that — you the one gets it for 'em." He narrowed his eyes. "You're about neck deep in this thing, you know. And I don't mean just lying to protect them boys, neither. I mean selling explosives illegally, to minors, Kirxy."

"I don't give a shit if I am!" Kirxy yelled. "Two dead boys in two days and you're worried about dynamite? You oughta be out there looking for Frank David."

"He ain't supposed to be here for another week or two," Goodloe said. "Paperwork —"

He fired his pistol then. Kirxy jumped, but the sheriff was looking past him, and when Kirxy followed his eyes he saw the dog that had been creeping in. It lay slumped in the mud, a hind leg kicking, blood coloring the water around it.

Goodloe backed away, smoke curling from the barrel of his pistol.

Around them the other dogs circled, heads low, moving sideways, the hair on their spines sticking up.

"Let's argue about this in the truck," Goodloe said.

At the store Kirxy put out the OPEN sign. He sat in his chair with his coffee and a cigarette. He'd read the same page three times when it occurred to him to phone Montgomery and get Frank David's office on the line. It took a few calls, but he soon got the number and dialed. The snippy young woman who answered told Kirxy that yes, Mr. David was supposed to take over the Lower Peach Tree district, but that he wasn't starting until next week, she thought.

Where was he now? Kirxy wanted to know.

"Florida?" she said. "No, Louisiana. Fishing." No sir, he couldn't be reached. He preferred his vacations private.

Kirxy slammed down the phone. He lit another cigarette and tried to think.

It was just a matter, he decided, of keeping Wayne alive until Frank David took over the district. There were probably other game wardens who'd testify that Frank David was over in Louisiana fishing right now. But once the son-of-a-bitch officially moved here, he'd have motive and his alibi wouldn't be as strong. If Wayne turned up dead, Frank David would be the chief suspect.

Kirxy inhaled smoke deeply and tried to imagine how Frank David would think. How he would act. The noise he would make or not make as he went through the woods. What he would say if you happened upon him. Or he upon you. What he would do if he came into the store. Certainly he wasn't the creature Kirxy had created to scare the boys, not some wild ghostly thing. He was just a man who'd had a hard life and grown bitter and angry. A man who chose to uphold the law because breaking it was no challenge. A man with no obligation to any other men or a family. Just to himself and his job. To some goddamn game warden code. His job was to protect the wild things the law had deemed worthy: dove, duck, owls, hawks, turkeys, alligators, squirrels, coons and deer. But how did the Gates boys fall into the category of trash animal — wildcats or possums or armadillos, snapping turtles, snakes? Things you could kill anytime, run over in your truck and not even look at in your mirror to see dying behind you? Christ. Why couldn't Frank David see that he, more than a match for the boys, was of their breed?

Kirxy drove to the highway. The big thirty-aught-six he hadn't touched in years was on the seat next to him, and as he steered he pushed cartridges into the clip, then shoved the clip into the gun's underbelly. He pulled the lever that injected a cartridge into the chamber and took a long drink of whiskey to wash down three of the pills that helped dull the ache in his knees, and the one in his gut.

It was almost dark when he arrived at the edge of a large field. He parked facing the grass. This was a place a few hundred yards from a fairly well-traveled blacktop, a spot no sane poacher would dare use. There were already two or three deer creeping into the open from the woods across the field. They came to eat the tall grass, looking up only when a car passed, their ears swiveling, jaws frozen, sprigs of grass twitching in their lips like the legs of insects.

Kirxy sat watching. He sipped his whiskey and lit a cigarette with a trembling hand. Both truck doors were locked and he knew this was a very stupid thing he was doing. Several times he told himself to go home, let things unfold as they would. Then he saw the faces of the two dead boys. And the face of the live one.

When Boo had killed himself, the oldest two had barely been teenagers, but it was twelve-year-old Wayne who'd found him. That truck still had windows then, and the back windshield had been sprayed red with blood. Flies had gathered at the top of the truck in what Wayne discovered was a twenty-two caliber hole. Kirxy frowned, thinking of it. Boo's hat still on his head, a small hole through the hat, too. The back of the truck was full of wood Boo'd been cutting, and the three boys had unloaded the wood and stacked it neatly beside the road. Kirxy shifted in his seat, imagining the boys pushing that truck for two miles over dirt roads, somehow finding the leverage or whatever, the goddamn strength, to get it home. To pull their father from inside and bury him. To clean out the truck. Kirxy shuddered and thought of Frank David, then made himself think of his wife instead. He rubbed his biceps and watched the shadows creep across the field, the treeline dimming, beginning to disappear.

Soon it was full dark. He unscrewed the interior light bulb from the ceiling, pushed the door lock up quietly. Holding his breath, he opened the door. Outside, he propped the rifle on the side mirror, flicked the safety off. He reached through the window, felt along the dash for the headlight switch, pulled it.

The field blazed with the eyes of deer — red hovering dots staring back at him. Kirxy aimed and squeezed the trigger at the first pair of eyes. Not waiting to see if he'd hit the deer, he moved the gun to another pair. He'd gotten off five shots before the eyes began to vanish. When the last echo from the gun faded, at least three deer lay dead or wounded in the glow of his headlights. One doe bleated weakly and bleated again. Kirxy coughed and took the gun back into the truck, closed the door and reloaded in the dark. Then he waited. The doe kept bleating and things in the woods took shape, detached and whisked toward Kirxy over the grass like spooks. And the little noises. Things like footsteps. And the stories. Frank David appearing in the bed of somebody's *moving* truck and punching through the back glass, grabbing and breaking the driver's arm. Leaping from the truck and watching while it wrecked.

"Quit it," Kirxy croaked. "You damn schoolgirl."

Several more times that night he summoned his nerve and flicked on the headlights, firing at any eyes he saw or firing at nothing. When he finally fell asleep at two A.M., his body numb with painkillers and whiskey, he dreamed of his wife on the day of her first miscarriage. The way the nurses couldn't find the vein in her arm, how they'd kept trying with the needle, the way she'd cried and held his fingers tightly, like a woman giving birth.

He started awake, terrified, as if he'd fallen asleep driving.

Caring less for silence, he stumbled from the truck and flicked on
the lights and fired at the eyes, though now they were doubling up,
floating in the air. He lowered the gun and for no good reason found
himself thinking of a time when he'd tried fly fishing, standing in his
yard with his wife watching from the porch, *Tarzan of the Apes* in her
lap, him whipping the line in the air, showing off, and then the strange
pulling you get when you catch a fish, Betty jumping to her feet, the
book falling and her yelling that he'd caught a bat, for heaven's sake,
a *bat!*

He climbed back into the truck. His hands shook so hard he had
trouble getting the door locked. He bowed his head, missing her so
much that he cried, softly, for a long time.

Dawn found him staring at a field littered with dead does, yearlings
and fawns. One of the deer, only wounded, tried to crawl toward the
safety of the trees. Kirxy got out of the truck and vomited colorless water, then stood looking around at the foggy morning. He lifted his rifle
and limped into the grass in the drizzle and, a quick hip shot, put the
deer out of its misery.

He was sitting on the open tailgate trying to light a cigarette when
Goodloe and a deputy passed in their Blazer and stopped.

The sheriff stepped out, signaling for the deputy to stay put. He sat
beside Kirxy on the tailgate, the truck dipping with his weight. His
stomach was growling and he patted it absently.

"You old fool," Goodloe said, staring at Kirxy and then at the field.
"You figured to make Frank David show himself?" He shook his head.
"Good Lord almighty, Kirxy. What'll it take to prove to you there ain't
no damn game warden out there? Not yet, anyhow."

Kirxy didn't answer. Goodloe went to the Blazer and told the deputy
to pick him up at Kirxy's store. Then he helped the old man into the
passenger seat and went around and got in the driver's side. He took the
rifle and unloaded it, put its clip in his pocket.

"We'll talk about them deer later," he said. "Now I'd better get you
back."

They'd gone a silent mile when Kirxy said, "Would you mind running me by Esther's?"

Goodloe shrugged and turned that way. His stomach made a stran-
gling noise. The rain and wind were picking up, rocking the truck. The
sheriff took a bottle of whiskey from his pocket. "Medicinal," he said,
handing the bottle to Kirxy. "It's just been two freak accidents, is all,
Kirxy. I've seen some strange shit, a lot stranger than this. Them Gateses

is just a unlucky bunch. Period. I ain't one to go believing in curses, but I swear to God if they ain't downright snake-bit."

Soon Goodloe had parked in front of Esther's and they sat waiting for the rain to slack. Kirxy rubbed his knees and looked out the windows where the trees were half submerged in the rising floodwaters.

"They say old Esther has her a root cellar," Goodloe said, taking a sip. "Shit. I expect it's full of water this time of year. She's probably got cottonmouths wrapped around her plumbing." He shuddered and offered the bottle. Kirxy took it and sipped. He gave it back and Goodloe took it and drank then drank again. "Lord if that don't hit the spot.

"When I was in the service," Goodloe went on, "over in Thailand? They had them little bitty snakes, them banded kraits. Poison as cobras, what they told us. Used to hide up under the commode lid. Every time you took you a shit, you had to lift up the lid, see was one there." He drank. "Yep. It was many a time I kicked one off in the water, flushed it down."

"Wait here," Kirxy said. He opened his door, his pants leg darkening as the rain poured in, cold as needles. He set his knee out deliberately, planted his cane in the mud and pulled himself up, stood in water to his ankles. He limped across the yard with his hand blocking the rain. There were two chickens on the front porch, their feathers fluffed out so that they looked strange, menacing. Kirxy climbed the porch steps with the pain so strong in his knees that stars popped near his face by the time he reached the top. He leaned against the house, breathing hard. Touched himself at the throat where a tie might've gone. Then he rapped gently with the hook of his cane. The door opened immediately. Dark inside. She stood there, looking at him.

"How come you don't ever stop by the store anymore?" he asked.

She folded her arms.

"Scott's dead," he said.

"I heard," Esther said. "And I'm leaving. Fuck this place and every one of you."

She closed the door and Kirxy would never see her again.

At the store, Goodloe nodded for the deputy to stay in the Blazer, then he took Kirxy by the elbow and helped him up the steps. He unlocked the door for him and held his hand as the old man sank in his chair.

"Want these boots off?" Goodloe asked, spreading a blanket over Kirxy's lap.

He bent and unlaced the left, then the right.

"Pick up your foot. Now the other one."

He set the wet boots by the stove.

"It's a little damp in here. I'll light this thing."

He found a box of kitchen matches on a shelf under the counter among the glass figurines Kirxy's wife had collected. The little deer. The figure skater. The unicorn. Goodloe got a fire going in the stove and stood warming the backs of his legs.

"I'll bring Wayne by a little later," he said, but Kirxy didn't seem to hear.

Goodloe sat in his office with his feet on his desk, rolling a cartridge between his fingers. Despite himself, he was beginning to think Kirxy might be right. Maybe Frank David was out there on the prowl. He stood, put on his pistol belt and walked to the back, pushed open the swinging door and had Roy buzz him through. So far he'd had zero luck getting anything out of Wayne. The boy just sat in his cell wrapped in a blanket, not talking to anybody. Goodloe had told him about his brother's death, and he'd seen no emotion cross the boy's face. Goodloe figured that it wasn't this youngest one who'd killed that game warden, it'd probably been the others. He knew that this boy wasn't carrying a full cylinder, the way he never talked, but he had most likely been a witness. He'd been considering calling in the state psychologist from the Searcy Mental Hospital to give the boy an evaluation.

"Come on," Goodloe said, stopping by Wayne's cell. "I'm fixing to put your talent to some good use."

He kept the boy cuffed as the deputy drove them toward the trestle.

"Turn your head, Dave," Goodloe said, handing Wayne a pint of Old Crow. The boy took it in both hands and unscrewed the lid, began to drink too fast.

"Slow down there, partner," Goodloe said, taking back the bottle. "You need to be alert."

Soon they stood near the trestle, gazing at the flat shapes of the boat on the bank. Wayne knelt and examined the ground. The deputy came up and started to say something, but Goodloe motioned for quiet.

"Just like a goddern bloodhound," he whispered. "Maybe I ought give him your job."

"Reckon what he's after?" the deputy asked.

Wayne scrabbled up the trestle, and the two men followed. The boy walked slowly over the rails, examining the spaces between the cross ties. He stopped, bent down and peered at something. Picked it up.

"What you got there, boy?" Goodloe called, going and squatting beside him. He took a sip of Old Crow.

When Wayne hit him, two-handed, the bottle flew one way and Goodloe the other. Both landed in the river, Goodloe with his hand clapped to his head to keep his hat on. He came up immediately, bobbing and sputtering. On the trestle, the deputy tackled Wayne and they went down fighting on the cross ties. Below, Goodloe dredged himself out of the water. He came ashore dripping and tugged his pistol from its holster. He held it up so that a thin trickle of orange water fell. He took off his hat and looked up to see the deputy disappear belly-first into the face of the river.

Wayne ran down the track, toward the swamp. The deputy came boiling ashore. He had his own pistol drawn and was looking around vengefully.

Goodloe climbed the trestle in time to see Wayne disappear into the woods. The sheriff chased him for a while, ducking limbs and vines, but stopped, breathing hard. The deputy passed him.

Wayne circled back through the woods and went quickly over the soft ground, scrambling up the sides of hills and sliding down the other sides. Two hollows over, he heard the deputy heading in the wrong direction. Wayne slowed a little and just trotted for a long time in the rain, the cuffs rubbing his wrists raw. He stopped once and looked at what he'd been carrying in one hand: a match, limp and black now with water, nearly dissolved. He stood looking at the trees around him, the hanging Spanish moss and the cypress knees rising from the stagnant creek to his left.

The hair on the back of his neck rose. He knelt, tilting his head, closing his eyes, and listened. He heard the rain, heard it hit leaves and wood and heard the puddles lapping at their tiny banks, but beyond those sounds there were other muffled noises. A mockingbird mocking a blue jay. A squirrel barking and another answering. The deputy falling, a quarter mile away. Then another sound, this one close. A match striking. Wayne began to run before opening his eyes and crashed into a tree. He rolled and ran again, tearing through limbs and briars. He leapt small creeks and slipped and got up and kept running. At every turn he expected Frank David, and he was near tears when he finally stumbled into his family graveyard.

The first thing he saw was that Kent had been dug up. Wooden stakes surrounded the hole and fenced it in with yellow tape that had words on it. Wayne approached slowly, hugging himself. Something floated in the grave. With his heart pounding, he peered inside. A dog.

Wary of the trees behind him, he crept toward their backyard, stopping at the edge. He crouched and blew into his hands to warm his cheeks. He gazed at the dark windows of their cabin, then circled the house, keeping to the woods. He saw the pine tree with the low limb they used for stringing up larger animals to clean, the rusty chain hanging and the iron pipe they stuck through the back legs of a deer or the rare wild pig. Kent and Scott had usually done the cleaning while Wayne fed the guts to their dogs and tried to keep them from fighting.

And there, past the tree, lay the rest of the dogs. Shot dead. Partially eaten. Buzzards standing in the mud, staring boldly at him with their heads bloody and their beaks open. Their tongues red.

It was dark when Kirxy woke in his chair, he'd heard the door creak. Someone stood there, and the storekeeper was afraid until he smelled the river.

"Hey, boy," he said.

Wayne ate two cans of potted meat with his fingers and a candy bar and a box of saltines. Kirxy gave him a Coke from the red cooler and he drank it and took another one while Kirxy got a hacksaw from the rack of tools behind the counter. He slipped the cardboard wrapping off and nodded for Wayne to sit. The storekeeper pulled up another chair and faced the boy and began sawing the handcuff chain. The match dropped out of Wayne's hand but neither saw it. Wayne sat with his head down and his palms up, his wrists on his knees, breathing heavily, while Kirxy worked and the silver shavings accumulated in a pile between their boots. The boy didn't lift his head the entire time, and he'd been asleep for quite a while when Kirxy finally sawed through. The old man rose, flexing his sore hands, and got a blanket from a shelf. He unfolded it, shook out the dust and spread it over Wayne. He went to the door and turned the dead bolt.

The phone rang later. It was Goodloe, asking about the boy and telling what had happened.

Kirxy laughed. "You been lost all this time, Sugarbaby?"

"That I have," Goodloe said, "and we still ain't found old Dave yet."

For a week they stayed there together. Kirxy could barely walk now, and at times the pain in his side was worse than ever. He put the boy to work, sweeping, dusting and scrubbing the shelves. He had Wayne pull a table next to his chair, and Kirxy did something he hadn't done in years: took inventory. With the boy's help, he counted and ledgered each item, marking them in his long green book. The back shelf contained canned soups, vegetables, sardines and tins of meat. Many of the cans were so old that the labels flaked off in Kirxy's hand, and so they were unmarked when Wayne replaced them in the rings they'd made not only in the dust but on the wood itself. In the back of that last shelf, Wayne discovered four tins of Underwood Deviled Ham, and as their labels fell away at Kirxy's touch, he remembered a time when he'd purposely unwrapped the paper from these cans because each label showed several red dancing devils, and some of his Negro customers had refused to buy anything that advertised the devil.

Kirxy now understood that his store was dead, that it no longer provided a service. His Negro customers had stopped coming years before. The same with Esther. For the past few years, except for the rare hunter, he'd been in business for the Gates boys alone. He looked across the room at Wayne, spraying the windows with Windex and wiping at them absently, gazing outside. The boy wore the last of the new denim overalls Kirxy had in stock. Once, when the store had thrived, he'd had many sizes, but for the longest time now the only ones he'd stocked were the boys'.

That night, beneath his standing lamp, Kirxy began again to read his wife's copy of *Tarzan of the Apes* to Wayne. He sipped his whiskey and spoke clearly, to be heard over the rain. When he paused to turn a page, he saw that the boy lay asleep across the row of chairs they'd arranged in the shape of a bed. Looking down through his bifocals, Kirxy flipped to the back of the book to the list of other Tarzan novels — twenty-four in all — and he decided to order them through the mail so Wayne would hear the complete adventures of Tarzan of the Apes.

In the morning, Goodloe called and said that Frank David had officially arrived — the sheriff had witnessed the swearing-in — and he was now this district's game warden.

"Pretty nice fellow," Goodloe said. "Kinda quiet. Polite. He asked me how the fishing was."

Then it's over, Kirxy thought.

A week later, Kirxy told Wayne he had to run some errands in Grove Hill. He'd spent the night before trying to decide whether to take the boy with him but had decided not to, that he couldn't watch him forever. Before he left he gave Wayne his thirty-aught-six and told him to stay put, not to leave for anything. For himself, Kirxy took an old twenty-two bolt action and placed it in the back window rack of his truck. He waved to Wayne and drove off.

He thought that if the boy wanted to run away, it was his own choice. Kirxy owed him the chance, at least.

At the doctor's office the young surgeon frowned and removed his glasses when he told Kirxy that the cancer was advancing, that he'd need to check into the hospital in Mobile immediately. It was way past time. "Just look at your color," the surgeon said. Kirxy stood, thanked the man, put on his hat and limped outside. He went by the post office and placed his order for the Tarzan books. He shopped for supplies in the Dollar Store and the Piggly Wiggly, had the checkout boys put the boxes in the front seat beside him. Coming out of the drugstore, he remembered that it was Saturday, that there'd be chicken fights today. And possible news about Frank David.

At Heflin's, Kirxy paid his five-dollar admission and let Heflin help him to a seat in the bottom of the stands. He poured some whiskey in his coffee and sat studying the crowd. Nobody had mentioned Frank David, but a few old-timers had offered their sympathies on the deaths of Kent and Scott. Down in the pit the Cajuns were back, and during the eighth match — one of the Louisiana whites versus a local red, the tall bald Cajun stooping and circling the tangled birds and licking his lips as his rooster swarmed the other and hooked it, the barn smoky and dark, rain splattering the tin roof — the door swung open.

Instantly the crowd hushed. Feathers settled to the ground. Even the Cajuns knew who he was. He stood at the door, unarmed, his hands on his hips. A wiry man. He lifted his chin and people tried to hide their drinks. His giant ears. The hooked nose. The eyes. Bird handlers reached over their shoulders, pulling at the numbered pieces of masking tape on their backs. The two handlers and the referee in the ring sidled out, leaving the roosters.

For a full minute Frank David stood staring. People stepped out the back door. Climbed out windows. Half naked boys in the rafters were frozen like monkeys hypnotized by a snake.

Frank David's gaze didn't stop on Kirxy but settled instead on the roosters, the white one pecking out the red's eyes. Outside, trucks roared to life, backfiring like gunshots. Kirxy placed his hands on his knees. He rose, turned up his coat collar and flung his coffee out. Frank

David still hadn't looked at him. Kirxy planted his cane and made his way out the back door and through the mud.

Not a person in sight, just tailgates vanishing into the woods.

From inside his truck, Kirxy watched Frank David walk away from the barn and head toward the trees. Now he was just a bow-legged man with white hair. Kirxy felt behind him for the twenty-two rifle with one hand while rolling down the window with the other. He had a little trouble aiming the gun with his shaky nerves. He pulled back the bolt and inserted a cartridge into the chamber. Flicked the safety off. The sight of the rifle wavered between Frank David's shoulders as he walked. As if an old man like Kirxy were nothing to fear. Kirxy ground his teeth: that was why the bastard hadn't come to his deer massacre — an old storekeeper wasn't worth it, wasn't dangerous.

Closing one eye, Kirxy pulled the trigger. He didn't hear the shot, though later he would notice his ears ringing.

Frank David's coat bloomed out to the side and he missed a step. He stopped and put his hand to his lower right side and looked over his shoulder at Kirxy, who was fumbling with the rifle's bolt action. Then Frank David was gone, just wasn't there, there were only the trees, bent in the rain, and shreds of fog in the air. For a moment, Kirxy wondered he'd even seen a man at all, if he'd shot at something out of his own imagination, if the cancer that had started in his pancreas had inched up along his spine into his brain and was deceiving him, forming men out of the air and walking them across fields, giving them hands and eyes and the power to disappear.

From inside the barn, a rooster crowed. Kirxy remembered Wayne. He hung the rifle in its rack and started his truck, gunned the engine. He banged over the field, flattening saplings and a fence, and though he couldn't feel his feet, he drove very fast.

Not until two days later, in the VA hospital in Mobile, would Kirxy finally begin to piece it all together. Parts of that afternoon were patchy and hard to remember: shooting Frank David, going back to the store and finding it empty, no sign of a struggle, the thirty-aught-six gone, as if Wayne had walked out on his own and taken the gun. Kirxy could remember getting back into his truck. He'd planned to drive to Grove Hill — the courthouse, the game warden's office — and find Frank David, but somewhere along the way he passed out behind the wheel and veered off the road into a ditch. He barely remembered the rescue workers and the sirens. Goodloe himself pulled Kirby out.

Later that night two coon hunters had stumbled across Wayne, wandering along the river, his face and shirt covered in blood, the thirty-ought-six nowhere to be found.

When Goodloe told the semiconscious Kirxy what happened, the storekeeper turned silently to the window, where he saw only the reflected face of an old, failed, dying man.

And later still, in the warm haze of morphine, Kirxy lowered his eyelids and let his imagination unravel and retwine the mystery of Frank David: it was as if Frank David himself appeared in the chair where Goodloe had sat, as if the game warden broke the seal on a bottle of Jim Beam and leaned forward on his elbows and touched the bottle to Kirxy's cracked lips and whispered to him a story about boots going over land and not making a sound, about rain washing the blood trail away even as the boots passed. About a tired old game warden taking his hand out of his coat and seeing the blood from Kirxy's bullet there, feeling it trickle down his side. About the boy in the back of the game warden's truck, handcuffed, gagged, blindfolded. About driving carefully through deep ruts in the road. Stopping behind Esther's empty house and carrying the kicking boy inside on his shoulder.

When the blindfold is removed, Wayne has trouble focusing but knows where he is because of her smell. Bacon and soap. Cigarettes, dust. Frank David holds what looks like a pillowcase. He comes across the room and puts the pillowcase down. He rubs his eyes and sits on the bed beside Wayne. He opens a book of matches and lights a cigarette. Holds the filtered end to Wayne's lips, but the boy doesn't inhale. Frank David puts the cigarette in his own lips, the embers glow. Then he drops it on the floor, crushes it out with his boot. Picks up the butt and slips it into his shirt pocket. He puts his hand over the boy's watery eyes, the skin of his palm dry and hard. Cool. Faint smell of blood. He moves his fingers over Wayne's nose, lips, chin. Stops at his throat and holds the boy tightly but not painfully. In a strange way Wayne can't understand, he finds it reassuring. His thudding heart slows. Something is struggling beside his shoulder and Frank David takes the thing from the bag. Now the smell in the room changes. Wayne begins to thrash and whip his head from side to side.

"Goddamn, son," Frank David whispers. "I hate to civilize you."

Goodloe began going to the veteran's hospital in Mobile once a week. He brought Kirxy cigarettes from his store. There weren't any private rooms available in the hospital, and the beds around the storekeeper were filled with dying ex-soldiers who never talked, but Kirxy was beside a window and Goodloe would raise the glass and prop it open with a novel. They smoked together and drank whiskey from paper cups, listening for nurses.

It was the tall mean one.

"One more time, goddamn it," she said, coming out of nowhere and plucking the cigarettes from their lips so quickly they were still puckered.

Sometimes Goodloe would push Kirxy down the hall when they could get a wheelchair, the IV rack attached by a stainless steel contraption with a black handle the shape of a flower. They would go to the elevator and ride down three floors to a covered area where people smoked and talked about the weather. There were nurses and black cafeteria workers in white uniforms and hair nets and people visiting other people and a few patients. Occasionally in the halls they'd see some mean old fart Kirxy knew and they'd talk about hospital food or chicken fighting. Or the fact that Frank David had surprised everyone by deciding to retire after only a month of quiet duty, that the new game warden was from Texas. And a nigger to boot.

Then Goodloe would wheel Kirxy back along a long window, out of which you could see the tops of oak trees.

On one visit, Goodloe told Kirxy they'd taken Wayne out of intensive care. Three weeks later he said the boy'd been discharged.

"I give him a ride to the store," Goodloe said. This was in late May and Kirxy was a yellow skeleton with hands that shook.

"I'll stop by and check on him every evening," Goodloe went on. "He'll be okay, the doctor says. Just needs to keep them bandages changed. I can do that, I reckon."

They were quiet then, for a time, just the coughs of the dying men and the soft swishing of nurses' thighs and the hum of IV machines.

"Goodloe," Kirxy whispered, "I'd like you to help me with something."

The sheriff leaned in to hear, an unlit cigarette behind his ear like a pencil.

Kirxy's tongue was white and cracked, his breath awful. "I'd like to change my will," he said, "make the boy beneficiary."

"All right," Goodloe said.

"I'm obliged," whispered Kirxy. He closed his eyes.

Near the end he was delirious. He said he saw a little black creature at the foot of his bed. Said it had him by the toe. In surprising fits of strength, he would throw his water pitcher at it, or his box of tissues, or the *Reader's Digest*. Restraints were called for. His coma was a relief to everyone, and he died quietly in the night.

In Kirxy's chair in the store, Wayne didn't seem to hear Goodloe's questions. The sheriff had done some looking in the Grove Hill public library — "research" was the trendy word — and discovered that one species of cobra spat venom at its victim's eyes, but there weren't such snakes in southern Alabama. Anyway, the hospital lab had confirmed that it was the venom of a cottonmouth that had blinded Wayne. The question, of course, was who had put the venom in his eyes. Goodloe shuddered to think of it, how they'd found Wayne staggering about, howling in pain, bleeding from his tear ducts, the skin around his eye sockets dissolving, exposing the white ridges of his skull.

In the investigation, several local blacks, including Euphrates Morrisette, stated to Goodloe that the youngest Gates boy and his two dead brothers had molested Euphrates' stepdaughter in her own house. There was a rumor that several black men dressed in white sheets with pillowcases for hoods had caught and punished Wayne as he lurked along the river, peeping in folks' windows and doing unwholesome things to himself. Others suggested that the conjure woman had cast a spell on the Gateses, that she'd summoned a swamp demon to chase them to hell. And still others attributed the happenings to Frank David. There were a few occurrences of violence between some of the local whites and the blacks — some fires, a broken jaw — but soon it died down and Goodloe filed the deaths of Kent and Scott Gates as accidental.

But he listed Wayne's blinding as unsolved. The snake venom had bleached his pupils white, and the skin around his eye sockets had required grafts. The doctors had had to use skin from his buttocks, and because his buttocks were hairy, the skin around his eyes grew hair, too.

In the years to come, the loggers who clear-cut the land along the river would occasionally stop in the store, less from a need to buy something than from a curiosity to see the hermit with the milky, hairy eyes. The store smelled horrible, like the inside of a bear's mouth, and dust lay thick and soft on the shelves. Because they had come in, the loggers felt obligated to buy something, but every item was moldy or stale beyond belief, except for the things in cans, which were all unlabeled so they never knew what they'd get. Nothing was marked as to price, either, and the blind man wouldn't talk. He just sat by the stove. So the loggers paid more (some less) than what they thought a can was worth, leaving the money on the counter by the telephone, which hadn't been connected in years. When plumper, grayer Goodloe came by on the occasional evening, he'd take the bills and coins and put them in Kirxy's cash drawer. He was no longer sheriff, having lost several elections back to one of his deputies, Roy or Dave. He still wore the same khaki uniform, but now he drove a Lance truck, his route including the hospitals in the county, and, every other month, the prison.

"Dern, boy," he once cracked to Wayne. "This store's doing a better business now than it ever has. You sure you don't want a cookie rack?"

When Goodloe left, Wayne listened to the rattle of the truck as it faded. "Sugarbaby," he whispered.

And many a night for years after, until his own death in his sleep, Wayne would rise from the chair and move across the floor, taking Kirxy's cane from where it stood by the coatrack. He would go outside, down the stairs like a man who could see, his beard nearly to his chest, and he would walk soundlessly the length of the building, knowing the woods even better now as he crept down the rain-rutted gully side toward the river whose smell never left the caves of his nostrils and the roof of his mouth. At the riverbank, he would stop and sit with his back against a small pine, and lifting his white eyes to the sky, he would listen to the clicks and hum and thrattle of the woods, seeking out each noise as its source and imagining it: an acorn nodding, detaching, its thin ricochet and the way it settled into the leaves. A bullfrog's bubbling throat and the things it said. The trickle of the river over rocks and around the bases of cattails and cypress knees and through the wet hanging roots of trees. And then another sound, familiar. The soft, precise footsteps of Frank David. Downwind. Not coming closer, not going away. Circling. The striking of a match and the sizzle of ember and the fall of ash. The ascent of smoke. A strange and terrifying comfort for the rest of Wayne Gates's life.

1999

DENNIS LEHANE

···

Running Out of Dog

THIS THING with Blue and the dogs and Elgin Bern happened a while back, a few years after some of our boys — like Elgin Bern and Cal Sears — came back from Vietnam, and a lot of others — like Eddie Vorey and Carl Joe Carol, the Stewart cousins — didn't. We don't know how it worked in other towns, but that war put something secret in our boys who returned. Something quiet and untouchable. You sensed they knew things they'd never say, did things on the sly you'd never discover. Great card players, those boys, able to bluff with the best, let no joy show in their face no matter what they were holding.

A small town is a hard place to keep a secret, and a small Southern town with all that heat and all those open windows is an even harder place than most. But those boys who came back from overseas, they seemed to have mastered the trick of privacy. And the way it's always been in this town, you get a sizable crop of young, hard men coming up at the same time, they sort of set the tone.

So, not long after the war, we were a quieter town, a less trusting one (or so some of us seemed to think), and that's right when tobacco money and textile money reached a sort of critical mass and created construction money and pretty soon there was talk that our small town should maybe get a little bigger, maybe build something that would bring in more tourist dollars than we'd been getting from fireworks and pecans.

That's when some folks came up with this Eden Falls idea — a big car-nival-type park with roller coasters and water slides and such. Why should all those Yankees spend all their money in Florida? South Carolina had sun too. Had golf courses and grapefruit and no end of KOA campgrounds.

So now a little town called Eden was going to have Eden Falls. We were

going to be on the map, people said. We were going to be in all the bro-
chures. We were small now, people said, but just you wait. Just you wait.

And that's how things stood back then, the year Perkin and Jewel Lut's
marriage hit a few bumps and Elgin Bern took up with Shelley Briggs and
no one seemed able to hold on to their dogs.

The problem with dogs in Eden, South Carolina, was that the owners
who bred them bred a lot of them. Or they allowed them to run free
where they met up with other dogs of opposite gender and achieved the
same result. This wouldn't have been so bad if Eden weren't so close to
I-95, and if the dogs weren't in the habit of bolting into traffic and
fucking up the bumpers of potential tourists.

The mayor, Big Bobby Vargas, went to a mayoral conference up in
Beaufort, where the governor made a surprise appearance to tell everyone how pissed off he was about this dog thing. Lot of money being
poured into Eden these days, the governor said, lot of steps being taken
to change her image, and he for one would be god-damned if a bunch
of misbehaving canines was going to mess all that up.

"Boys," he'd said, looking Big Bobby Vargas dead in the eye, "they're
starting to call this state the Devil's Kennel 'cause of all them pooch
corpses along the interstate. And I don't know about you all, but I don't
think that's a real pretty name."

Big Bobby told Elgin and Blue he'd never heard anyone call it the
Devil's Kennel in his life. Heard a lot worse, sure, but never that. Big
Bobby said the governor was full of shit. But, being the governor and
all, he was sort of entitled.

The dogs in Eden had been a problem going back to the twenties and
a part-time breeder named J. Mallon Ellenburg who, if his arms weren't
up to their elbows in the guts of the tractors and combines he repaired
for a living, was usually lashing out at something — his family when
they weren't quick enough, his dogs when the family was. J. Mallon
Ellenburg's dogs were mixed breeds and mongrels and they ran in
packs, as did their offspring, and several generations later, those packs
still moved through the Eden night like wolves, their bodies stripped to
muscle and gristle, tense and angry, growling in the dark at J. Mallon
Ellenburg's ghost.

Big Bobby went to the trouble of measuring exactly how much of 95
crossed through Eden, and he came up with 2.8 miles. Not much really,
but still an average of .74 dog a day or 4.9 dogs a week. Big Bobby

wanted the rest of the state funds the governor was going to be doling out at year's end, and if that meant getting rid of five dogs a week, give or take, then that's what was going to get done.

"On the QT," he said to Elgin and Blue, "on the QT, what we going to do, boys, is set up in some trees and shoot every canine who gets within barking distance of that interstate."

Elgin didn't much like this "we" stuff. First place, Big Bobby'd said "we" that time in Double O's four years ago. This was before he'd become mayor, when he was nothing more than a county tax assessor who shot pool at Double O's every other night, same as Elgin and Blue. But one night, after Harlan and Chub Uke had roughed him up over a matter of some pocket change, and knowing that neither Elgin nor Blue was too fond of the Uke family either, Big Bobby'd said, "We going to settle those boys' asses tonight," and started running his mouth the minute the brothers entered the bar.

Time the smoke cleared, Blue had a broken hand, Harlan and Chub were curled up on the floor, and Elgin's lip was busted. Big Bobby, meanwhile, was hiding under the pool table, and Cal Sears was asking who was going to pay for the pool stick Elgin had snapped across the back of Chub's head.

So Elgin heard Mayor Big Bobby saying "we" and remembered the ten dollars it had cost him for that pool stick, and he said, "No, sir, you can count me out this particular enterprise."

Big Bobby looked disappointed. Elgin was a veteran of a foreign war, former Marine, a marksman. "Shit," Big Bobby said, "what good are you, you don't use the skills Uncle Sam spent good money teaching you?"

Elgin shrugged. "Damn, Bobby. I guess not much."

But Blue kept his hand in, as both Big Bobby and Elgin knew he would. All the job required was a guy didn't mind sitting in a tree who liked to shoot things. Hell, Blue was home.

Elgin didn't have the time to be sitting up in a tree anyway. The past few months, he'd been working like crazy after they'd broke ground at Eden Falls — mixing cement, digging postholes, draining swamp water to shore up the foundation — with the real work still to come. There'd be several more months of drilling and bilging, spreading cement like cake icing, and erecting scaffolding to erect walls to erect facades. There'd be the hump-and-grind of rolling along in the dump trucks and drill trucks, the forklifts and cranes and industrial diggers, until the constant heave and jerk of them drove up his spine or into his kidneys like a corkscrew.

Time to sit up in a tree shooting dogs? Shit. Elgin didn't have time to take a piss some days.

And then on top of all the work, he'd been seeing Drew Briggs's ex-wife, Shelley, lately. Shelley was the receptionist at Perkin Lut's Auto Emporium, and one day Elgin had brought his Impala in for a tire rotation and they'd got to talking. She'd been divorced from Drew over a year, and they waited a couple of months to show respect, but after a while they began showing up at Double O's and down at the IHOP together.

Once they drove clear to Myrtle Beach together for the weekend. People asked them what it was like, and they said, "Just like the postcards." Since the postcards never mentioned the price of a room at the Hilton, Elgin and Shelley didn't mention that all they'd done was drive up and down the beach twice before settling in a motel a bit west in Conway. Nice, though; had a color TV and one of those switches turned the bathroom into a sauna if you let the shower run. They'd started making love in the sauna, finished up on the bed with the steam coiling out from the bathroom and brushing their heels. Afterward, he pushed her hair back off her forehead and looked in her eyes and told her he could get used to this.

She said, "But wouldn't it cost a lot to install a sauna in your trailer?" then waited a full thirty seconds before she smiled.

Elgin liked that about her, the way she let him know he was still just a man after all, always would take himself too seriously, part of his nature. Letting him know she might be around to keep him apprised of that fact every time he did. Keep him from pushing a bullet into the breech of a thirty-aught-six, slamming the bolt home, firing into the flank of some wild dog.

Sometimes, when they'd shut down the site early for the day — if it had rained real heavy and the soil loosened near a foundation, or if supplies were running late — he'd drop by Lut's to see her. She'd smile as if he'd brought her flowers, say, "Caught boozing on the job again?" or some other smartass thing, but it made him feel good, as if something in his chest suddenly realized it was free to breathe.

Before Shelley, Elgin had spent a long time without a woman he could publicly acknowledge as his. He'd gone with Mae Shiller from fifteen to nineteen, but she'd gotten lonely while he was overseas, and he'd returned to find her gone from Eden, married to a boy up in South of the Border, the two of them working a corn-dog concession stand, making a tidy profit, folks said. Elgin dated some, but it took him a while to get over Mae, to get over the loss of something he'd always expected to have, the sound of her laugh and an image of her stepping naked from Cooper's Lake, her pale flesh beaded with water, having been the things that got Elgin through the jungle, through the heat, through the ticking of his own death he'd heard in his ears every night he'd been over there.

About a year after he'd come home, Jewel Lut had come to visit her mother, who still lived in the trailer park where Jewel had grown up with Elgin and Blue, where Elgin still lived. On her way out, she'd dropped by Elgin's and they'd sat out front of his trailer in some folding chairs, had a few drinks, talked about old times. He told her a bit about Vietnam, and she told him a bit about marriage. How it wasn't what you expected, how Perkin Lut might know a lot of things but he didn't know a damn sight about having fun.

There was something about Jewel Lut that sank into men's flesh the way heat did. It wasn't just that she was pretty, had a beautiful body, moved in a loose, languid way that made you picture her naked no matter what she was wearing. No, there was more to it. Jewel, never the brightest girl in town and not even the most charming, had something in her eyes that none of the women Elgin had ever met had; it was a capacity for living, for taking moments — no matter how small or inconsequential — and squeezing every last thing you could out of them. Jewel gobbled up life, dove into it like it was a cool pond cut in the shade of a mountain on the hottest day of the year.

That look in her eyes — the one that never left — said, Let's have fun, goddammit. Let's eat. Now.

She and Elgin hadn't been stupid enough to do anything that night, not even after Elgin caught that look in her eyes, saw it was directed at him, saw she wanted to eat.

Elgin knew how small Eden was, how its people loved to insinuate and pry and talk. So he and Jewel worked it out, a once-a-week thing mostly that happened down in Carlyle, at a small cabin that had been in Elgin's family since before the War Between the States. There, Elgin and Jewel were free to partake of each other, squeeze and bite and swallow and inhale each other, to make love in the lake, on the porch, in the tiny kitchen.

They hardly ever talked, and when they did it was about nothing at all, really — the decline in quality of the meat at Billy's Butcher Shop, rumors that parking meters were going to be installed in front of the courthouse, if McGarrett and the rest of Five-O would ever put the cuffs on Wo Fat.

There was an unspoken understanding that he was free to date any woman he chose and that she'd never leave Perkin Lut. And that was just fine. This wasn't about love; it was about appetite.

Sometimes, Elgin would see her in town or hear Blue speak about her in that puppy-dog-love way he'd been speaking about her since high school, and he'd find himself surprised by the realization that he slept with this woman. That no one knew. That it could go on forever, if both of them remained careful, vigilant against the wrong look, the wrong tone in their voices when they spoke in public.

He couldn't entirely put his finger on what need she satisfied, only that he needed her in that lakefront cabin once a week, that it had something to do with walking out of the jungle alive, with the ticking of his own death he'd heard for a full year. Jewel was somehow reward for that, a fringe benefit. To be naked and spent with her lying atop him and seeing that look in her eyes that said she was ready to go again, ready to gobble him up like oxygen. He'd earned that by shooting at shapes in the night, pressed against those damp foxhole walls that never stayed shored up for long, only to come home to a woman who couldn't wait, who'd discarded him as easily as she would a once-favored doll she'd grown beyond, looked back upon with a wistful mix of nostalgia and disdain.

He'd always told himself that when he found the right woman, his passion for Jewel, his need for those nights at the lake, would disappear. And, truth was, since he'd been with Shelley Briggs, he and Jewel had cooled it. Shelley wasn't Perkin, he told Jewel; she'd figure it out soon enough if he left town once a week, came back with bite marks on his abdomen.

Jewel said, "Fine. We'll get back to it whenever you're ready."

Knowing there'd be a next time, even if Elgin wouldn't admit it to himself.

So Elgin, who'd been so lonely in the year after his discharge, now had two women. Sometimes, he didn't know what to think of that. When you were alone, the happiness of others boiled your insides. Beauty seemed ugly. Laughter seemed evil. The casual grazing of one lover's hand into another was enough to make you want to cut them off at the wrist. *I will never be loved,* you said. *I will never know joy.*

He wondered sometimes how Blue made it through. Blue, who'd

never had a girlfriend he hadn't rented by the half hour. Who was too ugly and small and just plain weird to evoke anything in women but fear or pity. Blue, who'd been carrying a torch for Jewel Lut since long before she married Perkin and kept carrying it with a quiet fever Elgin could only occasionally identify with. Blue, he knew, saw Jewel Lut as a queen, as the only woman who existed for him in Eden, South Carolina. All because she'd been nice to him, pals with him and Elgin, back about a thousand years ago, before sex, before breasts, before Elgin or Blue had even the smallest clue what that thing between their legs was for, before Perkin Lut had come along with his daddy's money and his nice smile and his bullshit stories about how many men he'd have killed in the war if only the draft board had seen fit to let him go.

Blue figured if he was nice enough, kind enough, waited long enough — then one day Jewel would see his decency, need to cling to it.

Elgin never bothered telling Blue that some women didn't want decency. Some women didn't want a nice guy. Some women, and some men too, wanted to get into a bed, turn out the lights, and feast on each other like animals until it hurt to move.

Blue would never guess that Jewel was that kind of woman, because she was always so sweet to him, treated him like a child really, and with every friendly hello she gave him, every pat on the shoulder, every "What you been up to, old bud?" Blue pushed her further and further up the pedestal he'd built in his mind.

"I seen him at the Emporium one time," Shelley told Elgin. "He just come in for no reason anyone understood and sat reading magazines until Jewel came in to see Perkin about something. And Blue, he just stared at her. Just stared at her talking to Perkin in the showroom. When she finally looked back, he stood up and left."

Elgin hated hearing about, talking about, or thinking about Jewel when he was with Shelley. It made him feel unclean and unworthy.

"Crazy love," he said to end the subject.

"Crazy something, babe."

Nights sometimes, Elgin would sit with Shelley in front of his trailer, listen to the cicadas hum through the scrawny pine, smell the night and the rock salt mixed with gravel; the piña colada shampoo Shelley used made him think of Hawaii though he'd never been, and he'd think how their love wasn't crazy love, wasn't burning so fast and furious it'd burn itself out they weren't careful. And that was fine with him. If he could just get his head around this Jewel Lut thing, stop seeing her naked and waiting and looking back over her shoulder at him in the cabin, then he could make something with Shelley. She was worth it. She might not be able to fuck like Jewel, and, truth be told, he didn't laugh as much with her, but Shelley was what you aspired to. A good woman, who'd be a good mother, who'd stick by you when times got tough. Sometimes he'd take her hand in his and hold it for no other reason but the doing of it. She caught him one night, some look in his eyes, maybe the way he tilted his head to look at her small white hand in his big brown one.

She said, "Damn, Elgin, if you ain't simple sometimes." Then she came out of her chair in a rush and straddled him, kissed him as if she were trying to take a piece of him back with her. She said, "Baby, we ain't getting any younger. You know?"

And he knew, somehow, at that moment why some men build families and others shoot dogs. He just wasn't sure where he fit in the equation.

He said, "We ain't, are we?"

Blue had been Elgin's best buddy since either of them could remember, but Elgin had been wondering about it lately. Blue'd always been a little different, something Elgin liked, sure, but there was more to it now. Blue was the kind of guy you never knew if he was quiet because he didn't have anything to say or, because what he had to say was so horrible, he knew enough not to send it out into the atmosphere.

When they'd been kids, growing up in the trailer park, Blue used to be out at all hours because his mother was either entertaining a man or had gone out and forgotten to leave him the key. Back then, Blue had this thing for cockroaches. He'd collect them in a jar, then drop bricks on them to test their resiliency. He told Elgin once, "That's what they are — resilient. Every generation, we have to come up with new ways to kill 'em because they get immune to the poisons we had before." After a while, Blue took to dousing them in gasoline, lighting them up, seeing how resilient they were then.

Elgin's folks told him to stay away from the strange, dirty kid with the white-trash mother, but Elgin felt sorry for Blue. He was half Elgin's size even though they were the same age; you could place your thumb and forefinger around Blue's biceps and meet them on the other side. Elgin hated how Blue seemed to have only two pairs of clothes, both usually dirty, and how sometimes they'd pass his trailer together and hear the animal sounds coming from inside, the grunts and moans, the slapping of flesh. Half the time you couldn't tell if Blue's old lady was in there fucking or fighting. And always the sound of country music mingled in with all that animal noise, Blue's mother and her man of the moment listening to it on the transistor radio she'd given Blue one Christmas.

"*My* fucking radio," Blue said once and shook his small head, the only time Elgin ever saw him react to what went on in that trailer.

Blue was a reader — knew more about science and ecology, about anatomy and blue whales and conversion tables than anyone Elgin knew. Most everyone figured the kid for a mute — hell, he'd been held back twice in fourth grade — but with Elgin he'd sometimes chat up a storm while they puffed smokes together down at the drainage ditch behind the park. He'd talk about whales, how they bore only one child, who they were fiercely protective of, but how if another child was orphaned, a mother whale would take it as her own, protect it as fiercely as she did the one she gave birth to. He told Elgin how sharks never slept, how electrical currents worked, what a depth charge was. Elgin, never much of a talker, just sat and listened, ate it up and waited for more.

The older they got, the more Elgin became Blue's protector, till finally, the year Blue's face exploded with acne, Elgin got in about two fights a day until there was no one left to fight. Everyone knew — they were brothers. And if Elgin didn't get you from the front, Blue was sure to take care of you from behind, like that time a can of acid fell on Roy Hubrist's arm in shop, or the time someone hit Carnell Lewis from behind with a brick, then cut his Achilles tendon with a razor while he lay out cold. Everyone knew it was Blue, even if no one actually saw him do it.

Elgin figured with Roy and Carnell, they'd had it coming. No great loss. It was since Elgin'd come back from Vietnam, though, that he'd noticed some things and kept them to himself, wondered what he was going to do the day he'd know he had to do something.

There was the owl someone had set afire and hung upside down from a telephone wire, the cats who turned up missing in the blocks that surrounded Blue's shack off Route 11. There were the small pink panties Elgin had seen sticking out from under Blue's bed one morning when he'd come to get him for some cleanup work at a site. He'd checked the missing-persons reports for days, but it hadn't come to anything, so he'd just decided Blue had picked them up himself, fed a fantasy or two. He didn't forget, though, couldn't shake the way those panties had curled upward out of the brown dust under Blue's bed, seemed to be pleading for something.

He'd never bothered asking Blue about any of this. That never worked. Blue just shut down at times like that, stared off somewhere as if something you couldn't hear was drowning out your words, something you couldn't see was taking up his line of vision. Blue, floating away on you, until you stopped cluttering up his mind with useless talk.

One Saturday, Elgin went into town with Shelley so she could get her hair done at Martha's Unisex on Main. In Martha's, as Dottie Leeds gave Shelley a shampoo and rinse, Elgin felt like he'd stumbled into a chapel of womanhood. There was Jim Hayder's teenage daughter, Sonny, getting one of those feathered cuts was growing popular these days and several older women who still wore beehives, getting them reset or plastered or whatever they did to keep them up like that. There was Joylene Covens and Lila Sims having their nails done while their husbands golfed and the black maids watched their kids, and Martha and Dottie and Esther and Gertrude and Hayley dancing and flitting, laughing and chattering among the chairs, calling everyone "Honey," and all of them — the young, the old, the rich, and Shelley — kicking back like they did this every day, knew each other more intimately than they did their husbands or children or boyfriends.

When Dottie Leeds looked up from Shelley's head and said, "Elgin, honey, can we get you a sports page or something?" the whole place burst out laughing, Shelley included. Elgin smiled though he didn't feel like it and gave them all a sheepish wave that got a bigger laugh, and he told Shelley he'd be back in a bit and left.

He headed up Main toward the town square, wondering what it was those women seemed to know so effortlessly that completely escaped him, and saw Perkin Lut walking in a circle outside Dexter Isley's Five & Dime. It was one of those days when the wet, white heat was so overpowering that unless you were in Martha's, the one place in town with central air-conditioning, most people stayed inside with their shades down and tried not to move much.

And there was Perkin Lut walking the soles of his shoes into the ground, turning in circles like a little kid trying to make himself dizzy.

Perkin and Elgin had known each other since kindergarten, but Elgin could never remember liking the man much. Perkin's old man, Mance Lut, had pretty much built Eden, and he'd spent a lot of money keeping Perkin out of the war, hid his son up in Chapel Hill, North Carolina, for so many semesters even Perkin couldn't remember what he'd majored in. A lot of men who'd gone overseas and come back hated Perkin for that, as did the families of most of the men who hadn't come back, but that wasn't Elgin's problem with Perkin. Hell, if Elgin'd had the money, he'd have stayed out of that shitty war too.

What Elgin couldn't abide was that there was something in Perkin that protected him from consequence. Something that made him look down on people who paid for their sins, who fell without a safety net to catch them.

It had happened more than once that Elgin had found himself thrusting in and out of Perkin's wife and thinking, Take that, Perkin. Take that.

But this afternoon, Perkin didn't have his salesman's smile or aloof glance. When Elgin stopped by him and said, "Hey, Perkin, how you?" Perkin looked up at him with eyes so wild they seemed about to jump out of their sockets.

"I'm not good, Elgin. Not good."

"What's the matter?"

Perkin nodded to himself several times, looked over Elgin's shoulder. "I'm fixing to do something about that."

"About what?"

"About that." Perkin's jaw gestured over Elgin's shoulder.

Elgin turned around, looked across Main and through the windows of Miller's Laundromat, saw Jewel Lut pulling her clothes from the dryer, saw Blue standing beside her, taking a pair of jeans from the pile and starting to fold. If either of them had looked up and over, they'd have seen Elgin and Perkin Lut easily enough, but Elgin knew they wouldn't. There was an air to the two of them that seemed to block out the rest of the world in that bright Laundromat as easily as it would in a dark bedroom. Blue's lips moved and Jewel laughed, flipped a T-shirt on his head.

"I'm fixing to do something right now," Perkin said.

Elgin looked at him, could see that was a lie, something Perkin was repeating to himself in hopes it would come true. Perkin was successful in business, and for more reasons than just his daddy's money, but he wasn't the kind of man who did things; he was the kind of man who had things done.

Elgin looked across the street again. Blue still had the T-shirt sitting atop his head. He said something else and Jewel covered her mouth with her hand when she laughed.

"Don't you have a washer and dryer at your house, Perkin?"

Perkin rocked back on his heels. "Washer broke. Jewel decides to come in town." He looked at Elgin. "We ain't getting along so well these days. She keeps reading those magazines, Elgin. You know the ones? Talking about liberation, leaving your bra at home, shit like that." He pointed across the street. "Your friend's a problem."

Your friend.

Elgin looked at Perkin, felt a sudden anger he couldn't completely understand, and with it a desire to say, That's my friend and he's talking to my fuck-buddy. Get it, Perkin?

Instead, he just shook his head and left Perkin there, walked across the street to the Laundromat.

Blue took the T-shirt off his head when he saw Elgin enter. A smile, half frozen on his pitted face, died as he blinked into the sunlight blaring through the windows.

Jewel said, "Hey, we got another helper!" She tossed a pair of men's briefs over Blue's head, hit Elgin in the chest with them.

"Hey, Jewel."

"Hey, Elgin. Long time." Her eyes dropped from his, settled on a towel.

Didn't seem like it at the moment to Elgin. Seemed almost as if he'd been out at the lake with her as recently as last night. He could taste her in his mouth, smell her skin damp with a light sweat.

And standing there with Blue, it also seemed like they were all three back in that trailer park, and Jewel hadn't aged a bit. Still wore her red hair long and messy, still dressed in clothes seemed to have been picked up, wrinkled, off her closet floor and nothing fancy about them in the first place, but draped over her body, they were sexier than clothes other rich women bought in New York once a year.

This afternoon, she wore a crinkly, paisley dress that might have been on the pink side once but had faded to a pasty newspaper color after years of washing. Nothing special about it, not too high up her thigh or down her chest, and loose — but something about her body made it appear like she might just ripen right out of it any second.

Elgin handed the briefs to Blue as he joined them at the folding table. For a while, none of them said anything. They picked clothes from the large pile and folded, and the only sound was Jewel whistling.

Then Jewel laughed.

"What?" Blue said.

"Aw, nothing." She shook her head. "Seems like we're just one happy family here, though, don't it?"

Blue looked stunned. He looked at Elgin. He looked at Jewel. He looked at the pair of small, light-blue socks he held in his hands, the monogram *JL* stitched in the cotton. He looked at Jewel again.

"Yeah," he said eventually, and Elgin heard a tremor in his voice he'd never heard before. "Yeah, it does."

Elgin looked up at one of the upper dryer doors. It had been swung out at eye level when the dryer had been emptied. The center of the door was a circle of glass, and Elgin could see Main Street reflected in it, the white posts that supported the wood awning over the Five & Dime, Perkin Lut walking in circles, his head down, heat shimmering in waves up and down Main.

The dog was green.

Blue had used some of the money Big Bobby'd paid him over the past few weeks to upgrade his target scope. The new scope was huge, twice the width of the rifle barrel, and because the days were getting shorter, it was outfitted with a light-amplification device. Elgin had used similar scopes in the jungle, and he'd never liked them, even when they'd saved his life and those of his platoon, picked up Charlie coming through the dense flora like icy gray ghosts. Night scopes — or LADs as they'd called them over there — were just plain unnatural, and Elgin always felt like he was looking through a telescope from the bottom of a lake. He had no idea where Blue would have gotten one, but hunters in Eden had been showing up with all sorts of weird Marine or army surplus shit these last few years; Elgin had even heard of a hunting party using grenades to scare up fish — blowing 'em up into the boat already half cooked, all you had to do was scale 'em.

The dog was green, the highway was beige, the top of the tree line was yellow, and the trunks were the color of army fatigues.

Blue said, "What you think?"

They were up in the tree house Blue'd built. Nice wood, two lawn chairs, a tarp hanging from the branch overhead, a cooler filled with Coors. Blue'd built a railing across the front, perfect for resting your elbows when you took aim. Along the tree trunk, he'd mounted a huge klieg light plugged to a portable generator, because while it was illegal to "shine" deer, nobody'd ever said anything about shining wild dogs. Blue was definitely home.

Elgin shrugged. Just like in the jungle, he wasn't sure he was meant to see the world this way — faded to the shades and textures of old photographs. The dog, too, seemed to sense that it had stepped out of time somehow, into this seaweed circle punched through the landscape. It sniffed the air with a misshapen snout, but the rest of its body was tensed into one tight muscle, leaning forward as if it smelled prey.

Blue said, "You wanna do it?"

The stock felt hard against Elgin's shoulder. The trigger, curled under his index finger, was cold and thick, something about it that itched his finger and the back of his head simultaneously, a voice back there with the itch in his head saying, "Fire."

What you could never talk about down at the bar to people who hadn't been there, to people who wanted to know, was what it had been like firing on human beings, on those icy gray ghosts in the dark jungle. Elgin had been in fourteen battles over the course of his twelve-month tour, and he couldn't say with certainty that he'd ever killed anyone. He'd shot some of those shapes, seen them go down, but never the blood, never their eyes when the bullets hit. It had all been a cluster-fuck of swift and sudden noise and color, an explosion of white lights and tracers, green bush, red fire, screams in the night. And afterward, if it was clear, you walked into the jungle and saw the corpses, wondered if you'd hit this body or that one or any at all.

And the only thing you were sure of was that you were too fucking hot and still — this was the terrible thing, but oddly exhilarating too — deeply afraid.

Elgin lowered Blue's rifle, stared across the interstate, now the color of seashell, at the dark mint tree line. The dog was barely noticeable, a soft dark shape amid other soft dark shapes.

He said, "No, Blue, thanks," and handed him the rifle.

Blue said, "Suit yourself, buddy." He reached behind them and pulled the beaded string on the klieg light. As the white light erupted across the highway and the dog froze, blinking in the brightness, Elgin found himself wondering what the fucking point of a LAD scope was when you were just going to shine the animal anyway.

Blue swung the rifle around, leaned into the railing, and put a round in the center of the animal, right by its rib cage. The dog jerked inward, as if someone had whacked it with a bat, and as it teetered on wobbly legs, Blue pulled back on the bolt, drove it home again, and shot the dog in the head. The dog flipped over on its side, most of its skull gone, back leg kicking at the road like it was trying to ride a bicycle.

"You think Jewel Lut might, I dunno, like me?" Blue said.

Elgin cleared his throat. "Sure. She's always liked you."

"But I mean . . ." Blue shrugged, seemed embarrassed suddenly, "How about this: You think a girl like that could take to Australia?"

"Australia?"

Blue smiled at Elgin. "Australia."

"Australia?" he said again.

Blue reached back and shut off the light. "Australia. They got some wild dingoes there, buddy. Could make some real money. Jewel told me the other day how they got real nice beaches. But dingoes, too. Big Bobby said people're starting to bitch about what's happening here, asking where Rover is and such, and anyway, ain't too many dogs left dumb enough to come this way anymore. Australia," he said, "they never run out of dog. Sooner or later, here, I'm gonna run out of dog."

Elgin nodded. Sooner or later, Blue would run out of dog. He wondered if Big Bobby'd thought that one through, if he had a contingency plan, if he had access to the National Guard.

"The boy's just, what you call it, zealous," Big Bobby told Elgin.

They were sitting in Phil's Barbershop on Main. Phil had gone to lunch, and Big Bobby'd drawn the shades so people'd think he was making some important decision of state.

Elgin said, "He ain't zealous, Big Bobby. He's losing it. Thinks he's in love with Jewel Lut."

"He's always thought that."

"Yeah, but now maybe he's thinking she might like him a bit, too."

Big Bobby said, "How come you never call me Mayor?"

Elgin sighed.

"All right, all right. Look," Big Bobby said, picking up one of the hair-tonic bottles on Phil's counter and sniffing it, "so Blue likes his job a little bit."

Elgin said, "There's more to it and you know it."

Playing with combs now. "I do?"

"Bobby, he's got a taste for shooting things now."

"Wait." He held up a pair of fat, stubby hands. "Blue always liked to shoot things. Everyone knows that. Shit, if he wasn't so short and didn't have six or seven million little health problems, he'd a been the first guy in this town to go to The 'Nam. 'Stead, he had to sit back here while you boys had all the fun."

Calling it The 'Nam. Like Big Bobby had any idea. Calling it fun. Shit.

"Dingoes," Elgin said.

"Dingoes?"

"Dingoes. He's saying he's going to Australia to shoot dingoes."

"Do him a world of good, too." Big Bobby sat back down in the barber's chair beside Elgin. "He can see the sights, that sort of thing."

"Bobby, he ain't going to Australia and you know it. Hell, Blue ain't never stepped over the county line in his life."

Big Bobby polished his belt buckle with the cuff of his sleeve. "Well, what you want me to do about it?"

"I don't know. I'm just telling you. Next time you see him, Bobby, you look in his fucking eyes."

"Yeah, What'll I see?"

Elgin turned his head, looked at him. "Nothing."

Bobby said, "He's your buddy."

Elgin thought of the small panties curling out of the dust under Blue's bed. "Yeah, but he's your problem."

Big Bobby put his hands behind his head, stretched in the chair. "Well, people getting suspicious about all the dogs disappearing, so I'm going to have to shut this operation down immediately anyway."

He wasn't getting it. "Bobby, you shut this operation down, someone's gonna get a world's worth of that nothing in Blue's eyes."

Big Bobby shrugged, a man who'd made a career out of knowing what was beyond him.

The first time Perkin Lut struck Jewel in public was at Chuck's Diner.

Elgin and Shelley were sitting just three booths away when they heard a racket of falling glasses and plates, and by the time they came out of their booth, Jewel was lying on the tile floor with shattered glass and chunks of bone china by her elbows and Perkin standing over her, his arms shaking, a look in his eyes that said he'd surprised himself as much as anyone else.

Elgin looked at Jewel, on her knees, the hem of her dress getting stained by the spilled food, and he looked away before she caught his eye, because if that happened he just might do something stupid, fuck Perkin up a couple-three ways.

"Aw, Perkin," Chuck Blade said, coming from behind the counter to help Jewel up, wiping gravy off his hands against his apron.

"We don't respect that kind of behavior 'round here, Mr. Lut," Clara Blade said. "Won't have it neither."

Chuck Blade helped Jewel to her feet, his eyes cast down at his broken plates, the half a steak lying in a soup of beans by his shoe. Jewel had a

welt growing on her right cheek, turning a bright red as she placed her
hand on the table for support.

"I didn't mean it," Perkin said.

Clara Blade snorted and pulled the pen from behind her ear, began
itemizing the damage on a cocktail napkin.

"I didn't." Perkin noticed Elgin and Shelley. He locked eyes with
Elgin, held out his hands. "I swear."

Elgin turned away and that's when he saw Blue coming through the
door. He had no idea where he'd come from, though it ran through his
head that Blue could have just been standing outside looking in, could
have been standing there for an hour.

Like a lot of small guys, Blue had speed, and he never seemed to walk
in a straight line. He moved as if he were constantly sidestepping tackles
or land mines — with sudden, unpredictable pivots that left you watching the space where he'd been, instead of the place he'd ended up.

Blue didn't say anything, but Elgin could see the determination for
homicide in his eyes and Perkin saw it too, backed up, and slipped on
the mess on the floor and stumbled back, trying to regain his balance as
Blue came past Shelley and tried to lunge past Elgin.

Elgin caught him at the waist, lifted him off the ground, and held on
tight because he knew how slippery Blue could be in these situations.
You'd think you had him and he'd just squirm away from you, hit somebody with a glass.

Elgin tucked his head down and headed for the door, Blue flopped
over his shoulder like a bag of cement mix, Blue screaming, "You see
me, Perkin? You see me? I'm a last face you see, Perkin! Real soon."

Elgin hit the open doorway, felt the night heat on his face as Blue
screamed, "Jewel! You all right? Jewel?"

Blue didn't say much back at Elgin's trailer.

He tried to explain to Shelley how pure Jewel was, how hitting something that innocent was like spitting on the Bible.

Shelley didn't say anything, and after a while Blue shut up, too.

Elgin just kept plying him with Beam, knowing Blue's lack of tolerance for it, and pretty soon Blue passed out on the couch, his pitted face
still red with rage.

"He's never been exactly right in the head, has he?" Shelley said.

Elgin ran his hand down her bare arm, pulled her shoulder in tighter against his chest, heard Blue snoring from the front of the trailer. "No, ma'am."

She rose above him, her dark hair falling to his face, tickling the corners of his eyes. "But you've been his friend."

Elgin nodded.

She touched his cheek with her hand. "Why?"

Elgin thought about it a bit, started talking to her about the little, dirty kid and his cockroach flambés, of the animal sounds that came from his mother's trailer. The way Blue used to sit by the drainage ditch, all pulled into himself, his body tight. Elgin thought of all those roaches and cats and rabbits and dogs, and he told Shelley that he'd always thought Blue was dying, ever since he'd met him, leaking away in front of his eyes.

"Everyone dies," she said.

"Yeah." He rose up on his elbow, rested his free hand on her warm hip. "Yeah, but with most of us it's like we're growing toward something and then we die. But with Blue, it's like he ain't never grown toward nothing. He's just been dying real slowly since he was born."

She shook her head. "I'm not getting you."

He thought of the mildew that used to soak the walls in Blue's mother's trailer, of the mold and dust in Blue's shack off Route 11, of the rotting smell that had grown out of the drainage ditch when they were kids. The way Blue looked at it all — seemed to be at one with it — as if he felt a bond.

Shelley said, "Babe, what do you think about getting out of here?"

"Where?"

"I dunno. Florida. Georgia. Someplace else."

"I got a job. You too."

"You can always get construction jobs other places. Receptionist jobs too."

"We grew up here."

She nodded. "But maybe it's time to start our life somewhere else."

He said, "Let me think about it."

She tilted his chin so she was looking in his eyes. "You've *been* thinking about it."

He nodded. "Maybe I want to think about it some more."

In the morning, when they woke up, Blue was gone.

Shelley looked at the rumpled couch, over at Elgin. For a good minute they just stood there, looking from the couch to each other, the couch to each other.

An hour later, Shelley called from work, told Elgin that Perkin Lut was in his office as always, no signs of physical damage.

Elgin said, "If you see Blue . . ."

"Yeah?"

Elgin thought about it. "I dunno. Call the cops. Tell Perkin to bail out a back door. That sound right?"

"Sure."

Big Bobby came to the site later that morning, said, "I go over to Blue's place to tell him we got to end this dog thing and —"

"Did you tell him it was over?" Elgin asked.

"Let me finish. Let me explain."

"Did you tell him?"

"Let me finish," Bobby wiped his face with a handkerchief. "I was gonna tell him, but —"

"You didn't tell him."

"But Jewel Lut was there."

"What?"

Big Bobby put his hand on Elgin's elbow, led him away from the other workers. "I said Jewel was there. The two of them sitting at the kitchen table, having breakfast."

"In Blue's place?"

Big Bobby nodded. "Biggest dump I ever seen. Smells like something I-don't-know-what. But bad. And there's Jewel, pretty as can be in her summer dress and soft skin and make-up, eating Eggos and grits with Blue, big brown shiner under here eye. She smiles at me, says, 'Hey, Big Bobby,' and goes back to eating."

"And that was it?"

"How come no one ever calls me Mayor?"

"And that was it?" Elgin repeated.

"Yeah. Blue asks me to take a seat, I say I got business. He says him, too."

"What's that mean?" Elgin heard his own voice, hard and sharp.

Big Bobby took a step back from it. "Hell do I know? Could mean he's going out to shoot more dog."

"So you never told him you were shutting down the operation."

Big Bobby's eyes were wide and confused. "You hear what I told you?

He was in there with Jewel. Her all doll-pretty and him looking, well, ugly as usual. Whole situation was too weird. I got out."

"Blue said he had business, too."

"He said he had business, too," Bobby said, and walked away.

The next week, they showed up in town together a couple of times, buying some groceries, toiletries for Jewel, boxes of shells for Blue.

They never held hands or kissed or did anything romantic, but they were together, and people talked. Said, Well, of all things. And I never thought I'd see the day. How do you like that? I guess this is the day the cows actually come home.

Blue called and invited Shelley and Elgin to join them one Sunday afternoon for a late breakfast at the IHOP. Shelley begged off, said something about coming down with the flu, but Elgin went. He was curious to see where this was going, what Jewel was thinking, how she thought her hanging around Blue was going to come to anything but bad.

He could feel the eyes of the whole place on them as they ate.

"See where he hit me?" Jewel tilted her head, tucked her beautiful red hair back behind her ear. The mark on her cheekbone, in the shape of a small rain puddle, was faded yellow now, its edges roped by a sallow beige.

Elgin nodded.

"Still can't believe the son of a bitch hit me," she said, but there was no rage in her voice anymore, just a mild sense of drama, as if she'd pushed the words out of her mouth the way she believed she should say them. But the emotion she must have felt when Perkin's hand hit her face, when she fell to the floor in front of people she'd known all her life — that seemed to have faded with the mark on her cheekbone.

"Perkin Lut," she said with a snort, then laughed.

Elgin looked at Blue. He'd never seemed so . . . fluid in all the time Elgin had known him. The way he cut into his pancakes, swept them off his plate with a smooth dip of the fork tines; the swift dab of the napkin against his lips after every bite; the attentive swivel of his head whenever Jewel spoke, usually in tandem with the lifting of his coffee mug to his mouth.

This was not a Blue Elgin recognized. Except when he was handling weapons, Blue moved in jerks and spasms. Tremors rippled through his limbs and caused his fingers to drop things, his elbows and knees to move too fast, crack against solid objects. Blue's blood seemed to move too quickly through his veins, made his muscles obey his brain after a quarter-second delay and then too rapidly, as if to catch up on lost time.

But now he moved in concert, like an athlete or a jungle cat.

That's what you do to men, Jewel: You give them a confidence so total it finds their limbs.

"Perkin," Blue said, and rolled his eyes at Jewel and they both laughed.

She not as hard as he did, though.

Elgin could see the root of doubt in her eyes, could feel her loneliness in the way she fiddled with the menu, touched her cheekbone, spoke too loudly, as if she wasn't just telling Elgin and Blue how Perkin had mistreated her, but the whole IHOP as well, so people could get it straight that she wasn't the villain, and if after she returned to Perkin she had to leave him again, they'd know why.

Of course she was going back to Perkin.

Elgin could tell by the glances she gave Blue — unsure, slightly embarrassed, maybe a bit repulsed. What had begun as a nighttime ride into the unknown had turned cold and stale during the hard yellow lurch into morning.

Blue wiped his mouth, said, "Be right back," and walked to the bathroom with surer strides than Elgin had ever seen on the man.

Elgin looked at Jewel.

She gripped the handle of her coffee cup between the tips of her thumb and index finger and turned the cup in slow revolutions around the saucer, made a soft scraping noise that climbed up Elgin's spine like a termite trapped under the skin.

"You ain't sleeping with him, are you?" Elgin said quietly.

Jewel's head jerked up and she looked over her shoulder, then back at Elgin. "What? God, no. We're just . . . He's my pal. That's all. Like when we were kids."

"We ain't kids."

"I know. Don't you know I know?" She fingered the coffee cup again. "I miss you," she said softly. "I miss you. When you coming back?"

Elgin kept his voice low. "Me and Shelley, we're getting pretty serious."

She gave him a small smile that he instantly hated. It seemed to know him; it seemed like everything he was and everything he wasn't was caught in the curl of her lips. "You miss the lake, Elgin. Don't lie."

He shrugged.

"You ain't ever going to marry Shelley Briggs, have babies, be an up-standing citizen."

"Yeah? Why's that?"

"Because you got too many demons in you, boy. And they need me. They need the lake. They need to cry out every now and then."

Elgin looked down at his own coffee cup. "You going back to Perkin?"

She shook her head hard. "No way. Uh-uh. No way."

Elgin nodded, even though he knew she was lying. If Elgin's demons needed the lake, needed to be unbridled, Jewel's needed Perkin. They needed security. They needed to know the money'd never run out, that she'd never go two full days without a solid meal, like she had so many times as a child in the trailer park.

Perkin was what she saw when she looked down at her empty coffee cup, when she touched her cheek. Perkin was at their nice home with his feet up, watching a game, petting the dog, and she was in the IHOP in the middle of a Sunday when the food was at its oldest and coldest, with one guy who loved her and one who fucked her, wondering how she got there.

Blue came back to the table, moving with that new sure stride, a broad smile in the wide swing of his arms.

"How we doing?" Blue said. "Huh? How we doing?" And his lips burst into a grin so huge Elgin expected it to keep going right off the sides of his face.

Jewel left Blue's place two days later, walked into Perkin Lut's Auto Emporium and into Perkin's office, and by the time anyone went to check, they'd left through the back door, gone home for the day.

Elgin tried to get a hold of Blue for three days — called constantly, went by his shack and knocked on the door, even staked out the tree house along I-95 where he fired on the dogs.

He'd decided to break into Blue's place, was fixing to do just that, when he tried one last call from his trailer that third night and Blue answered with a strangled "Hello."

"It's me. How you doing?"

"Can't talk now."

"Come on, Blue. It's me. You okay?"

"All alone," Blue said.

"I know. I'll come by."

"You do, I'll leave."

"Blue."

"Leave me alone for a spell, Elgin. Okay?"

That night Elgin sat alone in his trailer, smoking cigarettes, staring at the walls.

Blue'd never had much of anything his whole life — not a job he enjoyed, not a woman he could consider his — and then between the dogs and Jewel Lut he'd probably thought he'd got it all at once. Hit pay dirt.

Elgin remembered the dirty little kid sitting down by the drainage ditch, hugging himself. Six, maybe seven years old, waiting to die.

You had to wonder sometimes why some people were even born. You had to wonder what kind of creature threw bodies into the world, expected them to get along when they'd been given no tools, no capacity to get any either.

In Vietnam, this fat boy, name of Woodson from South Dakota, had been the least popular guy in the platoon. He wasn't smart, he wasn't athletic, he wasn't funny, he wasn't even personable. He just was. Elgin had been running beside him one day through a sea of rice paddies, their boots making sucking sounds every step they took, and someone fired a hell of a round from the other side of the paddies, ripped Woodson's head in half so completely all Elgin saw running beside him for a few seconds was the lower half of Woodson's face. No hair, no forehead, no eyes. Just half the nose, a mouth, a chin.

Thing was, Woodson kept running, kept plunging his feet in and out of the water, making those sucking sounds, M-15 hugged to his chest, for a good eight or ten steps. Kid was dead, he's still running. Kid had no reason to hold on, but he don't know it, he keeps running.

What spark of memory, hope, or dream had kept him going?

You had to wonder.

In Elgin's dream that night, a platoon of ice-gray Vietcong rose in a straight line from the center of Cooper's Lake while Elgin was inside the cabin with Shelley and Jewel. He penetrated them both somehow, their separate torsos branching out from the same pair of hips, their four legs clamping at the small of his back, this Shelley-Jewel creature crying out for more, more, more.

And Elgin could see the VC platoon drifting in formation toward the shore, their guns pointed, their faces hidden behind thin wisps of green fog.

The Shelley-Jewel creature arched her backs on the bed below him, and Woodson and Blue stood in the corner of the room watching as their dogs padded across the floor, letting out low growls and drooling.

Shelley dissolved into Jewel as the VC platoon reached the porch steps and released their safeties all at once, the sound like the ratcheting of a thousand shotguns. Sweat exploded in Elgin's hair, poured down his body like warm rain, and the VC fired in concert, the bullets shearing the walls of the cabin, lifting the roof off into the night. Elgin looked above him at the naked night sky, the stars zipping by like tracers, the yellow moon full and mean, the shivering branches of birch trees. Jewel rose and straddled him, bit his lip, and dug her nails into his back, and the bullets dance through his hair, and then Jewel was gone, her writhing flesh having dissolved into his own.

Elgin sat naked on the bed, his arms stretched wide, waiting for the bullets to find his back, to shear his head from his body the way they'd sheared the roof from the cabin, and the yellow moon burned above him as the dogs howled and Blue and Woodson held each other in the corner of the room and wept like children as the bullets drilled holes in their faces.

Big Bobby came by the trailer late the next morning, a Sunday, and said, "Blue's a bit put out about losing his job."

"What?" Elgin sat on the edge of his bed, pulled on his socks. "You picked now — now, Bobby — to fire him?"

"It's in his eyes," Big Bobby said. "Like you said. You can see it."

Elgin had seen Big Bobby scared before, plenty of times, but now the man was trembling.

Elgin said, "Where is he?"

Blue's front door was open, hanging half down the steps from a busted hinge. Elgin said, "Blue."

"Kitchen."

He sat in his Jockeys at the table, cleaning his rifle, each shiny black piece spread in front of him on the table. Elgin's eyes watered a bit because there was a stench coming from the back of the house that he felt might strip his nostrils bare. He realized then that he'd never asked Big Bobby or Blue what they'd done with all those dead dogs.

Blue said, "Have a seat, bud. Beer in the fridge if you're thirsty."

Elgin wasn't looking in that fridge. "Lost your job, huh?"

Blue wiped the bolt with a shammy cloth. "Happens." He looked at Elgin. "Where you been lately?"

"I called you last night."

"I mean in general."

"Working."

"No, I mean at night."

"Blue, you been" — he almost said "playing house with Jewel Lut" but caught himself — "up in a fucking tree, how do you know where I been at night?"

"I don't," Blue said. "Why I'm asking."

Elgin said, "I've been at my trailer or down at Doubles, same as usual."

"With Shelley Briggs, right?"

Slowly, Elgin said, "Yeah."

"I'm just asking, buddy. I mean, when we all going to go out? You, me, your new girl."

The pits that covered Blue's face like a layer of bad meat had faded some from all those nights in the tree.

Elgin said, "Anytime you want."

Blue put down the bolt. "How 'bout right now?" He stood and walked into the bedroom just off the kitchen. "Let me just throw on some duds."

"She's working now, Blue."

"At Perkin Lut's? Hell, it's almost noon. I'll talk to Perkin about that Dodge he sold me last year, and when she's ready we'll take her out someplace nice." He came back into the kitchen wearing a soiled brown T-shirt and jeans.

"Hell," Elgin said, "I don't want the girl thinking I've got some serious love for her or something. We come by for lunch, next thing she'll expect me to drop her off in the mornings, pick her up at night."

Blue was reassembling the rifle, snapping all those shiny pieces together so fast, Elgin figured he could do it blind. He said, "Elgin, you got to show them some affection sometimes. I mean, Jesus." He pulled a thin brass bullet from his T-shirt pocket and slipped it in the breech, followed it with four more, then slid the bolt home.

"Yeah, but you know what I'm saying, bud?" Elgin watched Blue nestle the stock in the space between his left hip and ribs, let the barrel point out into the kitchen.

"I know what you're saying," Blue said. "I know. But I got to talk to Perkin about my Dodge."

"What's wrong with it?"

"What's wrong with it?" Blue turned to look at him, and the barrel swung level with Elgin's belt buckle. "What's wrong with it, it's a piece of shit, what's wrong with it, Elgin. Hell, you know that. Perkin sold me a lemon. This is the situation." He blinked. "Beer for the ride?"

Elgin had a pistol in his glove compartment. A .32. He considered it.

"Elgin?"

"Yeah?"

"Why you looking at me funny?"

"You got a rifle pointed at me, Blue. You realize that?"

Blue looked at the rifle, and its presence seemed to surprise him. He dipped it toward the floor. "Shit, man, I'm sorry. I wasn't even thinking. It feels like my arm sometimes. I forget. Man, I am sorry." He held his arms out wide, the rifle rising with them.

"Lotta things deserve to die, don't they?"

Blue smiled. "Well, I wasn't quite thinking along those lines, but now you bring it up . . ."

Elgin said, "Who deserves to die, buddy?"

Blue laughed. "You got something on your mind, don't you?" He hoisted himself up on the table, cradled the rifle in his lap. "Hell, boy, who you got? Let's start with people who take two parking spaces."

"Okay." Elgin moved the chair by the table to a position slightly behind Blue, sat in it. "Let's."

"Then there's DJs talk through the first minute of a song. Fucking Guatos coming down here these days to pick tobacco, showing no respect. Women wearing all those tight clothes, look at you like you're a pervert when you stare at what they're advertising." He wiped his forehead with his arm. "Shit."

"Who else?" Elgin said quietly.

"Okay. Okay. You got people like the ones let their dogs run wild into the highway, get themselves killed. And you got dishonest people, people who lie and sell insurance and cars and bad food. You got a lot of things. Jane Fonda."

"Sure." Elgin nodded.

Blue's face was drawn, gray. He crossed his legs over each other like he used to down at the drainage ditch. "It's all out there." He nodded and his eyelids drooped.

"Perkin Lut?" Elgin said. "He deserve to die?"

"Not just Perkin," Blue said. "Not just. Lots of people. I mean, how many you kill over in the war?"

Elgin shrugged. "I don't know."

"But some. Some. Right? Had to. I mean, that's war — someone gets on your bad side, you kill them and all their friends till they stop bothering you." His eyelids drooped again, and he yawned so deeply he shuddered when he finished.

"Maybe you should get some sleep."

Blue looked over his shoulder at him. "You think? It's been a while."

A breeze rattled the thin walls at the back of the house, pushed that thick dank smell into the kitchen again, a rotting stench that found the back of Elgin's throat and stuck there. He said, "When's the last time?"

"I slept? Hell, a while. Days maybe." Blue twisted his body so he was facing Elgin. "You ever feel like you spend your whole life waiting for it to get going?"

Elgin nodded, not positive what Blue was saying, but knowing he should agree with him. "Sure."

"It's hard," Blue said. "Hard." He leaned back on the table, stared at the brown water marks in his ceiling.

Elgin took in a long stream of that stench through his nostrils. He kept his eyes open, felt that air entering his nostrils creep past into his corneas, tear at them. The urge to close his eyes and wish it all away was as strong an urge as he'd ever felt, but he knew now was that time he'd always known was coming.

He leaned in toward Blue, reached across him, and pulled the rifle off his lap.

Blue turned his head, looked at him.

"Go to sleep," Elgin said. "I'll take care of this a while. We'll go see Shelley tomorrow. Perkin Lut, too."

Blue blinked. "What if I can't sleep? Huh? I've been having that problem, you know. I put my head on the pillow and I try to sleep and it won't come and soon I'm just bawling like a fucking child till I got to get up and do something."

Elgin looked at the tears that had just then sprung into Blue's eyes, the red veins split across the whites, the desperate, savage need in his face that had always been there if anyone had looked close enough, and would never, Elgin knew, be satisfied.

"I'll stick right here, buddy. I'll sit here in the kitchen and you go in and sleep."

Blue turned his head and stared up at the ceiling again. Then he slid off the table, peeled off his T-shirt, and tossed it on top of the fridge. "All right. All right. I'm gonna try." He stopped at the bedroom doorway. "'Member — there's beer in the fridge. You be here when I wake up?"

Elgin looked at him. He was still so small, probably so thin you could still wrap your hand around his biceps, meet the fingers on the other side. He was still ugly and stupid-looking, still dying right in front of Elgin's eyes.

"I'll be here, Blue. Don't you worry."

"Good enough. Yes, sir."

Blue shut the door and Elgin heard the bedsprings grind, the rustle of pillows being arranged. He sat in the chair, with the smell of whatever decayed in the back of the house swirling around his head. The sun had hit the cheap tin roof now, heating the small house, and after a while he realized the buzzing he'd thought was in his head came from somewhere back in the house too.

He wondered if he had the strength to open the fridge. He wondered if he should call Perkin Lut's and tell Perkin to get the hell out of Eden for a bit. Maybe he'd just ask for Shelley, tell her to meet him tonight with her suitcases. They'd drive down 95 where the dogs wouldn't disturb them, drive clear to Jacksonville, Florida, before the sun came up again. See if they could outrun Blue and his tiny, dangerous wants, his dog corpses, and his smell; outrun people who took two parking spaces and telephone solicitors and Jane Fonda.

Jewel flashed through his mind then, an image of her sitting atop him, arching her back and shaking that long red hair, a look in her green eyes that said this was it, this was why we live.

He could stand up right now with this rifle in his hands, scratch the itch in the back of his head, and fire straight through the door, end what should never have been started.

He sat there staring at the door for quite a while, until he knew the exact number of places the paint had peeled in teardrop spots, and eventually he stood, went to the phone on the wall by the fridge, and dialed Perkin Lut's.

"Auto Emporium," Shelley said, and Elgin thanked God that in his present mood he hadn't gotten Glynnis Verdon, who snapped her gum and always placed him on hold, left him listening to Muzak versions of The Shirelles.

"Shelley?"

"People gonna talk, you keep calling me at work, boy."

He smiled, cradled the rifle like a baby, leaned against the wall. "How you doing?"

"Just fine, handsome. How 'bout yourself?"

Elgin turned his head, looked at the bedroom door. "I'm okay."

"Still like me?"

Elgin heard the springs creak in the bedroom, heard weight drop on the old floorboards. "Still like you."

"Well, then, it's all fine then, isn't it?"

Blue's footfalls crossed toward the bedroom door, and Elgin used his hip to push himself off the wall.

"It's all fine," he said. "I gotta go. I'll talk to you soon."

He hung up and stepped away from the wall.

"Elgin," Blue said from the other side of the door.

"Yeah, Blue?"

"I can't sleep. I just can't."

Elgin saw Woodson sloshing through the paddy, the top of his head gone. He saw the pink panties curling up from underneath Blue's bed and a shaft of sunlight hitting Shelley's face as she looked up from behind her desk at Perkin Lut's and smiled. He saw Jewel Lut dancing in the night rain by the lake and that dog lying dead on the shoulder of the interstate, kicking its leg like it was trying to ride a bicycle.

"Elgin," Blue said. "I just can't sleep. I got to do something."

"Try," Elgin said and cleared his throat.

"I just can't. I got to . . . do something. I got to go . . ." His voice cracked, and he cleared his throat. "I can't sleep."

The doorknob turned and Elgin raised the rifle, stared down the barrel.

"Sure, you can, Blue." He curled his finger around the trigger as the door opened. "Sure you can," he repeated and took a breath, held it in.

The skeleton of Eden Falls still sits on twenty-two acres of land just east of Brimmer's Point, covered in rust thick as flesh. Some say it was the levels of iodine an environmental inspector found in the groundwater that scared off the original investors. Others said it was the downswing of the state economy or the governor's failed reelection bid. Some say Eden Falls was just plain a dumb name, too Biblical. And then, of course, there were plenty who claimed it was Jewel Lut's ghost scared off all the workers.

They found her body hanging from the scaffolding they'd erected by the shell of the roller coaster. She was naked and hung upside down from a rope tied around her ankles. Her throat had been cut so deep the coroner said it was a miracle her head was still attached when they found her. The coroner's assistant, man by the name of Chris Gleason, would claim when he was in his cups that the head had fallen off in the hearse as they drove down Main toward the morgue. Said he heard it cry out.

This was the same day Elgin Bern called the sheriff's office, told them he'd shot his buddy Blue, fired two rounds into him at close range, the little guy dead before he hit his kitchen floor. Elgin told the deputy he was still sitting in the kitchen, right where he'd done it a few hours before. Said to send the hearse.

Due to the fact that Perkin Lut had no real alibi for his whereabouts when Jewel passed on and owing even more to the fact there'd been some very recent and very public discord in their marriage, Perkin was arrested and brought before a grand jury, but that jury decided not to indict. Perkin and Jewel had been patching things up, after all; he'd bought her a car (at cost, but still . . .).

Besides, we all knew it was Blue had killed Jewel. Hell, the Simmons boy, a retard ate paint and tree bark, could have told you that. Once all that stuff came out about what Blue and Big Bobby'd been doing with the dogs around here, well, that just sealed it. And everyone remembered how that week she'd been separated from Perkin, you could see the dream come alive in Blue's eyes, see him allow hope into his heart for the first time in his sorry life.

And when hope comes late to a man, it's quite a dangerous thing. Hope is for the young, the children. Hope in a full-grown man — particularly one with as little acquaintanceship with it or prospect for it as Blue — well, that kind of hope burns as it dies, boils blood white, and leaves something mean behind when it's done.

Blue killed Jewel Lut.

And Elgin Bern killed Blue. And ended up doing time. Not much, due to his war record and the circumstances of who Blue was, but time just the same. Everyone knew Blue probably had it coming, was probably on his way back into town to do to Perkin or some other poor soul what he'd done to Jewel. Once a man gets that look in his eyes — that boiled look, like a dog searching out a bone who's not going to stop until he finds it — well, sometimes he has to be put down like a dog. Don't he?

And it was sad how Elgin came out of prison to find Shelley Briggs gone, moved up North with Perkin Lut of all people, who'd lost his heart for the car business after Jewel died, took to selling home electronics imported from Japan and Germany, made himself a fortune. Not long after he got out of prison, Elgin left too, no one knows where, just gone, drifting.

See, the thing is — no one wanted to convict Elgin. We all understood. We did. Blue had to go. But he'd had no weapon in his hand when Elgin, standing just nine feet away, pulled that trigger. Twice. Once we might been able to overlook, but twice, that's something else again. Elgin offered no defense, even refused a fancy lawyer's attempt to get him to claim he'd suffered something called Post Traumatic Stress Disorder, which we're hearing a lot more about these days.

"I don't have that," Elgin said. "I shot a defenseless man. That's the long and the short of it, and that's a sin."

And he was right:

In the world, 'case you haven't noticed, you usually pay for your sins.

And in the South, always.

Biographical Notes

Frederick Irving Anderson (1877–1947), although he never wrote a novel, was for a time one of the most popular mystery writers in America. Readers followed his short stories avidly in the pages of *The Saturday Evening Post* and other popular fiction magazines. In addition to the ultimate criminal mastermind, the Infallible Godahl (all six of whose adventures were collected in *The Adventures of the Infallible Godahl,* 1914), Anderson created the notorious jewel thief Sophie Lang, whose exploits were recorded in a single volume in 1925 and in three 1930s movies, all starring Gertrude Michael as the attractive young woman with a penchant for diamonds. Anderson's *The Book of Murder* (1930) was selected for *Queen's Quorum,* Ellery Queen's list of the 106 greatest mystery short story collections of all time.

Lawrence Block (1938–), a prolific novelist and short story writer, has averaged about two books a year for most of the past thirty years, sometimes under a pseudonym (the best known being Chip Harrison and Paul Kavanagh). Although the earliest titles were undistinguished paperback originals, Block has developed into one of today's most versatile and popular mystery writers, with such lightly humorous works as his series about Bernie Rhodenbarr, a burglar, and the books about Matt Scudder, the former policeman who works as a sort of private eye — easily his darkest and finest work. Block has won several Edgars as well as the Grand Master Award for lifetime achievement. "By the Dawn's Early Light" won an Edgar in 1985; it was originally published in an anthology, *The Eyes Have It* (1984), and was later expanded into the novel *When the Sacred Gin Mill Closes* (1986).

Pearl S. Buck (1892–1973) was a popular novelist whose career reached its pinnacle with the publication of *The Good Earth* (1931), for which she won the Pulitzer Prize and, with subsequent work, the Nobel Prize for Literature in 1938. When she was elected to the American Academy of Arts and Letters in 1951, she was only the second woman to be accorded the honor. Having lived in China for some years, Buck set many of her books there, and she founded the East and West Association in 1941 to foster better understanding between the two hemispheres. "Ransom" was first published in *Cosmopolitan* in October 1938.

James M. Cain (1892–1977), one of the first and greatest hard-boiled novelists, never wrote a detective novel or story because he anarchically didn't like the idea of a criminal being caught in a tidy conclusion. His first novel was the immensely successful *The Postman Always Rings Twice* (1934), which was followed by *Serenade* (1937), *Mildred Pierce* (1941), *and Double Indemnity* (1943), among his more than twenty books. *Postman* and *Double Indemnity* also became classic noir movies. His tales of lust and greed remain remarkably readable today, and Cain has been described by Elmore Leonard as one of his two literary influences, the other being Hemingway. "The Baby in the Icebox" was originally published in *American Mercury,* January 1933.

Willa Cather (1876–1947), a novelist seldom associated with the mystery story, is best known for chronicles of pioneer life (*O Pioneers!*, 1913; *My Ántonia,* 1918), although she was born in Virginia and moved to the relatively unsettled area of Nebraska when she was eight. She was less successful when writing about contemporary events, though the now largely unread *One of Ours* won the Pulitzer Prize in 1922. She moved to New York to work at *McClure's Magazine* soon after the turn of the century and became the managing editor from 1906 to 1912, when the success of her novels enabled her to devote herself full-time to writing. "Paul's Case" was first published in *McClure's Magazine,* May 1905.

Raymond Chandler (1888–1959), perhaps America's greatest mystery novelist, was born in Chicago but lived in England until after World War II. His first six detective novels, all featuring Philip Marlowe, were filmed with varying levels of excellence, but the books rank among the absolute elite of the genre, as enjoyable today as when they first saw the light of day. Marlowe was introduced in *The Big Sleep* (1939) and became the model for most of the private eyes that followed, personifying the lone knight mentality that is so uniquely American. "Red Wind" was first published in *Dime Detective,* January 1938.

An argument could be made that **James Crumley**'s (1939–) second detective novel, *The Last Good Kiss* (1978), is the most compelling private eye novel ever written. Hard-boiled aficionados can quote its opening paragraph verbatim. Although his stories are not set in the mean streets of urban fear, but in the Big Sky part of America, mostly Montana, Crumley still defines himself as "the bastard child of Raymond Chandler," acknowledging that his work couldn't exist had Chandler not come before him. And while his detectives have a moral code, they are closer in mindset to criminals, paying little attention to the law on their quests to find or to save someone. "Hot Springs" was originally published in the anthology *Murder for Love* (1996).

After three novels in the Lewis Cole detective series, **Brendan DuBois** (1959–) broke out with a major "parallel universe" novel called *Resurrection Day* (1999), which postulated that the Cuban missile crisis blew up into a full-scale nuclear war between the United States and the Soviet Union. His short stories have been honored with three Edgar Award nominations and a Shamus, given by the Private Eye Writers of America for the best short story of the year. In 1994 it went to "The Necessary Brother." "The Dark Snow" was originally published in *Playboy,* November 1996.

Stanley Ellin (1916–1986), nominated for numerous Edgar Allan Poe Awards and a three-time winner, was one of the most distinguished short story writers and novelists in this century, yet curiously never attained quite the recognition that his varied and innovative work deserved. Two of his Edgars were for short stories ("The House Party," 1954, and "The Blessington Method," 1956) and one for the superb private eye novel *The Eighth Circle* (1958). His early short stories were collected in *Mystery Stories* (1956), which Julian Symons accurately described as "the finest collection of stories in the crime form published in the past half century." He was named a Grand Master by the Mystery Writers of America in 1981 for lifetime achievement. Although "The Specialty of the House" is Ellin's most famous story, "The Moment of Decision," which resonates in the memory, may be his masterpiece; it was first published in *Ellery Queen's Mystery Magazine,* March 1955.

Although it is as an author of fantasy and science fiction that **Harlan Ellison** (1934–) has gained the majority of his fame, he has had success in numerous genres. He wrote juvenile delinquent novels in the late 1950s and early 1960s, turning to fantastic landscapes and nightmares mainly in the short fiction that has made him one of the most honored (Hugos and Nebulas line his office) and frequently anthologized authors of the second half of the century. The anthology of stories that he commissioned on normally censored subjects, *Dangerous Visions* (1967), is without question the most famous anthology of speculative fiction ever published. Ellison has won Edgars for two short stories: "Soft Monkey" (1987) and "The Whimper of Whipped Dogs," which was inspired by the real-life attack on Kitty Genovese; it was originally published in an anthology, *Bad Moon Rising,* in 1973.

William Faulkner (1897–1962), generally regarded as one of the greatest of American writers, often employed elements of crime, mystery, and detection in his novels and short stories. His first popular success, *Sanctuary* (1931), is the grim tale of a young woman who is raped by a gangster and then falls in love with him. *Intruder in the Dust* (1948) was selected for "The Haycraft-Queen Definitive Library of Detective-Crime-Mystery Fiction." *Knight's Gambit* (1949), his short story collection featuring "Uncle" Gavin Stevens, the shrewd attorney of Yoknapatawpha County, was selected for *Queen's Quorum* as one of the 106 greatest mystery collections of all time. "An Error in Chemistry" was originally published in *Ellery Queen's Mystery Magazine*, June 1946.

Robert L. Fish (1912–1981), during his successful career as an engineer, tried his hand at producing some Sherlock Holmes parodies, and his Schlock Homes adventures became arguably the funniest ever written. He had even greater success with his novels and short stories about Kek Huuygens, the world's greatest smuggler, who has managed to cross borders with everything from an original Bach cantata to a two-ton Indian elephant, and Jose de Silva, a policeman in Rio de Janeiro. Under the pseudonym Robert L. Pike, he wrote *Mute Witness* (1963), later filmed as *Bullitt* (1968), starring Steve McQueen. "The Wager" was first published in *Playboy*, July 1973.

Tom Franklin (1963–), born and raised in southern Alabama, was neither a good hunter nor a good shot, but his years spent in the deep woods lend resonant reality to his early short stories. In 1997, he received his M.F.A. from the University of Arkansas before returning to teach English at the University of South Alabama in Mobile. With the success of his first book, *Poachers* (1999), he and his wife, the poet Beth Ann Fennelly, moved to Illinois so he could devote himself full-time to writing. "Poachers" won the Edgar Allan Poe Award; it was first published in *Texas Review*, Spring 1998.

Jacques Futrelle (1875–1912), in spite of his French-sounding name, was born and raised in Georgia, and became a theatrical manager before going to work for the *Boston American*, where much of his fiction first appeared. He died too young to have been prolific, but his reputation as a master storyteller endures through his creation of Professor Augustus S.F.X. Van Dusen, better known as the Thinking Machine because of his extraordinary cerebral faculties. In the several books about him, beginning with *The Chase of the Golden Plate* (1906) but at his best in *The Thinking Machine* (1907), a newspaper reporter brings him cases to solve, which he does simply by applying the rules of logic. Futrelle was on the *Titanic* when it sank, refusing to enter a lifeboat while helping his wife and other women to board. "The Problem of Cell 13" first appeared in the *Boston American*, October 30, 1905.

Susan Glaspell (1882–1948), the author of several novels and numerous short stories, is best remembered for her plays, one of which, *Alison's House*, was awarded the Pulitzer Prize for drama in 1931. Certainly her most celebrated work in any medium is "A Jury of Her Peers," a subtly brilliant short story that is regarded even today as a cornerstone of feminist writing. It began its life as a one-act play titled *Trifles*, which was published in 1916 by Shay in the United States and by Benn in London in 1926. "A Jury of Her Peers" was first published in short story form in *Every Week*, March 5, 1917, and was so highly regarded that Benn published it as a stand-alone short story in a limited edition of 250 copies in 1927.

Joe Gores (1931–), a versatile and prolific writer, has written more than a hundred short stories, about a dozen novels, numerous filmscripts, and countless teleplays. And it is not merely about numbers. Gores has won Edgars in three different categories: Best Short Story ("Goodbye, Pops"), Best First Novel (*A Time of Predators*, 1969), and Best Episode in a TV Series ("No Immunity for Murder" for *Kojak*, 1976). He has also written for *Columbo, Mickey Spillane's Mike Hammer, Magnum, P.I.*, and *Remington Steele*. His novel *Hammett* (1975) was filmed in 1978, but he is best known for his DKA series about a private investigation firm, bringing his twelve years of detective experience to the novels and stories that are realistically funny and gritty at the same time. "Goodbye, Pops" was first published in *Ellery Queen's Mystery Magazine*, December 1969.

Sue Grafton (1940–), although a successful television writer for more than a decade (with scripts for full-length made-for-television movies based on Agatha Christie's novels and for such series as *Rhoda* and *Seven Brides for Seven Brothers*), will be remembered for her creation of Kinsey Milhone, one of the seminal figures in the history of detective fiction. No woman author had successfully written a hard-boiled female private eye series until Grafton produced the novels featuring her smart-mouthed heroine. *"A" Is for Alibi* was published in 1982 and the famous alphabet books have continued to the most recent *"O" Is for Outlaw*, and is the all-time best-selling series about a female private eye. "The Parker Shotgun" was first published in an anthology packaged by the Private Eye Writers of America, *Mean Streets*, in 1986.

John Marshall Tanner, the hero of **Stephen Greenleaf**'s (1942–) novels, is very much like his creator, a former lawyer whose sense of honor and ethics drives his life and career. The early novels, beginning with *Grave Error* (1979), are utterly reminiscent of Ross Macdonald's work, with the resolution of contemporary crimes inexorably linked to family secrets from the past. The cynicism of Tanner, like Lew Archer, is expressed in witty one-liners and superb similes matched only by his mentor and Raymond Chandler. In the later novels, Greenleaf tackles a different complex social issue in each adventure. The shockingly poignant "Iris" is Greenleaf's only attempt at a short story; it was published in an anthology executed by the Private Eye Writers of America, *The Eyes Have It*, in 1984.

If not the greatest, **Dashiell Hammett** (1894–1961) is certainly the most important American mystery writer of the twentieth century and second in history only to Edgar Allan Poe, who essentially invented the genre. Hammett introduced realism to the crime story, bringing murder "back to the kind of people that commit it for reasons," as Raymond Chandler wrote, "not just to provide a corpse." He made popular the hard-boiled private eye hero invented by Carroll John Daly in *Black Mask* magazine, creating such giants of the literature as the Continental Op, the nameless operative of *Red Harvest* (1928), *The Dain Curse* (1929), and his best short stories; Sam Spade, perhaps the best-known private eye in fiction, in *The Maltese Falcon* (1929); Ned Beaumont, the loyal hero of Hammett's masterpiece, *The Glass Key* (1931); and Nick and Nora Charles, who starred in one book, *The Thin Man* (1935), and six memorable movies. "The Gutting of Couffignal" was first published in *Black Mask,* December 1925.

After being caught for embezzling funds from the bank at which he worked, William Sydney Porter served five years in the Ohio State Penitentiary, where a friendly guard named Orrin Henry is believed to have inspired the pseudonym **O. Henry** (1862–1910). A prolific and much loved short story writer, with more than six hundred stories to his credit, O. Henry was the master of the surprise, or twist, ending. Although lightly regarded by many critics for his extensive use of sentimentality, the Society of Arts and Sciences acknowledged his preeminence in the short story form by creating what quickly became the prestigious O. Henry Memorial Award for the best short story of the year. While many of O. Henry's tales feature crime and criminals (such as the kidnapers in "The Ransom of Red Chief"), there is little real violence or evil. "A Retrieved Reformation," originally published in *Cosmopolitan,* April 1903, is more famous as *Alias Jimmy Valentine,* the title of the successful Broadway play and several motion pictures.

Patricia Highsmith (1921–1995), in spite of the tremendous success of her first novel, *Strangers on a Train* (1950), and the film made by Alfred Hitchcock the following year, was always far more appreciated and understood in Europe than in her native America. Perhaps Europeans were more tolerant of work in which there are no good people, no hope for happiness, and no redeeming traits in even the lesser characters. Her best-known creation, Mr. Ripley, an amoral art collector, con man, and murderer, appeared in a series of novels beginning with *The Talented Mr. Ripley* (1955), which won the French Grand Prix de Littérature Policiere. "The Terrapin" was first published in *Ellery Queen's Mystery Magazine,* October 1962.

Evan Hunter (1926–), in addition to a hugely successful writing career under his own name, including such bestsellers as *The Blackboard Jungle* (1954), famously filmed the following year with Sidney Poitier and Glenn Ford, attained even longer-term success as Ed McBain, the creator of several series characters, including the members of the groundbreaking Eighty-seventh Precinct. In this series of police procedurals, the entire squad is the detective hero. *Hill Street Blues* and *NYPD Blue* made the concept of the team as the hero of a story familiar, but McBain was the first to popularize it, beginning with *Cop Hater*

(1956) and continuing with nearly fifty novels. Several of the Eighty-seventh Precinct novels have been filmed, but Hunter's most successful Hollywood foray was as the screenwriter for *The Birds* (1963), directed by Alfred Hitchcock. "First Offense" was first published in *Manhunt,* December 1955.

If someone keeps a record of such things, there is a strong possibility that the most anthologized short story of the past half century is **Shirley Jackson**'s (1920–1965) "The Lottery," one of the most subtle and shocking horror stories ever written. The author is equally frightening in the novel-length tale of bone-chilling suspense, as demonstrated with *The Haunting of Hill House* (1959), which was successfully filmed in 1963 as *The Haunting,* starring Julie Harris and Claire Bloom. Not given to histrionics, but no less scary than her peers (of which there are few) in the horror-writing world, Jackson focuses on psychological terror, rather than violence and gore, for her effects. "The Possibility of Evil" won an Edgar Allan Poe Award and was first published in *The Saturday Evening Post,* December 18, 1965.

Harry Kemelman's (1908–1996) eight Nicky Welt short stories are models of armchair detection, first-rate depictions of deduction with little characterization or social significance, while his other fictional creation, Rabbi David Small, is an interesting and sympathetic character who solves mysteries within the context of his community and the solutions of which are often connected to Jewish lore, the rabbi's training in Talmudic logic serving as ideal training for his role of detective. *Friday the Rabbi Slept Late* (1964) established Kemelman instantly, and his next several novels made the bestseller list. The first Nicky Welt story, "The Nine Mile Walk," was first published in *Ellery Queen's Mystery Magazine,* April 1947.

Stephen King (1947–), the most successful horror writer who ever lived, has become a household name due to his remarkable skill in taking popular fiction across every demographic that can be measured — men, women, young, old, rich, poor. Everyone has read King and been terrified by him. While his fame rests mainly on such supernatural tales as *Carrie* (1974), *Salem's Lot* (1975), *The Shining* (1977), and *Firestarter* (1980), he has turned his hand to rationally explained stories of suspense with equal skill. *Misery* (1987) shares his own nightmare with the rest of us. While King is not generally known for his subtle escalation of fear, his "Quitters, Inc." is as accomplished a story of that kind as has ever been written; it was first published in his collection *Night Shift* (1978).

Ring Lardner (1885–1933), one of the great humorists of twentieth-century America, was also one of its great pessimists. Having begun his career as a sportswriter, he used that background for many of his earliest works of short fiction, notably the Alibi Ike stories collected most famously in *You Know Me, Al* (1916). His colloquial usage helped him find a large readership, both for his journalism and for his fiction, but in retrospect it seems he was read mostly for his incredibly original humor while his own cynicism and despair lurked just beneath the surface. "Haircut," his most famous story, was first published in *Liberty,* March 28, 1925.

If anyone requires evidence that the present day is a golden age in mystery fiction, one need look no further than **Dennis Lehane** (1965–), the brilliant young writer who burst onto the stage in 1994 with *A Drink Before the War,* which won both the Shamus Award from the Private Eye Writers of America for best first novel, and the Anthony Award, voted by fans. This successful pairing of Boston private eyes Patrick Kenzie and Angela Gennaro was followed by *Darkness, Take My Hand* (1966), *Sacred* (1997), the achingly poignant *Gone, Baby, Gone* (1998), and *Prayers for Rain* (1999). Illustrating his versatility, Lehane's "Running Out of Dog" is set in the south and is told in an entirely different voice from the snappy Boston novels. It was first published in the anthology *Murder and Obsession,* 1999.

After returning from military service in World War II, **John D. MacDonald** (1916–1986) was a prolific contributor to the pulp magazines, both under his own name and numerous pseudonyms. Unusually for the era, he also sold frequently to the higher paying "slicks." As those markets withered, he was among the first to recognize the possibilities of the new mass market paperback book world and wrote numerous novels for Gold Medal and other paperback houses. His most famous character is Travis McGee, the Florida rogue who helped people get out of trouble, usually while enriching himself. His best-known book, *The Executioners* (1958), was twice filmed as the terrifying psychological thriller, *Cape Fear.* "The Homesick Buick" was first published in *Ellery Queen's Mystery Magazine,* September 1950.

Ross Macdonald (1915–1983) was one of the great American hard-boiled writers, generally the third in the chronological pantheon of Hammett-Chandler-Macdonald. After four moderately successful novels under his own name, Kenneth Millar, he took a pen name and created Lew Archer, the smart-mouthed southern California private eye who, along with Philip Marlowe, inspired so many imitators. The first Archer novel, *The Moving Target* (1949), was filmed as the excellent *Harper,* starring Paul Newman, in 1966. Virtually all of Macdonald's Lew Archer novels have two elements: an examination of an issue of social or political concern and a complex mystery that has its solution in an unearthed family secret from the distant past. The uniformly superb reviews of his books, which were (properly) treated as serious literature as well as popular fiction, eventually made him a national bestseller. "Gone Girl" was first published in *Manhunt,* February 1953.

Michael Malone (1942–) is noted primarily as a writer of intelligent humor in the manner of John Irving. His critically acclaimed works of mainstream fiction, particularly *Dingley Falls* (1980), *Handling Sin* (1986), and *Foolscap* (1991), ensured that his two superb southern detective novels, *Uncivil Seasons* (1983) and *Time's Witness* (1989), would receive the review attention they warranted. Rarely has a mystery writer so successfully combined two extreme opposites as partners and friends on a police force in a believable fashion as Malone has with the wealthy, aristocratic Justin Savile and the poor redneck who worked his way up to be police chief, Cudberth "Cuddy" Mangum. These two distinguished books have been compared to the work of Truman Capote and Walker Percy. "Red Clay" won the Edgar in 1997; it was first published in the anthology *Murder for Love* in 1996.

Margaret Millar (1915–1994), the critically acclaimed author of award-winning crime fiction (*Beast in View* won the Edgar for best mystery of 1955), was also an active conservationist, founding the Santa Barbara chapter of the Audubon Society and being named the *Los Angeles Times* "Woman of the Year" for her "outstanding achievements as a writer and citizen" in 1965. She was married to the mystery writer Kenneth Millar, who adopted the pseudonym Ross Macdonald so that his work would not be confused with his wife's. "The Couple Next Door" was first published in *Ellery Queen's Mystery Magazine*, July 1957.

Joyce Carol Oates (1938–), one of the most versatile, prolific, and justly honored authors working today, has written virtually every type of prose it is possible to imagine, including hundreds of short stories, an opera libretto, an essay on boxing, dozens of novels, and on and on, achieving not only great popular success but the (sometimes grudging) glowing reviews of critics who remain baffled that she can be so consistently excellent while producing such a large body of work. She has turned with increasing frequency to mystery and suspense in recent years, including several novels under the pseudonym Rosamund Smith. "Do with Me What You Will" was first published in *Playboy*, June 1973.

Flannery O'Connor (1925–1964) was noted equally as a Catholic writer and a southern writer. Her beautifully crafted stories and novels can only be described as Gothic. They deal with religious fanaticism, as in *Wise Blood* (1952) and *The Violent Bear It Away* (1960), and grotesque examinations of southern domestic life, notably in her short story collections *A Good Man Is Hard To Find* (1955) and *Everything That Rises Must Converge* (1965), which contains the first publication of the meticulously honed description of paranoia and psychosis with its cunningly deceptive title, "The Comforts of Home."

Sara Paretsky (1947–), along with Sue Grafton and Marcia Muller (whose first works preceded both of her sisters in crime), is largely responsible for the enormous growth in popularity of women's hard-boiled fiction, beginning with *Indemnity Only* (1982). Her series character, V. I. Warshawski, is a private eye working in Chicago whose cases invariably explore white-collar crime and corruption, with a deeper investigation of the pain those crimes bring to the less fortunate whose lives are intertwined with those in positions of power. Paretsky had the misfortune to have her character inspire a motion picture, *V. I. Warshawski* (1991), which starred Kathleen Turner in a memorably terrible and incoherent film. "Three-Dot Po" was first published in the anthology *The Eyes Have It*, 1984.

Melville Davisson Post (1869–1930), as a writer whose technical skill in plotting stories was unmatched, was perhaps the most commercially successful short story writer of his day. He is remembered nowadays for two characters he created: Uncle Abner, the morally upright Virginia squire whose biblical knowledge and beliefs help him to help God punish evildoers, and Randolph Mason, the utterly unscrupulous lawyer who maintains the position that if no law specifically forbids an act, then it must be legal; in that spirit, he once advised a client to commit murder. Erle Stanley Gardner named his famous lawyer, Perry Mason, after Post's. Both *The Strange Schemes of Randolph Mason* (1896) and *Uncle Abner: Master of Mysteries* were selected for *Queen's Quorum*. "Naboth's Vineyard" was first published in the *Illustrated Sunday Magazine*, June 4, 1916.

Entering a mystery novel contest sponsored by *McClure's*, the Brooklyn-born cousins Frederic Dannay (1915–1982) and Manfred B. Lee (1905–1971) submitted *The Roman Hat Mystery* (1929) and had the brilliant notion of giving the detective the same name as the book's byline, helping to cement the **Ellery Queen** name in the memory of millions. The character went on to appear in more than forty books, successful radio programs, a half dozen television series, and nearly a dozen motion pictures, with Queen played most frequently by Ralph Bellamy or William Gargan. In 1972, Orson Welles starred (not as Queen) in *10 Days' Wonder*. Dannay was also a noted scholar, collector, essayist, and bibliographer in the field of the mystery short story and helped found *Ellery Queen's Mystery Magazine* in 1941. "The Adventure of the President's Half Disme" was first published in *EQMM*, February 1947.

Ben Ray Redman (1896–1961), in addition to the two mystery novels featuring Colonel Winston Creevy which he wrote under the pseudonym Jeremy Lord, *The Bannerman Case* (1935) and *Sixty-Nine Diamonds* (1940), wrote in a variety of genres under his own name, including verse, journalism (a book column for the *New York Herald Tribune*), comedy, and translations of several French classics. He also worked as a member of the production staff of Universal Pictures. "The Perfect Crime" was first published in *Harper's*, August 1928.

Jack Ritchie (1922–1983), a short story writer of prodigious output, like O. Henry and Edgar Allan Poe, never wrote a full-length novel. Having written hundreds of stories, it is almost inevitable that there will have been a range of styles and subject matter, but he will forever be associated with the quirky, off-beat humor that dominates his best work, as collected in *The Adventures of Henry Turnbuckle* (1987) and *Little Boxes of Bewilderment* (1989). The only collection published in his lifetime was *A New Leaf and Other Stories* (1971), the title story being successfully filmed in 1971, starring Walter Matthau and Elaine May, who also wrote the screenplay and directed. "The Absence of Emily" won the Edgar for Best Short Story of the Year; it was first published in *Ellery Queen's Mystery Magazine,* January 28, 1981.

If Mark Twain had not lived into the twentieth century, **Damon Runyon** (1880–1946) would surely rank as its funniest author as the creator of Broadway lowlifes and chiselers who spoke in an idiom he invented. He began as a sportswriter and reporter (Arthur Brisbane called him "America's greatest reporter") and continued as a journalist for most of his life, during which he also wrote numerous short stories; a successful play, *A Slight Case of Murder* (1935) with Howard Lindsay; and several films, notably *Little Miss Marker* (1934), which launched the career of Shirley Temple. It is possible that the single most successful title in Runyan's career is *Guys and Dolls,* which had success as a book (1931), an often revived Broadway musical, and a motion picture. "Sense of Humor" was first published in *Cosmopolitan,* September 1934, and collected in *Money from Home* (1935).

Henry Slesar (1927–), the versatile copywriter for Young and Rubicam and other advertising agencies, had scores of short stories published in many magazines (mainly *Ellery Queen's Mystery Magazine* and *Alfred Hitchcock Mystery Magazine*), and wrote several novels (his first, *The Gray Flannel Shroud,* won the Edgar for Best First Mystery in 1960) and hundreds of television scripts (winning both an Edgar and an Emmy in his career), including for such shows as *The Twilight Zone* and *Alfred Hitchcock Presents* and as head writer for the daytime soap opera *The Edge of Night.* "The Day of the Execution" was first published in *Alfred Hitchcock Mystery Magazine,* June 1957, and collected in *Clean Crimes and Neat Murders* (1960).

Wilbur Daniel Steele (1886–1970), a serious writer who worked hard to achieve his accurate depictions of life in the west (though he was an easterner, living most of his life in Lyme, Connecticut), won first prize more than once in the prestigious O. Henry short story competitions. Many of his stories (the form in which he excelled to a greater degree than in novel-length works) have strong elements of crime, mystery, and suspense, managing the difficult trick of oblique detective work, which permits the reader to observe and deduce at the same rate, or slightly ahead of, the characters in the stories. "Blue Murder" was first published in *Harper's,* October 1925, and collected in *The Man Who Saw Through Heaven* (1927).

John Steinbeck (1902–1968), as the author of some of the twentieth century's most famous, popular, and significant novels, especially *The Grapes of Wrath*

(1939), *Of Mice and Men* (1937), *East of Eden* (1952), and *Cannery Row* (1945), has taken his place among the half dozen or so iconic authors whose critical and commercial success have combined to place him in the first rank of important novelists. Most of his major works have been filmed, often very well, and numerous literary honors have been bestowed on him, including a Pulitzer Prize for *The Grapes of Wrath* and the Nobel Prize for Literature. Although his novels are often peopled with drunks, prostitutes, and other minor criminals, it is only in a handful of short stories that Steinbeck has turned to the mystery. "The Murder" was first published in *North American Review,* December 1933, and collected in *The Long Valley* (1938).

James Thurber (1894–1961), a brilliant humorist and artist whose style (along with E. B. White's) defined *The New Yorker* from the 1920s through the next half century, was nearly blind for much of his remarkable career. While he may be better known for his drawings, which hilariously chronicle the battle between men and women in a style that is instantly recognizable but impossible to describe, he thought more of his work as a writer, which, in addition to his innumerable stories and sketches for *The New Yorker,* have appeared on the stage (*The Male Animal,* 1940, with Elliott Nugent) and on the screen (*The Secret Life of Walter Mitty,* 1947, starring Danny Kaye). His several mystery stories include "The White Rabbit Caper" and "The Catbird Seat," which was first published in *The New Yorker,* November 14, 1942.

The short story collected in this volume is a microcosm of most of **Jerome Weidman**'s (1913–1998) work, a depiction of the evil side of mankind. If a good person appears in one of his novels or stories, he inevitably will be destroyed by the terrible people with whom he comes in contact. Weidman's most famous works have been adapted for other media, including *I Can Get It for You Wholesale* (1937), filmed in 1951 with Susan Hayward and Dan Daily, and *I'll Never Go There Any More* (1941), filmed as *House of Strangers* in 1949 with Hayward and Edward G. Robinson. "Good Man, Bad Man" was first published in *The Saturday Evening Post,* July 1, 1967.

Donald E. Westlake (1933–), as the creator of the amoral criminal Parker under the pseudonym Richard Stark, has demonstrated an ability to write very hard-boiled, action-driven adventures that have been frequently made into motion pictures, most notably *The Hunter* (1963), filmed as *Point Blank* in 1967 starring Lee Marvin and Angie Dickinson, and remade as *Payback* (1998) with Mel Gibson as the protagonist. But Westlake's major contribution to mystery fiction is the humorous caper, often featuring John Dortmunder, the thief whose most ingenious plans always seem to go wrong for no reason of his own making, notably in *The Hot Rock* (1970), filmed in 1972 with Robert Redford; *Bank Shot* (1972), filmed in 1974 with George C. Scott; and many others. He was nominated for an Academy Award in 1991 for his screenplay of Jim Thompson's *The Grifters* and was honored with the Grand Master Award for lifetime achievement by the Mystery Writers of America. "Too Many Crooks" was first published in *Playboy,* August 1989.

Cornell Woolrich (1903–1968), after beginning his writing career as a romantic novelist whose work was compared with F. Scott Fitzgerald, turned to the novel of suspense, both under his own name and using the pseudonyms George Hopley and William Irish, which defined his work for the rest of his life. No author ever matched his consistent ability to create suspense in his novels and short stories, which depicted "the every-day gone wrong," as Anthony Boucher described them. Among his most famous works, all of which have been made into noir movies, are *Phantom Lady, The Bride Wore Black, Deadline at Dawn, Black Angel, The Night Has a Thousand Eyes,* and *Waltz into Darkness* (filmed as *Mississippi Mermaid* by François Truffaut). "Rear Window," wonderfully filmed by Alfred Hitchcock, was first published in *Dime Detective,* February 1942, under the title "It Had to Be Murder."